THE RHAPSODY PLAYERS

THE RHAPSODY PLAYERS

A NOVEL

BY JIM LYNCH

Copyright 2010 Jim Lynch

Paperback ISBN 978-0-557-50962-1

Hardback ISBN 978-0-557-53887-4

All inquiries with respect to The Rhapsody Players or Rhapsody Holdings should be directed to:
TRP@RhapsodyHoldings.com

Dedication

To my wife Debbie, with love

Disclaimer

Although all of the events and characters contained in this book are entirely creations of the author's imagination, there are certainly numerous parallels to events in the real world and I have drawn upon my perception of these events during the relevant time period to create this work of fiction.

In addition several Trademarked business names are utilized in the story. Each of these is marked (™) and footnoted the first time it is used in the novel. This has been done with the written permission of the owners and founders of Rhapsody Holdings. Repeated markings are omitted for artistic purposes.

-- JJL3

TABLE OF CONTENTS

FOREWARD

"Time is an illusion. There is no beginning. There is no end. Life is simply a series of snapshots without a plot. If you flip them together quickly the mind creates the mirage of motion and motion creates the illusion of time.

What occurs within the breach between two discreet points in a person's life is most commonly perceived as an effort to elongate the span between these points in some sort of meaningful way, while each person attempts to discover wisdom and understanding during his or her own aperture of life."[*]

The *Rhapsody Players* represent a subset of this human condition and this is their story. It spans a four year period, before and after which, thousands of episodes, for millions of people, have unfolded, and will continue to unfold. The Rhapsody Players define themselves by their desire to live longer, better lives.

Jim Lynch

---

[*] Anonymous

ACT ONE

THE RHAPSODY PLAYERS

Autumn of 2008

Chapter 1: *Flying East*

Fernando saw John Brady leaving through the front door of his King's Point house and he quickly jumped out of the driver's seat and opened the rear door on the passenger's side of Brady's limousine. Fernando had been Brady's corporate driver for more than three years but Brady never once asked Fernando about his personal life. It was just as well. It was strictly a business relationship. Brady gave the orders and Fernando followed his directions.

"We need to make good time getting to the airport," Brady stated flatly, without acknowledging that Fernando and the other passenger had been waiting in his driveway for the past forty minutes.

Brady slipped into the back seat next to Maria Cardoza, his executive assistant and mistress, and Fernando shut the door behind him. By the time Fernando got back in the driver's seat the glass partition between the seats was being raised. Fernando found it curious that Brady rarely raised the partition when he was in the car with his wife, Maureen, but he almost always raised the partition when he was with his EA, Maria. After all, it wasn't as though Fernando didn't know what the respective relationships entailed.

To the casual observer, John Brady was a reasonably happy man. At 48 years of age, he was a highly respected CEO of a multibillion-dollar computer company, Integrated Computer Devices (ICD.) He and his attractive second wife, Maureen, had three children, two in college and one a senior at a prestigious private high school. They lived in a well-manicured five-acre estate in Kings Point on Long Island's North Shore, and enjoyed a posh summer home in trendy Southampton. Over the years John Brady had invested quite well and even before his first eight-figure bonus as CEO of ICD, he had managed to amass a sizable personal portfolio. At a slightly tanned, but seemingly well toned, 6 feet 3 inches tall and 235 pounds, John had an athletic build and good looks that were accentuated by a middle aged graying at the temples and a spray of salt in his mostly pepper-colored full head of hair.

Brady, or JB as he was known to the business elite, traveled constantly as he perched atop his far-flung business empire. The corporate jet was always at his disposal, but this simply made it easier for him to work continually. Although Brady's company was doing well, the competition in his industry was fierce, and the business dilemma of the hour could easily cause his day to merge with his evening, as he toiled to maintain his status as a corporate titan. It was not unusual for Brady to work 80 hours a week. He seemed to have a very wide circle of friends, but a very large percentage of these people had a subtending business agenda.

Brady's oldest son, Mark, and his only daughter, Megan, were both attending Ivy League colleges, in the nearby northeastern states of Massachusetts and Connecticut, but he saw them less and less as they progressed through their undergraduate academic years. John's youngest son, Kenneth, was tall and handsome like his father, but gay like his Uncle Arthur. JB was unaware of his youngest son's sexual preferences, but he had subconsciously wrestled with the *"what if?"* question without ever dealing with it on the surface.

And then there was Maria. Maria traveled with JB more than his wife Maureen traveled with him, and Maria spent far more time talking sideways with John, than Maureen did in an upright position. John enjoyed the satisfaction and the convenience of the classical extramarital misdemeanors, and he believed that the pillow talk often helped him sort out his business agenda.

As Fernando sped through the side streets of Kings Point, Brady turned to Maria and inquired about their upcoming schedule in London. After she laid out a busy agenda for the next several days, JB asked, "Do we have any time to relax?"

"Not much, but I have booked a private dinner for just the two of us on Thursday evening before we fly back to New York." Maria answered. She humored JB but the reality was that recently his controlling attitude was beginning to irritate her.

Maria Cardoza had always prided herself in being her own woman. Her early childhood experiences in Italy included many attempts at indoctrination in the rudiments and teachings of the Roman Catholic Church, but somehow Maria felt that she had successfully resisted the attempts of her parents and extended family at making these teachings formative to the person she believed she wanted to be. It was not that she was openly disrespectful to "the Faith," but she silently felt that the context of the family religion was much too constrictive to the person she wanted to be.

Maria Cardoza had an enthralling quality about her. Most men found her physical beauty to be enchanting, and once enchanted by her beauty they were often entrapped by her sensuousness.

An odd dimension of Maria's past relationships with men was that her more enduring relationships had always been with *older* men, but the age gap was narrowing.

When Maria was nineteen years old, she had a four-year affair with an Arabian businessman, who had commercial interests in oil and munitions but had a passion for horses. She called him her Arabian Horseman. He died on a gambling weekend in Monte Carlo at the age of 68.

Three years later Maria's new man friend, Jorge Ortega, a Spanish Art dealer in his late fifties came into her life. Jorge gave her gifts and complimented her constantly. He would often step back and look at her from head to foot and then step much closer and stare deeply into her large brown eyes, the highlight of her olive skinned visage. He did this repeatedly, often angling his own cranium slightly as though he were assessing a work of art.

Maria had an appreciation for her own beauty and while in Spain she enjoyed both the beach and the mirror. She met some new friends who owned and operated a high end spa, known as Poco Pedazo di Ciela, overlooking the Mediterranean, and she became both a patron and a practitioner at the Spa. Before long Maria took over the daily management of Poco Pedazo de Ciela, but literally maintained a hands-on approach to the business and its high end customers.

Unfortunately both Maria and her art dealer paramour eventually became more preoccupied with their own pursuits than their interest in one another. It bothered neither Jorge nor Maria, when their five-year relationship wound down. That's when Maria met an American CEO in her Spanish Spa. She must have rubbed John Brady the right way because within six months she had moved to the United States and had become a capitalist, or at least, a capitalist aide. Along the way she acquired an affection for stylish business attire. She purchased a NYC co-op, and trimmed her long black hair to a more business- like, shoulder length with very slight highlights. Regardless, her appearance remained sensuous and very European.

Even with no formal education to buffer her new career, Maria spent her early thirties as the executive assistant to one of the most powerful men in the business world. JB was thirteen years older than Maria, but often acted younger. Even more intriguing was the fact that Maria occasionally felt older, or at least more mature, than JB. It was somewhat understandable, because John was Maria's youngest lover ever.

"I hope we can get a few hours sleep on the flight. That schedule for tomorrow seems challenging," said Brady. He seemed to be in an irritable mood, and Maria herself was annoyed that she had already spent so much time waiting in the driveway for JB, but she said nothing.

While Fernando sped them towards JFK Airport, the two would-be lovers sat in silent reflection, each contemplating some personal medical concerns.

JB had a sore back, occasional numbness in his hands, frequent headaches, "jellyneck," and occasional pain radiating from his shoulders to his arms and hands. During the past twelve months, he had seen his general practitioner, an orthopedic surgeon, a chiropractor, an acupuncturist, a neurologist, a neurosurgeon and a physical therapist in the hope that the seemingly core issue of back pain would dissipate. The pain persisted, and JB's frustration grew. Private massage therapy administered by Maria was a flop in more ways than one. And to exacerbate the issue, none of the practitioners worked in any coordinated way to document his dilemma.

Maria's healthcare concerns were less physically daunting and began more recently. It started with betrayal by one of Maria's closest allies, her mirror. Recently she stood in front of it and appraised her naked body, the way Jorge had so often done in the past, first from a full-length distance and then up close and personal. But the nuance was different. Where Jorge's eyes had savored perfection, Maria's self-perusal searched out imperfections, blemishes, faults and flaws. The first few gray hairs appeared amidst the highlights. Her muscle tone ebbed slightly. Her breasts appeared larger but somehow less natural; her nipples less spry and a less defined pink. Her shoulders seemed too narrow and her butt actually wrinkled slightly when she sat! She was 35. She was getting old! Worse yet, it bothered her, and she admitted it to her ever-confident self. She knew that for the first time she was experiencing depression.

Maria never cared much for doctors and never felt she needed their help. As a child her experience was that they administered inoculations, and checked your pulse. Adolescent physical examinations were bothersome at best, personally intrusive, at least, and downright embarrassing most of the time. When she came to New York she met an OB/GYN, by the name of Al Moses. She liked Moses and besides dealing with some complications of her menstrual cycle, he actually talked to her. And he examined what she said, as much as how she bled. Lately she was both speaking and bleeding a lot less frequently. Maybe it had something to do with her depression.

"We're only nine days away from the financial analysts call." JB finally broke up the silence. "We'll have a lot to in preparation for that call as soon as we return from London."

"You need to relax, John. Take things one at a time. You're already worrying about what you're going to do after the trip, before you've even left. Slow down."

****

Left behind in their Kings Point home, Maureen Brady made herself a cosmopolitan and sat down in her living room mindlessly thumbing through the magazines that she had brought in from the kitchen. She sat alone.

Maureen Brady's friends thought that she had it all. Her father's family traced the origins of their wealth back to late 19th century railroad money, and even before that her great great great grandfather on her mother's side was one of the largest plantation owners in the South and a classmate of Robert E Lee, when the Southern General attended West Point, in 1829. Many of the stories, some of the attitudes, and lots of the money had been handed down from her ancestors. Maureen was born into the pluperfect WASP establishment. She bathed twice a day, and had sex once a week invariably in the missionary position, and always with her husband, John.

Maureen was very soft spoken, but that did not mean that she was without her viewpoints. Her politics were stoically conservative, and her values had taken root with her two oldest children Mark and Megan. Lately however Maureen was beginning to quietly question some of the tenets of her conservative agenda. Much of this was triggered by the recent recognition of the fact that her youngest son, Kenneth, was gay. He was a very athletic swimmer, barely missing a spot on the US Olympic team, and had developed his golf and tennis skills, with the help of the club's professional coaches, to the point where he routinely beat his father and his brother in both sports.

Maureen loved Kenneth, but she worried. She wondered why Kenneth was gay, and why her brother, Arthur, was also gay. Is there a gay gene? Maureen had begun reading about "twin studies," "brain dissections," and gene "linkage" studies in an effort to learn more about why Kenneth was gay. She also worried about what John would think about Kenneth's sexual preferences if he found out.

Maureen Brady was now in her early forties, surrounded by people, but often feeling quite alone. He husband JB was totally absorbed in his business. He traveled constantly, and although Maureen occasionally accompanied him on his travels, she often felt more like part of the staff rather than like his wife. In fact he often spent more time talking to other members of his staff, like Maria Cardoza, than he spent talking to his wife, Maureen.

Maureen was not personally jealous of Maria. She was confident about her own physical attractiveness and even marveled when some people remarked about the similarity in appearance between Maria and herself. They were both dark-haired and shapely but Maureen believed the similarities stopped there. Besides, JB didn't seem to be overly interested in sex. Their own sexual relationship had started out rather passionately more than twenty years earlier, but had settled into what Maureen considered a comfortable routine in recent years. John was not very demanding of her and she was responsive enough when he expressed his physical desires. Sometimes though she did think back to the good old days when she and JB first began dating. They had sex anywhere and everywhere, and could not keep their hands off one another.

Maureen was proud of her husband. JB was a self made man. Some of Maureen's extended family had been suspicious of John and his latent Catholicism when they became engaged, but they too were rapidly won over by John's remarkable climb up the ladder of success. John never debated his positions in life. He demonstrated them.

If Maureen had one complaint about John, it was that he was hard to keep up with. Besides his constant travel, he was continuously bringing new people into their lives. It was almost destabilizing to Maureen. The people were all so different. Maureen's WASPY upbringing had been re-sensitized to now include relationships with Catholics, Jews, and Mormons. More recently some of John's crowd included Asians who were Muslims, Sikhs, Hindus and Buddhists. It was enough to drive a woman to drink. And so she did.

****

Dr Al Moses had spent his first day in London catching up on his sleep, after his flight from New York. He got out of bed about 11 AM. He was looking forward to having dinner that evening with his lifelong friend, Steven Struben. Moses was staying at the London Marriott Hotel, across from the Marble Arch in Hyde Park. Very typically, he was staying alone.

After a brisk walk in the park Moses went back into the hotel, took a swim in the indoor pool. After a refreshing shower, he went back down to the Park Lane Restaurant off the lobby of the hotel and had a light lunch.

"Would there be anything else for you today, sir?" the young waitress flashed a friendly smile.

"No, just a check, please." Al was in no particular hurry as he sat in the restaurant in silent refection. He simply didn't know where life might lead him next, but he was in no particular hurry to get there. He reflected back upon his life as he calmly waited for his check.

Dr Al Moses was born in Palestine in 1942 after his parents had fled from Germany, Hitler and the Holocaust in 1939. His family immigrated to the United States when Al was 10 years old. He learned English at his public high school in Williamsburg section of Brooklyn. After completing his undergraduate work at City College, Al went to medical school in Rome. It was a lot easier to get into school in Italy, than it would have been to get into a US Medical School. It was also a lot cheaper.

For the first fifteen years of his medical career he was known as Dr Moses. For the next fifteen years he was referred to as Dr Al Moses, and for the last dozen or so years he was simply Dr Al, or even just Al. Things were certainly less formal than ever. But he needed to go with the flow to keep his clientele. Over the years more and more female practitioners were entering the world of medicine and the OB/GYN specialty was particularly vulnerable to the trend of same gender election by patients. However Al's practice was not suffering from defections to female practitioners and this was evident by the age group of his clients. They seemed to be getting younger and younger, meaning that he was getting his fair share of the emerging market. Al believed that part of this was keeping up with the times and part of it was that he thought of the women who came to his practice as customers or clients rather than as patients or cases. He thought of them as healthy women with certain specialized needs. Unlike many of his professional colleagues, Al did not presuppose that he had all of the answers to those needs. Rather he decided that he would listen to the articulation of those needs, provide immediate assistance where possible and practical, and seek out answers for those needs that could not be immediately addressed. Al was an OB/GYN who did most of his work from the neck up.

Oddly Al never married. He truly loved women, in general, and had loved one particular woman for the better part of 25 years. However he never married, Anne … Dr. Anne, his former business partner … Dr Anne Mohr. Anne passed away seventeen years earlier from an aggressive case of breast cancer. There were many reasons why Al and Anne never married, but never a day went by that he didn't think about her, and pray for her spirit. When he went home at night, he spoke to her in the bedroom they once shared. Only one voice could be heard on this earth, but Al knew that it was a two-way discourse. And he knew that Anne took their shared secret to the grave with her, even though they now still discussed it occasionally in the privacy of Dr Al's bedroom.

Since Anne had died Moses had had an occasional female companion, but he never found any of them to be interesting enough to have an enduring relationship.

Recently one young lady came into his office concerned that she might be experiencing symptoms of menopause at a very early age. He was able to explain to her that POF (Premature Ovarian Failure) was probably not occurring because her estradiol levels weren't low and her FSH (Follicle Stimulating Hormone) levels weren't too high. However if he had more information about his patient, Maria Cardoza, he might have been able to help her more. He had taken a personal liking to Maria, because she reminded him physically of a young Anne Mohr. Maria had been coming to him for periodic check-ups for about three or four years, and he marveled at how she always seemed to be so serene. She was a very intelligent young woman, with an important executive job, and was probably too busy to think about a husband or a family. But when he saw her most recently, she seemed more distant, somewhat pensive and even a little sad. He wished he knew more so he could have helped.

Dr Al Moses enjoyed his work with his Park Avenue clientele and was not ready to retire. He had cut back on his hours a bit and was careful not to add many new patients even as others moved away from his practice. Dr Al realized that if he retired tomorrow, he would have more money than he would have time left to spend it. He had no close family members to whom he felt he should leave an inheritance, and he was somewhat skeptical of many of the charitable organizations that often solicited his support.

Moses' musings were interrupted as his waitress returned with the check. He quickly added a tip and signed his name and room number to the bill and slowly made his way out of the restaurant and back into the lobby, where he leisurely browsed through the shop and bought nothing before taking the elevator back up to his room.

When he got back to his room, he lay down on the bed once again and exhaled deeply. In spite of all of the traveling, and all of the ongoing interaction with interesting patients, and all of the reading and personal research that he had conducted, Al had recently admitted to himself that he was "lonely." The loneliness made him feel silly and embarrassed and helpless. The helplessness made him feel depressed. He was too depressed to talk about his depression. Maybe his friend, Stephen, could help.

****

Josh Struben's flight from New York had already landed at Heathrow Airport and his car service was whisking him into the city. He was talking non-stop on his cell phone. His first call was to his office. Then he called his parents at their London home and now he was calling Gina Alvarez, who had arrived in London a day earlier.

"Hey Gina, how did the concert go?"

"It was fabulous…..a great start to the tour. The people in London really know how to rock. So when do I get to see you in the flesh?

"I'm in London. We just landed. I'm having dinner with my mother. You told me that you would be tied up this evening."

"I'll be free by 10 PM."

Josh Struben surprised people when he told them that his mother was the famous singer/actress Danielle. Most people knew Danielle by her first name only, and occasionally by her full stage name of Danielle Dubonet, but rarely by her married name of Danielle Struben.

Therefore connections were rarely made to his somewhat famous and now somewhat reclusive mother.

However Josh remembered the frenetic days of his early childhood, sometimes being whisked from one city to another while his mother made concert appearances, and toiled long hours at recording studios. There were always lots of people around. Young Josh and his even younger brother, Adam, seemed to tolerate the chaotic pace much better than their mother. But when Dad was in town with them everything slowed down and everyone including Mom was happy. However, "in town" could be any town or city, because the Struben family was constantly on the go. Although he was born in New York City, Josh had grown up as a citizen of the world at large, having lived for a year or more in seven different countries, including France, England, Germany, and Switzerland in Europe, Canada and the United States in North America, and also in Hong Kong, China. He was fluent in the native language of every country in which he had lived, with the exception of China.

Now Josh's business career was in full bloom. Always an excellent student, Josh had completed secondary school at the age of sixteen and completed his undergraduate work in the USA just prior to his twentieth birthday. While working as a sales assistant at the elusive hedge fund known as Cromwell Parsons Resources, (CPR) he started his graduate degree in Mathematics. He never completed his graduate degree because the "math didn't work." The time spent learning anything new in mathematics was nowhere near the value of his time spent at his job. Although he had started work as a sales assistant, his technical analysis of certain complex sets of financial variables had allowed the firm to prosper. Josh got several offers from other firms, but the hedge fund owners in London were savvy enough to understand the value of his counsel and a seven figure bonus was awarded to Josh at the ripe old age of 23. A multi-million pound bonus was awarded to Josh at the age of 24 and an even larger bonus kept him in at Cromwell Parsons through his 27th birthday.

Things were going well for Josh. He was making money at an electric pace!!! He was partying at all hours of the day and night, and he was making new friends all the time. Unlike his mother he reveled in the velocity of life and didn't shy away from the bright lights when they shone nearby. His current romantic companion was Gina Alvarez, the super-hot lead singer of the female rock group the "Lay D's."

Josh and Gina had their picture plastered all over the Internet when a stalker had posted topless beach photos taken with a zoom lens off the remote Caribbean Island of Guadeloupe. The verbiage that attended the photo described Josh as "Gina Alvarez's Mega-Millionaire Financial Hotshot Hunk, the son of singer/actress, Danielle." His "hedgie buddies," were constantly busting his chops about this photo and began calling him Mr. Alvarez.

Truthfully, Josh was somewhat smitten by Gina. She was every bit as hot as her publicists said she was. Besides having four consecutive billboard smashes with the "Lay D's," Gina was the subject of multiple tabloid tales and was considered a great catch for any talk show that could get ten minutes or her time. She was beautiful, intelligent and oh sooooo sexy! At 22 years of age, she was considered more "sex kitten" than "seductress," more "pop idol" than "celebrity," more "bling" than "platinum," and more "toxic" than "tonic." A liaison with Gina was not fulfilling; it was draining. It was not complimentary; it was comprehensive. It was not so much fun, as it was entertainment. And in an uncanny way it was not as much an adventure as it was an addiction. Josh was along for the wild ride and was willing to hang on for dear life.

"I'll drop my mother off and meet you. Where do you want to meet?"

"I'm staying at The Four Seasons in Mayfair. I'll leave a room key for you at the front desk of the hotel."

Chapter 2: *Dinner in London*

"Hello Al. How was your flight from New York?"

"Uneventful, Stephen," Al answered. "But, you know, those are always the best kind."

As Stephen Struben stood up to greet his old friend, Dr. Al Moses, a younger man stood with him. Maksym Tkachuk was twenty years younger than both Struben and Moses, but all three men looked to be nearly the same age. Struben and Moses kept themselves in good physical shape, but Tkachuk paid no attention to fitness. And although Moses was physically fit, if a bit pudgy, he was not blessed with the native good looks of Stephen Struben. About 5' 10" inches tall and balding, Moses could easily get lost in a crowd of three.

"Glad to hear that, my friend," said Stephen as he vigorously pumped Moses' hand. "Al, I'd like you to meet Max Tkachuk. Al…Max; Max….Al"

The three men sat back down at the table of the posh restaurant in the Mayfair section of London, near the US Embassy. It was a pleasant autumn evening, and normally Al and Stephen would have gradually updated each other on their views of the world at a leisurely pace. This night was a little different in that Max Tkachuk was at dinner with them and had only one purpose in mind. Shortly after a wine list selection was made, Al turned to Max and inquired about his work.

"Stephen has told me a lot about your fascinating business career, Mr. Tkachuk." It was meant to be a patronizing statement, but still it was delivered in a manner that seemed like an effort to connect the well-dressed physician, with the nouveau-riche entrepreneur.

Maksym Tkachuk was born in 1962 in the Eastern Ukraine, when it was under Soviet rule. His grandparents and his parents hated everything Russian and admired many things about the USA. They all looked to Maksym or Max, as he was called to be the answer to their many years of prayer. They hoped that the world their protégée would inherit would be one of freedom and prosperity. His success would ensure that a long line of Tkachuk offspring would happily inhabit the vast regions of the earth.

Max had learned an awful lot at an early age and soon after the Ukraine's Declaration of State Sovereignty, on July 16th 1990, Max was able to secure a student visa to study in the United States. Max embraced two raging phenomena of the 1990s, entrepreneurism and the IT, Information Technology, Revolution.

Max honed his skills as a programmer working part time for several different IT companies, until the late nineties, when it became apparent with the run up to the Y2K scare that he could command top dollar for his programming skills if he formed his own company. Max hired other programmers, including many fellow Ukrainians. Before long his company had twenty programmers and he was billing his US client companies more than $3 Million dollars. To his surprise and delight, his company elicited buyout interest from a growing Indian company, that was also doing IT business in the US and Max quickly sold his company for $5 Million dollars cash!

Max, at first, thought that he had made a phenomenal deal. He later learned that he could have sold his company for a much higher multiple, given the skill set of his programmers, and the pedigree of his clientele.

By the day of his fortieth birthday in 2002, Max had started a new IT firm, which he named, Apakoh, which translated to Dragon in English, and was now dubbed a "serial entrepreneur." While working on an outsourced project for the German conglomerate, STRX, Max discovered that the industry most in need of IT renovation was Healthcare. Unlike the automotive industry, or the financial services industry, healthcare was completely underserved by IT. There was almost no electronic communication between healthcare providers and their patients and very limited communication between doctors, hospitals, labs and pharmacies. Patients were still entering their medical histories on clipboards that were later transcribed by office staff, and a large percentage of physicians were growing frustrated with the lack of timely information needed to treat their clientele. It was a mess. Max believed that this was the opportunity he had been searching for.

"Thank you. I'm honored that you find my career interesting."

"Very much so… I have always been intrigued by the role that entrepreneurs play in the development of industries. I'm just a semi-retired physician, with a modest investment portfolio. I know very little about business, other than what my investment advisor tells me," said Dr Al.

"Fair enough," Max replied, "but at least you have an investment advisor to guide you through your decisions. I don't have a medical advisor."

"What do you mean?"

"I know very little about the medical profession, and the more I speak to different doctors, the more confused I get. I don't have a healthcare advisor to guide me through all of my medical data, the way your investment guy helps you with your financial portfolio."

Al Moses listened but didn't comment. He wondered why Stephen found Tkachuk so interesting. Tkachuk wore a cheap suit that appeared to be a size too small. His shoes were poorly shined, but he wore a Patek Philippe watch. He was a man of contrasts.

"I agree the medical field can be a bit confusing," Stephen piped in. "I have difficulty staying up with everything also. There are many things to think about. Every couple of months I read about some new medical breakthrough that contradicts the old way of doing things and suggests a brand new approach.

"Take this whole notion of healthy red wines for example. In fact this bottle of Bordeaux that our waiter is about to pour for us contains the miracle elixir, Resveratrol."

Struben's tone was not cynical but it was intended to recognize an overstatement. He stopped for a glance at the label the waiter held in front of him. He nodded his assent to the selection and paused a few seconds as the waiter opened and decanted the bottle at Stephen's request.

"Resveratrol comes from the skin of the red grape and there are those that believe that it has significant anti-aging agents, and that it even reduces the chance of getting breast cancer. Some believe it kills cancer cells, controls cholesterol, promotes better sleep habits and reduces the risk of blood clots."

"If it does all those great things, our problems are solved," smirked Dr Al.

"Well there is some convincing evidence in support of the positive impacts of Resveratrol. At STRX we were doing research on this as far back as the early 1990s. Recently there have been a number of trials with very encouraging results. Of course, my wife, Danielle, is always kidding me about the 'French Paradox.'"

"What's that?" asked Max

"My wife is a native of France. The French eat the richest foods imaginable and remain so thin. They eat all of these saturated animal fats and have about a third of the number of heart attacks as Americans and Brits….and they also have a very low cancer rate I might add. Some have attributed these findings to the French devotion to red wine. Go figure."

"Maybe Anne should have drunk a little more Bordeaux." Dr Al said wistfully.

"Anne Mohr was Al's partner." Stephen explained. She passed away from breast cancer. We all loved her…..especially, my wife, Danielle."

"Well let's switch to a happier topic," Al suggested. "Stephen tells me your company is working on the development of new software for electronic healthcare records?" His voice trailed up with the interrogatory.

"We've been working on it for several years now," Max began proudly. Tkachuk shifted his ample body forward as he spoke. While both Al and Stephen had gotten together for dinner to relax, Max had come to dinner to discuss his software.

"But I'll tell you what our biggest issue is. It certainly isn't anything technical. Coding, technical infrastructure, large file transfers…these are all issues that my team deals with routinely….never a problem. The real issue is the application itself. What do people want to see in their healthcare record?"

"Oh I can believe that. Doctors never know what they want, and they certainly don't do a good job of communicating with one another." Al said.

"You're correct in a sense, Dr Moses, but you've missed the real problem."

"What is that?"

"All of the current technology that is out there … the electronic medical records or EMR's … they're sometimes called electronic healthcare records or EHR's … all of these software packages are geared toward the problem you referenced, doctors talking to doctors, or doctors interfacing with institutions. That's *a* problem, but it's not *the real* problem."

"We're listening."

"The real problem is that doctors need to communicate with their patients. It's bad enough that they communicate so poorly with one another. It's much worse that they communicate so poorly with their patients. After all their patients are their customers.

"Through one of our customers, a company called ™Rhapsody Holdings[1], we've been working with a marketing group back in your neck of the woods, in New York City, that has done a lot of research on what people want when it comes to healthcare."

"And what did they have to say?" Al asked.

"Some of the answers won't surprise you. For example they want access to the best physicians and they want the access immediately. They don't want to wait for appointments. They also expect to spend more time with the doctor and less time wading through the office bureaucracy. Of course they want more affordable care. Everyone thinks healthcare is way too expensive. But the most important thing that people want is a little more subtle, although also not really surprising."

"What is it?"

"They want *transparency*." Max stopped for a second to let that sink in. But he was still leaning forward over his plate. Both Al and Stephen were sitting back in their chairs but were absorbing Max's words thoughtfully.

The waiter took advantage of the pause and asked if he could tell them about the specials for the evening. After short discussion about a couple of the entrees, selections were made. As the waiter ambled back to the kitchen, Max took up the discussion once again

"This whole idea of *transparency* is simply the notion that the patients want in on the discussion. They don't want doctors to make decisions about their healthcare without their own input. And they also want to know a lot more about their available options for treatment.

"There seems to be this sentiment that a lot of physicians have a biased predisposition towards the type of treatment their patients should receive. If you see an orthopedic surgeon about pain, he will invariably see a surgical solution. It's not that he won't recommend physical therapy or medications or whatever other treatments that may be appropriate. But he will also recommend that you go to other specialists to pursue those options. If you end up back with the orthopedic surgeon, he will eventually operate. Patients want much more than this. First of all they want to be treated like people, not like

---

[1] *Rhapsody Holdings* is a trademark of Rhapsody Holdings, LLC and Rhapsody Holdings, Inc.

patients. Secondly they want to be able to better understand what all of their options are"

"Some of what you say may be true, Mr. Tkachuk, but in defense of my profession, most of the doctors I know, will always do what's right for their patient, not what's best for their practice," said Al.

"With all due respect, Dr. Moses, I am actually getting at something more basic. Do doctors always *know* what's best for their patients?"

Moses sat back and chuckled lightly to take the edge off the exchange before replying. "Yes. Well I think I understand what you're getting at. So what does this have to do with your medical record software? And how is this related to ... what did you call it *transparency*?"

"The software that we have been creating is much more consumer oriented. It is also much more comprehensive than the EMR's that are in the market place today. It includes wellness and fitness data in addition to the traditional healthcare data."

The conversation between Al Moses and Max Tkachuk was animated but not heated. They shared a common friend in Stephen Struben, but Moses and Tkachuk had more in common with one another than they did with their friend Struben. Both Tkachuk and Moses were unmarried and successful professionals. By contrast, Struben had been married for more than thirty years, and had two successful sons already embarking on their own careers. He considered himself, a semi-retired family man, who was ready to savor the fruits of his business accomplishments. Still he enjoyed being the catalyst for the meaningful interaction of other professionals.

Before long the entrees were served and the conversation picked up again a second bottle of Bordeaux was decanted.

"Let's go back to the discussion of the healthcare records for a minute or two," said Stephen. "To put some things in perspective, let me tell you why I thought it might be useful for you two to meet each other. Max, I have known Al since before you were born. Al and I went to high school together and have been friends ever since. I can assure you that throughout his career as a physician, he has always treated the women who come to his OB/GYN practice, as people first and patients secondly.

"And Al, let me tell you that Max, here, is the kind of entrepreneur that can bring many of your insights about treating the whole person to the forefront. Max and I met through some business colleagues at my company, STRX, and I know that they are pretty impressed with Max and his team.

"So anyway, to pick up where we were before, Max, you were explaining to us how your software deals with this issue of *transparency*."

"Yes Stephen. As I was saying, people want to have greater control of their own healthcare. What I mean by *transparency* is that patients want to see what the doctors see and be able to understand it. It is *their* health, and *their* healthcare. It should also be *their own* healthcare record. That is why the software that we are creating is not an EMR or an EHR that is used solely by interacting clinicians, it is PHR, or Personalized Healthcare Record that is owned by the person, not the clinician or institution."

"Our PHR is capable of receiving and storing lab tests, MRI's, X-rays EKG outputs...in fact, just about everything you can imagine. It's also capable of storing all of a person's historical medical data as well. Therefore your patient will in essence *own* her own healthcare. She will be able to view her records wherever she goes."

"Isn't this a little elaborate for a lay person? Even amongst physicians, there is a certification process for reading certain medical data. Are you telling me that the patients are capable of reading and interpreting their own MRI data, as well as a radiologist?"

"No. Of course not ... nothing like that. What we are saying is they will *own* and store this data, and that this data can then be sent to specialists of their choice. Then the clinician of choice can use this data, and add to it, to deliver the appropriate care for their client."

"Well that would undoubtedly broaden the conversation between the physician and his patient, and probably help the patient understand her own treatment."

"Exactly, and that is what we mean by *transparency*. In fact, to be precise, it is *portable transparency*. This is what the client truly wants. And that is why we are referring to our PHR as the *HealthPort*. We are developing this in conjunction with an emerging health and wellness group, who actually came up with the name *HealthPort*. We think that our healthcare clients will view their *HealthPort* in much the same way as they view their passport, as something that is essential to them when they travel around the world."

"Is this that Rhapsody Holdings group that you mentioned before?" Al inquired.

"Yes, it is."

"Okay, let's go back to this *HealthPort* thing. So how comprehensive is this *HealthPort*? What does it put at the patient's disposal that I don't capture now on my EMR at the office?"

"A lot....but first let's clear up this notion of *patient*. That word suggests remedial healthcare. It connotes illness. If we move away from the idea of *patient* to the concept of *healthcare client*, you'll get a better idea of the strength of our *HealthPort*. To repeat what Stephen said earlier, I know that you recognize the value of treating your client holistically and from what Stephen has told me about you, I know that you spend as much time talking to your clients as you do examining them. That's terrific. What our *HealthPort* will do is make those conversations much more meaningful.

"So in addition to the data that you have on your EMR, our *HealthPort* will include fitness and wellness data, dental records, personal grooming and beauty data, and much more. All of your prescription data will be there as well, whether it's for contact lenses or anticoagulants. Our developers have been dealing with doctors and practitioners on a worldwide basis to gather data and create interactive templates."

Even as he spoke, Max could feel the need for a *HealthPort* in his own life. He didn't know a dentist in town and he didn't have his dental records available. His teeth were beginning to bother him again, and he thought that it might be a good idea to pick up the pace of his alcoholic consumption, if he hoped to enjoy his dinner. He kept his problem to himself.

"Well it all sounds quite exciting, Mr. Tkachuk. I'd love to learn more."

"When you are back to NY, I can have someone give you a demo, if you'd like."

"That would be terrific." They started talking about the food and finished their meal at an unhurried pace. The plush surroundings of the restaurant helped Al and Stephen relax even more. But Max was still restless. He knew that the two friends wanted to spend at least a little time alone together and his tooth hurt anyway. Although Max rarely passed up dessert, he did so on this evening. Explaining that he had an early meeting in the morning, he excused himself without offering to pick up the tab. Stephen and Al stood to say good night to Max and then relaxed back into their seats.

"Thanks for agreeing to meet with Max," Stephen said.

"No problem .... Not at all ... He's an interesting guy. He does seem to be all business though. Does he have a personal side to him?"

Stephen laughed. "Not that I have seen. He's a very driven young man."

"I can see that. But he doesn't seem to be that young. He had a little trouble getting out of his seat and he walked with a little bit of limp or at least a hitch, or something as he was leaving."

"Always the good doctor....worrying about other people's health." Stephen kidded Al. "For the record he's only 46, 20 years younger than us, but I would agree with you he looks much older or at least he looks like he could use a good vacation. From what I hear he's a workaholic. The guys at STRX like him a lot though. They think he's on to something. I think so too. You ought to have a look at his software when you get back. I'd be interested in your opinion," said Struben.

"I will. But promise me this, that you'll have your friend see a doctor for a checkup soon. He's way overweight and talks as though he is in pain of some sort."

"Will do... How about a cognac?"

"Sounds great..." The two friends were quiet for a bit, making small talk mostly while their cognac was served and then Dr Al inquired about Stephen's family?

"So how are Danielle and the boys doing?"

"Pretty well, I think Al. Danielle is happy that she is not pestered as much by the media as she used to be. But as you may know, our son, Josh is now the subject of some of the same nonsense that Danielle had to put up with for years. He has been seeing that lead singer of the Lay D's for the last couple of months and the paparazzi have been all over the two of them wherever they go."

"Ah yes, so I've heard ... the lovely Gina Alvarez. Like father, like son. Have you met her yet?" Al was curious about his friend's son's superstar girlfriend.

"No. I didn't even know who Gina Alvarez was until Danielle showed me something in the paper about the two of them. Who knows when or if I'll meet her? You know how those Hollywood romances are." Stephen said it with a smug sense of humor and an air of self-deprecation alluding to his own long lasting "Hollywood Romance."

Moses chortled into his snifter, more the influence of the cognac than the impact of Stephen's wry humor. "Well it's good to see that the Struben family is still extending its influence into the arts."

"Actually Josh is in town this weekend. He has been spending more time back in the US of late, but tonight he's having dinner with Danielle while we are having dinner here."

"Oh really … I hope I didn't keep you from having dinner with your son."

"No don't be silly. I invited you to dinner, Remember? Besides Josh is in and out of town all the time. He's hard to keep up with. Same is true of his younger brother. Adam is just the same. Always on the go. But I'll catch up with them next time," Stephen said.

Al listened but looked down at the table as Stephen spoke. He sometimes wished that he had family of his own to discuss but there wasn't much to talk about in that regard so he was content to experience this part of life somewhat vicariously through Stephen's family.

****

Meanwhile across town Danielle and Josh were finishing up dinner as well. Their evening had been lovely. Mother and son had reminisced about Josh's childhood. They talked about the many places they had lived and visited and Josh also seemed to have a renewed interest in his mother's career. He had asked her a few questions about how she had coped with all of the unwanted media attention and Danielle had explained away the nuisance as simply one of the known hazards of the professional limelight.

Now in her early fifties, Danielle had very definitive opinions about people as well, even though she most often kept these opinions to herself. She had always sort of watched the world unfold around her. Earlier in her life, before she began her singing career, she lived for a short time in San Francisco. She lived in a tiny studio apartment, and while she was attempting to get singing gigs in local pubs at night, she worked as a mime on Fisherman's Wharf. She sang in French and she struggled to master the English language. No one knew her then. She was just an Indian Princess Statue that stood perfectly still and watched as people stopped, stared and occasionally threw a few coins in her leather woven purse. Some of the other mimes would silently move and make silent emotional contact with the public, by gesturing and making contorted facial expressions. Danielle was content to be the beautiful and immovable Indian Princess. The silent princess learned a lot about people in that short time. Now, much later in life, the lessons learned by the Silent Indian Princess, allowed the middle-aged mother/singer/actress to reflect and ruminate on the many types of people who roamed the earth and to select those with whom she chose to spend her time.

Danielle had very little knowledge about what her son, Josh did for his firm, and they almost never talked about his work. But what others had told her was that Josh had latched on as an expert analyst to a group of these "Hedgie" people and was instrumental in their making hundreds of millions of pounds in profit. She also recognized that like his father, Josh was a "Pond Jumper," and spent as much time at the Hedge Fund's office in Greenwich Connecticut as he did in their London Headquarters. But she would let others have dinner with the Hedge Fund Heavy; she just wanted to have dinner with her 27-year-old son Josh. Besides, Josh had recently begun seeing a very popular young singer and Danielle wanted to hear all about her. She thought that it was somewhat interesting that Josh was dating a singer, when he never seemed all that interested in his mother's singing career. She guessed that Gina Alvarez had a lot more going for her than a healthy set of lungs.

During their dinner, Danielle had gently probed about Josh's relationship with Gina Alvarez. Josh was not effusive at all and more or less stuck to a discussion of what they were doing and where they had been. Still Danielle's mother's intuition told her that Josh was more than casually involved with the leading Lay D.

Josh had called their driver, so that they could leave the restaurant without a fuss. It was rare that celebrity stalkers bothered Danielle in recent years, but his mother was still a strikingly good-looking woman, capable of turning the heads of males, both young and old. As they walked down the steps from the restaurant to the limousine, they presented an interesting picture of a family with many creature comforts. Josh wore a tailored black pin striped Dolce & Gabbana suit, that accented his tall, fit physique and his mother wore an olive colored short sleeved Oscar de la Renta suit. Danielle still appreciated looking good when she was out in public.

The driver held the door open and Danielle got in while Josh slid in from the other side. If anyone had listened to them converse with one another they might not think they were mother and son. Josh spoke with a neutral English accent that reflected neither an American nor a British dialect. Danielle spoke English with an evident French inflection. She still could not pronounce the letter "h" especially when it began a word, so that "hotel" sounded like 'otel. And "happy" came out of her mouth as 'appy. She also pronounced many of her short "I" sounds like long "ee" sounds so that the words "sit" and "little" sounded much like *seet* and *leetle*.

"Thank you for *deenner*, Josh. *Eet's* so nice to spend a few hours alone *weeth* you. *Eet* doesn't '*appen* too often anymore."

"Yes it was very nice, Mom. I enjoyed it too." Josh wondered about his mother. She talked very little about herself and only briefly about his father, who she said, was having dinner with Dr Moses. Although she smiled a lot throughout dinner Josh could sense that something was not right. He just couldn't seem to put his finger on what it was, and he didn't know how to ask.

Danielle was happy to have had a nice evening with her son, but she was not ready to tell him about her breast cancer. She hadn't even told Stephen yet. She wanted to think about it some more. Danielle was also happy that Josh hadn't lost perspective in his highly publicized romance with Gina Alvarez. He still seemed to have a very levelheaded attitude about the whole thing. Of course what did she know, she was only his mother. She smiled, looked over to Josh and grabbed his hand and simply said, "the three men *een* my life, you and Adam and Stephen, all make me a very '*appy* woman."

Josh just smiled back and they rode back toward the family townhouse in silence. He walked his mother into the foyer and kissed her good night. Josh didn't head back to his own apartment but he asked the driver to take him to Mayfair to the Four Seasons Hotel on Park Lane.

There was an envelope with a key in it waiting for him at the front desk. He checked the suite number and took the elevator up to the top floor.

****

Al and Stephen were getting up from the dinner table and walking toward the door, when a familiar and pretty face looked up at Al from a nearby table. There was brief eye contact and a lingering look of recognition on the face of the pretty young dark-haired woman, as well as on the face of Dr Al. It wasn't until after Al had said good night to Stephen and was in a cab back to his hotel room that he was able to place the face. Sure that's who it was, he realized, Maria Cardoza, the young business woman, who was worried about premature ovarian failure and who for some reason reminded him of Anne. He felt a sudden sadness that was oddly accompanied by a wry smile. The mixed emotions made him a bit jumpy and he wished that he had recognized Maria earlier, so that he could have said hello to her in a social setting. He thought back to the quick view he had of the man she was dining with. He looked familiar also. Who was he? The glimpse he had caught of Maria's tablemate was only a profile, but a familiar one that he couldn't quite place.

The cab pulled up in front of Al's hotel. He made perfunctory greeting acknowledgements to the hotel staff and went directly to his room. He undressed quickly and then sat in his underwear on the side of his bed and started his conversation aloud with his long deceased partner, Anne. These one-way conversations were becoming more common of late. But tonight's conversation was relatively short.

"Good evening, Anne, my love. How are you?"

"That's nice. I had an interesting dinner with Stephen Struben."

"No she wasn't there. She was having dinner with Josh."

"I don't think so. Why do you ask?"

"They've been married for more than thirty years. I sincerely doubt that."

"No, he didn't talk much about her either … says he hasn't even met her yet."

"She's very popular alright but Josh is no dope. I've always felt that he inherited the best selections from the gene pools of Stephen and Danielle."

"You know who else I saw tonight?"

"How do you always guess these things right?"

"Yes that's true. I did tell you that she reminded me of you."

"It's not that simple. I can't tell you what it is. Anyway she was with a good-looking dark haired businessman. At least I think he was a businessman. He looked familiar."

"You're right. That's who it was. John Brady, the CEO of ICD! Why didn't I think of that? Maria had told me that she worked closely with the CEO. I've seen his picture in a lot of magazines. In fact I think he was in Forbes just last month."

"Oh, you can sometimes have such a nasty mouth, my love. You never even knew the man. Maria seems to like him anyway."

"Yes, my love. Actually I will be traveling to Asia in a couple of months."

"No just another exploration of one of the fine corners of the earth. I'm not sure whom I'll be going with."

"Okay, okay, you've been on this topic a lot lately. I'll see someone who can help before I leave. I promise. Good night my love. And tell Sarah I love her."

Dr Al Moses took a deep breath and settled into one side of the bed. He never slept near the middle. He closed his eyes and awaited dawn.

****

Gina could always sing, and she could always rock. She never knew her father, but she appreciated her mother's efforts at giving her an education. She was one of the few in her group to get her high school diploma on time, even if she eventually got it in the Detroit. Her career precluded her from pursuing a college education, but that could always come later. Her marks were always among the best in her class.

Gina was born in Puerto Rico, where her mother worked as a chambermaid at various resorts in different parts of the island. Gina's mother never disclosed much to her about her father, but Gina held the belief that her golden blonde tresses and blue eyes must have been the result of an ill-fated union between her mother and a foreigner that she met at one of the resorts. Sometimes when her mother would work overtime as a waitress, Gina would wait for her down near the club. She would sneak out along the beach and watch the beach parties, and listen to the bands that played on the beach. She would sing along with them and she knew that she had a lot of gusto to her voice. She also didn't need a microphone because there was no one nearby to listen. She just danced and sang to her own beat in her own little corner of the beach.

By the age of sixteen, Gina had the body of woman. She also had the desire of a young lady destined to be successful at a very early age.

Everything happened so quickly. She had a brief encounter with a record company talent scout who was vacationing at the Puerto Rican resort. (This kind of tryst was apparently in her family genes.) The talent scout actually found her singing voice more exciting than her youthful body and soon thereafter brought Gina and her mother to Detroit where she finished high school. While in Detroit, she took an IQ test and registered a genius score of 171. They discussed this astoundingly high score with Gina's mother and she retook the test two more times, scoring 164 and 171 once again.

The talent scout stayed interested in Gina and brought her to NYC, where she was matched up with two other talented young ladies and the Lay D's were formed. Gina became tired of singing songs written by others and for others. She began writing her own music and it was raw, edgy and unique. Demo tapes led quickly to production contracts and before long the Lay D's were an overnight sensation. The group was hot, but Gina was oh so hot! Then the heat exploded and Gina's music was everywhere and her picture adorned the covers of magazines all over the country and before long all over the world

****

Josh inserted the key and turned the handle on the door to the suite. He stepped in and he could hear Gina singing in the bathroom. She never sang her own songs when she was alone but she also never stopped singing. Josh was happy that Gina allowed him to hear her sing her own private renditions of Mick Jagger or Sly Stone, efforts she would never attempt on a public stage. Obviously she trusted him.

He opened the bathroom door and saw Gina, up to her neck in bubbles with a bottle of Don Perignon standing in an ice bucket next to the tub. The champagne must have been a gift for him, because Gina didn't drink alcohol.

As Josh stood in the doorway, Gina stood up covered with soapy bubbles, and stepped over the side of the tub and onto the floor. She stopped singing and stretched her arms open wide and moved toward Josh. She wrapped her naked wet body tightly around Josh's pin striped suit.

"Gina, sweetheart…." He started.

Gina stopped him by staring her big blue eyes into Josh face, first to his lips and then to his eyes. She raised her right index finger to her own lips in a classic sign for silence, and Josh merely stared down at

Gina. She giggled a little and then raised her hand to his neck tie and wrenched it left, right, left, right, left in a quick motion that loosened the knot but did not undo the bow entirely.

Gina turned up Josh's collar and slipped his silk tie over his head, and then put it around her own neck but didn't tighten it.

"Gina, darling," Josh started again. This time she didn't stop him with a finger to her lips, but rather she arrested his protest by putting both hands near his waistband and unzippering his pants.

With little further protest Gina quickly undressed Josh and marched him back to the bedroom. She pushed him back playfully on the bed, and straddled his shins just below his knees. She moved both her hands to his erect fifth appendage and began rubbing it left and right in her hands as though she were warming her hands in front of a fire.

"Careful, careful," Josh warned. Gina leaned forward and once again looked deeply into Josh's eyes. Then she sat back again and said, "I'm wearing the tie." With that she flipped around so that she was still straddling Josh's shins but was now facing away from him. With a slight backward adjustment she then proceeded to plunge Josh deeply inside her, while she clasped the wide end of his silk tie tightly down against her femininity and rocked out for an energetic couple of minutes before exploding in a shrieking orgasm. Josh must have orgasmed somewhere along the way because he was able to catch his breath shortly after Gina screamed and asked her, "Whatever happened to foreplay?"

Gina just stood up glistening, no longer from soap but from sweat, and asked in her best imitation British accent. "How was dinner with Mummy?" She didn't return to the topic of being a Mom herself. She was still awaiting an answer from her last conversation with Josh.

****

Maria Alvarez and John Brady, CEO of ICD, were ready for bed. They had booked separate rooms at the company's luxury guest house in London, but the few insiders, who worked closest with John, realized that Maria would never go to her own room. John was smart enough not to ever discuss this with anyone. Some people just knew what they knew.

Maria slept in the nude and John slept in his boxer shorts. Although they had dinner alone that evening, they still talked mostly about business. It was more usual for them to discuss more personal moments when they were truly alone, usually in bed. They were both tired from their flight across the Atlantic, which was followed by multiple meetings and their dinner alone together. They had both slept a few hours on the flight which was the only way they could have tackled the days' work but now all the bouncing about was taking its toll.

"When we were at dinner earlier tonight I saw my Gynecologist."

"That's interesting. Why didn't you say something before?"

"He and another man were leaving when I spotted them. Besides, what was I going to say? 'Hi Dr Al. Meet my boss John Brady, who also happens to be my lover.' It's awkward."

"Why wouldn't you just leave it at, 'Meet my boss, John Brady?'"

"Because I like Dr. Al... He's very personable and I wouldn't want to be deceptive."

"Okay, then why not: 'Meet John Brady, my lover."

"People don't say those things. Besides, if I said that, you would have been absolutely pissed off. And I don't think that your wife, Maureen would appreciate such disclosures."

"I guess you're right about that," John said as he made an amorous approach by putting his hand near the top of Maria's left thigh.

"John, I'm a bit tired. Save it for the morning. Let's get some sleep."

"Whatever you say." John took his hand off her leg and tucked it up under his own pillow. He was happy that he at least made the move. He wasn't really in the mood for sex either, but he wanted it to be her choice. Besides, that usually meant better sex in the morning.

****

Maksym Tkachuk had left dinner with Stephen Struben and Al Moses early enough that he thought he would walk back to his hotel rather than take a cab. He gave himself several reasons that this decision seemed to make sense. His toothache was now quite severe and he wanted some fresh air so that he could think clearly about what to do about that problem. He also wanted to develop a game plan to deal with the diabetes issue that the NYC doctor had told him about. He was staying in a cheaper hotel that he had booked through one of the online travel sites, but it wasn't too far from the north end of the

Park, altogether about a twenty-five block walk. He thought the exercise would do him some good. But the real reason that Max was walking was that he didn't have anything else to do that evening and he was too cheap to pay for the cab.

When Max got to the hotel, he took the elevator up to his room, and flopped down on the bed fully clothed, and sweating profusely, but it was an odd cold kind of sweat. He thought about taking a shower, something that he did not do on a daily basis.

The pain came suddenly, first like a fist tightening in his chest. It spread quickly to his shoulders arms and legs. His chest felt first like it was on fire and then like an elephant was perched on top of it. Cognition came quickly to Max. He was having a massive heart attack! He was going to die! This *can't* be, his mind screamed. I'm Ukrainian. I should live to be one hundred or at least ninety-five! But it certainly *was* to be. The frightening cognition gave way to an unconscious temporary peaceful semi-awareness that finally gave way to death. Presently all that was left of Maksym Tkachuk was his cold sweaty flesh and his hot flashy software.

****

As midnight approached in the city of London, England, it was cocktail hour back on the North Shore of Long Island.

Maureen Brady, John's wife, had just finished reading the third novel she had started in less than two weeks. She enjoyed all kinds of reading and had even considered joining a book club where people discussed what they had read. The idea was a little too proletarian for her lot in life, so she ignored the impulse and just kept much of her literary insights to herself.

Maureen had hoped that John would call her earlier in the day, but realized it was close to midnight in London and the likelihood of a call after dinner was remote. John hadn't said much about the trip. He rarely did so in the last couple of years. All she knew was that the trip entailed a quick review of European operations and that he would be back in New York within three days. Still she wished he would call.

Maureen decided to have her dinner out on the back portico, and Jeannine, the family cook, would soon serve it to her. As she began sipping her first cosmopolitan she thought for a second and realized it was Monday evening. There was nothing special about the days of the week for Maureen lately, and she was often confused enough after a couple of cosmos to forget what day it was altogether. It was easier to keep track of the days during the summer when she left midday on Thursdays for their place in Southampton, and usually returned to their Kings Point home on the North Shore on Mondays. That schedule at least gave a little rhythm to her life.

This autumn evening still had the warmth of summer, and that's why she chose to have dinner out back. The back portico to the family home was a three level, one thousand, eight hundred square foot, stone floored work of art. Three stone steps separated each level, and evergreen trees lined the bottom level. A small paver style pathway led from the evergreens to the large vegetable garden that was cared for by the landscaping staff. Beyond the garden were the pool, the athletic changing rooms and the tennis court. Five years earlier all of these facilities had been used by Maureen's family and her children's friends. However after Mark and Megan went off to college, the sports areas became adjuncts to the home. They were opened in the spring and closed in the fall and rarely used in between. During the months of July and August, everyone simply spent more time in the Hamptons.

The portico was a little different. About two thirds of the floor space of the portico was open air space and about a third of the space was semi-enclosed and roofed. Both the enclosed area and the open area had eating tables for eight, and each had its own bar area as well, so it was the perfect place for parties. This was the area Maureen sat in as she began her personal cocktail hour.

By the time she was finishing her second cosmo, Maureen was deep into reflection about her family. She loved her children very much and she loved John also. But times were changing. As John kept getting more involved in his business life, Maureen was losing some interest in their personal relationship. The excitement wasn't there as it once had been.

She also worried about her son, Kenneth. While Mark and Megan were enjoying college life, her youngest child was more enigmatic. She reached into her handbag and pulled out a piece of paper that Kenneth had given her a week earlier. She had simply inquired about what John and Kenneth had been discussing on the golf course earlier in the day.

Kenneth's real time, one word answer, had been, "golf." But later that evening he gave her the piece of paper containing his poetic response to her inquiry. It was entitled "Son to Father Rejoinder."

"Don't just stand there. Do something," you say.
Well tell me "why," and I just may.
For I have no reason, not to do,
The things that you might ask me to.

But let me ask you quite sincerely,
"Why is action held so dearly?"
Could it be you just don't know?
And it's best to just keep on the go?

Well ponder this now, if you will
Even if its meaning's nil
Is it right for every man,
To work out his own master plan?

A rationale for his ineffectivity
Seems to be his continuous activity
But you may be right. So I chose to write,
These few words, this moment's delight.

Maureen tucked the poem back in her purse. She wondered if John would ever truly accept Kenneth for the true artist that he was. And she also wondered whether or not Kenneth could be as open with John as he was with her. For that matter would Kenneth ever truly open up to her entirely? Would Kenneth eventually tell her about Rickie? She felt certain that if John knew about Rickie and Kenneth, he would fire Rickie in a moment. But maybe she would never find out.

Soon Jeannine brought out a two-course dinner. The first course was a fresh Caesar salad and the second was a Beef Wellington. Dinner was accompanied by a bottle of California merlot. Maureen finished half of the salad and sampled the entrée. She drained about three quarters of the bottle of merlot and retired to her bedroom still without a call from her husband.

Chapter 3: *Decisions, Decisions, Decisions*

Back in his New York office, John Brady was well aware of the fact that his very stature as an international business leader was dependant on decisions he would make within the next two to three weeks at Integrated Computer Devices (ICD). He was also aware that the decisions would not be easy ones. They never were.

Many times economic melt downs seemed to be more connected to the general economic outlook and confidence of the ultimate consumers than to the underlying business plan fundamentals. However any business plan that did not take into consideration the confidence in its market's consumers was by definition a flawed plan. In addition, the Presidential campaigns in the US were coming down the home stretch just at the time when the banking system was going haywire.

Forty-eight year old JB walked briskly out of his office into the adjoining office of his assistant, Maria Cordoza.

"Maria, make sure that we have all hands on deck for the in house financial prep meeting. What we tell those bastards next Tuesday will have a major impact on the price of our stock. *How* we tell them will have an even bigger impact"

"Besides you, who do we want to talk on the conference call?" She asked.

"Let's get Neal Farmer to cover the specific financial guidance, and Izzy Fleckenstein can cover merger related performance issues in the Q&A. The upcoming forecast will be critical and we should have Monroe and Morgan ready to answer anything that might come up along those lines. Our Asian performance is over the top, so I don't think we will get many probes there, but we need to have Hasegawa prepared just in case." Brady paced back and forth while he spoke.

"Someone needs to prepare my opening remarks. And Maria, I suggest that you work with Rickie Van Dorfan on those comments, personally. Van Dorfan is a prissy little kid but he writes well. You can get all the data you need from Farmer and Fleckenstein.

"Okay, John, I'll start chasing people down and give you an update later in the afternoon."

Maria found it fascinating how John could be so decisive in his business life and so indecisive in his private life. Originally JB was going to be in Boston for the weekend with his family. Then he changed his mind and was going to blow that off and work in the city on Saturday. Now he was back to the original plan of going to Boston with his family. At times it made life with the CEO of ICD a bit trying.

Maria was well aware that John was married with a family and that he had no intentions of leaving Maureen. She was content sharing John. What she didn't like was when John stewed over personal issues in his family, and when he dragged those problems into the office. Maria felt that she had a "time share" portion of John's life, and when she was there with him she didn't want to see anyone else's baggage still in the room. She didn't mind sharing him with business colleagues. That was part of the deal. She just didn't like it when Maureen and her kids entered the equation. They never discussed it, but Maria knew when something was wrong. She had a sixth sense that John was having family issues and that they were driving him a little crazy.

John walked out of Maria's office and back toward his own. He was annoyed that Maureen had made such a big deal out of nothing the night before. He acknowledged that they had previously made plans to take Kenneth up to see Mark and Megan in Boston for the weekend, but the recent turmoil in the office required that he work on Saturday. He had appointments all week long and he needed some additional time to sort out his approach to the financial community the following week. ICD was about to significantly soften the bullish forecast of the previous quarter. John went back and forth on the Boston trip issue with Maureen. Finally he gave in and agreed to go to Boston after all. The debate with his wife had taken place over several cocktails and a couple of glasses of wine. He didn't like drinking during the week, but he was reluctant to let Maureen drink alone.

He had not returned either of Maureen's two calls earlier in the day, but his secretary, Alice, relayed the fact that "Mrs. Brady sounded very cheerful. She was heading out to a luncheon with some of the ladies from the club and said that she would see you this evening."

The third call from home could not be ignored. It didn't come from Maureen. It came from Jeannine, the family cook.

****

The afternoon had started out pleasantly enough for Maureen. John's driver, Fernando, had driven her to meet three other ladies for lunch at the club. Ostensibly the purpose of the luncheon was to discuss the leukemia fundraiser that would be held at the club the following month. The four women were co-chairs of the event, but, in fact, others including the staffs of their husbands' companies were doing most of the work.

None of the four women had ever held a salaried job, and each of them had come from family money before marrying their respective husbands. Maureen enjoyed the company of these women, who shared a common heritage of sorts. But she most enjoyed the fact that she was the youngest and prettiest of the group and the fact that that none of the women were opposed to the idea of having a cocktail or three over lunch.

Around 2:30 in the afternoon, Fernando picked her up at the club and drove her home. Maureen was more than a little tipsy, but she was pleased with herself. She had stuck to her guns the night before and John had finally agreed to go with her to New England for the weekend. She had listened with casual interest to the gossip of her luncheon companions and their hints of infidelity either on their own part or on the part of their husbands. She was happy that she was "above" that kind of thing. She had neither need nor desire to cheat on John and she was certain that he felt the same way. Still she wanted much more of his time and she wanted him to be more involved in her life. All of this she believed would come relatively soon, when he retired. For the time being it was important to keep herself fit and attractive for John so that he would be proud to call her his wife.

When they arrived back at the Brady estate, Fernando helped Maureen out of the back of the car and into the front of the house. Cara, the maid, took Maureen's linen jacket and whisked it away to be hung up in one of the many closets in the changing area of the master bedroom. Mrs. Brady was still wearing a linen skirt and a tight-fitting light white lace blouse.

Maureen continued walking through the double-storied foyer and hallway of the main floor, and out through the kitchen, past the massive family room where she kicked off her heels and continued barefoot outback onto the portico. It was her favorite part of the house. Except for Cara and Jeannine, no one was inside the house. No one was on the portico and the grounds keeping staff was working out beyond the pool area. Maureen could hear the low level hum of the power leaf-blowing machines in the distance beyond her view. The setting was very private. She didn't care much what the staff thought or did, as long as they left her alone.

Maureen hadn't heard from John but she thought that he might be home late because he had so much work to do. It was a sunny day and still somewhat warm, but Maureen was feeling light and loose, and almost carefree. Mrs. Brady decided that she would have one more cocktail and then go up to her bedroom for a late afternoon nap before sprucing up a bit for John's return from the office. She even felt sexy. Maybe she and John could get over their differences from the night before with an amorous interlude that would set the stage for a nice weekend. The thought of it made her smile and put a skip in her step as she kept walking down the portico steps to the bar on the bottom level.

Maureen went behind the bar and made herself a cosmopolitan, something she had only recently learned to do. In the past there was always the household help to do this. Maureen demonstrated her independence by mixing her own concoction. She then set the outdoor stereo on low and took the barrette out of her black hair. She shook her head to purposely loosen her locks. She also reached behind her back an undid the button at the top of her skirt and lowered the back zipper about two inches, at the same time pulling the shirt tail of her lace blouse from inside the skirt, making herself as comfortable as possible. Maureen hummed along with the music and uncharacteristically swung her hips back and forth in an exaggerated fashion, amusing no one but herself, but enjoying the moment nonetheless.

She filled the martini glass to the brim with her cosmopolitan and held it out daintily in front of her as she proceeded toward the stone steps leading up to the enclosed portion of the portico. That's when everything went wrong.

Maureen caught her stocking-covered big toe on a tiny rock projection on the stone floor. Normally this would have resulted in a torn stocking at worst, but in an effort to avoid spilling her cosmopolitan, she lost her balance completely and began to fall hard and fast, face down into the stone steps. She tried to catch herself with her left hand but missed the top step and plunged face first into the edge of that same top stone step. It hit Maureen about an inch below her left eye and gashed her face open in a bloody uproar. Her glass shattered, and a shard of glass lacerated the back side of her right hand. As her head hit the lip of the top step, her left breast and body slammed into the lip of the third step painfully pinching her breast and even more painfully cracking a rib near the sternum and making her breathing extremely painful.

Maureen gave a staccato scream as she moved her left hand to the gash below her left eye. She fainted as she pulled her hand down and saw it covered in blood.

****

John Brady listened to Jeannine as he tried to grasp the cause as well as the severity of his wife's calamity. His heart was beating rapidly and he tried hard to focus on what Jeannine was saying:

"It's bad Mr. Brady. No one saw it happen. I was in the kitchen and I heard her yell. It was very bloody. Her eye looks very bad. There is lots of blood on her face. She was unconscious at first but she is awake now. Cara is with her while I am calling you." Jeannine was weeping while she was talking. JB had never heard Jeannine cry. That alone made him queasy. "It looks like a very bad wound. I don't know. We called the ambulance, because we didn't know what to do. Then I called you. Wait, they are here now."

"Jeannine, listen to me. Let me talk to Maureen? Bring the phone over to Mrs. Brady?"

JB did not get a response. In the confusion with the arrival of the ambulance, Jeannine was in a state of panic, and wasn't terribly coherent in her explanations to JB or her response to the EMS crew that was inquiring about what happened.

"Jeannine, Jeannine, damn it," JB shouted into the phone.

Jeannine was talking to the EMS driver who said that he would take Maureen to the hospital in Great Neck 20 minutes away. Maureen was conscious but scared and crying.

Cara now came out on the portico also and heard JB shouting on the phone. She picked up the wireless extension and brought it over to Maureen who was lying flat on the portico with an iced paper bandage pressed against her face. Her left eye was swollen shut. Before giving the phone to Maureen, Cara spoke into it.

"Mr. Brady. This is Cara. I'm here with Mrs. Brady. The ambulance is getting her ready to go to the hospital. Do you want to talk to her first?"

"Christ Cara. Of course I want to talk to her. Put Maureen on the phone," he commanded. "Maureen, Maureen."

"Oh John, Help me please. Come home and help me." John was immediately alarmed by the tone of his wife's voice, and by her slurred speech. He still wasn't sure what happened, but he was very upset by the sound of her voice. She began sobbing uncontrollably at this point

"Maureen, are you okay?" The reverberation of Maureen's crying was his only answer.

John's first reaction was to search his own brain to see who could help. What doctor should he call? Did he need a plastic surgeon? Did he need a dermatologist? Did he need an ophthalmologist? For that matter did he need a psychiatrist? He heard Cara say that they were taking her to the hospital. He was familiar with the hospital, in Great Neck. In fact one of his employees sat on the Board of Trustees, but he wasn't sure whether this was the right place for his wife to be treated. He wasn't even sure where to begin with his decision-making.

Business decisions were far easier for JB to make. When making decisions about the health of Integrated Computer Devices (ICD). John Brady instinctively knew how to calculate risk and who to turn to for support. He was far more uncertain when it came to the health of his family. He was on a first name basis with many of the most preeminent doctors in New York. The group included cardiac surgeons, urologists, anesthesiologists, vascular surgeons, oncologists, plastic surgeons, neurologists, and physicians in just about every specialty practiced in the NYC area. Business triage was something he personally performed on a daily basis, many times instinctively. At that moment he was not sure whom he should turn to for medical triage. He needed more information.

"Maureen, listen to me. I will meet you at the hospital as fast as I can get there. Can you talk to me?"

Maureen was in shock. She wanted to keep her eyes closed and wake up as though it were all a bad dream. How clumsy and stupid could she be? Why had she had so much to drink in the middle of the day? She kept opening her right eye simply to prove to herself that she could see. But her left eye hurt, and the sight of her own blood made her nauseous. Her left breast and the left side of her chest were causing a lot of pain also. She found it very difficult to talk. It was even hard to moan. She simply handed the phone back to Cara.

* * * * * * * * * *

The warm-up band was winding down on Thursday night at the Olympic Stadium in Rome, Italy, and Gina Alvarez and the Lay D's were about to seize the stage. The other two members of the Lay D's, Marilyn

Mitchell and Karen Buffet, were already rocking back and forth, and getting ready to burst out into the open stadium. Gina was conserving her energy, even as her makeup man put the final touches on her exotic eye makeup.

Both Marilyn and Karen were still in their mid twenties but a few years older than Gina and had been singing professionally for a while longer than the lead singer. However neither of them resented Gina's celebrity. Their success together as the Lay D's had followed many false starts on the part of both Marilyn and Karen, and they were both experienced enough to realize that uniting behind Gina in the Lay D's had been the turning point of their careers.

Gina shared the financial success of the Lay D's generously with Marilyn and Karen, and they both realized that there would probably be a time when Gina would want to branch off on her own. Gina had never given them an indication that it would be any time soon, but she was beginning to exercise more creative independence in their performance. Gina was clearly in control of their destiny.

If there was any petty jealousy at all it probably revolved around Gina's uncanny ability to stay in perfect shape, never gaining an ounce, no matter what she ate. This was not an issue at all for Marilyn, but Karen seemed to be trying much too hard to keep up with Gina, and for the last six months, Karen had shown signs of bulimia. She had been using a lot of diet pills and laxatives, but had found them to be unsuccessful crutches in her fight against binge eating. Marilyn and Gina knew nothing about Karen's problem and she wanted to keep it that way.

The makeup artists finished their work and Gina joined Marilyn and Karen at the curtain as they heard their cue to explode onto the stage.

"Le signore ed i signori, accolgono favorevolmente prego dagli S.U.A. la Lay D's!!!!!"

The band exploded into a magnificent detonation of rock reverberation, as Gina and the Lay D's sashayed out on the stage for their Italian debut.

****

JB called across the corridor to Maria's office. In many sticky personnel situations, John Brady got quick ideas and solutions from Maria. She was an excellent executive assistant, and knew his likes and dislikes as well as any one of his direct reports. From time to time Maria even helped with the coordination of some of his agenda, although for the most part this was left to JB's secretary, Alice. But this time he called on Maria first.

"Maria, come into my office right away." He turned and reentered his office with Maria following close behind.

"Maureen has had an accident, and has been taken to the hospital. I want the chopper to be ready to take me to Great Neck in five minutes. They have a pad out at the hospital." He thought about having Maria call his children, but then changed his mind. "Also call the team and tell them that the financial prep call is off for tomorrow morning and to be ready for it tomorrow evening. No details."

"John, how is Maureen? Was she driving?" Maria was genuinely concerned. Regardless of the fact that she shared the affections of JB with Maureen, Maria felt that Maureen was a likable person. Their interactions over the last few years had always been cordial.

"No she had a fall. That's all I know for sure. I was able to talk to her, but she was in pain. I'll call you tonight and let you know what's what." John then stopped abruptly and just glared at Maria. She sensed that he wanted her to leave as abruptly as he had asked her to come in. Maria turned around and went back to arrange for the chopper. She wasn't going to leave this to Alice to do.

John's mind was churning. At first he had wanted to share more with Maria, and have her help him think through which of his doctor friends he should call first. Then he thought better of that idea and decided to give himself a minute or two to think. From what he had been able to learn over the phone, Maureen had apparently ripped open her face in a fall and bruised herself badly as well. He remembered that Maureen had been seeing a doctor in Manhattan who had performed a face lift for her four years earlier and had continued to treat her for other cosmetic facial issues ever since. Dr Vincent was regarded as the best in the business. JB didn't know him. He decided to call Mike Kelvey. Mike was a handsome, friendly young internist who networked very well and who knew all the other prominent NY doctors on a first name basis. He doubled as JB's personal physician. ICD paid Kelvey $50K a year just to be on call for JB. It was as good a place to start as any.

****

The Lay D's concert was proceeding well. It was their third city in three days, but they were planning on back-to-back shows in Rome. The

Olympic Stadium was rocking. Gina finished her newest number "Angel Feathers." And she flew off stage. The Italian crowd buzzed and yelled for more. The band increased the amperage and the ongoing light show continued to bedazzle the crowd.

Gina's fourth wardrobe change took place while Marilyn and Karen remained on stage waving and blowing kisses to the crowd. The band began playing a medley of the Lay D's hits, but had not yet played any of the music from the Lay D's signature hit, "My Kind of Love," the full throated pop sensation that crowds had taken to singing along with. Some in the crowd had begun to chant for their song.

Back stage, Gina's wardrobe team quickly removed her previous costume. Everything came off. The kinky black-beaded, high-thigh dress was tossed in a corner. The mesh stockings were quickly rolled down her legs and off her feet. The flesh colored backless bra, was removed from her breasts, ready to be replaced by invisible pasties for her next costume. In the brief few seconds that she stood naked, her sweaty body was quickly enclosed in cool wet towels, that were almost as quickly removed in place of warm dry towels that quickly absorbed as much of the moisture on her hot body as possible.

Gina was then rapidly redressed for her final act. It was all pink silk. A flesh colored thong was covered by low slung, hip hugging, pink silk pajama shorts, which in turn were covered by silk tear away mid-calf length pajama pants, but not before the obligatory matching pink knee pads were slipped into place. These were thinner than the other kneepads that she wore with some of the other costumes, but they were more functional than fashionable anyway.

Her pink silk spaghetti strap camisole style top was slipped over her head, and tightened slightly just below her breasts. The top stopped in mid torso and left her midriff and diamond studded naval exposed.

Another of Gina's wardrobe people carefully footed the rock star in pink medium heeled slipper-shoes that were wrapped tightly enough to ensure her dancing would be uninhibited.

Gina paused as her make-up adjustments were made and her final hairpiece was attached. She turned to no one in particular and asked, "the tie's behind the drummer, right?'

"It's there as you wanted it." A reply seemed to come from nowhere.

Gina was ready. She was not tired at all. Rome had reinvigorated her. Her youthful fitness was serving her well. She also knew that Josh was here for this concert and she was looking forward to giving him a special treat. Turnaround time for the costume change was three and a half minutes, her longest of the evening, but it had given Marilyn and Karen and the band time to build the crowd to a crescendo for the final act.

The band started moving toward a rhythmic beat that the crowd realized was the onset of the lyrics they were waiting to hear. Gina neared the curtain and was handed a remote hand held microphone, the first time all evening that she would use this amplifying device. It was really more of a prop than a technical aide for her final act anyway, but the microphone would perform well in both capacities.

Gina took a deep breath than sang out into the microphone. The repetitious inquiry that set off her signature song was accompanied by a quick moving and repetitious drum and guitar beat that captivated the crowd as they heard the pop star's voice ask "Are you ready? Are you ready? Are you ready? Are you ready? Are you ready for …?"

The enthusiastic crowd completed her inquiry in unison as she march-danced onto stage. "My kind of love?" They answered.

Gina was turned on by her audience. For most of the night it was hard to see the audience with all of the stage lighting, but she could definitely feel them. She was feeling them more now than ever.

"My kind of lu uh uh uve!" Gina dragged the word upward over the musical scale in a stutter of excitement that many in the crowd tried to imitate. "My kind of lu uh uh uve!" they echoed, knowing that they would be stair-step singing this word again and again.

Gina came straight toward the front of the stage in her march-dance fashion. Then she skip-danced to the left in front of Marilyn and Karen and sang, "If you're stickin'…If your stickn'… if your stickn' to…." She paused and aimed the microphone out into the audience off the left front of the stage as they responded, "my kind of lu uh uh uve." Marilyn and Karen both sang into a stand up microphone and completed Gina in unison with the audience near the right of the stage

Gina part skipped, part marched, part danced her way across the stage in a Jagger-esque manner, and sexually suggested."If you're clickin' if you're clickin' if you're clickin it's…?"

"My kind of lu uh uh uve!" The crowd answered into the outstretched microphone.

Gina turned and sang as she approached the band and sang, "If you're stricken…if you're stricken, if you're stricken, then it's…?" She turned around and flipped the microphone toward the crowd once again and they were getting louder still. "My kind of lu uh uh uve."

"If you're trickin'… if you're trickin' … if you're trickin' … It's …?"

"My kind of lu uh uh uve!"

"If you're tr_____ u're tripin'… If you're tripin'…It's …?"
"My kind o_____ve."
Gina move_____aight toward the audience again, and dug into her lyrics.

"He's an_____
"He's a_____know." echoed Marilyn and Karen
"He's a_____ Gina sang
"He's a_____I'm told," responded the Lay D's

"He's a_____d man,"
"But a lover so bold,'
"He's a Bad Boy,"
"As the night unfolds."

"But I don't care."
"No I don't care at all."
"Cause he's my lover."
"And it's my kind of love."

Gina and the Lay D's bounced back and forth between the lyrics and the evolving refrain. The Lay D's energetically danced in place while Gina continued to work her way back and forth across the stage. The words to the refrain kept changing slightly and both Gina and the audience sang them at a faster and faster pace.

"If you're hitchin…if you're hitchin…if you're hitchin. Then it's…?"

"My kind of lu uh uh uve." The Italian audience paid no attention to the ludicrous immaterial lyrics. They simply worshiped the sound of "my kind of lu uh uh uve." For their own part Gina and the Lay D's had sung this poppycock so often that they didn't care about the words they were simply into the emotion that it brought forth.

"If you're bitchin' … If you're bitchin' … If you're bitchin'… then it's …?"

"My kind of lu uh uh uve." The audience was in full throttle now, as Gina suddenly whipped off her tear away silk pajama pants, revealing her much shorter pink shorts and slim pink kneepads. Her legs glistened above her pink healed slipper-shoes from the captured heat of the silk, and her naval diamond glistened above her shorts.

"If you're kickin'….If you're kickin'….If you're kickin'… It's…"
"My kind of lu uh uh uve."

At first her bedtime attire seemed almost incongruous with her raucous rocking music. But now that her bedtime attire had been someone trimmed, the realization that Gina's pink silkies were bedroom ware, but not sleepwear, was quite apparent.

With her right hand she raised the microphone close to her lips and suggestively rolled her tongue around her lips and slowed the rhythm along with the band for one chorus of

"If you're lickin'...If you're lickin, if you're lickin' It's ...?"

"My kind of lu uh uh uve." The crowd had a little trouble slowing to the beat and staggered out their response this time. But the tempo picked up immediately and Gina repeated the chorus in a faster higher pitched tempo.

"If you're slickin'....If you're slickin' ... If your slicken' It's....?"

"My kind of lu uh uh uve." Faster ... Louder ... With more vigor than ever!

"My kind of lu uh uh uve." Gina stopped center stage and cried out to her audience. She was improvising now. *"My kind of lu uh uh uve."*

"My kind of lu uh uh uve." Gina turned again toward the band and sang out.

"My kind of lu uh uh uve," they answered her in unison, as she danced up behind the drummer and pulled out a tie which two weeks earlier had belonged to Josh Struben. It was still loosely knotted in a lopsided noose. She slipped the noose over her head, and let the tie swing loosely in front of her.

Gina danced back to the front center of the stage and brought the microphone back to her lips once again. She dropped to her knees and sang out.

"If you're flickin'...If you're flickin' ....If you're flickin' ... It's ...?"

"My kind of lu uh uh uve."

"My kind of lu uh uh uve." She answered them and began to tuck Josh's tie through the top of her camisole and between her breasts. The long wider end fell out through the bottom of the camisole and across her diamond-studded naval. Gina tucked it well into the top of her shorts. As she did so she propped up the hand held microphone between her knees, ball end up. Her voice could still be heard as she repeated: *"My kind of lu uh uh uve."*

The crowd went crazy as Gina snatched the microphone from between her thighs and spun on her right knee, until her back was to the crowd. With her right hand grasping the microphone tightly, Gina moved her left hand down to the wide tip of the tie and began to bounce on her knees, as she arched her back. She didn't miss a beat; in fact she picked up the tempo.

"My kind of lu uh uh uve." Stronger: *"My kind of lu uh uh uve."* Lustier: *"My kind of lu uh uh uve"* She fell limp. The lights went out for ten full seconds and then came back on as Gina skip-danced back toward the curtain.

About ten rows back from the stage, Josh Struben sat next to his brother Adam, and Adam's starry-eyed girlfriend, Celine. Josh had invited Adam and Celine to be his guests in Rome for the weekend, and all were enjoying themselves immensely. As Josh watched the final act unfold on stage, he flushed with the excitement of a naked déjà vu, and he realized that once again Gina was enjoying herself as well. He wasn't in a hurry to get his tie back

Meanwhile, Gina, Marilyn and Karen fell into one another's arms backstage. It had been another night and another successful gig for the Lay D's. Karen however became almost instantly heavy in Gina's arms and it was all Gina could do to hold Karen slightly aloft as she slipped to the floor in a semi-conscious state.

****

Back in New York City, Maria made sure that John got on the chopper and then she returned slowly to the office. It was not yet 5:30 PM on Thursday afternoon, and there was still a lot to do. However, she was suddenly a bit melancholy and not in the mood for work. She was legitimately concerned about Maureen. Maria never expected that John would leave Maureen for her. Ironically Maria believed that if she herself ever considered getting married, she would never marry someone like John. He was a cheater! The more she thought about it the more she thought it might be time to move forward in her love life. The sex with John was good, but it was sporadic. She didn't always have John when she wanted him. Maybe it was time for someone new.

Maria sat behind her desk and thought about her situation a little longer. For the first time in her life she thought that she might profit from some professional counseling. She had never seen a shrink before, but she knew several people who had benefited from this type of help. Was it time to move on? Was it time to end her relationship with John? But what would she do about her job? She really liked her job. She didn't see how it would be possible to keep her job as JB's

EA, without sleeping with him. Hell, they often talked about business in bed, never as foreplay, but certainly as a replacement for the after sex smoke.

Well if she needed some help with this, maybe Dr Moses could recommend someone. She thought that maybe there was enough of a connection between her physical issues and her emotional issues that using someone that Dr Al might recommend could provide some overall synergies to addressing her general health.

Maria picked up the phone and called Dr Moses' office.

"I'd like to speak to Dr Moses, please."

"I'm sorry. Dr Moses is out of the country this week. May I ask who is calling?"

"Yes, this is Maria Cordoza."

"Oh, Hi Maria ... This is Charlotte." What Maria liked most about seeing Dr Moses was that his staff was so streamlined. It enabled them to be on a first name basis with the narrowing number of patients in his practice.

"Hi Charlotte, could you have him give me a call when he gets back? I'm looking for a recommendation to see a specialist, and am interested in seeing someone Dr Al recommends." She didn't bother mentioning that she had actually spotted Dr Al earlier in the week when they both were in London.

"Is there something I can help you with?" There were obviously some drawbacks about the intimacy of Dr Moses practice.

"No just have him call me when he returns."

****

John Brady was not a man to be taken lightly. Although it had been less than an hour since he had spoken to his wife on the phone and less than forty-five minutes since he began a telephonic search for medical help from physician friends, he had not heard back from any of them yet and he was arriving at the hospital with little recourse other than to listen to what the emergency room physicians would tell him. He was worried about Maureen, but he was aggravated about the lack of responsiveness amongst his medical contacts. Had any direct report of his been so unresponsive they would have been looking for a job the following day.

Finally John got a call from on his cell from Dr Mike Kelvey, his personal physician, just as he was about to enter the emergency room.

"Hello John, I got your message just a few minutes back? How is Maureen?"

"I just got to the hospital Mike," JB snapped in an annoyed voice. "I haven't seen Maureen or any of the doctors yet. I don't know how she is. Let me call you back when I know more. Gotta go."

"Okay, call me, when you can." Even as he walked into the emergency room, JB felt some satisfaction that Kelvey had called. But at the same time he was annoyed that Kelvey wasn't on his way to the hospital. And why was ICD paying this young punk doctor 50 grand, anyway?

* * * * * * * * *

Stephen Struben looked across the table at his wife, Danielle. He loved her very much, and could tell that something had been bothering her lately. Both of their sons called earlier in the week and Stephen knew that they were together in Rome for the weekend. Stephen knew that family was as important to Danielle as it was to him, but he didn't believe that Danielle's recent melancholy had anything to do with their sons. He wanted to come right out and ask her about it, but something told him that it was best to wait for her to bring up whatever it was that bothered her. He decided to talk about the things that bothered him instead.

"I still haven't been able to get over what happened to Max Tkachuk."

"What was *'e* like?"

"He was a brilliant guy. It's sad. He had so much to offer."

"From the newspaper story, I read, *eet* sounds as though *'e deedn't 'ave* any close *fameely* … unmarried … no children … *deedn't* even mention anything about brothers and *seesters.*"

"I didn't know that much about him personally. I just knew him as an enterprising young man, who worked hard at his profession and accomplished a lot."

"What *deed 'e accompleesh* that was so special? … seems like *'e* was just another computer guy who made a few quid, or Euros or whatever." Danielle picked at her late night dinner and moved her food around the plate a bit as she spoke.

"He was working on a software program that could help bring a lot of organizational symmetry to the health and wellness industries. He had the potential to bring a lot of help to an industry that really needs it."

"So what *'appens* now? They find *thees* guy dead of an apparent *'eart* attack *een* a cheesy *'otel* room. *'E* doesn't seem to *'ave* any family *eenvolved een 'ees buseeness*, and there *ees* no one quoted from *'ees* company, Apakoh, that said anything about what the company might be doing. Seems to me that whatever *'e* was working on could have just died *weeth 'eem*."

"Maybe, I'm not sure. Most of the work he was doing was for a specific customer, Rhapsody Holdings, but he never talked that much about them. I'm sure some of the folks at STRX will know more about it." Stephen was struck by Danielle's cynicism. She was not normally that skeptical about people. He, himself, was shocked when he heard about Max. It took the police two days to find him and ask routine questions about their dinner. There was no question about the cause of death. The police were merely looking to locate his next of kin, although they were intrigued by the fact that Tkachuk had nearly 2,000 Euros in his shabby hotel room when they found his body. Stephen had called his friends at STRX in Germany, to tell them of Tkachuk's unfortunate demise. They said that they would see what the company knew about Tkachuk's family, and they would logically follow up with someone at Apakoh with respect to Tkachuk's work.

"What *deed* Al Moses *theenk* about Max?"

"He was shocked, like everyone else."

"No, I mean what did *'e theenk* about *'eem*? Did *'e* like *'eem*? Did *'e* think *'e* was *eenteresting*? Was *'e* glad you *eenvited 'eem* to *deenner*?"

"Funny that you should ask … I don't think that Al was overly fond of Max, but he could at least see that Max was working on something of value to his profession. After Max left the dinner, Al made a few comments about the fact that Max didn't seem very healthy and even commented on the fact that Max looked and seemed a bit older than he was."

"*Eenteresteeng*, two guys *een* their *meed seexties, talkeeng* like a couple of cats about someone twenty years younger."

"You mean someone who is now dead. I don't think there was anything at all catty about our commentary on Tkachuk's health."

Danielle let the topic drop without responding. She stood up to put her plate in the sink, and Stephen couldn't help but notice that his wife was still a remarkably attractive woman. Danielle was fourteen years younger than Stephen, and he had begun to wonder whether or not the age difference was beginning to matter. His ruminations were interrupted when Danielle sat back down across the table and looked into his eyes in a piercing manner and said. "Stephen, I *'ave sometheeng eemportant* I want to talk about."

"Yes, Danielle, darling. What is it?"

"I *'ave* breast cancer," she said simply, and then added, "I'm not sure who to see about *eet*. I went to an *'arley* Street doctor and *'e* wants to do *sometheeng queeckly*. I'm not sure what to do. I'm scared."

****

Gina and Marilyn helped Karen over to a couch in the dressing room and although Karen was now awake, she seemed quite weak. As soon as they got her settled, Karen stood and wobbled toward the bathroom, where she proceeded to vomit, while grasping her stomach.

"What's this all about?" Gina was looking after Karen at the doorway to the bathroom but she was asking Marilyn, who was standing next to her.

"Didn't notice any problem on stage."

"Me neither."

"She was puking earlier before we went on stage though. I just thought it was nerves. You know how our girl gets some times."

Karen Buffet continued to moan and hold her stomach. Bruce Heilman, the tour manager came over and said, "I think we ought to get her to see a doctor ASAP. She doesn't look good. And we have another concert tomorrow night."

Gina looked at Heilman and said, "Great, how do you know who's a good doctor in Rome?"

Heilman answered, "Don't worry we'll get someone."

Gina retorted "Not just someone, Bruce. Our girl needs help."

****

John Brady listened intently to the words of Dr. Abramson.

"Mrs. Brady has a severe laceration on her face and will probably require multiple stitches to close the wound below her left eye. The bleeding has been stopped, but she will need to see a plastic surgeon to rehabilitate the whole area. A more immediate concern is that your wife has been experiencing significant difficulty breathing deeply. We believe that because of her rib injury she has suffered what is known as a tension pneumothorax."

"What is that?"

"Because of her fall she has some trapped air under pressure that is compressing her lung. It is making it difficult for her to breathe. My colleague, Shiv Chattopadhyay will be treating this shortly."

"How serious is this?"

"Dr. Chattopadhyay will be treating your wife under local anesthesia. He has expressed concern that she also has a haemothorax. This is something like the pneumothorax except blood is trapped near the base of the lung instead of air being trapped. Shiv is also treating the haemothorax. Both conditions can be quite serious if not treated, but your wife was brought here quickly and she should recover fully after her injuries are treated. One other concern is that Mrs. Brady has acknowledged that she has had a considerable amount to drink this afternoon."

JB had never met Dr Abramson before and he had no idea about the skill level of Dr. Chattopadhyay. He wasn't afraid to admit to himself that he was biased against a doctor with an Indian surname. He had no rational reason for this bias. However, Kelvey had called him back to tell him that Chattopadhway was the department head and an excellent physician. He wondered how Kelvey came to that conclusion. He just wished that an American doctor were treating his wife. Little did John Brady know! Dr. Chattopadhyay was born in Westchester County and had been to India only once in his life. He was every bit as American as Brady was!

Chapter 4: *A Higher Order*

Climbing into the sky above the Mediterranean, soaring towards the Atlantic Ocean and on toward the USA, Dr Al Moses sat in seat 3A in a wide-bodied Boeing 767, reading <u>Harry Potter and the Deathly Hallows.</u> He didn't think of it as a child's book. It was categorized as "fantasy," and that's how he fancied it.

The jumbo jet had left Rome nearly filled to capacity, and was now reaching cruising altitude of 36,000 feet. Dr Al put his book in his lap for a second and thought back over the two legs of his most recent trip. He had initially flown to London to have dinner with Stephen Struben and Max Tkachuk. Then he'd flown on to attend a reunion in Rome for a few days with his medical school classmate, Dr Paolo Grassani.

The stopover in London was not everything he had hoped it would be. He wanted to spend more quality time alone with his friend Stephen. But putting aside the Tkachuk tragedy, the London stopover hadn't quite lived up to Dr Al's expectations anyway. He and Stephen never got to the point in their discussion that Al felt comfortable mentioning his own depression. They barely talked at all about the good old days when Stephen and Danielle and Al and Anne were constantly together, and at the top of the social scene in Manhattan. Stephen and Danielle were now spending most of their time in London, and even when they made an occasional trip back to the States, they often spent their time in Westchester, rather than Manhattan.

The four days in Rome with Paolo were more fun than he expected. As usual the restaurants that Paolo selected were fabulous. Paolo was one of those wonderfully charismatic people who were always surrounded by a large group of new friends. This time was no exception. Dr Grassani spent much of his time these days in research pursuit at the University. He stayed young by chasing his young research assistants. Even after four marriages, Paolo was still scurrying after the fountain of youth. Then again, Paolo would never refer to his past nuptials as "failed marriages;" they were simply "lezioni continue di amore," or "ongoing lessons of love."

Al grudgingly admitted to himself that he envied Paolo Grassani. Maybe he just needed to force himself to be more outgoing. With that in mind he closed the book on his lap and placed it in the proverbial "seat back in front of him." He then took the unusual step of noting the reading matter of the young man sitting next to him.

Sitting in seat 3B was a good looking dark haired young man, who was reading a well-worn leather bound text of some sort. Dr Al took a chance and began a conversation.

"Looks like we could make up some time in flight if the weather stays good."

The younger man put his book down and inclined his head toward Dr Al while turning it about a quarter of the way and as he responded. "Let's hope so. I'm just glad we're airborne. Nothing worse than sitting around waiting in the terminal,"

"I know what you mean."

A full minute or two went by, and the flight attendant came by to begin the mid day service. Dr Al noted that the young man bowed his head as though he were saying a silent blessing over his meal, as the first course was being laid out for them.

"As far as I know even divine intervention won't make this meal taste any better," Al joked hopefully.

The young man took the bait and answered humorously, "I was just praying that they would keep the bar open for the whole flight. Whatever they serve can't be too bad if you can wash it down with a toddy or two." Dr Al detected the ever distinctive Boston accent as his seat mate omitted the telltale "r" from the end of "bar," and the end of "whatever."

Moses forced a laugh and the two just sat in silence for a minute or so. Then the Bostonian broke the silence by pointing at the book in front of Al. "You enjoy that Harry Potter stuff? I thought that was children's literature."

"I guess it is meant for children, but I find the books to be a great escape from everyday life."

"What's everyday life for you?'

"I'm a physician…currently a vacationing physician. How about yourself'

"I'm Brian Flaherty. I'm a Catholic priest."

Al was mildly flummoxed, and then said. "Oh. I didn't realize that you were a priest." When he spoke it sounded as though he were talking to a different species. Then realizing how surprised he sounded, he stuck out his hand in friendship and said. "Well, hi Father Flaherty, I'm Al Moses."

"Just call me Brian and I'll refrain from calling you Dr. Moses, if that works for you."

"Okay. Sorry if I seemed a bit confused. Usually if I see a priest on an airplane, he's wearing a black suit and a Roman collar. I'm not used to seeing priests in civvies."

"Normally, I would wear my collar. But I was in Rome on vacation also. The trip was a gift from my parents. They gave me first class tickets. I wouldn't want others to see a priest flying first class and wondering why the money isn't going to some better cause."

"I see," said Al but he didn't. There was too much pretending in everything in life, he thought. However, he didn't get bogged down in the reflection but simply moved on to another topic.

"Was that one of the classics that you were reading?" Al nodded toward the leather bound text that was now folded over on the seat beside Brian.

"I guess you could say that. I was actually reading my breviary. It's a daily prayer book that priests read from every day."

"Is it a classic in a sense that the writing goes back to the time of Christ?"

"Yes, part of it goes back to writings that predate Christ by more than a thousand years. The Psalter is part of the daily breviary readings and they are drawn from the Psalms that were part of the liturgy of the Jews for more than twelve centuries before Christ. So you might say that I'm reading the wisdom of some ancient thinkers."

"Is any of it still relevant today?"

"Absolutely, the breviary itself is somewhat prescriptive and prayer-like in a priest's daily execution of his duties, but the individual readings themselves hold many universal truths that transcend time and culture. The prescriptive part is that there are different readings for different parts of the day, based on the old Roman divisions of the day into three hour segments, and different readings for the different liturgical seasons of the year, but I find the content to be very moving at times."

"That's quite interesting, Brian. You seem to be well suited to be a 'man of the cloth'."

"Thank you. I guess. Are you a God-fearing man yourself?"

"I'm a Jew. I don't know whether that qualifies me as God-fearing. Most of us are just mother-fearing first, and if there is room in later life we become God-fearing." He joked.

"What is it with Jews and their mothers?" Both men were now warming to one another, and beginning to enjoy their dialogue.

"I don't know what it is. We keep them on pedestals. Can you believe it, there once was a Jew who believed his mother was a virgin?"

Flaherty laughed. "Oh yeah, I remember that story. All the other Jewish kids got so pissed off about it, that they nailed the guy to a cross." Both men laughed comfortably at the sacrilegious humor but managed to restrain themselves from further commentary.

"To answer your question more seriously, Brian, I've never been deeply religious, although I observe the major holidays and occasionally go to synagogue. But I have to tell you, living in New York; I have a lot of friends from all kinds of religious and ethnic backgrounds. We all manage to get along."

"That's not only attributable to where you live, but also probably to your profession. Everybody has health needs, right?" Dr Al was aware that this line of discussion could get less comfortable quickly, if he disclosed his OB/GYN specialty and the conversation turned into an abortion debate, but he persevered and pressed the conversation forward.

"That's true to a certain extent. My practice has a much wider ethnic diversity today than it did when I first started out. But I bet that's a bit different for you. The very nature of your work would seem to lend itself to a slightly more narrow perspective."

"Not necessarily. There are lots of issues that the Church has to deal with these days, but the official mission of the Catholic Church is to spread the word of Christ, administer the sacraments and to exercise charity towards all men and women. All of that probably sounds very parochial. But the devil is in the details, you might say. In order to do any of these things effectively, the church and its ministers need to have an acute understanding of the non-Catholic world, and especially the theologies of the non- Christian world."

The two men settled back into their chairs and continued their conversation over lunch. They liked one another instinctively and respected their differences. The conversation wandered back and forth over debatable topics, and they each stated their opinions on medical and theological issues and the crossroads between the two. As they grew more comfortable with each other, Al did tell Brian that his specialty was OB/GYN and they did discuss abortion. They also tackled embryonic stem cell research, euthanasia, celibacy in the priesthood, spiritual healing and many other potentially contentious topics. They were able to voice their opinions ardently but without rancor, and at 36,000 feet a friendship was being formed.

Dr Al was very pleased with himself for simply being himself.

****

On the opposite side of the 767 cabin, toward the rear of the first class section, Josh Struben sat across from his brother Adam and Adam's girlfriend, Celine. They were returning from their short excursion to Rome. Together they had enjoyed a double dose of the Lay D's concerts, and partied well into the early morning hours. Gina flew on to Zurich that morning with her entourage, following the second concert and a tour of Rome's trendy nightspots. The brothers Struben were returning to the USA later this same day.

They had all arrived in Rome on different paths. Gina and Josh had been together in London earlier in the week and in Rome the last two nights. They went their respective ways in between.

Josh was busy at the London office with his hedgie mates and Gina and the Lay D's went from London to Amsterdam to Paris before flying on to Rome.

Adam and Celine arrived in Rome three days earlier. It was a busy week but after each of the two shows in Rome, the group had partied hard into early morning hours. The only respite from the raucous partying was on the afternoon between the concerts when Josh went with Gina to the Vatican Museum.

Celine was exhausted by the excursion but Adam and Josh were still upbeat and excited by the wild Italian three-day jaunt. So while Celine stretched out sleepily and pulled a blanket over herself in her window seat, Adam and Josh talked across the aisle.

"I guess you were the good son, this week, stopping to see mother on your trip." Adam cracked. "How is she doing? Did she get to meet Gina?"

It was the first time the brothers had talked *family* during the last couple of days.

"No I didn't want to go down that path, with Mum, this time through. Besides Gina was only in London for a day and a half before she scooted off to Holland." Josh paused and then added, "Mom seemed alright, maybe a little quiet. She was her usual self, I would say. I didn't get a chance to see Dad, but I talked to him on the phone yesterday for a bit … a dreadful story about a colleague of his dying of a heart attack in some obscure hotel room."

"Yes he told me some things about that guy, Tkachuk, also. I think Dad was trying to help him out, before the poor chap up and died."

"Some kind of software maven … if I've got the story straight," Josh added.

"Yea, Dad called me a couple of weeks back on another matter and mentioned this guy was trying to get some additional financial backing through the strategic equity fund guys at STRX. I don't know how well it was going because he hinted that he might want me to talk to some of the venture group at our bank to see if they could help." Adam said.

"I guess that was before this massive banking meltdown started."

"Well there is no money moving in any direction now."

"It will bounce back. Not everyone got smoked."

"I was almost afraid to ask over the last two days, but how are you and your hedgie buddies holding up. Lots of talk about additional blow ups … Everything okay?"

"Yeah we're a lot better off than a lot of guys. Can't say that we saw the meltdown coming … but we did get out of the CDO/CMO trap early and we have been shorting the hell out of the subprime mortgage market. We also have been shorting equities since the end of last year."

"The SEC put an end to that strategy, at least temporarily."

"That's a short term problem. Because nothing's moving … backwards, forwards … not even aggressively treading water. It just isn't happening. So I guess you're right. We could see a few more blow-ups. But I think we're fine. Equities are going to bounce back anyway. The mortgage mess will take a hell of a lot longer to rebound. In the war of attrition the fat man always wins."

"I guess that depends on how fat you are." Adam remarked. "Seems to me that even the fat man gets blown up if he gets too close to the action. If the fat guy ate the skinny guy's lunch, he may have gotten poisoned in the process."

"We've been thinking about that, for more than a year, so it's been a simple strategy of "purge baby purge.""

Both brothers allowed a common nervous laugh.

"Change of topic?" Adam suggested.

"Absolutely," Josh agreed. "Portfolio evaporations are not a pleasant discussion."

The two young men sat back for a second or two sipping their martinis as Adam casually eased in to his change of topics.

"I liked Gina a lot … not at all what I anticipated." Adam offered.

"How so?"

"First of all, she's even better looking in person. What skin! And what a body! Nice catch Joshua, ole boy."

"Thanks bro."

The flight attendant served two Martinis to the Struben brothers and smiled a warm friendly smile. She glanced towards the apparently sleeping Celine and asked Adam in a soft voice. "Do you think she wants something?"

"Not now. I should think," Adam answered in an equally soft voice. They were now officially kicking back.

"The thing that surprised me is that she isn't full of herself, like a lot of these entertainment types."

"Careful bro. We've got Mumsy to remember. She's one of those 'entertainment types.'"

"No she's not. In fact that points out exactly what I mean. When we were growing up, Mom had a lot of weird friends in the entertainment field."

"Not so much weird….just assholes."

"Well you know what I mean. There were a lot of people that thought that they were the most important people on the face of the earth. Mum wasn't like that at all. And that's what I like about Gina. She is genuine."

"You need to knock off the comparisons to Mum. I don't have an Oedipus Complex." Josh laughed. "But you're right; Gina's not at all pretentious. The playful Lay'D you see on stage is the same fun loving lady offstage." Josh saw no real parallel between his mother and his girl friend, other than they were both singers. Danielle Dubonet Struben was pensive and even reserved. Gina Alvarez was purposefully bold and flashy.

"Well she certainly seems to be a tough business person as well. She got a replacement for Karen Buffet for the Friday night show and didn't miss a beat." Adam noted.

"Apparently, as it turns out, Karen has a severe eating disorder. Gina made sure she was flown back to London to see someone there who specializes in that kind of thing. She cares about Karen. But yeah you're right. The beat goes on. They needed a new singer and they had a back up ready in Rome the very next night."

"Good management team, I guess."

"For sure, but don't kid yourself. Gina calls the shots. For someone with only a high school education, she has a hell of a good gut for the business side of entertainment. She knows that she can be the lead, the star, the celeb. But she also helped create the Lay D's brand. And she knows what it's worth, and doesn't want to squander any of that brand equity."

"So the brand is hurt less by replacing Karen than it would have been by canceling part of the tour."

"Absolutely."

"Like I said, you've got a real good score there, Josh…a fascinating woman. What drives her? I mean, besides the money."

"Oh I think the money plays less of a role in what drives her engine now. I'm sure the money was important at one time. But she's raking in the quid, no doubt about it. Look at these concerts in Rome. Average ticket price is 200 euro. The Olympic Stadium is sold out. The place holds 85,000 for sports and they wall off about half of the place for the concerts. Still they sell over 45,000 tickets each night. You do the math and it comes to nine million euro a night. There are twenty-four concerts on the tour, granted most of them at smaller venues, but any way you slice it, the tour will gross more than one hundred million euros in about two months."

"Okay, got it. What else besides the money? She's what twenty-four years old?"

"Would you believe twenty-two?"

"Wow seems like the Gina and the Lay D's have been at it for a while. She's only twenty-two?"

"Yep. And I'll tell you what I think is really driving her. She is inherently insatiable when it comes to her need for self-affirmation. No matter how well she does something, she always expresses a need to do it better."

"That's deep stuff, Josh." Adam laughed as he took a sip of his martini. "I hope you know what you're getting into. Didn't I read in one of the gossip mags that she has a genius IQ of 171, or something ridiculously off the charts like that?"

"Who knows about that IQ stuff? She's never mentioned anything like that to me, although I read the same thing. But to answer your question … yeah … I know what I'm getting into, and I'm learning a few things along the way as well."

"Like what?"

"Some stuff that I haven't given much thought to before…..like Health and Spirituality."

"Health and Spirituality are two pretty different things, aren't they?"

"Normally I'd say they are very different. However Gina has a somewhat different outlook on it. I think that she gets some of these ideas from her yoga instructor, but I'm not sure that she doesn't come up with certain concepts just through her own personal exploration."

"From what I could tell, Gina doesn't seem to be one to get caught up in someone else's abstractions. She seems to be a pretty free thinker. What kinds of things is she coming at you with?"

"Well first of all, she has asked me to take a yoga class with her, so that I can get a sense of why it is so important to her. I'm all for that. Back in NYC we already have the same fitness trainer."

"So what's the big deal? Seems like everyone is into yoga these days."

"But then Gina has also been talking a lot about reincarnation, afterlife, longevity, and cognitive transmigration. It's almost as if she is searching for some exotic blissful state, a rhapsody of sorts, where she can pursue perfection in physical, mental, social, sexual and spiritual matters, a heaven on earth, if you will."

"So is she challenging you sexually bro? Is that what this is all about?" Adam laughed and tried to lighten his brother's heavy rap.

Josh smiled sheepishly. "No not all. The sex is unbelievably great. I could say that she is an animal in bed, but that wouldn't do her justice. You see, it's a lot more than just sex, even though she certainly can communicate with her body, and believe me we communicate a lot. Sex is part of something bigger with Gina." Josh just stopped at this point, not knowing what else to say.

Both brothers paused and Adam just looked at his smitten brother and shrugged his broad shoulders with a smile.

Josh had exposed more of his feelings to his brother than he had wanted. They both sipped their drinks in silence for a few seconds and then Josh tried to engage Adam in a reciprocal kind of discussion. He leaned closer across the aisle toward his brother and nodded toward the sleeping Celine. He whispered his question.

"Okay, Adam, so what's the story with Celine?"

"Met her at the office … gives good head."

****

It was early Saturday afternoon at the headquarters office of ICD in New York City. JB was furious with Maria. He had asked her to meet him in the office at noon so that they could review his comments for the upcoming analysts call on Tuesday. She left a message that said she would be there by 1PM, because she was at the Goddamn Spa. That wasn't the name of it but that's what JB called it. It wasn't the Gotham Spa. It was the Goddamn Spa.

Nothing was going right for Brady. His wife, Maureen, was at home with Dr. Mike Kelvey, and together they were talking with several different physicians in order to address a number of Maureen's problems.

Maureen had been released from the hospital early that morning, but by the looks of JB's north shore mansion, it appeared that Maureen had just moved the hospital to her home. By 11 AM, Dr Kelvey seemed to have things under control so JB had Jeannine fix him a quick brunch and then Fernando drove him to the office.

"Mr. Brady?"

It was no other than the man that JB had referred to as "prissy." Rickie Van Dorfan.

"Come on in Rickie. Thank you for coming in on Saturday. I appreciate it."

"Sure Mr. Brady. How is Mrs. Brady doing?"

"I guess you heard she had a fall?"

"Yes, Maria told me about it. I hope she's feeling better."

"A bit bruised and a nasty cut below her eye, but she'll be fine, I'm sure."

Even though JB believed that Rickie was gay, he included him on his staff, or at least he allowed Maria to include him on her staff. It was not that Brady was at all open-minded or tolerant of alternative life styles; he just recognized it as good business to allow "a few flits" in the office environment. And although the CEO of ICD was indeed prejudiced, he did think that Rickie did a commendable job when asked to produce press releases, short speeches, and executive "talk from" pieces.

But it was Saturday afternoon, and there wasn't anyone else in the office, and JB was still pissed off waiting for Maria to get her ass out of the spa and into the office. The ugly side of the CEO was looming in the air and he decided to play a little game with Rickie.

"So here you are working hard on a Saturday afternoon, while your boss is off at some spa. Doesn't that piss you off, Rickie?"

Van Dorfan didn't know what to say. He was not prepared for this line of questioning from Mr. Brady. Any questions JB had ever asked him before revolved directly around business, not people in the office. He didn't know where this line of questioning was going, but his antenna was up.

"Well not really Mr. Brady. I know that Maria works hard, and I just look at this as an opportunity to help her out."

"Do you really? That's good of you Rickie. If I were a young man like you, with an attractive female boss, I'd be wondering what she is *really* doing while I'm here slaving away at the office."

"Like you said, she's at the spa. She should be here soon," Rickie said nervously.

"Well I guess I'd be thinking that here I am saving her bacon with her boss, while she's getting a massage from some muscular pool boy type. She's lying there naked with just her privates covered by a thin sheet or a towel or something, while Mr. Pool Boy rubs away to his heart's content. Then she'll come in here in a few minutes after being rubbed, scrubbed and serviced in whatever other ways she had scheduled for the afternoon and make slight changes to what you've done and call it her own work. Doesn't that bother you Rickie?"

JB knew he was way out of line, but there was no one there at the office at that time, who would be able to corroborate any allegations that Rickie might make, so he just kept playing mind games with Van Dorfan.

"It's all right Rickie. Just two good 'ole boys here, you and me. You can tell me if Maria is mistreating you, by getting her massage from the pool boy. Or I don't know maybe you *like* the pool boy thought. Can't tell the way people think any more."

Rickie was every bit as embarrassed as JB wanted him to be. There was no good reason for it. JB was angry with Maria, but he was taking it out on Rickie. Fortunately before Rickie had a chance to answer, Maria's footsteps were heard approaching the office.

"Cardoza you're late," boomed Brady.

"Sorry John. I had a gift certificate for a day at the spa, and I wanted to use it. I had everything scheduled for today. I was looking forward to it. Besides you didn't leave a message for me to come into the office until late last night. Anyway I'm only an hour late. Let's get going."

****

In London, seven miles below the westbound 767, Josh and Adam's parents sat together in a private consultation room, awaiting the appearance of Dr Neville Roorback, for their late afternoon appointment.

Danielle was not an overly vain person, but she felt that she should always look as attractive as she could. She didn't know what "beauty" meant anymore. During her active singing and acting career days she had had several cosmetic procedures performed on her face as well as her figure. Part of the job … comes with the turf, she thought. As she gradually languished into professional retirement, she wanted to maintain her sense of "beauty," without some of the excesses of her past "work." It seemed to take a lot of effort to maintain her "look:" A little Restylane here to help with the wrinkles; a little Botox there to eliminate the frown lines; occasionally a facial peel to ensure age spots evaporate. The hair color and cut needed to be just right also. She wanted it all to be much more natural, but she would settle for it being much more under control. "Staying pretty" involved a lot of people. Of course these days, "staying pretty," was taking a back seat to "staying alive."

For more than thirty years of marriage, Stephen and Danielle had maintained a faithful loving relationship in spite of the fact, or maybe because of the fact, that their professional pursuits occupied very different space and led them to interact with very different groups of people.

Both Stephen and Danielle had traveled the world, achieving sufficient success in their respective fields. Danielle had never won an Oscar or an Emmy and Stephen had never won a Nobel Prize, but neither was the type of person who sought such acclaim.

The Strubens shared a committed personal relationship and were open about their professional interests, but didn't discuss them in much detail. They had always been content to allow each other the space to pursue their careers separately, and yet would always be supportive of each other when it was important.

Normally there were no secrets between Stephen and Danielle, although from time to time there had been a "delayed disclosure." Danielle's cancer fit into that category. She didn't want to tell Stephen right away, because she knew that he would be hurt by the news. When she finally told him, he was hurt more by the fact that she hadn't told him sooner and he worried that Danielle was letting fear get the best of her.

Dr Roorback entered the room and exchanged perfunctory pleasantries with the Strubens. Neville was a gangling middle-aged man with poor posture and a mouth full of crooked teeth. Roorback carried a clipboard and a pen that seemed to be useless props that he dropped on his desk. A stethoscope hung around his neck and over his white pullover shirt. Stephen Struben hoped that Roorback cared more about his clientele than he did about his appearance.

After the short greetings, Roorback got down to the discussion of the lab test findings. "Mrs. Struben as we started to discuss last time, there are three generally recognized forms of breast cancer. Ductal breast cancer and Lobular breast cancer are by far the most common forms of breast cancer and they are named because of where the malignancy is found in the breast or breasts. Ducts connect the lobes and lobules of the breast. In very simple terms if the malignant cells are found in the lobes it is called lobular cancer and if the malignant cells are found in the ducts it is known as ductal breast cancer. The technical terms for these two types of cancer in their earliest stage are *Ductal Carcinoma in Situ* and *Lobular Carcinoma in Situ*. I don't want to oversimplify these cancers because they can become quite complex if they go untreated and then metastasize, meaning that they spread throughout the breast and to other parts of the body. These cancers then unfortunately reach stages 2, 3 and 4 and are quite dangerous potentially even fatal."

"But you *eendeecated* that these are not the types of breast cancer that I *'ave*."

"Yes. That's correct. I only quickly point out these other cancers so that we can distinguish the kind of cancer that you have, and the treatments that you should anticipate."

"What kind of cancer does Danielle have?" asked Stephen. He wanted to grasp what his wife's cancer was as quickly as possible.

"Danielle, what you have is known as Inflammatory Breast Cancer or IBC. It is different from the other cancers I just mentioned." Roorback answered Stephen's question but addressed his answer to his patient.

"It doesn't show itself with the typical tumor in the breast, and so it is sometimes harder to detect. Classic cases of IBC will present with external warmth and ridges on the breast and sometimes the nipple flattens out or it looks like it is inverted, but a lot of these cases, including yours, don't present as obviously."

" *'Ow deed thees 'appen* so *queeckly*? I go *een* for a mammogram annually and *'ave* routine checkups every *seex* months. In fact I checked my calendar and my last mammogram was only five months ago."

"Unfortunately IBC is not like the other kinds of breast cancer. There is no lump or tumor that can be detected by a mammogram or for that matter by an MRI of the breast. The first tipoff is usually painful swelling and redness. The other disturbing part about IBC is that it is aggressive and develops much more rapidly than some of the other types of breast cancer. Having said all of that, it is treatable. But I have to tell you that we should begin the treatment immediately."

"When you say *eet ees* treatable, does that mean I *weell 'ave* to *'ave* surgery?"

"Yes." He allowed the definitive answer to register for a full second or two before continuing. "And if the underlying question is: 'Do we need to remove the breast?' the answer to that is also unfortunately, yes."

"Can't something be done with chemotherapy or radiation?" Stephen asked the question, but again Neville Roorback addressed his answer to Danielle.

"Actually we will incorporate chemotherapy in our treatment. It is what we will need to do first, prior to the surgery. After surgery we will utilize radiation to eliminate any remaining cancer cells."

Danielle looked down for a second in the direction of her right breast and then looked up at Dr. Roorback. "A lumpectomy *ees* not *posseeble*? You *weell* need to remove the whole breast? What *eef* the chemotherapy works? *Weell* that obviate the need for surgery?"

"No Danielle, unfortunately that's not how this all works. In the case of IBC, chemotherapy, surgery and radiation, in that order, are all part of the combination treatment process. The presurgical chemo is called neoadjuvant therapy. This takes care of some of the surface problems and effectively shrinks or mitigates the cancer, but doesn't eliminate it. This prepares your body for the surgical removal of your breast. A lumpectomy is something that is done for the other forms of cancer that I mentioned that present with a tumor in a duct or a lobe. Inflammatory breast cancer does not lend itself to this type of remedy because that type of tumor is not normally present. At any rate, following the breast removal, we will need to radiate the area of the breast and under the arm to reduce the possibility of any recurrence."

It was a lot to digest for both Danielle and Stephen, but Dr Roorback had laid it out in black and white. They all knew that there was only one important question left to ask. Roorback waited patiently for either Stephen or Danielle to ask it. Danielle finally complied.

"What are my chances for beating *thees* cancer? I guess I'm asking, what are the survival rates for women *weeth* IBC?"

"Roughly 50% of women diagnosed with IBC live to the 5 year mark." Roorback answered.

****

Back up on the Boeing 767, they were now out over the Atlantic Ocean, the main meal had been served, and the brothers Struben had switched from martinis to single malt scotch. They were intent on enjoying every minute of their trip.

Sitting next to Adam, his friend Celine was now sitting up straight and staring out the window with her arms folded across her ample chest. Earlier she had been quiet and drowsy, but not asleep as she eavesdropped on the Struben brothers conversation, and she was pissed off. *"Met her at the office ... Gives good head."* The phrase kept running through her mind. After all their commentary on the wonderful and enigmatic Gina Alvarez, could Adam at least have said: *"Celine is a smart woman"* or *"an interesting lady."* No it was simply: *"Met her at the office ... Gives good head."* Celine would have even accepted: *"Celine's an animal in bed,"* the throwaway phrase they didn't want to pin on Gina. None of that though, just: *"Met her at the office... Gives good head."* The more the phrase rang through her brain the more irate Celine became. For Christ's sake: *"Met her at the office.... Gives good head!!!!"* Couldn't that asshole at least have said: *"Met her at the office.... Gives GREAT head!!!"* She was absolutely furious. And she couldn't wait to get away from Adam when the plane landed. She hated Adam and she also hated Josh but mostly she hated the "perfect" Gina Alvarez.

****

On the other side of the plane Dr. Moses and Father Flaherty were also enjoying an after dinner cocktail. This had already been a highly unusual flight for Al Moses. Instead of simply enjoying his normal contemplative solitude, he had been engaging in an active and interesting discourse with his new friend, Brian Flaherty.

When there was a short silence for a moment or two, Al asked to get by to go use the men's room. Al walked back toward the galley way at the rear of the section.

They were more than six hours into the flight before they ran into one another. As Dr Al had walked to the rest room at the rear of the first class cabin, he almost looked right past the young man exiting the facility. He had a glint of recognition. When Josh looked over his shoulder and saw Dr Moses, his recognition was more absolute.

"Dr. Moses?" he said. "Do you remember me, Josh Struben?"

"Yes, of course, Josh. How are you? I just had dinner with your Dad on Sunday night! He gave me the run down on you and your brother. Both spending a lot of time in New York, I hear."

"Yes, Adam lives there. In fact he's on the plane also. We were just together in Rome for a few days. Actually the night you were having dinner with Dad, I was having dinner with Mom, and then I flew over to Rome to meet up with Adam and his friend, Celine. What a coincidence running into you a few days later.

"It's been a long time since I saw you and your brother. A few years anyway… Adam's graduation, maybe? I saw you boys then."

"That could be it." The plane bounced a little bit as it hit an air bump, and then the flight attendant could be heard giving her instructions in Italian and English

"Signore e signori, Ladies and gentlemen. We are experiencing slight turbulence. The captain has turned on the seat belt sign. Please return to your seats."

Josh and Dr Al ignored the flight attendants warning and kept on talking.

"So what brings you boys to Rome?" Dr Al inquired.

"Just a little vacationing … I have a friend who is doing a concert tour in Europe and she was in Rome for a couple of shows."

"Ah yes, so I have heard. Gina Alvarez. Quite a sensation! I saw a picture of the two of you in a magazine in my office. Didn't do either of you justice."

Just as Josh was wondering what picture that might be the plane took a much heavier bounce, and the flight attendant came up to them and said, "We are hitting some unexpected bad weather, gentlemen, I have to ask you to please return to your seats, now."

Another still bigger bump punctuated her request and Dr Al said, "I'll stop by your seat a little later to say hello to Adam." Then he quickly ducked into the restroom so that he wouldn't have to return to his seat without taking care of business. Josh walked back to his seat on the right of the plane.

As Josh slipped into his seat he noticed that Adam and Celine were having a rather heated discussion, with Adam on the receiving end of the heat. As Josh approached from behind they stopped talking, and Celine turned and glared out the window once again. Just as Josh flopped down in his seat, the big aircraft lurched once again and it felt as though a giant hand was on top of the plane and just pushed the huge 767 downward ten to twenty feet. There was some rattling of pots from the galley that accompanied the repositioning of the jumbo jet.

"Signore e signori; Ladies and gentlemen. This is your Captain speaking. We apologize for the bumpy ride. We will try to find a different altitude with a smoother flight. Meanwhile please stay in your seats with your seatbelts buckled."

Josh looked across the plane and noticed Dr Al wobbling back to seat 3A near the very front of the first class cabin. Al was seated for less than three seconds, when the plane lurched once again. Now the giant hand seemed to be on the right of the plane moving the plane three feet to the left.

Up front, Brian Flaherty said to Dr Al. "I'm glad you made it back. This is starting to get a little rough."

"I'd say so. Did you feel that last one? Seemed to push the whole plane… Bad news is they temporarily closed the bar."

The huge invisible hand now seemed to be behind the plane pushing it forward. And then quickly it was like the Hand of God. It was on the top front end of the plane and with a sudden push it sent the nose of the plane hurtling downward in a steep angled plummet. The oxygen masks popped out of the overhead compartment, and stomachs reached toward the ceiling of the plane.

****

Back in New York, it was about 4 PM and John and Maria were finishing up their work. Rickie Van Dorfan had left about an hour earlier.

"Where would you like to go for dinner tonight, Maria?"

"I don't know. I didn't know that you would be staying in the city for dinner tonight. I thought that you might be out on Long Island with Maureen."

"Maureen is taken care of. Mike Kelvey's at the house with her. I thought that maybe we'd have dinner and a drink or two and that I would just stay in the city tonight. It's been a long week."

"I don't know John. If you don't mind, I think I'd just rather be alone tonight. You're right. It has been a long week.

They were still sitting in JB's conference room as they discussed how to spend the evening, and neither John nor Maria had anticipated a confrontation beforehand. Maria really had thought that John would return home to his wife and John had believed that Maria would want to see him because he had been particularly preoccupied with his domestic problems over the past two days.

"Okay, I get it. You're not too happy that I haven't called or said much to you for the last two days. But what you have to understand, Maria, is that Maureen took quite a spill. She actually could have died. She had some severe lung problems until we got them straightened out. She messed up her face pretty good as well. I couldn't just leave her."

It finally dawned on Maria what a buffoon John Brady actually was. It was one thing to be so callous and inconsiderate of his wife. It was something entirely different to grossly misunderstand Maria's conception of their relationship as well as her concern for his wife. Anger was an emotion that rarely visited Maria's face. She was now flushed red with rage.

"John, what do you mean you couldn't just leave her? Why, on earth, are you leaving her now? You need to be with Maureen." There was an uncharacteristic emotion to Maria's protest. John mistook Maria's anger for misdirected ardor. He was being turned on by it.

He stood up behind his seat at the head of conference table and took a hard look at the flushing Maria. Her breasts were bulging against her thin black cashmere sweater. Suddenly JB felt like *doing* his executive assistant right there on his conference table. It wouldn't have been the first time.

"Maria, remember the time we worked late after the Rillings & Charm acquisition....?" John reached down with his left hand toward Maria's right breast, as she was getting up out of her seat.

"John. Sometimes you can be such as asshole!!" Maria avoided his grasp and moved toward the conference room door. She looked over her shoulder and said. "I'm going home!" Then she looked back and for good measure cautioned "Alone!"

John stared after her, taking notice of the delicate curvature of Maria's derriere and said to himself, "I'll never understand women."

****

The Strubens had returned home to their London townhouse mostly in silence, holding hands in the back of the taxi. The cab driver had recognized Danielle and made a comment about how much he enjoyed her music, but after accepting a polite "Thank you," he didn't press the conversation further. They got out of the cab and entered the townhouse still silently holding hands most of the way.

They both wandered around their spacious townhouse, neither talking at first as they occupied space in separate rooms, Stephen staring at the books on the shelves of the library and Danielle tinkering aimlessly in the kitchen. They both finally wandered into the living room and sat next to each other on the couch.

"This all seems to be happening so fast," Stephen said.

"The chemo starts Tuesday. I *'ave* to tell the boys *sometheeng*. Don't you *theenk*?"

"Of course."

"I'm not *lookeeng* forward to *telleeng* them. I could *'ave* told Josh last Sunday, but I *'adn't* told you yet."

"I understand, Danielle. I'll tell the boys if it will be any easier on you."

"No Stephen. I *weell* tell them. *Eet weell* be soon. But *eet* may not be before Tuesday."

"As you wish, Danielle … With some of these things, there is no right and wrong way. You just do what you do."

"I know, Stephen. But I'm very *'appy* that you are always there for me."

"How could it be any other way? You are the love of my life." They looked deeply into one another's eyes and held the moment for more than a minute, almost two. No one was counting.

****

The Captain had found a new altitude all right. The plane had been in a free fall for more than a thousand feet before he managed to bring it out of its nosedive. Two of the overhead bin doors were cracked and some loose bottles had smashed in the galley. A trickle of water ran out below the door of the restroom. Inside the 767, passengers grabbed for the oxygen masks and some were groaning in fear. However the aircraft had straightened out for about thirty seconds and then started a much less precipitous decline. There was no news from the cockpit yet.

Near the left rear of the first class cabin, Celine clutched onto Adam's arm with both of her own arms and had buried her head against his chest. Adam just looked across the aisle at his brother Josh. The few martinis and single malts that they had consumed along the way had helped keep both brothers calm. The aircraft's emergence from the downward spiral had enabled everyone to breathe slightly deeper, but almost everyone kept their oxygen masks in place. The plane had not lost cabin pressure, but most of the passengers were not willing to take chances.

In seat 3B Brian Flaherty had turned ashen, but was recovering his color as the flight trajectory flattened out somewhat.

Dr Al turned to Brian and asked, "Does your breviary have any prayers for times like this?"

"We'll be fine, Al. It looks like it's okay!" His words were meant to be reassuring. His tone was shaky.

"They haven't said anything." As Moses said this, the intercom made a gargling noise of its own and all of the passengers stopped moaning in a hope to hear what had happened or worse what was happening.

The familiar start to the announcement began again: "Signore e signori; Ladies and gentlemen; Ciò è vostro parlare del capitano; This is your Captain speaking. We have encountered a severe wind shear. The loss of altitude that you experienced was unanticipated. We are now moving at a controlled pace. We do not expect further difficulty. However, please remain in your seats with your seatbelts buckled. There has been no loss of cabin pressure, but as a precaution we are moving down to a lower altitude."

"Do you think they know what they're doing?" Al looked at Brian when he asked this question, and responded with equal uncertainty. "It seems to me no one ever truly knows what they're doing,"

"Refreshing thought."

Across the first class cabin, Josh, Adam and Celine all listened intently as the Captain came back on the intercom and declared,

"Signore e signori; Ladies and Gentlemen. We are currently flying over the Atlantic Ocean on a flight plan that has us 780 miles away from Newark Airport. We have arranged for priority landing clearance and will be making our way straight into Newark, and should be landing in an hour and twenty minutes."

"So Josh, what do you think? Are we in trouble here or not?"

"Damned if I can tell you Adam, we really are at the mercy of those guys up front,"

"I think it's more like we're at the mercy of that guy up there." Adam pointed skyward.

****

Saturday night on the north shore of Long Island brought with it a whole new perspective to Maureen Brady's life. Her husband, John had just arrived home but had not as yet come upstairs to see her. She sat before the mirror in her dressing room antechamber, and stared at the bandages that partially covered her swollen face, below her left eye. They were a dire reminder of how fleeting life could be. "I need help." She said aloud to the mirror. *And I need it now*. She said to herself under her breath. She took the bottle of Percocet that Dr Kelvey had given her, and thought for a second about taking a double dose, or more. Then she decided that this was not the kind of help she needed. Maureen determined that she would definitely get *real* help. She took the prescribed dosage and went to bed alone.

Chapter 5: *Tuesday*

The call came at 7:30 AM on Tuesday morning, and Danielle wasn't quite sure what to make of it, so she went into the study to discuss it with Stephen.

"Neville Roorback's office just called. They don't want me to go to the *cleeneec* at 8:30. They said that I should meet Dr Roorback at *'ees* office, where we met *'eem* on Saturday and they want to do *eet* at 2:30 PM *thees* afternoon."

"Are you going to get the chemo at his office instead? I wonder what that's all about."

"I asked the woman who called *eef* that was what was going to *'appen* and she said 'no' and that Dr Roorback would be *deescusseeng* a change *een* treatment *weeth* me."

"What on earth is this all about? Did she say?"

"She *deedn't* seem to know, or at least she gave me the *eempression* that she *deedn't* know. She just said that *eet* was *eemportant* that I speak *weeth* Roorback, before going to the *cleeneec* and that *eet* was *eemportant* that I speak *weeth 'eem* as soon as *posseeble*"

"Did she seem to think it was good news or bad news?"

"*Eet* was *'ard* to tell. But *theenk* of *eet thees* way. We *'aven't 'ad* a lot of good news *een thees* regard lately, so let's *theenk poseeteevely*." Danielle was glad that she had Stephen to talk to. Her attempts to keep Stephen composed were in fact calming to herself.

"So if he wanted you to talk to him as soon as possible, why didn't he just call you himself?"

"I don't know."

"Did you tell this woman that we could go over to Roorback's office right away? We've been ready to go to the clinic. We'll just change directions and go to his office and meet him there at 8:30."

"We'll apparently *'e* wasn't *goeeng* to be at the *cleeneec* when I received the chemo anyway and now *'e's* not available until *thees* afternoon."

"This is not something we want to be held in suspense about."

"I know, *darleeng*. But what am I supposed to do?"

"I'm sorry, Danielle. I didn't mean to sound that way to you. I'm a bit jumpy this morning. That's all. It's not your fault."

Stephen made a pot of coffee and also began to boil some water for Danielle's tea. Stephen then retrieved the newspaper from the front doorstep. He shared a section with Danielle and the two of them tried to think about other things for a little while before they got ready to leave for Roorback's office but they were not able to concentrate on the national news. They were only thinking about the news they would get from Roorback.

****

It was Tuesday afternoon in Poland and Gina Alvarez was at the finest spa in Warsaw. She'd spent more than two hours with her yoga instructor. And this was after spending more than an hour and a half in the fitness center in the morning. Over the last few years Gina had become a spa-junky and she went to the best spas throughout the world whenever she was on tour. It was her attempt to relax.

Early in life Gina had begun reading the philosophical teachings of the great Greek philosophers, Aristotle, Plato and Socrates. There was a built in ethos to all of their writings that emphasized a sound mind, in a sound body, with a sound spirit. She had reread these works many times since. Gina recognized that she had trouble with the spiritual side of things. However she believed that if she worked hard enough to ensure that she had a sound mind and body, the spiritual part would eventually unfold for her.

She was careful about her body. She observed a daily exercise routine faithfully. Yoga classes were an add-on to this routine. It provided her with a comfortable marriage of Greek and Hindu philosophies.

Gina was also wary of drugs of all kinds, including prescription drugs and over the counter medications, as well as the recreational drugs used by many people in her profession. After some adolescent experiences, she also abhorred alcohol use, and this was the only bone of contention between Josh and her.

Gina didn't believe that she needed to create any artificially induced emotional states. She was searching for a natural bliss that could be a free extension of her mind/body experiences. The closest she had come to this was through her sexual experiences. Her muscle tone allowed her to pursue the physical pleasures of sex in a multi-orgasmic array of ever escalating sensation. However her sexual partners had sometimes seemed to be mere joists in her sexual exploration. That was the one most magnificent difference in her relationship with Josh. Not only was he her match physically, but he was also an intellectual stalwart, able to share her journey to true joy. In her search for rhapsody, Josh was a perfect partner.

Gina also knew how fortunate she was. She was well aware of the God-given attributes that helped make her different. And she was also well aware that even these gifts were not enough to make a substantial difference when she was a child.

Growing up fatherless on the beaches of Puerto Rico, she was often left to her own devices by a mother who cared very much but worked very hard. As a young teenager, Gina had multiple passions. She always had her music and her books, but she also loved sports. At fourteen years old, she filled out a bikini, and had no trouble sneaking into pickup beach volley ball games at the resorts where her mother worked. After school each day, she would sneak along the beach to the nearby resort and easily mingled amongst the crowd. She befriended many vacationers, who never recognized her as a local. She never had money to buy food or drinks, but accepted graciously when others bought meals for her.

As a fifteen year old, a miscalculated volleyball wager with a spring-break vacationing college student cost Gina the top to her bikini. The same student taught Gina her original lessons in sex. As she sometimes reflected back on these memories they seemed long ago. But in reality it was a mere seven years that had transpired since her initiation to intimacy. She had learned a lot since then.

But this was now a different day, a different country and even a somewhat different Gina. It was still quite early in the day and Gina wanted some time to relax. For the next hour and a half she had scheduled a "fourhanded massage." Two massage therapists would simultaneously knead Gina's body in symmetric strokes of equivalent pressure working on both the left and right sides, of her body, in a balanced ballet of therapeutic muscle manipulation. It was a growing favorite for Gina amongst the many forms of massage that she had experienced in the last couple of years. Gina craved intensity even in her efforts to relax.

Dressed in a terrycloth robe Gina walked from the sauna and shower area into her treatment room where her two male masseurs greeted her. The lighting was low and the soft and sensitive in the backdrop. The massage table was in the center of the dark paneled treatment facility, and about two dozen candles were burning atop a wooden chests filled with creams and oils lining the back and sides of the chamber.

"Good afternoon Miss Gina. I am Stan and this is Henryk." One of the two young masseurs greeted Gina in unbroken but heavily accented English, "We will be administering your massage today. Have you experienced a fourhanded massage before? Is there any particular area of your body that you would like us to attend to, in any more delicate or more aggressive way, than normal?"

Stan was well aware of who his client was, and had often catered to famous clientele in the past. However both he and Henryk were both immediately captivated by the sheer aura that Gina exuded. They wanted to be polite and welcoming, but did not want to seem in awe of Gina either.

"My thigh muscles are a bit sore, but I don't want you to change anything you do. Just proceed as normal." Gina then added. "My right shoulder is also a bit fatigued, but like I said, nothing but your usual approach."

Gina didn't wait for the two men to leave the room as they normally did while she readied herself for her treatment. She simply untied the front of her robe and removed it; stood stark naked for a second and then said; "Let's just get started." She then laid face down on the massage table while Henryk covered her lower extremities with the sheet up to her lower back. He glanced across Gina's prone body at Stan with a surprised shy smile that said; "This is a very different and very beautiful woman."

****

The Wall Street conference call had not gone smoothly for JB. Too many questions went unanswered or were inadequately addressed. Way too many questions about cost controls were asked. He knew that the markets were plummeting all around him, but he didn't think that the general economic slowdown was being fairly factored into the overall results for ICD. Sure they were giving Wall Street new guidance about their expected performance. And yes the outlook was much dimmer than it had been last quarter. But wasn't this true just about everywhere? Didn't they deserve some credit for a solid performance in the Asian markets?

No. It just didn't go well, and John Brady knew it. The stock had already slipped from 98 to 79 over the first three quarters of the year and this was with a much more optimistic outlook. By the time he left the conference call and went back to his office, he could see that the stock watch monitor on his computer showed ICB down to 76.87 at the open. A half hour into trading ICD was selling at 76 even, down $3 on the day, bringing the overall slump for the year to more than 20%. He took no solace in the fact that the overall market itself was in a freefall. He was John Brady, CEO of ICD. He should have been more personally assertive on the call.

John closed the door to his office and buzzed his secretary.

"Alice, hold all of my calls for a half hour or so, and then come in and we'll go over the appointments for the rest of the week. Any Wall Street calls should be sent to Neil Farmer. All internal calls should be sent to Maria. Send the customer calls to Monroe or Morgan. Any external business calls we'll get back to later in the day as appropriate."

"Maria left after the conference call, Mr. Brady. She had a doctor's appointment."

"Did she say what time she would be back?"

"She said that she should be back by 1 o'clock, Mr. Brady"

"Okay, then have Van Dorfan work the internal nonsense until she gets back."

JB then just leaned back in his chair, put his feet up on his desk, and folded his hands together behind his head. It was simply Brady's thinking position. His reading glasses were unused on his desk and intermittently he would unlock his hands and run them both through his hair simultaneously, and then once again lock them behind his head.

His ruminations veered from his business concerns to his personal concerns. To start with he was annoyed with Maria. Who the hell did she think she was? He plucked her out of a European spa and made a successful businessperson out of her. Where was her gratitude? She blew off dinner on Saturday night, right when he needed her. And then she had the audacity to suggest that he should be at home with his wife. As he leaned back in his chair his annoyance with Maria flared toward anger. He put the anger aside and aimed at resolution. Regardless of her impertinence the last few days, he had to admit she was still a fine piece of ass, and although no one talked openly about it, he knew that his colleagues and competitors alike admired his trophy. But as attractive as Maria was, there were other trophies out there to be had, and so maybe it was time to move on. He thought that he would have one last good fuck-fest with her in the next week or two and then tell her it was over.

He sat up in his chair and then got up and stood behind it while contemplating what business event over the next couple of weeks would provide the opportunity for his final rendezvous with Maria. He walked toward the window and as he did so he felt a sharp twinge in the lower right side of his back. This twinge quickly morphed into a familiar dull discomfort that had plagued JB periodically over the last year. As he felt the oncoming symptoms, he realized that they appeared most often at times of particularly acute stress. The pain also seemed to be most resolute on the relatively infrequent times that he was irritated by Maria.

The variant thought that quickly crossed John Brady's mind with respect to Maria, was that she had become a valuable business asset as well as his personal passion interest. He thought a bit about how he was able to utilize Maria as a sounding board. She had a sixth sense when it came to evaluating people, their motivations and their intentions. He often relied on her counsel on multiple business issues. Operating as both his executive assistant and his intimate interest allowed John the luxury of getting unfiltered feedback from Maria. He would miss that. He knew that Maria had no financial needs whatsoever because of past liaisons, so he suspected that she would have no reason to want to retain her job, once their personal relationship was terminated. Her business termination would come with an attractive exit package from ICD so it should all be amicable. Okay, that decision was made, he thought.

Now with both hands above his hips and supporting his lower back John just stared out the window and changed his reflections. Thoughts about Maureen brought more immediate action. He walked back over to his desk and buzzed Alice.

"Get my wife on the phone, Alice, and let me know when you've got her."

A few seconds later JB heard the intercom buzz, "Mrs. Brady on line 2."

"How are you feeling Maureen?"

"Much better John ... My face still is very sore from the operation yesterday. Dr Vincent said that everything should heel nicely over time, and Fernando is driving me back to Dr. Vincent's office later this morning. Dr. Vincent said that I was lucky that the cut was deep but it was clean and not jagged and that there was no broken facial bone. The bone is just severely bruised."

"Well he knows your face as well as anyone. This isn't the first surgery he has performed on it."

"Is that your idea of sarcasm, John? Why are you so mean spirited?"

"Just stating the facts … How long before you're back to looking normal?"

"Oh John, you're so damn unpleasant. I didn't fall on purpose. Sometimes I think you go out of your way to sound callous."

As John paced around his office still holding his painful back while he barked at his speakerphone he couldn't help noticing the difference between his wife Maureen and his mistress, Maria. Even though English was not her native language, Maria spoke the language fluently. But she would never use words like "unpleasant" and "callous." That was the verbiage of the American patrician class that Maureen grew up in. Maria would have just told him that he was an "asshole and that he could just go fuck himself." Regardless of her methods and tactics, Maria was a self-made woman.

"I'm not trying to be *unpleasant*, Maureen. I'm just trying to get a worthwhile estimate about timeframes for your healing process."

"Dr Vincent was a bit vague yesterday. He said that I would need to have a good make-up person for a while and that it was possible that I would need some more work in about eight weeks. I'll probably know more after I see him today."

"Well I guess that takes you out of the benefit dinner circuit for a while."

"Does that bother you? You can just take Maria or one of your office assistants to those things. They seem to enjoy them more than I do anyway."

"No, that's not a problem. It's just that you are my wife and from time to time, it helps to have you available for some of these business dinners, and recognition functions. That's all."

"Well John. I'm not going to be available for a while anyway. I am going to Costa Rica for the next two months."

"What do you mean, you're going to Costa Rica?"

"Just what I said … I'm going for a stay at 'Solace in the Sun'."

"Isn't that the rehab place where all those Hollywood types go?"

"Yes John. It's a rehabilitation facility. I need the kind of help that I can get there."

"Whose idea was this?"

"What do you mean? It was my idea of course."

"You're going to take a two month vacation? What about the kids? What about me? This was your idea? Are you sure?"

"Yes. I talked it over with Dr Kelvey and he assured me that 'SIS' as they call it is a wonderful caring place and that I could recover from my wounds while I was rehabilitating my alcohol addiction."

"Kelvey told you that? Kelvey told you that he thought you were an alcoholic?" John was incredulous. Now he was ready to hang Mike Kelvey. He was supposed to be helping her with this mess she had made, and now it appeared he was making it even worse. Well at least JB now knew where he could reduce ICD's costs by $50K.

"John, stop thinking about yourself all the time. I don't know how I got myself into this predicament but I'm going to get myself out of it. I have a drinking problem, and unless I can help myself, how can I be of any help to Mark, Megan and Kenneth or for that matter, to you John. I can't help anyone if I can't help myself."

"I don't need your help, Maureen and for that matter neither does Mark and Megan. But Kenneth is still at home. He needs you."

"He has a father. Doesn't he? Besides John, what's with all the melodrama? Kenneth is seventeen years old. He'll be fine. And it's not like I won't see my family for two months. The program has a lot of flexibility built into it."

"How do we know this is the best place for you? Did Kelvey pick this place?"

"No John. I keep telling you that this is my choice. Actually I looked at the possibility of doing something there a month before my fall. I've been thinking about it for a while. I did discuss it with Dr Kelvey and he was making the preparations for me this morning."

"Is Kelvey out there at the house?"

"Yes, he's in your office making calls."

"All right. Tell him to call me when we finish talking."

"What else do you want to talk about, dear?' There was no sarcasm in her voice. She was generally open to a change of topic. In fact it would be nice to have a more general conversation in the middle of a business day. That type of conversation seemed to be a relic of the distant past."

John didn't answer Maureen right away and he seemed ready to hang up and move on, when Maureen gave life to further dialogue. "How did your call with the financial analysts go?"

John was slightly befuddled. Maureen never asked any questions about ICD. He was surprised that she even knew of the importance of the morning financial guidance call. "It didn't go very well. They don't like the early returns from the merger and are indicating that our costs are out of line. We lowered projections and the market hadn't previously factored that into our share price. In short, we're getting hammered."

"Don't worry about it, John. You have a strong management team. It's just a cyclical thing."

Rather than express his frustrations at Maureen's lack of business acumen, John, for once, listened to his wife's intuition and then answered her in a quiet voice, but with a tone that was respectful of that intuition. "Maureen, the world financial markets are crumbling. The US economy is in recession, and all of the financial gurus seem to be out of new ideas. Why shouldn't I be worried? Frankly, I am worried."

"John, just remember … it's only money." *How I wish that were true. John thought to himself.* John was well aware of the fact that it wasn't the money. It was the power and excitement that he craved. He was impossibly addicted to both.

"I've got to go Maureen. We'll talk more about this Costa Rican excursion when I get home tonight."

"Oh good … you'll be home for dinner? I'll let Jeannine know. I think Kenneth will be around for dinner also. It will be nice."

"Yes plan on dinner around eight." Then as an afterthought he inquired, "Have you heard from Mark or Megan?"

"I haven't heard from Mark since we told him all about the fall last week. He's pretty busy with his midterms. Megan has called every day. She's thinking about coming home to see me this weekend. She has also talked to Kenneth a lot, and she has asked how you were doing with all of this market turmoil."

"What did you tell her?"

"The same thing that I told you."

"And what was that, may I ask?"

"It's only money."

"Fine … just have Kelvey call me."

"See you this evening. Good bye."

"Bye."

John picked up the Wall Street Journal from his desk but didn't sit down. He stretched and twisted his back slightly to try to find a comfortable position. He couldn't quite find it. Just as he was reaching for his reading glasses, Alice buzzed in again on the intercom.

"Dr Kelvey on line 2 … Mr. Brady."

That was good, John mused. The great and mighty Dr Michael Kelvey being responsive for a change and thereby showing some respect. After all what good would it be to be acknowledged as a captain of commerce, by what had become a skittish Wall Street crowd, if the hired professional help was unresponsive?

"Hello Mike, what's this I hear about Maureen going to Costa Rica?"

"Hi John … oh yes … 'Solace in the Sun.' It's a great place. It's got …"

"Have you ever been there?" JB interrupted.

"No, but I …"

"Have you ever sent anyone there before? What were the results?"

"John I've never had a patient go there before, but SIS has an absolutely fabulous reputation. I'm sure you've heard about it. I just got off the phone with their director. They take a holistic approach to medical issues. They have a terrific staff. They're extremely discreet and …"

"Christ Mike, you sound like a fucking commercial for the place. 'Holistic this…Discreet that.' I don't know what any of that shit means. All I want to know is that if Maureen needs to go dry out somewhere is this SIS place, the right place?"

"Yes John. I think it is."

"Okay, fine. I'm not even going to bother asking you *why* you think that." He paused for about two seconds and let his semi-veiled reprimand set in. Then he continued in another direction. "Another thing Mike, my back is still killing me. I've seen just about every last doctor and witchdoctor on the list. This has been more than a year now, and I still get these pains, and now they're more frequent than ever."

"Is your back bothering you right now?"

"You bet your ass it is. I have a hard time even sitting down, much less getting work done. And I've got that jelly-neck feeling again, like my neck can't hold my head on straight." JB didn't realize and didn't care how absurd and silly his description sounded.

"Are you coming out to Long Island tonight or will you be staying in the city?"

"I'm going to the Island. I plan on having dinner with Maureen and Kenneth and then going to bed."

"Okay, good I'll prescribe something for you and have it delivered to the house. Read the directions. OK?"

"Okay, Okay."

"If you still have the pain tomorrow, call me. Okay?"

"Okay, okay. I've got to go, Mike." JB hung up the phone without officially saying goodbye or waiting for similar sentiments to be uttered by Dr Kelvey. But the thought went through his mind that Kelvey's solution was like the old medical dogma of "take two aspirin and call me in the morning."

Here he was perched in a beautifully appointed, mahogany lined office, high above the streets of Manhattan. He was one of the world's most prominent business leaders, and yet after eleven months of pain and agony and disparate X-rays, MRI's CAT scans and assorted other medical diagnostic nonsense, he was still getting the old cure "take two aspirin and call me in the morning. What was next? Chicken-fucking soup?

He ignored the pain and stopped rubbing his back. Work would be his immediate panacea. He buzzed Alice. "Come on in, Alice, let's work the calendar. As he did so he glanced at his stock watch: ICD 73.125, and falling.

****

Al Moses was happy just to be at work. The Saturday evening flight from Rome had thoroughly shaken him. The final two hours had been a harrowing event. The frequent updates from the Captain had been reassuring, not because of anything he said but because of the way he said it. He kept repeating his updates in Italian and then in English, but his voice always remained calm. The interesting part about updates from the Captain was that he was every bit as much at peril as was any of the passengers. But he was the one with more information, and if the Captain wasn't too worried than the passengers didn't need to be too worried either.

Doctor Al tried to put the weekend behind him as he began his appointments. He was happy to see that Maria Cordoza was amongst his clients for the day. He looked at her chart and it helped him recall the details of her last visit. She had been experiencing menstrual cycle interruptions and his notes reflected that she seemed saddened by something that she didn't discuss. During the recent economic downturn several of his clients had seemed somewhat depressed, but his notes said that Maria had multiple addresses worldwide and that she enjoyed prosperity, and was interested in medical philanthropy. The economic crisis probably wasn't concerning her very much. Maria had set up this appointment by persuading his assistant, Charlotte, to have Al start his day an hour earlier than he had planned. He would give her whatever time she needed.

****

Stephen and Danielle were at Dr Roorback's office a half hour early, but he didn't keep them waiting any longer. When Neville Roorback entered the familiar conference room he appeared even more disheveled than usual. His white coat looked like it was one or two sizes too small. His shoes appeared as though they hadn't been polished in a month, and his eyes looked sleepier than they had in the past. It was the eyes that Stephen noticed first. Besides their normal sleepy expression, they now appeared to be sad and somewhat downcast. He had the usual stethoscope straddling his neck for no apparent reason, other than doubling for a tie. Stephen and Danielle both began to rise out of their seats to greet Roorback.

"No no don't get up." Roorback started. He himself went over and sat on the edge of the large desk so that he was half standing and half sitting when he talked. "Thank you for coming in today. I wanted to deliver some information to you in person, because of the nature of what I am going to tell you."

Stephen seethed and thought *if this is what this clown believes to be bedside manner, he needs another few years in med school. Don't prevaricate and delay. Tell us what we need to know.* However he said nothing at first. He just listened.

"I have what is essentially good news for you, Danielle." Another maddening pause ensued and Dr Roorback neither smiled nor looked directly at Danielle as he finally delivered his news. "You don't have cancer."

"I don't 'ave IBC? I don't 'ave Inflammatory Breast Cancer?"

"As of now you don't have any kind of breast cancer, or any cancer period, at least, as far as our tests go." Roorback was hemming and hawing. It was as though he were making an excuse for being definitive. It was almost paradoxical.

"What are you *talkeeng* about Dr Roorback, when you say 'as far as our tests go?' What do you mean? I thought that you took a biopsy on my breast *teessue* and *eet* came back *poseeteeve*. Did you perform some *addeetional* tests that negated the first tests? How does *thees* all work?" Danielle's voice was uncharacteristically aggressive.

Roorback thought about what Danielle had asked. He wondered if there was something in Danielle's question that would allow him to soften the impact of the admission he was slowly unfolding.

"Well it's not any additional tests that we did." He paused again and then continued. "Let me say this first. I want to reinforce the fact that you don't have cancer." He was attempting to hammer home the good news. "You may recall that we did have you take a mammogram and an ultrasound scan and that these tests were somewhat preliminary in that nothing definitive would be detected. We were just looking to get an additional picture of the breast and attempt to detect any changes in the breast."

"Yes. Sure. I recall that you said that the only *defeeneeteeve* way to *determeene* that I *'ad* IBC was to do the biopsy. I remember all that *deescussion* clearly, and I also remember that you said the tests came back *poseeteeve* and that the biopsy clearly *eendeecated* that I had IBC. I guess I'm very *'appy* and relieved to *'ear* you say that the *diagnosees* of the biopsy is now *negateeve* and that I don't *'ave* cancer. But *ees* the evaluation of the biopsy so *deeffeecult* to make. Should I *steell* be worried?"

"No. Let me repeat the good news. You don't have cancer. Definitely." Roorback then delivered the difficult, embarrassing and negligent part of his news. "The diagnosis of biopsy was correct. We just got back the wrong lab results. The biopsy was of another patient's breast tissue. The biopsy of your breast tissue, the core biopsy, the skin biopsy and the lymph node biopsy all were negative."

The immediate reaction of Stephen and Danielle was enormous, deep-sighing relief. The emotion took root in both Strubens' consciousness, and then it was rapidly replaced by concern, bordering on anger. Stephen spoke first.

"How could something like this happen?"

"*'ow* can I be sure you *'ave* the right answer *thees* time? 'Ow do I know you're not *steell makeeng meestakes*?" Danielle added. "What I *'ear* you *sayeeng ees* that *thees ees* a case of 'right *diagnosees*, wrong chart.' *Ees* that correct?"

"That's one way of putting it." Roorback answered defensively. "We simply got the data transposed incorrectly from the lab."

Danielle was perplexed more than pleased, but the combination of emotions had her totally off balance. She needed more clarity.

"All right Dr Roorback, I understand that you now believe that my biopsy tests were *negateeve* and that I don't *'ave* cancer. The problem *ees* that my breast *ees steell* very red, very sore and very *'ot*. What *ees* wrong *weeth* me? I'm a wreck over all of *thees*. My breast feels a *leettle* better over the last couple of days, but *eet ees steell*, for lack of a better word, *eenflamed!*"

"Well that's part of the reason why I wanted you to come in. Let's have another look at the problem and see what now seems reasonable. We may even want to do another biopsy to be on the safe side. But my guess is that you simply have some kind of breast infection that we can treat with antibiotics. But before we jump to any conclusions let's have you go in the examination room and see where we are at."

"There *ees* no chance *een 'ell* that I'm *goeeng* to *'ave* another exam *een thees offeece*, Dr Roorback. I want to see someone else. Can I get a copy of my test results and all of my records? I'll want to bring them *weeth* me." Danielle was now almost out of her chair, as she sat on its very front edge.

"Certainly I understand, Mrs. Struben. We'll do what we can to help you with the records."

"I don't think you do understand, Dr Roorback. My wife wants to bring her records with her and she wants to take them *now*." Stephen was himself inflamed, and now standing.

"As I said we'll do what we can to accommodate you Mrs. Struben." Roorback continued his annoying habit of speaking only to Danielle, and not addressing Stephen when he spoke. "We will have to make copies of a few things. It will take a couple of days. Besides I'm sure that whomever you see will want to do their own tests and create their own files."

Neville Roorback remained sitting on the edge of the desk when he was speaking, with one unshined shoe touching the floor and the other suspended about a foot off the floor. As Stephen stood up, Roorback also stood back up and believing the conversation was coming to an end, he turned as though he were going to leave the room. Stephen stopped him and said.

"One other question Dr Roorback ... well actually two questions ... when did you realize your mistake, and why didn't you see Danielle right away after your secretary called? We have been anxious all day long."

"We learned about the error at the labs yesterday afternoon and then took the time to make sure that we now have the patients' lab results and records correctly assigned. We were all straightened out last night, and that's why we called you this morning. Obviously we also called the clinic so that they wouldn't begin your treatment, if we had been unable to reach you."

"And what about Stephen's other question? Why *deed* we *'ave* to wait? Why *deedn't* you see me *thees morneeng*?"

"Remember Mrs. Struben. You are the lucky one. You don't have cancer. I had another patient to see this morning, who thought her biopsy was negative and now learned that she has cancer. I thought it would be best to see her first."

****

Doctor Al Moses had completed his physical examination of Maria Cardoza and she had closed her gown and was sitting on the edge of the examining table. Dr Al had his back to Maria but he spoke over his shoulder and said "I have some time before the regularly scheduled day begins and I know you wanted to talk about some things. Why don't you get dressed and we can talk in my office. You might be a bit more comfortable there. I have one quick call to make and then we can chat."

He could have simply continued the discussion with Maria in the examination room. But the physical examinations required that he have an assistant in the room at all times and his clinical staff was constantly at the ready. Offering to continue the discussion in his office afforded Maria the privacy that he felt Maria wanted.

It was the kind of decision that made Dr Moses different from many of his colleagues. It was unusual and time consuming, but in his mind it was good medical practice. He was always trying to make people comfortable.

Moses realized instinctively that Maria wanted to talk about an issue more than she felt the need for ongoing gynecological therapy. Ms Cardoza had called while he was away and told his assistant

Charlotte that he wanted to talk about a referral. Then she had called back and made an appointment rather than call on the phone.

Five minutes later, Maria came into his office and sat down across the desk from Dr Al. She was very pleasing to look at. Her business attire could not conceal her shapeliness. Her shoulder length black hair accentuated her olive colored complexion, and large deep brown eyes. She looked very Italian, but yet much more beautiful than the young research assistants that his buddy Paolo Grassani was chasing all over Rome.

"As I indicated to you in the other room, physically everything appears to be fine. The pelvic exams don't show any overt problems. The Pap smear tests were negative and the blood tests that we ran show no signs of irregular hormone levels. I see no need for a progestin challenge test at this time. You're still a healthy young woman. The fact that you have had your second consecutive normally spaced period a couple of weeks back could mean that some of the past irregularity will clear up, especially since you indicated that symptomatically these periods were what you had been experiencing most of your adult life…these are good signs."

"I'm glad to hear that but what might have caused these problems in the first place? Am I just getting older?"

"There are lots of potential causes besides aging. The fact that you were so regular for so long is what may have you worried. But the symptoms you exhibited are not at all unusual for normal healthy women, like yourself."

"It still bothers me." Maria obviously wanted to hear more from Dr Al so he offered some additional information.

"We can rule out pregnancy, cancer, uterine scarring and complications from contraceptive use, based on your tests and our discussions. I see that you're not on any medications that might trigger the problem and we now know that there are no hormonal imbalance problems. That leaves us with a variety of different lifestyle issues. Sometimes excessive exercise or extremely low body weight can make a difference, but remarkably your weight has not fluctuated more than three pounds in the last four years. The most common lifestyle issue may be the problem."

"What is that?"

"Stress."

"Okay. I guess there have been a few stressful times over the last year. But to be honest I have not felt stressed as often as I've felt depressed." Maria paused as though she did not know where this conversation was headed.

"So tell me what is it that has you depressed?"

"I know this may be an odd thing to complain about but I feel like I'm getting old."

"You're still a very young lady. My records show that you just turned 35 earlier this year. And remember the problems with your period are not age related if that was what your concerns were about. The hormone tests are quite clear in that regard. So tell me why do you feel old and why does it matter to you?"

"I don't know what it is exactly, but I have been a bit depressed lately. I think it would be helpful if I could see someone to talk about it. I trust you and I was hoping that you might be able to recommend someone."

"Let me give it some thought. There are a few different people that I could recommend depending on what you feel you need. Tell me a little more about what depresses you." Moses was well aware of the irony of trying to counsel someone about depression, when he himself was constantly battling the painful isolated feelings that accompany depression.

"It's actually almost embarrassing. I feel like I am getting old and that I am no longer attractive. In the past I have felt beautiful. I don't feel beautiful anymore."

"Really."

"Yes I know it sounds banal but that's truly what it is. I'm not young and I'm not beautiful."

"Interesting."

"The fact that my cycle is messed up just adds to the problem. I guess that's part of getting old."

"Maria, you're right in one sense. Sometimes these things can be very interconnected. But let me stop you right there. You are a young and very beautiful woman. Understand that beauty and youth are somewhat relative but not necessarily related concepts, so it matters whose opinion you are listening to. The best opinion to heed is your own."

"But isn't my own opinion based, at least in part, by what others tell me?"

"Sometimes it can be. So who is telling you that you are not beautiful, and who is telling you you're old?"

"Actually no one is coming right out and telling me that."

"I see. I know from our ongoing discussions of your physical health that you have maintained normal, healthy sexual activity. Are there any difficulties along those lines that you want to discuss? Are your relationships for the most part monogamous? Sometimes there is an added level of complexity that is brought on by the uncertainty of multiple relationships. On the other had there can be a level of complacency that is brought on when your relationship is more singular in focus."

"I don't have sexual difficulties that are a problem although I will say that I don't enjoy sex as much as I may have when I was much younger."

"That could be an issue of sorts. As I said, Maria, you are a young woman. You should be at the apex of your sexuality. I am asking these things so that I can determine who might be best suited to help you."

"I understand. And I think you are probing the right issue. Maybe if I told you a little more about myself it would be helpful?" Maria's inflection let Dr Al know that it was a question.

"Certainly. Whatever you feel like sharing...."

"As I think you know from our past discussions, I am unmarried. And I have never been married. I don't have any children either."

"Yes some of that is reflected here in your record. I think I recall also that you recently lost both of your parents."

"Yes that's right. I went back to Italy twice this year to bury my father and then my mother."

"I hope your flights were less adventurous than the flight I just took back from Rome, last week."

"You were on that flight? The one that lost altitude and had to have an emergency landing...the one that was on the news?"

"Yes as a matter of fact I was."

"And that flight came from Rome. Right?"

"Yes, I was over visiting a medical school colleague."

"Were you in London earlier in the week?"

"Yes."

"You know I have to ask you something. Last week I was in London on business and I thought I saw someone, who looked a lot like you, when I was at a restaurant in the Mayfair area."

"Yes, that was me. I have to confess. I saw you also. I just didn't make the connection right away. Seeing you there was out of context. I didn't realize it was you until I was in the cab. I'm sorry. I should have mentioned it. I just didn't want to say anything until I knew what you wanted to talk about today. I wanted to respect your privacy. I guess."

Maria peered imploringly at Dr Al. She was unsure what to do with that statement. It didn't seem that there was that much room for privacy between a gynecologist and his patient.

"Well, I saw you as you were leaving with the other doctor, but you were across the room and it happened very fast."

"It's such a small world isn't it? I was having dinner with an old friend…. He's a business executive though, not a doctor….and I'm a whole continent away from my practice and I run into someone I know. What makes it even more bizarre, is that on my flight home from Italy I ran into the same fellow's two sons on the plane."

"Oh that's very strange. It's almost like some spirit or something is setting your agenda for you."

"If that's the case then I'm glad that spirit was watching out to make sure our plane arrived safely. Believe me it was just awful. But enough about me … We're here to talk about you and how to get you some help for things…"

"Oh I don't mind. I enjoy talking to you, Dr Al, about anything." Maria smiled fully for the first time that morning and the room lit up. Her eyes sparkled and Moses remembered where he was with respect to their discussion of Maria's issues.

"I want to go back to this notion that you don't feel pretty. And you were telling me a little bit more about your background. You were saying that you had never married before I sidetracked you with the discussion of adventures in Europe." Moses said this with a smile of his own and he was effectively putting Maria at ease. She felt comfortable talking to him about things that she couldn't discuss with others.

"That's okay. In fact, I'm glad we cleared the air about London. I don't know if you noticed the man I was having dinner with. That was my boss, John Brady. He is the CEO of ICD."

"I know who he is. I mean I've read about him in the papers. But I've never met him."

"He is also my lover, or maybe I should say my love interest. Frankly I don't know what to call him. I don't have a specific name for our relationship, I guess."

"I see." He didn't really.

"John is married. But he and I have a sexual relationship, and have had one for more than four years. But I think it's about to wind down."

"And why do you think that will happen."

"It just isn't the same as it once was. John isn't the same person he once was, and I imagine I'm not the same person either." Maria stopped for a second or two as though she were visiting the situation real time in her mind. "John can be so immature. He doesn't think of anyone but himself. His wife, Maureen, is actually a very nice woman. I've known her for almost as long as I've known John, and we've been to a number of charity dinners and such together."

"Does she know about you and John?" Dr Al twisted his mouth and raised his eyebrows in an inquisitive manner.

"I seriously doubt it. She is much more civilized than John, but I doubt that she would put up with his other relationships if she knew about them. I know it sounds strange but I try not to think too much about John and Maureen's relationship."

"You mean you don't want to think about them having sex."

"That too."

"I see." He still didn't, but he was trying.

"Anyway I think, John and I will soon become a thing of the past,"

"Will you still keep your job?"

"I've been thinking about that. I really like my job. But it would be next to impossible to keep doing my job, the way I'm doing it, and not have a personal relationship with John. We actually talk about work in bed."

"I see." Now he thought he did. "That certainly presents the possibility of disenchantment with your sexuality."

"Maybe but I still don't think that's the problem. I simply need to move on. And that more than likely means leaving ICD as well."

"Does John make you feel less than beautiful?"

"No just the opposite, actually. John wants sex pretty much all of the time, except when his back hurts. If I were to simply use his lust as a barometer, I guess I'd feel pretty desirable. I think I just want something more."

Dr Al Moses leaned back in his chair for a moment and reflected about where this discussion had taken them. Maria was concerned about her youth; concerned about her sexuality; concerned about her beauty and concerned about her overall depression. Was there a common thread? Who could he recommend that she see?

At the same time Maria Cardoza glanced across the desk at Dr Al and thought that he was both affable and wise. He knew how to talk to a woman in a no nonsense manner. She liked the fact that Dr Moses was able to comment on her emotional issues with full understanding of her physiology as part of the equation. Maria didn't have many female friends and none with whom she cared to discuss very personal issues. She would be interested in seeing whom Dr Moses might suggest to her as an emotional therapist.

"Maria, before I suggest someone that you might want to see to discuss all of these issues further, is there anything else you think I should know?"

Maria thought for a moment about the best way to phrase her answer and then just said what was on her mind, "I have been thinking lately about the fact that I don't have children and that if I ever wanted to have a child of my own I would have to do so relatively soon. I know that in this day and age there are optional ways to conceive if I wasn't in a relationship with someone who wanted to have a child, but I still think it's something that I would like to resolve in my own mind. I'm not sure if I want to be a parent. I'm just not sure one way or the other. That's all."

"Maria, you are still young. But you're right; it's not a decision you should take lightly. There is a woman I met about two years ago that I think you might want to speak with. Her name is Angelique Lefebvre. She is a French psychologist, and she is married to an Indian yoga instructor."

****

Josh hung up the phone in the Connecticut office of Cromwell Parsons Resources, CPR. the once bullish, now bearish, hedge fund that he had helped grow into a trend setting wealth creating behemoth over the last several years. Positions were crashing everywhere. The sales guys and traders were looking for help or looking for the exit. Everyone's personal portfolio had taken major hits over the past two months. The season was aptly named: Fall.

Jonathan Cromwell appeared at the door to the visitor's office that was becoming more of the regular office for Josh Struben of late. The three principal offices were in New York, Greenwich (Connecticut) and London. But they also had a smaller office in Hong Kong.

"Heard you had quite a flight back to the US, Josh?"

"Nothing I want to dwell on, to be honest."

"Fair enough ... I've got something else I want to tackle anyway."

"Good because even the wild ride on the market is easier to talk about than my ride home from Rome." Cromwell nodded. He was never one for small talk, especially during market hours. Any non-business related repartee would always have to wait until the market closed and the bars opened.

The market was already down another two hundred points on the day after being up almost a hundred points shortly after the opening bell. Cromwell was only forty-four years old. He had never seen volatility like this in his twenty years of investing. The hedge fund that bore his name was actually a series of seven different funds, and they had performed much better than the competition over the last two years but two of the seven funds were in significant trouble and each of the other five funds was hemorrhaging value substantially. Cromwell had realized significant personal wealth atrophy as well. However Jonathan Cromwell and CPR had one terrific asset. They had a rock solid investor base. CPR's funding sources were some of the most substantial family trusts in all of Europe, Asia, the Middle East and the USA. The Cromwell funds were actually private equity funds as well as hedge funds, and many of their clients were looking at hedge fund redemptions of substantial size. The trick was to get them into Cromwell's private equity funds and not lose the investors to someone else on the Street.

Irrespective of the worldwide financial turmoil, Cromwell did not appear flustered. He was tall and lean with jet-black hair combed straight back without even a fleck of gray. His custom tailored dress shirt cost $350 and his custom made black loafers set him back another $900, but none of his apparel seemed ostentatious. Everything about Cromwell seemed focused.

"We need some help on the new fund. Pritchard left ... resigned this morning ... personal reasons."

Josh knew that it would be utterly useless to ask Cromwell what personal reasons would have Paul Pritchard leaving CPR, but he also knew that it didn't really matter. Pritchard's work would have to be picked up and moved along. Cromwell was standing in Josh's doorway to discuss just that.

"Paul said that we were almost ready to go out the door with the life sciences fund. But I haven't talked to him about it for weeks."

"I'm not sure what you'll be able to get from Pritchard, but talk to Susan and Percy back in London. They know what was going on. With Pritchard gone I want you to run this thing. It could get very big. Everyone's talking healthcare. $300 million at get go, and we'll see where that takes us. Figure it out. The big boys want to do some bottom feeding, but there's also some appetite for risk with the new stuff. Just remember that you now own the rodeo, you're no longer a cowboy."

"How much of the $300 million do we have committed from investors?"

"Half."

"And how much do we have placed so far?"

"About $50 million promised, half that placed."

"Susan and Percy are working on the rest of the portfolio?"

"All the time. They're vetting stuff on a regular basis. I'm not up on all of it. Call them. They know Pritchard left."

"Where's Pritchard going? Susan and Percy are not flight risks. Right?"

"No Pritchard's packing it in. Heading to the beach or something … lost his stomach … whole bunch of shit … wife left him … .girlfriend suing him for child support. He has pissed off more than a few people, including me. He's just taking his money to the beach. He also needs to drop about 50 pounds, and grow some hair on his balls as well as on his head … has a bad ticker, I think. That could be part of it. Forget about Pritchard. Let's just get this thing out the door."

****

Her limousine picked her up after her evening concert and brought her back to the hotel. Even with her large circular sunglasses and dark silk scarf covering her eyes and hair respectively, Gina was still recognized as she scooted into the hotel, in front of her bodyguard. A young couple with a camera took a picture and several others followed suit until she was in the door of the hotel and walking brusquely across to the elevator. She reached her room and locked the door.

The concert had gone extremely well. They rocked the place. The other good news was that The Lay D's new single "Mind me," was shooting up the charts in both the USA and in Great Britain. It was becoming a monster hit already. And other than "My Kind of Love," it drew the loudest reaction from the crowd earlier that evening. She was not as exhausted as she had been earlier in the tour, and when she flopped on the bed, her mind was still back at the concert. She flipped on the TV, and whirly-birded her way through the channels. A local channel was covering the news about the concert in Polish. Gina had no idea what the commentator was saying, however it was obvious that she was pumped up about the concert, because she rolled her shoulders a bit as she reported the news and then cut away to a twenty second clip from the concert,

Gina stared at the TV and laughed at herself as she saw the clip with her singing, with her hands by her head:

"Mind me. Mind me
Don't let me loose and you won't
Find me Find me
Don't turn my head or you will
Blind me Blind me
Don't tie me up, yeah just don't
Bind me Bind me
Don't mix me up or you will
Grind me Grind me
Get off my back and don't you
Hind me. Hind me
Can start me up yes you can
Wind me. Wind me
But think it through and you will
Mind me. Mind me."

The Polish newscaster was back again imitating Gina's new hit, with a quick giggle amidst teasing in Polish from her fellow newscasters. And then, just like that, they moved on to coverage of local weather. Gina appreciated the twenty seconds of news coverage. It was more than the Lay D's been allotted in the past. She kept flipping the channels and then decided to try to reach Josh. She picked up the receiver for the phone in the room and gave the operator Josh's cell phone number back in the States.

"Struben." Josh's voice on the phone sounded like it was right next-door.

"Hello Struben. Guess who?"

"Hi. How did the concert go?"

"We rocked. The usual."

"Did you do the tie thing or is that a special treat for visiting groupies from the financial world?"

"I hate to disappoint you, but I did the necktie thing without you."

"Do you mean on stage?"

"Very funny."

"I thought so."

"So what's new? Where are you by the way?"

"I'm in Greenwich Connecticut. And there is a lot new today. As you may or may not know, the market was down another 400 points on the day. A lot of investors are getting very antsy. We've been bearish for a while, but we're now looking for buys all over the lot. One of our principal fund managers left today and Cromwell gave me the job. Barring a total collapse of capitalism on a worldwide basis, this should be the best damn opportunity of my career. I'll be running our new life sciences and healthcare fund."

"Congratulations Josh. I always knew you were hot!"

"Lucky for me. You weren't the only one."

"Don't say that. I'll have to fly home and jump your bones."

"Sounds good to me ..." He laughed, but he was very much into the sound of her voice. She was in his head big time and he knew it was dangerous. "Where are you off to next, by the way?"

"Athens, Greece. Why does Joshie-boy want to come out and play again?"

"I need to hunker down for the next week or so. But I'll probably be in London again for the weekend. Do you get a day off on this tour deal? Maybe we could meet half way. We could go back to that same hotel in London. I've got some new ties."

"That might be a little too crazy. We do have next Monday off. You know come to think of it, I wouldn't mind seeing Karen Buffet. She's still in recovery in London."

"How's the new girl working out by the way?"

"She's not Karen."

"Let's see what the next 24 hours brings, and let's keep a London soirée in the mix of possibilities. I could easily work out of our London office the early part of next week. The new job will require that I spend some time with a number of the salespeople, analysts and traders in London that I haven't dealt with in the past."

"You know Josh. I thought you told me that London was your home office. By the way, I never really asked you this before. I know you live in both places but technically are you an American or are you a Brit?"

"I'll tell you when I see you in London."

"What's the big secret?"

"Nothing really. If you must know I am an American. Now you're not going to ask me whether I am a Democrat or a Republican. Are you?" Josh kidded her.

"No big deal. I was just curious, that's all.... seems like something I should have known about you by now."

"I was born in New York. I think that still counts as American." He said wryly.

"Okay. I get it. Let me change the subject. No one else will be with me if I go to London, so why don't we skip the hotel in Mayfair and just go to your flat?"

"Why? Oh I know… because you know I have more ties there?"

"As good a reason as any."

"Let's talk about it tomorrow."

"Good night."

"It's only 6 o'clock here. What do you mean good night?"

"Good night, Josh." Gina hung up the phone and got ready for bed. She was happy.

Chapter 6: *Coming Together*

Friday night signaled the end of a long work week for Josh. He decided to wait until Saturday to fly back to London, so that he could have dinner with Adam in the city on Friday. There was no one better to talk to than family when one's life was speckled with uncertainties. Adam was not only a good listener; he also had great insights and ideas. Adam chose the venue for dinner, a place called Tao an Asian Fusion hotspot in the upper fifties just east of Fifth Avenue.

Although the décor was kept dark and the music was loud but not noisy, most of the young people were able to zone in on one another without much difficulty. The hook-up rate was recognized as a bacchanal bonanza.

The dining area in the restaurant was frenetic. It was a two story room with a separate stairwell at the back of the dining area that lead to the balcony. The open space area between the first and second floor dining was filled with a two-story statue of Buddha. The Struben brothers had a reserved table at the rear of the balcony dining area.

Josh normally drank red wine, but he ordered a bottle of Cakebread Chardonnay partially out of deference to Adam's preference for California white wine, and partially because the cuisine at Tao lent itself more to a lighter white wine. There was a lot of nibble food including every kind of sushi ever concocted.

"Did you hear anything more from Mom?" Adam inquired as the waitress brought their wine glasses and an ice bucket, and took their order.

"Not since Wednesday morning. I had no clue that she might have a problem in the first place. I had dinner with her less than two weeks back and she said nothing about it at all."

"I don't think that she even told Dad until just last week. It's scary that she was all set to start chemo, and had no idea that they mixed up the lab tests. She was seeing someone else today though."

"She still could have a problem, I guess. If that guy Roorback fucked up the diagnosis as much as they said he did, he could have just as easily given her a false negative this time through." The disgust was evident in Josh's voice. "I'm glad she's seeing someone else."

"If it's bothering her that much, she should come to NYC. There are several places here that are world renowned for cancer diagnosis and treatment."

"There are a lot of good places to go in London too. She'll be okay. If it weren't in the middle of the night over there I'd just give her a call and see what's up."

"Should have thought about that a few hours back," said Adam.

Josh rolled his glass of chardonnay in his hand a bit as he spoke. "I'll be over there tomorrow night. I'll see her Sunday morning at the latest. I'll call you after I talk to both of them. Dad also seems pretty upset about all of this."

Adam looked around the crowded balcony dining room, scanning the smartly dressed twenty-something and thirty-something year old crowd. Most tables had four or more at a table and there was animated conversation going on everywhere. There was one table with four eye-catching females, all attractively dressed in a manner that best displayed their individual physical assets, two with low cut tops, one with tight fitting pants and one with a short black skirt that exposed a lot of thigh as she sat at an angle to the table. He nodded in their direction and said to Josh, "Lots of eye candy in this place."

"You're a letch, bro. We haven't even ordered dinner yet and you're checking out the local talent."

"Yes, those four over there are looking good." Adam nodded once again in their direction and Josh twisted in his seat to get a look across the room.

"Dressed for success, I would say." Josh offered.

"Dressed for suck-sex, did you say brother Josh?"

"Come on, Adam, give it a rest will you." He turned back toward his brother but not before the brunette with the high thighs glanced furtively in their direction. "By the way whatever happened with Celine? She didn't seem too happy with you by the time we landed last Saturday."

"She was okay until the flight home. I think she thought we were making fun of her when we were bullshitting while we were ripping through those martinis. I'm not sure what offended her, but by the time we landed in Newark, you would have thought that the wind shear thing was my fault. Not a big deal. She's been telling everyone at the bank about you and Gina and the monster bash in Rome. She's made quite an epic story out of the trip home. I hear this from others; she isn't talking much to me. That's fine … no big whoop … better this way. She'll be back looking for action in a few weeks. Meanwhile I can zoom in on those big tatas across the room.

"So anyway," Adam changed the topic, "tell me about the new job. Pretty stud-ly, running the whole gig on the new private equity fund. My brother the financial All Star, or what was it they called you with that Internet picture 'Gina Alvarez's Mega-Millionaire Financial Hotshot Hunk.' How apropos !."

"Yeah the last few days have been absolutely crazy. The market is down big time for the week, for the month and for the year. Everything seems to be a bust and I'm leading the hunt for new investments. Cromwell wants to keep the hedge fund money in the house so he's pumping the private equity stuff. It's not the same 'two and twenty' take, like the hedge funds, but it beats insolvency. Lots and lots of opportunity in the life sciences stuff. I can't believe that this guy Pritchard bolted when he did. Something seems odd there. I know that he and Cromwell didn't get along. The inside skinny is that it has nothing to do with business … more to do with Cromwell humping Pritchard's old lady behind his back."

"Is he going to a competitor or starting his own fund?"

"Cromwell doesn't seem to think so … just another beached whale." Josh shrugged.

"Okay, so you get this new fund to run. What are you backing that's new?"

"There are several different types of companies we're looking at. The field of neutraceuticals, functional foods that aid in maintaining positive heath trajectories has some appealing opportunities for us. Then there are more than a few opportunities with the genome area, once they work out some of the ethical kinks. Stem cell research companies will be the rage in a few more years. In the very near term IT opportunities in healthcare and the life sciences may have the most immediate return.

"An interesting tidbit along those lines…. I came across the company, called Apakoh, that was run by that guy Dad knew who died last week."

"The Ukrainian guy?'

"Yes, Maksym Tkachuk. I wouldn't have remembered the name either, because our guys accent his name differently. But of course, the memorable part about the company is that the founder and CEO just passed away. Apakoh, I was told, is Ukrainian for 'Dragon.' Anyway, this guy Tkachuk apparently was doing work with some other company,

Rhapsody, or something like that, which is run by a group of physicians out of New York and Thailand. They were commissioning a lot of the work that Tkachuk and Apakoh were doing and they intend to use this software in a few different clinics in the US and Asia.

"The interesting part is that they are trying to do something on a global basis. In what I know of healthcare, no one does anything on a global basis. And yet this these folks apparently have some traction with STRX. If so, I'm sure Dad must know something about it. Our people liked what they heard about Apakoh, and Rhapsody preliminarily, but Tkachuk was the key link and now he's dead. From what we have heard about Rhapsody, however, there's more to their business than just the software that Apakoh was developing for them. There's a dermatologist out of New York … somebody named Alison McDuffee. She and her sister run this Rhapsody business. There's another doctor who works in Thailand who is also somehow involved. Our folks will be meeting with this group in a few weeks to ferret out what the opportunity is all about."

"So the net-net of all of this is that you see this equity fund as a major opportunity and you're having fun playing God and deciding who gets money and who gets squat."

"That's not far off. But I've only been at this for three days. What's going on at the bank?"

"Well, we keep getting bigger, but it's starting to feel more bureaucratic than ever. Now that we are bailing out the brokerage firm, we've got to go through this whole mating dance where we look at their people and our own people and decide who to keep and who to let go. A lot of the guys on their sales and trading desks are wired in the industry, so it won't be simply a matter of keeping our own people and adding a few of them. Overall, they have better talent than we do."

"You aren't at any risk, are you?"

"Not really. I'm pretty junior and the main flesh trading is going on higher up in the firm. I'm pretty wired on the banking side. However, I've been thinking about doing something else anyway. I'm not sure I'm cut out for the bureaucracy that is about to run the bank."

"Cromwell's got a 'no nepotism rule' but I have a pretty good network on the street, if you need my help."

"I'm fine for now. As you're looking at all those new medical technology firms let me know what you find interesting."

****

Further to the west side of town and about twenty blocks south. Maria Cardoza and John Brady were getting into the ICD helicopter and heading to Atlantic City. This trip was a last minute addition to Brady's agenda. His northeast sales region was having a weekend sales rally to celebrate their success over the first three quarters of 2008, when they were leading the country in production. John would normally not have agreed to speak to such a small segment of his sales force that had achieved partial year leadership recognition in an off year. JB just wanted to have a chance to take care of "the Maria thing."

Maria had been feeling better about herself almost all week. Since her chat with Dr. Moses, she was beginning to see things in a new light. "The John thing" was about to end and she was finally ready to move on. The odd part about it was that Brady didn't annoy her anymore. They worked hard and well together in addressing the recent damage, and although the stock had fallen to 70 ½, it had rebounded slightly to close at 72 ½ by the Friday close. Given the current market conditions it could have been much worse.

In spite of a long day's work, Maria was able to freshen up at the office before Fernando drove them over to the chopper pad and she knew that she looked pretty good. She had changed her skirt and blouse and let her hair down. She knew she had a nice shape that was naturally well endowed without being out of balance in any one dimension.

JB took note of how good Maria looked. He was careful to keep the mood cheerful, because he was beginning to anticipate his one final dalliance with Maria. He was no longer in a mood for business. He wanted to get laid.

Maria stepped into the helicopter first. This was the larger of the two helicopters that ICD kept in New York. It was a Sikorsky SK-76 and was set up to seat six people although it was large enough to accommodate eight. This evening the only passengers would be JB and Maria. The pilot and the copilot could get the chopper's twin engines up to about 175 miles per hour and the ride was always very smooth. It would be about an hour from the westside heliport to the strip in Atlantic City.

As Maria was ducking into her seat in the chopper, JB was following close behind and he resisted the temptation of pinching her proffered rear end. He would enjoy the night but he wouldn't force things until an appropriate hour.

The plan for the evening was that John and Maria would arrive at Atlantic City at about 8:30 and then they would be whisked over to the casino where the regional sales manager was holding his dinner for about 150 sales people. JB was now scheduled to be the after dinner speaker. The sales people would be thrilled to see their corporate leader, and the regional manager would probably be nervous as hell. John would simply tell a few corporate war stories; thank them for a job well done; give them a little rah rah and then call it a night. Maria would stay in the background and take notes on any follow up promises that John might make during the Q&A. For JB and Maria it would be an easy night.

If the crowd was enthusiastic, John might even stay around after he spoke and grab a cocktail or two with the sales team. He would act like one of the guys, and also be on the alert to see if might be some pretty young sales skirt that might be the logical heir apparent to Maria. He kept that last thought to himself.

The chopper lifted off the ground and headed south along the East River. Lower Manhattan loomed off the left of the chopper. The view had not been the same over the last seven years since the twin towers had been attacked. They could look down at a slight angle into "Ground Zero." From the air it appeared to be a large blank spot on a screen of skyscrapers. They flew past the Statue of Liberty and Ellis Island and then over the Verrazano Bridge before continuing on their way down the Jersey shore to Atlantic City. It was a clear and beautiful night and no matter how many times they had choppered out of Manhattan in the past, neither John nor Maria tired of the spectacular view.

Before they had reached Lady Liberty, John had already fixed drinks. He had a sense that with a very light business agenda ahead of him, it wouldn't hurt to start drinking early. Maria was happy to indulge. She believed it would be an interesting night, however it unfolded. She too wanted the evening to begin in a civilized fashion.

JB and his executive team at ICD customized the interior of the Sikorsky SK-76 for his use. The two seated area where the pilot and copilot sat was standard issue for the aircraft. However in the passenger area, the wood paneling was upgraded to match the paneling in JB's Manhattan office. The leather seating was soft and plush and gave one the feeling of sinking into the lap of comfort. The first two seats of the passenger area were slightly further back in the cabin to allow for the placement of a full bar and service area, as well as a small but functional PC work station that JB had never used but which Maria occasionally did use. There was an overhead magazine rack and a collapsible wooden table that was removable to allow additional passenger access to the four additional seats, to the rear of the aircraft.

"Maureen should be arriving at that SIS place right about now. I'm not sure how that's all going to work out. She seems determined to conquer her demons but I don't think she needs two months to do it." John didn't want to discuss business and he didn't want to talk to Maria about their relationship, so he chose to personalize the conversation by talking about his wife.

"You don't know John, That's for the professionals to determine."

"Sure. Let's see how this works. If I'm running the place and I have an affluent woman appear on my doorstep. I charge $2,000 a day. Money's no object to my guest. Do I let her stay at my resort for *two weeks* for $28,000 or do I let her stay for *two months* for $120,000? I say, the more money she has; the sicker she is."

"Don't be so cynical, John. It's not a resort. It's a rehabilitation center."

"I'm not being cynical at all. The only difference is that they don't put booze in the umbrella drinks."

"Well, I sent Rickie down on the Cessna with her so that he makes sure she gets settled in okay." Marie said indicating the ICD Corporate jet was their mode of transportation.

"Maureen said that Kenneth was going to go down to this place to get her squared away. So now Van Dorfan is going down there too? Maureen has a regular little entourage, just like a rock star."

"I wouldn't go that far. Maureen does still have some visible injuries. There is a full time dermatologist who works at the 'Solace in the Sun Spa' and he has been talking all week to Dr Vincent about the creams and ointments that he has prescribed for Maureen. In fact Dr. Vincent went down there on the Cessna along with Maureen and Kenneth and Rickie."

"Christ all-fucking Mighty!" JB said it loud enough so that the pilot and co-pilot overheard him.

"Everything okay back there, Mr. Brady?"

"Yes, fine … fine." He shouted back up at the pilot. Then he turned back and took a gulp out of his Bombay Safire on the rocks before addressing Maria in a lower tone.

"How the hell do you know all of this stuff?"

"It's my job to know all this."

"Don't be a smart ass."

"No seriously. I have to know these things and take care of these matters so that you can run the business. You told me that was my job the day you hired me."

JB kept his drink in his right hand and waved his left hand dismissively but didn't respond.

"To answer your question specifically, I talked to Dr Vincent last night, when he called looking for you. I left this information on both your voice mail and your email by the way."

"I don't use that stuff. You know that. That's like sending a message to yourself." He interrupted,

"You had already left for dinner with your lawyer." Maria countered. "Anyway, I figured I'd tell you today."

"So how did Vincent end up on ICD's jet?"

"Well when he called I told him that I was your executive assistant and gave him enough information to let him know that I was conversant with Maureen's problems, and asked if I could help, because you were unavailable. He didn't go into much detail but said something about how he had several conversations with the folks at SIS, and how they in fact had invited him down for a visit whenever he wanted to go. I had already booked Maureen, Rickie and Kenneth. So half-kiddingly I asked Dr Vincent if he wanted to hitch a ride down with them. He said he would love to go."

"Did you ask Maureen about this?"

"Of course. I called her to see if she was okay with Dr Vincent going along for the ride. She thought it was a great idea."

"Sounds like a great party, they're all having. I'm surprised that Mike Kelvey didn't ask if he could go along too,"

"Well it's obvious you didn't get any of my messages. Kelvey is also on the Cessna. As a favor to you, he wanted to ensure that there was a coordinated approach to Maureen's health issues, down in Costa Rico."

"Did we send along a band, a publicist, and selected members of the media as well?"

"Of course not. The Cessna Citation 2 only holds twelve." Maria couldn't resist poking a little humor into the situation. JB thought that this was really funny and he quickly turned to look out the window so Maria wouldn't see the smile that he couldn't repress.

"John, oh John," She laughed and sung his name as she tried to get him to turn and face her. "Come on John, I can see that smile." She reached over and tugged on his arm and JB knew he'd been had.

"Okay. I'll admit it. That *was* funny."

"Good I'm glad to see that you are relaxing." Maria had taken a liking to Bombay Safire gin herself over the last few years of traveling with JB, and she took a healthy swig out of her glass as they soared toward the gambling Mecca of the eastern seaboard.

****

It was some god-awful hour in the middle of the night, and Stephen Struben couldn't sleep. He just kept rolling around in bed unable to find a comfortable position. This had not happened to him in a few years. Insomnia was not one of his problems. He had always worked hard, played hard and let the chips fall where they may. For most of his life this had been a successful strategy. Sure there were critical junctures in his business career that led to worry and maybe just a little sleeplessness. But this hadn't happened very often.

Tonight was different. No matter what way he tossed and turned he could not find the comfort of slumber. He got out a bed and stood up on his way to the bathroom. He gazed down at Danielle. She looked so quiet and peaceful, more the silent Indian Princess than the sophisticated singer/actress. He was lucky and he knew it. He was very much in love with his wife.

Still what was keeping Stephen up at night was his concern about her. Dr Snyder, Danielle's new physician, indicated that it was appropriate to be aware of the larger risks but to treat the visible symptoms while investigating the causes. He gave her an ultrasound and took some cultures and ran another precautionary biopsy. Given her prior problems all of the testing was expedited and Dr Snyder's diagnosis was that Danielle was suffering from a chronic mastitis. Normally mastitis occurs when women were breast-feeding, but in some cases, apparently Danielle's being one of them, it can occur in women after menopause. He had prescribed an antibiotic and Danielle seemed to be much more at ease.

But there was more to all of this that added to Stephen's sleeplessness and chagrin. He was very concerned about the way his wife had suffered because of all of the medical misinformation. He thought a lot about the efforts that Max Tkachuk had been undertaking and wondered what would become of Tkachuk's company, Apakoh. He decided that he would call one of the EVP's over at STRX and see where things stood.

He came back out of the bathroom and went back to his side of the bed. Danielle had said that Josh was going to stop by over the weekend. He had heard from Josh that his new fund was interested in medical technology plays. He looked forward talking to his son. He climbed back under the covers and finally fell asleep.

****

The chopper lifted off high above the city of Athens and started circling the city. Gina was wired. Her long blonde hair hung loose over the shoulders of her bombshell tight body. The chopper was a small Bell Jet Ranger but there was only the pilot and his two female passengers taking this flight. Although the chopper was a bit on the noisy side, Gina and Marilyn could hear the pilot as he pointed out some of the sights below him. He spoke perfect English and turned his head when he pointed out the Parthenon looming high above the Acropolis,

"Off to the left there is the National Archaeological Museum. Every work of art in the whole museum is Greek. There over to the side of the Acropolis," He added pointing down and to his right, "you can see Lykavittos Hill. You can get some spectacular views of the city from that point as well."

As he spoke the pilot kept turning around so that he could get his own spectacular view of two perky members of the Lay D's jiggling around and teasing one another about their shorts outfits. The early fall weather was still around 80 degrees Fahrenheit (27 Celsius) and the ladies were wearing midsummer attire. Gina had on a pair of white cotton shorts, a powder blue tank top, large round sunglasses and a broad floppy hat. Marilyn had on very short frayed edged denim shorts and a gold colored faux-wrap tee, sunglasses and a New York Yankee baseball cap. Both of the Lay D's wore sandals. Neither of them wore a bra.

It was very early Saturday morning in Greece and the plan for the day was to do a quick trip out to Mykonos and Delos and to be back into Athens before 5 PM to get ready for their performance that evening. It was typical of Gina to crunch as much into a day as she possibly could. This was her first time in Greece and she wanted to get a flavor for what the country was like outside of the urban settings for their shows. She was able to convince Marilyn get up at 6 AM to tag along, but unable to get Sophia, Karen's replacement, out of bed for the outing.

"I'm not sure how you talked me into this, Gina baby. It is real early, and this girl didn't get much beauty sleep. And this helicopter isn't exactly the easiest thing on my stomach" Marilyn managed a toothy smile that lit up her African American features. Her high cheekbones and enormous eyes seemed to flash a 'fun' sign to anyone who was near her.

Gina gave Marilyn a playful shove and said, "You're fine, girl. Besides this is your first trip to Greece too isn't it?"

"Yes, but that doesn't mean I have to see everything there is to see in seventy-two hours. I've lived in the US for all my twenty-seven years and there are plenty of places I haven't seen. Never seen the Grand Canyon; never seen Niagara Falls; never been to Mount Rushmore; never been to Yosemite, and I've sure as hell never been to Alaska. So I'll be damned if I can figure out why you talked me into this whirlybird whirlwind tour of Greece in twelve hours."

"Don't worry you're going to love it."

"Girl, that's your answer to everything! That's your favorite way to get people going. I don't know how you do it. Everything's always so positive. Don't you ever have a negative thought?"

"I don't have *time* for negative thoughts. And the closest thing that I have to a negative thought *is*..." Gina paused to add emphasis. "...that I don't have enough *time*."

"Much too heavy for me at this hour." Marilyn knew Gina too well to try to break through her impenetrable optimism about life. As usual she decided to go wherever Gina led the way. It always turned out to be fun.

"I think it's important to get what you can out of every day, that's all." She smiled back at Marilyn's smile. "And every night too." She then added, as an afterthought.

"Seems like we have a game plan for the nights." Marilyn said. "Gina, you keep up a more hectic pace than anyone I know."

"I *do* like to keep busy. I'm flying back to London on our off day on Monday."

"You seeing, your man, Josh?"

"Yes, but I'll probably see Karen too. Want to come with me?"

"Nothing against Karen. Give her my love. But I'll take a pass and meet you in Prague on Tuesday."

The sun was starting to make them feel warm and cozy as it shone through the chopper's windshield and side windows. They cruised over the smaller nearby islands just south of Athens and Gina and Marilyn just stared out the windows as the pilot tilted the aircraft into a due south direction.

Marilyn broke the silence "So what are we going to do when we get to Mykonos?"

"We can go to the beach or we can shop. I'm up for anything."

"If we go to the beach, we'll have to shop first anyway, unless you brought a bathing suit."

"Not to worry about that," their pilot casually interjected. "Many of the beaches allow you to go nude."

"I think we'll stick with the shopping, thank you," Marilyn answered him.

The three occupants of the Bell Jet Ranger then fell silent for a little while as the chopper glided out over the Aegean Sea. On the beautiful morning ride to Mykonos, Gina began to think a bit about her earlier clipped conversation with Marilyn. She did sometimes worry that she wouldn't have enough time to do everything she wanted to do in life

Gina loved life and wanted to live forever. Recently she had been collecting information on longevity and anti-aging, and knew that if she started addressing lifestyle issues early enough, the likelihood of living a longer better life would be enhanced.

Although Gina was rebuked whenever she brought these topics up with Marilyn, or other friends, she enjoyed talking about it with Josh. She was looking forward to Monday. For now however it was on to Mykonos and Delos. But even as they charged toward the Aegean Islands, music rang inside Gina's head and it was the words from the musical "Fame." "I'm going to live forever! I'm going to learn how to fly!"

****

While it was the very early hours of Saturday morning in Greece, it was just past midnight on Friday night in New York City. And it had been another lonely night for Dr Al Moses. He had finished his office hours around 6:30 pm and, in no hurry to go anywhere, he remained at the office for another hour and a half catching up on his reading. Then he took a cab downtown to 14th Street and treated himself to a steak dinner at a restaurant he hadn't been to in about two years. He no longer was self conscious about dining out alone. He just made sure that he went to different restaurants all the time so that no one would pity him for his long sequence of solo suppers.

After dinner, he wandered around the west Village, window-shopping and people watching. He sauntered aimlessly down 8th Avenue, past W 4th Street to the intersection with Bleeker Street and then turned and walked southwest on Bleeker Street as it cut through the heart of the Village.

Greenwich Village is an interesting part of New York City. It exists at the opposite end of the city, geographically as well as culturally, from Moses' Upper East Side home and his Park Avenue medical practice. It has a well-deserved reputation for counter cultural types that goes back almost two centuries.

Even the layout of the streets of Greenwich Village defies order. Whereas most of Manhattan is laid out in a grid with numbered *streets* going east to west and numbered *avenues* running north and south, the Village has many twisting streets, some bearing names and others bearing numbers that are often out of sequence. At different points in the Village, W 4th Street runs both south of W 5th street, and north of W 12th street. The buildings themselves also seem to be from a different era. Unlike the high-rise office and apartment buildings that cover a good bit of the island of Manhattan, the Village has always been different. It is, in fact, a village ensconced within a city. There are row houses and two story walk-ups throughout the village and the retail shops are individual entrepreneurships, rather than corporate America's chain stores.

The village has long been the home to aspiring artists, many of them malcontents. Amongst those famous residents of the village was Edgar Allen Poe, who wrote his poetry in the Village after his court-martial and dismissal from West Point in the nineteenth century. Poet/singer/songwriter Woodie Guthrie ended his wanderlust in the 1950's and settled down in the Village to compose and perform before being committed to Greystone Park Psychiatric Center. Bob Dylan and Joan Baez were artistic activists who called the West Village home. Beat generation writer Jack Kerouac composed his classic <u>On The Road</u> from his Greenwich Village loft. Contemporary artists like Sarah Jessica Parker and Gina Alvarez were also known to make their New York City homes in the Greenwich Village.

The restaurants in the village were some of the finest in all of Manhattan. There was just about any kind of cuisine a person could want within the village neighborhood between the SoHo and Chelsea sections of the city. There also are several private clubs in the village that helped establish its eclectic reputation. A hundred-year-old Italian American club is located just north of Houston Street. In this club you can shoot handguns at targets in the basement while other club members dine on fabulous food upstairs. A few blocks away there is a Transgender Club that meets weekly at a restaurant on Bedford Street owned by the club's President.

The Village is known to have many gay and alternative life style residents. It harbors many different cultures, lifestyles and political ideologies, and philosophies all in an open and welcoming atmosphere that makes it an interesting venue for visitors and residents alike. The high cost of living in the Village in the 21st Century has changed the resident population from fledgling artists like the penniless Mommas and the Papas before their California Dreaming fame to the established artists of the 21st Century such as the Blue Man Group at the Astor theatre, and the money minting machine known as the Lay D's.

None of this was news to Al Moses. As he continued down Bleeker Street Al passed two "heavy leather," retail shops that featured sado masochistic paraphernalia in the front window. A little further down there was a store with all sorts of sex toys and apparatus. He stopped in front of the store and was greeted by a small chubby man with a Van Dyke Beard and a shaved head.

"See anything that interests you?"

"Well I guess everything is interesting." Al said.

"Why don't you come inside and I can show you something for you?"

The little man beamed at Moses and he wasn't sure what to make of him. He just peered inside the small shop from the doorway and saw that there were anatomically correct sculptures draped in revealing lingerie, another whole wall was lined with triple X rated videos, and there was a section in the back that was called "creative marital aides," whatever that was. Fear of nothing in particular, but fear nonetheless overcame Moses curiosity and he stepped back from the door front, with the odd rejoinder, "Just looking, thanks."

"If you're just a gawker you ought to come down here next weekend for the Halloween parade. You'll see everything imaginable."

"I've heard about that. But I have never seen it." Al said this in an interested way. He was lonely for anyone's friendship, even a fellow like this.

"It's not just the Village people, who parade around. There are people like you, from the Upper East Side … Right?"

"Right." Al laughed. He wasn't sure what it was that so readily identified him as a "foreigner" to the Village but he accepted it.

"Plenty of Wall Street types dressed kind of funky…. There's a Madison Avenue Public Relations tycoon that comes to the parade every year in a big bunny costume. Lots of drag queens that don't normally frequent the village…. Other people dressed only in body paint…and not a stitch of anything else. You'll love it. You ought to come back."

"I'll think about it." said Al and he continued his walk down Bleeker Street, turned left on Christopher Street and thought that the people of the Village seemed to have Halloween every week, and they loved it.

Dr Al enjoyed his stroll through the village and was ready to go home. He hailed a cab, which took him back up to his East side apartment.

Back in his bedroom, he sat in the old comfortable reading chair that had rested under his antique lamp for the past twenty-five years. But he didn't fell like reading. He wanted to talk to Anne Mohr. He hadn't spoken to her all week long.

"Good evening Anne, my love. How are you?" He always started these conversations the same way.

"I'm home, now." He said to the empty bedroom.

"I had an interesting evening." There was a perceptible pause, but no one there except Al to perceive it.

"Yes I miss you too."

"Yes, everyone's talking about the election in a couple of weeks."

"I don't know. What do you think?"

"Interesting perspective. I hadn't thought about it that way."

"I'm still not sure." There was a much longer pause during which Dr Al alternatively smiled slightly and then frowned.

"So much to think about … let's change the subject. I haven't talked to you since the flight home from Italy last week."

"I thought so too. But it wasn't to be. I'm still here."

"Yes. It surprised me too. He seemed like a nice guy … for most of the flight. He was a priest, you know."

"Yes, I wasn't happy that he called me a 'nut job' but I guess I've been called worse."

"I agree. So anyway, he's saying his prayers, or 'talking to God.' Meanwhile, I'm just talking to you. He's asking God to let everyone survive and he was annoyed that I told you I'd be with you soon."

"No. They only talked to me for a minute. Father Flaherty actually helped out with them … told them that the flight attendants were wrong. I was okay, just stressed out."

"I doubt it. He lives in Boston. He told the Irish cop at the airport that I was simply a mother-fearing Jew. They both got a good laugh about it. And that was that."

"Something else."

"No. Something else about that patient … Maria, the one I almost ran into in London, the one that reminds me of you."

"That's right. Maria Cardoza. Well, I think she wants to have a baby. She says she is depressed. That's not a good reason to have a baby."

"But of course we both loved Sarah. We both wanted her to be with us."

"Yes I know. But we wanted her with us on the outside as well. She was taken from us before ….."

"Okay, but be sure to tell her how much I love her. Tell her I'll be there soon."

Dr Moses abruptly ended his conversation with Anne. He never liked rehashing the circumstances around Anne's miscarriage. It was depressing and he was annoyed whenever it came up in his "conversations." He was annoyed with himself. He also was annoyed that he never asked Anne to marry him. She was going to have their child. And then they lost their child. They thought about getting married, but Al never got around to asking Anne for her hand until after she was diagnosed with terminal breast cancer. She said that she didn't want a marriage of pity, and that their relationship should remain what it always had been, one of mutual love and respect without a need for legal confirmation.

Moses was unhappy. He walked over to the large framed picture of the two of them that had been taken when they were in Acapulco together. He lifted it off the wall and exposed the safe behind the picture. After spinning the combination lock to its familiar settings he withdrew his loaded Smith and Wesson 38 caliber handgun.

He walked around the bed again and sat back down in his favorite chair. He had an awkward moment or two and his mind became a blur of many faces, Anne, Maria, the bald guy at the adult store, Father Flaherty, Stephen Struben, the doorman to his apartment, the Big Bunny in the parade that he had never really seen, Max Tkachuk and others. He put the four-inch gun barrel in his mouth, and cocked the trigger. His heart beat at a crazy rate. He didn't do it. He put the gun down and didn't get up out of the chair until his heartbeat returned to normal. That makes three times, he thought to himself. Until that moment he had conveniently forgotten about the other two times. There was an awful lot he was forgetting lately. Some of it was good and some of it wasn't.

****

John Brady was an effective after dinner speaker. His audience laughed at all of his jokes, listened as he spoke about the outlook for the future, and seemed generally happy that the company's CEO felt their success warranted a personal visit to their sales rally. When it came time for Q&A, Brady was on his game. He effectively deflected questions about revenue slow down and stock market pricing and any potential layoffs that might be forthcoming. He focused on the positive and charged the sales team to commit to having a stronger fourth quarter than the results from the previous three.

Maria stood off to the side and jotted down a few notes.

"Mr. Brady, if understanding our customers in detail is so important to our success, why are we organized in a regional fashion instead of by industry? The main similarity between the customers we serve is the location of their headquarters. Wouldn't we be better off if we sold to customers in the same industry? We could have a sales team for healthcare or a sales team for financial services. In this way we could get more depth and understanding of each customer."

"Excellent question. We have a task force looking at that very possibility as I speak. We will run a trial in January to see where this leads us." JB could have cared less about organizational design. ICD had several large consulting firms on retainer who studied these things continuously. However if he wasn't really interested in the question, he certainly had some interest in the questioner. She was a drop dead gorgeous redhead, with a breezy voice that managed to sound both sensuous and sensible. She was tall, maybe even 5' 10" and JB was already sizing her up as an erstwhile candidate to replace Maria. "Give Maria your name and number and we'll see if we can't get you some advance information about the industry trial."

Brady took about ten more minutes of questions and then ended the Q&A by saying. "Okay. That's about it. I know enough not to be the last man standing between a salesman and a night on the town. Thanks for all your good questions and for a great start to 2008. Now let's finish strong."

Brady walked over to Maria and said, "Let's go have a cocktail or two before turning in. It's good for the morale of the team." They stayed in the private dining area with some of the salespeople for another half an hour, and JB got a chance to ogle the redhead up closer. *Very smooth skin. Very pretty face,* he thought *Seems bright also.*

As they always did, JB slipped away first and went to his room. Maria always had another room at the various hotels where they stayed and she always at least checked in. Usually she would then wait twenty minutes and go to John's room to spend the night. Tonight she had a different agenda in mind. She would go to his room and have their usual nightcap over which she would tell him that she wanted to end their personal relationship. Wherever it went from there, she would just have to wait to see.

Twenty minutes after JB had left the cocktail crowd, Maria knocked on his door. He was oblivious to the fact that she had left her overnight bag in her own room. He merely opened the door and walked back into his suite where he had been reading.

Someone on his staff had ordered a bar set-up with all of the usual accompaniments. Actually it was probably someone on Maria's staff who did the ordering. There was always a bottle of red wine, a bottle of white wine and a bottle of Bombay Safire gin. No questions asked. If JB needed anything else there was room service. They had been drinking gin all night, so Brady stuck with the program and poured a couple of glasses of gin on the rocks. At ICD this was known as a Brady Martini. No one ever thought of even whistling the vermouth by the glass.

Maria steeled herself for what she wanted to say.

John readied himself to discuss his decision.

Both were feeling the effects of the multiple Brady Martinis they had consumed throughout the night. Without giving it much thought, Maria had unbuttoned the top couple of buttons to her blouse. She was feeling a bit woozy but she knew that she would get through it.

John knew what he wanted to say, but the animal in him instinctively knew what he wanted to do. Experience told him the order they should come in.

John walked over to Maria and put his arms around her from behind, clasping his hand in front of her at her waist. He whispered. "Why don't we put this long week behind us the right way?"

The effect of the alcohol was now strengthening and Maria was starting to lose it a bit. She rolled her head backwards toward John's shoulder and said, "I'm tired, John." John didn't listen and he just held her up from behind while his fingers began to unbutton her blouse the rest of the way. Maria didn't resist, but she was resigned.

In short order John removed the rest of Maria's clothing, and the two soon-to-be ex-lovers fell on the bed in an alcohol induced state of amore. Maria was face down on the bed and John put his hands under her hips and entered her from behind. Maria was merely going through the motions and when that wasn't enough for JB, he playfully slapped her on the buttocks as he repeatedly drove into her. A full-length mirrored door to a nearby closet reflected his sexual conquest. It appeared more like an oversized jockey spurring a smallish mare toward the finish line, than like any shared human passion.

It was not as though JB and Maria could hear Tony Bennett in the background singing "That's amore," but there was a perverse pleasure that each of them derived. Maria was glad that she could still arouse such ardor in the loins of her boss, irrational as the thought might have been in those circumstances. John's thoughts were much different. With each thrust of excitement he was not thinking at all about Maria. He was fantasizing that he was banging the long stemmed redhead from the Q&A session.

****

Maureen Brady and her entourage arrived in Costa Rica in the early evening on Friday and were greeted by Chipper Geld himself.

Geld was the entrepreneur/owner/operator and original concept person who put together the SIS project in the early nineties. Originally thought of as a "fugitive financier" in all of the media, he had reinvented himself as wellness guru.

Seven years before the advent of SIS, Geld had fled to Costa Rica in the late eighties to avoid extradition to the United States on tax fraud charges. It was a major news story at the time, but lost steam over the ensuing years and the matter was eventually settled financially with the US government during the early years of the Clinton administration. It was one of many confirming points in Chipper's career that told him "everything in this world is for sale." And Chipper Geld continued to live his life just that way; Money was his god; Money was his code; Money was his law; Money was even his name.

As much as he loved money, there were many things that Geld despised. He hated the USA, because they had too many laws and regulations that got in the way of making a profit. He hated women, because to him they were "soft-minded and spineless." Yet, as one of his "outside interests," Geld secretly trafficked in importing women from Russia into New York, California and Florida to work as prostitutes in his silent empire of topless bars. And he frequently and freely sampled his own product. He hated drug; they are for the weak willed lazy fools of the world. Yet he trafficked in drugs as well. Although much of his financial empire was well hidden and guised through a series of offshore corporate shells, the front or face of Chipper Geld's realm was "Solace in the Sun." His whole media image was carefully crafted as a born again health and wellness genius. His overt behavior was that of charming and sophisticated middle-aged bachelor, a persona he worked hard to cultivate. The hatred that frequently threatened to consume him, was hidden from this public persona.

"Hello Mrs. Brady. Welcome to 'Solace in the Sun.'" Chipper Geld had a smile that certainly appeared genuine. He turned to the other members of the group and asked, "So which of you is Dr. Vincent and which of you may I address as Dr Kelvey?" The greeting process was quickly finished, but not without Geld taking note of the fact that the last two of his guests/customers Kenneth Brady and Rickie Van Dorfan had an interesting rapport. Chipper Geld never missed this kind of thing. Others might never pick up on information that went unspoken and wasn't nuanced by non-verbal suggestion. Part of the notorious genius of Chipper Geld is that he never missed these things and he almost always found a way to benefit personally from this intuitive advantage. Kenneth was not externally effeminate, and Rickie knew how and when to tone down any overt signals about his sexual orientation. However, Chipper knew they were gay. And he was already devising ways to use this information to his advantage.

"How nice of you to greet us personally Mr. Geld." Maureen said. "As you can see I wasn't sure what to bring so I have a lot of baggage." Geld smirked a little but didn't say what was on his mind: *Do you mean the suitcases or this motley crew you brought along with you?*

"Perfectly natural, Maureen." He went right to a more casual address without asking. "And please call me Chipper. We will have your bags delivered to your room. You will be staying here at SIS. We have arranged rooms for the rest of your party, at our visitor's lodge, the Solace Support Station, just outside our main gate."

He looked quickly at some cards that he had gotten from the bellboy who seemed to materialize almost the moment that Geld began talking. Thinking for a second he then said. "Please change the rooms for Mr Van Dorfan and Mr. Brady to 301 and 303. The rooms for Dr Vincent and Dr. Kelvey will be just fine." He gave no reason to anyone right away, but when he noticed a slightly quizzical look on Mrs. Brady's face, he simply said to no one in particular. "There, now I have you all on the same side of the building" He said it as if was important to someone. In reality it was important to Geld. Information was power and he had ways of gathering information.

Geld then turned to the two doctors and said, "Dr. Chow will be meeting you both inside the main foyer of the lodge after you are in your rooms." Then he turned to Kenneth and said, "Kenneth, I will be showing your mother around our facility personally. You are free to come with us or I will have someone show you and Rickie around separately."

Kenneth was forthright and direct. He was a stunningly handsome young man and when he spoke his tone was deep, resonant, and direct. It surprised Geld somewhat. "You can show my mother around, Mr. Geld. Personally I'd like to talk to the program director about communication during my mother's stay. I spoke briefly with Mr. Ashburn on the phone earlier this week. Where is his office?"

"I'm sorry but I believe he has left for the day. Why don't you just come with us then, and I can show you all around. I'll have your bags brought to the lodge. You are staying until Sunday. Is that correct?"

"Yes. Rickie, the doctors and I will all be leaving around noon on Sunday. Meanwhile I think I will accompany you and Mom on the tour."

"I'm just going to go check in," said Rickie.

A small open sided transport cart came and picked up Rickie and the two doctors while Geld ushered Maureen and Kenneth inside the main lobby of SIS. He then proceeded to walk them to the front desk and down a long row of small conference rooms.

"These are individual consult rooms, where you can meet with our councilors or for that matter with our other guests, and engage in therapy and therapy related discussions with privacy." He opened the door to one such room.

"You'll see that we have these conference rooms set up more like living rooms, because that's exactly what they are. They are designed to help you work with others on your strategy for living. They are quite comfortable by design. You will find that there is nothing austere at Solace in the Sun. Unlike some of the other rehabilitation facilities that you may have heard about we're not big on things like chores, making your own bed and other such ploys." He said this with an air of distain towards any and all competition.

"SIS is designed for people of substantial means. We are not set up for people of various economic strata, and we offer no free stays to any rehabilitating individuals. We make no excuses for who we are and how we do what we do. We don't ask you to make your own bed, because you won't be making your own bed when you return to your home. We want you to relearn how to live within the existing framework of the place you came from because that's the environment you will be going back to when you leave here. Most of our clientele have assistance in their daily lives when they are home, so we have to recognize that and ensure that it will be the same when they return. We do not want to turn their lives inside out. We are only seeking to remove an addiction from their lives."

Geld said all this as if he were talking to someone who was not herself an addict. He seemed to be talking about others, but not necessarily about Maureen. Maureen found this tactic to be more confusing than comforting. She had admitted her problem to herself and now really wanted to begin fixing it. She wondered if everyone else here felt the same way.

Geld didn't bother showing Maureen and Kenneth around the spa itself but merely walked back out past the pool area and slowly the threesome walked back to the rotunda and made a right and walked down to the suite area. He stopped and opened the door to Maureen's suite and walked inside.

"This will be your home during your stay with us. It will not be as spacious and functional as what you have at home, but most of our guests feel that is more than adequate to avoid any feeling of confinement one might have."

The suite was brightly colored and had a large bedroom complete with a king-sized bed and a long triple dresser. There was an armoire that housed a large flat screen plasma TV, and two comfortable sitting chairs as well. The bathroom was modern and spacious and included both a shower stall and a Jacuzzi tub. The living room to the suite had a separate flat screen TV, and two love seats that surrounded a small minibar that was stocked with fruit juices and power bars.

Geld handed Maureen the key to her room. "Let me give this to you now so you have it and I will take you out to the other side of our complex where we have our three dining areas, our gym facilities, our nature trails and much more. I just thought that I would show you to your room first to make sure that it met with your approval."

"Thank you Chipper. This seems very nice. Do you like it, Kenneth?"

"What I like is not so important, Mom. You need to feel comfortable. It's what you think that counts. Are all of the rooms similar to this?" Kenneth asked Chipper.

"For the most part, yes. Unlike many other rehabilitation and detoxification facilities that you may have heard about, we do not recommend a system with roommates. Some of these facilities say that they have roommates to avoid letting their patients feel isolated. We don't believe that being alone is being isolated. We feel that our patients have enough interaction all day long with our medical staff and other recovering patients, and that they don't need to be surrounded by others 24/7, because it won't be that way when they return home. We can accommodate 120 guests at a time at SIS and we are normally at capacity year round."

There was no further discourse in the room. They simply went back on the tour and ventured over to the other side of the facility. As they passed a well appointed fitness facility, Geld turned and asked Kenneth.

"Kenneth, you will be attending our family day program tomorrow. Is that correct?"

"Yes, I want to get an idea about what Mom will be doing while she's here."

"Good. And I know we have a number of folks for the two doctors to meet and talk with. I hope that Mr Van Dorfan will be able to find some time to relax before you all leave on Sunday. But please be sure to mention to them that my staff will be more than willing to help if they can be of any assistance."

Geld watched to see what Kenneth's expression would be as he casually mentioned Van Dorfan, but Kenneth seemed to be generally more concerned about his mother and didn't seem to be at all concerned with Van Dorfan's comfort. *Well maybe I'm wrong*, he thought. *Not too worry I'll know for sure later* Chipper resolved to himself.

****

Sometime between the late-night drunken sexual encounter with her boss and the early morning reality that things didn't go exactly as she had planned, Maria woke up in John Brady's suite. Brady was sleeping on his back and snoring loudly. Maria got dressed quickly without showering or cleaning up. She could do that in her own room.

She took a piece of casino stationery out of the desk drawer and wrote a note to Brady.

Dear John. The moment she wrote it, it struck her as funny. This was going to actually be a *Dear John* letter in the classic sense.

Dear John,

Tonight was not what I expected it to be. Although I wanted the evening to be pleasant, I also meant for us to have a serious conversation. And most assuredly I did not expect to end up in bed with you. In fact I left my clothes in the other room.

Bluntly, I've decided it's time to end our personal relationship. I don't think it has been working well for either of us lately. I didn't plan on doing this by writing a note, but now I know of no other way.

I fully understand that this may also mean that I will have to move on in my professional career and that I will no longer work at ICD. That will be your decision.

I am very grateful for all you have taught me, John, but I know the best thing for both of us, now, is to move on.

I will be taking a car service back to NYC and will meet you in the office at 9 AM on Monday to cover several lingering business issues. My decision is final.
Affectionately,
Maria.

When JB awoke at about 6 AM, he found the note and was furious. He called the other room but Maria was gone. Thoughts raged through JB's mind. *She can't just dump me like that. I was going to dump her ass. What an ungrateful bitch. She will regret her insolence; she will never work another day at ICD. There will be no severance package. There will be no references to friends. There will be no references period.* And JB determined that he would call security and make sure she wasn't allowed in the building on Monday. Nobody treated John Brady with such disrespect. It may have been 6 AM but he had a middle of the day anger brewing. He stood up quickly and felt the pain soaring across his lower back.

"Fuck!" He slammed his hand down on the desk and it began to hurt as much as his back. He painfully wobbled across the room. His back hurt. His hand hurt. And his pride hurt. He already had plans to assuage his injured pride. He suddenly wanted a quick fix for his painful back. He tried Kelvey's cell phone. He got voice mail and remembered that Kelvey was in Costa Rica with his wife.

"Fuck, fuck, fuck,"

****

There had been no time for the nude sun bathing on the island of Mykonos. Gina and Marilyn simply enjoyed their shopping spree too much. Cabs proved easy enough to get so they didn't regret wearing sandals as much as their pilot had told them they would. However secure, soft, flat shoes were still one of the first purchases of the day and helped the Lay D's negotiate the stone cobbled streets around town. Local jewelry and perfumes also made up part of the shopping spree and Gina and Marilyn stored all of their acquisitions with the concierge at a downtown hotel before taking the 20-minute taxi-boat over to Delos. They seemed to hear sirtaki music near every street corner beside the beachfront ferry stop and they appreciated the musical variance from their own compositions. The music on Mykonos was supplanted by a silent reverence on Delos, the mythical birthplace of the god Apollo; ironically, it now seemed the god of music, truth and light.

Gina and Marilyn were liberal with the sun tanning lotion before they climbed amongst the ruins at Delos as the sun was hot and the sky was cloudless. Somehow they both managed to avoid getting burned. Gina made sure they made the most of their time on Delos as they visited *The Agora of the Competaliasts* near the *Sacred Harbor* and *Stoivadeion Temple*. They learned much about the gods of the Greek Pantheon as Gina had expected they would. They discovered that as far back as the ancient days of Greece no one was ever allowed to be born or to die on the island of Delos. It was the birthplace of Apollo and his twin sister, Artemis. Supposedly the two illegitimate offspring of the greatest of the Greek gods, Zeus, were the only true natives of Delos.

Following their early afternoon crawl amongst the ruins, Marilyn and Gina took the taxi-boat back to Mykonos, retrieved their shopping bags from the hotel concierge and taxied back to their rented helicopter.

Gina gave the word. "Let's rock." And then they were airborne within minutes, with another somewhat frenzied excursion under their belts.

As they choppered back toward Athens the pilot got his bearings set and his radio contacts established and then turned and asked his passengers about their day.

"I see you did some shopping, did you hit any of the clubs."

"Not really."

"So you went to the beaches?"

"Too windy, but we enjoyed our time among the ruins at Delos." Gina offered cheerily.

"Our girl is trying to turn me into a culture freak. I keep thinking we're going to do some partying somewhere along the line and this is my third 'day of the dead kind of deal' with Gina. We did it in Rome too. I don't know what it is with her fascination with all of these ghosts of the past." Marilyn laughed as she said it and it was obvious that she had also enjoyed her day of sightseeing.

Gina listened to the chatter between the pilot and Marilyn, but didn't join in. She thought that their pilot might be a logical person for Marilyn to party with after their gig that night anyway. Her own mind was in a different place.

Gina wasn't treating her day amongst the ruins of Greece lightly. She was thinking about the people of the past. Were these souls possibly people of the present as well? Was there such a thing as reincarnation? Polytheism was somewhat haunting for her. It was difficult enough to deal with monotheistic ideas about an almighty God. But at least in those situations it was possible to attribute eternally positive attributes and characteristics to that one God. When dealing with the many gods of ancient Greece, she was dealing with greater gods and lesser gods. What was that all about? And so many of these gods exhibited human like characteristics. Were they supposed to *be* human? And if they were human, in any way, were they to be respected any less because they lived at an earlier time. None of the Greek gods seemed to be omnipotent. In fact many of them exhibited very human failings ….mostly based upon their interactions with other gods. What did it mean to be God? What did it mean to be a god or a goddess? What did Gina have to know to figure this all out?

Between Mykonos and Athens it was simply the sky above and the ocean below once again. But Gina was still fascinated about the sheer fame of the Greek gods. They had endured for more than thirty centuries. And then she could hear the music again and she was happy. "Fame! I'm going to live forever. I'm going to learn how to fly!"

****

Act Two

THE RHAPSODY TEAM
Winter of 2008

Chapter 7: *Hong Kong Day 1*

The changing face of Hong Kong was not lost on Abby McDuffee. It was a little more than five years since her last trip to the Big Lychee, and its face had continued to evolve. This trip was to be different from past excursions to the Asian commercial hub. When she had been with the computer conglomerate, ICD, there was always a jam-packed agenda; an existing supplier network to meet with; performance reviews for the local team and numerous Asian customers to meet.

This trip was not about running an existing business. It was all about putting a new business in motion. Abby and her twin sister Dr. Alison McDuffee had flown together on a non-stop flight from Newark to Hong Kong that landed in the still new Hong Kong International Airport. Like so many of the newer airports around the world, Hong Kong International seemed more like a huge shopping mall with runways than a lift off and landing arena for travelers. For all its modern amenities, the ten-year-old Hong Kong International had none of the charm and excitement of Kai Tak Airport, the official international airport for Hong Kong for most of the twentieth century.

Alison and Abby moved methodically through Hong Kong International and avoided most of the shopping mall that would greet them again on the way out of the city. Their driver was ready with a sign that read A & A McDuffee, and both women found the sign to be clever.

"Sounds like a name for a fast food chain." Abby said.

"I'm tired enough from the flight that I could care less how I get there, I just want to get to my hotel room and go to bed," Alison answered.

Their uniformed driver did a double take when he saw his passengers. After the thirteen hour flight the women looked somewhat tired. However even at the age of 48, they looked very much alike. They were both 5'7 inches tall and a wiry 115 pounds. Their uncommon dark red hair was cut in similar styles, and their large standout blue eyes, showed their fatigue in an oddly similar manner. Even as they walked across the open terminal area, their gait and stride was about the same.

Alison (Allie) McDuffee was born the identical twin sister of Abigail (Abby) McDuffee on the 4th of July 1960. Allie was older and wiser than her sister, or at least she thought she was for the entire first 48 years of her life.

Fair haired, freckled faced and flat chested, in the early 70s, Allie was not a young teenager who turned the heads of young men and boys with her looks. However as she matured from nubile youth to college coed, her fair red hair darkened to raven red and her full face of freckles faded to a less pronounced sparse sprinkle of Irish identifiers. Meanwhile her legs stretched out even if her chest never much did, and she blossomed into a tall thin beauty, somewhat shapely and statuesque rather than curvaceous and buxom. She also jettisoned her childhood nickname of Allie and began to introduce herself as Alison. The only person who continued to refer to her as Allie was her twin sister, Abby.

Although she grew up in the Midwest and went to college in New England, Alison chose a west coast school to pursue her medical degree. She had her choice of several schools but chose to gain her medical education in southern California, because she believed that schools in that region were more open to alternative medicine and personalized medical approaches.

Alison trained as a dermatologist and did internships in California followed by a residency in Washington DC. Along the way her personable nature allowed her the opportunity to assemble a wide circle of friends and colleagues spanning many different fields of interest.

During her med school years she dated and then married the man she called husband for the ensuing 20 plus years, Tom Singleberry, an African-American professional baseball pitcher. Singleberry was a first round draft choice, who was the talk of tinsel town's baseball beat as he rose through the minor leagues, before blowing out his arm after "a cup of coffee" with the big club. He met Alison during his stint in the big leagues in LA, and they married two years later after he was out of baseball for good. The name Alison McDuffee-Singleberry was not on Alison's wish list of "gotta-haves," so Tom was perfectly content to let Alison maintain her maiden name.

By her early thirties Alison's New York City practice was thriving and her cosmetic surgery reputation was soaring. She and her partners opened another practice in LA and she was a budding bi-coastal. She and Tom had two sons and the family made its home in the NJ suburb of Bernardsville, where Tom coached his sons and opened a small juvenile athletic complex. However Tom and Alison still had a large number of friends in colleagues in the LA area from the early days of their marriage, so they maintained a condominium in Manhattan Beach in Southern Los Angeles County.

Always very liberal in her political outlook on life, Alison had many friends with similar interests in New York, New Jersey and California. However most of those with similar ideologies were not amongst her medical colleagues. And most of their neighbors in Bernardsville as well as in Manhattan Beach were political conservatives but it never stopped Alison from voicing her more liberal minded viewpoints.

Alison hated the way medicine was practiced in the United States. She felt that it was a bold-faced sham run as an attempt to aggrandize, the wealth of the large medical insurance companies. She was quick to cite the other culprits in the industry amongst whom she believed were some of the large healthcare providing systems, the monolithic pharmaceutical companies and for sure the US government. In short she felt that there was enough blame to go around for everyone. It was a twisted web of a mess and neither political party had an adequate solution to fix it.

Alison's bicoastal practice was not financially impacted by the crude payments systems that the insurance companies spun out to their *networks* because she wasn't associated with any of these *networks*. She practiced what was known as *concierge medicine,* a pay as you go approach that was very popular in NYC and LA. She realized that this was paradoxical with respect to her liberal leanings that begged for affordable healthcare for everyone. However she reconciled her personal inconsistencies by believing that she and many other high-income earning individuals should be taxed at a much higher rate to pay for the care for the masses. She also believed that there was a fundamental responsibility of generosity, benevolence and philanthropy that was appropriate for people of means.

These inclinations led Alison to the basic belief that if change was going to come to health and wellness, those with ample financial assets bore the responsibility to be leaders in pursuing this change. It was this kind of thinking that led Alison to envision what would come to be known as the ™*Rhapsody Philosophy*[2] and to create ™*Rhapsody Lifestyle Memberships.*[3]

"You ladies are going to the Ritz Carlton in Central, correct?"

"Yes, and the sooner we get there the better," Alison answered for the both of them.

Soon after they left the airport they saw the exit marked for Penny's Bay on Lantau Island, one of the ever expanding landfills in the area. This one housed a piece of Americana known as Disneyland Hong Kong. It had opened in 2005, a couple of years after Abby's last visit to China.

"Now there's something I didn't think I'd ever see in this country. Have you been there?" Abby asked the driver.

"Yes, I took my children. People who know these things say that it is much like the United States."

Abby let the answer hang in the air for a bit. She was too tired to question whether the driver meant that the park was like the United States, or like the Disneyland Park in the United States.

Abigail McDuffee was to the business world what her sister Alison McDuffee was to health and wellness, an agitator, or what her politically conservative friends and colleagues now fashionably referred to as a "Maverick." She didn't like the term. She thought it had no real meaning. Abby McDuffee preferred that everything in life have meaning.

Born seven minutes after her sister Alison, Abby shared so many physical traits that the nurses recalled that soon after their births the two babies actually started crying in unison. The shared DNA that Abby and Allie exhibited at birth remained a factor throughout their lives. However one trait common to their DNA ironically took them down separate paths. Both girls were born with the makeup of a fiercely independent personality. So at many stages in life they both wittingly and unwittingly pursued separate passages to success. Both loved politics and political activism but they supported different parties and political viewpoints.

---

[2] *The Rhapsody Philosophy* is a Trademark of Rhapsody Holdings, LLC and Rhapsody Holdings, Inc.

[3] *The Rhapsody Lifestyle Memberships* is a Trademark of Rhapsody Holdings, LLC and Rhapsody Holdings, Inc.

Along with their differences the two successful women enjoyed many similarities. Both were excellent students. Both had voracious appetites for all types of food and never gained a pound. Neither girl had a steady boyfriend in high school. And neither girl was sexually active until college.

Only when they went off to separate colleges did the girls begin to see things differently. When Alison went to school in New England, Abby set off for college in North Carolina.

After graduation Abby stayed in North Carolina and studied for another two years to get her MBA. While there she met a law student named Bo Blanchard, who five years later became her husband. The lengthy courtship was interrupted in the middle for about two years when Abby moved to New York and began her business career, working for the computer conglomerate, ICD. Later, Bo moved to New York himself to take a job in the Manhattan office of a national law firm.

The twin sisters remained very close throughout. Abby was the Maid of Honor at Alison's wedding, and when Abby got married there was no thought of anyone other than Allie becoming her Matron of Honor. Their younger sister served as a very young bridesmaid in both weddings.

Abby proved to be a natural leader of men and women, and began to show this leadership strength soon after she arrived at ICD. She started in sales and immediately achieved "President's Club" status in her first year in the company. She transferred and became a sales manager in the Pittsburgh Office and then within three years she became the regional sales manager back in New York. During the Pittsburgh days she commuted weekly so that she could be home on weekends to be with Bo.

Abby managed to catch the eye of the aging CEO of ICD, who transferred her out of sales and into the headquarters complex in Westchester County. She became a Vice President of Marketing and Distribution at the age of 34. At the time she became the youngest Vice President in the company. When she secured this prime position she beat out an individual by the name of John Brady. At the time Brady didn't take lightly the fact that he got passed over for someone, "who is obviously making her career on her back." Brady made sure that others recognized his inference, and Abby made certain that her ethics were beyond reproach. Still she despised Brady and from that time forward Brady and Abby were bitter adversaries, rivals and enemies while both continued to move up the corporate ladder.

Aside from her mid career run in with John Brady, Abby enjoyed her work at ICD. For the most part she was good for the company and the company was good for her. After becoming a VP, Abby led the international marketing effort for ICD. She managed to prepare a doctoral thesis on global labor markets while trotting around the world for several years.

Things happened quickly, after Abby received her PhD. She became an officer of ICD and a board member of two small IT firms that were looking for operational guidance. Abby also joined two non-profit boards in Westchester County. One of these was a performing arts group and the other was a hospital system board. She learned from every endeavor.

Bo and Abby had thriving careers but they were having difficulty conceiving children. Nothing seemed to be physically wrong, except for Bo's lower than normal sperm count. At the age of thirty-seven, Abby finally conceived and nine months later gave birth to a beautiful baby girl, Melinda, whom they nicknamed Mindy.

Life was good for Dr Abby McDuffee, but after Mindy was born, she began to feel guilty about the business trips, the Board meetings and the succession of nannies. Shortly after Mindy turned six, the ICD Board met and elected John Brady as its new Chairman and CEO. Abby didn't need a push. She resigned at the age of forty-three after an eighteen year run, and for the next three years thereafter, Abby became a full time mother and she limited her business life to board work.

Abby was always close to her sister Alison, and Allie had a vision that was beginning to come together about this concept of Rhapsody. Alison thought this symphony of ideas that she called Rhapsody was actually the yogurt for a business that could do a lot of good and also make a lot of money. Alison knew just the person who could pull the ideas together into a vibrant business model, her sister Abby. After three years as a stay at home Mom, Abby accepted her sister's challenge and the two of them along with another physician, formed the Rhapsody Group and went into business together.

It was nighttime as they travelled into Hong Kong, and there seemed to be very little traffic. The journey was a little less than 50 kilometers and moving rapidly they made it into town in a little more than half an hour. The two McDuffee sisters went to their rooms shortly after their arrival. Tomorrow would be an important day. It held the promise that Rhapsody, the project they had been working on for several years, could be on its way to its launch date very soon.

****

The morning was off to a good start for Dr Moses. He was still bothered by the horrible flight that he had taken from Italy a month earlier, but he had conveniently forgotten about his subsequent bouts with depression and his near suicide. Sometimes it was like there were two separate Al Moses. This Al Moses was in a good mood on a mid November morning. He had a cancellation that freed up a half an hour on his calendar, and he spent the time on the phone talking to his friend, Stephen Struben, who was in Germany for a conference. Al learned all about Danielle's harrowing experience with a false positive reading on a biopsy and he was happy to hear that she had now been given a clean bill of health and that an apparent breast infection was also now cleared up.

When Al hung up the phone he had two thoughts. One was the usual melancholy that he felt for Anne Mohr, any time he heard about anyone having, or potentially having, breast cancer. The other thought was about what Stephen had told him about the survival of Max Tkachuk's software company, Apakoh. Apparently there were some people who might be able to pick up the pieces of the company and carry Max' work forward. This was good news. Dr Al's own electronic medical record system was a bit primitive when compared with the plans that Max Tkachuk had in mind, but at least it did allow him to share some patient data with some clinicians, with whom he dealt on a regular basis.

Al Moses clicked through his patient files and looked for an update that might be of interest. There was an entry on the file of Maria Cardoza that was made by Dr Angelique Lefebvre. Even before he read the text, the lovely face of Maria, the dark haired, olive skinned beauty came to mind. What was it about her that interested him so much? He read the file and the entry was short and to the point, indicating that Maria had been to see Angelique twice already and that she was taking Yoga lessons to help her reduce apparent job related stress. There was an additional reference to the fact that Maria had been referred by Dr Al Moses.

Al then took out his calendar and noticed that Thanksgiving was just a few weeks away. He marked his calendar with his usual plan. For about the tenth year running, Dr Al would help out at a downtown soup kitchen as they prepared Thanksgiving dinner for those who didn't have so much to be thankful about.

****

John Brady was about to pull his hair out. Or at least that's how he felt. Maybe he shouldn't have dumped Cardoza so fast. While he was looking for her replacement, he was stuck with Rickie Van Dorfan. It wasn't going well.

On his first day in his new job, Van Dorfan was faced with the fact that his mentor and supervisor, Maria Cardoza, was no longer with the company. He also was surprised that JB didn't ask any questions about his wife, other than whether or not she seemed ready to spend two months in a "posh rehab center." JB was certainly aware that Rickie had accompanied his wife on her trip to Costa Rica. But the topic was hardly mentioned.

Meanwhile JB just wasn't used to the fact that Maria wasn't there for him. Over the past several years she had exhibited a sort of sixth sense about what JB needed to do in many different business situations. She didn't need to be informed. She developed her own informal sources. Van Dorfan needed to be spoon-fed on every issue. He couldn't or didn't work well with Alice to get the important meetings on his calendar and there were too many trivial matters occupying his daily agenda.

And to top all of this off, market conditions were just awful. ICD stock had begun to slip again with the rest of the market. It was now selling at 66 dollars per share. Even more troubling was the fact that the worldwide financial slump was beginning to have an effect on the sales forecast for 2009. This was soon after ICD guidance had retreated from its initial forecast just four weeks earlier. Another correction would be a disaster. The analysts never took kindly to a downturn in a forecast, but they would be absolutely unforgiving of companies that showed that they couldn't even forecast accurately on a quarter to quarter basis, much less on a month to month basis. Farmer and Fleckenstein, ICD's CFO and Treasurer, pointed the finger at the sales and marketing people, Morgan and Monroe. Morgan and Monroe were blaming the worldwide economic slump, and no one had offered up any real solutions. In the past, he would sometimes derive his own inspired solutions while relaxing in post-coital calm with Maria. Since he terminated Maria, JB was uninspired.

****

Maria Cardoza's morning routine had changed dramatically. She no longer reported to the midtown headquarters of ICD, to check both her own calendar and that of John Brady. Now she didn't even make constant calendar entries on her Blackberry. She simply adjusted to a slower pace, and she found it remarkable how pleasant that feeling of freedom was.

She was angry at John Brady and had not seen him since she left him naked in his hotel room in Atlantic City, a couple of weeks earlier. There had been a voice mail on Sunday from an ICD HR attorney indicating that she need not report to work the following day and she didn't. She had contacted her own employment attorney and turned the situation over to her to work through. Maria felt certain that they would work out some effective severance package over time and she didn't need the money anyway so she didn't give it another thought. More importantly she could now do whatever she wanted to do.

One other matter that drew her attention was the recommendation that had been made by Dr Moses. He suggested that she consult with Dr Angelique Lefebvre, the French psychiatrist, whose husband was Yogi Vijay, a prominent New York practitioner of the yoga principals developed and dispersed by Aurobindo Ghose. She saw both wife and husband within days of her departure from ICD, and she was currently enrolled in a course with Yogi Vijay that met twice a week at 7AM. In many ways this was a return to her life before John Brady.

Back in the days when she worked in Poco Pedazo de Ciela, the Spa on the Mediterranean coast of Spain, she had spent many hours in the pursuit of the spirituality that emanated from Integral Yoga and the teachings of Aurobindo Ghose. She was delighted to find that Yogi Vijay was also a practitioner of this same Integral Yoga. The classes brought back a time in her life when her spirit was open and inquisitive. Although she had lost a relationship with her lover of the time, art dealer, Jorge Ortega, Maria was much happier with herself, and she felt much more beautiful back then. She was grateful that these days seemed to be reemerging, and she knew that she had Dr Al to thank for understanding her and making the appropriate introductions to Angelique and Vijay.

Maria now believed that she wanted to stay in the USA. She had no real interest in returning to her native Italian roots. She had learned a lot about the business world in the last five years and for that she was grateful to JB. She had plenty of money and for that she was grateful to an earlier lover, her Arabian Horseman. But when she thought things through, she realized that she had been happiest when she was working at Poco Pedazo de Ciela in Spain. Maybe she could combine her business skills and her money and open her own spa. The question was where to open it. Maybe she could discuss it with Angelique or even with Vijay.

Just about everything seemed to be better for Maria lately, except for the fact that once again she had missed her period. She just couldn't seem to shake that problem. Dr Al had made her less concerned the last time he saw her. Maybe she would make another appointment. She wanted to thank him anyway for recommending Angelique.

****

The meeting convened at 7:30 AM in the Cromwell Conference room at the Hong Kong offices of Cromwell Parsons Resources. Josh Struben had been in Hong Kong for ten days, meeting with both investors and some Asian business leaders who were looking for funding for their various projects. He was also happily awaiting the arrival of Gina Alvarez and the Lay D's as their world tour was moving into Asia. Gina was due to arrive in Hong Kong that evening.

But for now it was business first and he had been looking forward to meeting the members of the Rhapsody Group. His staff's briefing notes told him that he would be meeting with four people two of whom were named Dr. A. McDuffee, one was an MD and the other was a PhD. This should be interesting.

"Good morning ladies and gentlemen. Thanks for your willingness to get an early start. I'm Josh Struben by the way. Come into our conference room."

"Hello, Josh. I've heard a lot about you. I'm Abby McDuffee, and this is my sister Allie McDuffee. Let me also introduce you to Ben Hui Zhang, who is our CFO and who lives right here in Hong Kong. And I would also like you to meet Sandeep Mehra, our Chief

Information Officer. Sandeep got into Hong Kong last night as did Allie and I." The four members of the Rhapsody team came into the conference room together and sat along the conference table that overlooked Victoria Harbor. It was an exotic view out towards Kowloon and the New Territories sections of Hong Kong. The meeting participants exchanged business cards in the perfunctory Asian manner, where they gripped the cards with both hands and actually made a pretext at reading them.

Josh was startled as were most people when they met the McDuffee twins together for the first time. The physical similarities were that stunning. They were dressed differently, Abby in a navy blue skirt and light blue blouse and Alison in a dark striped pants suit, but there was no mistaking their sisterhood regardless of the fact that Abby's heels made her appear taller than her sibling.

Josh noticed that both women were clothes-hanger-thin, in a style that most women either envied or admired. This was the same style that most men found just a bit too frail to frolic with. Josh's open friendly smile put everyone at ease, as they prepared to get down to work. Ben and Sandeep were quiet but ready to answer the many questions that they anticipated from Josh and his two person staff.

"So let me tell you what little I know about the Rhapsody Group and then maybe I can ask you to fill in the enormous gaps in my information so that we can have a meaningful discussion about how Cromwell Parsons might help.

"I first learned about your team a few weeks back from some discussions with folks in our London office. I may have this a bit skewed, but I believe that you are establishing a global health and wellness business, with operations in 50 cities around the world. Am I all right so far?"

"I don't mean to interrupt, but that's slightly out of focus." Alison jumped right into the discussion. "Our business is not a global health and wellness business. As you will see, we are really a membership business that facilitates global health and wellness."

"Okay. I'll defer to your description. I also understand that part of the business involves electronic medical records. I may actually have a personal connection there to your team member who passed away."

"Do you mean Max Tkachuk?" Abby looked over her shoulder at Sandeep, who was the team's primary contact with Tkachuk.

"Yes."

"Max wasn't actually part of the Rhapsody Group. But we were very interested in some of the work he and his company, Apakoh, were doing on our behalf. How did you know Max?" The question came from Sandeep, who spoke in heavily Indian-accented English, in which he juxtaposed the sounds of the "w" and the "v" so that "we were very interested" sounded like *"ve ver wery intwested."*

"I didn't know him. My father knew him. My father was with STRX but is retired now. He still does some consulting work for them and he knew Mr. Tkachuk very well. In fact he had dinner with him the night that he died." This information brought an astonished look from the four members of the Rhapsody Group. The meeting had been arranged through a mutual contact at STRX. And they knew that Cromwell Parsons interest in Rhapsody was in some ways tied to their IT platform. However they were unaware that the relationship between Tkachuk and Cromwell Parsons was personal.

"Wow! We didn't know that." Abby said. "He was working on something we refer to as the '*HealthPort,*' for us, and that remains an important part of our membership product. We will miss Max' contribution, and it sounds as though your father may have lost a friend. Max was also a friend of Sandeep's sister. That's how he and his team started to work with us." Abby nodded in the direction of her youthful CIO.

Josh didn't care to take this line of conversation any further. He felt that it was no longer relevant. At one end of the table there were blue lined pads. Josh began to reach in that direction, and one of his staffers got up and grabbed a pad and handed it to Josh as he began to speak.

"Why don't we take it from the top, and you can explain to us exactly what Rhapsody is or what Rhapsody does?"

Alison passed around copies of a preprinted presentation while Abby began to speak. "The idea for Rhapsody was originally Allie's idea so before we describe the business let me allow Allie to tell you a little about the market and why we formed Rhapsody." Josh's gaze ping ponged back and forth between the two sisters as they fluidly shifted the conversation between them. Even their voices had almost the same pitch. However Josh began to observe a more confident tone when Abby spoke and it was becoming clear that she was the businesswoman and Alison was the visionary. In the instant before Alison spoke, Josh glanced at their business cards and noted the reflection of that nuance. Abby was the CEO and Alison was the EVP of Strategy.

"There seems to be an endless stream of information as well as misinformation in the marketplace about health, medicine, wellness, fitness, beauty, and generally about what people want, when it comes to their body."

There was a certain sensuousness about Alison as she said this that underscored her deep feelings on the topic. She continued. "This stream of information also spills over into spirituality and the impact that a person's mind and spirit play in the process of remaining healthy throughout a long lifetime. We believe that there is a way to corral all of this information into an important new business. This business will serve our clientele in a proactive holistic manner that will allow practitioner and client alike to explore all of the options that life has to offer, and to select an individualized pathway to their own happiness."

Alison said all of this as if she had practiced it many times. She wasn't halting or hesitant. She appeared to be speaking from the heart. Her twin Abby then picked up the drum beat.

"Allie has discussed her feelings on these issues many times over the last several years, and although she is a physician, and I am a business person with a layman's understanding of many of these issues, I certainly have felt frustrated in the past by the lack of a truly holistic global offering." The two sisters weren't exactly finishing each other sentences, but they were sharing the storyline effectively.

At this point Abby simply continued. "We founded our business on the principle that there are four major opportunities that need to be addressed." Sandeep clicked through the PowerPoint presentation as Abby spoke. "First there are no truly global players in the health and wellness industry today. Secondly the industry is totally underserved by IT, that is, information technology. Third, access to best of breed healthcare professionals is irregular and limited, and finally the industry, as it is now, is set up to service institutions and practitioners rather than customers. Together these four macro issues provide an enormous business opportunity."

Abby paused for several seconds to make sure that the Cromwell Parsons people, particularly Josh Struben, had digested her points. She noticed that his eyes were fixed on her face and mouth and what she was saying, rather than on the PowerPoint slide. Her business experience told her that this was a good thing. Struben could look at the slides later on. He was obviously more interested in the conviction and persona of the presenter.

As Josh took in the words of Abby McDuffee he thought that she seemed to be an activist promoter. This was good. Whoever would be running the business had to have a visceral passion about it. In order for the business to succeed the leaders had to have the *will* not just the *words*. Josh saw that quality immediately in both McDuffee sisters. Neither looked a day over forty. But their youthful appearance and enthusiasm seemed to be tempered with wisdom and experience. He knew that he would continue to listen to the plan, but more importantly he would listen to the planners.

"So with these problems plaguing the industry, we asked ourselves, 'What do people want? How can we serve the consumer in the health and wellness arena?' The answer to these questions became the fundamental building blocks of Rhapsody."

"And what do people actually want?" The question came from one of Struben's staff, almost like a perfect straight man for Abby.

"It turns out that they want a lot of things. And realistically these are things they could have. First and foremost they want timely access to their doctors. Secondly they want the broadest possible set of solutions to their issues"

"In other words they want choices?"

"Exactly, but they want this broad set of choices to span many sectors. They want choices in healthcare, choices in wellness, choices in fitness, choices in dentistry, choices in beauty and beauty products. They want to know what all of the alternatives are in every facet of life, including their sexuality and their spirituality. And they want to know about all of the interrelationships of these facets of life, and how they affect their happiness and their longevity."

Abby paused in a very professional way to allow her statement to sink in. As she did so she looked around the table at every other set of eyes in the room. When she was satisfied that they had at least digested her words, she continued without taking any questions. Meanwhile Sandeep was clicking through slides with bullet items that matched up with Abby's words. When Abby nodded to Sandeep he clicked to a slide that depicted four columns holding up a trapezoid shaped roof. Inside the trapezoid roof were the words, "*Rhapsody Lifestyle Memberships.*" Abby then referenced the slide as she began to speak once again.

"After assessing what our clientele wanted, we put together our business based on these four pillars. The first pillar is *the* ™*Rhapsody*

HealthPort.[4] You know a little bit about this already, if you know what Max Tkachuk was working on for us. The second pillar is our ™*Rhapsody Global Practitioner Society*[5], the acronym for which is *GPS*. I'll have to admit that this is *not* meant to be subliminal. This is meant to very overtly give our members a method to find the route to the appropriate practitioners. We are in the process of putting together a worldwide society of practitioners that will be ™*Rhapsody Certified*[6] and who will be available to service our membership. The third pillar of our business is the *Rhapsody Centers*. This is the bricks and mortar portion of our business, and potentially the most capital intensive part of the plan. We will be opening fifty ™*Rhapsody Centers*[7] in the major cities of the world over the next seven years. I'll say more about the centers themselves a little later."

Josh had actually moved his gaze from Abby to the PowerPoint slide that showed the pillars of the Rhapsody business. He had heard her tick off the first three pillars, and was beginning to get an idea of the enormous size and scope of the Rhapsody plan. There had been no discussion at all about the financing of this plan, and he was curious about how they had managed to finance the work that they had done so far, and how they intended to finance the full blown business. He parked these thoughts in the corner of his mind as he turned his attention back to Abby and listened to her explain the final pillar of the business.

"The three pillars that I have mentioned so far are moving forward at a rapid pace. The plan is in place, and execution of the plan has begun. You might say that the cement for the pillars is already poured in form and is hardening. The fourth pillar of our business may be the most important pillar of all. In addition to our first three pillars, *the HealthPort, the GPS and the Centers*, we have a fourth pillar that we call ™*RhapsodyCare*[8]. I indicated that the cement in the other

---

[4] *The Rhapsody HealthPort* is a Trademark of Rhapsody Holdings, LLC and Rhapsody Holdings, Inc.
[5] The *Rhapsody Global Practitioner Society* (GPS) is a Trademark of Rhapsody Holdings, LLC, and Rhapsody Holdings, Inc.
[6] Rhapsody Certification is a Trademark of Rhapsody Holdings, LLC and Rhapsody Holdings, Inc.
[7] Rhapsody Center is a Trademark of Rhapsody Holdings, LLC and Rhapsody Holdings, Inc
[8] RhapsodyCare is a Trademark of Rhapsody Holdings, LLC and Rhapsody Holdings, Inc

pillars was hardening. By design we're still mixing the cement for the *RhapsodyCare* pillar. However the essence of *RhapsodyCare* is that every one of the Rhapsody members will have an individualized health and wellness program that is supported by a personal healthcare concierge."

"What does that concierge do?" Josh was curious about how extensive this element of the business would be.

"That's a very important question. First of all the term *concierge* is a working title. We will come up with a better name for these important folks as the plan unfolds. The concierge will be responsible for co-developing a ™*Rhapsody HealthMap.*[9] These *HealthMaps* will be different for each member and will obviously be dependent on many apparent variables like age, gender, genetics, and general physical health. They will also be co-developed with the member and therefore, lifestyle preference oriented. Obviously this is not the work of a single practitioner, but each member will have a lead concierge, who will be backed up by others. This Healthcare Concierge will also be supported by a 24/7/365 contact center that a member can communicate with from anywhere in the world, through just about any communications medium."

Abby made her points while smiling only slightly. Her hand gestures helped support her explanation of the pillars, and she spoke at a measured yet confident pace that allowed her audience time for comprehension. They were all seated. The aura that Abby conveyed was one of confident success.

"So let me see if I have this straight. If I'm reading your slide correctly, your four pillars support something that you refer to as *The Rhapsody Lifestyle.*"

"Correct."

"And from what you've told me, a member would be able to get access to physicians throughout the world, through your GPS, and I'm assuming these physicians would use the *Rhapsody HealthPort* to access medical records and other relevant information on a real-time basis, while tracking and monitoring the member's progress using the HealthMap, and that this access is facilitated by the ™*Rhapsody*

---

[9] Rhapsody HealthMap is a Trademark of Rhapsody Holdings, LLC and Rhapsody Holdings, Inc

Concierge[10] and is likely to take place at any one of 50 centers in different parts of the world. Do I have it all right?"

"Nice summary. However there is much more detail within each of the pillars. For example the GPS is not just physicians. We were originally going to refer to it as the Global Physician Society, but changed it to the Global Practitioner Society in order to be much more encompassing."

"Okay. I understand that."

"And then with respect to the *Rhapsody Centers*, they are a lot more than a Health and Wellness facility, they also include spa services. In fact more than half of the physical space is devoted to spa services."

"So I can get a massage at the same facility where I get my check up completed or I can have a laceration stitched."

"Yes absolutely. But the list of services available at each center is very long. You will be able to get your hair cut or your dental work done. There is a wide range of beauty services as well as cosmetic surgery services. Actually dermatology and cosmetic medical procedures are elements of the medical practice that Alison has back in New York." She nodded briefly in her sister's direction. "In addition there will be a wide range of complementary or alternative medical services. These are too numerous to list but include chiropractic services, acupuncture, Ayurveda medical practices, aromatherapy and a long list of other approaches to health and wellness."

Josh was growing more intrigued as the presentation went along, but he was mindful of the time that they had allotted to the discussion today. The agreement with the Rhapsody folks was that they would meet for ninety minutes today to get an overview of where their specific intersections of interest might be. Then if everyone was agreeable they would have another meeting the following day. He could see that even though they were only twenty minutes into their meeting that there was an awful lot here to discuss, and he believed that they would not be able to reach any meaningful conclusions in the short timeframe they had allotted this morning. He put both hands out on the table and stretched them in Abby's direction.

---

[10] The Rhapsody Concierge is a Trademark of Rhapsody Holdings, LLC and Rhapsody Holdings, Inc

"Dr. McDuffee, let's just pause here for a second. I don't mean to interrupt …..in fact I want to hear every bit of your presentation… but maybe I should have framed our discussion here this morning a little tighter."

Josh stood up and gazed out the window at the bustling boat traffic along Victoria Harbor. There were hundreds of boats moving in every direction, seemingly without order. Sailboats and yachts, big and small, bounced in the choppy waters between Kowloon and Central. The scene from the conference window seemed as energetic, diverse and complex as the business that the McDuffee sisters were describing, and yet on both accounts Josh Struben was just trying to take it all in. He turned back to the table and continued his statement.

"Before we get much further into the particulars of the Rhapsody business, it might behoove us to frame up the rest of the time we have here this morning. Your business seems to be quite ambitious in its scope, and will probably not lend itself to adequate description in one brief meeting. On the other hand, we here at Cromwell Parsons Resources are interested in investments of many different types and sizes. The private equity fund that we are referring to as Blue and Green, or just B&G, houses our healthcare portfolio of companies. I manage this fund for Cromwell, and we anticipate the size of our fund to be about 350 million dollars, when fully funded and invested.

"We haven't discussed the current funding for Rhapsody yet. And we haven't discussed your short term and long term financial needs. We also haven't discussed whether or not there would be a financing opportunity that meets the objectives of both Rhapsody and of Cromwell's B&G fund. However as I see the multiple facets of your business….What did you call them? Pillars…….the multiple pillars of your business…… I see many crossover opportunities between your business and the other businesses that are supported by the B&G fund."

By now Josh had the full attention of the four members of the Rhapsody Group and he took his time to look squarely from one face to another. He was by far the youngest person in the room, and he was less experienced in running aspects of a business than several others in the room. However his confidence emanated from the golden rule, "He who has the gold rules." Therefore the particulars of the interactions between the firms were going to unfold as Josh saw fit. He continued to address the table.

"What I would like to understand over the next hour or so includes several things. Before I tick off those items, I just want to be certain that we will be able to continue this meeting tomorrow as we originally agreed." He looked around the table and saw no dissent so he continued, "Mostly what I'd like to hear about for the rest of this morning is the background and experience of the leaders of the business including yourselves, and then I'd like to get a high level understanding of the financials of the business to date and the financial projections that you see as probable in the business plan. Does that sound okay to you?"

"I'm glad you want to use both days, and we'd be happy to go about our presentation in the manner that you have requested," said Abby. "Just so you know, Ben will handle the financial projections, Allie can answer any GPS related questions, and Sandeep will be happy to address any of the IT issues that you may have."

Josh sat back down in his chair and said, "Okay. Then let's get back to work." For the next hour or so the McDuffee sisters, Sandeep Mehra, and Ben Hui Zhang provided Josh Struben and his colleagues at Cromwell Parsons Resources with a litany of background information on about twenty or so influential people who were the business leaders of Rhapsody. Ben also gave a synopsis of the funding and projections for the company.

They were running about fifteen minutes over the allotted time for the meeting and Josh had another group waiting to come in, so he stood up to summarize where he thought they were at.

"We're a bit into the next meeting here, so let's stop and pick this up again tomorrow around 10 AM. Will that work for all of you?"

"Yes, we all will still be here, but Abby and I will be getting a flight out tomorrow afternoon." Alison answered for the group.

"Okay. What I heard in the last hour or so is that your group has self-funded all of your progress to date, with sweat equity and a few million dollars in cash. You are in the process of securing $300 million to launch the business. You don't expect to see any revenue for the next year and you don't expect to show a profit until the latter half of year two, when you will have two centers up and running, and four more sites selected. Right so far?"

"Yes." Ben Hui Zhang answered, as he had been the one presenting the numbers over the last hour.

"All right so what we would like to discuss tomorrow is the sales and marketing plan that you intend to deploy, a lot more detail on the operations of a single center, and the corporate and financial structure that you envision as you grow towards your multibillion dollar revenue targets."

There was not even the slightest hint of sarcasm or cynicism in Josh's voice as he summarized the morning's discussion and set the agenda for the following day. He knew of many people who would scoff at an entrepreneurial group that was hoping to drive billions of dollars in revenues before they even had their first sale. But even though he was only twenty-seven, Josh had seen enough instant wealth creation in his business career to doubt nothing. Besides one of the most salient business lessons that Josh had learned was embodied in something his father, Stephen Struben, had taught him:

"If you set out to create a ten million dollar business, you may, in fact, get to ten million. Alternatively you may come close and need be satisfied with an eight or nine million-dollar business. But there was one certainty. You were not going to have a hundred million dollar business. Unless you set your *targets high*, you cannot hit high *targets*." There was something about this Rhapsody Group that brought his father's lesson back to mind.

They said their goodbyes at the doorway and the Rhapsody Group walked toward the elevator bank. Alison McDuffee reached out and gave her sister Abby an undisciplined high-five. This was accompanied by four smiles as the group entered the elevator. Rhapsody had moved one step further and they weren't even sure what that step entailed.

****

Maureen Brady lay down on the plush sheets of her king size bed. She had the air conditioning on high, and she didn't worry at all about the eighty-five degree heat outside on the balcony to her suite. She felt good. In so many ways she felt better than she had in some time. She was tired after her day long interactions with the other guests of SIS, but she felt an inner peace that she hadn't felt in a long time. As she stretched out on her bed she was looking forward to reading herself to sleep.

She thought back on her day and for whatever reason she first thought about her meals. To start with there were three of them. She ate breakfast, lunch and dinner and enjoyed each meal. The food at SIS was good, but it was the way that she ate that made her *feel* good. She had not made a ritual of eating three meals a day since she was ten years old. At SIS she ate small portions but tried most everything. It had been a long time since she had paid a lot of attention to the taste of her food. She had never had an eating disorder. In the past she simply ate small portions to avoid gaining weight. Now she was still eating small portions but it was so she could enjoy the variety.

Her discussion group for the day was made up of a number of people with different addictions. Some were fighting multiple addictive demons. They all shared the common desire to be rid of these demons. The discussions and the sharing were healthy, but Maureen also appreciated the quiet time, the contemplative solitude that made SIS such a departure from her "normal" life.

She had lots to read both from the program and some casual entertaining reading that she brought along to help her relax. However before she began her reading, she wanted to figure out a few things. When she first decided to go to Solace in the Sun, she knew that she had an alcohol problem and she was convinced that once she had stopped drinking cold turkey, she would be fine. That was the way it was when she was younger and smoked cigarettes. Once she quit, she quit forever. She was beginning to understand that it wouldn't be the same with her alcohol addiction. The alcohol addiction came with a lot more emotional baggage.

Maureen was surprised and hurt by how little she had heard from her husband, John. Although he had called several times, he didn't talk for long, and he talked more about what was wrong with the economy, and about the upcoming presidential election than he did about her. Invariably the few calls that she had gotten from John were interrupted by business emergencies and call backs were either delayed or deferred to next time. John shared the news that Maria had abruptly resigned, and Maureen was sad to hear this, because she knew that John relied on Maria, and that might have been the reason for his jumpiness on the few phone calls that they had shared recently.

Maureen worried about her relationship with John. Maybe she had been expecting too much, and not giving enough of herself. As a stumbling, bumbling alcoholic she sure couldn't have helped him very much over the last few years. She resolved to make it up to him once she was cured. She hoped that John would keep his promise and visit her this coming weekend.

The children had been responsive. Megan called often from school and Mark called as well, less than Megan but more than her husband, John. Kenneth called her almost every day and emailed her and texted her multiple times daily. One side benefit of her stay at SIS was that she was finally getting her computer skills up to speed.

She missed life back on Long Island, but not as much as she thought she would. She had heard nothing from her friends except three get well cards that had been forwarded from home. She had met some interesting people at SIS, but she doubted any would blossom into a longer friendship. On the other hand, she had gotten a lot of attention from the staff. Even Chipper Geld had made a point of constantly checking with her about how she was feeling. Just two nights before he had sat down and spoken to her after dinner for about an hour. He was such a nice man and he seemed to want to know everything about her and her family. He said nice things about Kenneth, and inquired about his two siblings. He even seemed concerned about John, asking a lot of questions about how he and ICD were faring during the economic downturn. He also commented on the fact that her facial wounds seemed to be healing nicely and he made sure that she had the full attention of the staff dermatologist.

As well as she was being treated, Maureen realized that she still had a way to go, and that she wouldn't leave SIS until just before Christmas. The family had collectively agreed to forego a traditional Thanksgiving dinner together this year, but Maureen thought that Kenneth might fly into Costa Rico to see her anyway. Maureen knew that she was healing but she also knew that the process needed to run its course. That was about all the introspection she was ready for tonight. She picked up her book and began to read.

****

Another long business day had neared the end for many people but not for John Brady. JB was determined to see ICD through to the other side of the recent meltdown no matter what it took. He didn't get to be the CEO by sloughing off. If it took twelve hours a day, seven days a week to re-erect the stature of ICD, then he would just have to do it. He had spent the better part of the day poring over reports that members of his team had sent to him.

The only area of the business that showed any sign of life whatsoever was the Essential Solutions Division run by Jason Tobin, a young VP out of Atlanta. It was now close to 7 PM. He wondered if Tobin would still be in the office.

"Alice, get me Jason Tobin in Atlanta." All day long, JB had been barking into the intercom and Alice had been lining up the phone calls. She had been JB's secretary since before he became CEO, and she was infinitely loyal to him. She didn't always stay late at the office, but when things were rough around the office Alice always made certain that she was available to help. She knew that times were tough of late for JB.

"Jason Tobin on Line 1, Mr. Brady."

"Tobin, John Brady here."

"Hello John. Good to hear from you." He was nervous about the nature of the call, but tried not to sound that way. Brady had never called him directly before, and it was late in the day.

"I was looking through the results of the various business units today," Brady wasted no time whatsoever with small talk. This was partly for effect but it was also partly because he didn't give a damn about a lot of personal nonsense in a time of business crisis. "and I noticed that your unit is the only one with five quarters of consecutive double digit growth."

"Thank you for noticing that John." Tobin was temporarily relieved.

"Not much to notice, Tobin. The growth is significantly below what we targeted even though you are riding ahead of the pack."

"I certainly recognize there is much room for improvement." Tobin knew how to run the race. He also knew he had a three or four length lead.

"Good. So now tell me about growth. What are you doing correctly to sustain growth, even if it is below target?"

Tobin ignored the stick and went with the carrot. He saw an opening and was intent on taking advantage of it. He started down a well-trod path of platitudes that were familiar to those who worked in his shop, but may not have been as familiar to his CEO John Brady. He tried to sound unrehearsed by dropping John's name a few times in the middle of his soliloquy. "There are a few things that make us different, John. First of all we make use of a lot of suppliers and don't use ICD products exclusively. Secondly we try to provide total solutions for our clients, not simply hardware products. As I'm sure you know, John, we use many different software providers, big and small, to make our hardware run effectively in our customers' technical environments."

"You don't sell our own software. You just use others' software to grease the skids so to speak. Am I correct?"

"Yes you might say that." *I would never say it that way but you're the CEO, JB, so you can say it whatever fucking way you want,* thought Tobin

"That makes us very dependent on these other companies to do what we do for our customers. Doesn't it?"

"Not really, John. In the Essential Solutions Division we provide comprehensive answers for our clients' complex business issues. Therefore we need software to be comprehensive, but, of course, we're not limited to any one software company."

"Cut the bullshit, Tobin. Here's a simple question. Whose margins are better on these deals - the software suppliers or ours?"

"Probably the software suppliers have better margins."

"Right answer, but a bad answer....but at least you were straight about it. Let me know in less than one week, why we can't develop some of this software in-house. ICD has thousands of software engineers. I want to know what it would take."

"Yes sir."

"Next item, Jason." It was the first time he called Tobin by his first name. "Here's your chance. Tell me what the one thing your division does differently, that makes you more successful than the rest of the divisions we have."

Tobin didn't know what to make of the inquiry at first. So he thought for a split second and gave a direct answer. "Our teams are aligned vertically by industry, because we need to understand our customers within the context of their businesses. I don't believe any of the other divisions are aligned that way. I think they are more aligned around our products and services."

"Thanks Tobin. That's helpful. Get a plane up here and we'll talk some more tomorrow in person." Brady hung up the phone and thought for a second. He had heard about this industry-aligned issue somewhere else recently, but couldn't quite remember where at first. Then it came to him; the tall redhead in Atlantic City.

****

It was nearing the end of the business day in Hong Kong, but still the morning hours in London. Josh picked up the phone and called his father.

"Hi Dad. It's Josh."

"Oh hi, son." Then in the background you could hear him say over his shoulder to his wife. "It's Josh, Danielle."

"Dad?"

"Yes Josh. How are you? In fact where are you?"

"I'm fine Dad and I am in Hong Kong. How's Mom doing?"

"She's doing fine … much better in fact. She's right here. Do you want to talk to her?"

"In a minute, Dad." Josh shook his head silently on the other end. Sometimes his worldly wise father could be so insecure when it came to his children. "How are *you* doing, Dad?"

"I'm doing great … just terrific. Healthy as a horse you might say."

"Good to hear it. I have a business issue I'd like to ask you about."

"Is this about Max Tkachuk's company, Apakoh?"

"Yes. As I said I'm in our Hong Kong office for a couple of weeks, and our folks set up a meeting with a group called Rhapsody Holdings. Apparently they were contracting with Tkachuk to create something called the *Rhapsody HealthPort*. Are you familiar with this?"

"To some degree, yes. Tkachuk was working with Rhapsody on behalf of STRX. STRX likes Tkachuk's company, Apakoh, a lot, but they have an even stronger interest in Rhapsody. As I understand it the IT development for Rhapsody's HealthPort concept was being contracted out to STRX who subcontracted it to Tkachuk. I think Max and the Rhapsody people hit it off well."

"I'm surprised that Rhapsody didn't just contract directly with Tkachuk."

"You've still got a lot to learn about business, son. First of all STRX probably introduced Rhapsody to Tkachuk. Secondly STRX's medical device business sees Rhapsody as a potentially large customer that can purchase their heavy metal, like CAT scans, MRI magnets and the like, to be used in their Rhapsody Centers. And finally, Rhapsody wants to connect all of the inputs and outputs from their *HealthPort* to all of the medical toys that STRX wants to sell, everything from digital scales and blood pressure readings to cardiograms and other sophisticated radiological reports. That's why this was shaping up as a multiple party contract."

"What happens now that Tkachuk is dead?"

"Good question. What is Rhapsody saying about that?"

"I'm not sure. But we're meeting with them again tomorrow. I'll ask them. Thanks for the input"

"Are you thinking of investing in these Rhapsody people?"

"Don't know yet, Dad. And you know that if I did know that we would be investing, I'd have to be very careful with that information."

"They're not a public company."

"STRX is though."

"I guess so. Well anything I can do to help let me know. Here's your mother."

"Hi, Josh. *'ow* are you?"

"Hi Mom I'm fine. And Dad said you're feeling a lot better also. Right?"

Mother and son continued to talk for about fifteen minutes before Josh promised to spend several weeks in the London office in December around the holidays. It was always a bit hard for Danielle to believe that Josh actually worked out of London, because he seemed to spend so much more time in New York, Hong Kong and other places. But when she remembered how her sons were raised - as showbiz nomads - she just let the thought drop.

Josh finally hung up the phone. He looked through the glass window of his office to see almost all of the people in the office, seem to freeze.

She wasn't expected to arrive in Hong Kong until later that evening, but when Gina Alvarez walked into the office of Cromwell Parsons Resources and asked for Josh, everyone in the office seemed to hear the request, stop what they were doing and listen for a response. It was like a scene from the old EF Hutton commercials in the 1980s that said "When EF Hutton talks; People listen."

Everyone was interested in Gina Alvarez. As her world tour was making her more popular than ever, she was making Josh into a mini-celebrity along the way. The media had caught up with them when they were in Rome together and spotted them again when Gina flew in from Greece for a London rendezvous ten days later. Now another three weeks had passed and Gina and the Lay D's had played throughout Europe and made a two day swing through Moscow on their way to China. They were setting all kinds of records at the gate everywhere they played, and the paparazzi were dying to know more about the personal lives of Gina Alvarez and her friend, Josh Struben. Josh had never granted an interview, nor stopped to say anything to the paparazzi. He and Gina both travelled almost exclusively by private jet and thereby avoided being seen at large public airport terminals. But the Asian paparazzi seemed to be even more persistent than their American and European counterparts. At the very least there were more of them.

Gina arrived at the Cromwell Parsons office alone, and that was unusual. Her agent, Carl Gordon, had provided security in every city along the tour, but Gina was not always so easy to keep up with. Josh had planned to meet her at her hotel later that night, and was surprised when she came to the office. He stepped out of the visiting executive office and greeted Gina in the reception area. She was dressed casually, but stunningly. She wore low-rise jeans that clung to her lower torso and came up to hipbone level. They might as well have been painted on. Her tight white silk and cashmere scoop-necked sweater top strained to contain her cleavage that somehow seemed to have swollen a bit over the last few weeks. Her shoulder length thick blonde hair was parted in the middle and pulled down over her ears, then loosely wrapped around the back of her neck, where it was gathered in a gold clasp. The large round sunglasses were more of a signature style piece than a disguise of meager means, and she had removed them after entering the building anyway. She carried a small purse in one hand and her sunglasses in the other, as Josh came out to see her.

With Gina there was never any true sense of decorum, so when Josh entered the reception area, she simply threw her arms around his neck crossing her hands, purse, and sunglasses in the caressing process.

"So are you glad to see me?" She squealed, paying no attention to the gathering audience of about a dozen people.

"Sure, sure, come on in." Josh ushered her quickly into the visiting executive office without making any awkward introductions. He closed the door.

"So what brings you to the office? I thought I'd be meeting you back at the hotel."

"I just couldn't wait to see you. I have some great news."

"Really? What is it?"

"I'm pregnant!"

Chapter 8: *Hong Kong Day 2*

Ben Hui Zhang was born in Hong Kong and had been involved in the financial circles of that mystical eastern city for most of his adult life. His father and mother were native to Shanghai in Mainland China, but had immigrated to Hong Kong to avoid the oppressive policies of the People's Republic of China after the Communists took charge in the late 40's. The Zhangs arrived in the city of Hong Kong shortly after a combination of British and Chinese troops ended the occupation of the Asian port by the Japanese during World War II

Zhang's parents united with other Chinese refugees to develop a fledgling textile industry that began to flourish in the late 1950's. They learned to speak English from a Brit who was a high ranking aide to the British Governor of Hong Kong, and who also sponsored textile exports to the UK. The Zhang family textile business blossomed in the waterfront section of Kowloon. When the Zhangs' only son was born in 1959, they western-styled his name in the hope that he would benefit from the change. Ben Hui Zhang did just that. He was a capitalist of the first order from his youthful days in the retail clothing business to his formal education on the other side of the world.

The Zhang family business survived the political upheavals in Hong Kong in the sixties, but nine-year-old Ben Hui Zhang almost didn't survive the Hong Kong Flu epidemic of 1968. In fact it was only with the assistance of their British friends that young Ben was allowed to leave Hong Kong to be treated for his severe weight loss in a London Hospital. It would be the first of many trips to England for the young heir to the Zhang textile business.

After spending nearly seven months in London, Ben returned home to Hong Kong and developed a very serious approach to his studies. He worked seven days a week for several hours a day measuring textiles to fit foreigners, and spent five days a week in school measuring the time and money it would take to break loose and go to school in London or the USA. Fortunately for young Zhang, his parents shared his dream and helped him cultivate his desire.

The extraordinary growth of Hong Kong throughout the 1970s allowed many of its citizens to profit from their industriousness. With the help of British partners the Zhang family did just that. Their goal of gaining an education for their son was abetted by their business dealings with the British and in 1975 and the age of sixteen, Ben Hui Zhang was once again on his way to the UK. This time he was able to complete his secondary education on a cultural exchange program that nurtured his native intelligence and allowed his curious mind to develop. Ben returned home to Hong Kong in 1977 and worked for another year in the family business while saving every dollar he could so that the next phase of his dream would come true. The Zhang family now had twelve retail store outlets for their textile business, ten in Kowloon and more importantly two in Central, just outside the new hotels that were growing up near the waterfront. Selling custom made suits and shoes to businessmen in Central was far more profitable than the same business in Kowloon. Ben was well versed in the differences because since his return from secondary school in London, he was the one responsible for keeping the books of the family business.

Ben and his parents were keenly aware that Ben had been destined to continue his education in the United States. It was something that they had talked about from the time Ben was 6 years old. They just never knew exactly how they were going to accomplish this feat. The family textile business provided the answer. Several large American shipping companies were now competing to establish a foothold in Asia. The package delivery business derived a lot of money from a mail order retail textile business that was growing up rapidly in Hong Kong. Ben was befriended by the Asian representative of Global Express Shipping, who told him about an education/internship that GES was offering to prospective Asian employees, who could study in the USA under a student visa, while working at GES headquarters in Nashville, Tennessee.

Although he was a few years older than the other college freshman in his class, his age was far less of a diversifying factor than his Chinese heritage. Still Ben Hui Zhang never felt like Middle America was discriminating against him. Zhang finished in the middle of his class but felt as though he had gained more knowledge and wisdom than many of his Middle American peers. Through it all he was gainfully employed by a multinational corporation that was growing in worldwide prominence.

During the mid eighties, Zhang continued to work in the United States, returning to Hong Kong once a year for an extended holiday with his parents. They often discussed the future of the United States as well as the future of Hong Kong. There was a relatively cooperative climate between the People's Republic of China and the British government under Margaret Thatcher, and a growing acceptance by the PRC of democratic and capitalistic policies for Hong Kong. However, the long promised "Hand Over" of Hong Kong from the British to the Chinese in 1997 loomed on the horizon. Many native Chinese families such as the Zhangs worried that the "Hand Over" might result in repatriation of their assets. They began to emigrate in droves, to San Francisco and Seattle in the United States, to Vancouver in Canada and to London and Scotland in the UK. The Zhangs had been hedging their bets in the textile business with a small partnership with another Chinese family that had gone on to live in Singapore. In 1990, Ben's parents moved out of Hong Kong to Singapore themselves and took more than 50 % of their textile business with them.

Meanwhile Ben Hui Zhang had negotiated the green card process in the United States throughout the 1980s and became an American citizen in 1990. He accomplished this after working for more than eleven years with GES, first as a student intern, then as an accountant, and accounting manager, and then as an Assistant Vice President of Finance.

In 1993, armed with his American citizenship, Zhang became Vice President of Finance for GES Asian operations group, and he moved back to Hong Kong. He was the CFO and the right hand man to the Asian Group Executive, as they embarked on a roll up of nine different package delivery companies throughout Asia and one in Australia. By the end of the century the Asian Group had become the Far Eastern Group and now encompassed both continents. The handover of Hong Kong from the British to the Chinese in 1997 proved to be much less upsetting than any of the predictions, and it had little impact on the business of GES. Ben Hui Zhang became the CFO of the Far Eastern Group of GES in 1999 and three years later became the Group Executive when his predecessor died.

Ben's personal life did not move at the same speed as did his professional career. Slight of stature and relatively nondescript to the casual observer, Ben only stood out in a crowd when it came to his business prowess. Never one to be led by his libido, Ben still sometimes pined for the social acceptance and personal comfort that a spouse might provide. He dated infrequently, and didn't have any enduring hobbies, that would lead him to interact with others in a social gathering. Although early in life his parents had taught him the Five Precepts of Taoism, "*No Murdering; No Stealing; No Sexual Misconduct; No False Speech; and No Taking of Intoxicants,*" he practiced no formal religion after he moved to the United States.

At the age of 42, Ben began dating a Buddhist co-worker who was a dozen years younger. He married Charini in a Buddhist ceremony in Hong Kong, and the two went about setting up their home in a small apartment on Hong Kong Island. When they vacationed together it was typically a visit to Singapore to see Ben's parents or an occasional trip to the resorts in Phuket, Thailand. Ben and Charini never expressed a serious interest in having children. They kept to themselves and to their respective jobs while working in the Hong Kong offices of GES. Ben's job required that he travel a good deal, both within the region and occasionally back to the United States. Charini's job was entirely within Hong Kong.

After Ben Hui Zhang became the Group Executive of the Far Eastern Group of Global Express Shipping (GES), people began to realize for the first time that Charini and Ben were man and wife. Charini didn't appreciate the unwanted celebrity that came with being the Group Executive's spouse, and so she resigned. Ben continued to work hard and traveled even more. One day he came back from a business trip only to find that Charini had run off to live with a younger Chinese man who lived in the New Territories. Strangely, he didn't miss Charini, nor was he jealous in any way about her new life. He just wanted to move on with his own life.

Ben began to make his vacation sojourns to the resorts in Phuket by himself. He found this a relaxing way to get away from the growing monotony of work. His vacations began to elongate from the typical five days that he would spend with Charini to a week and then ten days when he went there by himself. He enrolled in yoga retreats and spent a good deal of time considering his station in life and what made him happy and unhappy. He came to realize that his position as Group Executive was not all he hoped it would be. While he was proud of the fact that he had reached the top rung of the ladder, he also came to realize that it was lonely at the top. He was essentially a lot happier when he was contributing to the advancement of a group than he was leading the group. He found this personal revelation inspiring in a way, and he started the search for a change, He wanted to be a key player on a team, but he didn't want to lead the team. He was perfectly content with this realization.

Ben Hui Zhang began meeting new people in the restaurants, bars, and beaches of Phuket and on one such occasion he took a Dharma meditation class and met a female physician from Bangkok, Dr Dao Diskul, who interested him in a project that she was working on with two American sisters. A month later on a business trip to the USA Ben Hui Zhang met with a very charismatic woman named Dr Alison McDuffee, who explained the Rhapsody project to Ben. It took him about three weeks to button up the last of his business efforts at GES and join forces with the entrepreneurial Rhapsody Holdings group as their CFO.

****

Abby thought the small coffee shop in the Central Mall was a good place for the Rhapsody team to convene before going back for another meeting with Josh Struben and his people at Cromwell Parsons. She and Alison got there first. Ben and Sandeep were a few minutes behind. They were about a half an hour early for their follow up meeting, but they weren't meeting to discuss the upcoming conference with Josh Struben. They had discussed everything yesterday afternoon and they all felt that today's meeting was meant to simply solidify Cromwell Parsons interest in Rhapsody. They expected to make no specific proposals, nor did they expect to hear any specific offers. It was too early in the relationship building process for any of that to occur.

The banter was light as they discussed some of the shopping and sightseeing they had done the day before, and the terrific dinner they had in a quaint Kowloon restaurant. Being a native of Hong Kong, Ben Hui Zhang hosted the city tour as well as the dinner. He was pleased that his colleagues enjoyed his home city so much.

"This city will be perfect for one of the Rhapsody Centers and the sooner the better." Sandeep offered and Ben smiled happily. "There's lots of action in this town."

"Our plan calls for Hong Kong or Singapore to be our regional headquarters, but both will have a center by the end of year three of the plan," said Abby. "But some of the discussions we have been having with the people in Taiwan, may make that country a logical regional headquarters as well. We have some time yet to make that decision."

They were an odd looking group as they stood around the high top table, sipping their teas and their juices. As thin as the McDuffee sisters were, they were still taller and heavier than Sandeep, who was just a little over 5'4 inches tall and weighed a little over one hundred pounds. Ben Hui Zhang was not tall but he was a lot thicker through his mid section. Together they looked like three string beans and a Brussels sprout. However once they began any business discussions they had poise and presence and their intellects commanded respect. In a conference room they were all able to stand tall upon their experience and success in their respective business endeavors. The coffee shop venue was simply an equalizer.

Alison McDuffee had walked away for a few seconds and returned clutching a local tabloid. "I hope our friend Josh is able to stay focused this morning. It looks like he had an interesting night out on the town." She flipped the English language version of the tabloid onto the small round high top table around which the others were still standing. There was a picture of Gina Alvarez and Josh Struben leaving a Hong Kong nightclub surrounded by security guards. The caption said "Rocker Gina Alvarez and her regular squeeze, Josh Struben, leave club in Central." The picture had Gina dead center and Josh off to her right and seemingly a half step behind her. The shoulder of one of Gina's security people partially obscured the couple, but there was no doubt who they were. And both Gina and Josh were smiling as though they were enjoying themselves.

There was a short article about Gina's worldwide tour and the fact that she and the Lay D's would be playing in Hong Kong over the next two nights. The shows had both been sold out for several months.

The fact that Josh Struben was dating Gina Alvarez was not news to the Rhapsody Group. They knew about this before they ever arrived in Hong Kong. It had appeared many times when they did some Internet background checking on Struben. Alison also knew that Josh's mother was singer/actress Danielle Dubonet Struben, more commonly just known simply as, Danielle. Abby was much less attentive to such details. Josh Struben's connections to the entertainment world did not enter into any of the business discussions they had among themselves to this point. It was just an interesting sidelight. However Alison had a thought as she plunked down the tabloid paper.

"Wouldn't it be great if our relationship with Josh and the Cromwell Parsons group progressed to the point where we could get an introduction to Gina? Think what a great spokesperson she would make for us and for our centers."

"Wonderful idea Alison," said Ben. "They love that lady everywhere. She is famous on every continent, and she has a perfect body. Just gorgeous." Ben's comment actually struck the women as funny. He was not normally one to express his opinions on people's appearances.

"I know what she does for you men. But she also has enormous appeal with us women," Alison said excitedly. "She is one hell of a business person, and I heard somewhere that she has a genius IQ. Not only that, she is regarded by the show biz crowd as an icon at a very early age. To have that kind of respect from people who are used to having their asses kissed all the time is what really makes Gina so different."

"I also read that Gina is *wery* much into health and *vellness*. She doesn't drink and do drugs, and she's a bit of a Spa junky to boot." Sandeep added his opinion. Everyone seemed to be very conversant on the lifestyle of the pop icon.

Abby picked up the paper that her sister had thrown on the table and stared at the picture of Josh and Gina and then said "Very sexy people….very beautiful people…that's exactly who we want as our members….the beautiful people…..It would be great if both Josh and Gina were actually *Rhapsody Lifestyle Members*….but I'm not sure we want them to be spokespersons. I'd rather they be role models of the kind of member we will attract. When you make them spokespersons you run the risk of demeaning the product. People will think that it's just another business venture for Gina rather than something she truly believes in."

The four Rhapsody colleagues finished their juices and headed toward the elevator in the nearby building that led up to the offices of Cromwell Parsons Resources.

****

John Brady looked across his office at Rickie Van Dorfan standing in the doorway, but he didn't stand up or ask him to come further into the office. There was no attempt whatsoever to make Van

Dorfan feel comfortable. Rickie had simply been summoned to take a few directions from his boss.

"A few weeks ago, when Cordoza and I went down to Atlantic City, we had a Q & A session with the sales team. There was a young lady who asked a question about our sales structure. Find out who she is and get me some background on her. Find out where she went to school; how long she has been with the company; what kind of production numbers she has, and any personal information that you can dig up. Is she married? Does she have kids? … that sort of thing."

"Sure Mr. Brady. What's her name?"

"If I knew her name I'd have all this information in front of me already. Go find out."

Van Dorfan retreated back the half step it took him to be out of Brady's office entirely. He wished he would have had the courage to tell JB to go to hell but he just didn't. He didn't like Brady at all. Here was someone who had driven his wife to the bottle, paid little to no attention to his children, and a person who seemed to believe that when anything went wrong in his life or in his business, it was someone else's fault. Van Dorfan had heard all the rumors about Brady and Maria but had refused to believe any of it. It wasn't that he thought Brady wouldn't cheat on his wife; it was simply that he believed that Maria was too smart to get mixed up with a pig like John Brady. Although he didn't like Brady he stopped just short of hating him because of Kenneth. Rickie believed that Kenneth was blind to his father's foibles.

Still, Rickie had the task of finding an obscure sales person, who asked an isolated question, in the middle of a sales meeting, that took place several weeks earlier. He had no description and no name. He had talked to Maria twice since she left the company. Both conversations were impersonal and dealt with work that needed to get done. Maybe she could help once again. It was a shot in the dark but maybe she remembered something about the woman who asked John some dopey question.

As soon as Van Dorfan left his office John knew that Rickie would call Maria. This would accomplish several objectives. First it would piss off Maria when she learned that John might replace her with a low level saleswoman. Secondly, it just might bother Maria to know that he had paid attention to the redhead. Finally he might be able to find out through Van Dorfan what Maria was up to.

Brady walked around his desk and entered his private bathroom. He splashed a little water on his face and looked in the mirror. He saw the determined countenance of a man who shouldn't be crossed, a man who would stop at nothing to succeed where others had failed. He saw a very capable leader, who needed to straighten out a flagging computer device business, in a down market. He stiffened up and adjusted his tie and went back to work at his desk.

****

Gina had gotten out of bed a little later than usual. Josh had already left for the office, and Gina called down to another room in the hotel to tell Leon, her personal trainer, that she would meet him at the gym in half an hour. She noticed for the first time that the message light on her phone was lit. She picked up the receiver and dialed *88 to get her messages.

The recorded voice filled the room. "Gina, it's Carl Gordon. Sorry to have to leave you a message on the hotel voice mail, but I've tried your cell phone number and couldn't get through. Don't be alarmed but your mother had to go to the hospital today. She is okay. Everything is fine. She'll be just fine. Anyway I wanted to track you down so I could give you some of the detail so call me when you get this. I'm in my LA office this week so we're about fifteen hours behind you. But just call me whenever you can. I wanted you to hear from me, but don't worry your mother is doing fine"

Carl Gordon was a Motown mogul. He and his former partner Merv Bernstein were known throughout the music world as S&P, which was short for Salt and Pepper. They had formed a music talent agency that was second to none. It was Bernstein that initially discovered Gina on the beaches of Puerto Rico and brought her to the United States, first in Detroit and then on to New York. Bernstein who had been "Salt" had died in an auto accident almost three years earlier and Carl "Pepper" Gordon had taken over the management of S&P on his own. He had a stable of talented performers, but by far the most famous and the most productive was Gina Alvarez and the Lay D's.

Gina had planned on calling her mother today to check in with her. Her mother stayed out of her business affairs, and now lived in Detroit. She hadn't planned on telling her mother about her pregnancy just yet but she did want to bring her up to date on how well everything was going with Josh. Now she was concerned that her mother might have had some significant medical problem. There was only one way to find out. Gina thought for a second and knew it would be about 6 PM in LA so she picked up the phone in the room and asked the operator to dial Carl Gordon's cell number.

"Gordon, here."

"Carl, hi. It's Gina. I just got your message."

"Yea. I didn't want to alarm you, but your Mom went to the hospital this morning. Seems she has some sort of respiratory problem brought on by her diaphragm being displaced. She's doing well from what they told me at the hospital, but I thought you ought to know."

"How did you hear about it?"

"Your mom listed you and your NYC number as her emergency contact. When they couldn't get through to you they went looking for your agent."

"Are you sure she's okay?"

"She's doing fine. I have a number at the hospital for her. You can talk to her yourself. Got a pen?" He then proceeded to read her the phone number for her mother's hospital room. "I'll be flying back to Detroit tomorrow. I will check everything out for you."

"Thank you, Carl. I can always count on you." Gina was already contemplating flying to Detroit herself, but didn't want to say that to Carl.

Within minutes Gina was on the phone to her mother.

"Hello Gina, how is Hong Kong?" Gina and her mother talked about once a week and her mother kept close track of her tour.

"Just fine Mama. How are you doing? Is everything alright?" Gina could sense a fatigue from the very first words she heard from her mother.

"I'm okay I guess. Some of this might be my own fault. I don't know who to listen to when it comes to medical things."

"What exactly is the problem?"

"A few months ago I was reading an article in some women's health magazine that was talking about blood transfusions. It said that they were now screening blood in ways they never did twenty to twenty-five years ago. It also said that women who received blood transfusions during that time frame were at a risk for Hepatitis C, and that this could cause some health risks downstream."

"But you never had any health problems and you didn't have a blood transfusion, did you?"

"Until now I haven't had any health issues, but I did have a blood transfusion when I gave birth to you."

"Oh, I didn't know that."

"Well it never seemed like a big deal until I read that article. So when I went for a routine checkup I also had my blood checked for remnants of Hepatitis C and sure enough the tests came back positive."

"But you weren't showing any ill effects from this. Were You?"

"No but I asked the doctor and he did some checking and said that it could cause some serious liver problems later in life and so he suggested that I take this Interferon drug to avoid any of these problems."

"That was a while back, right?"

"Yes, but one of the side effects of Interferon is that it could cause a loss in bone density. So you're right I knew all this nine or ten months ago. But this morning I was lifting some boxes to place on the shelf in the closet and somehow or other I broke a bone in my back. The pain was very severe and in the process I have displaced my diaphragm, which has made it difficult to breathe, and so here I am in the hospital."

"What are they telling you, Mom? Are you getting out or will you be in the hospital for a while." Gina was incredulous about the bizarre chain of medical events but she maintained a calm demeanor so as not to alarm her mother.

"They're not telling me very much. But they sure are asking a lot of questions.....everything from my age to whether I have gone through menopause yet....to have I ever harbored any thoughts about violence."

"That's nuts. What did you tell them?"

"I told them that I am fifty-three years old, post menopausal and that I haven't harbored any thoughts about violence but that could change soon if they asked me any more stupid questions." Gina was glad to see that her mother still had her sense of humor.

"Nothing about a prognosis? Nothing about how long you will be in there?"

"They haven't told me a lot. I'm not even sure who is best to ask. There have been a few different doctors and nurses, X-ray technicians and other people. I'm not sure who is in charge. There is one nice young doctor who seems very competent, but they told me he was an intern and only worked nights."

"I'm going to come back there. I can cancel part of the tour."

"Don't be silly. That's why I'm glad you called. You need to just finish the tour, and call me when you can. Besides Carl is coming here tomorrow. I'm sure he'll be able to help me straighten things out. By the time you could get back here I hope to be out of the hospital. Just call me, because it's harder for me to contact you."

Gina listened carefully to what her mother said and the way she said it. It helped her defray her sense of panic. She took a deep breath and then said, "Okay for now. I'm happy that Carl is on his way to help. I just got off the phone with him."

They spoke for a few more minutes and Gina's anxiety about her mother dissipated slightly. She was still very much concerned. Her mother was the only family she had.

Gina wanted to tell her mother about her pregnancy, but she hadn't planned on telling her over the phone. She wanted to wait a month until her tour was over. Then she planned on seeing her in Detroit, where they could be together in person to enjoy the moment. She had confirmed her beliefs about her pregnancy by using an over the counter pregnancy test kit, so for now the only person in the world that knew of her joy was Josh. Her tour had five more weeks to go. She wasn't sure she wanted to continue, but she wasn't yet sure when she would cut it short. The last three weeks were scheduled for the United States and were being built up to be the crescendo, culmination and victorious conclusion to the tour. Pepper Gordon was already working to set up a selective post tour interview circuit, which would undoubtedly take her career to an even higher level. She wasn't sure how Carl would handle the pregnancy. However she had experienced one person's reaction already. That reaction made her feel great. Josh was thrilled when she told him that he was going to be a father.

She put on her gym clothes and went down to meet Leon for her workout. The workout would be less vigorous than usual.

****

"Thanks for seeing me on such short notice, Dr Al." Al Moses was once again seeing Maria Cordoza in his office and not in his examining room. Of course the majority of the time patient visits started and ended in the examining room, but Al made frequent exceptions and was not at all reluctant to be different from other physicians in this regard. In made no difference financially where he saw his patients. He billed them by the quarter hour rather than by the procedures he may or may not perform. He didn't take insurance. His clientele paid cash. He had no complaints and no collection problems. It was good business and it was good care.

In the particular case of Maria Cardoza, he knew that it was more important just to spend ten to fifteen minutes talking to her as a follow up to previous conversations, without necessarily going through a normal full examination. Having a closed and manageable practice made it easier for Dr Al to accommodate this type of visit without throwing his daily schedule into chaos. His clients almost never waited more than 5 minutes to see him. When Maria came to the office she first went to see one of Dr Al's physician assistants, who drew blood and collected a urine sample so that they could run the normal body fluid tests and make comparisons to past tests.

"It's always good to see you Maria. You look very relaxed. Have you been on vacation?"

Maria gave Dr Al a very full smile, the kind that had been difficult to muster in recent months. "You might say that," she answered.

Moses simply responded to her answer by widening his eyes and dropping his chin slightly in a facial gesture that seemed to say, *tell me more.*

"I resigned from my job at ICD," she continued. "And I took your advice and have been going to see your friend Dr Lefebvre. She has been very helpful to me in sorting through some of my life. I am also actually taking a yoga class with her husband."

"Wonderful. They are both talented professionals. I'm glad you are making progress." Even as he said this there was part of Al that wished he were the one talking Maria through her problems. He wouldn't quite admit it but he was actually developing an emotional attachment to Maria that was like a teenage crush. He wanted her attention as much as she wanted his help. As she sat across the desk from him she looked more beautiful than ever. It was not that he had been oblivious to her physical beauty in the past. There were lots of attractive women in his practice. It was something beyond physical beauty that portrayed itself through her countenance. There was more eye contact. Their voices were quieter. A more personal bond was building.

An awkward moment lasted a matter of a mere few seconds when neither Maria nor Dr Al spoke, but they simply looked at one another. Then Dr Al looked down at his chart and got back to business. "I see you are still having some difficulty with your menstrual cycle...." As he was talking there was a quick two-tap knock on the half-open door to his office and Charlotte his assistant peeked in.

"Dr Moses, I think you might want to see this." She walked in and handed Moses a printed page of data from Maria's electronic record. Near the bottom of the page there was a new notation that was circled with a red marking pen. Charlotte didn't wait for any comment from Dr Moses and didn't say anything to Maria whom she had greeted earlier when Maria first arrived. She merely turned around and left the office, carefully making sure the office door was fully closed behind her.

Al looked down at the circled notation on the bottom of the page. He raised his eyebrows in surprise. He was startled by the circled memo. However he was not dispassionate, as he might have been with many of his patients.

"Maria, we just ran some simple tests while you were here. It appears we may have a cause for the current interruption of your menstrual cycle. You are pregnant."

Dr Moses watched the vivacity drain from Maria's face. As with nearly all of his patients, he could tell almost instantly whether he was delivering good news or bad news.

"How could that be?" Her only sexual partner for the last several years had been John Brady. She had been taking birth control pills until the last year when she started to fear the side effects of the pills. Even so, John had commonly practiced protected sex by use of a condom, to the point where Maria had sometimes found the practice insulting, given the other parameters of their relationship. However, when she thought about her last sexual encounter with Brady, she reddened in anger. And as if the particulars of any given episode are impressed in some databank in the recesses of the brain, she recalled that John hadn't bothered to use a condom.

"I can tell you are surprised. And that sometimes is the case with some of my patients. I can talk to you about this now, for as long as you'd like." Dr Al was also surprised, because of some of the peripheral details of Maria's sexual relationships that she had shared previously. He knew that she had been thinking about having a baby, but she hadn't really convinced herself that she was ready for motherhood. He did not want to appear to be making any assumptions about the veracity of those details. He just wanted to listen first.

"The problem is that this is John Brady's baby. In addition to resigning from ICD, I have ended my relationship with John." Dr Al had watched Maria's face redden dramatically. He was unsure whether the emotion causing it was embarrassment, anger or something else. "I did have sexual relations with John recently, and I haven't had sex with anyone else."

****

They were back again in the same conference room that they had been in the day before. This time only Josh and one junior assistant represented Cromwell. Josh did not look at all like he had had a wild night out on the town. Even the news that he was going to be a father hadn't changed his even-tempered approach to business. He had learned early on how to separate his personal life from his professional life. Therefore when the Rhapsody team arrived, he had a very businesslike demeanor and seemed to be in a hard working mid-day frame of mind.

"Let's pick up where we left off yesterday. You were going to tell me a little bit about your sales and marketing efforts and also provide some detail about the individual centers." He ended the declarative statement with an upward intonation and a smile in the direction of Abby McDuffee.

Abby began, "The *Rhapsody Centers* were the original brainchild of Allie, so she will take us through what a typical center looks like. We are already looking at space in New York City for our first center." Abby made a short almost imperceptible nod in Alison's direction and her sister picked up the discussion.

"That's right. Each of the Centers will be located in a major metropolitan area. The plan is for us to open centers in NY and London in year two and then to open centers in Los Angeles, two Asian cities and one more European city in year three."

"I see from your slide that there are no centers in year one of your plan. Is that correct?"

"Yes. Year one actually is an amalgam of all of time and work that has been done so far, plus twelve more months starting with our date of funding. There is obviously a lot of work to be done before we actually open our first center. We will not begin to sell memberships until about three months before the opening in NYC."

"And this is work you already have under way?"

"Oh yes, of course. For example we spoke yesterday about our Global Practitioner Society, our GPS...well we have been talking with practitioners on four different continents already about joining our society. And we have already done a great deal of work with STRX on the rudiments and building blocks of our *HealthPort*. But there is a lot more to do, obviously."

"So in your NYC center....give me an idea of the type of services you will provide for your members." Josh wanted to understand the project thoroughly.

"Each center is designed with 40,000 usable square feet, and as you can see from our design about half of the footage is used for spa and spa-like treatments. The other 20.000 square feet is set up for a variety of medical treatments and consultations including alternative and traditional medicine as well as conventional medicine. The floor plan takes into consideration placement of heavy medical equipment, including a whole array of radiological instruments and devices."

Alison's voice was animated and enthusiastic. Josh could tell that the center itself was a big part of her dream. In fact it was originally the crux of her dream, a center where people could receive holistic care in a luxury setting.

"Now that I've shown you what a center looks like let's go back to your question about what kind of services we will offer. On the spa side of the Center we will offer a wide selection of relaxation and beauty aids. There will be massage and facial treatments as well as beauty and grooming services. Yoga and Pilates classes will be available as well. Among the many beauty services, we will include a facility for the dentals arts." Alison paused long enough to ensure that much was digested and then continued.

"With respect to the medical half of the Center, there will also be a wide spectrum of services. These will include minimally invasive surgery, a full range of radiological services such as CT, MRI Mammograms, X-rays, sonography and densitometry. These services will be supported by laboratory services that will deal with genetic and fertility issues as well as general clinical tests."

"These are traditional medical services. You mentioned that you would also offer alternative medical services. Is that right?"

"Yes for sure." Alison seemed very happy that Josh had asked this question. She could see that he understood the scope of what the *Rhapsody Lifestyle Membership* and the *Rhapsody Centers* would include. "We will offer access to a wide range of alternative medicine including ayurveda, acupuncture, aromatherapy …"

"You're not even out of the A's. Are there that many different kinds of alternative medical approaches?"

"A simple answer? Yes. Sometimes these are referred to as complementary medicine and in fact some of these therapies are offered in conjunction with traditional medical approaches. There are techniques involved such as biofeedback, meditation, and hypnosis that sometimes work quite well with traditional evidence-based medicine. I'm sure for example you have heard of the success that hypnosis has had with respect to smoking cessation."

"Yes certainly." Josh now had his elbows on the table leaning forward and staring at the computer projection that Sandeep had put on the wall. It listed a whole litany of different alternative medical practices. He allowed himself time to read the list slowly and also take in the aura of the Rhapsody team around him. While Abby and Alison effectively shared the lead in the presentation, he knew from his briefing package that Ben Hui Zhang was a prominent Hong Kong businessman and that Sandeep Mehra was also quite accomplished, even at his young age. The Rhapsody team had a lot of horsepower at the table, and it was good to know that there were many others that shared their vision. After finishing his perusal of the slide he turned back to Alison.

"So then you will offer these services in the same center as the traditional services?" His inflection indicated a question but he didn't wait for an answer. "It seems like you are taking the idea of holistic treatment to a whole new plateau."

"Yes and no. First the 'no.' You mention a plateau. We'd like to believe that this does not represent a *plateau* or any kind of new *level*. We'd rather think of this as an ongoing and upwardly focused quest for new knowledge about our humanity. Also we believe that our members need to *own* their own health. We will not determine what is right for any individual, without input from the member. And now the 'yes.' Yes we will make all of these services available side-by-side at the same center. We will facilitate access to all of the best practitioners who can aid in this quest to own your own health."

Josh began jotting down comments on his blue-lined pad and then asked a few questions about the scalability of the center. These included several questions with respect to utilization and costs. Ben Hui Zhang, the Rhapsody CFO, fielded many of these questions and

Sandeep Mehra addressed some of the technical questions in his role as CIO and chief technology officer. When most of Josh's questions had been answered, he paused and then said to Alison.

"I think I have a good handle on what goes on in the typical center; I imagine that the exact mix of service utilization may depend upon the area of the world where a center is located. Am I right?"

"Yes you are." Alison waited until the declaration set in and then said, "Let's move away from the Centers."

Josh smiled and said, "Okay, where do we go next?"

"It's important to recognize that the centers are only a part of the *Rhapsody Lifestyle Membership*. They are facilities at which a member can take advantage of all of the elements of the plan. However, many of the elements of membership are independent of the centers."

"So I can get treatment from one of your GPS practitioners at some place other than a Rhapsody Center?"

"Yes that's right. That's a big part of the plan. We will have groups of Rhapsody certified practitioners working at our Centers, but we will also have GPS practitioners working out of their own facilities in other venues. The common linkage will be the *Rhapsody HealthPort*, the *RhapsodyCare* team and the *Rhapsody HealthMap*. Any of these practitioners who will be working out of their own facilities will also be Rhapsody certified."

"Take me through how this might work. Say I am a *Rhapsody Lifestyle Member*, and I am on vacation in Aruba and I fall and break a few bones in my hand playing tennis. And now, for conversation sake, say you don't have a Rhapsody Center in Aruba, but you do have a Rhapsody certified orthopedic physician who has his own office in Aruba. How would I know who that physician is and whether or not I should go to see him?"

"Your *RhapsodyCare* concierge is the point of triage for this kind of situation. He or she will be able to put you in touch with a *GPS* practitioner in Aruba, and you will be comfortable knowing that the particular practitioner has been Rhapsody certified. In a more serious situation we also have an air ambulance capability to get our members to a hospital or a clinic in a major metropolitan area, or even back to a facility near their home. All of this would be captured on the *Rhapsody HealthPort* for the member."

"Okay. I think I've got the Center part down and I see how the other pillars of the membership fit in. Now we also want to talk about the marketing plan, your financials, and your funding. Are we together on all of that?"

Josh was a very organized man, and obviously a quick study. He took copious notes on blue lined pads, but still managed to pay rapt attention to the details that the Rhapsody team was laying out. Even though the McDuffee sisters were in general control of the flow of the meeting, Josh made every effort to make certain that all of his questions were answered.

"I think we're all on the same page." Abby McDuffee now took over from her older sister. "In discussing our marketing plans it's important to understand that our lifestyle memberships are targeted at the very high end of the market. The price of an annual membership is between $35,000 and $50,000. We will not be directly addressing healthcare access for the general public. Our *Rhapsody Lifestyle Memberships will* only be offered to a very exclusive group of consumers."

"Doesn't this cause some perception problems, in that you are offering healthcare services to the rich that aren't available to the general public?"

"That one question begs a few additional questions as well. I'll try to answer them all together. First, as I mentioned earlier, we are not in the business of providing healthcare services. We are in the business of providing a membership that among many other things, facilitates *access* to healthcare. The physicians who work at our centers, as well as those who are aligned in our Global Practitioner Society all have their own professional corporations. They merely pay us a fee to use our medical information tools and equipment or facilities. They are not employees of the *Rhapsody Center.*"

Josh took careful notice of Abby McDuffee's demeanor. She had a powerful way of speaking for such a slightly built woman. She was also able to disagree or provide a conflicting opinion on a topic without ever appearing confrontational. She exuded a level of confidence that had probably been an important contributor to her professional success over the years of her career. He noticed also that her personality was almost magnetic and that she had a certain charisma about her that both men and women would find appealing. For the first time he was beginning to sense a subtle difference between the McDuffee sisters. Where Alison was passionate, Abby was pragmatic. Where Alison was expansive and imaginative, Abby was focused and resourceful.

Abby continued her answer. "So now that I have clarified the fact that we do not *directly* provide healthcare to anyone, let me go back to the issue about marketing to the high end instead of the general public. The people who can afford a membership are concentrated in the major cities of the world, but they tend to travel extensively, have multiple residences and may belong to two or more health or athletic clubs. They tend to be conscientious about their health and fitness and keenly aware of their personal appearance. They are already living the good life and they want to live it for a considerable time longer. When we think about marketing to this affluent group we think about reaching them at openings at art galleries, yacht shows, fund raising benefits. We have also developed co-marketing agreements with some other firms that sell to the same market that we will reach."

"I think I understand that but how will you avoid criticism for providing something to the wealthy that will not be offered to the general public?"

"First we will be donating 5 % of our profits to the ™*Rhapsody Foundation*[11], which in turn will fund healthcare research that is geared toward preventative measures rather than remedial treatment. Secondly, many of the products and processes we develop, as well as the proactive approach that we will spawn, will have a trickle down impact on society as a whole over time."

Josh nodded his concurrence and then went back to more detailed questions about the sales and marketing plan for the company. Over the next half hour Abby described Rhapsody's multi-channel marketing plan and included data that demonstrated that there were more than ten million people worldwide with investment assets of more than a million dollars. She also allowed that there were more than 100,000 individuals worldwide with financial assets in excess of $30,000,000. Neither of these figures included non-liquid wealth such as cars, homes, jewelry and such. When Josh was satisfied that Rhapsody had done its homework on both the market and the marketing, he turned his questions to the funding for the business.

"Let's probe the current status of funding for your business. We don't want to lose sight of what has brought us together in the first

---

[11] *The Rhapsody Foundation* is a Trademark of Rhapsody Holdings, LLC and Rhapsody Holdings, Inc

place. Why don't you take me through what you've done so far, and then we can bridge to how Cromwell, Parsons may be able to help."

Abby began their story. "Allie called me about a year and a half ago and asked me to join with her and another of our founders, Dr Dao Diskul, in this integrated health and wellness project that has now become known as Rhapsody Holdings ... Dr Diskul, by the way, is from Thailand and Allie is flying to Bangkok this evening to see her.

"After many discussions with financial institutions, hedge funds, and private equity groups, we have gotten to the stage where our launch is near. We are currently waiting to consummate an agreement that will allow us to avail ourselves of a little less than $300 Million in debt financing. Our deal is based upon an asset-backed note that is guaranteed by gas and oil lease rights.....hard assets... as opposed to the subprime mortgages that underpinned the lion's share of the CDO market over the last few years."

"Interesting. So assuming that you secure the $300 Million relatively soon, what would you anticipate the business interest would be for Cromwell Parsons?"

"We regard the $300 Million as seed money. We will need to consider multiple sources of money in order to realize our vision of 50 Centers in seven years. Over time we will obviously use other sources of money. The key thing is for us to do this synergistically. We are far better off using funds from a source that has similar interests to Rhapsody's interests. That is why we want to talk to you about the investments that you are making from your PE Fund for healthcare."

"So if I understand you correctly, you haven't yet diluted the original Founders Equity, except for the warrants that are part of the current funding contract."

"That's correct."

"Have you considered the possibility of any additional equity funding?"

"We are open to all ideas about expanding our funding horizons, but raising funds through an equity sale at the holding company level doesn't seem to be practical at this juncture. However we might consider such an investment in one of the sub elements of the plan."

"You mean investment in one of the pillars?"

"Yes for example an investment in ownership of one or more of the *Rhapsody Centers,* or possibly an investment in the *Rhapsody HealthPort.* It will depend in some ways on the revamping of our corporate structure, which we will do when we close our initial funding deal"

It was becoming increasingly apparent to Josh that Abby McDuffee had a clear idea of where she wanted to take the business and that Alison McDuffee had a specific service vision in mind for their customers. The plan was very ambitious, but their team appeared to be a veteran group with good experience and a common bond. He liked the project a lot, but was uncertain if they could help out within the constructs of what they had planned for the B&G Fund. Any investment from the healthcare fund would be minor, and this opportunity might inspire more bold participation on the part of Cromwell Parsons, at the enterprise level, maybe through one or more of the others funds in conjunction with B&G.

The two days of business discussions wound down without a clear understanding of next steps, other than the fact that both parties agreed to meet again in three weeks time. The purpose of the follow up would be to discuss relative progress, after Cromwell Parsons Resources did some additional due diligence.

As they were leaving, Alison turned to Josh and said, "On a social note I couldn't help but notice your picture in the paper today with Gina Alvarez. I'm quite a fan."

Josh smiled and said, "of me or of Gina?"

Alison laughed at Josh's easygoing humor and said, "I guess we'll know the answer to that in about three weeks." Josh laughed at what seemed to be a throwaway remark, but he also took away the fact that the Rhapsody group still wanted something significant from Cromwell Parsons Resources and/or from Josh Struben, and it might be more than just money.

**********.

Danielle Struben arrived back at her town house after a vigorous walk through the park. It was only the last few years that she had been able to take such an excursion without being swarmed by celebrity gawkers or the dreaded paparazzi. She now relished her position as a second tier celebrity. Danielle felt good this morning. She was thankful for the many blessings that she had been given in life, starting with her husband and her two sons. So many of her friends had gone through life, cycling through marriages and blended families in a way that defied any sort of permanence, that she wondered how they maintained any real sense of direction.

She was also grateful for the wonderful professional life she had enjoyed. More recently, Danielle had reason to give thanks for the fact that the breast cancer scare she had experienced was just that, a scare, nothing more. It even had some positive side effects; most notably it had brought her closer to her husband Stephen. It was nice to know that she could always count on Stephen.

Her sons were also there for her, and she was happy they were prosperous, and that they were close to each other. The only worry that she had was that the level of success that Josh was experiencing was so rapid. She just hoped he wouldn't lose his way. She hadn't yet met his girlfriend, Gina Alvarez, and she assumed that she would meet her if and when Josh deemed such a meeting to be appropriate. Danielle had read a few of the gossip stories about how Gina was "Livin' La Vida Loca," and that Josh was the man of Gina's life at that time, but she also knew that Josh was not the kind of person to be awed by celebrity or enthralled by the craziness that accompanied fame. If Josh was spending time with Gina it was undoubtedly because he found her company fulfilling. Danielle suspected that there was a lot more to Gina Alvarez than what she read in the papers and saw on the news. She was looking forward to meeting her.

****

The day had gone a little better than some of his recent days. JB decided early that it would be a day of decisions. Several sources had suggested he ramp up the software development efforts of ICD in conjunction with newest version of the company's hardware. He also wanted to get his company closer to its customers so he wanted to realign many of his profit centers.

JB also needed to cut costs, so he had issued the usual end of year edicts about limiting travel, curtailing business entertainment, avoiding all unnecessary in-year expenditures and terminating all external consulting contracts. In order to show the appropriate leadership he announced that he was closing the executive dining room at the Manhattan headquarters and was eliminating limousine service for corporate officers. The latter measures were window dressing at best. However one more robust decision he made, got less publicity, but had a greater financial impact. He terminated the negotiations on a new contract with the world-renowned strategic consulting firm, McGreavy and Little. McGreavy, it turns out, had billed various ICD entities more than $60 million in the past year, and seemed to have permeated every nook and cranny of the company. They had been pushing for some of the changes that he was now looking to execute, and their advice was realistic and forward looking. However JB felt that his executive team was abdicating its responsibilities by allowing an eternal firm to make all of the strategic suggestions for change. Plus $60 million dollars was one hell of a big ticket. It never appeared on a monthly bill but rather was billed to individual ICD units. When he finally saw the audited numbers he nearly choked in exasperation.

To punctuate the decisions he was making, JB also announced several management changes that he had been contemplating for weeks and indicated that more would soon follow. Therefore anyone who had a sudden command appearance for a meeting with JB, had reason for concern. Jason Tobin the head of the Essential Solutions Division, waited in the executive conference room. He was totally unsure whether his meeting was going to be a good one or a bad one, but he had been gathering information throughout the day that he believed might aid his cause. The night before JB had asked him to get information with respect to what if would take to have the Essential Services Division develop its own software and Tobin was already gathering information with phone calls to his staff during the day. However JB was not ready to see Tobin just yet, because he had Rickie Van Dorfan shuffling in an out of his office all day long and he called him in once again.

"So what do we know about the redhead from Atlantic City?" Van Dorfan wondered why Brady hadn't provided this little descriptive hint earlier in the day. Was it some kind of perverse test? Maybe Brady was simply in a better mood now. It had been a very active day and the whole company seemed to be waiting for Brady's next pronouncement, Brady himself seemed to take pleasure in having everyone up tight. The good news was that Van Dorfan had managed to track down the sales woman from Atlantic City. Her name was Caitlin Browning. She was 32 years old, married with no children. Her husband, Scott Browning had formerly worked at ICD but had moved on to another company two years earlier. She also had an older sister that had worked at ICD, but that sister had also left the company. Browning had graduated magna cum laude from Notre Dame University in Indiana and had received her MBA in the Executive MBA program at Columbia. Caitlin had been with the company for six years, was the second highest producer in the northeastern region. Her performance evaluations were stellar and she was rated as "promote now" and was also noted as potential "flight risk."

"I have some details for you Mr. Brady." He then handed Brady his one page summary memo detailing what he had learned about Caitlin Browning. Brady frowned but was secretly amused at his good fortune for having a reason to beckon Browning to New York.

"You know what Rickie? We always screw up and wait until the last minute to move our good people up. This young lady has a track record of success and we're just allowing her be overlooked by being buried in the sales organization, Says here that she has been on the 'promote now' list for two years and her husband has already left the company. Let's get her up here for an interview."

"For what job, Mr. Brady?"

"For Cardoza's old job. This Browning woman could be your new boss." Van Dorfan had mixed emotions about Brady's answer. It wasn't that he himself wanted to be Maria's replacement. The last couple of weeks of abuse from JB had squelched any designs he may have had on that job. However he was hoping to make enough of an impression on Brady to secure a promotion elsewhere in the ICD superstructure. Brady's dismissive way of answering his question had actually answered a few questions at once. It might be time to put his resume out on the street. It was a bold thought, but Rickie was not a bold person. He knew that he would just end up doing JB's bidding whatever that might be. At least he was about to get a buffer.

****

Many of the American patients at Solace in the Sun were going home before Thanksgiving. No one was scheduled to start rehab in the days before Thanksgiving. There would be fewer staff members and fewer patients at SIS starting the weekend before the holiday. Maureen Brady was one of the few ongoing residents left to pursue her recovery throughout the holiday weekend. The group classes were recombined and somewhat limited for the upcoming week, and there would be more time for reflection and assessment. The good news for Maureen Brady was that she was feeling much better about herself.

It had been several weeks since she had hoisted her last cosmopolitan lipward. The first few evenings had been difficult. She remembered feeling that she wanted to replay her days at night over a martini glass, and that it had seemed awkward to handle her reflections without her Cosmo prop. Once she negotiated her way past those first few evenings, there was a period of about ten days when she was depressed and disappointed with respect to the self-inflicted mistakes and mistreatments that she had endured. But she continued to learn from her classes and from others in rehab to leave the past behind and to focus on what she had to offer in the future. Then there seemed to be a turning point of sorts when she recaptured her self-respect. She was now in the process of building from that turning point.

There were things to be grateful for all day long. First each day started without a hangover. Then as soon as she ate her breakfast she experienced a new level of energy unlike anything she had felt in more than five years. She enjoyed reading, exercising and just conversing with her fellow recovering alcoholics. She was grateful that her facial injuries seemed to be healing rapidly and fully. Dr Vincent had come down from New York to visit, and indicated that additional surgery was unwarranted and that they should simply continue to monitor the healing process.

Maureen felt clean and emotionally unencumbered except for the guilt. Even the guilt was beginning to dissipate a bit. The memories that she now had from the past were from a more distant past, a time when she and JB were young and in love. She wanted to recapture that part of her past and transport it into the future. During the last week or so she had also begun thinking more and more about sex. She was only 42, but didn't have much of a sex life. She remembered having sex with John three or four times in the month before her accident but she couldn't recall her last orgasm.

Many of the residents at SIS discussed sex on an ongoing basis. Some had sexual transgressions that were fueled by their addictions and some just liked talking about sex. Regardless, the topic was a daily agenda item in one forum or another. Maureen hoped that when she was finished with her rehab at SIS, she would be able to be more sexually expressive with her husband John.

On this particular warm November evening, Maureen had left her room and was walking through the reception area when she spotted Chipper Geld, and his program manager, Paul Ashburn, discussing something that was obviously amusing to them. When Geld saw Maureen he quickly toned down his hilarity, but still greeted Maureen with a big smile.

"Hi Maureen, I hope that your stay is going well. I haven't seen you in a few days." He moved toward Maureen as he spoke and half waved to Ashburn in a low sideways manner that was clearly dismissive, indicating that their conversation was now over.

"Hi Chipper. Yes things are going pretty much as planned….check that….better than planned. I'm certainly feeling a lot better."

"Good, good…..very good." Geld had a way of intoning his satisfaction in a low volume, almost slippery manner that was not as readily apparent to Maureen as it might have been to others.

"Yes it is good. I'm starting to get home sick, though. I am resigned to spending Thanksgiving here but I think I'd like to go home earlier than the two months we originally planned."

"Those are normal feelings at this point…..good healthy feelings in fact. Actually, if you don't mind my saying so, I would say that you look terrific. Even though I, myself, am not a professional therapist, I am certainly able to see visual signs of progress. I'm sure you have always been a very beautiful woman, but I would have to say that you look extraordinarily beautiful after your first few weeks here at SIS. It does my heart good to know that we may have helped somewhat, in that regard."

"Thank you, that's very nice. I think I'm actually blushing at your comments." She was indeed. "And I am very grateful for your terrific staff. I know I am well on my way to a bit of a personal transformation." Maureen liked Geld and she was not at all wary of his motives, but she couldn't help but feel that Geld was flirting with her. It was okay. It made her feel sexy. She hadn't felt sexy in a long time.

****

Dr Al Moses was home again, and had a lot on his mind. He hung his coat in the front closet and the conversation started almost as soon as he walked through the door.

"Good evening, Anne, my love. How are you?" There was an interim silence in the room, but Dr Al kept responding to the voice that went unheard by others

"Yes I know, my love. I'm sorry. I know it's been several weeks. I'm just busier than usual at the office. I think I need to see fewer patients. I never seem to have enough time for the ones I have"

"No. Never too busy for you, my love"

"It doesn't matter. I didn't do it. Did I? It was just some kind of test." He responded to the unheard inquiry.

"It's different now. I feel better."

"There's something I want to talk to you about." Dr Al was wandering around his apartment as he spoke to his deceased lover. In the past he had usually confined these "conversations" to the bedroom. But his perspective was evolving. Anne Mohr was walking with him from room to room.

"You're so perceptive. Yes it's about Maria Cardoza."

"Yes that's right the lady who reminds me of you. And guess what? She's pregnant."

"Yes that's true. She wasn't sure whether she wanted a baby or not. I don't think she had made up her mind before. But now I'm worried for her. I don't think she wants to keep the baby."

"I know. Yes. That's true. But in an odd way she seemed happy before I told her."

"Well she was very surprised, because even though she missed her period, she didn't think she was pregnant."

"That could be true. However he's a grown man and I assume that he didn't want to have a child with Maria. However even some of these supposedly intelligent men can do some pretty stupid things. God knows I've seen that often enough over the years."

"No. She didn't say one way or the other. I think she was a bit shocked. The other thing that makes it difficult is that she just broke off her relationship with the father,"

"Yes, that's right, John Brady."

"Well sometimes people can transform anger to passion very quickly. I don't know the exact circumstances nor did I ask."

"No I am not at all curious."

Dr Al had made his way into the bedroom and removed his clothing and was now sitting on the end of his bed in his undershorts and had stopped talking aloud. He was just staring ahead for the better part of two minutes. And then he heard his former lover and restarted his conversation again with Anne.

"Not at all quiet… Just thinking. That's all."

"I'm not sure I want to talk about it just yet."

"No, I don't have anything else to say. Let me think about it."

"My thoughts are much more expensive than a penny." He laughed, not fully realizing there was no one else in the room to see his snicker. He paused for a long moment and then abruptly just said "Good night, my love, and give Sarah my love as well." He pulled himself under the bed covers and went to sleep.

Chapter 9: *Two Financial Conversations*

The sun was setting in late afternoon in Hong Kong and it was mid morning in London. The financial markets were still several hours away from opening in New York. As he gazed out the window of his Hong Kong office, Josh Struben had a lot on his mind. His Rhapsody guests from earlier in the day were each going their respective ways and were probably in the air already. Josh was too busy to attend the Lay D's concert that evening. However he did plan on leaving with Gina the following morning to catch the opening night concert in Tokyo. Then he planned to fly back to London from Tokyo so that he could meet with Jonathan Cromwell. He didn't want to wait until he was in London to talk with Cromwell about Rhapsody because it was potentially good news and in this market good news shouldn't wait. He picked up the phone and got right through to Cromwell in the office.

"Jonathan, what's breaking?"

"Hey Josh...what do you mean breaking? Do you mean, 'What's new?' or do you mean: What's now on the floor in pieces?"

"These days that seems to be a difference without a distinction."

"Always a wise ass, Struben. Maybe that's why I like you." Josh actually thought this was true. He always believed that Cromwell had one of those wry sense-of-humors that allowed him to laugh in the face of adversity. That combined with the nerves and straight face of a riverboat gambler had made Jonathan Cromwell, the toast of the financial markets. Of course these days that image was surely a half-baked double entendre. But then again Cromwell's personal earnings over the past six years had been in excess of $375 million. His former partner Paul Pritchard, by comparison, had made a piddling $135 million over the same period.

"I'm finishing up here. We got a lot done. We have a few concerned clients but I think they believe that we understand what's going on better than the rest of the financial world. So, that's a plus. In short I've sent your regards to our clients and I think we may have minimized potential redemptions."

"Good. Wish I could say the same here. Redemptions are starting to drill a hole in the bow of the 'good ship Cromwell' and we're taking on water as much as some of those who have already sunk. We need to bail the redemption money into new assets Jonathan. Right now everyone's just buying treasuries. So tell me about our healthcare fund."

"There's a lot of action in the bioscience arena … lots of companies making projections predicated on their research in the human genome area. I've got a good list we can pick from. We'll go over all that when I get back to the UK. But I wanted to alert you to one other company that I spent some time with today and yesterday."

"Who's that?"

"Rhapsody Holdings."

"Refresh my memory."

"Best way to summarize their story is that they are a creative marketing group that has figured out a way to make a lot of money by providing health and wellness care to the rich and famous."

"I thought these were the guys that were working with STRX on electronic medical records and putting advanced medical devices into clinics. What's all this about marketing to the rich and famous?"

"They're a lot more than that. I just wanted to get your attention." For the next twenty minutes or so Josh relayed all that he had been told about the various pillars of the *Rhapsody Lifestyle Membership,* and about Rhapsody Holdings, in general.

"Sounds like an interesting business but what do you see in it for Cromwell. These folks don't have a current revenue stream and we don't do venture capital work. Besides you said that they have already secured $300 million in debt financing. Certainly they're not looking for $10-$15 million investment from the Blue & Green Fund. Are they? We're looking at B&G to be $350 Million tops for *all* of the investments." Cromwell was intrigued but perplexed as to what Struben saw as the opportunity for his B&G Fund.

"I had the same concern originally. But I see two potential opportunities. First of all they have not yet closed the deal on the debt financing and you and I both know how tight those markets are at this moment. Even though they think they're very close they could still be a few months away."

"So you *do* see an investment from us?"

"Possibly … maybe a minor equity play … something to get us in the game with these people. But that probably won't happen. The real opportunity I see is for us to use this *Rhapsody Lifestyle Membership* as a launching pad for all of the other projects that we have B&G investing in. Rhapsody will be developing a consumer platform that could be the jet fuel we need for some of the other B&G companies. Rhapsody could be a big customer for some of our other businesses."

"You've got to remember we're an investment firm not a management company."

"I know Jonathan, But I'll tell you this much. In light of the current financial meltdown, our investors now expect a lot more from us. They don't want us to simply *place* their bets, they want us to *ensure* their bets."

"No one can do that Josh."

"Well then expect more redemptions." This was about as directly as Josh had ever disagreed with Cromwell, and he expected some backwash but got none.

"You may be right Josh. I don't know. I just don't know. But as our investors continue to liquidate, they will need to do something other than put the money in their mattresses."

"Isn't that why we have our PE Funds including the B&G Fund. I thought that this was our way of keeping the funds in house so to speak."

"Well that's certainly part of the equation. Back to this Rhapsody thing … What kind of investment do you see being practical?"

"We didn't get that far and I want to talk more to you about it in London. But the way I see it, if they are anywhere near as successful as they are projecting, they will need and will attract, more money. One member of their team referred to the $300 Million as 'seed funding.' And I think that's exactly what it is. When I had some of our guys go through their plan numbers, we can see a potential need for at least four times that much money. It would certainly be useful in getting them to grow faster."

"Are you suggesting that we look at a much bigger investment?"

"Potentially, yes. We need to find a way to get in on the ground floor, first and then we can figure out where to go from there. But I think we should be prepared to look across our funds and as we work to head off redemptions that could send money out of our group entirely. We ought to be looking at this as a cross fund opportunity. Let's talk more when I'm in London."

"When will you get here?"

"I'm going up to Tokyo tomorrow and then on to London."

"What's going on in Tokyo?"

"I need a day off."

"The Lay D's?"

"Yes."

"Figures. All right, Josh. Say hello to Gina. I'd love to meet her some day. Let me think about the rest of these things. The open in New York today could be awful. It's this Citibank mess. The crybabies in Detroit aren't helping much either."

"Alright Jon, we'll talk later."

Jonathan Cromwell hung up the phone on what he thought was a two party conversation, but every word of this conversation and most of the other phone conversations from his London office were being tapped and taped by none other than his former business partner Paul Pritchard.

****

Ben Hui Zhang was growing frustrated with the lack of communication from the Louisiana Group, the gruff, but resilient dealmakers, who insisted upon secrecy and flying below the radar screen.

The most recent communication from the Louisiana Group had been more than ten days earlier, even though Ben and Abby had both called and emailed and left voice mail messages. Ben was making this call from his Skype account on his computer at the airport VIP lounge, as he got ready to fly on to Bangkok with Alison to meet Dao Diskul. At the same time Abby and Sandeep were already on their flight to Germany, so Ben figured that he would summarize the call in an email to Abby after the call concluded. It wasn't the most opportune time, but Ben was determined to make the most of the call, because the Rhapsody staff was looking to him to give them a positive update on the Louisiana Group efforts.

Bob Johnstone was the spokesperson for the Louisiana Group and he took the Skype call immediately even though Ben dialed in three minutes before the appointed time.

"This is Ben Hui Zhang."

"This is Johnstone. Are any other members of your team going to join us?"

"No. Abby McDuffee is in the air on her way up to Munich. I'll report for the team. How are we doing? Are we getting any closer?"

"We are closer for sure. However everything takes a lot more time these days. We are coming down the home stretch though. I am taking this call from Switzerland."

"Based upon our last conversation, your group was going to establish its own line with a bank, and then finance our project and other projects from that line. Is that correct? You are no longer going to be issuing an asset backed note. I want to make sure I've got the process straight so I can explain it to our team."

Johnstone took a deep breath and then said. "We've been working on this thing twelve hours a day, six and seven days a week for the last month to get all of the assets pledged and deposited, with a consortium of banks here in Europe. The valuation process for the deposits has been ongoing for the last few weeks. They're killing us with the LTV. They are offering us about forty-five cents on the dollar." Ben realized that this loan-to-value concern meant that more of the Louisiana Group's assets would be tied up in the eventual transaction. However he chose not to acknowledge this complaint.

"Well we were certainly wondering how this was going, since we hadn't heard from you guys in ten days. The most important thing for us to hear is the time frame to funding. Do you have a better idea than you did two weeks ago?"

"I am very optimistic that *we* will have our line very soon and then *you* will have your line in a matter of weeks not months. I think we'll have the funding set by the end of December. But again, I want to caution you. Read the papers. Turn on the news. As of now no one is getting credit. There is some intrigue because of the new President-elect Obama, but no one really knows what impact his election will have. Call me again this time next week. Got to go." Johnstone clicked the hang up button and was gone as fast as he had appeared.

Chapter 10: *Team Building*

GINA! GINA! GINA! The chants were loud and lusty. The Lay D's had just whipped the Japanese crowd into an absolute frenzy. The performance veered from the usual two and a half hour format and lasted almost three and a half hours. It was fascinating that the crowd in Tokyo was more enthusiastic than any of the promoters could possibly have anticipated. There were some new wrinkles in the performance including some enhanced pyrotechnics that were added for outdoor performances. The Tokyo Dome was an indoor facility but it was large enough to accommodate the enhanced pyrotechnics anyway. The stadium held 55,000 for sporting events but it was set up to accommodate 35,000 for the Lay D's Concert, special effects and all.

Gina seemed to be in another world. It was uncanny professionalism that allowed her performance to exude such raw sexuality, while her true emotions were cycling back and forth around concern for her mother back in Detroit, and love for the child growing in her uterus. In an interesting way, Gina's ability to go through rigorous singing and dancing routines while her emotions were in a different place, caused her performance to be almost mystical. Her audience was trying to reach through her physicality and find wherever it was, that the real Gina was at. Like many of life's searchers and seekers the crowd was unable to attain its goal. Gina's psyche remained allusive just barely out of the reach of the crowd who stretched out their arms and screamed her name, "GINA, GINA, GINA."

Josh Struben had seen the Lay D's performance several times from the audience vantage point. This was his first time seeing it from backstage. He had watched his lover excite and entice audiences in many different cities. This was the first time he had seen the mother of his child engage a frenzied crowd. "GINA, GINA, GINA." It sounded odd to hear her voice screamed by a Japanese speaking audience, and as they yelled her name it sounded more like it rhymed with China, and when they yelled it rapidly several times in succession it echoed as though they were yelling an anatomical term for the female private part.

As Gina raced off stage, she was wearing a large smile. But it was not her professional stage countenance and so Josh knew that after three encores, the Lay D's were finally done for the evening. He moved over to embrace Gina and she literally jumped into his arms, and wrapped both legs around him with her feet banging up against the back of his upper calves. Her head was slightly above his face and as he held her, she bent her head down and French-kissed him deeply. She was very hot and very sexy, and was delivering an embrace that said 'Why don't we just do it here up against the wall?'

Josh enfolded his arms around Gina tightly as he returned the passionate embrace. And as he squeezed her moist body up against him he could feel her heart pounding. He knew that the heart pounding was more from the just completed hard-thumbing encores, than it was a sign of sexual passion, but he didn't let that stop him from enjoying the mutual squeeze. They stayed interlocked for almost half a minute before he eased her back to a standing position on the floor.

"Wow. That was terrific."

"The kiss or the show?"

Josh meant the show but he said, "The kiss." It was simply a better answer.

The crowd noise had dissipated only slightly and so they had to talk lips to ears, leaning back and forth to be heard for the next minute or so and then the crowd began to gradually realize that the show had indeed ended.

"It seems like every night is more fun than the night before. I think we are actually improving our gig as the tour goes on. No one is tired yet."

Josh was still talking in a relatively loud voice but could be heard only by Gina, and so he was unconcerned about being overheard. "You need to take it a little easier, now that you're carrying the baby." He smiled as he said it and she smiled back.

"It's Okay. I'm healthy and the baby's healthy, and that's what matters. You need to be healthy to be happy and happy to be healthy. Any way you slice it, everything's good." Gina's jumble of double talk actually made some kind of sense to both of them, and they continued to stare into one another's eyes until they were assured of their mutual cognitive connection. Josh's gaze then fell to Gina's perspiring body. She was still breathing deeply from the exertion of her performance, and her pink camisole clung to her breasts in a sensuous and partially transparent fashion. Over the past few performances the silk camisole had been replaced by a silk-like synthetic fabric that retained less of the body heat that Gina generated. Gina had retained the tie as a prop in the final wardrobe act, and it was now a much talked about signature part of her attire.

Josh changed the subject. "Did you talk to your mother at all today?"

"I talked to both Mom and also to Carl Gordon. Both of them are telling me that Mom is fine. But she is still in the hospital and she is still on oxygen. So I'm not real thrilled by the fact that they are both telling me to just continue the tour and that everything will be fine. In fact I'm beginning to hate the word 'fine.' I'm never quite sure what it means anymore."

"Did you mention anything about the baby?"

"No. As I told you before, I want to do that in person." Gina began walking back toward her dressing room and noticed that the rest of the performers had begun drinking beer and wine and they were in a celebratory mood. She too was feeling pretty upbeat, but she thought that she would do her celebrating back at the hotel with Josh, the father of her baby. She was looking forward to the final stages of the tour. After Tokyo, it would be back to the USA, with a one-night stopover in Hawaii before opening the mainland tour in Los Angeles, in five days. She started stripping off her costume even before she made it to the dressing room, but she closed the door behind Josh and herself soon after entering. Josh began to realize that maybe they were going to do some celebrating backstage at the Tokyo Dome after all.

****

Other than that one most important fact of her impending motherhood, Maria Cardoza had been quite open with Dr Angelique Lefebvre in exploring the past as a way of making the future more satisfying. Maria freely discussed past relationships with men, right up through her breakup with John Brady. She didn't leave anything out, the sexual satisfaction, the emotional bonding, even the emotionless distancing that sometimes occurred. It was all open for examination. Discussions about her parents were not as deep, but they provided background, and both Maria and Angelique had been satisfied that there had been closure following Maria's parents somewhat recent deaths.

Since leaving ICD she had had this idea about owning her own spa. She had come to realize that although she had some excellent connections there was still much to learn and so she had adjusted her sights and decided that she would get a job in the front office of a spa company for a year or so and learn what hazards needed to be avoided. She discussed this also with Angelique who thought it was a great idea, because there would be less pressure as an employee, and it might be worth enjoying a time period of reduced business stress.

Angelique also counseled Maria that she would need to embrace her friends, new and old, in order to fully appreciate what it was she wanted out of life. Maria wondered if Angelique would be giving her different advice if she knew of her pregnancy.

And of course that was the biggest thing in her life. She had never wanted to have a child, but now that she was pregnant, Maria was experiencing some difficulty making the appointment to have the pregnancy terminated. Dr Al had said that it was okay to just think about things for a little while and see how she felt after she came to grips with this change. What he had neglected to tell her was that she might feel very differently about potential parenthood, now that a child was growing within her.

There was an interesting irony to all of this. She pitied John Brady, now that she was no longer seeing him on a daily basis, but she didn't hate him. It didn't even bother her that Brady was the father of her unborn child. She herself had to take at least part of the responsibility for conception. But Maria thought Brady was foolishly chasing his tail in a never-ending loop of business problems. Didn't he realize how good he had it? Not only did John have a nice wife and three children, but also he had an exciting job and more than enough resources to do a lot of good in the world.

But in her heart, Maria knew that if she had still been working at ICD, she would already have had an abortion. Brady would have insisted on it. It was nice to take her *own* time to make her *own* decisions. She would make another appointment with Dr Moses. He was older and wiser and had a lot of experience with women like herself. He would help her decide how best to interpret her feelings in order to make her decision. Yes. Dr Al Moses. Now there was a man who was in control of his life!

****

When Alison McDuffee was putting together the rudimentary philosophies behind Rhapsody Holdings the first person she turned to for help in vetting her ideas was Dr Dao Diskul. This was even before Alison turned to her sister Abby for help. Dao embraced the concept of the Rhapsody Lifestyle wholeheartedly and joined forces with her good friend almost immediately. Dao managed to keep her practice in Bangkok strong while she spent every free hour she could find, supporting the Rhapsody dream that she shared with Alison, Abby and the rest of the team.

Dr Dao Diskul and her good friend Alison McDuffee were as close as two friends could be. As much as Alison and her sister, Abby, looked alike and truly loved, trusted and respected each other as sisters, Alison and Dao had the kind of relationship that was rooted in common outlook, values and experience. Dao had often invited Alison to visit her in Bangkok. Dao was thrilled that the Rhapsody project had finally made this visit a reality.

Both women had highly successful careers. Alison had a bicoastal practice in Los Angeles and New York. And Dao had a rapidly expanding medical tourism practice in Thailand. Money was not a problem for either physician and it was no longer a prime motivating factor in either of their lives. Both women had medical colleagues who complained long and loud about the state of medicine in their respective parts of the world, but the complaints were different in their two countries. In the United States the complaints centered on the industry infrastructure, laws, and insurance payments. In Thailand the controversy was geared more toward the practice of providing better healthcare for wealthy foreigners than for the Thai citizenry.

Dao and Alison had heard the complaints that were indigenous to their respective countries and still managed to be successful in spite of the problems. However they both knew that there was a chance to make things much better. The Rhapsody project was their chance to create a paradigm shift in the industry. They would be the physician architects of the globalization of Healthcare, and with Alison's sister Abby running the business their success would be assured.

Dao picked up Alison and Ben Hui Zhang from Suvarnabhumi Airport the night before and brought them to the hotel without much discourse. Both Alison and Ben seemed a bit drained by a long day of travel and business meetings and wanted to go sleep off the day before getting down to business.

Alison wondered about the relationship between Dao and Ben. Alison knew that Dao had a very open attitude towards sex. In fact Dao had more sexual partners than anyone Alison knew. So she speculated that the friendship between Dao and Ben was more than just business. It didn't bother Alison at all. She just would rather have it out in the open. She also realized that it would be just that way if it were Dao's decision. She was not at all shy about her attitudes towards sex. She simply drew a line at disclosures that would make her partners uncomfortable. At present that's where the relationship between Dao and Ben Hui Zhang resided.

However they were not all gathered in Bangkok to discuss Dao's willful promiscuity. They were here to discuss the development of the *Rhapsody Global Practitioner Society* otherwise known as the *Rhapsody GPS.*

The threesome walked across Lumpini Park in the direction of the Dusit Thani Hotel, just stretching their legs and opening their minds to the discussion of the many things that needed to be considered.

"What kind of targets is Abby looking at in terms of GPS locations in Year One?" Dao threw the question out to be answered by either Alison or Ben, but Alison jumped on it first.

"It's not just the sheer number of locations that is important, but it is also the depth of services that we can offer at any one location. For example it will *not* be sufficient, or for that matter efficient, to have a cardiologist on board in Bangkok and a neurologist on board in Osaka, a breast surgeon in Sydney Australia and claim we have a GPS presence in 3 cities."

"That makes sense," Dao responded. "However isn't it a reality that we will add practitioners in this manner? Won't it be true that we will have a smattering of different specialties scattered across the globe and then try to add the depth over time?"

"No. It won't work that way. That's what we are here to work through over the next couple of days. We already have some ideas about how to go about fleshing out the GPS, but we will have to consider the budget for everything as well. Ben will need to keep us honest in that regard." Alison was walking stiffly now, but standing straight and tall. Dao waddled a bit as she walked next to Alison, but she garnered more of Ben's attention than did her American associate. Alison continued anyway.

"Let's review what we have already decided, and then we can put more meat on the bones." Alison was going over ground that they had ploughed through already, but it was helpful for her to reiterate their decisions so that she could get her elevator speech about the *GPS* down pat.

"We have to think about the *GPS* in two different buckets. The first bucket is what we refer to as the *CAP* or the *Center Aligned Practitioners*. And the second bucket is what we call the *ALP* or the *At-Large Practitioners*. Within the *CAP* we will need to have as many varieties of practitioner as possible ready to serve our members at our *Rhapsody Centers,* whereas an *ALP* practitioner, can be a purveyor of any specialty or health/wellness discipline anywhere in the world, and can offer these services to our members at their own facilities in a standalone fashion. Of course the ALP practitioners will utilize our *Rhapsody HealthPort* and will go through a *Rhapsody Certification* process with the same rigor as the CAP group."

"Yes, and so we will need to have a very extensive team available to us for the CAP at each of the 50 centers we will be building around the world." Dao echoed her understanding.

"And that's over seven years." Ben chimed in.

"You're both right. So think of it this way. In year one, we will have two Centers, one in NYC and one in London. We will need to build a deep, multi-disciplined CAP in each of these two cities."

"Sounds like a lot of work," said Zhang.

"I'm not so sure," said Dao. I could put together a CAP here in Bangkok in a heartbeat.

"I'll bet you could Dao," Alison continued. "Let's come back to that thought when we talk about the ALP rather than the CAP."

The three Rhapsody executives were now passing some very old banyan trees and heading in the direction of the ancient Chinese Clock Tower. Dao was eager to point out landmarks as they walked through the park, but they were able to return to the important discussion at hand without much prompting from one another.

"So let's talk about putting together a *GPS CAP* for NYC. The real secret is to get a broad brush at all of the necessary specialties. The way we do that is by striking an agreement with one of the university affiliated medical groups. There are several reasons for this. First and foremost these groups have excellent reputations and generally have cutting edge technology in place. Secondly they usually have additional capacity among their doctors, who are salaried by the university. Thirdly, they are always looking for new sources of income to support their research."

"These university groups will be the backbone to our centre aligned GPS. That's it. Right?" Ben queried Alison to demonstrate that he was on the same page as she was.

"Yes. The interesting fact is that, in many locales, individual doctors do not have strong brand or name recognition. However institutions that employ doctors often *do* have a strong brand. This is what makes selecting an individual physician such a nosebleed in today's environment. Everything is word of mouth. You don't generally know who the best spinal surgeon is in a given city, until you need spinal surgery, and begin to ask around. However, certain institutions have reputations that would lead you to believe that the physicians associated with the institution are top notch. In New York City for example you might think of Sloan Kettering for cancer or the Hospital for Special Surgery for orthopedic work. These places have the reputation rather than Dr Smith or Dr Jones who may work there."

"These university groups generally practice more conventional and less integrated medicine. Right?" Ben wasn't sure.

"It depends. That is generally the case for New York and London. However outside of the western world the university groups get further away from allopathic medicine and have practitioners who employ all kinds of alternative medicine. So to answer your question, it depends on the city and it depends on the university group that we will choose as the backbone for our GPS CAP."

"But we will still offer alternative medicine in our New York and London centers. Is that correct?"

"Absolutely, yes. The answer is simple. We will be open to any type of alternative medicine that our members would like. Our job will then be to secure the services of the top practitioner in each of these fields and align them with the Rhapsody Center, so that our members are both happy and satisfied."

"So that we understand ourselves and are all on the same page, the New York Center will be served by our GPS Center Aligned Practitioners or CAP. The same is true with our London Center when we open it up. However, we may have Rhapsody GPS practitioners in a hundred locations throughout the world by the end of year one. These practitioners, who are in cities where we don't have a *Rhapsody Center,* will be part of the *GPS ALP,* or the *GPS At-Large Practitioners"*

"Then that is a goal that we will need to set. Right? We want to set a goal in terms of how many locations will be GPS ALP locations."

"Correct. By the way if you talk to Abby about this, she will tell you that the hundred locations number I threw out, is a good number for year one. So yes we certainly have our work cut out for us."

"I'm not worried about it," said Dao. "I have regular contact with several different networks of physicians in multiple cities around the world. I'm sure you have the same kind of network, Alison. Don't you think so?"

"I've already discussed this with a lot of physicians that I know and they're excited about the possibilities. But I would have to say that your network is much broader than mine."

"There's one other thing that we need to keep in mind when we talk about the GPS. We need to remember that the 'P' in GPS stands for Practitioner, not for Physician. We will have a large number of non-physician practitioners on the spa side of the business, who make our service offerings truly holistic." Dao made this point as she often had during the past few months. The nomenclature for the GPS had been her contribution and the subtle word change allowed the team to think and plan much more expansively. "Our practitioners include stylists, masseuses, dentists, personal physical trainers, occupational therapists, acupuncturists, ayurvedic medicine specialists, herbalists ... the whole spectrum."

"Yes that is important," said Alison. "And every one of these practitioners is either *aligned,* CAP, or *at-large,* ALP, depending upon whether or not we have a center nearby for them to be aligned with."

As the Rhapsody team walked through the park, they could see all of the Bangkok skyscrapers in the background. Lumpini Park was right in the center of the city and it reminded Alison somewhat of Central Park in New York. It was a rural-like oasis in the midst of a teeming metropolis. Alison was glad that Dao had suggested the walk through the park for their discussion because she was growing weary of conference rooms and PowerPoint presentations. They came to a resting spot with a few empty bench seats, and they sat down, not out of fatigue, but merely to be able to look at each other as they talked.

"I think we all share the same enthusiasm for getting the project launched," Ben put his thoughts on record. "But until we get the funding in place, we will be stuck with simply enjoying each other's company."

Dao playfully grabbed Ben's hand and swung in back and forth like a young schoolgirl. She affected a put-upon voice and simply said, "... And that's not all that bad ... now is it Ben?" Alison looked at her colleagues and smiled simply and shook her head. Ben smiled sheepishly, as though he had not meant to be party to the outing of his personal relationship with Dao. Dao just smiled.

****

Hard work had always been the hallmark of Sandeep Mehra. He grew up poor in Bombay (Mumbai) India, and he never forgot the experience of being poor. His family valued education and made sure that Sandeep understood the sacrifices that had to be made in order to secure the educational tools needed for success.

Like so many other young Indian students Sandeep selected the rapidly growing field of Information Technology as the domain interest within which he would pursue his career. And like so many other young Indians Sandeep went down an entrepreneurial route in pursuit of his dreams. However he struggled mightily to make ends meet while he watched other Indian companies grow and prosper off American contracts.

In the mid nineties, while Sandeep was still in his early thirties, he finally got the break he needed. He was subcontracting work through a Ukrainian entrepreneur Max Tkachuk, who had befriended Sandeep's sister, Ameena. Tkachuk had many contacts in the United States and Europe and was quite adept at securing business contracts from large corporations looking to outsource to Asia. Max introduced Sandeep to two large firms that would be willing to do business directly with Sandeep and his small team. One of these companies was STRX in Germany and the other was Global Express Shipping out of Nashville Tennessee in the US.

Sandeep and his company did an excellent job for both STRX and for Global Express Shipping and Sandeep made friends along the way. With Max Tkachuk as his mentor, Sandeep learned to network with people and negotiate with businesses. When the Far East Group of Global Express Shipping wanted to bring most of its programming back in house, the company negotiated with Sandeep Mehra to buy his company. Sandeep and his team then became employees of GES in the process. A byproduct of the buyout of his firm was a growing friendship between Sandeep and the Group Executive of GES, Ben Hui Zhang. When Zhang left GES to join the Rhapsody Holdings group, he knew that Rhapsody would need a good CIO, and although the position might be a stretch for Sandeep, Ben convinced Abby McDuffee to trust him and to hire Sandeep. She did on both counts.

****

When Abby and Alison left Hong Kong, they went in opposite directions. Alison went on to see her friend, Dao Diskul, and brought

Ben Hui Zhang along with her and Abby went on to Germany, accompanied by her young CIO, Sandeep Mehra. The latter two individuals had business meetings set with various STRX officials in order to reconvene the working team that was developing aspects of the *HealthPort* and determining the equipment needs of the Rhapsody Centers. Abby was always ready to engage with persons of interest among her potential suppliers as they might prove to be effective hires in the near future.

Abby knew that the Rhapsody business would eventually employ thousands of people, but for the start of the business it was important to get a highly talented executive team in place and they had done a good job so far. The three principal Founders of the business, the McDuffee sisters and Dao Diskul all had achieved business success, but Abby was the only one of the three that had any large corporate experience. Therefore the additions of Ben Hui Zhang and Sandeep Mehra were very critical; later they became known as the "Band of Five."

As Abby rode in the cab with Sandeep to STRX headquarters, she was checking her emails and voicemails on her blackberry. There was a message from Ben concerning his discussion with the Louisiana Group. She frowned as she listened to the message as Ben indicated the general demeanor of Bob Johnstone and the information that indicated that they still did not have a date certain for funding.

Abby and Sandeep's first two meetings with STRX were simply information sharing sessions. However the afternoon meetings were more eventful. STRX showed the Rhapsody team a prototype of the first release of the *HealthPort*. They included in the demonstration thirty-seven different medical devices that contained a digital information port that downloaded test results and other data directly into the *HealthPort*. These devices included everything imaginable from electronic scales that calibrated and recorded a patient's weight, to electronic blood pressure devices, and on to EKG's; MRI readouts and CAT scan outputs. STRX also claimed that multiple other devices were under development that would also utilize similar electronic downloads.

STRX had given Abby and Sandeep a private conference room to use between their meetings with the STRX employees. Abby turned to Sandeep and asked, "So after listening to all of these presentations today, what do you think the probability of these folks delivering the *HealthPort* in less than nine months?"

"That depends on *vhat* our expectations *vould* be for the first release. They have been *vorking* on EMR prototypes for a *vhile*, long before Rhapsody came to them for help." The slim Indian CIO answered.

"But what they have been talking about seems to be more of a traditional Electronic Medical Record. It seems to be geared more towards medical practitioners and institutions than towards individuals such as our members. You've known these people for some time, Sandeep. Do they get it? Do they understand how important it is for us to have our *HealthPort* up and running for a pilot in about nine months?"

"You have *vorked* for a big company, Abby. You know how it is. They fiddle around for a *vhile*, trying to get things straight. But if you give them a deadline, they are *wery* capable of throwing enough resource at the task to get it done on time. The most important thing is to get it done right."

"And you have confidence that they will, in fact, get it done right?"

"Yes. As you said I have known this company for a *vhile*. I did some *vork* for them as far back as twelve years ago *vhen* I had my own company. That was after Ameena, introduced me to Max Tkachuk. Max helped me get in the door as a contractor to STRX. But Max always maintained the most important relationships. He was the one who knew Josh Struben's father, Stephen Struben. It's a small *vorld*, as they say."

"Good. We will need to rebuild the senior relationships however because Max is no longer with us."

"And a lot of our contacts have changed. We'll get a leg up on that tonight because Stephen Struben has flown in from London with his wife and they will have dinner with us tonight. He no longer *vorks* for STRX but he consults for them and still has a lot of influence."

"That's good work, Sandeep. Things all seem to be falling in place."

****

There was something about Caitlin Browning that made JB nervous. As she sat across from him in his office, she was even more attractive then he remembered from his trip to Atlantic City. Maybe it was because he "fantasy-fucked" her the last time he did Maria. Or maybe it was because he hadn't prepared his offer to her about the executive assistant job well enough in advance. Most ICD employees would be cowed by merely being in the same room with JB, ICD's CEO. But Caitlin Browning was different. She kept asking innocuous questions about what the job entailed and why she was selected to interview for the job. She said that she always felt that her career was in sales, and that if she were to be promoted she expected that it would be to a management spot in sales. Caitlin seemed unsure about taking a job as executive assistant to the CEO. And the more she seemed to equivocate, the more JB wanted her for the job. But he was frustrated by the fact that she had not rolled over easily. By the time she accepted the job, she had negotiated a significant move bonus, six months living expenses and a guaranteed annual bonus for the first year.

JB felt more than a little bit foolish. Normally he would have had one of his HR vice presidents negotiate with a lower level employee like Browning. But he wanted to demonstrate that he was a hands-on boss and that he didn't need others to do his bidding for him. In the course of recruiting Caitlin Browning, JB merely demonstrated to himself why he has an HR staff in the first place. However as he glanced across the desk at Browning he thought that it might all be worth it in the long run. She might be a challenge, but he felt that he would ultimately make a conquest. Still there was something about his new executive assistant that reminded him of someone from his past. He just couldn't quite put a finger on it. He was still ruminating in an uneasy manner when he stood up from his desk and walked her to the door.

"So you'll be able to start on Monday after Thanksgiving. Right?"

"I don't see why not. I may have to commute from Princeton until we can get an apartment in the city. My husband works downtown so he'll be happy with the move anyway." Caitlin had not let this tidbit be known as she was negotiating, and JB was annoyed that he hadn't yet thought about what to do with the husband. He remembered something from Van Dorfan's briefing that indicated that Browning's husband had once worked for ICD. He thought he remembered something about a sister who left the company also. He made a mental note to get more information on these people

As Caitlin turned and moved through the doorway to his office, Brady surveyed her lithe body. He decided that she probably had had a boob job, because her shapeliness was a little too perfect to be natural.

Her conservative attire hid any suggestion of sexiness, and she seemed almost a little bratty to Brady, but these were all things that he could work on, he assured himself silently. Caitlin Browning, he decided, was at the very minimum a big time upgrade over the temporary services he was getting from Rickie Van Dorfan. Brady also held out hope that she would supply services that would surpass what Maria Cardoza had provided in the past. In fact he hoped that Caitlin would help him forget that bitch Cardoza, entirely.

He wasn't quite ready to forget Cardoza however. In fact he had just learned from Van Dorfan that Maria was looking to open up her own spa. He hoped she fell flat on her face and he wondered if there was any way he could help assure such a failure.

After Caitlin Browning was gone, JB walked over to the long glass window looking northwest toward Central Park. He didn't currently have a personal residence in Manhattan because he preferred to keep his family out on Long Island. In this way he could sleep wherever he liked when he stayed in the city. ICD had three corporate suites available, but JB let others use those quarters. If he stayed in the city during the last few years he had stayed with Maria, either at her place or at the Waldorf Astoria. During the last couple of weeks, he had spent many nights alone at the Waldorf rather than returning to his Kings Point home.

Even with all of the comforts of the Waldorf Astoria, he was not sleeping well. His back had been bothering him more than ever and the stress of the financial markets had just added to his discomfort. JB's personal portfolio was getting hammered even harder than his ICD Stock. He couldn't even look at his portfolio without cringing. The last time he looked his nine figure net worth was beginning to ebb towards an eight-figure reality. He had been putting off a call to Paul Pritchard for weeks, and that was just plain stupid on his part. Pritchard and his partners at Cromwell Parsons Resources had more than doubled the value of his portfolio in the last four years but that value creation had been swallowed up in the last six months, to the point that the twenty million dollars that he had originally placed in the hedge fund was once again worth merely twenty million dollars. His financial and real estate investments elsewhere were also suffering rapid depreciation.

Another thing bothered him with respect to Pritchard. One of JB's Greenwich friends had told him that Pritchard had very recently left Cromwell Parsons, and rumor had it that the reason was that Jonathan Cromwell had been seeing Mrs. Pritchard for "nooners" on slow days in the market. Brady also wondered if Pritchard ever suspected that JB had also taken a tango or two between the sheets with Mrs. Pritchard a few years back. Regardless of the sexual misadventures of Pritchard's wife, Brady wanted to discuss redemptions in his portfolio with Paul Pritchard, before Pritchard was totally out of the loop.

Brady put these musings aside and got ready for his next meeting. He was about to tell Jason Tobin that he would now have free reign on developing software in-house in the Essential Services Division. Furthermore he wanted Tobin to work with Caitlin Browning his new Executive Assistant to implement an industry aligned cross product line restructuring of ICD's business units. He wanted to start with two industries, financial services and healthcare.

****

It had taken him some time to make the decision but Al Moses was determined to get the much-needed help that his problems required.

Dr Al made an appointment with a popular young psychiatrist by the name of Greg Mendelsohn. His very first session with Mendelsohn had produced excellent results. Dr Al was able to identify many of the symptoms of his sadness and depression. He also was more than a little surprised at the revelations that unfolded by viewing his own actions through the lens of another man's perspective. Generally he had some problems but they were solvable. The one, two, three of his problems were that he was lonely, he was depressed and he was fantasizing about a past lover and suicide. Okay, now that all of that was out in the open he needed to determine what he was going to do about it.

Dr Mendelsohn took a behaviorist approach to therapy. Although he was a medical doctor he indicated that he was slow to medicate. He didn't believe it was a good starting point. And he suggested that Al go down the path of Psychodynamic Therapy. Mendelsohn explained that there were many causes and types of depression and many different curative approaches for the array of depression problems. Each case was somewhat different, and needed to be treated on its own merits.

Sometimes the issue was related to a chemical imbalance in the brain. When this occurred the approach was usually to regain the appropriate level of serotonin or norepinephrine or dopamine through antidepressant drugs that disallowed the brain to overtax these neurotransmitters. Mendelsohn said that they could evaluate those possibilities over time, but he wanted to get to know Al Moses much better before testing for chemical imbalances.

Mendelsohn and Moses had an effective discussion about the efficacy of these drugs that bordered on odd. It was more of a discussion between two physicians than it was a discussion between a physician and a patient. However Moses relented and became the patient in short order because he truly wanted help.

The psychodynamic therapy that Mendelsohn was suggesting would be expensive and time consuming. But Moses had the resources he needed to get this kind of help and they had agreed that Al would see Mendelsohn three times a week. Mendelsohn was worried about Al's solo conversations with his deceased colleague Dr. Anne Mohr. These conversations were all the more troubling mostly because Al didn't always acknowledge to himself that they existed. Moses told him this forthrightly in the first fifteen minutes of their conversation.

The two men had discussed the nature of psychodynamic therapy, that it is based upon the assumption that people have a subconscious that parallels the experience of the conscious mind. The subconscious also can be a vehicle that carries painful memories that are simply too difficult to deal with in the conscious mind. Mendelsohn saw that Dr. Ann Mohr's death had taken a long lasting toll on her lover, Dr Al Moses. However he was unsure what recent events were triggering Moses' unconscious mind to contemplate suicide, and then to forget about these incidents for days on end and go about business as usual.

Moses himself, felt much relieved after his initial session with Mendelsohn. He had taken an important step by making the appointment, then a bigger step by keeping the appointment and then took the most important step of all by opening his mind to a stranger. In short order, Mendelsohn was no longer a stranger. And Al Moses was sure that Mendelsohn would be able to help him.

****

Maureen Brady walked next to her handsome son, Kenneth. They strolled slowly along the boardwalk that adjoined the beach at Solace in the Sun. It was the day before Thanksgiving holiday back in New York, but it was simply another sunny day in Costa Rica, with the temperature in the mid 80s and calm blue ocean quietly lapping at the white sand beach. The cloudless mid afternoon sky made sunglasses and sunscreen creams important accessories. Mother and son were both wearing shorts and polo shirts in lieu of bathing attire, and were walking in the general direction of the fruit bar near the border of the property. Their destination was located where one of the pools at SIS was separated from the ocean sand by a small hutched structure that enclosed the water sports gear, a beach towel station and rest rooms in addition to the aforementioned fruit bar.

"You look good, Mom. You seem rested and relaxed."

"I'm very happy that you came down to join me. Kenneth. I'm anxious to get home but I need a little more time." They were standing still and facing each other for a brief second and then continued the very slow pace across the beachfront. "I have learned that I am an alcoholic. I have not learned the cause. I don't believe it matters that much. I just need to make sure I am recovering on a daily basis."

"You can see the difference in your eyes."

"Thank you."

"Everyone misses you at home. Dad and Mark and Megan all send their love." This was one message that Maureen knew was half sent and half concocted by Kenneth. There was part of her that resented it and part of her that believed she hadn't earned much better. She also knew that Kenneth was probably trying to convince himself that his father and siblings cared that much for his mother. Anyway none of her resentment was directed towards Kenneth.

"How has your writing been going?" Maureen wanted to change the topic so that they could enjoy being together without belaboring the many faceted details of her recovery.

"It's been intermittent. Sometimes I write a lot but don't keep a lot. I don't really share a lot. It just makes me feel good to express myself sometimes."

"Kenneth you shouldn't destroy what you write." The mother was admonishing in tone but not severely. Then she inquired of her son, "Is it still mostly poetry that you write?"

"Yes. Although I have tried to write a short story or two, but I don't think I'm particularly good at writing prose in general. Mostly just poetry…"

"Well the few examples you've shared with me are quite good. I hope you will share more."

"Okay" It sounded more like complying acquiescence than a true interest in sharing.

They were once again strolling toward the juice bar and were now within hailing distance of the server.

"Do you want something to drink? Surprisingly non-alcoholic drinks make up most, but not all, of what is on the menu, at this particular bar. They do have beer available for non-rehab guests."

"That is surprising!"

"The attitude at SIS is that it is important to prepare you for an inevitable return to the world you left before rehab. In that world there will be plenty of alcohol around. We just have to realize that it is there for others, but not for those of us, who are recovering alcoholics."

They reached the juice and fruit bar and immediately recognized the man on the barstool as none other than the seemingly omnipresent Chipper Geld.

"Hello Kenneth. Nice to see you came to see your mother. She is doing terrifically well, and making wonderful progress."

"Nice to see you again, Mr. Geld." There was something about Geld that Kenneth didn't find trustworthy, but he had difficulty putting his finger on just what the issue was. Maybe it was simply his manner of always seeming so.....well, in a word, chipper. He was a little too quick with the friendly greeting, a little too quick to dismiss his existing conversations with staff members, and a little too quick to profess his satisfaction with things in general. As a result Kenneth's radar was always on alert. He thought that Geld had motives that went beyond the success of his rehab resort, or whatever SIS was supposed to be. He was glad that his mother seemed to be regaining her self-esteem, but he remained leery of Chipper Geld.

"Sit down, please make yourself at home." Geld motioned to the row of bar stools.

"No. But thank you. Mom and I are just going to keep walking for a bit. We've got a few things to catch up on." Kenneth was direct in his answer, but he surprised Maureen a bit. Maureen had none of the same feelings of trepidation around Geld, that Kenneth felt, but she was happy enough that her son wanted to keep their conversation going in private, so she agreed.

"Yes Chipper, maybe we'll see you later. We're just going to enjoy our beautiful sunshine walk for a bit."

"How is your friend, Rickie Van Dorfan doing?" It was too much of a left field inquiry to be taken any other way than as an intended embarrassment. Even Maureen was dumbfounded to hear this query.

"Mr. Van Dorfan works for my father at ICD," was the only answer Kenneth offered.

"Oh I was under the impression, you were personal friends."

"We are. Mr. Geld. Have a nice afternoon." The air of finality was not challenged by Geld as Kenneth and his mother stepped toward the beach.

"What was that all about?" Maureen wanted to rescind the question almost before she asked it, but it just came out.

"He is, of course, insinuating that Rickie is gay, and that by extrapolation so am I. Why he would care, I haven't the slightest idea."

"I can't imagine what would cause …" Maureen hesitated. "Does that bother you?" Maureen was upset and didn't know quite what to say. They had never openly discussed Kenneth's sexual preference, and Maureen believed it was not a topic that came up easily between a parent and a child in most circumstances anyway.

"The fact of the matter is that I am bisexual. So there I said it." He stopped for several strides along the sand and then continued. "I am not uncomfortable with my decisions along these lines. Am I making you uncomfortable, Mom?"

"No … not at all." It was the first lie she had told in several weeks. "Does your father know?"

Kenneth Brady pulled himself up straight and tall and laughed. "Come on Mom. Dad is clueless. We both know that."

"You know, Kenneth, your father and I have a lot of broken ground to repair."

"I hope Dad realizes his part in all of that. Why isn't he here? Why hasn't he been here?"

"I don't know the answer to those questions. But when you love someone, you need to give him the opportunity to love you also. I'm not so sure I have been providing that opportunity of late."

They walked along the beach silently for a while, but each of them was glad that they had shared their emotions. However Maureen was concerned about Kenneth. She only cared that he was happy. Was he truly as contented in his relationships as he said he was? Time would tell, she told herself. Time would tell a lot for her too.

****

It was the early hours of the morning in Tokyo and Gina Alvarez felt about as sick as she had ever felt. She was sitting near the edge of the king sized bed in a VIP suite at the Imperial Hotel. She felt a nauseous knot in the pit of her stomach and was afraid to move without risking the regurgitation of the contents of her stomach. She looked at the man sleeping soundly on the other side of the bed and realized that Josh was going to be able to do very little to help with morning sickness.

Gina got up quickly and ran to the bathroom. It was a good ten minutes before she felt anything near normal and she had vomited repeatedly to the point of being almost breathless. She was beginning to have doubts about finishing the tour.

****

JB took a careful look at the most recent email he had received from his HR director, Lois Haverstraw.

> *Mr. Brady,*
>
> *Pursuant to your inquiry with respect to Caitlin Browning, you were correct in your assumption that Ms Browning had two close relatives, who formerly worked for ICD. Her husband, Scott Browning, was employed by ICD from 1999 through June of 2007. His position at the time of his resignation was that of Senior Systems Director in our web hosting division. His ratings were always in the top 20 % and he left to go work for a competitor.*
>
> *Caitlin Browning (nee McDuffee) also had a sister who worked for ICD in a senior capacity. Abigail McDuffee, is someone whom I am sure you recall. She was a corporate officer of ICD until she left in 2005, to pursue other personal interests. Ms McDuffee is currently the CEO of a start-up company known as Rhapsody Holdings.*
>
> *If I can be of any additional assistance please call or Email me at the below listed contact addresses and numbers.*
>
> *Lois Haverstraw.*

"I knew she reminded me of someone. I'm surprised I didn't notice it earlier." JB said to Rickie Van Dorfan. "Go out and track down everything you can find out about Rhapsody Holdings." After Rickie left, JB pounded his right fist into the palm of his left hand, and thought to himself: *that bitch Abby McDuffee was a pain in the ass when she was here. Maybe now I can be a pain in the ass for her. I knew she had a twin sister but I never knew she had a younger sister working right under my nose. Soon enough I'll make it right under my desk!*

****

After spending an absolutely perfect day with her youngest son, Maureen Brady was retiring to her suite at Solace in the Sun. She knew that the days were getting shorter in number until the time that she could renew her relationship with her husband, John Brady. She was looking forward to giving the relationship every effort possible.

Maureen showered and put on her nightgown and prepared for bed. Just before turning in she checked her email and found a note from Kenneth thanking her for a wonderful day. He also said that he was happy that she had showed interest in his poetry and he even attached a poem that he felt was germane. He said that the original piece contained one changed spelling of a word, and that he might re-change it, after he recited it in his head a few more times. He said that the poem was meant as a message for lovers.

Maureen opened the attachment and read her son's work. She was able to reflect on it without thinking about being Kenneth's mother. This was a newly learned talent. She brought no baggage to her perception of art or to the artist. She just contemplated the piece.

> *If loving were having*
> *You'd be so sincere.*
> *But loving's not having.*
> *I'm sorry, my dear.*
>
> *So keep you the fire*
> *Of your own self-respect*
> *Though the heat of desire*
> *Is so hard to neglect.*
>
> *The trap; You must set it.*
> *The bait; It must be you.*
> *When hunter is hunted,*
> *You've followed the cue.*

Then trust, you can trust,
With no worry at all.
And just motion emotion,
To come have a ball.

Maureen replied in her own email "Thank you for sharing. By the way I would opt for the three-letter spelling of the word. No sense in changing things just for your mother. I love you and will see you in the morning."

Chapter 11: *The Holiday Season*

Ben Hui Zhang went through the projected numbers on the phone with Josh Struben. The call was cell phone to cell phone, Bangkok to London. Zhang was lying in his hotel bed as he was taking the call, and he wasn't alone, so he didn't want to use a video Skype call from his computer. The due diligence team for Cromwell Parsons Resources had gone back and forth with Zhang for over three weeks, digging into every detail and every assumption that had been made by the Rhapsody team, and had rendered a very favorable opinion to Struben.

"The market sensing that you have done indicates that you may eventually have as many as 3,000 members associated with each of the centers that you set up in different venues around the world. Is that correct?"

"Yes, but you must remember that the members are global members and not really associated solely with a single center."

"With an eventual target of at least 100,000 members, across your spectrum of 50 centers, that would give you annual membership revenue of between 3.5 and 5 Billion dollars. This assumes that your price points stay between the targeted range of $35,000 to $50,000, annually."

"Yes and we view these membership sales numbers as conservative."

"From what our team has been told the revenues from spa services are a separate source of revenue as is the revenue that accrues from fees charged to physician groups for billing and facilities management. Correct?"

"Yes that's right."

"So if I read all of your cost estimates correctly, and if our team has vetted your assumptions meticulously, we are looking at more than a billion dollars in profit by the end of year 4. Am I reading this right?"

"Yes you are."

"These are certainly very ambitious numbers, but the Cromwell team is rating your efforts as having a good probability of passing the hurdle rates we have established for success. It's intriguing because…..well just because…"

"What are your doubts, Josh?"

"They aren't really doubts at all Ben. I trust the analytic team we have here implicitly. After all I put the team together. It's more amazement than doubt. You know what they say: 'Rome wasn't built in a day."

"That's because Rhapsody didn't build it!" retorted Zhang.

The two businessmen continued their give and take and when they were near the end of the call, both men were feeling quite satisfied that they would be able to work together on an ongoing basis.

After he hung up the phone, Ben rolled over in bed and caressed the side of Dao Diskul's pie-shaped face. What she lacked in physical beauty, Dao more than made up for in intelligence, humor and sexual prowess.

"Sounds like that call went well," said Dao as she reached out for Ben to see how fast he could switch from business to pleasure. Ben's physical transition was instantaneous and it simply made Dao realize just how much fun it was going to be putting Rhapsody in motion.

****

Danielle was happy that both of her sons and her husband were home in London for the holidays. It was all about family. She knew it and they knew it. And that was a very good thing. Adam and Josh were both coming over for dinner, but neither of the boys was bringing a date. It was just as well. She liked playing the role of mother. She wasn't so sure about how she'd feel about playing the role of mother-in-law, when the time came. And the idea of playing the role of grandmother was even more foreign to her. The woman in her liked the idea of having the men in her life to herself a little bit longer.

There were still a few hours before her sons showed up, and so she was into playing the role of loving wife to her husband, Stephen Struben. This had already included a protracted sexual encounter earlier in the afternoon, followed by a short nap before cocktail hour. Life was good.

There was a roaring fire in the fireplace of their townhouse living room and Danielle was dressed in a festive seasonal long red skirt and a black cashmere top. She felt warm inside and out. Stephen wore a less stylish gray cardigan sweater, but he also was enjoying the warmth of home and hearth. He looked up from his 18 year old

Macallan single malt Scotch and reflected back on their dinner in Germany a few weeks earlier.

"I forgot to mention to you that I got a call from Dr. McDuffee yesterday."

"Abby? ... oh. *'Ow ees* she *doeeng*? I really like that woman."

"She has asked me to sit on the board of Rhapsody Holdings. She believes that I will add a good deal of value to their business."

"What *deed* you say?"

"It was an interesting conversation. Naturally I acknowledged that I was flattered that she believed that I would add value to her team. And you know that Abby McDuffee is no dope. She realizes that if she gets me to join the Board, she will also get you in the process. You never know they may need a celebrity spokesperson downstream. I told her that I would have to review the potential conflict of interest issues with my attorney, but I am interested and I told her as much."

"I've been *theenkeeng* about what Rhapsody *ees tryeeng* to *accompleesh*, ever *seence* our *deenner*. I *theenk eet's* a great *theeng* for you to be *eenvolved* with, Stephen. Just *theenk* about the mess that was created by Neville Roorback's *meesdiagnosees* of my breast *eenfection*. I *'ave* to wonder *'ow* many other people suffer through similar horrors." Danielle worked hard at pronouncing the 'h in 'horrors and was able to spit it out somewhat gutturally.

"Believe me I've been thinking about the same thing. Have you read the stuff that Abby sent us regarding the *Rhapsody Lifestyle Philosophy?*"

"Yes, the *preventateeve* and the *proacteeve* versus the *remedeeal* approach; the *eveedence*-based *eentegrative* options rather than an *excluseeve seengular* method that might not take *eento* account the whole *eendiveedual* – body, mind and soul....I read all of that and I'm also *eentrigued* by the *eemportance* their *pheelosophy* attaches to beauty and *sexualeety* and how it all connects to *longeveety*. The meaning of these elements of life *ees* more *eentrinsic* than *pereepheral* to the *Rhapsody Pheelosophy*. Others talk about *longeveety* but these folks let you know that a prolonged *exeestence 'as* a chance to be a more *meaneengful longeveety*. I'm *een* my fifties and could possibly be only *'alfway* through my life. I really want the rest of my life to be *feelled* with even more *'appiness* than the first *'alf*, and I want to be able to share *eet*. They get *eet*! The *Rhapsody Lifestyle* is what we all want whether we know *eet* or not, or should I say whether we acknowledge *eet* or not. I *theenk eet* would be a great idea for you to join their board."

"I agree. I just need to clear the potential conflicts with STRX."

" 'Ow about *confleects weeth* Josh and potential *eessues weeth* Cromwell Parsons, *eef* they *eenvest.*"

"That's why we have attorneys. They'll help us sort all of that out. Frankly however I don't see any real issues, so there is a high probability that I will accept the offer. We'll just have to make all of the appropriate disclosures."

Danielle smiled and thought about how lucky she had been and continued to be. At 52 years of age, she enjoyed a successful career, raised two successful sons and had been married to the same man for more than 30 years. She wondered how the next 50 years could possibly be better.

****

John Brady had many things to do. First he wanted to clear the decks of the dysfunctional female relationships in his life.

Maureen was due to return from Solace in the Sun this weekend, and JB planned on taking the corporate jet down to pick her up. He then had to figure out what kind of shape Maureen would be in to attend a few Christmas parties. Maybe he would try to work harder at his marriage….or maybe not. Meanwhile his daughter Megan was returning from Yale for Christmas vacation and it would be nice to see her again, because he had only spent a few hours with her on the Thanksgiving weekend.

Some of the other female relationships needed to be acted upon as well. He wanted to make sure that no one settled the wrongful dismissal lawsuit that Maria Cardoza had brought against himself and ICD. He also wanted to make sure that his new EA, Caitlin Browning was not privy to his hatred for her older sister, Abby McDuffee. So far Browning was working out rather well, but he wanted to take a shot at getting in her pants before the year was over. What the hell. It's all a game. He was the boss and he needed to underline his superiority every once in a while with a new conquest. Besides such a conquest would have double the impact because he would be, in a way, repaying Abby McDuffee at the same time. Women like McDuffee, Cardoza, and Browning needed to know their place. If they were intent on having their eyes on the glass ceiling, he wanted to make sure they were on their backs when they were looking through it.

These things were all running through his mind as was heading into Madison Square Garden to meet Paul Pritchard at his Sky Box before the Knicks game. He took the escalator up from the street level and then walked around to the elevator that led up to the top of the Garden where a circle of private executive boxes lined the top of the stadium. He hadn't seen Pritchard in almost a year, and he could never figure out what Pritchard liked about the Knicks. They had been a god-awful team for a number of years, and the future didn't look any better. In addition the skyboxes at Madison Square Garden were not nearly as nice as those of other sports arenas. They were perched above the nosebleed section of the cheapest seats in the house, and were not really meant for the true sports fan. Yet the executive boxes were all very posh, with high definition digital TV inside the suites, so that you could get a close up view of what was a relatively distant basketball game on the Garden floor. Each suite had a full bar and servers were available. The suite was preset with a spread of fancy hor d'ouvres and snacks.

On this occasion the box, which had twelve exterior seats and could accommodate more guests inside, was being used by two people, Paul Pritchard, the host and John Brady the guest. When Brady arrived at the suite, Pritchard was already inside and he was speaking on his cell phone. JB simply grabbed a set of tongs and scooted a few shrimp onto a serving plate and doused them with cocktail sauce, while the financier continued his conversation, but greeted Brady with a half wave.

Brady fixed himself a gin and tonic in a tumbler to help him digest the shrimp and walked through the doorway to the front of the suite and sat in one of the rear seats that overlooked the court. A minute or two later Pritchard joined him and they both sat a seat apart watching the warm-ups below.

"How've you been, John?"

"About what you might suspect. Pretty shitty actually."

"You're not alone."

"Doesn't really help…..in fact I'd rather be alone…but at the top of this financial disaster…..not suffering along with all of the other peons."

"I know how you feel, John. Believe me I do."

"Somehow I doubt it Paul. You know you Wall Street guys built this financial house of cards with other people's money that was earned by building businesses. Every one of you fuckers belongs in jail."

"Nice seeing you too, JB."

Brady took a gulp of his gin and tonic and glared at Pritchard. He thought of Pritchard as one of those weasels that would scramble about and manage not to get squashed when everyone around him was getting hurt big time. So although he didn't like Pritchard personally, he had taken a lot of investment tips from him in the past that had panned out well. He had also indulged in the many excessive perks that came with the territory. Brady secretly knew that one of the perks that he procured from Pritchard was not freely given. Several years earlier, he had engaged in a bit of fabulous fornicating with a rather promiscuous Mrs. Pritchard, but fortunately his act of dipping the wicket had not been in flagrante delicto as had been a similar offense committed by Paul Pritchard's former partner, Jonathan Cromwell. As this background surfaced in JB's consciousness, he calmed a bit before responding to Pritchard.

"Okay Paul, let's get right to it. How do I play through this mess and how can you help me. I'm assuming that you didn't invite me here as a thank you note for past business, or to see a halfway decent basketball game. Neither of those scenarios is remotely possible."

"Well I do have a thought or two. First let me clear the deck on the Cromwell Parsons Resources situation. I no longer have anything to do with the firm personally, although I will say that there are some people over there that I do respect. Also like everyone else I have had my personal portfolio torched over the past six months. Contrary to what you may have heard, I am not retiring from the capital markets jungle to simply enjoy the benefits of capitalistic success. I will just be going about it differently."

Brady ran the fingers of both hands simultaneously straight back through his mane of black hair, and then interlocked his fingers behind his head. It was a gesture that said, "All right I'm listening," without the need for articulation.

The horn blew at courtside indicating that the game was nearing tip-off and Brady got up and walked back into the suite. Pritchard followed him inside and closed the glass door shutting out ninety percent of the Garden noise. Almost simultaneously there was a light tapping on the hallway door at the opposite side of the suite, and the door opened partially. JB didn't turn around to see who was looking to gain entry, but Pritchard immediately went to the doorway and said to the one visible and very attractive young lady. "Give us a little privacy for about fifteen minutes."

"You got it. We'll be back, in a few," There was a breathless young voice answering through the doorway and the sound of others talking behind her. Pritchard closed the door and walked back over to the bar where Brady was fixing himself another gin and tonic.

"As I said, JB, I am out of the picture at Cromwell Parsons, but I'm not out of the loop. I do know what they are up to. They are trying to move money into their Private Equity funds as fast as they possibly can. They're doing a good bit of combined debt/equity deals and they've got a lot of convertible bond instruments that they're investing in as well. They are very much into value creation for the time being. And frankly value investing doesn't mean they want to underwrite the expansion efforts of companies like ICD. There's not enough return in it for them."

"So how do you know all of this?"

"We have ways, John. We have ways."

"You've got a mole inside your old company?"

"Not exactly. But just as good. Maybe better. Moles leave holes."

"What does all of this have to do with me? Cromwell Parsons has $20 million of my money or whatever is left of it now."

"I still have a few associate/friends inside Cromwell and I am looking out for client/friends like you." JB listened and cynically wondered if Pritchard had any true friend/friends.

Pritchard continued, "In light of the fact that you have requested a full redemption, you should be receiving your money as it becomes contractually available to you." Pritchard maintained good body language even though he was merely relating some information that he had learned through the wiretapping of Cromwell's offices and taking educated guesses at the rest. He had to guess at what was left of Brady's portfolio. He knew that at one time the value was considerably more than the $20 Million that JB cited as his best guess of current valuation.

"So you still haven't answered my question. If I wanted to get out of investing with CPR entirely, why would I care about what they want to do now? What does this have to do with me?"

"One of the strategies that Cromwell is chasing is to align their investments with certain industries, one of them being Health and Wellness. They are fiddling around with several emerging companies in the Biobusiness arena … you know, genomic engineering, stem cell cures that sort of thing. Most of their investments are relatively small, the largest so far being about $32 million. However they have been flirting with one interesting company that is not on the radar screen of most analysts, a company called Rhapsody Holdings."

"What do they do? It seems to me that I've heard that name someplace else recently." The context didn't come to JB immediately but he knew he had a negative feeling for some reason toward the name Rhapsody Holdings.

"I've got my feelers out but it isn't easy to come up with anything on them. They seem to be a company that is operating at the crossroads of medical innovation and global information technology, and then they are purveying their products and services through membership sales at centers that are planned for various large cities around the world. It seems that they are doing this in conjunction with some kind of global network of doctors. That part is a little unclear."

"Why do they interest Cromwell Parsons?"

"Several reasons…first there seems to be a lot of very bright people involved in the planning process. Secondly, if Rhapsody succeeds, it provides an excellent sales and marketing channel for the products and services of Cromwell Parson's other companies in the healthcare business. And thirdly, if Rhapsody meets its business plan it will be creating a business valued at more than $10 Billion and it will also get to the billion dollar value threshold faster than any company in business history, faster than Amazon, faster than EBay; faster than Facebook and way way faster than ICD."

"Good for them. I can see why CPR is interested, you still haven't answered why John Brady and ICD should be interested. You know I hear financial pump ups from you financial sales fuckers on a regular basis. If you want me to invest in Rhapsody the answer is 'No' Do I need to be clearer?"

Pritchard ignored both Brady's tone and his inferences. It was his time to light a fire under JB's ass and he knew just what he was going to say, and exactly how JB would react.

"I don't want you simply to *invest* in Rhapsody, JB. I want you to help me *stop* Rhapsody. So before you ask your questions about why you should do so, I'll give you several good reasons why I know you *will* help:

"First, if we steal the market from Rhapsody, we get the big money, and I do mean *big* money. Secondly, you will develop a very strategic relationship with every wealthy businessperson in the world who will want to become a member of this new healthcare initiative……the one we'll set up to compete with Rhapsody. Third you'll get some measure of revenge against Cromwell Parsons for mismanaging your money. And lastly you will stick it to the CEO of Rhapsody Holdings, someone you have crossed swords with in the past."

"Who is the CEO? There aren't many guys that I have crossed swords with that are still standing."

"It's not a guy, JB. It's a woman. Rhapsody's CEO is Abby McDuffee!!"

The ice rattled around in Brady's gin and tonic and he was clearly disturbed, just as Pritchard wanted him to be. Suddenly JB remembered Lois Haverstraw's email and the reference to the current whereabouts of Caitlin Browning's sister, Abby McDuffee. She had said something about a startup called Rhapsody Holdings He drained the rest of his drink and said, "So what do you want me to do? I don't personally have the financial resources to compete with a company in a business I know very little about."

Inside the suite there were three strategically placed television sets hanging from the ceiling in three of the four corners of the room. The sound was usually turned down low or was on mute, as it was now, so that people in the room could carry on conversations and at least see the game. Paul Pritchard looked up at the screen before he answered Brady's question. He noted that they were only three minutes into the game and the Knicks were already trailing 13-4 and had called a time out.

"It's important to start quickly. We're behind a bit but it's still very early in the game. We've got some good players that I'll tell you about in a second. But first let me answer your question about what you personally can do, and how I might be able to help.

"A modest investment from John Brady, say $1 million or $1.5 Million won't help much and might represent a conflict with what I want to propose. However downstream such an investment might be wise, and I'm sure we will be able to work out something that allows that later investment to come at advantaged prices.

"But that's not what we're talking about here. We will need a lot more money than just a few million to get us a quick start. We will need to tap into ICD's strategic equity fund."

"That's not feasible Paul." Brady's tone had softened considerably almost to the point where it belied his words. "ICD's strategic equity vehicle is funded for a total of $100 million in investments and is set up to invest in businesses that are potentially synergistic with the direction of the firm. We're not in the healthcare business. Besides the largest investment we ever made from the fund was $22 million. Won't this new company need a lot more than that?"

"Rhapsody is raising $300 million, but we won't need that much initially, especially if we can tap into the sweat equity of ICD employees.

"Here's what I see. $50 million from ICD's strategic equity fund, and I'll raise another $50 million from other investors. That will get us started. We won't need this all day one of course, but we'll need to move fast." On the TV the Knicks just hit consecutive three pointers and closed the gap by two-thirds of the deficit coming out of the time out.

"Of course we will also need some help from ICD programmers, mid-level managers and the like, and I'll need your personal help in sitting on the board and helping us attract physicians to our network. I already know many people who can help in this regard. But I'm sure your network will help. Certainly using your name will be an enormous help. Some of your other Board affiliations can also be quite helpful."

Brady seemed to be taking all of this in slowly, as he fixed himself another gin and tonic. The he said, "Who is going to run this company? Who will be the CEO? Don't you need to be recruiting someone now? You need someone who knows something about healthcare and running healthcare facilities. Don't you?"

"Actually I have an answer for all of that. Cromwell has another investor who has been torched a bit lately. He is someone that I brought into the fund and who I am helping to extract from the fund right now, as I am with you. We've been talking about this for more than a month."

"Is this someone I know? Is this someone I have met?"

"He says that he has never met you personally. But of course he knows who you are. He has met members of your family however, and he tells me that he will probably be meeting you this weekend."

"That's not possible. I'll be flying to Costa Rica to pick up my wife this weekend."

"I know that already. And when you are down there picking up Maureen, you will meet our CEO in waiting, Chipper Geld. He owns and runs Solace in the Sun."

Brady shook his head but he didn't mean 'no.' He simply wanted to ruminate a bit without talking to Pritchard. "Let me think about all of this, Paul. I'm going to invoke my three cocktail rule, which means I won't talk business after I finish this drink." Brady always made up the rules as he went along. It was part of his personality. "How are the Knicks making out?"

"Looks like they just tied it up."

There was another tap on the door and this time Pritchard gave entry to four lovely young ladies, in form fitting attire. Brady gulped down most of his drink and smiled.

"Speaking of being tied up...."

"Yeah. If that's what you want, JB, I like your chances."

"I always get what I want," said JB as he wrapped an arm around the waist of one of their new guests. "Can I get you a drink?"

****

Gina Alvarez and the Lay D's had finally brought their tour back to the United States. The financial success of the tour was breaking records with each passing day. The five nights they had played in LA and San Diego were all sell outs, as was the concert in San Francisco. The popularity of the group was at an all time high, and pictures of the blonde haired lead singer were everywhere, on magazine covers, tabloid pages, internet sites, downtown billboards, airport book shops, bus stop benches, just about everywhere.

Gina's publicist, Seth Silverstein, made sure that the rare interview was short and well targeted. The combination of overexposing her image and underexposing her persona was helping to create a mystifying and enigmatic aura around the mega star. People had an ongoing craving to learn more about her personal life, and Silverstein was doling these details out in small doses.

Through all of the tour stops and the traveling, Gina was constantly thinking about her baby. The morning sickness had gone away as quickly as it had come and that was an enormous relief. She was beginning to feel a little puffy but she only had four more performances to make it through, including the last two in NYC. She knew that she would have many stories to tell her child later in life, about the "very beginnings of his or her life." Josh had arranged for Gina to see a female OB/GYN when she was in Los Angeles, and Gina had half expected the rumors to fly right after that. However as far as she knew only three people shared her secret, Josh, the LA physician and herself. Ironically there had been rumors of her pregnancy several times before she actually became pregnant. She was not yet certain of the baby's gender but she was able to discern the baby's general good health. The doctor advised her to take it easy, but was open minded about her finishing the last two weeks of her tour.

Her baby was not the only issue occupying her thoughts. Gina was constantly concerned about her mother's health. On this rare free day on the tour, Gina had flown from Chicago to Detroit to visit her mother.

Gina's agent Pepper Gordon had picked her up at the airport and whisked her to her mother's modest two-story home. Gina was surprised when she saw her mother. Her mom was taking oxygen through a cannula into her nose. To see her mother chained to the oxygen tank was frightening to Gina.

"Mama." Gina's tone could not disguise her surprise.

"Gina, my one and only lovely daughter … I'm so glad you are here. And Carl, thank you for picking Gina up and bringing her here." Adriana Alvarez had not let her daughter's fame alter her life in any way. Although Gina purchased a home and cars for her mother and Gina's agent, Pepper Gordon, made certain that Adriana Alvarez received a personal management income derived from Gina's entertainment earnings, Adriana never aspired for additional material things. She understood that she had to accept a certain amount of living expenses from her daughter in order to avoid an unflattering image of living near the poverty line while her daughter took in mega millions of dollars. However she resisted, even rejected, gifts of expensive designer clothing and jewelry. She held steadfast to the notion that it was her prerogative to live simply. Nonetheless, she felt that Gina could live as lavishly as she wished as long as she maintained a sense of who she was and where she came from.

"You don't look so good." Gina said this frankly but with a pained and somewhat guilty expression. "I didn't know you were so sick. I would have come home sooner."

"I told Carl to make sure that didn't happen. It's not as bad as it looks. And there was nothing you could do. Besides you're here now and that makes me happy."

The two women just stared at one another in silence for almost a minute. Carl realized what a rare moment it was. Although the two women bore only a slight familial resemblance, they shared the same strong personality, and were both very opinionated and rarely quiet. Adriana's facial features were more rounded and less defined than those of her daughter. Adriana had brown hair and eyes. Gina had obviously inherited the recessive genes of her father, with her blonde hair and blue eyes and narrower frame.

So as Carl stood there observing his client and her mother, he found the moment of silence more unusual than did either of the two ladies. All three of them came to attention however as a fourth individual entered the room.

"Hello Ms. Alvarez. I'm very happy to meet you. I'm Dr. Gonzalez. I have been treating your mother over the last several weeks. She's been a very sick lady. However she has been coming around a lot of late." Dr. Gonzalez was a small wiry man no more than 5'6" tall and no more than 140 pounds after Thanksgiving dinner. But he had a manner about him that was very much a take-charge kind of approach. Therefore Carl, Gina and Adriana all listened to what he had to say.

"I've been talking with your mom over the last several days about the operation I think we should perform. Through a series of unusual events your mother has come to have a displaced diaphragm. The result is that your mother is experiencing significant difficulty breathing in a normal fashion." There was no doubt about the fact that Dr. Gonzalez was addressing his commentary to Gina. However he made no attempt to acknowledge her celebrity or to treat her any differently than the daughter of any other patient he might have had. This made Gina trust him instantly.

"When I last saw my mother three months ago she was the picture of health. It's hard for me to fathom what has gone on since then and to see my mother breathing through a tube. Can you explain to me in layman's terms what the diaphragm is and why she will need an operation?"

"Certainly. The diaphragm is a rib cage muscle located just below the lungs. Its function is to help the lungs expand and contract and help pull air into the body. When the air is sucked into the lungs it contains the oxygen that our bodies need to live. When we exhale the diaphragm relaxes and the body expels carbon dioxide and other unwanted waste gas. Because your mom has suffered a displacement to the diaphragm muscle, she is experiencing much more difficulty breathing normally and that's why she is on oxygen. We have run a number of tests and we believe that your mom is an excellent candidate for a surgical procedure to readjust the positioning of the diaphragm."

"Thank you for that explanation. So if I hear you correctly, if mom has this operation and it is successful, she should be able to go back to leading a normal life and certainly be off this oxygen tube."

"That's exactly right."

"So when exactly will mom have this operation?"

"We'd like to schedule it for the first week in January."

Dr. Gonzalez continued to discuss Adriana Alvarez's health with Adriana and with her daughter while Carl Gordon stood in the background. After about fifteen minutes of further discussion, both Adriana and Gina felt that Dr. Gonzalez was a competent professional who knew exactly what he was doing. They agreed that Mrs. Alvarez would undergo surgery at the beginning of the year.

Gina had not seen Dr. Gonzalez when he entered the room from elsewhere in the house. However she made a point to walk him to the door as he was leaving. Carl Gordon left along with Dr. Gonzalez and indicated that he would return to pick up Gina in a couple of hours, so that he could bring her back to the airport.

When Gina reentered the room she could sense that her mother was calmer and more at ease. However as they talked about many different things over the next several hours, including Gina's world tour and the growing publicity about her relationship with Josh Struben, Gina purposely avoided mentioning that she was carrying Josh's child.

Gina was simply happy to be with her mother and her mother was happy that she was there.

****

The discussion between Dr Al Moses and his patient, Maria Cardoza was frank and straight forward. The options had been laid out for Maria in a non-judgmental manner. Maria was healthy and the baby growing within her was healthy as well. There were no indications of any problems and her physical and emotional health seemed to be at a point in time when a decision about her pregnancy could be made without significant complications. Why then, Maria asked herself, had this become such a difficult decision for her to make? She had wrestled with the idea of being a mother, without seeking parenthood. Now when parenthood was thrust upon her she was reluctant to let go so easily. This was her fourth visit with Dr Moses since she became pregnant, and she knew that it was time to make some decisions but she was unsure what those decisions would be.

"Maria, you know that we are coming up on one of the first decisions you will need to make. The ultra sound that we ran indicates that you are about seven weeks pregnant today. If you decide to terminate your pregnancy medically through the use of mifepristone the time to do so is now. If you want to terminate your pregnancy in the next couple of months, the procedure will be surgical and will grow a bit more complex the longer you wait. And of course if you take the baby to term, you will have options to give up the baby for adoption, or to nurture your child as a fully responsible parent." Dr Al tried to be as explicit as possible in his explanation, but managed to convey the information in a soft tone and a nonjudgmental fashion.

"We have discussed these issues and options before but it is still difficult for me to decide what to do."

"Have you discussed this at all with the child's father?"

"I haven't talked to John Brady since the moment of conception." There was terseness to her reply.

"Yes, I understand."

For the next forty-five minutes or so they went back and forth about the details of Maria's situation. Only one thing was established and that was that Maria was not going to have a medical abortion, at this time, which basically meant that, unless she had a rapid change of heart, her options were down to surgical abortion, adoption or parenthood. Dr Al didn't want to influence any of these options unduly but he had an opinion about what Maria would eventually decide.

As they were wrapping up the medical visit, Dr Moses did something that he had never done before in his 40 plus year of practice.

"Maria, I feel as though you need more time, but just remember that I am available to talk about this anytime you want. In fact, I do have a full schedule today, but I would be happy to continue our discussion over dinner tonight or anytime soon, if you would honor me with your company."

Surprisingly, Maria wasn't surprised. Dr Moses was the most caring medical professional she had ever met, and he seemed determined to see her through her decision in a very personal way, that went well beyond the normal attributes of professional care.

"I'm free tonight." As she accepted his offer, Maria realized that she was free a lot lately.

$$**********$$

Sandeep Mehra was concerned about Rhapsody's relationship with Max Tkachuk's old IT firm. After meeting with STRX in Germany, he had traveled to the Ukraine to open discussions with the heirs to Max Tkachuk's estate. They were a confused group of people.

They never realized how much money Max had actually made or what his estate might be worth. They had secretly whispered that Max might be fairly wealthy, but they never realized that Max's estate was worth $18 million, mostly on deposit in Europe and the USA. This figure included no value whatsoever for Apakoh, the most recent IT company that Max had started a few years back.

The Tkachuk heirs also didn't have the vaguest clue as to what to do with Apakoh, the company they now owned. No blood relatives were involved in the business, and a family friend who was a Ukrainian based programmer was their closest tie to the operations of the business There was no one ready to step in and run the company and the family had no idea how to sell it or what it was worth.

As Rhapsody Holdings CIO, Sandeep Mehra had flown to the Ukraine for two purposes. The first reason was to see who was continuing to run the company and in particular who was responsible for working with STRX on the *HealthPort* development for Rhapsody. The second reason was to meet with Tkachuk's family to inquire about the potential purchase of Apakoh. The first mission was of most immediate importance, because Sandeep needed to feel comfortable that the *HealthPort* project would continue to move forward irrespective of the ownership of the company. On this score he felt things were stable. Apakoh had an accountant who was now doubling as the relationship manager with STRX, and work had continued unabated over the past two months.

The second issue was of more concern to Sandeep. It was clear to him that Max's family was not interested in Apakoh, at all. They were much more interested in receiving the proceeds from the liquid assets of Max's estate, than they were in running any income generating asset. Acknowledging as much, Sandeep realized Apakoh might be acquired for much less than its true value, if someone acted quickly, or on the other hand the company could rapidly become worthless, if Apakoh lost its contracts or its staff. Sandeep had evaluated the staff and found them to be a very competent team of IT development engineers. Rhapsody would eventually need such a staff internally, and he believed that this may be an opportunity to fulfill that need.

Sandeep came to the conclusion that the right decision would be for Rhapsody to acquire Apakoh. But, at what price? And, with what money? He would need to discuss this with Abby and with Ben Hui Zhang. An acquisition of Apakoh would also create the strange circumstance that Rhapsody had outsourced the *HealthPort* development to STRX, who in turn had subcontracted with Apakoh. Therefore, an acquisition would have the strange short term consequence of Rhapsody outsourcing to itself. This, of course, could be ameliorated quickly through a renegotiation with STRX, but that was for others to decide. He knew that Abby would want to be fair and the last he heard from Ben Hui Zhang, they still had not finalized the corporate funding through the Louisiana Group.

Sandeep knew they would have to move fast.

****

Abby McDuffee was back in New York and preparing to experience another joyful Christmas season. Her husband Bo and their ten-year-old daughter, Mindy, were happy that Abby would be spending a couple of weeks at home without any serious traveling. However Abby knew that she would need to balance the business and the family a bit better than she had been doing over the last couple of months. The best way for her to do this was by working from home, making her phone calls in and around the time she was making her Christmas cookies. Abby was happy to be spending some face time with her husband and daughter and she was also excited that Rhapsody was progressing on multiple fronts and that they would soon be able to begin operations out of their NYC offices.

It was still a few days before Christmas but on this particular Saturday night Abby was hosting a family party at her Scarsdale home. Her twin sister Alison and her husband, Tom had come up from New Jersey with their two teenage sons. Abby and Alison's younger sister, Caitlin, and her husband, Scott, also came up to Westchester County for the party, from their new apartment in the city.

Bo and Abby's home was an interesting old colonial house that had been built out and built upon several times over the years including the recent addition of a large two story family room at the rear of the old structure. The house was not massive in size but it was much larger than it appeared from the street. With the addition of the family room, which was done in conjunction with an expansion and renovation of the kitchen and pantry, the house was a little more than 4500 square feet of living space and it sat on a relatively modest sized one and a quarter acre piece of property, in an affluent section of Scarsdale, in Westchester County. The neighbors were mostly professional people, mostly of Jewish or Christian heritage.

The original structure to the house was more than eighty years old and had a small parlor off the front door that preceded a spacious living room that in turn sat across the hall from a large dining room. The remodeled kitchen and butler's pantry provided two-sided entry to the new family room. A family that was generally unpretentious, pompously referred to the finished basement area as the lower family room. This lower extremity of the home, housed a large collection of indoor sports and hobby items, including a pool table, a ping-pong table, a 48" plasma TV and an X Box set up for video games. On the far side of the lower family room there was an iron door that led to a modest sized 800-bottle wine cellar.

Inside and outside the house, the McDuffee-Blanchard residence heralded the Christmas season. Multicolored lights trimmed the various evergreens that wrinkled along the 150-foot long driveway leading up to the house. After walking through the center hallway of the main floor and into the spacious rear family room, the family guests were greeted by a fifteen foot high Christmas tree that was erected across from a large stone fireplace that was always roaring with a fire during the winter months. On one side of the family room there was a set of double sliding glass doors that led out to a rear deck for use during the summer months. On the other side of the room, across from the deck doors, there was a wet bar with four bar stools. Four couches arranged in a squared off pattern in the middle of the room semi-enclosed a six foot square marble coffee table. A ten-foot high custom designed wall unit warmly lined the wall adjacent to the sliding doors.

Abby and Bo varied the decorations on the coffee table and the wall unit to fit the changing seasons, and on this cold December evening, the wall unit was decorated with lighted model ceramic homes and the coffee table exhibited a large and stylish Lladro nativity scene. The figurines were lavishly displayed on a bed of straw that sat atop a white foot square table linen that covered the center of the marble top.

The three children got along well enough and they had sequestered themselves in the lower family room with the Xbox. The husbands shared an interest in sports and had grabbed the center seating in the upper family room that best allowed viewing of the NFL game that was airing in the background. The sisters had taken up positions on the bar stools and were making general conversation about myriad topics.

While their husbands all had different occupations, the three sisters shared some common business interests. The twins, Abby and Alison had brought their differing expertise together in the formation of Rhapsody Holdings and Caitlin was now employed by the same company, ICD, where Abby had spent the better part of her business career. It was natural that in relatively short order, the conversation would move from the social aspects of sisterhood to some of the more daunting details of business.

"So tell me about your trip to Hong Kong. You two must have been an interesting phenomenon for the Chinese to deal with. As I understand it, lots of Asians aren't quite ready for the prominence of the American businesswoman just yet."

Caitlin seemed genuinely intrigued by her big sisters' business agenda. Caitlin was sixteen years younger than her sisters but there was a strong family resemblance. At 5' 10" tall she was a full three inches taller than her older sisters, and although she was thin, she was not nearly as slight as her twin sisters. Caitlin was a little more into fashion and beauty than her sisters. She had a breast augmentation done when she was in college, and she had taken ready advantage of Botox and Restylane treatments, as periodic refreshenings for minor wrinkle removal, and beauty restoration. She often kidded her sisters about their super thin physiques, indicating that Alison probably had only two stripes on her striped pajamas and that Abby could not have more than a half dozen thistles in her toothbrush. The older sisters usually dismissed the good-natured ribbing with jokes about their sister's silicone cleavage, and they would gradually settle into more meaningful conversation.

"Actually we spent more time with transplanted Europeans and Americans when we were in Asia than we did with Asians, but we had a fascinating trip nonetheless." Alison responded. "You might also be surprised by how well women are received in business in Asia. As I understand it, other than in Japan and Korea, women do quite well in Asian businesses. Just take a look at how many Asian women are on the Forbes list of top executives worldwide. Anyway, it was my first time in that part of the world and frankly I'd like to go back and spend more time there before too long."

"Be careful what you wish for. I think that you'll be spending a lot more time in Asia over the next couple of years than you have bargained for," said Abby.

"So the business is going well, then I take it?" Caitlin inquired with a good deal of interest and was looking forward to a more detailed update. The three sisters were close and talked often, and although Alison and Abby were virtually inseparable with respect to the Rhapsody project, they also kept their sister well informed and made no secret about the fact that they would love to have her join them at some time in the future once they had the business up and running. Abby valued Caitlin's business drive and Alison could see that Caitlin would instinctively understand the market place for memberships, and could be a superb adjunct to the sales effort, and crafting the set of offerings that went into a membership.

"Yes things are going very well, After Allie and I went to Hong Kong to meet with some folks there, I went on to Thailand and Abby went to Germany. We needed to tie up some loose ends, and to begin creating more loose ends to be tied up later........ You know about our *GPS*. Well, Allie and Dao are starting to recruit and certify members beginning in January. When I was in Germany I checked up on our progress on the *HealthPort* and that seems to be moving along as well."

"How about your funding?"

"We're almost there. And on top of that there has been a significant amount of secondary interest ....that is interest from others who might want to invest after the initial funding is in place." Abby answered her younger sister's questions with enthusiasm.

"That's great."

"So now what we have to do next is flesh out the executive team at the holding company level and start to add workers to the operating company team to get things in place prior to starting work on the first center." Abby was animated as she spoke. Her long angular fingers dangled from her smooth thin hands like fringe on a baby blanket, and then periodically her hands would tighten into angular projectiles, as she would make a point. Her loose fitting long sleeved black dress simply amplified her lanky look. While Alison also gravitated toward a gangling appearance, she appeared a bit less so this evening as she wore a bright and bulky multicolored Christmas sweater and black wool pants.

Alison was also excited about Rhapsody Holdings and was quick to repeat a common theme amongst the sisters. "You know, Caitlin, it's only a matter of time before you leave that stodgy old firm. ICD, and come join us at Rhapsody."

"I'm still learning a few things where I am. But of course I'm flattered that my sisters think I can help. We'll see as time goes on. Right now I have my hands full dealing with JB and the other executives in the company. Scott and I just got our new place in Manhattan, and we're making all of the normal adjustments to living in the city again."

"Don't get too close to Brady. He's a real asshole, and I wouldn't trust him as far as I could throw him. When I worked at ICD, he was one of the most hated executives in the company. I still find it amazing that he managed to bamboozle his way to the top and even more amazing that he has managed to stay there." Abby and Caitlin had had this conversation or elements of it several times over the past three weeks. Abby gave Caitlin as much background as she could about John Brady saying that he would stop at nothing to get his way in any negotiation. Although Caitlin felt that she had negotiated her promotion reasonably well with JB, she took her sister's repeated warnings seriously and planned on being careful around John Brady while at the same time broadening her experience and enhancing her resume.

"Don't worry about me. I'm a big girl. I think I know what I'm doing with respect to Brady. I've also had some conversations with my predecessor over the last few weeks, and she has been very helpful. By the way she says that she remembers you from your time at ICD. It sounds as though she held you in very high regard."

"Are we talking about Maria Cardoza? Is she still with Brady as his EA?"

"Well, not any more. That's my job now."

"Of course … but you know what I mean. Was she still his EA, when you took over?"

"More or less… She resigned, or was pushed out. I'm not quite sure which. The lady has a lot of class. She isn't bad-mouthing Brady. However she has told me to make sure that I always understand what Brady wants from me. She has also warned me that Brady is very opportunistic and will take a mile if you give him as much as an inch. Maria said that sometimes she was working 80 hour weeks, and that Brady treated her as though it was to be expected."

"I remember Maria, very well. She came to ICD and was immediately hired as John's EA. I never saw the paper work on her but I understand that she was working at a resort in Spain, and that she supposedly had a lot of money. None of that really mattered once she began working for John, because she was quite competent. Even though I hated Brady, I liked Maria a lot. In fact we got along pretty well. But I left shortly after she came on board so I didn't get to know her real well. What's the skinny on her?"

"Rumor has it that she and Brady were lovers... Doesn't make much sense to me... She seems so refined and he can certainly be crass. But you just never know with these things. Anyway, if anything was going on in the past, I'm sure it's over. Brady speaks about Maria as though she were meaningless. But you can tell that he doesn't like her. He tries to hide it, but he seems peeved that she left the company."

The conversation between Abby and Caitlin left Alison out of the loop a bit, and so she remarked, "Sounds a little bit like the two of you are giving an unwarranted pass to a jerk."

"Count me out of that. Remember that I already told Caitlin that Brady is an asshole."

"Hey hey hey ... Come on now... that's my boss we're talking about," Caitlin giggled. "However if the truth be known, Abby's right. He's an asshole."

"Great!" said Alison. "That means that you'll be coming to work for us sooner rather than later." Alison was looking to push Caitlin every chance she got. Abby wasn't as adamant. She was more willing to let events run their course.

"So when you talked to Maria, what is she up to now?"

"We got into that a little bit, but not much. When we spoke she was sincerely trying to help me out, and didn't say a lot about what she was doing next, and nothing at all about why she left. Remember Maria Cardoza is a wealthy woman in her own right. She did mention something about wanting to buy into a spa or set up her own facility. That may be where she made her money in the past."

"We're looking for someone to run our spa business at Rhapsody. She may have some ideas. Maybe I'll give her a call and wish her luck in her post-ICD days. That won't cause you any trouble will it?"

"No. Not at all. By the way, she strikes me as a very competent person. You might want to give some serious thought to having her join your team in some capacity."

"That's what I was referring to when I asked if that would cause you any trouble. I just can't imagine John Brady liking the idea of his former EA going to work for the sister of his current EA, especially when that sister is a former rival who hates his guts."

"I'm pretty sure that Brady doesn't know that you are my sister. For the whole time I have been working for ICD, my name has been Browning, not McDuffee. And he has never once mentioned you."

"If he doesn't know yet, you can be sure he'll find out sooner rather than later."

****

John Brady sat next to Dr Kelvey as the ICD jet prepared for landing at the airport in Costa Rica. Brady had brought Kelvey along for two reasons. First he wanted Kelvey to talk to all of the SIS doctors to make certain that his wife was ready to resume her routine back on Long Island. He didn't really care much about Maureen's feelings. He was more concerned with whether or not she could resume her "role" as his wife. Secondly he wanted to discuss his own physical issues with Kelvey. There seemed to be no better time to do this than on the flight to Costa Rica.

"So Mike, I want to ask you about this back problem. I just can't take this shit anymore. It's been several years now and it just keeps getting worse. They tell me my problem is called cervical spondylosis. I've been to more fucking doctors that I can shake a stick at, and not one of these pricks has a solution for me. I asked you about it a number of times and besides the meds you gave me I really haven't gotten any help from you either. Now the pain seems to be coming more and more often and lasting longer and longer. Last week I went to talk to the neurosurgeon person that you recommended to me a few years back. Of course he wanted to operate then, and his solution hasn't changed. What do you think?"

"John only you know your body. Everybody has to know his or her own body. It is important. Everyone's threshold for pain is different. What might seem intolerable to you could be very tolerable for another patient, or vice versa."

"Knock off the nonsense Mike. It's me you are talking to. Should I have the fucking operation or not?" Brady could never seem to understand the value that Kelvey provided. He was all image – a good looking, well spoken young doctor, who dressed in expensive suits, wore fashionable ties and dispensed superficial advice and good drugs. For some unfathomable reason, however, JB continued to retain his services.

"I will tell you what John. I will make a few calls and get a few answers. Then there's one more neurosurgeon you could see. After that you can make the call about whether or not you want to go for a surgical fix."

The ICD jet landed on the runway in Costa Rica and taxied straightaway to the gate. John Brady and Mike Kelvey were whisked through customs and on their way to Solace in the Sun in a matter of moments. When they arrived at SIS none other than the great Chipper Geld greeted them.

"Hello Mr. Brady I have been looking forward to meeting you very much. I'm Chipper Geld." Geld, more or less completely ignored Mike Kelvey whom he had met on a previous occasion. "We are all happy that you are here with us and I know Maureen can't wait to see you. She knows that you've arrived. And I know she is more than ready to leave us. Would you like me to show you directly to her room?"

"That would be nice. This is quite an attractive facility that you have here. Have you been operating it for a long time?"

"Long enough to know what we're doing. That's for sure." Both men knew the value of specific information and danced around the opportunity to provide it to one another. Finally Brady made a specific point.

"I understand we have a financial advisor in common. Paul Pritchard says to say hello."

"Yes Pritchard has told me a lot about you. In fact I understand that he may be cooking up a business venture or two that he believes might interest both of us. Of course that can wait. Today is all about reuniting you and Maureen."

They had been walking across the lobby and down the hallway as they were talking. Mike Kelvey had been walking several steps behind him. A few doors down from Maureen's room, Geld stopped and turned around and said to Kelvey, "I'm sorry Dr. Kelvey; I should have pointed out the offices to our physician staff as we just went by them off to the right. Let me just get John and Maureen reunited and then I'll be happy to show you where our staff physicians are located."

"That's okay, Mr. Geld. I'll just retrace my steps here a little bit. I'm sure I can find my way." With that Mike Kelvey turned around and scampered towards the physician staff area. Geld walked Brady directly up to his wife's door, tapped lightly on it, and then turned to walk back toward the lobby.

Maureen swung the door open wide and looked up at her husband apprehensively. She wasn't sure what he was feeling. She wasn't even sure what she was feeling herself. She just said, "John."

"Maureen, you look absolutely fabulous." John was never that effusive. Maureen beamed.

****

Maria and Al met at Cafe Cielo, a small Italian restaurant on Eighth Avenue near 53rd Street. Although it was near the theatre district, it had a much less frenetic pace, and Al remembered the restaurant having excellent food, that was served in an unrushed manner. The restaurant was also conducive to quiet conversations.

Al arrived first and stood as Maria was shown over to his rear corner table. The square table had four chairs, and Maria could have chosen to sit across from Al or next to him on an angle. She chose the seat next to him on his right.

"Such a gentlemen..." Maria said as Al pushed the seat in for her. "Have you been here before?"

"Yes, a few times." Dr Al gazed at his dinner companion and felt young once again. He knew he was in uncharted territory but continued his conversation as though he had dinner with his patients every night of the week.

"It seems like a very nice place." They continued the perfunctory small talk as they both nestled into their respective seats and grew comfortable with the fact that they were having dinner together. Maria was a naturally beautiful woman and didn't need any makeup. However she had applied just enough to make her feel dressed up. Mostly it was eyeliner, a little eye shadow and a soft but distinct perfume. She wore an attractive black and gray dress that fit her form loosely but attractively without being overly sensual. Moses for his part had showered, shaved and cleaned up and put on a fresh blue suit after his office hours had concluded.

"You look especially attractive this evening, Maria," said Dr. Al. "Thank you for joining me for dinner."

"Well thank you for inviting me"

"How are you feeling?"

"To be honest I feel very good. In many ways I am happy about where I am in life and frankly I'm happy about the baby as well. I wanted to tell you that as soon as possible tonight, because we left that topic sort of up in the air when I was in your office earlier today."

"So Maria, your decision then, is to keep the baby?"

"Yes Al, I think is the right thing to do for everyone. And I know it's the right thing for me." It was the first time that Moses had heard Maria refer to him as just "Al" and not as "Dr Al." With others he had regarded this is as somewhat too familiar but with Maria he regarded the familiarity as almost intimate. He liked it.

"I am happy for you Maria, very happy. To be honest I wasn't sure what your decision would be. But I'm happy for you. As I mentioned to you in the office, all indications are that the baby is very healthy and that you should have no problem delivering your child in another seven months. For my part, I look forward to seeing you on a regular basis during your pregnancy."

"I guess that finishes the business part of our dinner and we haven't even ordered drinks yet." Maria smiled warmly and tilted her head slightly towards her shoulder as she spoke tenderly to her tablemate.

"Maybe so," said Dr. Al. "However I guess I never believed this dinner was all about business. In many ways it's more about friendship. Isn't it?"

"I am happy you feel that way," said Maria. "I actually have come to think of you as much more than just my physician. I certainly would like to believe that you're also my friend. When I go to your office I feel confident that I will be getting the opinion of a friend as well as that of a professional. It's always nice to feel special."

"I always try to make all the women who come to my office feel comfortable. I believe in the basic human goodness of all of my patients and therefore try to treat each of them with the respect they deserve."

"You are very good at doing just that." Maria reached across the tabletop and touched Al's right hand with her left hand, briefly. The electricity of the moment had been felt by both. It was interrupted slightly as the waiter came to the table and inquired about cocktails. Maria ordered an iced tea and Dr. Al asked for a Diet Coke.

And when the waiter moved off to fill their order, Maria inquired about her own drink selection. "We haven't talked at all about alcohol during pregnancy. I'm assuming it's taboo?"

"The problem with rules is that there are always exceptions. My personal belief is that an occasional glass of wine or two is not harmful. But the prevailing wisdom of today is abstinence with respect to alcohol and pregnancy. For sure any kind of over indulgence would be a problem. From time to time I've had to make this point much clearer with certain patients. But as I said, an occasional glass of wine is probably not going to be a problem. So by the way, if you're so inclined, be my guest, have a glass of wine."

"Well, I'm probably better off without it anyway. But of course if you feel like having a drink please go ahead don't let my condition stop you."

"Iced tea is fine. But maybe I'll have a little red wine with dinner."

The 30 year difference in their ages seemed to soften in the atmosphere. For sure, Maria was used to dating older men. For her whole life she had appreciated the experience that older men were able to bring to her life. Other than her recent relationship with John Brady, Maria had never had a serious relationship with anyone remotely close to her age.

On the other hand, Dr. Al had had few serious relationships, period. The one enduring love of his life, Anne Mohr, had been dead for more than seventeen years. Al had dated a few women since he lost Anne. The difficulty was that Al held them all to such a high standard. They were all being compared to Anne. That is not to say that Al didn't enjoy the company of many of these women. Several of them enlivened his sex life and kept him physically young. He never felt like he was using them, but the emotional stimulation was rarely there and when it was present, it wasn't enduring.

Al wasn't sure what it was that made Maria Cardoza different from these other women and frankly he didn't care. He was simply enjoying the moment in a way that had been all too rare in recent years. This was the new Al! He was determined to turn the corner. He was determined to enjoy a new approach to life. He was determined to make more out of his dinner with Maria. However Dr. Al Moses was not yet prepared to tell Maria Cardoza his plan. He wasn't even sure he was prepared to tell himself.

****

It had been a long day for Gina Alvarez. First it was the early morning flight from Chicago to Detroit. Then Carl drove her in and out of the city for her visit with her mother. This was followed by a flight out to New York and a limousine ride into the city, followed by VIP access to her hotel room. It was almost 10 PM by the time she was getting ready for bed. She thought about calling Josh, but she recognized that it was now 3 AM the following morning in London. So she simply showered and got ready for bed. That's when the trouble began. It started with a wrenching pain in her lower midsection that seemed to abate shortly thereafter. There was more pain in the early hours of the morning, and there were some bleeding as well. Several hours later Gina Alvarez had a miscarriage.

Chapter 12: *Help Is On The Way*

Josh Struben never realized how much he wanted to be a father. When he got the phone call from Gina he was shocked. He had grown accustomed to the notion of impending fatherhood without ever realizing what the responsibilities of the role would be. He had never discussed his impending fatherhood with anyone other than Gina, so Josh did not know where to turn when his girlfriend informed him of her miscarriage. After all Gina Alvarez was not your ordinary girlfriend.

The holiday season was still in full swing in London and although the Struben family was not particularly religious, they did celebrate both Christmas and Chanukah. Stephen Struben had grown up Jewish and Danielle Dubonet had grown-up as a Christian and their London townhouse was decorated with both a Christmas tree and a menorah. It was now just a week before Christmas and only a few days before the beginning of Chanukah, and Josh had just received news that wasn't at all pleasant. Although he had promised his mother that he would spend the rest of the year in London, it now became imperative that he catch the next flight to New York City. Rather than gloss over the news that might hit the tabloids within 48 hours, Josh decided to tell his parents about Gina and the baby. Conveniently they were currently sitting in the parlor having afternoon tea. This way he could tell them both at the same time.

"Mum, Dad, I just got a call from Gina in New York City. She has a problem or should I say she and I have a problem that I would like to discuss with you."

"Of course Josh. What *ees eet?*" Danielle's tone was anxious.

"I don't know quite how to say this so I might as well just blurt it out. Gina had a miscarriage. I know that you didn't realize that she was pregnant. I realize that I never told you about our baby or that you might soon be grandparents. Now I'm sorry about that. But you've never even met Gina and I had hoped that I would be able to accomplish that much before giving you the news that you would be grandparents. Now, of course, all that has changed. I need to leave today to go to Manhattan. I don't know what time the flights are early this evening, but I would like to get one out as soon as possible." Josh was uncharacteristically shaken and his eyes were moist with emotion.

"Josh, *darleeng*, I don't know what to say," said Danielle. Her man/child was standing boyishly upset in front of her. Danielle's motherly instinct caused her to jump up and hug her son. Then she looked back and forth between her son and her husband trying to ascertain whether or not Stephen had known this but hadn't told her. Satisfied that that was not the case she continued, "You know that your father and I *weell* do whatever we can to *'elp* you out. What can we do to *'elp*, Josh?"

"Josh, maybe your mother and I should go with you to New York. Adam hasn't left yet to come to London, so maybe we can celebrate the holidays in New York together instead. I don't mean to misuse the word celebrate, given what you just told us, but I think we'd all like to be there for you and for Gina. And if she feels up to it I would very much like to meet her sooner rather than later."

Stephen Struben stood up from where he was sitting in the parlor and walked over and put his arms around Josh while Danielle was still standing less than three feet away. It was not normal for Stephen to exhibit an outward expression of affection or emotion. However it was the kind of fatherly hug that seemed appropriate for the circumstances. Stephen was telling Josh that he and Danielle would stand behind him. Josh was physically a bigger man than his father. However his posture looked shaken and his demeanor was dour. He appreciated his parents' physical and emotional support.

A decision was made collectively by the Strubens and in short order Josh called his brother Adam while Danielle made airline reservations for herself Stephen and Josh to fly to New York within hours.

****

John Brady was sitting in the back of his limousine, accompanied by his EA Caitlin Browning. They were going over many of the end-of-year issues that needed to be resolved for ICD. Caitlin was taking copious notes, while at the same time considering to whom she might assign many of the tasks that JB was listing for her. However they were not on their way to a business meeting. Rather JB was on his way to an appointment with a neurosurgeon across town. JB frequently interlocked his personal agenda with his business calendar. He was able to do this as long as he could multitask as he traveled between appointments. A large part of his success in so doing was the constant accompaniment by his EA.

"What have we heard from Tobin? When will he be moving up from Atlanta? Have you and he begun putting together the rudiments of realignment for our emerging software business?"

"Jason will be moving up from Atlanta after the new year. He said probably that his family will be here around the middle of January. Of course he'll be up here right after New Year's Day. He's been spending most of December up in New York anyway. Jump starting the new business will take a lot more people than just Jason Tobin and whatever help I can give him." Caitlin spoke firmly and with resolve. She wasn't at all cowed by JB's superior attitude. She also wasn't about to make promises that she couldn't deliver on. As she spoke she pushed her long slender hands from her lap out towards her knees straightening her skirt in a gesture that said, "*I don't want to be a part of anything that's not tidy.*"

Brady noticed the distancing gesture, but didn't allow it to sway him one bit. He also noticed, as he had several times over the last few weeks, that Caitlin Browning had very nice legs.

Caitlin wanted to change the topic from business to ascertain how long she might have to wait for Brady while he was at the physician's office. She also had a vested interest in knowing just how painful her boss's back problem might be. She didn't know whether this would have an impact on any of his upcoming appointments and whether she should look to reschedule any of them based upon the outcome of JB's consultation with the neurosurgeon.

"What are you hoping to achieve when you see this physician today? It's about your back problem … Right?"

"Yes… In a word, yes. That's what I'm looking to achieve today. I'm looking to get to yes. I want to be able to agree with someone about the appropriate course of action to take with respect to my back problem. I've been dealing with this for years now and it's just about driving me crazy. Frankly, if this guy tells me that he can operate on the problem and have me back on my feet in a matter of weeks, I'm just going to go forward with it."

"That's a mighty important decision to make. I know this isn't the first person that you've seen about the problem, but you seem to be resigned to go with his opinion regardless of what that might be." This was the first time that Caitlin had been this forward with her boss. It was certainly within her nature to speak this way. She was generally forthcoming. However to this point, her relationship with JB had been strictly business. This was very different from the JB that she had been warned about by both Maria Cardoza and by her sister Abby McDuffee. The fact of the matter was that her respect for John Brady was growing, and Caitlin felt very comfortable making her own decisions about people.

"I want to get out of this doctor's office pretty quickly. What do I have on the calendar late this afternoon?" Before Caitlin could answer, JB's cell phone rang. He glared at the caller ID for a second and then decided to answer the call.

"Hello Pritchard. How are you doing? I met your buddy, Chipper Geld, over the weekend when I was down in Costa Rica. He seems to be an upbeat kind of guy. We didn't get much of a chance to talk about your ideas about your new healthcare fund, but I understand that might be coming up. Is that right?"

There was a pause in the conversation for more than a minute while JB listened to what Pritchard had to say on the other end of the phone, and then he responded.

"Well it's not something I want to talk about right here and now. I'm pulling up outside of the doctor's office. However I will be able to make dinner on Wednesday night and will be looking forward to spending a little more time getting to know Chipper Geld." He was careful not to mention anything about Rhapsody or the opposition to Rhapsody over the phone within the ear shot of Caitlin Browning, the sister of Rhapsody's CEO. As far as Caitlin knew, he, John Brady, was unaware of the relationship between the two women. He wanted to maintain that veneer for a while longer.

****

Dao Diskul and Ben Hui Zhang were enjoying their time together in Bangkok. Ben could just as easily have operated out of Hong Kong but he chose Bangkok simply to be near Dao. During the days Dao spent her time in surgery. Her practice was still thriving and she enjoyed literally living on the cutting edge. But Dao was also eagerly waiting the day that her practice would become part of the Rhapsody GPS. She was also looking forward to spending more time working with her longtime friend Alison McDuffee and her newfound boyfriend Ben Hui Zhang.

Ben was quite curious as to why Dao wanted to leave her thriving practice to join Rhapsody. He knew that she found certain aspects of her current business less than satisfying. However he wondered if Dao would be truly satisfied with the work environment of Rhapsody, even if she helped design the environment herself. He knew that Dao was a restless spirit, who was never truly satisfied by the status quo. In fact he wondered if Dao was ever satisfied by anything, or anyone. He certainly had been making a yeoman's effort at helping her achieve sexual satisfaction while he was working in Bangkok. He was already pushing his own creativity and stamina to the borders of his coital aptitude. And while he certainly enjoyed the fruits of his efforts, there was a certain amount of emasculation that accompanied his ardor. He had learned that multi orgasmic individuals knew of no such thing as a climax. He was about ready to take a vacation from his vacation. A few days earlier he had made plans to travel back to Hong Kong, to welcome in the New Year with some friends. He had invited Dao to come along with him, but Dao declined, opting instead to use her vacation time to travel to New York to spend some time with Alison between Christmas and New Year's Day.

Their month long sexual fantasy was coming to an end, and Ben was surprised that the principal emotion he felt was one of relief. He needed to recharge his batteries. He was looking forward to some rest at home. They traveled out to the airport together and Ben saw Dao off on her flight to New York before taking his flight back to Hong Kong.

As she was leaving him at the gate, the moon faced Thai physician turned to Ben, kissed him on the lips and said, "Get some rest. 2009 is going to be a year you will never forget, and all of us will need all of the energy we can muster."

****

The 6 PM flight from London to New York had arrived at JFK after 9 PM local time, and by the time the Struben family arrived in Manhattan they were quite tired because the local time back in London was in the wee hours of the morning. For convenience sake Stephen and Danielle simply grabbed a hotel room on the east side. They were careful not to choose the same hotel where Gina was staying, in order to avoid any additional publicity. Josh didn't bother going to his own apartment but rather went to be with Gina immediately.

Although the hour was very late and the mood was very somber, Josh and Gina were able to share the rest of the night privately. They had a chance to discuss their loss, as well as to discuss how they might deal with the inevitable prying from the press, who would be craving some sort of explanation for the cancellation of the concerts scheduled for New York City. All that had been said so far was that "tonight's performance of the Lay D's concert has been canceled due to illness of the lead singer, Gina Alvarez."

Gina's business manager, Carl Gordon was being a real prince. For the past fourteen hours Pepper had fielded all of the major business issues, not the least of which was dealing with the other two performers who currently comprised the "Lay D's." Carl knew that Gina's mysterious ailment could not be kept a secret for too long, but he wanted to afford Gina and Josh the opportunity to handle this in their own way. He didn't actually cancel the concert until 4 PM that afternoon. He had not as yet canceled the remaining concerts scheduled for New York City over the next two nights.

The complications of a celebrity lifestyle did not diminish in any way the reality that two human hearts were suffering. In some ways the jet set lifestyle of Josh and Gina had allowed them little privacy. But at this hour it was not privacy that they were seeking as much as it was intimacy. The young couple needed the opportunity to explore their emotions in an intimate way without having to explain their ruminations to anyone other than themselves.

Before they went to sleep, they discussed the fact that Josh's parents had come into town and that Stephen and Danielle wanted to be with them for support, but Josh also understood that Gina might not want to meet them right now.

"They will do whatever we would like them to do. It could be a bit awkward for all of us," Josh allowed.

"There never seems to be a perfect time and place. And I have been thinking about meeting your parents ever since I learned I was pregnant. I know that they have been married for 30 years and they are different from our generation in many ways. I was hoping they would accept me as the mother of their grandchild. Now I guess they will just have to accept me as me."

"I'm not worried about that one bit. They will love you."

"I'm glad they're here. I'm glad they came with you. I'd like to meet them. There's no sense in waiting. I'd like to meet them in the morning. Your parents are important to you and so therefore they are important to me as well. Not everyone has such a close family. You are lucky. You are close to Adam and you're close to your parents. It's part of what makes you who you are."

"You are also close to your mother ... Right? Isn't that part of what makes you who you are?"

"Absolutely ... And that's a whole other issue. I was on the phone with her, explaining things, just before you arrived this evening. It wasn't all that easy, because she has been so ill herself. I was just in Detroit yesterday visiting with her, and never told her that I was pregnant. We spoke for a while this evening though, and I believe that she's dealing with this pretty well. She did ask me to come back to Detroit to see her again. I told her I would return as soon as I could. I didn't make any specific promises, but I would like to go back there early next week. She is also being scheduled for her operation very soon. So that's something else that I'll need to get my hands around."

They never really ended their conversation. They just gradually prepared for bed and continued chatting until they both faded off to sleep. They nestled close to one another in the center of a king size bed and Josh kept his arm wrapped around his lover's body until they were both unconscious. They had very similar dreams and when they awakened in the morning they shared these dreams with each other. Then they came to a very similar conclusion.

****

Alison and Abby McDuffee were waiting in the Park Avenue conference room of Silverstein Associates for the appearance of the legendary Seth Silverstein. He was running about fifteen minutes late. Abby thumbed through a number of magazines. She noticed that many of them contained ads and articles about people and businesses, which were clients of Silverstein Associates. Silverstein's range of clients was very interesting. There were actresses and actors, athletes, restaurants and spas, religious leaders, book authors, small businesses and products, and large businesses and brands. It was an eclectic clientele, and it was difficult to see any specific theme surrounding the various clients. Amongst the very wide range of celebrities there were two interesting names; Gina Alvarez and Danielle Dubonet.

Before too long the door to the conference room opened and in walked Seth Silverstein. He had neatly groomed dark hair and was wearing a dark pinstripe suit and a wide full-toothed smile. He was thick-bodied and had a rotund boisterous presence that made all of his guests and clients instantly like him. His unusual warmth and radiance were either an innate personality trait or a well-developed professional skill, but either way Seth Silverstein was simply a very engaging individual.

"Now which one of you is Abby? Which one of you is the person who met one of my favorite people in the world, Danielle?"

"I guess that would be me," indicated Abby. "We met a couple of weeks back in Germany. She was with her husband at a business dinner that we held to discuss the Rhapsody project. It was such a pleasant surprise for me. I didn't know that she was married to Stephen Struben. I knew that Stephen was bringing his wife to dinner, but I was absolutely fascinated to find out who his wife was."

"I thought that Abby was losing it, when she told me she didn't know they were related. Not only is the connection between Josh, Gina and Danielle all over the TV and the Internet but also I could have sworn we talked about it when we were in Hong Kong. But you'll have to excuse my sister; she doesn't pay much attention to the celebrity scene."

"Well, I guess I will have to see what we can do to fix that." Seth beamed a broad smile."

"They were actually very down-to-earth people," Abby offered. "Very nice people….. And of course they gave us your name." Abby was attempting to bridge to the business at hand, but Seth was still interested in friendly chitchat.

"Aren't they just wonderful people though, Stephen and Danielle? I just absolutely love that couple. They are a real rarity in this day and age. Do you know that they've been married for more than 30 years? I would do just about anything for Danielle. I have known her for many many years, and I've never heard her say a bad thing about anyone. And he's the same way. Stephen is always out to help, always trying to assist others, and never looking for a thing in return. Wonderful people… just wonderful people!"

"You should know that we have asked Stephen to be on the board of Rhapsody Holdings. He hasn't yet accepted but we anticipate that we'll get a positive response as long as he can clear any potential business conflicts that he might have with respect to the consulting work that he does for STRX."

"That's wonderful. For your sake I hope he accepts."

The conference room door opened and Seth's personal assistant came into the room and after apologizing for the interruption, handed Seth a note and gave him a look that indicated the contents were important. Seth read the note and shrugged his shoulders and said; "Move things around. Fit him into my schedule later this afternoon." His assistant then turned and left the room.

Silverstein looked at his two guests and said, "It really is a small world. Isn't it now? That note was actually concerning Stephen and Danielle's son, Josh. I've never met him, although I do know that he's a very successful investment banker type. And as fate would have it, he is also quite friendly with another one of my clients."

"That would be none other than Gina Alvarez I guess." Alison finally added her two cents to the conversation.

Silverstein gave a full body-shaking chortle, without having it seem like a guffaw. He had the uncanny aptitude to smile broadly and speak at the same time. But he was careful not to directly confirm Alison's assumption. "There really is no *new* news in the world today is there? I'm not sure what Josh wants, but I certainly will be very interested in meeting him. And as you indicated earlier there are more than a few Internet stories circulating about Josh."

Alison stared directly at Seth and stated, "Actually both Abby and I have met Josh. In fact we met Josh, before Abby met Stephen and Danielle. That's part of the way we got to meet the Struben's in the first place. We were discussing some secondary funding options with Josh while we were in Hong Kong. Josh was over there for a number of weeks representing Cromwell Parsons Resources and we met with him a couple of times over the course of two days. He is one very impressive young man. I'm sure that you will find him to be every bit as interesting as your clients."

The conversation flowed back and forth and no notes were taken either by the McDuffees or by Silverstein. They truly were accomplishing the objective of the meeting, which was to simply get to know one another. However a lot more was going on. Abby felt a growing rapport with Silverstein and Silverstein was beginning to understand that McDuffee sisters and Rhapsody Holdings were very marketable assets.

The level of service that Rhapsody intended to provide for its clientele fascinated Silverstein. Unlike others who had concerns about the scope of the project, Silverstein seemed to bask in the very magnitude of the undertaking. The more questions he asked the more answers the McDuffee sisters delivered. This was obviously an effort that had been thought through over and over again. But Silverstein was concerned that the project didn't readily lend itself to an elevator speech for explanation and clarification. He thought about all of the anecdotes that had been presented during their meeting and how best these might be captured, digested and understood by the high-end consumer. Then he had an idea.

"You know what you should do? Write a book!"

****

Dr. Al Moses was not accustomed to being the patient. He was more familiar with the role of healer than he was with the role of patient. Nonetheless Dr. Al looked forward to his session with Dr Greg Mendelsohn, his psychiatrist. There seemed to be so much to talk about. He wanted to talk about the fact that he was no longer speaking unilaterally to Dr. Anne Mohr before he went to bed at night. He also wanted to discuss the fact that he was actually dating one of his patients. And he wanted to see if Dr. Mendelsohn regarded his relationship with Maria Cardoza as being in any way illicit.

As Al Moses entered Mendelsohn's office he was sitting on the bay window staring out at the park. Mendelsohn stood and greeted Al, inviting him to be seated anywhere he wished. Al looked around the expansive high-ceilinged office, and had a feeling that someone would be watching them from above whenever the two men decided to sit down together and talk. Al chose a comfortable beige couch, with three throw pillows and sat down near one end of it, pulling one of the pillows on to his lap as he sat. Mendelsohn sat down on another couch catty cornered to the couch that Al had selected.

"So how have the holidays been going for you, Al?"

"Very well thanks. In fact I've been more active this year over the holiday season than I have been in recent years. It's been a combination of more work and a little more social life."

"It's great to hear. So does that mean that you have begun to confront your loneliness, or should I say your shyness?"

"Yes absolutely. I have begun to behave in a way that no one would ever believe that I would've ever complained about being shy or lonely. I'm seeing a few more patients than I normally have, and my days are filled with interesting people. I think part of the problem that I've been experiencing, has come from cutting back on my practice over the last few years. I feel better seeing more people. That is to say I feel better seeing more people, as long as I can give them all the attention they deserve. I'm sure that you can relate to that."

"In a way I can now. However my practice is relatively structured in one-hour segments, 4 1/2 days a week. But let's talk about you. How are you making out with your discussions with Anne Mohr?"

"Good, I guess … What I mean is … I'm not having those conversations anymore. At least I haven't had any of them recently."

"And how do you feel about that? Do you miss them? Do you miss those conversations? Do you miss Anne Mohr?"

"The best way to express how I feel is to tell you that the conversations that I was having with Anne were beginning to bother me a lot. Over the years it was just a simple game that made me happy. But I knew they had to stop. And frankly I'm glad they have stopped."

"When did you realize that these conversations had to stop and what triggered your decision to get help with respect to these conversations?"

"I've resisted telling you this until now, but I did have an incident, that as you say *triggered* my decision. One night when I came home after a relatively routine day, I put a gun in my mouth and cocked the trigger. That wasn't a good night."

"Had you ever done that before?"

Al was prepared to reflexively answer, "No." However he stopped himself and answered the question truthfully, "I think that was the fourth time…obviously always with the same result."

"Maybe not. This time you decided to come here. This time you are looking for help. That's a different outcome from the other times, I take it?" Mendelsohn was trying to help Al add more outcome options to the bipolarity of life or death.

"That's true," Al readily accepted Mendelsohn's premise.

"So assuming that you felt you that you had good reason to do what you did, or almost did, what made you stop?"

"As strange as it may seem it was one of my patients. I felt that I would be letting down one of my patients in particular. I imagine that my decision was by the narrowest of margins, but I had just begun to become closer to this particular patient. And I guess that relationship had meaning to me. Obviously what I needed was meaning beyond what I could conjure up in my conversations with Anne."

"Interesting …Tell me more."

"More about what …? More about the conversations with Anne again …? Or more about the patient?"

"The latter."

"There's a young lady who has been a patient of mine for several years. However prior to the last year or so, I was only seeing her for routine checkups. About a year ago she began having difficulties with her menstrual cycle, and I started seeing her more frequently. She was concerned that she may be suffering a case of POF, that's 'premature ovarian failure.' We ran the normal tests and her results showed that her FSH levels weren't very high and so we were not really concerned that there was a serious physical problem involved."

"Go on," Mendelsohn encouraged him.

"Now let me tell you this is a particularly beautiful young woman. Her name is Maria Cardoza."

"No need for full names Al. Let's just call her Maria for now."

"Okay."

"Remember our only interest in Maria is her impact, or potential impact, on my therapy for you."

"Of course."

"All right … so you started to tell me that Maria was a strikingly lovely young lady. How young is young? May I ask?"

"Maria is thirty-five, I believe … and I am sixty-six years old … so thirty-five … to me … is very young."

"I guess it depends on the context in which you see Maria. Doesn't it?"

"Yes. And this is where we get to some of the reasons why she is important to me … Or I guess why she is important to my therapy. Maria began seeing me, as I said, because of issues with her menstrual cycle. Over a period of time we developed a personal relationship wherein she began to ask me for advice.

"She had just left a business … or at least a job … where she had worked for more than four years. She wasn't unhappy about leaving the job. In fact she quit. But she was a little unsettled about what she wanted to do next. I recommended that she see Angelique Lefebvre. I don't know if you know Angelique?"

"I know of her. But I don't know her. At least we've never met."

"Well Angelique is a therapist, and her husband is a yoga instructor, actually a rather prominent yoga instructor. So I recommended that Maria see Angelique and in the process she also started taking yoga lessons with Yogi Vijay."

"Sounds as though that all worked out very well for both you and for Maria. As I said we want to discuss you not one of your patients. But I get the feeling that I haven't heard this entire story. Correct?"

"That's right. I continued to see Maria about her gynecological issues, and in the process I made some relatively routine inquiries about her sexuality. It seems that she has been involved in a monogamous relationship with one man for the past several years, and that man was her married boss. When she left the employ of the company where she was working, there was also a breakup of her relationship with her former boss."

"Maybe we're going a little too far off track here. I don't yet quite see how this involves you and your therapy." Mendelsohn gave Dr. Al a thoughtful glance and at the same time he stroked both sides of his beard with his right hand.

"It's coming, believe me, it's coming. To cut to the chase, at the very hour of her departure from her company, her boss impregnated her. Since that time I have been counseling her with respect to the various options that she might have regarding her child. For the record, Maria has elected to keep her baby."

"Quite a compelling story, but I have to say I'm still not certain about the impact of this patient upon you as her doctor. What I mean to say is that I'm not sure why this particular situation is so compelling to you. You must deal with these kinds of situations on a relatively regular and routine basis."

"I know you're pushing for this answer so I'll give it to you. Maria Cardoza reminds me very much of my former partner, Anne Mohr. They both are very beautiful women, and in some ways….. I have to admit it….. Maria is filling a hole in my heart that has been there since Anne died. Recently I just took Anne … I mean Maria … out to dinner and we had a lovely time."

"Okay!!! Now I get it. It took a little while to get that out. Now, didn't it?"

"Yes it did. But please understand that there are many similarities between Anne and Maria. One major similarity is that Anne also became pregnant out of wedlock. She became pregnant with my daughter. But she miscarried."

"You know, Al … that you are on very dangerous ground here. It's not just that you are dating one of your patients; this can also complicate your own personal therapy. Frankly I don't see anything positive that can emanate from this relationship. But of course that's just my opinion…..for what it's worth. You're both adults and obviously you'll both make your own decisions. However as you have already indicated you are 33 years older than Maria. Do you think that the age difference comes into play here in any way?"

"I'm not sure, Greg. I'm just not sure."

Dr Al Moses was not worried. Dr Greg Mendelsohn was very concerned.

****

"So you see John, the options that you have are not limited but they certainly are defined. You may elect to continue to treat your pain, as you have been over the last several years. And this treatment may include some new therapies, or maybe even a more aggressive physical therapy routine. Or then again the other option that we discussed is to have surgery." The neurosurgeon, Dr Thomas Madison, peered out over his reading glasses and gestured with an open palm. He wore a large loose unbuttoned white surgical coat that covered his shirt and tie. He appeared quite professional as he spoke.

"Can I be certain that I will be pain free after this operation?"

"No, you can't. Unfortunately life is not filled with such certainties. However statistically speaking there is a high probability that the operation we discussed will alleviate the pain that you have been feeling, after the initial recovery period."

"I don't really want to hear about *statistically speaking*' People are always quoting me statistics. Sometimes I think they do that to obfuscate the truth. Let's deal with this in best case/worst-case scenarios. I already know the best case: no pain. What's the worst case?" JB snapped at the doctor as though he were a summer intern at ICD.

"I heard that you were going to be a difficult person to deal with. Now I know why." The surgeon chuckled as he spoke, more to put himself at ease than to calm John. "Okay … worst case of course is that you don't make it through the operation … that we have a problem with the anesthesia … or the surgery itself … and your body goes into trauma … and you die. Is that what you wanted to hear?"

"I've got news for you. That's not the worst case. The worst case is that I still have this god-awful pain."

"Okay John, I understand. But just to clear the decks on all of the risk factors … There is also a risk of paralysis that might occur about once in every six thousand cases like yours."

"How many of these operations have you done personally?"

"More than twelve hundred."

"How many of your patients have been paralyzed?"

"None. Thank God."

"I hope that doesn't mean that your number is up, or should I say that my number is up. You know what I mean, *statistically speaking*."

"John … you are just going to have to be more positive about all this. It's the only way that you should be thinking. Positive! Positive! Positive!"

About a half-hour later, John left the office of the neurosurgeon and returned to his limousine Caitlin Browning was waiting for him. He had decided to go ahead with the surgery sometime in mid January. The moment he had made the decision his back started feeling better.

****

Maria Cardoza was determined that this would be her last session with Angelique Lefebvre. Maria liked Angelique and she thought that she was as competent as any other therapist. The reality was that her sessions with Angelique could be compromised because her friendship with Al Moses was developing and Al had referred Maria to Angelique in a professional context. Another reality was that Maria was gaining significantly more satisfaction from her yoga sessions with Yogi Vijay than she was from the couch counseling that she was receiving from Angelique.

"Maria, I always begin my sessions with you by telling you how beautiful you are. You have mentioned this as a concern of yours in the past and I think it's a good idea to simply confirm your attractiveness on an ongoing basis. You are truly a beautiful physical specimen. Now we want to work on letting your inner beauty emerge as well." Angelique said all of this as if she were reciting from a manual. But she wanted it to have just that effect. She wanted Maria to see her external beauty as an asset, not as a concern.

"Thank you Angelique. That's very nice of you to say. But to be quite candid I am going through a physical transformation of sorts. I am pregnant." Maria didn't waste any time getting to the point. However she shocked Dr Lefebvre a bit by the bold pronouncement.

"Really! How long have you known?" Angelique's eyes narrowed as she spoke. She was careful to observe without staring.

"I am about two months along. The baby is healthy and I'm happy with the idea of motherhood." Maria took the time to establish eye contact and to be certain that Angelique understood the unambiguous nature of her resolve. Maria kept her hands folded daintily in her lap and Angelique fiddled with a Montblanc pen, holding it with the first three fingers of both hands and twirling it as she spoke.

"Would you like to discuss the child's father?"

"We *have* discussed the father in many of our previous sessions. The father is John Brady. And before you ask I will tell you. John does not know about the baby, yet, and probably never will know."

Angelique continued to twirl her pen and thoughtfully twisted her facial features as though she had tasted a lemon. "Well Maria, the first thing I should say to you is congratulations. The second thing I want to say is that you certainly brought us an interesting topic of conversation for our session today. Have you shared your news with anyone else?"

"Dr Al knows."

"Of course." Angelique said this in a dismissive way, readily acknowledging that Maria's gynecologist would obviously be privy to the fact that she was pregnant.

"There really isn't anyone else that I believe has a need to know. I don't have any extended family anymore. I'm trying *not* to spend much time with friends from my ICD days. I am very much trying to look forward rather than backward. And for the most part I think I have been successful in doing just that. Besides my sessions with you and my daily sessions with Vijay, I've been filling my days looking for opportunities in the spa business. So I have had a luncheon or two with some people that my lawyer has introduced me to."

"Doesn't your decision to become a mother have some impact on these other professional decisions that you will be making?"

"I'm sure there will be opportunities that a pregnant woman could pursue just as easily as any other professional woman. I'm not sure it makes a difference. Would you be practicing your profession any differently if you were pregnant?" Maria stewed a bit and was a little indignant and she wanted it to sound that way.

"Possibly. For example, in that hypothetical situation, I would have to make time for gynecological appointments and the like. I would probably cut back on my hours slightly. And then as I got closer to my delivery date I would probably opt to take a leave of absence. And then after delivery I would need to make the necessary adjustments that come with balancing career and motherhood. But those were never adjustments that I got the opportunity to make. And my childbearing years are now behind me. Let's focus on you. What are some of the things that you have been thinking about when you think about motherhood?"

"First and foremost I want to deliver a healthy baby. I will do everything within my power to ensure that happens. I do think beyond the birth of my child, however. I realize that I will have to do some growing on my own to learn to become a good mother."

"And just how would you define a 'good mother'?"

"I'll start by saying that I need to provide a loving environment where my child would be able to learn to be a productive member of society. And most of all I would want my child to be happy and to feel loved, by me, and by others, as she grew older."

"You said 'she.' Do you know that it's going to be girl?"

"No. I don't actually know the gender of my child yet, although I will know soon. But for whatever reason, in my mind, I have a feeling that my child is a girl."

"Well as you said you will know soon enough. Have you given consideration to who else may love your child? Do you think the child's father will love him or her?"

"Yes. I have thought a lot about this. I am certain that I will love my child and I am reasonably sure that John would rather not be bothered."

"Do you intend to give him that option?"

"No. Frankly I do not."

They wrapped up the session with some additional discussion about Maria's daily activities. Maria did not mention anything about having dinner with Dr. Al Moses, or how she felt about that dinner. That was the one important issue, besides her child, that had been occupying her consciousness for the last few days.

After Maria left her office Angelique looked at her pad and the one and only note that she had written: "*Maria's hiding something.*" She decided that they would get to that next time. However, Maria didn't think there would be a next time.

* * * * * * * * *

Alison McDuffee and Dao Diskul sat in the lobby of the Sheraton on Avenue of the Americas, and talked with Mark Candu. Dao had just arrived in the city and Candu was on his way out of town, so the hotel lobby was the most convenient meeting space for the threesome. Candu was a very interesting young man. Although still in his early

30s he had already earned two PhD's, and had a strong interest in what was right and wrong in the healthcare industry. He also was completely unabashed about offering his opinions on these topics.

Dao and Alison shared the responsibility of building a broad-based GPS for Rhapsody Holdings. They knew that they would need lots of help. And they were aware of the fact that there were people like Mark Candu who were wired into large groups of practitioners. They spent a lot of time speaking at conventions. Candu had two specific areas of interest, genomic testing and stem cell research. A self-described "geek" Candu's research had led him to believe that many of the medical approaches that existed in 2008 would become obsolete within the next decade. Therefore he had a strong interest in what Dao and Alison and her team at Rhapsody Holdings wanted to achieve. He had received an overview of Rhapsody's business from Josh Struben, who had recently agreed to invest in one of Candu's businesses. Struben believed that there would be some synergies between the businesses and Candu was following up on that.

"We heard that Cromwell Parsons has recently made an investment in one of your companies. Congratulations. In this day and age it's hard to get anyone to invest in anything." Alison's tone was friendly and her smile conveyed warmth and confidence. Dao sat comfortably by her side and listened. She was a bit tired from her long flight in from Bangkok, but she was determined to make it through several meetings that were planned for the next 24 hours.

"Yes one of the business initiatives that we have undertaken with a few colleagues is to build a business that offers genetic testing and genetic screening for things such as predisposition to a given disease, or a predetermined treatment course based upon one's genetic makeup. Based upon what Josh told me, there may be an opportunity for us to co-venture some of our products by working with or through Rhapsody."

"We are very interested in "personalized medicine," and the kinds of preventative tests that can enhance the possibility of living a longer life."

"So I've heard. Is this something that you are going to be offering to your membership?"

"Yes absolutely. In fact we have a significant interest in providing the widest range of services possible to our clientele. And we also want to provide the most advanced information and healthcare assessment possibilities that are available on the market today, and for that matter that will be available tomorrow, next week, next month or next year.

"Part of our product line is something we call the *Rhapsody HealthMap.* We realize that not all of our members will want to take advantage of our genomic testing as part of their particular *HealthMap*, but we expect a high percentage of our members will want such a service."

"My colleagues and I have found that lots of people are somewhat confused by the rapidly evolving area of predictive medicine, as a subset of personalized medicine. In particular the approaches of genomics and proteomics need to be fleshed out a good bit more to fulfill the promise of the new medical age that was supposed to have been ushered in by the completion of the mapping of the human genome. It's not only consumers who are confused. Physicians are not up to speed either. For example they continue to prescribe drugs for patients who can't benefit from them. If they had done a genetic screening ahead of time they would have realized this. Then they would not have prescribed the particular drug for the particular malady, even though it might have been effective for another patient with the same health problem. They would then have avoided all the risks associated with the side effects of the drug."

Mark Candu looked down at his shoes for a moment as he spoke, but his tone was full of confidence. He seemed to believe that they were on the right track but that there was a lot of track in front of them before they got to their destination.

Dao Diskul believed that Mark Candu was just the type of person that they needed as part of Rhapsody's scientific community. Even though he was a little dorky looking, he was young and energetic. She knew enough about his previous success to realize that he was also both pragmatic and the progressive. It was just the combination they needed to knit together the many disparate opinions that would come from various members of the Rhapsody GPS.

Mark Candu wanted to get across another point before they moved on.

"What interests me about Rhapsody is the opportunity to provide our services directly to the retail marketplace. Candidly the kind of testing that we do today is provided to institutions, so that they can provide information to their clients. To a degree this is not a bad model. At least it has some built-in efficiencies. But what I don't like about it is that my company is not talking directly to the consumer.

The end consumer is educated through the practitioner, who may or may not be up to date on the available screenings. The consumer remains unaware of the wide range of tests that are available.

"If we were able to interact directly with the consumer we all might be able to move a little faster." Candu was suggesting something that at first sounded radical. He seemed to be questioning the efficacy, maybe even the ethics, of physicians, whom he simply regarded as a middleman. His suggestion sounded liked a classic business school case of disintermediation. This was pretty direct talk considering his audience consisted of two physicians.

Alison stretched her long legs out in front of her and exhaled before responding. "Dr Candu, you seem to be suggesting that most physicians don't have their patients' best interests at heart, or that they are not keeping up with the scientific breakthroughs that will help their patients. Those are rather strong assertations." Alison purposely recognized Mark Candu's PhD when addressing him, so as to indicate that pomposity was not limited to the medical profession. However she was really just testing him. She agreed with almost everything he was saying.

"Please don't take this the wrong way. I believe that the vast majority of physicians want to do the right thing. But they have trouble keeping up. They also deal with a wide spectrum of different clientele. The reason that Rhapsody interests me is that the GPS provides a forum for us to educate practitioners worldwide. And secondly Rhapsody's members will be the precise clientele that we would like to serve. In general they are educated, health-conscious, and financially secure. This is the ideal group to help us roll out many of our genomic breakthroughs. Once the Rhapsody Membership embraces what can be done in the area of personalized healthcare, it will trickle down market effectively over time."

"That's exactly how we see it also," said Alison. "We plan on convening the first meeting of the GPS leadership team in California next month. We'd like you to join us if you can."

"Flip me an email with the dates and the details. I live up in the Silicon Valley area, so I can get there easily enough."

The two women talked with the young biologist for a little while longer until he had to get a cab to the airport. They wondered how many similar conversations with other scientists and physicians they would have in the next twelve months. They also wondered how they would balance the activities of their respective practices until the funding was secure and they could work the Rhapsody business full time. They would have to discuss this with Abby.

****

Neither Stephen nor Danielle felt awkward about the situation. They felt that they were needed and that helped alleviate any uncomfortable feelings that they may have had. Nevertheless when Josh opened the door with Gina by his side, he surprised his parents with this introductory salutation.

"Come on in Mum and Dad. I'd like you to meet my fiancée, Gina."

"Fiancée? Did you say fiancée? What have we missed?" Stephen said this in a manner that was not at all challenging, but rather engaging and hopeful.

"Yes I know things are happening pretty fast around here," said Josh. "But you and Mum might as well be the first to know that Gina and I have decided to marry."

"That's *terreefeec* news! But let us get *een* the door before you bowl us over with new news *eef* you *weell.*" Danielle moved quickly across the threshold, then past her son, and reached out with both hands towards Gina's hands in a warm and friendly greeting. The two singers made an immediate electronic bond. They looked at one another eyeball to eyeball and there was an instantaneous almost eerie cosmic connection. There was a shared realization of an unspoken something or other that united them in spirit from this very moment when they met. The bonding was woman-to-woman; artist-to-artist and certainly anything but daughter-in-law to mother-in-law.

"Hello Danielle. Hello Stephen. Please come in and sit down. Thank you for coming over this morning. I think things may get pretty busy around here before too long and I apologize for that. But I hope that we get some time to spend with one another before the phone starts ringing off the hook."

"Gina, we just want to be *'ere* to *'elp* you and Josh. So whatever needs to be done, don't be afraid to just do *eet.* We certainly won't be at all offended. As I said we're *'ere* to *'elp een* whatever way we can. Stephen and I are *threelled* to hear about your engagement. Josh *ees* our son, and we want our son to be *'appy.* He *ees* obviously *'appy* to be engaged to you, and so even though we are just *meeteeng* for the first time, we are pleased that the two of you seem to know what you're *doeeng.* Congratulations."

"Thank you Danielle. You don't know how good that makes me feel. It certainly is a little awkward meeting you and Stephen for the first time under these circumstances. I'm still glad we're meeting. Josh and I are still dealing with our loss. But it appears that even in our loss we have found each other in a way that we have underappreciated over the past several months."

"That's right," Josh chimed in. "When we both woke up this morning, we had a similar thing on our minds. While we both felt the loss of our child, we also both felt the rebirth of our love for one another. About three hours ago, I asked Gina to marry me and about two hours and 59 minutes ago she said yes."

Danielle and Stephen Struben sat down on the couch in the antechamber to the suite and Josh and Gina reclined across from them. The emotions of the moment swirled around the room like dandelion seeds being blown from their stalk in a stiff summer breeze.

After the drama of the opening introductions, Stephen tried to break the ice with a simple question about Gina's tour. "Are you ready to settle down and take a little vacation after the hectic tour that you have been on? It has been almost three months. Hasn't it?"

"Yes it has, but honestly, it's been an absolute ball. And if I'm tired from rocking out in all of these cities around the world, it's news to me. We have had a great time. People have been wonderful to us just about everywhere we went. I have no complaints at all. The press coverage can be a bit smothering, but they have their job to do also. So I tend to look at that as just a simple game of hide and seek. I do all the hiding and they do all the seeking. But frankly, it works."

"I know *eet's* not easy *dealeeng weeth* the media. And we all recognize, Gina, that they *weell* be very aggressive *een* the next 48+ hours. *'ave* you contacted Seth Silverstein yet, to *'elp* you *weeth* all of *thees*?"

Josh didn't wait for Gina to answer. He jumped in and said, "I just called his office right before you came, Mum. I wanted to introduce myself to him and make sure that he knows all of the facts so that he can help us avoid any negative press. I'm going to meet him a little later this afternoon and I'll be sure to pass along your regards."

"Seth *ees* the best. *Ee'll* be able to *'elp* you, I'm sure. Just trust *heem* because *'e ees* very trustworthy. *Ee'll* make sure that *everytheeng* gets *'andled* in the right way."

"So, now that you kids are engaged, do you have a wedding date planned?" Stephen asked his question in an innocuous way.

"Sorry Dad. We've only been engaged for three hours. We haven't even gotten an engagement ring yet. It's a simple story. We are engaged....details to follow." They all had a laugh at this and they were beginning to grow a little more comfortable with one another.

Josh walked into the bedroom area and picked up the telephone. He called down for room service and asked that they bring up some sandwiches and beverages. He didn't bother to inquire about the preferences of the others. He just ordered a variety of sandwiches and fruits sufficient to satisfy their lunch needs.

"By the way," Danielle said after a while. "Josh tells me that your mother *'as* been quite *eell*. *'Ow ees* she *doeeng*?"

"Yes. Thank you for asking. She is doing okay for now. But it looks as though she will have to have an operation in a little more than a week. The doctors say that her prognosis for a full recovery is good. But frankly I want to know a lot more. And speaking of health issues, how are you doing? Josh told me that you had a bit of a scare. I'm sorry I didn't ask about it earlier. Sometimes I can get caught up a little bit in my own issues."

"Don't be *seelly*. You *'ave* a real-time *eessue* that you needed to deal *weeth*, particularly because you *'ave* the media watching your every step. Believe me I understand. Besides, the *diagnosees eendeecating* I had breast cancer, turned out to be just a scare. But *eet* has certainly made me *theenk* a lot about healthcare *een* general. *Eet's* so *deeffeecult* these days to find out what's right to do, whether *eet's* your *meescarriage*, your mother's *respeeratory* problems, or my fantasy breast cancer. I have been *theenkeeng* about all these *theengs* quite a *beet* lately. Stephen has been *theenkeeng* about them as well."

"When we were in Hong Kong together, Josh mentioned something about a company called Rhapsody, that he was working with, and had some very good ideas about how to pull all these disparate problems together. I thought he mentioned that Stephen might be involved with these folks in some way also. Is that right?"

"Yes. *Een* fact Stephen and I had *deenner* not too long ago *weeth* two of the *executeeves* of the *buseeness*. I like them a lot and I'm encouraging Stephen to get more *eenvolved weeth* them. You should ask Josh a *leettle beet* more about them. *Eet's* all very *eenteresting*. You never know. Maybe we can all *'elp* them out *een* some way. I'd like to do *anytheeng* I can to advance the cause of *haveeng* greater access to my own healthcare *eenformation*."

"I will ask Josh more about Rhapsody. Once we get past the next few days I'm sure I'll have more time. From what Josh has told me this group is also very involved in longevity and has a strong emphasis on wellness, fitness and preventative care. These are all issues that are important to me. I think about them a lot. And in my spare time I've been reading a lot about 'mind-body-spirit' approaches to overall happiness. It's all very fascinating."

The lunch hour spilled into the early afternoon. Adam came by the suite with his on-again, off-again girl friend, Celine, and Gina put in another call to her mother and they spoke privately. Josh fielded a call from Pepper Gordon and placed another call to Seth Silverstein. Stephen Struben spoke with Adam and Celine and there was a general hubbub around the suite that made Gina feel much more comfortable. It was the type of frenzy to which she had grown accustomed.

Chapter 13: *The Battle Lines are Drawn*

The 2009 New Year arrived with much new hope that the financial struggles of 2008 would begin to dissipate. Worldwide credit markets were still tight but the New Year began with a few new debt offerings issued by blue-chip multinational corporations. However the financial crisis was continuing to cost jobs around the world and confidence was shaky at best. The Rhapsody Holdings team was concerned about having enough cash on hand to get through to a time when they would be able to draw down on the line of credit that was being arranged with European banks through the intermediary work of the Louisiana Group. Meanwhile it was business as usual as they kept the ball moving forward on all aspects of the business.

Abby McDuffee called for a three day meeting of the executive team and several interested advisers to take place in the warmth of Southern California. It was the first week in January and it was time to divvy up the workload that was in front of them. The conference room where they were planning their work was large and spacious, and had a conference table that could sit as many as eighteen people. They started their meeting with seven people, but they expected others to join them over the course of the three-day meeting.

Abby McDuffee flew into LAX after spending the holidays with her family back in New York. Alison McDuffee and her husband and their two children spent New Year's Eve at their West Coast home where Dao Diskul joined them as a houseguest. Sandeep Mehra and Ben Hui Zhang flew in from India and two new additions to the executive team had also come into town for the meeting as well. Maria Cardoza had accepted a role as the executive director of Rhapsody's Spa businesses and Stephen Struben came out to the meeting as an "advisor," as he was still seeking clearance to join the team as a Board Member.

"Good morning everyone and welcome to sunny Southern California. Those of us who live in the northeast part of the US might be interested to hear that New York City is experiencing temperatures in the teens with the prospects of 3 to 4 inches of snow. It's nice to be enjoying the seventy-degree temperatures here in Orange County." Abby was starting off the meeting by making everyone comfortable.

After her introductions of the people at the table Abby continued to describe the work plan for the next three days.

"We are not short on challenges at this point in the short history of our company. However our long suit is significant business acumen and a strong will to succeed. With that in mind we need to lay out some of the tasks in front of us. Some of these may seem like I'm overstating the obvious; other items may seem more monumental in scope. However taking all of these items together, they will serve as a starting to-do list for the executive team. From there we will need to devise our Critical Success Factors (CSF's) and the subtending Key Performance Indicators (KPI's)

"In a few minutes we will have an update from the Louisiana Group with respect to the funding. Assuming that we will have our credit line approved and advanced, we will need to spring into action. We have a number of legal issues that outside counsel will be helping us resolve.

"As you all are aware, we have been operating on a bit of a shoestring the last two years. We haven't generated any revenue to speak of and for that matter don't intend to generate significant revenues for another nine months. Therefore we are very much dependent upon getting closure with the Louisiana Group on our $300 million line of credit with the European banks. The line of credit will be secured by the Louisiana Group's oil and gas lease assets. We hope to have the first tranche of our funding available later this week and with that we will officially launch the deployment of the Rhapsody Holdings. Other major items on our list in the short term include putting employment contracts in place for each of the executives and starting the revamped budgeting process, from which we will develop critical path timeline for the business.

"In the IT area we need to rapidly renegotiate our contract with STRX and if appropriate with Apakoh, in the Ukraine, to complete the *Rhapsody HealthPort* project. We will also need to revamp our website, reinitialize our ERP systems and re-create our membership accounts database. The *HealthMap* analytical engine, graphical interface and multiple-level dashboard capabilities will also need to be developed in collaboration with a strong IT/integration partner. These are just a few of the major tasks that we have to undertake in the IT arena.

"We will continue our negotiations for real estate for our first centre in New York, and we will work with architectural partners to make sure that our centre design is everything that we planned for. The good news there is that the lease rates for property in NYC are dropping precipitously as we speak.

"With respect to our GPS, negotiations have to be closed out with one of the three university aligned medical groups that we have been speaking with in New York, so they are ready to support our pilot phase which we will roll out this summer. We also need to contractualize agreements with one hundred or so physicians, hospital/specialist group practices and practitioners around the world. As some of you are aware, Allie and Dao have been working on this already for quite some time. However in addition to completing the contracts we will certify the practitioners through the Rhapsody certification program that has been under development for the last four months. None of this is simple. We certainly have our work cut out for us and we do want every member of the team to execute flawlessly and rapidly.

"Our *RhapsodyCare* program is still not anywhere near ready for prime time. For sure this is one of the items that we will move up on the critical path, in order for us to be ready with the pilot during the summer months. This includes staffing and manning a 24/7 call center that we will initially outsource."

Abby's voice did not shake at all while she laid out many of the tasks that were ahead of the team. Although she didn't mince any words while addressing the many challenges that they faced, she also spoke with the confident air of a leader who had met big challenges in the past during her career. She looked from face-to-face around the table as she spoke and watched as her teammates nodded in recognition as she made her points.

"Let's get Bob Johnstone on the phone and see what he and the Louisiana Group have to say by way of an update."

"Check your blackberry, Abby. We just got an email from Johnstone fifteen minutes ago. He says that he is still working with the European banks and that he will not have an update for another week," Ben said.

Abby was disappointed but she did her best not to show any negative reaction to Johnstone's email. They had work to do and sooner or later that work would get funded.

The rest of the morning and early afternoon was taken up by a variety of updates from people, who were added by way of conference call. Seth Silverstein called in from New York and a representative from STRX made a PowerPoint presentation remotely from Munich. Others called with questions and/or answers related to the execution plan of the business. The afternoon was spent collaboratively working on a set of 5 Critical Success Factors for the business. When they broke late in the day the process was nearly half completed and they decided to take up the work again the following morning.

****

John Brady finished his Board Meeting and was ready to meet with Paul Pritchard and Chipper Geld, who were waiting downtown at Pritchard's newly-leased office space. JB purposely didn't bring his EA, Caitlin Browning, with him to the meeting. And Browning was also not at the ICD board meeting when the board discussed and approved a $50 million funding from the strategic equity fund of ICD. JB had been selective about what he chose his EA to see and hear in meetings in the past and therefore it was not regarded as noteworthy when she was not invited to take notes at the meeting.

Brady intended to inform Caitlin of selected details following the meetings. When Brady pulled up outside of Pritchard's new offices, he instructed Fernando, his driver, to pick him up in ninety minutes. When Brady entered Pritchard's office, he noticed two other men waiting with Geld and Pritchard. Pritchard quickly introduced the two as Mel Geist and Eric Mallory. Geist was a financier who was now working with Pritchard on their new private equity fund. Mallory was a recruited executive, who was potentially slated to become the CEO of the new business that Pritchard, Geld and Brady were forming. Geld himself was serving as acting CEO in the interim, for the purpose of pacifying the other investors from Paul Pritchard's new fund. The company had recently been incorporated under the name of Fundamental Health Resources, or FHR. The mission of the new company was to put together a membership offering for health and wellness services.

"How did you make out at the board meeting John?" Pritchard didn't waste any time with small talk but got right to the point.

"I usually get what I want when I go before the board. Today was no different." JB had a certain innate arrogance when he spoke. His tone rarely varied and his posture always portrayed an "I am the boss," type of attitude. Most of this attitude had evolved since he became

CEO of ICD. When he was working his way up the chain of command he had his moments when he was required to be deferential to others. He never liked those moments and so in some ways they added to his arrogance once he became the head man.

"I feel that we have commitments for up to $40 million from the fund that we are managing together. So our target of $50 million appears very reasonable. Together with the $50 million committed from ICD's strategic equity fund we will have all the capital needed to get a leg up on the competition. To be candid, even though we have the necessary commitments for financial backing, we have not totally structured the business plan in a final form. So it remains to be negotiated between us, meaning between the Pritchard group and ICD, as to what our respective equity stakes will be and which portions of the committed funding will be equity stakes and which portions will be convertible debt. We will need to hammer these details out within the next couple of weeks so that Mallory here can get started on the process of hiring his team." Pritchard attempted to lay out the details of their meeting, so that there would be no mistake about the challenges that lay in front of them.

"I already have more than two dozen feelers out in the field with respect to executive hires," said Mallory. "And I believe we can put the senior team together in less than six weeks while concurrently starting down the execution path so that we get ahead of the competition." Eric Mallory seemed to be a relatively strong personality in his own right and was not at all concerned by the officious attitudes of Pritchard and Brady.

"Putting the executive team together is only a small part of what needs to get done," said Chipper Geld. "If we intend to beat Rhapsody Holdings to the punch, we better be prepared to hire a high quality team of individuals to run our first Spa. That facility will go a long way to defining the caliber and quality of all the facilities that will be part of the FHR brand. I know a few people who may be able to help on that front.

"John, one of the things that we are counting on getting from ICD is a significant amount of IT talent, that will help us get our electronic medical record system up and running in less than eight or nine months. From what people tell me that means we should have started three months ago. So this becomes a major issue on the critical path to success. What can you tell us about ICD's willingness to commit IT resources to the project?"

"This is a bit of a slippery slope, Chipper. I've got a new organization ramping up to sell software services to our customer base immediately. They have goals that have already been set for 2009. Normally they would be hoping to sell to a company such as FHR, rather than collaborating with FHR. This is not a slam-dunk. This is something I want to discuss in more detail with my executive staff before I make a final decision on committing human resources of the company as well as the financial resources that we have been discussing, and of course this will have an impact on our equity stake."

Brady looked at the other four men in the room and wanted them to realize that they would have to do their fair share of the planning and execution for the business to work. It was certainly not going to be done entirely on the back of ICD. He finally rested his glare squarely on Paul Pritchard, and waited for him to respond.

"I can think of three really good reasons why you'd want to commit resources to guarantee success. First of all ICD has a major stake in FHR no matter how we structure the cash infusion. Secondly you have reinvested some of your personal redemption money from Cromwell Parsons into the new private equity fund that Mel and I have started … And the third reason is personal. I'm sure you don't want to read about the success of Abigail McDuffee in the Wall Street Journal." Paul Pritchard definitely knew how to push Brady's buttons.

"Oh, by the way," Pritchard continued, "I understand that another ex-ICDer has joined Rhapsody."

"Who is that?"

"Your former EA, Maria Cardoza. She has joined their team as the director of their Spa program. Apparently she has some experience in this area in her past business career."

"How the fuck do you know all these things, Pritchard?"

"Let's just say, I have my sources, and leave it at that." He didn't bother confiding that his sources were illegal electronic eavesdropping devices.

Brady regained his composure and said, "I need to be careful about my personal involvement in this FHR project. We have all kinds of disclosure requirements for officers and directors. Remember I am not directly investing in FHR. I am investing in the Pritchard fund and you and Geist here, and your fund is investing in the FHR. I have no say whatsoever in what the Pritchard Fund invests in. Correct?"

"JB I think you're being overly wary. FHR is going to be an excellent investment for John Brady as well as for ICD. The Pritchard fund is simply an intermediary vehicle for people like you and Chipper to realize the greatest possible personal return."

"What is your real interest in this Geld?" JB stared at Chipper Geld and waited for an answer that would help him understand Geld's keen interest in Fundamental Health Resources. He already knew a few things about Geld. He knew that there was much more to Chipper Geld than what appeared in his occasional PR releases and other periodic puff pieces that appeared in health and wellness trade magazines. In doing some of his background checking on Geld, Brady came to realize that it was highly probable that Chipper Geld was trafficking in prostitution and drugs. Those were the rumors but there was no overt proof.

"I don't imagine that my interest in Fundamental Health Resources is much different from yours, JB. We both see an opportunity to make a big buck. Frankly this business is more like what I do for a living than what you do at ICD. But certainly we are grateful to have the resources of ICD working for us all." Geld was content to appear to be only an investor in the project, but privately he fully intended to run the project. If this business helped to shroud his lucrative, if illegal, other interests, then so much the better.

"I have a very bright young manager in Atlanta, Jason Tobin. Tobin heads up ESD, our Essential Solutions Division I have already charged him with ramping up our internal programming staff. I'll see what I can do that allows him to redirect resources to work with FHR. You may be right, Paul. Our investment in FHR may prove to be a very prudent placement of funds for ICD. However we will need some kind of commercial relationship between FHR and ICD in order for us to pass the red face test."

Brady wasn't thrilled by the way things were lining up. However he accepted the fact that FHR would move much faster with significant support from ICD. He knew that they would have to move very rapidly in order to catch the first wave of progress with healthcare globalization. One thing was certain. Brady was not going to allow Abby McDuffee beat him to the punch. And he also didn't want to hear anything positive about that ungrateful bitch, Maria Cardoza.

Pritchard stared at Brady as though he were reading his mind and said, "Don't worry at all about Rhapsody. We will be aware of every step they take."

****

"Gina Alvarez and her hedge fund hunk Josh Struben had been expecting a child, conceived during Gina's red hot rock tour, probably

in Italy but maybe in London. Unfortunately Gina has miscarried. The magnetic mega couple however will soon be married. Details are unknown at this time." Both Josh and Gina were very happy that Seth Silverstein had managed to get the story out correctly. Josh was still working 60 hour weeks, but Gina had returned to Detroit to be with her mother and to kick back a little bit before re-engaging with the talk show hosts and other media outlets that could further her career.

Gina also had a new friend. She talked with Josh's mother Danielle almost as much as she talked to her own mother. They had many similar interests and had hit it off while they were together in New York City. Sometimes it's hard to say what causes a relationship to blossom as this one had, but there was no question that the two women had a deep affection for one another. In particular, Danielle had expressed an ongoing concern about the health of Gina's mother. She was concerned enough to call on a daily basis to offer her support and counsel.

Gina returned from the Henry Ford Medical Center after a short visit with her mother. Adriana Alvarez had just been released from ICU after successful surgery to reposition her diaphragm, and Gina was relieved that her mother would once again be able to resume a normal life style. In an attempt to avoid the prying eyes of a curious public, Gina was staying at one of the upscale condos that were owned by her agent Carl Gordon, while she was in Detroit for a couple of weeks. Pepper had made certain that she had round the clock security with her.

When the young singer arrived back at the condo it was still only 1 PM. It felt like a lot later after the early morning surgery and then the waiting period while her mother recovered. Gina decided to return a number of phone calls and text messages that had piled up on her blackberry. There was a message from Carl and one from Josh inquiring about her mother. She returned both calls and got voice mails and left messages. There was another call from London. This one was Danielle and when Gina returned the call Danielle picked up.

"Hello, Danielle. It's Gina."

"Hi Dear, *'Ow ees* Adriana *doeeng?"* Danielle's voice was soft and soothing. It was obvious she really cared and was not just making small talk. Gina took it as a personal reflection, because Danielle had never met Gina's mother, Adriana. Gina could feel the same soft-spoken strength of character in Danielle that she felt from her son, Josh.

"She's doing quite well thanks. The doctors indicated that the operation was a total success. There were no problems with the procedure and everything went according to plan. She should be in the hospital for another 48 hours and then should be able to return home."

"That's excellent news. I'll make sure that I pass *eet* along to Stephen when *'e* calls me. *'ave* you spoken to Josh yet?"

"I just tried to reach him but only got his cell phone voicemail. I left a message and I'm sure he'll call me back soon. What else is new with you?"

"Not too much. *Theengs 'a*ve been a *leettle* quiet around here. Stephen *ees een* Los Angeles for a *meeteeng weeth* the people from that Rhapsody company. From there *'e ees goeeng* on to Germany and should be back *'ome* by the weekend. We are *tryeeng* to plan a vacation for someplace south *dureeng* February, but we are not sure where to go yet. We just need to get to someplace warm."

"Rhapsody is that longevity company that we talked about in New York. Right?"

"Yes, although that's probably not the way they would refer to themselves." She thought for a second and then added, "On second thought they probably *do* refer to themselves that way. I'm not sure what you'd call *eet*. But yes you are right. *Eef* they are successful een *doeeng everytheeng* they set out to achieve, their company *ees* basically about *leeveeng* a longer better life. At least that's the way I see *eet*. *Eef* you talk to Stephen, or for that matter *eef* you talk to Josh, they also see *thees* as a very *seegneefeecant buseeness opportuneety*. But I like the way you *theenk* about *eet*. Rhapsody *ees* all about *longeveety*. But of course *eet* also *eencludes* better healthcare so that one can *leeve* a better life as well as a longer life."

"Yes, surely. By the way, what exactly is Stephen's involvement with them?"

"They asked *heem* to be on their board of directors."

"Oh yes, you mentioned that to me before. Josh has talked about Rhapsody several times also. I don't think he has any direct involvement with them at this point, but I know that he is intrigued by what they are trying to achieve. He told me that they will have the most advanced medical technology, combined with the world's best physicians, aesthetics experts, and fitness and wellness gurus. I think they're supposed to start selling memberships sometime later this year. That sounds like something I would want to have at my disposal."

"I agree. *Eet's 'a*rd enough to get *eentegrated medeecal* advice. *Eef* that can be combined with *feetness*, wellness and beauty, everyone *weel* want a *membersheep*. I *weesh* I *'ad* one already. I certainly could *'ave* used the *'elp* when I was *goeeng* through that mess with the false readings on my breast biopsy.

"The way I look at *eet, eef* I can gain some modicum of control over all of these *eessues,* I'm sure *eet'll 'elp* me *leeve* longer and healthier."

"Actually, I'm reading an interesting new book about longevity, that was written by a doctor who estimates that if someone my age takes good care of herself, she may be able to live to be 130 or older, and that during that lifetime, she could actually stay beautiful and vigorous, with an enhanced mental capacity."

"What does *eet* say about someone *een* her *feefties?*"

"I knew you'd ask that." Gina and Danielle both laughed and they felt very comfortable in their dialog with one another. "It's sort of a sliding scale, based upon how well you have taken care of yourself at any moment in life. You're in great shape so you would be at the high end of this guy's longevity scale. However based upon your current age, you might not see as many medical breakthroughs as someone who is younger. It is a mathematical probability game."

"So for example, *eef* I *'ad* actually contracted *eenflammatory* breast cancer and died from *eet,* I wouldn't *'ave leeved* long enough to see the cure. Therefore I would not be captured *een* the data that would correlate to a higher likelihood of *leeveeng* to a more advanced age."

"Exactly. The book gives a lot of examples of exactly that kind of breakthrough. For example it talks about testicular cancer in young men. It almost always affects young men between the ages of sixteen and twenty-five. In the 1980s testicular cancer was almost 100% fatal, if it wasn't detected and surgically treated before it metastasized. Now, due to breakthroughs over the last twenty-five years, testicular cancer is nearly 98% curable, even if it has metastasized. It can be treated by very effective chemo and radiation therapies as well as through surgery. All those young men who previously would have died are now living on average almost 60 years longer."

"That's quite *eenteresteeng. Eesn't* that what Lance Armstrong *'ad?*"

"Yes. And what's more interesting about that particular disease is that they still don't know what causes testicular cancer to occur, they simply know how to treat it when they find it. According to this writer, this is true of most cancers. They are unsure of their origins, even when they have effective treatments. All of which goes to demonstrate that if you can eliminate some of the causes of cancer so people don't get it in the first place, they will then have the opportunity to live a lot longer on average."

"The one *theeng* that concerns me about *leeveeng* longer *ees* that I don't know for sure that I *weell* be healthy *een* my old age. The last *theeng* that I would like to *'ave* occur *ees* to live for a long time *een* an unhealthy *condeetion*. At some point I would just say enough *ees* enough. I have led a good life and *eet's* time to move on."

"What do you mean by *move on*?" Gina wanted to know.

"That *ees* a very *eemportant* question, I guess. I am not sure and I really don't spend a lot of time *contemplateeng* what comes after life. I guess at *thees* point I *steell* feel like I *'ave* a lot of life to *leeve*. I've never been very *releegious*, and the *speereetualeety*, which I embrace, *'as* always been more focused on the *speereetual eempact* on my daily life rather than on some abstract after-life. What *ees* your perception?"

"I'm not sure. I think on some level I may have a fear of death. I certainly don't let it interfere with what I do on a daily basis. If anything along these lines captivates my attention, it's probably the idea of finding heaven on earth. I love life and I love sharing my life with a select group of people. I just hope that I will always feel the same way about life regardless of my chronological age. And I actually do back up those perceptions with actions. I try to keep myself in the best physical shape possible, and I try to keep my mind sharp."

"That's *eemportant* for all of us. What do you do to keep your mind sharp?"

"Besides reading, and the meditation that goes along with my yoga classes, I like to keep my mind sharp by contemplating the art of others, whether that art is literature, sculpture, paintings, music or whatever. I just feel that people communicate best with one another through their art. I think that their *true* essence is expressed through their art, and that art is what makes people interesting. I also believe that everybody is an artist of one form or another. It's just that not everyone takes the time and effort to express their art for the benefit of others."

"That's actually a very *beauteeful* thought, Gina. What I wonder about *ees* whether or not there *ees* a supreme *arteest* who has created us all. *Eet* seems to me, sometimes, that the greatest work of art *ees* the human being herself."

****

Dr Al Moses was a different man. Maria Cardoza was the catalyst for the change in outlook that had overtaken his life lately. He didn't understand why things were happening as they were, but he accepted his new perspective on life without questioning its permanence. Maria was out of town on a business trip this week, but she had called him. And when she called it wasn't related to their professional relationship. It was personal.

Al was happy that Maria was keeping her baby. There was a time almost eighteen years earlier when Al himself was getting ready for parenthood. He remembered when Anne Mohr was pregnant as a time when he was younger in spirit and somewhat wide-eyed with respect to the possibilities of life. He and Anne were already living together and they saw no particular need to get married. But they were both looking forward to the birth of their daughter, After Anne miscarried, neither Al nor Anne ever got over the loss. And then to make matters much much worse, Anne discovered that she had developed breast cancer soon thereafter. The cancer was aggressive and terminal. The love between the two physicians that had bloomed and flowered over many years came to a tragic end when Anne died.

Dr. Al was feeling pretty good about his new relationship with Maria before he went to see his psychiatrist Dr. Craig Mendelsohn for his regular visit.

"So Al, tell me if you have figured out what it is that you want from this relationship with your patient, Maria."

"It's not that simple Greg. Then again maybe it's simpler than I think. Maria and I have found one another at an important time in each of our lives. I, myself, have been in somewhat of a rut for much too long. On the other hand Maria was actively seeking change in her life. She was looking for new things and new people. It just so happened that we had reciprocal needs. These needs were underlined by a fondness for one another that has blossomed into something much more meaningful for both of us."

"That all sounds so romantic Al. But will it last? What happens when this tenuous relationship comes under some stress?"

"Think about that for a second Greg. What could be more stressful than watching the one you love grow more and more pregnant each day with another man's child?"

"We are both physicians Al. But you don't have to be a physician to realize the fact that you don't grow more and more pregnant. Either you're pregnant or you're not. I don't think this puts any new stress at all on your relationship. You knew she was pregnant before you started to date her. Possibly you liked the fact that she is pregnant. You yourself said that that is part of the reason why she reminds you of Anne Mohr. But you should be certain to yourself… and sincere with Maria… when you acknowledge that your relationship with Maria is truly all about you and her and not about you and Anne Mohr."

"That sounds better to me than the last time we discussed this. Last week you were critical of my relationship with Maria. Now you seem as though you have accepted it. Why is that?"

"This is not for me to accept or reject. I'm just an innocent third party here. I'm trying to help you see what decisions you have already made and what decisions you are yet to make and what the implications of both these might be. It is not my role to be judgmental. I only aim to help you to clarify any ambiguity that you might feel. I also want to help you understand some of the potential complications of your decisions. That is all that we are looking to accomplish here…understanding, just understanding."

"Isn't that what life is all about Greg? Isn't it all about the search for understanding, just understanding?"

****

Maureen Brady made some changes at her King's Point home on the north shore of Long Island. It was now the middle of winter and she was no longer spending time on the stone portico behind the house. The staff had decorated the house for the holidays, but Maureen had instructed them to take down the decorations right after New Year's Eve. She also ordered some renovations of the sauna and steam room areas in the basement area of her home. Maureen had utilized these facilities on a daily basis a few years back, but in recent years had barely entered this area of her home. Maureen also hired a personal trainer who would work with her four days a week.

Maureen's new personal trainer was a young man by the name of Grant but she wasn't sure whether that was his first name or his last name. All she knew or cared about was that Grant worked her hard, and that she continued to sweat out the toxins of the last few years.

Grant himself seemed to be an individual with a singular purpose. He was about 6'4" with very broad shoulders, and a V shaped trunk of a body, that tapered to a very narrow waist, and then broadened again across thick buttocks, thighs and calves. He had very large hands and feet and gave the overall impression that he could just as easily have had a career as a covert assassin rather than his chosen career as a convivial trainer.

Maureen felt that Grant was the perfect trainer for her. He pushed her and gave very direct instructions without engaging in much social banter. He worked her for about two hours each day in the small dark paneled workout room that was adjacent to the downstairs bathroom sauna and steam room facilities of her home.

"You're coming along very well Mrs. Brady," said Grant. "Your stamina has improved very quickly and your musculature is also being reconstructed properly. When I come again tomorrow we are going to take some time to sit down and revisit your initial goals to reflect the progress that you have already made. I'm going to take off now and be back at 8 AM." Grant wrapped his towel around his neck and held on to both ends in a manner that caused his biceps to bulge as he was speaking. Maureen didn't notice the slightest bit of fat on his body.

"Thank you, Grant. I'll see you tomorrow. I'm feeling a lot better already and I look forward to pushing the envelope a little harder in the next few weeks."

Cara, the Brady housekeeper, came downstairs as they were speaking and stood waiting to escort Grant to the front door. Grant quickly pulled his sweat suit over his workout shorts and T-shirt and got ready to leave. He and Cara turned and walked up the stairs, as Maureen walked back toward the shower and sauna facilities. She chose the steam room instead of the sauna, and quickly stripped off her clothes, grabbed a couple of towels, and entered the steam room naked.

As she sat in the steam room Maureen conjured up many images from the past. She thought about several of the functions that she had attended with JB over the years, and actually remembered what she wore, who she talked to, and why she went. Each of these memories was one where she herself played one distinct role. Her role had simply been that of Mrs. John Brady, supportive and loving wife. She had never disliked that role, and she didn't mind the fact that many people accorded her respect only because she was JB's wife. The fact that she was respected was all that really mattered to her. However she was beginning to grasp a new reality. In the past she had hoped that John would get his fill of the corporate life and finally retire, so that together they could enjoy the Long Island social scene, both in Kings

Point and in Southampton, on a full-time basis. What was beginning to surprise Maureen was not only that John Brady wanted more out of life, but also she herself, Maureen Brady, was now beginning to expect much more out of life. Being a mother to Mark, Megan and Kenneth was certainly a meaningful role. And being Mrs. John Brady was what it was. For the first time in her life Maureen began to wonder, "Is that all there is?" She got out of the steam room and took a cool shower.

****

It was amazing how JB's back had stopped bothering him the moment he made the decision to have neurosurgery. He had gone more than a week now without the slightest bit of pain. In fact his back felt about as good as it had in a year. He also didn't have the pinched nerve pain that radiated down his left arm and into his fingers. Gone also was the "jellyneck" feeling that drove him bonkers from time to time. He likened it to when he was a kid with a toothache. The toothache disappeared the moment he got to the dentist's office. Regardless, and for whatever reason, JB was just happy to be temporarily pain-free.

It was a new year and JB was determined that it would be a much better year than 2008. But he knew he had to make changes. And he had many of these changes underway already. One thing he wasn't going to change however was spending time with the executives of his largest customers. He had been invited by one of his customers to their reception at the Obama inauguration in two weeks. That was one customer event that he was going to blow off. It wasn't that he disliked the new President, Barack Obama. JB had managed to play both sides of the political fence and had been very adept at doing so for many years. It was simply that he didn't believe that he would be recovered from his operation in time to spend three days partying in Washington DC.

This was to be Brady's last night out before undergoing surgery in two days. He had started his day at 6:30 AM in a meeting with his executive committee on plans for 2009. He wrapped up this meeting in time for the 9AM start to the board meeting that went through until 4 PM. After the Board meeting he had scooted downtown to meet with Paul Pritchard and Chipper Geld. Following his meeting downtown, JB returned to midtown to have dinner with his staff.

Dinner was being held in the wine cellar at the Oceana restaurant and although the room could hold up to 25 people, Brady and his team of a dozen merely paid the extra fare and commandeered the room. JB was starting to get a little nervous about his upcoming operation and proceeded to drink a little more than he normally would. All those at dinner were part of his direct reporting management team and therefore he wasn't at all concerned about having a little too much to drink. The night before he had been much better behaved while dining with his Board of Directors.

The dinner went along smoothly without much business discussion. Brady seemed to be in a much more convivial mood than he normally was when meeting or dining with his direct reports.

Before too long the dinner meeting was breaking up and several of the team members said goodnight and left for the evening. Brady's eyes were getting a little glassy. His driver, Fernando, was waiting outside to take Brady either to his Kings Point home on Long Island, or to the company's apartment on Sutton Place.

Caitlin Browning had been biding her time and mostly observing the behavior of the other staff members in anticipation of getting some of the usual "go do's" from JB, before the night was over. Since taking her new job in December, Caitlin was getting quite used to last-minute requests from her boss. These requests often had very tight deadlines. Caitlin and her husband were now living in the city, so even though it was now almost 11 PM she knew that she could be home within fifteen minutes of the end of the dinner.

As the final few members of Brady's team began to leave for the evening JB turned to Caitlin and asked her to stand by.

"Caitlin I just need you for a few minutes. I want to talk to you about a couple of things before I retire for the evening. Maybe we can just ride together and I can drop you off at your apartment." Brady's request sounded innocent enough and Caitlin was not at all concerned about the perception of others. However other members of the senior team recognized the familiar pattern that had been in place for a half dozen years with Maria Cardoza.

When Brady and Browning got into the back of Brady's limousine, JB immediately made an attempt to alter their destination. It was then that Caitlin realized that John Brady was much like many other men. Once he had more than his fair share of alcohol, he began to think with his lower brain.

"Fernando, why don't you take us over to Sutton Place? I think I'm going to stay in the city this evening. Caitlin you can come up to the apartment for a few minutes so we can go over a few items. Can't you?"

"It's been a long night John. I think we would all be better served by just getting up very early so that we can start early in the morning. I'm willing to meet you at the office as early as you'd like."

"Come on Caitlin. You and I both know that this will be a lot easier on all of us, if we just get a head start on our work before the night is over. Just come up for a few minutes."

"John in case you didn't notice, it's zeroing in on midnight now. In effect the night is over." The back of the limousine was very spacious and Caitlin turned to face John Brady as she spoke to him. In so doing her back was actually up against the rear door behind the driver. She was effectively as far away from John Brady as she could get in the back of the limousine, but she made very direct eye contact with him so that there would be no mistaking of anything she said or intended. She had her legs crossed at her knees and she tugged a bit at her skirt to bring it back down to knee level from where it had ridden up slightly on her thigh. She was wearing a mink coat over her dress, but the coat had parted slightly when she sat down. Now she repositioned the bottom of her coat over her dress and over her thighs and knees.

Brady was now glaring back at Caitlin. His glossy eyes roamed over her body even though it was almost entirely covered up. He took note of the fact that Caitlin had very attractive feminine curves irrespective of the issue of whether they were natural or artificially enhanced.

"You know Caitlin; you are much more attractive than your sister."

"Than my sister?"

"Yes, you are much more attractive than your sister Abby McDuffee. In fact McDuffee isn't even in the same league you are in. What's she doing with herself these days anyway? Rumor has it that she has started some kind of spa or group of spas or some such nonsense."

"I didn't realize that you knew that Abby was my sister. Did you also know that Abby is a twin? My other sister Alison is a physician. She and Abby are working on a project together. I don't know that much about it. If you say it's a spa business, well then I guess it's a spa business. It's not what I do, so I don't really know that much about it. By the way how did you know about the business?"

"Oh I have a way of knowing these things. Trust me not much gets by my radar screen. But I don't want to talk about your sister. I want to talk about you. And I want to talk about me. And I want to talk about you and me." With that said, JB reached one drunken hand in the direction of Caitlin's lap. Caitlin pushed away his attempt at groping with disdain and disgust. Her sister's warnings went through her mind rapidly. She was embarrassed by the fact that Brady made no attempt to be discreet or to hide any of his arduous advances from Fernando. She felt that Brady had cheapened their relationship. It made her feel like taking a shower. He was just that gross.

"Fernando, please pull over and let me out at the next light."

Fernando did as he was instructed. He was smart enough to realize that Brady was pushing his luck, and he didn't want to be party to holding someone against their will. It was obvious to Caitlin, that Fernando had been in this situation before and had a practiced response to the dilemma of the evening.

As Caitlin was getting out of the limousine, an obviously intoxicated John Brady called after her, "Tell your sister that the Rhapsody thing that she's trying to do will never fly. There are a lot of big boys who will make sure of that."

Caitlin slammed the door to the limousine and flagged down a cab heading in the opposite direction. She was very annoyed, not just at John Brady but also at herself for being so gullible.

****

Josh Struben finally got through to his fiancée Gina. They had been playing telephone tag for most of the day. Within a few minutes Gina got Josh caught up on a number of different items. She told him that her mother was doing much better. And she also told him about the lengthy conversation that she had had earlier in the day with Josh's mother, Danielle. They discussed getting together for the weekend but didn't resolve the venue. The conversation then wandered to a variety of different topics until Gina came back to one of the topics that she had discussed with Danielle earlier today.

"I was speaking with your mother about our interest in the longevity company, Rhapsody. I told her I didn't know whether or not you had any further involvement with them since you met them in Hong Kong. And Danielle told me that both she and Stephen had met a few of the Rhapsody executives in Germany, and that they have asked your father to sit on their board of directors. I didn't know any of the details about this until Danielle clued me in, but apparently your father is out meeting with them someplace in California this week."

"Yes they are very interesting company. I know that Dad has an interest in their success that dates back to his relationship with the IT guy, Max Tkachuk, who has since passed away. That also told me that they have asked him to be on their board. Cromwell Parsons is very interested in what Rhapsody is doing and will continue to monitor their performance over the coming months. Personally I like their executive team very much. Not only are they nice people, but they also seem to have their heads screwed on right. The McDuffee twins are quite a treat. It is almost impossible to tell them apart visually. And you only get to understand the difference between the two of them when they sit down to discuss business and their respective responsibilities. Why are you so interested in them?"

"I'm interested in them because *you* are interested in them. And from what you told me the last time we talked about Rhapsody I think they're heading down the right path. You just repeated the fact that the people who are running the business know what they're doing. Once they get all of their products and centers and records and all of the rest of things that are looking to do ready for consumption, they will have a product that many people will want to buy. In fact, both Danielle and I were discussing the fact that we would love to have memberships as soon as they become available. I could even see trying to help them out in other ways, if these people are as talented as you think they are. So anyway those are my thoughts on that topic. No big deal. Just thought I would ask you what you thought."

"I'm not sure what I think about them. That's why we will continue to monitor their progress. But I do agree with you. If they can do everything they say they can do, then I want a membership also. Beyond that, if they achieve anything close to their projections, it would make sense to invest in their success on an ongoing basis. By the way the second center that they want to open up will be located in London."

"A place in New York and a place in London; that's perfect."

"And many more to follow, apparently."

****

Alison McDuffee returned to her hotel room at the end of what had been an interesting cocktail hour. She was too tired to stay around for dinner with the others. Besides she wanted to call home to talk to her husband, Tom, who was packing up at their Manhattan Beach condo to return to their East Coast home in Bernardsville, New Jersey. Alison was going to be relying on Tom more and more in the coming months and she was well aware of the fact that Tom would be the parent most responsible for getting their two teenage sons to and from school and the long litany of after school activities in which they participated.

Sometimes Alison was grateful for the fact that her children were boys. She admitted to herself on more than one occasion that without Tom she would be lost when it came to raising her sons. She believed that it was a bit easier for Tom to be raising boys than it would have been if they had daughters. There was a time when she and Tom thought about having another child, hopefully a daughter. The time seemed to expire quickly. They were happy with the two boys. Besides her medical practice had always consumed a good bit of Alison's time, particularly as she shuttled back and forth between New Jersey and California. But she was beginning to believe that her business career was about to go into overdrive with the launch of Rhapsody and she was just very happy to have someone as understanding as Tom to be her husband and the father of her boys.

"How's everything going at home, Tom?"

"Everything is fine here Alison. The boys are getting ready to see their friends back in New Jersey and we are going to catch the 9 AM plane out tomorrow. I guess we'll see you when you get home on Thursday. How is your meeting going?"

"Pretty well actually. I thought about driving home tonight and then back here in the morning, but it was a long day. We got a lot done. Abby took the lead, so I'm sure she's even more tired than I am. Everyone seemed pretty excited about the opportunities in front of us and it was one of those sessions where we just rolled up our sleeves and got right to work. Abby is unbelievable. She is still down at the bar having a couple more cocktails before having dinner with the rest of the team. I don't know where she gets the energy from sometimes."

"Are you the only one who didn't go to dinner?"

"I'm not sure. I think Stephen Struben also begged off early. And Maria Cardoza, who is our new spa director, didn't go to the cocktail hour. She said that she was going to go down for dinner, however. This was the first time that I met her I think she's really a great addition to our team. The only difficulty at all is that she's three and a half months pregnant, and so we will be missing her for some time over the summer. I get the feeling, however, that she has a great sense of how to balance her time and I'm sure she'll continue to make a significant contribution even when she's out on maternity leave."

"How's your friend Dao doing? She certainly enjoyed herself at a few of the parties here in LA over the holidays. She's quite a character. She entertained a number of my buddies with her stories about Thailand. She isn't a shy one."

"That's for sure. You're right. No one ever accused Dao of being shy. But she has been our friend forever. She thinks the world of you, Tom. And, you know, she is who she is. I'm never going to try to change Dao. Besides I don't think that I could change her even if I wanted to. The other thing that's important to remember is that Rhapsody was her dream as much as it was mine. We are both happy that Abby has taken control of the running the business, but we both know that as physicians and healthcare professionals we still retain a good deal of responsibility for ensuring that the Rhapsody vision is fulfilled in its entirety. Dao didn't come to Los Angeles just to have fun at our parties. She came out here to help launch the business. She's a great friend and a tremendous business colleague."

"Well I for one can't wait for the day that you folks open up your first center in New York. I think, though, that when you eventually open up a centre in Los Angeles your ultimate success will be ensured. People out here just seem to be a lot more involved in this health and wellness movement than they are other places in the world."

"Well get yourself a good night's sleep before your trip tomorrow. I'm going to turn in early myself because frankly I'm just exhausted. Love you, sweetheart."

Alison hung up the phone with Tom and noticed that the message light was blinking. She called out for her messages and listen to the one voicemail had been left. It was from her sister Caitlin.

"Alison this is Caitlin. Give me a call when you get a chance. I want to talk to you about something that John Brady let out of the bag tonight. It may be a problem."

Chapter 14: *Lovers, Liaisons, Funding and Fun*

It was Monday, February 16, 2009 and Abby, Alison and Dao were in three separate parts of the world. Dao had just returned from a rigorous walk in the park near her home in Bangkok. It was closing in on 9 PM. Abby was returning to her hotel room from a meeting in Paris, France. And Alison was about to go to her surgery center in New York City to perform three scheduled procedures for patients later in the day.

But the first order of business for the three Rhapsody colleagues on this Monday night/afternoon/morning was to get together via a Skype conference so that they could reconnect on various different open issues. The three women were not conferenced together for more than five minutes when Abby noted a new call coming into her computer via a separate Skype line. The call was from Bob Johnstone of the Louisiana Group. Johnstone was not in the habit of calling unless he had something to say, so Abby immediately excused herself to her two colleagues to answer the call from Johnstone.

"Hello Bob what's new?"

"Good morning, Abby." He obviously thought that Abby was in NYC, where it was still morning. "This is a call that you have been waiting for." He paused for effect and then said, "We have secured our line with the banks and have agreed and signed all of the term sheets and so we're ready to go. What we have to do next is simply to agree on the covenants that we have been discussing with you during the past year so that we can begin funding your business directly from the Louisiana Group's line with the banks.

"In addition, you will be happy to hear that the third party that we have been speaking to, Mr. Sun Feng, has agreed to front $5 million in bridge money to Rhapsody until such time as Rhapsody and the Louisiana Group have reached and signed our own accord. So before I forget about it, be sure to send along your bank's wiring instructions, because I anticipate having the $5 million ready to be wired to you by Thursday."

"That's fantastic news Bob. I am thrilled and I'm sure the rest of the team is going to be thrilled as soon as I can tell them. Where are you now?"

"I'm in London currently but I plan on returning to the states tomorrow morning. I can meet you in New York if that's convenient for you." Bob Johnstone was not an overly accommodating person by nature, so the offer to meet Abby in New York surprised her.

"Actually right now I'm taking this call from Paris. I'm over here meeting with a couple of people who will be instrumental in helping us put together some of the dietary regimen that will be an integral part of Rhapsody. Of course we want to move forward with the funding as rapidly as possible so I'm more than willing to fly back to New York tonight to meet you there, if that's best. Or I could just fly to London and we could meet there."

"Better yet why don't you just stay put in Paris. I haven't been to Paris in a number of years. Paris seems to me to be as good a place as any to indulge in a celebratory glass of wine and to begin to lay out the groundwork for the funding of the first tranche. Besides as fate would have it, Mr. Feng just happens to be in Monte Carlo at the current moment. He is Chinese and his office is in Beijing but he's on a gambling junket for the week. I'll ask him to fly up to Paris to meet us."

"That would be great! We've all waited such a long time for this funding to come through, that none of us want to wait another moment longer than necessary. If we can get started here in Paris, so much the better."

"Okay just stay put for now. We'll plan on getting there sometime tomorrow in the early afternoon. To be on the safe side, let's plan on dinner. I'm not sure what time Mr. Feng will be able to make it up there if I can convince him to come. If there's any change in our plans I'll call you right away. Make sure your computer forwards to your cell. Bye for now."

Abby clicked off her Skype connection with Johnstone and clicked on to her conversation with Allie and Dao.

"Well ladies you won't believe what I just heard."

"Oh yeah, Try us," said Dao.

"So don't keep us in suspense what did he have to say?" added Alison.

"Johnstone said that the funding is ready. He went so far as to ask me for our wiring information at the bank. I'll have to get back to him right away on that. He told me that they would have some money in our account by Thursday."

"That is absolutely wonderful news!" Alison seemed to be jumping through the computer phone with her exuberance. "We'll need to round up the rest of the executive team on the conference call ASAP to give them the good news."

"How did he sound?" Dao asked. "Is he as excited about this as we are?"

"No one is as excited about this as we are, Dao."

"But what did he say exactly? And how did he say it?"

"It was pretty straightforward. He acknowledged the fact that this had been a long time coming and he understood that we wanted to get started on the paperwork as soon as possible. To that end he's actually going to fly here to meet me tomorrow."

"In Paris?"

"Yes in Paris. In fact he also indicated that he was going to try to get the man who is responsible for our bridge loan to fly into Paris as well. He said that this person, Sun Feng, is already in France. He is down in Monte Carlo and apparently Johnstone has been in regular contact him. That seems to be the game plan for now, unless I hear differently."

"Congratulations … Abby. Here we go!"

* * * * * * * * * *

Gina Alvarez taped her late night talk show appearance in the afternoon and met Josh at his East side apartment after work. Gina preferred living in the artsy section of Greenwich Village, rather than in the uppity East Side. On the other hand, Josh made his NY home in the high rent district near Fifth Avenue overlooking Central Park, which separates the East Side from the West Side of Manhattan. They intended to go to dinner down in the SoHo section of the city, near Gina's Greenwich Village loft. It was a lot easier to come and go from her NYC home now that she wasn't on tour.

Soon after she arrived Gina and Josh were out of their clothing and into bed making love. They didn't waste a lot of time on preliminary discussion, they just allowed the passionate instincts within them to take control. After their lovemaking they nestled close to one another and talked about their respective days. They were both so comfortable snuggling that they discussed the possibility of forgetting about dinner and just remaining in bed. However, Gina had not eaten all day long and by eight o'clock she was getting hungry, so they got dressed and called for a car service to take them downtown, as per their original plan.

They arrived at the Tribeca Grill just before 9 PM and were seated immediately. They had dined there several times in the past and were always afforded a modicum of privacy to go along with the excellent food. The restaurant was owned by the actor, Robert DeNiro, and the staff was well aware of how to handle VIP clientele with discretion.

Josh ordered a glass of Cabernet, as Gina settled for a glass of sparkling water. The couple perused the menu ordered a light meal and began discussing the financial market meltdown. When their meals arrived they altered the topic slightly. They continued their conversation in quiet tones despite the spirited noise coming from the large bar area in the adjacent room.

"You know if I hadn't become a rocker, I think I would have been a banker!" Gina said with a giggle. Josh smiled back at Gina and shook his head slightly, giving a nonverbal response that seemed to say, *I believe you. You're not kidding!*

"Well, I'm sure that when you have the final tally from your tour, no one's going to have to pass the hat to bail out the Lay D's. If the tabloids have it correct your tour has grossed nine figures, and the first figure is a crooked one."

"Is there any reason you had to refer to the first figure as a *crooked* figure? We are really just making an *honest* buck for an honest day's work. There's nothing crooked about it."

"Touchy, touchy, now … Aren't we? Just a figure of speech … that's all"

"Is that a *crooked figure* of speech?" Gina punned. She hesitated and then added, "Okay I guess I deserve that." She laughed, and then began to sip her water thoughtfully.

"But you know money often causes many more problems than it solves. I didn't tell you this yet, but we have a bit of a debate going on about the respective split among Marilyn, Karen and Sophia. Once Karen rejoined the tour, Sophia stayed with us as backup. Karen didn't want her anywhere near the tour, but Carl insisted that Sophia stay on even after Karen was back on stage. And then on top of all of that, of course we cancelled the NYC concerts. So anyway Carl is working all of that out as best he can. I'm staying out of it as much as possible. But honestly, I hate to see money causing such a mess of things. There's plenty to go around for everyone. It's not like we were singing on the beaches in Puerto Rico for free."

"I think your attitude is spot on. Nonetheless you can't argue with the fact that people will be talking about your big payday, as much as they will be discussing your singing. That's just the way it is in the world today."

The young couple talked about myriad topics throughout dinner. They had yet to set an exact date for their wedding but spent some time discussing where it might take place.

When they arrived back at Gina's Greenwich Village townhouse, they didn't go directly to the bedroom, but instead Gina walked over to one side of the living room and looked back at Josh with a playful countenance.

"So now that we've solved all the problems of the world over dinner, I'll bet you just want to get laid again."

"Well you certainly have a way with words, Gina my dear."

"I don't think it's time for words anymore. Of course if you're too tired …"

Gina was standing about as far away from Josh as she could get, within the confines of the living area on the third floor. She had her back up against the wall and there were 20 feet and two couches between her and Josh. He began weaving around the furniture and closing the distance between them. As he approached her, Gina moved from one wall to another, but kept her back and the palms of her hands against the wall.

Josh continued moving towards Gina, and he was beginning to understand that his lover was in one of her game-playing moods. He knew that their earlier sexual escapade at his apartment was simply Gina's warm-up act. Josh himself was ready for an encore. Gina loved encores, sometimes performing several in a single evening. But she did have this preference for playing games. He kept circling closer and closer to her and said, "Tired? Who's tired?"

Now there was one armchair between the two of them. Josh faked a move to his left and circled to the right around the armchair and was on top of the Gina pinning her against the wall in one quick strong movement. He put both of his open hands on either side of Gina's thin waist, as she stretched her arms up straight towards the ceiling. He lifted her about a foot off the ground and nestled his face between her breasts.

"So what'cha gunna do big boy?" She lowered her voice in a pathetically poor Mae West type imitation of a gun moll. "Take me right here up against the wall?"

Josh never gave her a verbal response, but she was thrilled with his answer.

****

Al and Maria left the theater together and walked slowly down the great White Way. As a native New Yorker Al Moses felt that a stroll down Broadway was like a walk in his backyard. But now he was simply happy to have a good friend with him as he made that journey.

"What did you think of the show?" Maria looked up at Al as she asked the question.

"I have to confess it is not the first time as I've seen *Mama Mia*. But I will tell you this; I enjoy it every time I see it and I enjoyed it tonight more than ever."

"Exactly how many times have you seen it?"

"I think this was my third time."

"To be perfectly honest, it's the second time I've seen it as well. And I will have to admit also that I enjoyed it much more this evening."

Maria and Al were still learning a lot about one another, about their likes and dislikes, about their tastes in food, in art and in people. As they continued their stroll Al changed the topic.

"So how is the new job going? You seemed very excited about everything when you came back from California last month. Is everything still on track?"

"We have a very aggressive schedule but things appear to be progressing as planned. I really like the people that I'm working with and so the job is very energizing."

"Actually I have something I want to tell you about your friends at Rhapsody. This will have to go under the 'it's a small world' category. But it just so happens that I am close personal friends with one of the folks who were with you out in Orange County."

"Really! And who would that be?"

"Stephen Struben has been a friend of mine for more than 50 years. We went to high school together in Brooklyn."

"Amazing! Why didn't you say something before this? How did you find out about Stephen being out in California?"

"Like I said it's a small world, a very very small world. If you can believe this Stephen and I had dinner together in London several months back. He knew that I had an avid interest in electronic medical records and so he invited another man to dinner with us, a person by the name of Max Tkachuk. Max had a company called Apakoh, operating out of the Ukraine. Apakoh apparently was doing some work for Rhapsody. I didn't know anything about Rhapsody at the time. I only knew what Max told Stephen and me about his company Apakoh. The sad and bizarre twist to all of this is that after our dinner poor Max went back to his hotel room and suffered a massive cardiac arrest and died."

"That's absolutely horrible. You know I heard something at the meeting about Rhapsody doing business with Apakoh, and that the Apakoh owner had passed away. And I also heard Stephen mention that this fellow was a friend of his, and that was partly why he was involved with Rhapsody at this point. And now to hear that you and Stephen have been friends forever is just startling! It seems as though everything is webbed together by some 'Guiding Hand.' It makes me feel as though we are absolutely doing the right thing."

They turned left and walked past Avenue of the Americas and approached Fifth Avenue. Then they turned left again on Fifth Avenue and proceeded back uptown. A brisk snow flurry was beginning to light up the night and moisten the tips of their noses. Still neither Al nor Maria made any mention of a destination. For the moment they were content to simply walk and talk together. Maria was quiet for a moment or two as she thought about the social networking theories of six degrees of separation. She wondered how many other pathways might have led her to this same position in life. Her life now included a home in the United States; a broad portfolio of financial assets; a new job in an exciting industry; a new relationship with an interesting man, who also served in the role of her gynecologist; and a baby growing in her uterus, who was the child of someone she had grown to detest. In spite of all of these relationships Maria thought of herself as free and independent. She felt lucky, even blessed, to have choices in life. She recognized that not everyone was so fortunate. As these thoughts were going through her mind she reached over and took Dr. Al's arm. She looked up at him and said, "Thank You, Al."

"Thank you for what?"

"Thank you for dinner. Thank you for the show. Thank you for being there for me when I needed you. And thank you for being here for me now when I want you."

Dr. Al hailed a cab and he and Maria went back to his apartment. The rest of the night was magical for both of them. The 'Guiding Hand' was once again working overtime.

****

John Brady was very aggravated. The time had come to finally have the operation. He had recently moved it back a month but he couldn't deal with the intermittent pain any longer. One day there was no pain. The next day there was excruciating pain. This was no to live. He needed to take charge.

Brady didn't even bother to confer with Mike Kelvey, who was on vacation in Europe someplace. He was beginning to find Kelvey more useless than ever. He never seemed to have a definite opinion on anything. JB wouldn't tolerate such indecision from any of his business managers. Why should he take such a vacillating and vacant attitude from someone who was supposed to be vigilant about his health care? It appeared to Brady that the role of general practitioner in the medical field had been reduced to being simply a call director. Yes that's what Kelvey was. He was nothing more than a highly paid prompt. *Touch 1 for the orthopedist. Touch 2 for the neurosurgeon. Touch 3 for the psychiatrist. To hear these prompts again please renew my contract by touching zero.*

But JB was nervous. In addition to his apprehension about the upcoming operation, Brady had other concerns. He was worried about the continuing deterioration of ICD's stock price, although they had managed to hold their own among the blue chips on the Dow. He also wanted to know a lot more about the initial development of Fundamental Health Resources, and what amount of control that Jason Tobin had been able to exert. He wasn't able to count on his EA Caitlin Browning, to help him calibrate the progress of FHR. His relationship with Browning was a concern. For the past three weeks she had been showing up later than usual and leaving before he was ready to dismiss her. They had not discussed the limousine ride a few weeks back. In fact Browning had not been in the car with him since that time. She had not traveled with him either to the inauguration or to the Super Bowl, and when JB was in need of accompaniment for evening dinners, his wife Maureen had become a willing participant once again. There had been no need for stand-in guests/escorts.

JB wasn't certain what he wanted to do with Browning. He could move her to another position easily enough. He believed that she probably wanted that anyway. But then again Caitlin Browning presented somewhat of a challenge to JB. With the re-aggravation of his back problems over the last three weeks, Brady was less inclined to do any skirt chasing. However he believed that once his back problems were resolved through his upcoming operation, he would make another effort to bed his EA. For now his pining for a lascivious liaison with his long legged, redheaded subordinate would simply have to wait.

****

Danielle and Stephen Struben were very much in love. There was never a moment when either of them questioned their love for one another, but if they were to look at their relationship honestly they would acknowledge that over the years there were times when the physical distances that separated them also impacted the fervor of their physical and emotional rapport. Recently they had several reasons to check and recheck their love for one another and happily they didn't find it lacking in any way. In fact just the opposite was true. Their love for one another seemed to be growing in recent months as they dealt with a few family issues like Danielle's false positive for cancer and their son Josh's fiancée Gina's miscarriage. Through it all, there was constancy to their commitment to family life, and they hoped that the example they set was not lost on their sons Josh and Adam.

Throughout some of the stressful issues Stephen and Danielle had stayed pretty much in character with respect to their daily endeavors. Danielle remained focused on her two sons while filling some of the daytime hours of her life with charitable endeavors and some personal introspection. She took good care of herself physically and intellectually. She exercised daily and read voraciously. Her small group of intimate friendships now included her future daughter-in-law, whom she spoke to a couple of times a week. This was a new and different kind of family relationship for Danielle. She had two sons and always wanted a daughter. She never hoped that she would find a kindred spirit like Gina to embrace. In some ways it was almost too good to be true.

As 2009 unfolded and spilled into its second month, the Strubens got away from the cold weather in London and New York for a week-long vacation on a remote southern Caribbean island called Parker Cay.

Danielle had learned about Parker Cay from Gina and Josh, who had spent four days on the atoll the summer before. Recently Parker Cay had gained some momentum as an isolated honeymoon spot for newlyweds of substantial means, and for celebrities who were seeking to avoid the publicity that might attend their vacationing at a more populated destination. It was quite possible to spend a week at Parker Cay without ever seeing more than a couple of people outside of your own party during the entire week. For that reason, there were also stories, shared amongst the locals at the larger nearby islands, of wealthy individuals who actually came to the Cay alone and simply spent a few days or a week in private meditation.

Danielle sat down on the middle of one of the reclining chairs and retrieved her tanning lotion. She sat upright facing her husband and she used her right hand to spread the protection over the exposed parts of her body that she could reach, with the exception of her face.

"I can certainly see why Josh and Gina like *theese* place so much. *Eet's* very private." She looked around and could see no one except Stephen.

"Have they gotten any closer to picking a wedding date?" asked Stephen. "What did she have to say about that when you spoke with her? I'm sure you asked her."

"Naturally I brought the *topeec* up. But I *deedn't* push too *'ard*. Her mother *ees recovereeng* nicely from her operation and I'm sure we'll *'ear* from the *keeds* soon about what their plans are *goeeng* to be. All I know so far *ees* that *eet weell* be very small and very private."

Danielle wiped off the excess suntan oil from her hands onto one of the towels and then reached into her bag to get a separate ointment for her face. She went through a ritualistic application of the face cream to her cheeks, chin, forehead and ears. When she was finally through with the application to her face, she took the original suntan lotion and handed it to Stephen. Then she flipped face down on the lounge chair and asked her husband to apply the suntan lotion to her back.

Stephen sat up in his chair and squeezed some of the ointment into each of the palms of his two hands. He then reached across to Danielle and began lightly applying the lotion to her back. He pulled himself closer to her and began massaging the oil into her shoulders with the palms of his hands, and into the base of her neck with his thumbs.

"That feels nice, Stephen."

Stephen slid one hand down each side of her rib cage while keeping his thumbs close to the center of her backbone, all the while gently massaging the suntan lotion into her skin. The breadth of his large hands covered the width of her tapered back near the bottom of her ribs, and he rubbed firmly as he applied lotion and pressure downward until he reached the pink polka dots of her bikini bottom.

The temperature at Parkers Cay on this particular February morning had already reached the high 70s, and it appeared that it would be at least 80° before noontime. Both Stephen and Danielle could feel the hot Caribbean sun baking down on them as they began to truly relax.

"Just keep *doeeng* that. *Eet* feels so good. Soooo Good! Make sure you get the backs of my legs also," Danielle said.

"Don't worry. I'll get there. We've got all day." Josh said this very softly as he applied more suntan lotion to his wife's thighs, calves, feet and toes. By the time his fingers were soothingly massaging the area between Danielle's toes, she was extraordinarily relaxed. She closed her eyes and simply wanted her husband to keep kneading her body.

Stephen finally removed his hands from Danielle's legs and her feet and sat back slightly away from her chair. His wife rolled over on her back and said to him, "I'm not sure that I put enough lotion on the front."

"You know, Danielle, I do worry about you getting too much sun exposure, given the problems that you just have just gotten over." He then proceeded to apply more lotion to his wife's body. She found her husband's touch to be entirely soothing.

They were quiet for a couple of minutes as Stephen remained seated upright next to Gina's motionless horizontal body. He let his thoughts roam a bit across a number of different topics. He had decided that he would join the board of Rhapsody Holdings, and had been cleared to do so by STRX. He thought back to the meeting, which they had a few weeks earlier in California and the subsequent phone conversation about Rhapsody, which he had with his friend Al Moses. He then suddenly recalled the coincidental fact that Al had confided in him.

"I forgot to tell you about an interesting conversation that I recently had with Al Moses."

"So *'Ow ees* Al *doeeng*? I *'aven't 'eard* you mention him *een* a while. *Ees* he *steell traveleeng* a lot?"

"Actually no, he's not traveling very much at all lately. He seems to be much happier, though, than he was when I saw him before the holidays."

"I'm not sure about Al. I don't *theenk 'e 'as* been *'appy* since Anne died. He was a fool for not *marryeeng 'er een* the *feerst* place. Frankly, I *'ave* always felt rather bad about that. I was very fond of Anne."

"I know you were. And to some degree I think you're absolutely right. It's been a long time since Anne passed away but Al has never gotten over it. That's why I'm going to tell you something that should be very interesting to you. At least I think it'll be interesting to you. It certainly was interesting to me."

"Okay. I'm *leesteneeng.*"

"When I was out in California with the Rhapsody folks, I met a woman by the name of Maria Cardoza. Maria is their director for spa services. Apparently she was just hired on. Another interesting sidelight is that she was about three months pregnant at the time. She seemed like a very nice lady, quite accomplished and intelligent. I didn't think much about her personal life at the time. I was much more interested in significant contributions that she was able to make to the business discussions that we were having."

"So *thees* does *'ave sometheeng* to do *weeth* Al Moses. Yes?"

"Give me a chance. I'm getting to that. After my return from the conference, I had a conversation on the phone with Al. Remember how Al was with me when we met Max Tkachuk on the night that Max passed away? Well anyway, Al has had this ongoing interest in electronic medical records and such, so I mentioned to him that I had been asked to sit on the Rhapsody board, and I explained to him the relationship between Rhapsody and Apakoh. This of course immediately piqued his interest and he explained to me that Maria Cardoza had just gone to work for Rhapsody. He also explained to me that he was Maria's obstetrician."

"Wow that *ees fasceenateeng!*" Stephen had stopped rubbing Danielle for a few minutes while they went through the explanation about Al Moses. Danielle's interest was now very much piqued. While still lying on her back she rose up slightly from the chair sliding her elbows backward for support, while turning her head towards Stephen.

"Wait there is more. Apparently Maria reminds Al very much of Anne Mohr."

"I'm not sure I know … Check that … I'm not sure I *want* to know where *thees ees goeeng.*"

"Hold on a second. Don't make any judgments until you hear everything I have to say." Danielle was now sitting upright and had swung her legs off the lounge chair to the space between her chair and Stephen's chair. The only sound besides their voices was the gentle lapping of the ocean against the sand, 30 feet from where they sat.

Stephen continued, "Apparently Al has taken quite a liking to Maria. In addition, Maria isn't married, and she isn't even seeing the father of her child at all. And so Al has apparently begun to play the role of friend and confidante for Maria."

"'*E* told you all of *thees*? '*Ow* much *deed* he actually say and '*ow* much are you just *surmiseeng*?"

"Well I could tell from his tone of voice that he was more than just a little bit interested in Maria. It certainly is not simply a professional relationship. He mentioned that he has taken her out to dinner on several occasions. What else should I have asked him?"

"There are certainly ways that you could '*ave* learned more, *eef* you wanted to. I'm not sure you wanted to know. And I don't want to ask. '*Owever* let me ask you *these*; Al said that this Maria woman reminds '*eem* a lot of Anne Mohr. Does she look *anytheeng* like Anne?"

"Not really. Anne was an attractive woman and Maria is extremely attractive in her own right."

"What does *thees* mean … 'extremely *attracteeve een* '*er* own right?' And by the way, '*ow* old *ees thees* woman? *Ees* Al *eenfatuated weeth* '*er*? '*E* is probably old enough to be '*er* father. I would imagine. Tell me. What *ees* the story with your friend Al?"

"Well that's a lot of questions. So let me try to provide some answers. I'm not sure how old Maria is, and I certainly wasn't giving it much thought when I met her. I'm assuming she's probably in her mid-30s. And yes, she is a very pretty woman. She also strikes me as a very nice woman. There is no question in my mind that she also is a very reasonable and intelligent person."

"Regardless of what you think about Al Moses, he has been my friend for almost 50 years and he will always be my friend. I have to admit that from time to time I have worried about Al. But in general I regard Al as a man of character and integrity, and I have always thought that way. If he is finding some kind of fulfillment through his relationship with Maria then so be it. I think you need to give Al a chance. Remember you really liked Al when we were younger … when he was with Anne. What changed?"

The sun was very bright now and so Danielle quickly added a baseball cap to her wardrobe and pulled it down to just above her sunglasses, giving her a three-piece ensemble. She reached into the cooler and pulled out a bottle of water and unscrewed the cap before answering. She took a long swig of the water and handed the bottle to Stephen.

"*Eet's 'ard* to say, Stephen. *Eet's* not that I don't like Al … as you just said, we *deed* a lot together earlier *een* our lives when *'e* was together *weeth* Anne. But when she lost the baby and then they *deedn't* get married … and then Anne died … I was somehow angry *weeth* Al. I guess I *theenk* about *'im* as a dowdy *leettle* old man, who threw away *'ees* one great *'ope* for *'appiness*. And *een* many ways, *eet's* understandable why *'e 'as* been so *meeserable* ever *seence*."

"I don't think that you're being fair to Al. If he had married Anne, it wouldn't have mattered. She would still have contracted breast cancer and, unfortunately, she still would have died. Those are the facts. And those facts are not Al's fault. In many ways Al has been the victim of destiny. And now, I for one, hope that destiny is about to shine on Al Moses once again."

"Maybe you are right. I need to be much more open-minded about these *theengs*."

Stephen handed the water bottle back to Danielle after he had taken a swig of water himself. She promptly drank the rest of the water and said,

"It really is *'ot*. The water seems to be *goeeng* right through me." Droplets of perspiration began to appear near her clavicle, moistening the top of the valley between her exposed breasts.

Stephen took a long look at his lovely wife. To him she was a fascinating creature. She stood up and began walking towards the surf. He noticed that her nearly nude body was one that a 25-year-old woman would be proud to call her own. Her muscles were taut and tight and her skin was entirely unwrinkled. Although she had some minor cosmetic adjustments made in recent years, most of the form that was moving away from him towards the ocean was simply her natural French beauty. Stephen himself was not nearly as zealous about staying in shape, as was Danielle. However he was generally fit and healthy and had every intention of staying that way. He stood up and peeled off his jacket and followed his wife down to the shoreline. He caught up with her when she was about waist high in the surf. They held hands for a second and then both of them dove under an incoming wave, resurfacing on the other side smiling and splashing one another.

"God, the ocean certainly does feel *refresheeng*," Danielle said as she bounced up near her husband.

Stephen reached out and put both arms around his wife pulling her chest against his own chest. With one eye on the lookout for the next wave, he ducked his head down and kissed his wife on her lips. Then he quickly let go as they both once again dove beneath the oncoming surf.

This time when they resurfaced it was Stephen who spoke. "Yes it certainly feels good. You'll have to be careful about the sun though. The ocean will wash away all of the suntan lotion."

"That *ees* fine by me. We *weell* just *'ave* to go back on the beach and you can redo me."

****

Abby was excited. After finally deciding to be dressed comfortably in black slacks and a long sleeved, off-white silk blouse, she made her way to the hotel lobby to meet with Johnstone. When she arrived in the lobby, Johnstone was already there. Bob Johnstone was a big beefy American. He made no pretense that he subscribed to the 'dress for success' approach to business. He looked as though he hadn't shaved in a week His shirt and pants were wrinkled, and his sport jacket looked as though he had worn it every day for a week. No one would've ever suspected that Bob Johnstone was a wealthy man. At least they wouldn't have suspected that by just seeing him. But the moment Johnstone began to talk people began to listen.

"Well hello there, Abby. I'm glad to see that you made it on time. You know how I hate to wait for anything, or for anyone. I hate wasting time."

"Back at you, Bob … I'm on time, five minutes early in fact, so what's the problem?" It was literally an out of body experience for Abby to listen to her own words. These are not the kinds of things that she usually said in her normal business discourse. This time though she had decided to play according to rules that were set by Johnstone. If he wanted to be gruff, she could be gruff. If he wanted to be tough, she could be tough. None of this really mattered. It was all about securing the funding that was needed to launch Rhapsody Holdings. This preliminary meeting to secure the bridge loan that fronted Rhapsody's ability to take down a line of credit that was much more significant, than this initial $5 million.

"Why don't we go over and have a drink in the bar, Abby? We can probably discuss the objectives of the evening pretty sanely over a martini or two. Does that work for you?"

"You bet."

Johnstone hauled his ample girth toward the bar. At 6 foot five, and 325 pounds, he was nearly 3 times the size of Abby McDuffee.

When the two of them moved towards a corner table, a few heads turned to catch a glimpse of the odd couple. The svelte Abby and the less than svelte Bob comprised the dynamic duo that captured the attention of the servers who were quick to fetch them a white wine and a dry martini, respectively. After a couple of sips of his martini, Johnstone turned to Abby and explained the rules of the game.

"Let me tell you a couple of things about Sun Feng, who will be joining us for dinner. Mr. Feng is an interesting dude. We have shared with him the major elements of your business plan over the last twelve months or so, and he has been consistently interested in your progress. He loves the idea that you are 'thinking big.' He also loves the idea of bringing the *Rhapsody Lifestyle* philosophy to Asia. He definitely wants to be part of that effort. And I have to tell you; you definitely *want* to have him be part of that effort. And it's not just about his money. Of course there's no denying that Sun Feng is one of the wealthiest people in the entire world. In fact Mr. Feng has actually written off investments in other health and wellness opportunities in the past. He has simply treated them as charitable donations. It's not about making money, per se. However he will ask for a fair interest rate on his loan He has an avid interest in what you are doing. He also has an avid interest in living as long as he can possibly live and enjoying every minute of his life for however long it lasts. Mr. Feng is not about to loan Rhapsody Holdings $5 million without believing that your company can make a significant difference, a significant contribution for that matter, to the leadership of a new social order with respect to health and wellness worldwide."

"That's fine. I wouldn't ask him for the money if I didn't believe that also."

"By the way I got your e-mail with your wiring instructions to your bank. I have forwarded that information to one of Feng's people, who will be handling the transfer once Feng gives them the go-ahead."

Abby and Johnstone talked for a little while longer about the particulars of what needed to be done by the Rhapsody team and the time frames involved in executing various elements of the plan. Johnstone seem to listen carefully but made no attempt to take any notes or to query Abby in deep detail about any single element of the plan. After a while they got up from the bar and went out in front of the hotel to grab a taxi cab over to the Champs-Elysees. When they pulled up in front of the restaurant they noticed a long black limousine directly in front of the door.

As they stepped across the front portal, Sun Feng got out of the car and followed them inside. Johnstone greeted Sun Feng and introduced him to Abby and they were all escorted to a rear table. Abby immediately noticed how different Sun Feng was from Bob Johnstone. Whereas Johnstone was gruff and studiously unkempt, Sun Feng had a very refined appearance. He was slim and well groomed and he appeared to be a few years younger than Abby herself. If she had to guess she would've put Sun Feng's age at somewhere in his early 40s. He was wearing an expensive gray Caraceni suit, custom made in Milan and a stunning red silk tie. Abby felt uncomfortably underdressed, and immediately wished she had worn her black dress or her gray business suit. The threesome looked like an interesting group of unfamiliar individuals, with very little in common personally, who were simply coming together for a common business purpose. And that, in fact, is exactly who they were.

"So, Dr. McDuffee, I have been following your progress through my discussions with members of the Louisiana Group for more than a year now. I find your plan for Rhapsody Holdings quite fascinating. Besides the many therapies and services you intend to offer to your members, you have managed to think through how you intend to deliver your product. I know of no other business that has spent as much time developing such a broad range of ideas before deploying any of them. I'm not sure whether that's a good thing or a bad thing. What do you think?"

"Thank you for your compliments Mr. Feng, and let me address your concerns. Yes we have spent a good deal of time developing our membership product but we have a long way to go. We may never know what the optimal time to start is. We keep learning more every day. However we have reached a juncture where we recognize that the pace of our progress will be impeded without the infusion of the capital that is called for in the business plan."

"Yes of course. And from what Mr. Johnstone here has told me the funding arrangements with the banks here in Europe are now all in place and your funding should be flowing to you as per your agreement with Mr. Johnstone and his team."

"Exactly. And I was told that you personally will be willing to advance us some funds immediately, while we are working out the details of a long-term arrangement with the Louisiana Group."

"Yes. That's very direct. I like that. That's why we're having dinner here this evening. Is it not? So before we order we ought to get some of these minor business details out of the way. I like that approach. So what do you believe an effective short term interest rate should be, Dr McDuffee?"

"Mr. Feng, I wouldn't pretend to know the market as well as you do. What do you believe would be a fair rate to ensure Rhapsody's success, and to give you a fair short term rate of return?" Abby wanted Feng to put the first stake in the ground, and didn't want it to be a stake through her heart.

"In view of the fact that we all want Rhapsody to be a blue chip company at some point in the future, I think that we should look at the bridge loan rates that blue chip companies are currently paying for loans on various transactions. The debt for Altria's acquisition of UST was set at 6 points above the comparable treasury rates. The rate for Verizon's bridge loan to facilitate its acquisition of Alltel is 3 points above LIBOR. And rumor has it that Pfizer may have to pay a rate of as much as 7 to 9 points above treasuries for the bridge funds it needs to acquire Wyeth, in spite of Pfizer's AAA credit rating."

The negotiation went back and forth for about a half an hour until Mr. Feng was generally satisfied that Abby was an intelligent and reasonable businessperson. That was all he really wanted to know. He truly didn't care as much about the rate of return that he would achieve on such a small loan for such a short time period. He was more fixated on what Rhapsody would be able to achieve in the long run. Besides it was really Bob Johnstone and the Louisiana Group who would be bearing all of the long-term risk. It was their assets that were pledged to back the line of credit at the banks. And Johnstone had a business relationship with Feng's father that dated back almost twenty years. Feng knew that his quick cash infusion was what was needed, as Rhapsody and the Louisiana Group forged their final agreement. He planned on providing the bridge loan at a rate that would be much less than the Blue Chip rates that they discussed.

Before dinner was served they had agreed on an effective, actually very attractive, short-term rate for the bridge loan. The rate was LIBOR plus three percentage points and Feng sent a text message to his staff to release the $5 Million in bridge funding after they signed some simple documentation in the morning. The rest of dinner was delightful, although Abby could barely wait to share her good news with the team.

****

Alison was sitting at her computer ready to shoot off a few quick e-mails when her cell phone rang. It was Seth Silverstein, the "Dream Weaver" himself.

"Hello Seth how are you doing today?"

"Not bad, Alison. How about you and your team?"

"We're actually doing quite well thank you. Abby is in Paris and will be meeting with the financial people about the funding for our business. We are hoping that the bridge loan, that will get us through to our first tranche of senior debt funding, will be available to us as soon as Thursday. Abby is working on that as we speak. We're all thrilled! You are on my list to call this morning but it looks like you beat me to the punch."

"That's excellent news Alison. Excellent, excellent news! I was just calling to ask you about a couple of items that we discussed when you folks were all out in California at your meeting. Your team gave me an update on the number of items on our conference call. One of the things that we talked about was the status of the book about Rhapsody. I just want to make sure that I have my time frames straight. You think that we will be able to publish it before the summer. Correct?"

"Yes, absolutely. As we told you a couple weeks back, we already have a ghostwriter working on the story … in fact we have three ghost writers working on the story … and they should have the transcript ready for editing in another month."

"Good. Remember I mentioned to you that I have a very good relationship with Dr. Zoë Mansfield, or as she's known on TV just Dr. Zoë. I've arranged for you to have dinner with her in two weeks. As you know Dr. Zoë is extremely close to Omar. Omar is also very interested in health and wellness. It seems like every other day he has someone on his show who has written a book on one health care topic or another. I don't have to tell you that Omar is the single most influential person in the world when it comes to publicizing a book.

"I realize that this is only one pathway on our publicity trail, but take my word for it it's a very important one. I know you'll get along very well with Zoë. Some of her critics whisper that she's no more than a TV Dr. Don't believe it for one minute. I have to tell you that most of the physicians that I know, who know Zoë personally, think that she's a wonderful human being, and is an extremely competent physician. And more importantly, she's one step from Omar."

"Do you know Omar personally?"

"I've met him several times, but we're really just casual acquaintances. But we do have numerous friends in common. Of course Omar is a triple A+ celebrity. Besides being extraordinarily wealthy and enormously generous, he counts among his friends almost every big name in New York and Hollywood. He's a powerhouse. No doubt about it. But his bully pulpit is the media. Make no mistake about it; What Omar wants Omar gets. The good news about all of this is that the "Big O" has a gigantic heart. He always wants to help people as long as they're willing to help themselves. Bluntly speaking, it is a business imperative to have Omar on our side. He's not easy to get to. That's why it's best to get to him through Dr. Zoë. In addition to other things, she more or less vets all of the health and wellness people who appear on Omar's talk show."

"Thank you Seth. You've been wonderful to us. I can't tell you how much we appreciate your support in helping us launch this business. We will have the book completed on schedule, and I look forward to meeting Dr. Zoë in a couple of weeks."

"Great Alison. And congratulations once again on closing in on your funding. I look forward to seeing you and Abby sometime soon. Say hello to the rest of the team for me if you would."

Alison put down the phone and smiled. Things are really beginning to move fast, she thought. She opened her computer and began to craft the few e-mails to be sent to different members of the extended team. Before long she noticed the incoming call indicator for a Skype call on her computer coming from Sandeep Mehra. She clicked on his icon.

"Sandeep, did you get my e-mail? Did you hear our good news?"

"Yes Alison. I got the message. This is *wery vonderful* news! And I have more good news to share. I am back over in the Ukraine and it appears that Max Tkachuk's family is *villing* to sell Apakoh. So the funding could not have come at a better time. After Abby meets *vith* Johnstone and Mr. Feng today, *ve vill* need to get together on a conference call tomorrow to talk about Apakoh. *Ve vill* also need to have Ben on the call with us. I know *ve* talked about trying to acquire Apakoh from the Tkachuk family in a stock *svap* but I have to tell you in *adwance* they seem *wery* much more interested in a cash transaction."

"I'm not worried about that at all. In fact that may work out very well for us. By the time we finish the negotiation and agree upon the deal we will have more than enough cash to make the acquisition, as long as the Tkachuk family's expectations are reasonable."

"Okay Alison I just *vanted* to check in *vith* you. I didn't *vant* to bother Abby *vith* this right now because she could be meeting *vith* Johnstone and Feng real time and I'm sure she has other things on her mind." Alison could detect a strong sense of excitement on the part of the small Indian man, with the big appetite for challenge. She knew that Ben was right when he pushed Abby to hire the young entrepreneur.

"All right Sandeep. Thank you very much. I appreciate the call. I will get back to you as soon as I hear anything at all from Abby."

Alison was getting truly excited. Things were happening very quickly and everything seemed to be falling in place naturally. She marveled at what seemed to be a preordained set of circumstances that were about to permit her to realize her dream.

****

Fernando had driven both Maureen and John Brady to the hospital in Manhattan from their Kings Point home. They left at a little past 6 AM so that they could be at the hospital by 7 AM. Brady's surgery was scheduled to begin at 8:30 AM. However the hospital staff wanted him there by 7 AM in order to go through the regular routine of pre-operative prepping. JB was brought to a private VIP waiting room, and Maureen stayed by his side until about 7:30 AM. Then she kissed him on the lips and squeezed his hand and told him that she would be waiting for him when his surgery was completed.

Maureen waited at the hospital for the news that her husband's operation had been successful and that he was recovering comfortably. She expected to hear this news within a few hours after he had gone in for surgery. The surgical procedure itself was scheduled to take a little over two hours from the original administration of anesthesia to the time when JB returned to consciousness. It was logical that it might take as much as one additional hour before she would hear from his surgeon.

"Mrs. Brady?"

"Yes?"

"Dr Madison would like to see you in his office. He has just come out of surgery for Mr Brady."

"How is he doing? How did the surgery go? Can I see John? When can I see John?"

"Dr. Madison would like to talk with you directly Mrs. Brady. Only Doctor Madison can comment on the surgery. Please come with me. He is right around the corner in his office."

Dr. Madison and Dr. Adams were both standing inside Dr. Madison's office, which really was not Dr. Madison's personal office at all, but merely a shared facility for physicians who operated at the hospital.

"Mrs. Brady please come in and sit down." Madison actually picked up an armchair and turned it about an inch in Maureen's direction in a gesture that emphasized his desire that she be seated."

"How is my husband? How is John? How did the surgery go?" By now Maureen was a nervous wreck and it was very obvious from the urgency of her inquiries.

"Your husband is in our intensive care unit Mrs. Brady. His condition is not immediately life-threatening but the outcome of his operation is troubling. I'm sorry to have to tell you that Mr. Brady's spinal cord was severed during the operation, and unfortunately Mr. Brady is paralyzed. The prognosis is not good."

ACT THREE

THE RHAPSODY MEMBERSHIP

Chapter 15: *The New Beginnings –*
April 2010

Alison and Abby McDuffee stood up close to the giant ribbon near the fifth floor entranceway to the brand-new Rhapsody center on Park Avenue in New York City. The ribbon-cutting ceremony was something that the McDuffees and their Rhapsody team had envisioned for quite some time. Dao Diskul had wanted to attend in person, but was pressing forward with developments for Rhapsody's prospective Asian headquarters in Singapore. The opening of the first center in New York City in April of 2010 signaled the beginning of the 50-city rollout of centers worldwide.

Several members of the executive team of Rhapsody flanked the McDuffee sisters for the ribbon cutting, including two of the original "Band of Five," Ben Hui Zhang and Sandeep Mehra. Also standing two spaces away from Abby, was a thin Ukrainian man dressed in a new suit that didn't fit his narrow frame.

The mayor of New York City was not in the habit of showing up at the openings of spas and health centers. However the Rhapsody center opening was an exception to the rule. The city had experienced a significant economic downturn in 2009 and was just now beginning to turn the corner in 2010 as the financial markets finally started to show some signs of life and the mayor's many austerity programs began to be lifted. New York City was the worldwide headquarters for Rhapsody Holdings. The mayor was uncertain how many jobs that would mean for the city in the coming years, but he was sure that the global image that Rhapsody had already begun to create would have a positive inflection on the business environment in Manhattan.

The New York City media was out in full force as were a number of international reporters. Celebrity talk show host, Omar, had taped an interview with the McDuffee sisters for his show earlier in the day. It was the fifth time that the Rhapsody executives had appeared on the "Omar" show during the last few months, and Omar was one of the very special guests to be invited to the Rhapsody opening. Omar's cute young fiancée was by his side as was his ever-present friend and colleague Dr. Zoë Mansfield, and her husband, Peter.

The guests for the opening day celebration included many of the people who were instrumental in getting Rhapsody off the ground, including a mixture of A-list celebrities like newlyweds Josh and Gina Struben and Josh's parents, Stephen Struben and Danielle Dubonet. Mingling with the Struben party were Dr. Al Moses and his new live-in girlfriend, Maria Cardoza, who had left her baby daughter, Duffy, one floor below at the Rhapsody childcare center, "Raffies." Maria was doing double duty as a young mother and also as the director of Rhapsody's Spa services. The Struben group also included Josh's younger brother, Adam, and his on-again off-again girlfriend, Celine, of GGH infamy.

Also invited to the grand opening were a number of well-known physicians and health and wellness practitioners from the New York area, and a group of practitioners from London who were looking to get a head start on the London center which was scheduled to open up in the fall. The New York City physicians included the aforementioned Dr. Zoë Mansfield and one of her professional colleagues Dr. Thomas Madison. Madison had recently been exposed to a fair bit of criticism involving a somewhat sensationalized story surrounding the ill-fated surgery of former ICD CEO, John Brady.

Psychiatrist, Dr Angelique Lefebvre and her husband, Yogi Vijay, both of whom had joined Rhapsody's Global Practitioner Society (GPS) in recent months, at the invitation of Maria Cardoza, were also in attendance. Another leading psychiatrist who had been recruited into the GPS, Dr. Greg Mendelsohn, was also at the party, with his pretty young girlfriend. Several cardiologists, oncologists, neurologists and orthopedic surgeons rounded out some of the allopathic medical talent that was assembled. There also was a chiropractor, a nutritionist, a craniosacral therapist, an acupuncturist and an ayurvedic practitioner amongst the alternative medical practitioners in attendance.

Other prominent individuals at the opening included several business luminaries from the area, including highly regarded publicist Seth Silverstein, who seemed to know every individual in the room personally. Also making an appearance was Jonathan Cromwell, the well-known former proprietor of Cromwell Parsons resources, and recently appointed by the mayor to head up New York City's economic resurgence board. The CEO of supplier/partner STRX, Kurt

Gutfreund, was in town from Germany and also came to the opening. Local sports stars from the Knicks, Yankees and football Giants, who were also *Rhapsody Lifestyle Members,* mingled at the exclusive cocktail hour.

Gina Alvarez-Struben, had been pushing her agent Carl "Pepper" Gordon and her publicist, Seth Silverstein, to remove the hyphen from her name without much success. It seemed as though neither Gordon nor Silverstein felt that this was such a great idea, as she was looking to firmly establish her solo act, following her amicable split with the Lay D's.

The one place where Gina was able to see her name reflected as simply Gina Struben was on the membership rolls of the *Rhapsody Lifestyle Membership.* Both Josh and Gina had become "Cornerstone Members" five months earlier at the time of the initial membership sales. They were also discussing a significant personal investment in the London center to be opened later in the year as well as one that they hoped would be opened in either Paris or Rome in 2011. Their personal relationship with the McDuffee sisters had blossomed in the last twelve months and the twins treated them almost like family

In a back corner of the lobby Alison and Abby's husbands, Tom Singleberry and Bo Blanchard laughed spiritedly with their sister-in-law Caitlin Browning and her husband, Scott. They were enjoying the party, which was the capstone for a lot of hard work that had been done by the twins over the last three years. Caitlin was now leading Rhapsody's corporate sales effort to the large multinational corporations, several of whom have expressed significant interest in getting group memberships for their executive teams. Her days at ICD were now almost 9 months in her past.

The group that stood behind the ribbon waiting for Abby and Alison to cut it was being photographed so many times that they began to laugh among themselves and finally the Mayor turned to Abby and said, "Just cut the darn thing or they will be taking pictures until the end of my seventh term." Everyone laughed, and Rickie Van Dorfan hustled over with the giant scissors. Rickie had come over to fill the role of EA for Alison McDuffee, earlier in the year, at the request of his former boss at ICD, Maria Cardoza. Collectively Abby and Alison and the mayor managed to all hold onto the oversize scissors and finally severed the ribbon to the sound of applause from the 250 or so guests and the flashing of media cameras around the room. Abby looked around the room and then began to speak.

"Allie and I did not want to be long-winded with our remarks here at the opening. So we decided that one or the other of us would take the lead and welcome all of you to the grand opening of our first Rhapsody center.

"Thank you all for coming to our beautiful facility here on Park Avenue in the heart of New York City. This day has been a long time coming and has been the work of hundreds of Rhapsody employees, as well as our contracting partners, our strategic marketing partners, our supplier partners, and their financiers. A simple thank you is never an adequate way to express the deep gratitude that all of us feel towards all of you.

"In a few moments we will make a tour of the facility available to all of you in small groups. But before we get on with tours I'd also like to give a very special thank you to many of our Cornerstone Members who are here with us this evening. Our membership is a simple reason for our existence. Those of us who are members of the management team at Rhapsody, look forward to serving our *Rhapsody Lifestyle Members* in a manner that delivers to them service second to none. In fact, *Service Second to None*, has become the in house mantra amongst the *RhapsodyCare* team. In order to deliver that kind of service we will need to hear from you regularly so that we can exceed your expectations.

"As we build our global collection of Rhapsody Centers around the world, we will look to recognize individuals who have made a major contribution to the holistic healthcare movement that Rhapsody embodies. Each of our Rhapsody Centres will therefore bear the name of a person who we feel has brought honor to our efforts. With that in mind, I would like to tell you that our first center here in New York City is being named after someone who grew up far away from the bright lights of Manhattan, and who later became a very successful entrepreneur in the information technology arena.

"Most of you have probably never heard of a gentleman by the name of Maksym Tkachuk. However Max goes far back with the Rhapsody concept and has worked with our CIO Sandeep Mehra for many years. Through Mr. Tkachuk's Ukrainian IT company, Apakoh, Max has had an enduring impact on the Rhapsody dream. His team has been instrumental in helping us develop the *Rhapsody HealthPort* and they also have helped put together some elements of *HealthMap*, starting as far back as four years ago. Max was thinking about personalized healthcare records long before President Obama and many others popularized the idea. The collaboration between Apakoh, STRX, and Rhapsody is the longest standing business relationship in company's short history.

"Unfortunately, in the autumn of 2008 Max Tkachuk was taken from us before we had a chance to realize our dream together. He died in a London hotel room of a massive heart attack. However we know that his spirit is with us here today. The employees of Apakoh became part of our team here at Rhapsody in the spring of last year. And although Max can't be here physically with us today his brother Vladimir Tkachuk is standing over there near the glass elevator. Vladimir, would you come on up here to the podium so that we can have a few more photos taken together as we formally announce the name of our new *Rhapsody Center* here in New York City, the *Tkachuk Center for the Rhapsody Lifestyle.*"

As Abby posed for pictures with Vladimir Tkachuk she remembered how Max's brother had negotiated the naming rights as part of the deal when Rhapsody acquired Apakoh. Although Max had certainly played an early role in one pillar of the Rhapsody Lifestyle, Tkachuk was not the first name Abby would've had in mind for the center. In fact she, herself, had never met the man. But it wasn't a terrible choice either. She knew it wouldn't be the last compromise that she would make as CEO of the company and if it made some people happy then it wasn't all that bad a deal. After a few seconds of picture taking and a brief round of applause, Abby continued her commentary.

"I said I'd be brief but I want to make one other announcement before we let you get back to your cocktails and we begin some of the tours of our facility. Some of you may know that our business plan calls for us to donate 5% of our corporate profits to the Rhapsody Foundation. We expect to make the crossover to profitability in the not-too-distant future and therefore we want to announce the formal creation of the *Rhapsody Foundation,* and the appointment of Alex Trager as the President of the Foundation. His philanthropy is well known throughout the New York metropolitan area as well as throughout the healthcare business world.

"The Foundation itself will be focused on making donations to research dedicated to disease prevention and health promotion. In the past ninety cents out of every dollar of healthcare research has gone toward remedial treatment options. In keeping with our mission to find ways for our members to live longer healthier lives, we want to focus our resources and the resources of our foundation on the *elimination* of disease wherever possible."

Near the back of the room two interested men stood listening to Abby talk. Sun Feng turned to Bob Johnstone and said, "The only problem I see is that she needs to move faster. I would like to see the Beijing Center in operation sooner and I would also like to see a center in the works for Moscow. The more rapid development of Rhapsody Holdings and the wider its footprint of centers, the more good it will be able to do."

"I agree," said Johnstone.

Feng continued. "Faster is better. Over the last year Chinese investment in the United States has become more pervasive than ever before. The Rhapsody concept provides an opportunity for us to underscore the positive benefits of this cooperation to the people of both countries. Together with our friends in Moscow, we can demonstrate world leadership in something of benefit to all the people of the world. I would like to talk with Dr. McDuffee about these things, so that Rhapsody can be developed at a much faster pace."

"Yes. We need to accelerate everything. I'll arrange a meeting for us with Abby." Johnstone and Feng then walked over to the bar area to share a celebratory cocktail, as Abby completed her remarks.

****

Downtown, Paul Pritchard was fighting mad. He was not, and never had been, an operating executive. But over the years he had done enough investment and business initiatives to know the difference between a firm that was on the upswing, and the firm that needed a radical infusion of new talent to be at all successful. He was concerned and angry, in fact more angry than concerned.

Fundamental Health Resources had been given a shot in the arm in early 2008 with a sweetheart contract that they had negotiated with ICD, one of the most successful blue chip companies on the global stage. Pritchard felt that the management team led by Jason Tobin from ICD and Eric Mallory, his own recruited executive, was failing miserably with the task at hand. They had squandered what should have been "first mover advantage" in the marketplace and managed to sell less than 2000 memberships even though that they were selling memberships at less than half the price of the Rhapsody Center. He didn't realize or recognize the fact that Rhapsody was not selling memberships in its centers. They were selling memberships in the *Rhapsody Lifestyle*. The more he heard that excuse from his sales team, the more agitated he became. Pritchard felt that he had the right facility, located in the right neighborhood, attacking a broader marketplace, and yet he still could not explain why they had not garnered a much bigger share of the market before Rhapsody was out chasing members. The sales team was making the rounds of all the large MNCs in the New York City area, imploring the leadership of these companies to buy memberships for their executives. Although they were able to make some sales in this manner they were deeply discounted, at $15,000 to $20,000, compared to the Rhapsody prices that were more than double those rates.

There were a number of other business issues that also angered Pritchard. There was a significant cost overrun and the turnover amongst the physicians that they had hired for the center was high. These physicians felt that the electronic medical record system that was purchased for the center was woefully inadequate and difficult to use. Pritchard was also feeling a significant amount of pressure from Chipper Geld to make changes at the top of the executive management team. As two members of the FHR board, Geld and Pritchard had tried to provide some operational guidance to the management team for FHR. Until the last few months, John Brady had been totally out of the loop.

Pritchard was about to engage in a very unpleasant meeting with John Brady, former CEO of ICD, who was now a paraplegic. Nothing about this upcoming meeting would allow Pritchard to feel remotely comfortable. To begin with he understood the fact that Brady would be rolled into his downtown office in some device that defied description, but that would enable JB to bring his acute mental presence into a meeting, that didn't require physical prominence. JB was still very wealthy, and was more preoccupied than ever with the success of Fundamental Health Resources, now that he had been replaced as the CEO of ICD. Fundamental Health Resources was the vehicle by which JB intended to reassert his prominence. Paul Pritchard felt that JB's reemergence as a business force was a secondary consideration to the importance of earning a double-digit return on investment for all of the investors in the Pritchard Fund who had backed Fundamental Health Resources.

Following John Brady's disastrous surgery in February of 2008, it was only a matter of time before there would be a change of control at the helm of ICD. In deference to the tragic nature of JB's disability, the ICD board had named an interim CEO in March of 2008, and after months of negotiation, she was able to shed the interim designation, and become full-fledged CEO of ICD. Pritchard's negotiations with Susan Sheedy were a back burner item until the end of August. FHR had lost a lot of headway in the interim, but they were fortunate to have a solid group of workers from ICD who supported their goals and objectives without regard to the tenuous nature of the relationship between the two firms. Sheedy was also making it a priority to unwind the financial investment aspects of that relationship as soon as possible, while agreeing to support the project as a supplier.

But there were many other problems that concerned Pritchard. Many of these problems were associated with the other prominent investor in FHR, Chipper Geld. Geld seemed to be much more interested in the independent success of Solace in the Sun than he was in the FHR venture itself. The liberal terms of the deal that had been struck between FHR and Solace in the Sun allowed Geld to win regardless of the struggles of FHR. It was incredibly aggravating to Pritchard to have Geld complaining to him about FHR management and poor results of the investments through the Pritchard fund. At the same time, Geld's operation and expansion of Solace in the Sun, as a supplier of Spa services to FHR, was earning Geld significant financial windfalls. Pritchard had a hard time understanding how Geld could actually be greedier than he was himself. Pritchard also realized that Geld and Brady were rapidly becoming mortal enemies rather than trusted partners. Brady believed that Geld was ripping off FHR, and Geld claimed that the team that Brady had put in place from ICD was mismanaging the FHR operation. In short it was a mess. There was no trust. There was no profit. Value was dwindling. And FHR was having a significant overall impact on the Pritchard Funds.

The most galling part of the lackluster performance of FHR was the fact that its perceived competition, Rhapsody Holdings, was making significant positive inroads and was rumored to be already generating positive cash flow and profits. He also knew from his electronic surveillance that his former partner Jonathan Cromwell had made a significant investment in Rhapsody, and Jonathan's protégé Josh Struben and his wife, pop icon, Gina Alvarez were about to make a significant personal investment in the upcoming London center for Rhapsody. Nothing seemed to be going right for Pritchard.

John Brady entered the room on an electric wheelchair. His body was strapped onto the chair around both of his legs and both of his arms. He was able to move his head slightly and pivot his neck a total of 30 degrees. Brady was able to be expressive with his facial movements particularly around his eyes and eyebrows. This included the endless wrinkling of his nose and forehead. His breathing was labored and there was no movement whatsoever from any of his appendages from his neck down to his toes. He had an oxygen tube feeding oxygen through his nostrils from a tank attached to the back of his chair.

"Good afternoon John. Thanks for making the effort to come down to the office this afternoon." It was difficult for Pritchard to look at Brady when he spoke. At the same time he was astounded at Brady's ability to reengage in business endeavors so rapidly after his tragic operation. It had been a little more than a year since he became paralyzed, but he had been back to work for more than two months. Work now consisted of managing his own personal portfolio with the help of financial advisors, and digging in wherever he could with the overall direction of FHR. JB had not cut his ties with ICD entirely because he still owned a very significant amount of ICD stock. However he was no longer CEO and he was no longer chairman of the board. His influence was limited to a few ongoing personal relationships with ICD executives with whom he had worked over the years.

"Hello Pritchard. We need to make this meeting decisive. I'm very concerned that ICD wants to get out of the FHR investment, and I think that Sheedy bitch is still laying the blame for FHR's underperformance right at my feet. If I could manage it, I'd kick the ball under your feet." John Brady's voice was very raspy and much labored. However there was a strange power that emanated from an indefatigable will that had always been a hallmark of John Brady's character. His eyes flashed. His eyebrows danced. His forehead wrinkled and he conveyed all of his points.

"John, you and I have known each other forever. We've had many successes together over the years and we've met more than a few challenges head-on. Times are tough everywhere. Nonetheless we need to stay the course. We believed that FHR was a great concept and a great business opportunity. None of that has changed. We simply need to execute better. If the people we have in place now can't get the job done, then fuck-em, we'll go with someone else."

"Mallory was your guy and Tobin was from ICD. But neither of them has been getting the job done. I think that part of the problem is that you can't have two people in charge. Therefore my suggestion is very direct. I think I should run FHR myself. I'll keep Mallory and Tobin on board because they know where the bodies are buried. But all of the major decisions will now be mine."

"It won't work, John. Let's be very direct and realistic. A turnaround leader for FHR will need to work sixty or seventy hours a week. There will undoubtedly be a good bit of travel involved. We also will need to think carefully about the public relations issues surrounding a new leadership team. And candidly I don't believe that Chipper would support you taking control personally."

"Fuck Geld. Does he have a solution of his own? What does he want to do? Does he want to run the business himself? That was the original plan and he backed out." The agitation was beginning to show on John Brady's brow. The mere raising of his voice was an exertion of enough energy to make sweat appear across his forehead. His face, and for that matter his whole head, seem to redden like an isolated warning light, somehow turning itself on above a larger immobile mass of human bones and flesh. There was no mistaking the intensity of Brady's anger.

"John, let's face facts. Chipper is in a much better position to lead the team personally than you are. We are going to have to renegotiate our contractual agreements with ICD and with SIS. You and I both know that Sheedy wants out of this deal as soon as possible."

"Listen to me Paul and listen closely. I will deal with Sheedy and ICD and I will also deal with that greedy prick Chipper Geld." Although his arms and legs and torso didn't move even a fraction of an inch, JB conveyed the appearance of leaping out of his seat. "We want to open the second center in San Francisco by the end of this year and we're not going to give the spa contract to SIS. With your help we can get the money together to get rid of Geld. We still need ICD's help for a little while longer so I'll play my cards with Sheedy to maintain both their investment and their manpower until the San Francisco center is completed and sold out. I want to get rid of Geld before the end of the month. Once we right the ship we'll take on the McDuffees and Rhapsody."

Pritchard shook his head slowly as though he felt great compassion for John Brady, but he said softly, "It won't work JB. It just won't work. We need a different plan."

****

Singapore Changi Airport handled a record volume of passenger traffic in 2009, and the Rhapsody team had made their share of visits to the City-State by the equator. Dao Diskul and Ben Hui Zhang led the charge for the Rhapsody team. Singapore also had many leading-edge technologies in the medical field, and was conducting a good bit of breakthrough research with respect to genetics and genomic engineering.

This most recent trip to Singapore was very eye opening for Dao. She was accompanied on her trip by Mark Candu, the genomic PhD. Candu had been working as a part of Rhapsody's advisory board for the past year. They were a little late in getting some of the details of the *Rhapsody HealthMap* in place in time for the membership pilot that ran during the fall of 2009 but they managed to catch up before the main sales drive began. Then recently their focus on the *HealthMap* was enabling them to create intellectual property that would add significant value for the company. They were sitting at a coffee shop near the crossroads of two different terminal wings, which would lead Candu and Diskul in different directions on different flights within the next hour.

"Thanks for all your help on this trip, Mark. Not only were we able to recruit a good number of practitioners to the Rhapsody GPS, but I think we made some significant inroads in convincing a number of people that they ought to become *Rhapsody Lifestyle Members*."

"I agree with you. I think the people here in Singapore, in particular, are anxious to see us begin to build a Rhapsody center here as soon as possible. I can sense that they look to you personally Dao, as an advocate within the firm to solidify Singapore as Rhapsody's Asian headquarters. They want nothing less."

"It will be very interesting to see what the take rate for programmatic genetic profiling will be within the Rhapsody membership. What trends have you seen in your business so far, Mark?"

"As you know we are expecting the take rate to have a significant uptick as a result of our association with Rhapsody. We believe that the *Rhapsody Lifestyle Members* will be a very fertile test class for the many things that we like to do with respect to genetic profiling on an ongoing basis. The early returns from the *Rhapsody Cornerstone Membership* group show a significant interest in this type of testing. At least the take rate is at a much higher level than it has been in the general population of the Silicon Valley test groups that we have canvassed in the last few years. We are very excited about the possibilities going forward."

Dao looked at her watch and realized it was nearly time for her to move down towards the gate. She brought the topic of conversation to a more mundane level. "So what's next for you Mark? You're heading back to California now. Will you be out to New York to see the new center soon? I'm kind of eager to see it myself now that the opening is behind us."

"Actually I will be there early next week. I'm also am eager to see it. And Abby has asked me to meet with a couple of geneticists that she's been working with in New York to further develop the programmatic approach for the membership beyond what's already been done. She'll be sending me some information by e-mail. In fact I may already have it on my computer. That would be nice, because then I could read it on the plane on my way to California."

Dao got up from the table and said goodbye to Candu, and then hustled down towards the gate for her flight to Bangkok. Mark Candu soon got up and walked in the opposite direction for his flight back to San Francisco. Although they were headed in opposite directions, they were following similar paths.

****

The first 35 to 40 years of Maureen Brady's life read like something out of a romance novel. She grew up on the North Shore of Long Island, never knowing what it was like to worry about anything financial. She and her girlfriends talked mostly about finding "Prince Charming." Soon after four years of high school and four years at Vassar College, Maureen met John Brady and for two years they had an off again, on again relationship. John had been recently divorced, and Maureen's parents didn't care much for his working-class family background. When John met Maureen he was just starting up the ladder at ICD and Maureen was fresh out of college. They were from significantly different backgrounds, but Maureen convinced her parents that she was in love and soon thereafter she and John Brady married. Three children came quickly, and John's career moved up the corporate ladder. But that was then and this was now

In the last five years Maureen Brady's life had changed dramatically. She wasn't sure of the exact cause of her problems with alcohol, but now she fully recognized that those problems were a disease that had to be reckoned with. She was gratified that she had taken the appropriate actions to remedy this malady.

Maureen now had one significant goal. She wanted to get her body into the best possible physical shape that her 44 years of age would allow. Her personal trainer Grant was now working with her six days a week. Her husband John, had a physical therapist working with him seven days a week, and so their Kings Point home had become a destination point for a dozen or more health and wellness practitioners. Not a day went by when there wasn't a car or two in the long driveway that had been driven there by a healthcare professional of one sort or another. But recently JB was making it a point to get out of the house much more frequently and so most of his physical therapy regimen took place in the early morning hours.

John's new business partner, Chipper Geld, had recently purchased a co-op on the East side of Manhattan, and was a regular attendee at some of the celebrated philanthropic functions. Tonight's dinner was a black-tie affair and Maureen would be sitting at Chipper Geld's table. She wouldn't admit it to others, but she found Geld attractive. He had always treated her with kindness and respect, since they first met eighteen months earlier in Costa Rica at Solace in the Sun.

There were many oddities to all of this self-absorption on Maureen's part. Immediately following JB's disastrous operation, Maureen had been very attentive, spending a great deal of her personal time in a guilt-ridden obsession with trying to make her husband's life endurable, even meaningful. However JB reacted to this attention in a less than loving manner. He treated Maureen's attentiveness as though she were a paid caregiver rather than a loving spouse. As a result of Maureen began to respond in kind. The relationship between her and her husband evolved to being a marriage more of form than of substance. This was not at all what she had intended when she returned from Solace in the Sun after conquering her own demons. However her resolve to make her own life a better one surpassed her resolve to simply renew her marital vows. She wanted to be a better person regardless of the obstacles that life might have thrown her way. Her husband John Brady, a quadriplegic, had served himself up as being simply one of those obstacles.

She finished touching up her hair and makeup and entered her tripartite walk-in closet, ambling towards the section that held the collection of evening dresses and formal wear. There were at least a dozen dresses that had never been worn. She had an idea about the dress she was looking for, but managed to find something that she liked a little more but that she had forgotten she owned. Maureen selected this strapless dark purple dress and walked into the secondary area of the closet that held hundreds of color-coded boxes that contained shoes, handbags and other accessories. Almost as though she had a genetic homing-device sense for such things, she managed to migrate to the appropriate boxes containing the necessary items to complement her newly found dress. With her arms loaded, she walked back out of the closet and into the master bedroom and threw her selected wardrobe items on her bed. She then reentered her tripartite closet and walked to the rear right chamber where several randomly arranged dressers held a variety of undergarments. Remembering the words of her mother, "the right look requires the right undergarments," she rapidly selected what she needed and changed right there in the closet before going back into the bedroom to get into her dress.

About a half-hour later Maureen's bathing, makeup, grooming and dressing routine was finally completed to her satisfaction. Almost as though she were turning a switch, she started moving at a more rapid pace. She quickly grabbed a white cashmere pashmina to keep her shoulders warm and came down the stairway. Cara met her at the foot of the stairs and helped her put on her Black Gama mid-calf length mink coat, and opened the front door to the house for her.

As part of his severance agreement with ICD, John Brady and his family were able to keep their car and driver, Fernando, for the next five years. The new limousine had been outfitted to accommodate JB's disability, and Brady made full use of the stretch, going in and out of Manhattan on a regular basis. The car was not available for Maureen this evening however because Fernando was in the city with JB at a business meeting. However a silver Mercedes Mayback *was* available and the Mayback and its driver, who was waiting for Maureen in her driveway, both came to her courtesy of Chipper Geld.

****

The reception at the *Tkachuk Center for the Rhapsody Lifestyle* was now in full swing. The formalities had been dispensed with and the building tours were an adjunct to the general merrymaking on the part of the Rhapsody team and their guests.

    The Tkachuk Center occupied floors two through five in the Park Avenue building and also some retail space on the ground floor. Members had their own private entrance to the building and had access to the fifth floor reception area by walking over to a circular glass elevator located in the center of the building. This elevator made only two stops, one on the retail level and one at the fifth floor reception area. There were another two elevators of more classic design at the back of the reception area and they made stops on all five floors. One other elevator was located near the back of the reception area adjacent to the internal Rhapsody elevators. This elevator stopped at the retail level, the fifth floor reception area for Rhapsody, and then at all of the other floors of the other tenants throughout the multistoried edifice. This enabled the Rhapsody lifestyle members to have an appropriate level of privacy and security as they entered and exited the building.

    At the grand opening of the Tkachuk Center, Alison McDuffee and her husband, Tom, made a point of accompanying several of the groups as they took the tour of the premises. After listening to her sister address their guests at the start of the reception, Alison was now interested in seeing how these people would react to the beautifully designed center. They were now outside of the reception area on the fifth floor of the building, which was the top floor of the Tkachuk Center. The tour guide was explaining the layout of the floor space to the guests and Alison frequently added information as they went along.

    "This floor …and the three floors directly below us … are each approximately ten thousand square ft. of usable space. As you have already seen, members who enter the Center on the retail or ground level of the building will come directly up to our main reception area here on the fifth floor on the central glass elevator. The main reception area is the space where we were just having cocktails. Also on this floor is a large seminar room, which we are walking past on the right of the hallway. The door is open and you can look inside. On the left of the hallway you will see a conference rooms and two consultation rooms where practitioners can meet with members. Just beyond the conference room there is a fruit bar area and the adjoining library." The guide continued to lead the small group down the hallway walking backwards as he spoke. Alison paid close attention to the reactions of her guests to the lush wood trim and moldings that adorned the hallway and she noticed some of the guests start to take note of the paintings on the walls.

"The men's spa comprises the rest of the space here on the fifth floor. The space includes private lockers, tanning and relaxation rooms, steam baths, sauna and Jacuzzi facilities as well as individual treatment rooms for massages and other spa treatments. Toward the back of the spa is an administrative area including several computers for members use. All of these resources and more are replicated on the fourth floor just below us in the women's spa. But as you'll see when we get down to the fourth floor there are some additional areas adjacent to the women's spa that are dedicated to the Center's salon and aesthetics center. This area has stations for hairstyling and hair drying as well as stations for hair coloring and shampooing. Other stations are offered for makeup, manicure and pedicure within the salon area. And to the front of the fourth floor, you will also see our childcare facility 'Rhaffies,' where some of our members might choose to leave their young children while they use services."

They then took the spiral staircase near the center of the floor down to the fourth floor and toured the women's spa as well, before once again taking the stairway down to the third floor and the fitness part of the center.

"Is this part of the center open to both men and women?" One of the female guests asked?

"Technically all floors of the center are open to both men and women. Although the men's spa is on the fifth floor, as you saw the floor also houses seminar rooms and conferences as well as our juice bar. And although we recognize that more women than men will probably utilize the salon on the fourth floor, the guys will still make good use of the salon as well. But you are right. This floor, the third floor, generally will be more of a blend of men and women. Like the other floors it is approximately 10,000 ft.² of usable space. And as we walk around you'll see areas devoted to personal training, Pilates, yoga and dance studios and exercise rooms. This floor also houses our smaller unisex spa facilities for such activities like ayurvedic oil baths, Balinese massage, aromatherapy, foot massage, hydrotherapy, hyperbaric oxygen therapy, colonic washout and other therapies. Each of these rooms is outfitted with the latest equipment that will be continuously updated. Rhapsody has negotiated obsolescence insurance into contracts with each of our suppliers to ensure that we always have the latest equipment, whether we're talking about a treadmill on this floor, or an MRI machine like you will see on the medical floor which is just below us.

"There is one other thing that you should know about our equipment," Alison continued. "Every piece of equipment will collect personalized data for our members that will feed directly into our *HealthPort* and this will enable our practitioners to work with our members to continuously define and refine each members individual *HealthMap*. If anyone has any specific questions about that, I would suggest that you speak with Sandeep Mehra, our CIO who is here at the reception with us today. Sandeep was instrumental in designing the *Rhapsody HealthPort* and the *HealthMapping* algorithms and process interfaces, and would like nothing better than to discuss his work with any of you who would care to speak with him."

The group looked around the floor and walked past the general fitness areas. Then they passed the staff lockers and two rooms designated as "couples' rooms," which were in essence, multipurpose facilities that could accommodate concurrent message or other joint therapies. Toward the rear of this floor there were twelve separate personal examination rooms, where practitioners would be able to consider and evaluate members' health and wellness. In fact, at Rhapsody, we combine the two concerns and call it *healthness*, instead of health and wellness. There were three additional treatment rooms, six consultation rooms and an in-house pharmacy dedicated to personal compounding for vitamins and prescription drugs. After touring the third floor space they once again made their way over to the circular stairway and descended to the second floor of the building, which was the bottom floor of *The Tkachuk Center for the Rhapsody Lifestyle*. Once more the guide took over the narrative.

"On this floor we house all of our 'heavy medical iron' so to speak. We will have all the latest and most sophisticated equipment with respect to diagnostic radiology and our members' analytical needs. You'll see CT machines, MRI magnets, mammography equipment, ultrasound equipment, infra-red thermagraphy and densitometry and x-ray machines. Also towards the front of the floor, you'll see our section dedicated to the dental arts, complete with six dental chairs and our own dental lab, so that the dental procedures can be completed all in the same day. This floor also houses our operating suite and recovery rooms, which will be used for a variety of 'same-day surgical procedures,' including numerous cosmetic surgery processes. We also have a fertility lab and a general clinical lab located on this floor, just beyond the lounge area where we are now standing."

When they finished looking around the main medical floor, the group moved back over in the direction of the enclosed elevator bank. Alison pointed out that one of the elevators only traveled between the second floor and the small, twenty-car private garage, located one floor below the street level of the building. This was designed to ensure maximum privacy and security for any of the members who might want to enter and exit confidentially after receiving various treatments in the Center.

Alison and her husband Tom took the elevator with the rest of the group back up to the fifth floor reception area where she once again met up with her sister Abby, and Abby's husband, Bo. Another small tour group was leaving the area accompanied by Ben Hui Zhang and Sandeep Mehra. It was quite apparent that each of the business leaders was truly enjoying the rewards of several years of hard work.

Just after Alison reached her sister's small circle of celebrants, they were joined by Bob Johnstone and Sun Feng, who had also just arrived back in the main reception area from a tour of the facilities. Feng looked directly at Abby and asked a simple question in a very soft and unassuming tone. Nevertheless there was no mistaking his intention or his intensity.

"So, Dr. McDuffee, when will Rhapsody open a center in Beijing?"

****

Josh and Gina arrived back at their East side apartment shortly after 10 PM. They still kept two residences in the city. It was not a good time to sell, and they enjoyed the convenience of having options on any given evening. Josh felt that something was different with Gina recently. Uncharacteristically quiet, she seemed to be wrestling with a decision about something that she was reluctant to discuss. Josh had come to know his wife better than anyone in the world. He knew when to probe and when to leave her alone with her thoughts. Gina was a very engaging woman and throughout their relationship she rarely held back on her emotions. Josh knew that she trusted him implicitly. Therefore he would simply wait for her to tell him what was on her mind.

"Did you enjoy the opening?" Josh was just trying to make conversation. Gina was hanging her mink in the front hall closet and walked back towards him in the living room area.

"Absolutely. I enjoyed the party. I really like all of the Rhapsody people. Abby and Alison are great and it was nice to spend some time with your parents. It's just that I have something else in mind. It's something that my mother mentioned to me last week."

"Tell me about it. How is she feeling? Is she having any recurrence of her past respiratory problems?"

"No she is fine….. and healthy again. However when I went to see her last week she told me something that she has been keeping secret from me for my whole life."

"Really? So what might that be?"

"She actually does know who my father is. She just never told me about him before. It was shocking and I just had to think about it a while before sharing it. Until last week I never knew anything about my father other than the fact that he was never around when I was young. I believed that he left my mother before I was even born. That isn't exactly true. It appears that my father was with us in Puerto Rico until I was almost 2 years old. He left to go to the United States when he discovered that he had an unusual and incurable disease, called Huntington's Chorea."

"Isn't that the disease that causes people to slowly lose their mind? They become spastic and lose body control right?"

"Yes you're right. But that's just part of it. Over the last several days I've been doing some research on Huntington's disease and the picture is rather grim."

"As terrible as that is, you haven't seen your father in more than twenty years and you don't even remember him. Do you want to find him now? Is he even alive?"

"I don't know the answer to any of those questions. But there's a lot more to this issue than just locating a long lost parent."

"Like what?"

"Huntington's is hereditary. There is about a fifty per cent chance that I personally have the disease."

"Oh." Josh was speechless.

"My mother has been harboring this secret for a long time. It has been particularly hard on her over the last year. She said that she tried to tell me about it more than a dozen times but couldn't get up the courage to do so. When I was younger she simply made the decision not to tell me so that I could enjoy my youth without being concerned about the potential onset of Huntington's Chorea.

"It usually doesn't manifest itself until someone is at least 30. However after my miscarriage, she began to feel guilty about not telling me, in case I had the disease, and would potentially pass it along to our children. She simply had a hard time getting up the courage to tell me until last week. And now I have mustered the courage to tell you."

****

Chipper Geld's dinner table in the ballroom of the Waldorf Astoria Hotel was located off to the left of the dais and near the corner of the room. There were eight people seated at the table but the only one that Maureen had met before was Geld himself. Surprisingly Geld had brought an escort with him whereas he usually came to these events solo. Maureen was seated directly across from Geld.

Maureen couldn't help occasionally staring across the table at Geld's companion, "Natasha-something-or-other." She seemed inappropriately attired for the evening. She was one of the few women at the dinner who wore a short dress, and then her idea of a short dress was a next-to-nothing cheap black number that squeezed across her assets in a less than subtle manner. She appeared to be about a size 4, but had large standup Barbie Doll like breasts that seemed incongruous with the rest of her body. She had a smile that revealed less than perfect teeth that might have been a work in process as part of an ongoing makeover. The word that kept coming to mind for Maureen was "sleazy." The introductions by Geld had been brief and Maureen knew little about Natasha other than her first name. Natasha spoke with a heavy Russian accent whenever she could be heard making inane small talk with Chipper. For the most part Natasha just ignored the doctor seated to her left who had a hard time removing his eyeballs from her Barbie Doll assets.

Dinner was finally winding down and Maureen was happily ready to call it an evening. Chipper walked around the table to speak with Maureen with the Russian bombshell trailing close behind.

"We barely had a chance to talk, Maureen. Did you have a nice evening?"

"Yes Chipper. It was very nice," Maureen lied. "And by the way, thank you so much for sending the car. It made things a lot easier for me. I hope you had a nice evening as well."

"I know your car and driver are waiting downstairs for you, but if you are not too tired, why don't you come back to my apartment for a nightcap. Of course, I realize, that would be a non-alcoholic nightcap.

My place is right around the corner, five minutes away, tops. But I would like to show you the plans for the new center that Fundamental Health Resources will be opening in San Francisco later this year. Your husband has been very instrumental in the growth of the company in spite of his condition. He's quite a man. Don't you think?"

"Yes. John is very motivated." Maureen thought that Geld's question was a bit strange. Why would he ask her whether or not she thought her husband was "quite a man?" The truth of the matter was that Maureen and John were growing apart. It certainly wasn't what she had intended after she completed her rehabilitation at Solace in the Sun. But there was no getting around the fact that John's misfortune had a negative impact on their marriage in some unexpected ways as well as the expected ways. Maureen knew that their sex life would be terminated. What was unexpected, to her, was how much she would miss it. "Yes I think I will stop by for a couple of minutes," she answered Geld.

Maureen had no idea whether or not the Russian bombshell, Natasha, would also be coming back to Geld's apartment. For the first time ever in her life, Maureen Brady decided that it was okay to live life a little dangerously.

****

It was still early in the evening when Dr. Al Moses and his significant other, Maria Cardoza, picked up Maria's nine month old daughter, Duffy, from *Rhaffies* on the fourth floor of the *Tkachuk Center* and headed home from the grand opening of the center. Their car was waiting for them at the Park Avenue entrance to the building and they quickly jumped inside with Maria holding Duffy.

"I didn't want to stay there very long tonight but I'm glad we went. It was kind of thrilling to have everyone there in one place for a change. Everyone has worked so hard for so long that it was just great to be there. Don't you think so?" Maria turned towards Al as she spoke, looking for some reaction to the evening's events.

"Yes it was a very nice time. In some ways I didn't feel like leaving. It is interesting to watch the rapport between you and the McDuffee sisters. You all seem to get along so well."

"They have been unbelievably supportive of me throughout the past year. There have been so many changes in my life and Abby and Alison have made the transition very easy for me to make. That's why I named my daughter Duffy."

"She'll never have to worry about two people in her class being named Duffy Cardoza. That's for sure. An interesting combination of Irish and Italian ..." Moses caught himself before continuing, realizing that he had inadvertently commented on the natural parentage of the baby, when he only meant to underscore the beauty of her name. He realized that Maria had never told John Brady about Duffy, and as everyone knew Brady had other significant personal issues to absorb him.

"Honestly I never thought that I would enjoy being a mother is much as I do. However I have to admit that I also enjoy my job more than I've ever enjoyed any other job that I have held in the past. That's why I'm also so grateful that I have you, Al. You have been so wonderful to me in so many ways and I can't thank you enough. I don't know how I would've been able to manage being a businesswoman and mother at the same time if I hadn't had you helping me at every step along the way. I am truly grateful, Al.

"Then maybe one day soon, you'll reconsider my marriage proposal?"

Maria averted her eyes and then looking down at Duffy said softly, "Maybe."

"And just what does maybe mean? Does it mean maybe yes? Or maybe no?"

Still looking down at Duffy, Maria simply answered, "Maybe just means maybe."

Dr. Al turned and looked out the side window. He thought that his life had also changed dramatically for the better over the last year. But he also realized that he wasn't getting any younger. He was now 68 years old and had never been married. For whatever reason he wanted that condition to change. However he knew that it was not himself that he had to sell on the idea, it was Maria.

****

Danielle and Stephen Struben were among the last to leave the grand opening. Both Stephen and Danielle had enjoyed themselves more than they had thought they would. For some reason it seemed that the Rhapsody businesspeople, the Rhapsody physicians, and the Rhapsody members all got along very well with one another and it made for an interesting and fun filled evening. The only concern that Stephen had about Rhapsody was that its programs were currently helping a very elite and focused group of well-heeled client-members. In his heart Stephen believed that Rhapsody's true mission would not be fulfilled until the benefits of the Rhapsody program were available to everyone. He believed that his role on the Board of Directors would help ensure that this vision was eventually realized.

All of these thoughts and more were going through Stephen's mind as he and Danielle returned to their hotel room. As Stephen shut the door behind them, Danielle quickly sat down in an armchair, removed her high heels, and rubbed her sore feet.

"I guess I am *getteeng* old. My feet get very sore when I stand on them for too long."

"You're not getting old. You're every bit as beautiful as the day I met you. By the way, what did you think about Al's girlfriend, Maria?"

"Well *eet* was nice to finally meet 'er. I know you've been *eempressed weeth 'er abeeleety*, since you first met 'er at your *meeteeng* last year *een Caleefornia*. But *buseeness abeeleeties* aside, she seemed like a very nice young lady. So you tell me. What *ees* she doing *weeth* your good friend Al Moses? I'm sure she could do a lot better for *'erself*."

"Wow! How about another saucer of milk? That's about as catty a comment as you have made in a while. I guess some things just don't change. I know you think that Al is a bit dull, but he is my friend, and he'll always be my friend."

Danielle got up from the chair and walked over to her husband turning her back towards him so that he could unzip her dress for her. Facing away from him she said, "I know *'e weell* always be your friend. That *ees* just the way you are, Stephen … loyal. And I love you for who you are, and I always *weell*."

After he unzipped her dress, Stephen put a hand on each of his wife's shoulders and spun her around slowly. He then bent down and kissed her on the lips. He pulled away briefly and said, "I love you too."

Chapter 16: *Membership Has Meaning –* June 2010

It was now the sixth week of operation for the *Tkachuk Center for the Rhapsody Lifestyle* in New York City and the Rhapsody team was almost overwhelmed.

Abby looked around the room at the members of her executive team who were present for the meeting. Not all of the team was there, but enough of the executives were present to get a lot accomplished. The company's Chief Medical Officer, Dao Diskul was in from Bangkok and had visited the center for the first time over the weekend. Ben Hui Zhang was also in town and had been poring over the financials for the past 48 hours and was anxious to deliver the good news with respect to the balance sheet, income statement and the company's cash flow. Sandeep Mehra was a bit more reserved. He wanted to discuss the continued rollout of the *Rhapsody HealthPort* and *HealthMap* including the schedule for the next two releases due before the end of the year. The status of the ongoing growth of the *GPS* association was also on the agenda to be addressed by the GPS President Zoë Mansfield and by the Chief Strategic Officer, Alison McDuffee. Later in the day they were due to hear from Sun Feng and from Bob Johnstone who were working together in Beijing. They didn't anticipate getting that call much before 5 PM, which would be the following morning at 5 AM in Beijing, China.

"There's a lot that we need to get done in a very short period of time today. So let's get right into the agenda. In addition to the formal presentations that we have scheduled during the day we have a laundry list of problems/issues that need to be put on the table. For now we just want a list."

"I'll throw one up right away," said Alison. "We are falling behind on our training program for GPS practitioners."

"We're also behind in getting the latest member surveys data compiled and analyzed appropriately. We're asking our members what they want; they're completing the surveys and getting them to us. And we haven't yet begun to do interpret the data. It's just stupid." Maria added. "And another thing that I'll throw out there is that the salon is very underutilized. Maybe we should open it for Day-Members or something."

"There also are some issues with the take rate in our dental arts area. It has been picking up in the last few weeks and bookings are starting to look a little better, but scheduling is a bit off." Once again Alison was throwing another issue into the cauldron.

"The dental business should pick up *vith* the next release of our *HealthPort's* dental application. It *vill* be fully integrated at that point." Sandeep Mehra offered a potential solution to the problem almost immediately after it was put on the table.

"Remember what we are doing here. We're venting as many issues as possible. We are not trying to solve all the problems, or debate them, until we have a pretty good list to work. Okay? By the way, you *are* capturing all of this stuff. Aren't you Rickie?" Abby turned to Rickie Van Dorfan, her executive assistant to make sure he was not missing any of the issues.

"I've got them all right here." He was writing on an easel near the end of the table. Rickie had only been working with Abby and her team for a short while after coming over from ICD on a recommendation from Maria Cardoza. So far it was working out without any problems.

"Another issue I'd like to get out for us all to consider," said Ben, "is the fact that we all are getting some pressure in a big way to make the final decisions for the locations for our Asian centers in 2011. Dao has been running around like crazy throughout Asia, trying to satisfy a lot of different people." Dao nodded silently in tired agreement to Ben's statement. The two former lovers were no longer sharing each other's boudoir, but they were still quite friendly.

"That's a rather substantive issue, Ben. I know it's something that you get pressed on a lot, probably more than the rest of us. It's something that we will spend a good bit of time on later today. And I expect that we will make a decision on that sometime this week. However what we're looking to get out in front of us right now are some of the more tactical issues that we can make immediate progress on today. So anyway, good issue ... we will get to it. I promise."

"We need to find a way to update our website content more regularly. We are having a difficult time keeping it current with the many changes that are occurring every day." Alison added

"Okay website changes. Got it. What else?" Abby was clearly pushing for the list.

"HR issues. I've got a lot of them in my shop. *Ve* are adding people *wery* rapidly to maximize our output, but I *hawen't* personally been *ower* to see our IT group in Delhi, India or the people in the Ukraine who came *ower* as part of the Apakoh acquisition." Sandeep sounded off on an issue that all of the executives could relate to. The growth in personnel within Rhapsody was a significant challenge.

"I don't want to belabor Sandeep's point, but we have a number of HR on-boarding and training issues in the center as well," said Maria. "These issues are only going to multiply as we begin operations in a few months in London."

Over the next half hour or so the members of the executive team threw out a variety of different issues, some big, some small. Some issues were small enough to be resolved right on the spot. Usually these were issues where there was a simple misunderstanding on the part of one executive or another. When she was satisfied that she had a reasonable compendium of workable issues Abby then ask Rickie Van Dorfan to flip over a couple of pages and put a new heading on the board that said, "Things that are going well."

"So now that we've got the list of problems to tackle over the next several weeks, let's just make a list of the things that are going well and see what we can learn from them. Of course we also want to ensure that whatever is going well, stays on track. So let's hear it. What are we doing right? How are we making our members happy?"

"I know that our members are happy that they don't have to wait. A couple of them have commented on the courtesy of our staff as well," said Maria.

"People like the fact that we always have fresh flowers throughout the building." This comment came from Rickie and surprised some of the other team members a bit. Van Dorfan's role at the meeting was meant to be that of scribe. However his contribution was acknowledged as acceptable with a nod from Abby and a smile from Maria, so Rickie gleefully posted his own point and waited for additional commentary.

"I think that people are generally very happy with the ambiance of the center itself. But we mustn't lose sight of the fact that the center -- and for that matter all of the centers as we build them -- is only one pillar of the product. Our product is our memberships and our memberships are represented by the platinum and diamond keys that our members hold." Zoë Mansfield made the comment. However it could have been made by any one of the assembled business leaders. Abby was glad that it was Zoë who spoke up.

The team made a point of reminding each other about the true purpose of their business -- -- membership longevity, not center membership. With all of the excitement that was sure to be generated around the opening of centers throughout the world, there was a genuine concern that the ideal of "longer, better lives for Rhapsody Members," might be under emphasized. The executive team's job was to make certain that that did not happen.

"Another good thing is that people seem to be generally surprised and happy with the wide range of services that we offer." The team was back on track with the sound bite approach to brainstorming. This time it was Maria who spoke up.

"We are also ahead of where we had planned to be, with respect to the number of GPS locations. That was a big worry for Rhapsody last year," said Zoë. "I even remember when Omar asked you to explain how we would be able to roll out more than a hundred GPS locations and two full-blown *Rhapsody Lifestyle Centers* in less than a year. You did a great dance on that question on national TV, Abby."

"I guess I wasn't dancing after all, Zoë. Remember it's all about thinking big and acting big, having big plans, and achieving those plans. So it's good to see that we're ahead slightly in that arena, but as we noted earlier there are number of concerns yet to be resolved with respect to the GPS. But let's move on. What else can we say that we are doing correctly?"

"Well, following up on what I just said, Omar wants to have you and Alison back on his show next month. People want to know about our progress." Zoë was smart and understood the power of the televised media better than anyone on the Rhapsody team. She actually wore two hats for the group, one as the leader of the GPS and the other as the in-house PR czar. In the latter role she worked closely with her good friend Seth Silverstein, the Public Relations titan who had helped bring Gina Alvarez-Struben into the fold as a major part of the PR effort.

"That's great. Omar is a blast. Thanks, Zoë. Let's talk more about that at dinner tonight. What else do we have that's going well for us?" Abby inquired.

Abby McDuffee, Rhapsody's CEO continued in her role of coach and cheerleader and went around the table several more times as prissy

Rickie Van Dorfan wrote down many examples where the business seemed to be ahead of plan. Abby viewed this exercise as important, so that the team could realize how much progress they actually had made. She knew from experience that it was sometimes discomforting if they only looked at their problems and didn't take time to reflect upon the significant progress that they had made. She was proud of that progress and thought that the team should be proud as well.

****

Maureen Brady was having a difficult time with everything lately. After the diabetes dinner that she attended with Chipper Geld in April, she had become a different woman. But the woman she had become was not the woman she wanted to be. It wasn't that she had a sense of desperation. No, that would be describing her distress too heavy-handedly. It was more like an inner sadness had taken over her personality in a very pervasive way. She no longer viewed herself as a good judge of character. And she wasn't quite sure where her life was heading. Ever since she'd been a young girl, the direction of her life was somewhat defined by her relationships with the men in her life. That was now changing, and it needed to change. But still, she felt this inner sadness.

Following the charity dinner in April she had returned to Chipper Geld's Manhattan apartment, ostensibly to see the model for Fundamental Health Resources new Medi-Spa that was due to be built in suburban San Francisco. What occurred at Geld's apartment had nothing to do with viewing models, unless that's what the Russian tramp Natasha represented herself to be.

But Maureen didn't want to reflect on that evening too deeply. She had managed to escape and return home without being physically assaulted. However her dignity had taken a bit of a beating and there was an hour of that night that she would like to forget forever, as Chipper Geld attempted to force her to have a sordid three-way with him and his misanthropic Muscovite.

There were many other things on her mind. Her husband had become more of a challenge than ever before. He had twin obsessions, which drove him harder than any goals he had ever set for himself during his days at ICD. One of these goals she could readily understand. She realized why JB would be obsessed with research that might reverse his paraplegic existence. But the other obsession

Maureen found much more difficult to understand. John was a very rich man. Even after a couple of years of market downturn, he still had a net worth that exceeded $130 million. So why was he so obsessed with the success of this new company Fundamental Health Resources?

Her children all seemed to be doing okay. Maureen was only slightly concerned that she didn't talk to Kenneth as regularly as she had in the past. This was probably simply a sign that he was growing up. At least he still sent her regular e-mails and even if the tone of his communications had become a bit more acerbic of late, she was still always glad to hear from him. However she could tell from the tenor of his correspondence that Kenneth was having a hard time relating to his father.

Through all of these emotional changes in her life, Maureen had maintained a consistency with respect to her fitness regimen. During the last few weeks she had spent more time at her Kings Point home and she had doubled the time that she spent in fitness and tripled the time she spent reading. Her personal trainer, Grant, had increased the difficulty of her workout to match her interests. She had also retained a martial arts tutor, who accompanied Grant to her home and assisted in her work out. Her attitude towards her conditioning had become much more aggressive, and when she was through with her workout each day, she maximized the amount of time that she would spend in either her steam room or her sauna, before dressing and getting ready for the rest of the day. She was beginning to understand that she was suffering from depression. Worse yet, she didn't know who to turn to for help.

Maureen had just finished her shower following her morning workout and was back up in her bedroom slipping on some jeans and a tank top and running a comb through her long black hair, when the phone rang.

"Happy Birthday, Mom." The citation was echoed twice more as her three children all wished her well. They had patched together a conference call and rang through to her to wish her the best. She chatted with her children for a few minutes and then let them get back to their respective activities. She had mixed emotions of happiness and melancholy. She was glad that her children took the time to call her together, and yet she believed that that would be the last expression of goodwill that she would receive on her 45th birthday.

It was also the first time anyone had expressed good wishes to her on this significant birthday. Her husband John had left earlier that morning without saying a word. Although two dozen roses had arrived for her earlier, she knew that they were part of an automatic product renewal that JB had charged to his credit card several years earlier, so that he could never be accused of forgetting her. The same two dozen red roses, from the same florist, arrived at the same time of the morning each year, with the same salutation that said simply, "Happy Birthday to my dear wife, Love John." It occurred to Maureen a few years back that if John ever decided to divorce her and remarry, he would only have to change the delivery address and the date of delivery.

Maureen decided to go out for a drive. She had no particular destination in mind as she climbed into her Mercedes SL 65 AMG Roadster, and pulled out of her driveway. As often as she rode in the rear of a limousine, Maureen also cherished the few private times that she was able to get behind the wheel of her powerful V12 vehicle with its awesome 6.0 Liter engine. The silver colored convertible was a birthday present that she had given to herself a year earlier on her 44th birthday, and had driven less than a dozen times since. She wasn't sure what she would get herself for this birthday.

Maureen zoomed out of the driveway and away from Long Island Sound. She cruised southwest on Kings Point Road, and alongside Kings Point Park, going about 20 miles above the allotted speed limit. She turned left sharply on Steamboat Road and followed it around the park to Wood Road, where she made a right hand turn toward Great Neck. Her drive then twisted and turned along Arrandale Ave, Saddle Rock Boulevard, West Shore Road and eventually onto Bayview Avenue heading south. She drove past Northern Boulevard and kept heading south until she came to the Long Island Expressway.

Maureen was wearing dark sunglasses and had the top down on her Mercedes. Her long black hair was blowing wildly behind her. She had barely run a comb through it once or twice before receiving the phone call from her children and now she was paying no attention to it whatsoever. Her hair became a wild tangled mess as she shifted into fifth gear and pulled into the left lane of the Expressway, heading eastbound. It was the middle of the day and the middle of the week. The traffic was not nearly as heavy as it might have been. Maureen took advantage of the lighter traffic and weaved in and out of the eastbound vehicles. This was not an unusual route for Maureen to travel. In fact it was a well-traveled passage for the Brady family between their two Long Island homes, one in Kings Point and the other in Southampton. However Maureen rarely drove the route herself and in recent years she had just as often traveled between her two houses by helicopter. But for now, Maureen was directionless. She had no particular destination in mind, but she wanted to get there fast, wherever *there* was.

Even during the midweek the traffic was heavy enough to keep Maureen's speed under 75 miles an hour through Nassau County. It was a bright sunny day and once she passed into Suffolk County the traffic lightened up considerably. The further east she drove the lighter the traffic became. The lighter the traffic became, the faster Maureen drove. Most of the vehicles around her were traveling at about 70-75 mph. Maureen began passing some of these cars like they were standing still. Her speed crept up to 95, then 105 and when she hit a patch of open road she let the engine open up and briefly saw the needle show 125 mph! She was hot! She was excited! She knew that if she crashed at this speed, she was dead! And then she rapidly approached a section of the road where three cars were casually passing one another at much lower speeds. She was coming up on them fast, maybe much too fast!

She had to hit the brake hard in order to avoid a rear end collision with the car in front of her. Fortunately she was driving a well-balanced Benz and it decelerated as she hit the brake without a significant swerve. Nevertheless she came within two feet of rear-ending the GMC Yukon in the left hand lane. She continued to slow down as the Yukon passed another SUV in the middle lane. The driver gave her the finger. That was when Maureen first noticed the flashing lights that were gaining on her rapidly. Instead of slowing down she again hit the gas pedal and roared past the two SUVs with the police car in hot pursuit. She again saw the needle hit triple digits on the dashboard, 103mph, 108mph, 115mph, but then she quickly came upon another dangerously congested clump of cars that were about 100 yards in front of her. She was forced to slow down and the police vehicle rapidly closed the gap to about a half dozen car lengths. Maureen heard the officer tell her to pull over on his microphone and she slowed and gradually moved towards the right lane and eventually pulled over on the right shoulder.

"Stay in the car ma'am." The officer delayed for about two minutes while he called in her plates and then got out of the car and started to approach Maureen's vehicle. For a moment she had the urge to simply step on the gas pedal and peel out once again. She resisted the temptation as a State Police officer approached the driver's side door.

"License and registration." The officer took a moment before looking quickly at the driver's license for her name. "So Ms. Brady, you seem to be in quite a hurry."

"And you officer, seem to be quite observant!" Right around this time a second police vehicle pulled off the Expressway just in front of Maureen Brady's Mercedes.

"Let's try this again, Ms. Brady."

"It's Mrs. Brady, officer."

"Okay. Let's try this again, Mrs. Brady. Do you want to tell me why you were driving 110 mph?"

Maureen sucked in her breath so that her chest pushed out against her tank top and she held her breath for about three seconds before exhaling. Then she simply said, "I was just a little depressed. That's all. And for the record I wasn't going 110."

"I'm sorry to inform you Mrs. Brady that you were *definitely* going 110 mph and we are going to charge you with reckless driving and because you tried to outrun the police, we are going to impound your vehicle."

Maureen reached over and grabbed her cell phone and pushed the speed dial number for her attorney. Before the phone began to ring, she once again looked up at the police officer said, "I told you I wasn't driving 110. However you clocked me, you got it wrong. I was going 125, and by the way, you can go fuck yourself, asshole."

****

Gina Struben stepped out of the glass elevator at the fifth floor reception area of the *Tkachuk Center*. The pretty young receptionist who greeted her with a smile was secretly a huge fan of Gina Struben, and had been since Gina's days with the Lay D's. However the receptionist was trained well and she knew enough not to overreact to the arrival of any of the celebrity members of the *Rhapsody Lifestyle*. During the first couple of months of operation many celebrity members had visited the center. In fact just one half hour earlier, Tom Garrett, the famous network news anchor had arrived and was currently receiving a massage in one of the treatment rooms on the same floor. And Omar, the celebrity of celebrities himself, was also in the building consulting with his personal concierge down on the second floor. Pete Toohey, the Yankees rookie second baseman, was in the center the day before having an MRI done on his wrist, which he injured when he couldn't get out of the way of an inside fastball thrown by a Red Sox hurler.

"Hello Mrs. Struben. How are you doing today? You have a concierge appointment with Jedediah scheduled for 11:30? Correct? And I also see that you are scheduled for a hot stone massage at one o'clock. Is that right?"

Not only was Jenny, the receptionist, a pretty and bright young lady but she also had a megawatt smile that made all of the *Rhapsody Members* feel right at home as soon as they entered the building, She had been working at the center since its opening and her demeanor was illustrative of type of service personnel that Rhapsody was hiring. Jenny had been personally interviewed and hired by Maria Cardoza, Rhapsody's Spa Director, after being vetted and downselected by the HR staff. Maria had convinced Abby that the receptionist was a much more important position in their business than in a lot of other businesses and had insisted upon getting someone who was career oriented and not simply someone looking for a job.

Jenny was actually a 22-year-old college graduate, who had her sights set on medical school, when she was recruited into the business. She was also rotating through a Rhapsody training program, which would teach her the nuances of Rhapsody's service character and deportment. This was as important in the receptionist role as it was for one of the ™Rhapsody PALs (Personal Advocates for Longevity,)[12] like Jedediah. The strategic team had finally conceptualized and named the position for the concierge who coordinated *RhapsodyCare* and the *Rhapsody HealthMap* for each individual member.

Jenny knew that Gina would be arriving at the fifth floor reception area, the moment Gina put her *Diamond Membership Key* in the entrance slot for the glass elevator on the ground floor of the building. That simple action had triggered a named notification to light up on the tool bar at the bottom of Jenny's computer screen.

The key itself was an amazing device that served many purposes. *Diamond Members*, like Gina Struben, were given a platinum key adorned with tiny diamonds arranged in the shape of the *Rhapsody Logo*. Just behind the tip of the key there was a tiny computer chip that contained first level security information about the member. For the

---

[12] *Rhapsody PALs (Personal Advocates for Longevity) is* a Trademark of Rhapsody Holdings, LLC and Rhapsody Holdings, Inc.

most part this was simply rudimentary access to data. However coupled with iris scanning equipment located in other parts of the center, it provided for second and third level security clearance. These higher level security clearances enabled members to access personal account information and access to the *Rhapsody HealthPort*, including their own health and wellness data as well as their own personal *HealthMap*. In addition, there was a small data storage capability on the key, not unlike a thumb memory stick. *Rhapsody's Platinum Members* also received a key with all of the same identification, security clearance, and data storage capabilities of the *Diamond Key*. However, the Rhapsody logo was engraved in the platinum itself, and not detailed with diamonds. The *Diamond Key* signified certain additional services, but didn't actually directly render any differentiation with respect to data access and security clearance.

"Hi Jenny... It's good to see you. Before you call Jed, I'd like to retrieve an Internet file that I was looking at a couple of days ago, so I'm just going to go back into the admin section for a few minutes. You can tell Jed that I'm here, and that I'll be with him in a few minutes." Gina didn't need to see Jenny's name tag to know her name, because she remembered her from several previous visits, as a sweet individual. They were also nearly the same age, and Gina had asked her once before to simply call her as Gina.

"Take your time Mrs. Struben. I'll let Jed know that you are here."

Gina walked past the reception area and down the hallway to the area that was designated as the study. She inserted her member key into the computer and the Rhapsody security page appeared and inquired whether she would like her security clearance to be achieved through iris scanning or through fingertip scanning. She clicked on fingertip scanning and inserted her right thumb into the small access kiosk, wired to the computer. Immediately the Rhapsody home page flashed up on the computer screen with a replica of her *Diamond Key* on the left side of the screen and a series of options arrayed along the right side of the screen with checkboxes. Above the options list there was a short greeting that said, "Good morning, Gina. What would you like to do?" She smiled as she realized that at least she had been able to convince the computer to call her by her first name. Her list of options included: Access the *Rhapsody HealthPort*; View your *HealthMap*; Make an appointment; Access your account; Access the Internet; Membership News & *Rhapsody MemberLinks*; and Log Out.

Gina selected the box next to "Access the Internet" and was immediately afforded secure access behind the Rhapsody firewall. She quickly found a couple of articles that she had come across the week before, regarding research on Huntington's Chorea. She hit the save button and captured the data on her *Rhapsody Diamond Key*, and then clicked and entered the *Rhapsody MemberLinks* section. She quickly found her husband's icon and sent him a chat message: "I'm over at the center, and I am forwarding these two files that we discussed earlier today. I'll call you when I leave. L&K. Gina." She then pasted the files into the dialog box for Josh on his *MemberLinks* page. Gina quickly got a response from Josh's Blackberry, which had access to *Rhapsody MemberLinks*: "Okay Gina. On the golf course, with Dad. Talk later, Josh" Gina marveled at the quick response from her husband who was in London with his father. She would be flying over to meet him in the morning.

The pop icon quickly removed her *Diamond Key* and started walking towards the reception area. She met up with Jed halfway down the hall and they both turned around and went into the nearby consultation room. Jedediah Miller served as Gina's PAL and as such was responsible for the overall coordination of health and wellness information dissemination, as well as the coordination of access to the practitioners within the *Rhapsody GPS*. At the time a new member joined the *Rhapsody Lifestyle*, the PAL would also be the person who coordinated the collection of the new member's medical history and arranged for the member's initial check up. The PAL then also coordinated the entry of inputs into the member's individualized baseline *HealthMap* assessment.

All of the Rhapsody PALs were well-versed in the needs of their member/clients. They came from a number of different backgrounds but they all were trained and licensed in some aspect of healthcare. Most of them were medical doctors, who had left GP or Internist practices to join the Rhapsody team. The PALs were the heart and soul of *RhapsodyCare* and the group was growing. There was a strong push among the Rhapsody executive team to bolster the internal training program and to broaden the skill set of the PALs even further.

The PAL team was empowered to do many different things, and they were not limited to simply practicing medicine in the classical sense. In addition to their medical training they were wired to the concept of customer service. This was as important as the dispensing of medicine or prescriptions. Their specific role was to help the member/client coordinate their thoughts, feelings, emotions, and activities with respect to ultimately achieving a longer, better life. In order to do so the PAL would often coordinate access to specific medical specialists, or to specific physical therapists, or even help the member attain access to an alternative medical practitioner as appropriate or necessary. They would also help the member coordinate the compilation of medical files and inputs into their *HealthPort* and advise the member about a variety of ™*Rhapsody Healthness*[13] related services. They would also research various health and wellness topics and procedures and ensure that the information was readily available to the members so that they could make informed personal decisions with respect to their own health. Part of the training for the PAL position included indoctrination in the *Rhapsody Lifestyle* philosophy. The PALs frequently underscored the most important tenant of that philosophy, "own your own health and wellness," as they worked with their clientele. Because each PAL had only 50 individual clients, they were able to provide a significantly broader array of services than a general practitioner who might see thousands of patients annually.

Jedediah sat down across from Gina and opened up his note pad. Meanwhile he took his *Rhapsody Practitioner Key* and put it in the computer that sat on the table between the two of them. Gina also handed him her key and he quickly entered her key into the kiosk as well. Both Jedediah and Gina also casually registered thumb print verification into the kiosk so that they would have total access to her records during their discussion.

"There are several things that we have scheduled to discuss today, Mrs. Struben. You had a number of questions that you wanted to get answered with respect to Huntington's disease. I think that was paramount among your concerns when we spoke last week."

"Yes Jed. And please I know they encourage you to address your clients formally, but if you don't mind, I just prefer being called 'Gina,' even if I do love *being*-- Mrs. Struben."

"Sure Gina." Jedediah Miller tried not to be too overwhelmed by the beautiful woman sitting across from him. He was a 30-year-old physician, who had grown up in Western New Jersey. He had been assigned to work with Gina Alvarez-Struben through an internal

---

[13] *Rhapsody Healthness* is a Trademark of Rhapsody Holdings, LLC and Rhapsody Holdings, Inc.

matchmaking algorithm that Rhapsody was using to match up its PALs with *Rhapsody Members*.

"I brought a couple of articles I found about Huntington's disease," Gina said. "I'm not sure whether or not these are things that you might have seen, or research that you might have heard about but they don't help me feel much more comfortable about my prospects for developing the disease."

"As you know from our previous discussions Gina, all the research indicates that you really don't develop or contract the disease, as much as you fulfill your genetic disposition to having the disease. You're either born with it, or you are not. For more than 20 years now there has been a simple genetic test that can determine whether or not you will eventually suffer from Huntington's."

"And from what you have told me I can have that test right here at the Tkachuk Center."

"Yes you can. You can have that test performed today, next week, next year, or never. It, of course, is your decision. There are many ethical discussions ongoing on this topic particularly as it pertains to Huntington's Chorea because of the very specific deterministic attributes of the disease.

"And you should know that there is new research done on Huntington's almost on a daily basis. And the findings have been quite definitive. The disease is linked to a gene located on chromosome 4. There is a certain code that is repeated on this gene multiple times in all human beings. The code, which is called a 'CAG repeat,' is easily identifiable and traceable, and is quite definitive in its ability to predict whether or not a person will develop the disease. Depending upon the number of sequential repetitions of this code, the timeframe for the initial onset of the disease can be determined. If the code is repeated 39 times or more there is a virtual certainty that the patient will develop this disease sometime in mid life. If the code is repeated less than 35 times sequentially, the patient will not ever suffer from the disease. The more sequential instances of the CAG repeat - 50, 60, 70 or more, - the earlier the onset of the disease. Some people are known to display symptoms of the disease as early as age 30. Then the ensuing loss of motor control, speech debilitation and the onset of dementia all seem to occur at an earlier age. So the predictability of the actual age of death from Huntington's also becomes an ethical issue. The real question is, if you could be told 'you definitely will develop Huntington's disease and this is *when* you will die,' would you want to know?"

Gina thought for a second but didn't answer Jedediah's question directly. "There are really three questions for me to get answered. First, did my father actually have Huntington's? Secondly, do I have it? And thirdly, if I have it, what are the chances that any children that I have will inherit it?"

"As we sit here right this second, I can only answer the third question. If you do have Huntington's disease, or what is sometimes called Huntington's Chorea, then the probability of any of your children inheriting it is precisely, 50%. Your second question can be answered with or without knowing anything about your father. A simple genetic test can determine whether you have Huntington's disease or not. And of course the first question could only be answered conclusively by finding your father."

"From everything you've told me, in conjunction with everything I've read, I think I want to have the test performed."

"All right. We can arrange for that whenever you're ready."

"How about today?"

"I'll arrange it. Will you be here at the center for a while?"

"I'm scheduled for a massage early this afternoon. I could do it after that."

"Sure. Let's change gears here for a second or two." Jedediah hit a few keys on the keyboard and they both watched as Gina's *HealthMap* appeared on the screen. They then began a lengthy discourse on a variety of different topics relative to Gina's approach to "owning her own health." She had recently changed personal trainers and had put a bit more emphasis on aerobic conditioning than on muscle building. There was also a notation that she wanted to speak to a specific Rhapsody dietitian who was out of the country for a few weeks. The note indicated that Jedediah had offered to establish a videoconference with the dietitian, but that Gina had opted to wait until he returned to the US from his vacation in Africa.

At the end of their discussion about the various options for services available at the center, Jedediah made one more offer open to Gina. "During our last couple sessions you've been expressing some significant interest in genetics as it pertains to disease and to disease control. Within the Rhapsody family we have a group of scientists who are always eager to share their perspectives on these topics with the bright men and women who make up our membership. The leader of our scientific community, Mark Candu is here in the city today and will be meeting with a couple of our members with similar interests later in the day. If you'd like to join them, I can arrange that."

"That would be great. Just leave me a message on my member page so that I know where to go after my massage."

Before long, Jedediah and Gina finished their conversation and Gina walked down the spiral staircase to the women's spa. Jedediah couldn't help but notice how confidently Gina carried herself, and how cheerful she appeared to be, even with a very heavy inquiry yet to be resolved. She was an admirable young woman.

****

There are times in life when the roles people play can become confused. This might have been the case as Dr. Al Moses sat across from his psychotherapist, Dr. Greg Mendelsohn. Both Dr. Moses and Dr. Mendelsohn were physicians with the *Rhapsody Global Practitioner Society*, the so-called *GPS*. In addition, both Dr. Moses and Dr. Mendelsohn had purchased *Platinum Keys* in the *Rhapsody Lifestyle Membership*. Interestingly Dr. Mendelsohn had been providing therapeutic care to Dr. Moses for more than a year before either of them became platinum members at the end of 2009. And all of that was a curious part of the initial discussions that they were having this morning.

"How are you this morning, Al?"

"I'm doing just fine, Greg. Thank you." Al Moses was now comfortably seated on a plush cloth couch in a second-floor consultation room at the *Tkachuk Center for the Rhapsody Lifestyle*. This was the second session that they had held in this building. Dr. Mendelsohn still maintained his own office on Fifth Avenue overlooking Central Park, but more and more frequently over the last month he was seeing clientele at the *Tkachuk Center*. Those of his clients who were Rhapsody members preferred to see Mendelsohn during the same day that they might have a hairstylist appointment, or might be getting some dental work done. But the odd part about Moses seeing Mendelsohn in this environment was that Al was seeing some of his own patients in the very same building, sometimes on the very same floor. It seemed a little unusual to Al, at first, but by the time of the second session he merely appreciated the convenience.

"You see some of your clients here as well. Don't you, Al? Some of your patients are *Rhapsody Lifestyle Members*. Are they not?"

"Yes in fact I have four members with scheduled gynecological appointments this afternoon. It's actually quite convenient. How about you? You are a member here also. Aren't you?"

"Well, yes I am. But I haven't used any of the facilities at all just yet. My PAL is helping me assemble my own medical history, and is working on scheduling a full day's checkup for me in about three weeks. I couldn't get in any sooner because my own practice is pretty heavily booked between now and then. But enough about me, let's talk about you, Al. How is your lovely friend, Maria, doing? And how is the baby? Duffy? Right?"

"Yes Duffy. She and Maria have made my life totally different over the last year. I can't believe what a different person I have become. See, you *can* teach old dogs new tricks."

"Tell me about the tricks, Al."

"Well, how about this for starters. Until this year I had never changed a diaper in my whole life."

"Well now that's an interesting place for you to start telling me about your new tricks. How does that make you feel?"

"Younger."

"Tell me more."

"It really is amazing. Throughout my career, I have delivered many babies.... I really have no idea how many.... But I never diapered a single one of them. And, I guess, in order to keep my professional distance, I never really became that attached to any one of them either. I never thought that much about how a loving adult could influence the life of the newborn child. I thought that that was the work of parents, possibly with the help of pediatrician, a teacher or whomever. But from a professional standpoint, being an OB/GYN, I needed to detach myself somewhat from the emotional bond that a baby sparks."

"Tell me about Duffy."

"Duffy is wonderful! She'll celebrate her first birthday next month. She is happy and cheerful. She smiles all the time. And it is just a fabulous experience to look into her eyes and see the goodness and the wonder that will be around on earth for the next hundred years or so. I don't know if I would have appreciated someone like Duffy, when I was in my 20s or 30s or for that matter in my 40s or 50s. But I sure do appreciate having her as part of my life right now."

"And why is that, Al? After all, she is not your child. Does that bother you at all?"

"Well Duffy is Maria's child, and I love Maria. And very simply, I love Duffy too. Truthfully, I never even think about John Brady's involvement in all of this. And of course as everyone knows, Brady has his own problems."

"I hear what you're saying, Al. But hasn't it crossed your mind, that even in his current condition, John Brady might have a right to know that he has another child?"

"No. You have brought this up several times in the past. And I know you think that this concerns me. But, I don't think about it at all." Al Moses said this in a definitive manner that simply told his therapist that he wanted to change topics. He didn't say it in a way that convinced Mendelsohn that he was telling the truth. Regardless Dr. Mendelsohn changed the subject.

"Al, I have noticed that you've lost a little bit of weight. You look quite good actually. I'm assuming that you might be on some kind of program?"

"Yeah I have dropped a few pounds. So now I am no longer short, fat and balding. Now I am just short and balding."

"Well maybe short and balding, with a renewed sense of self-deprecating humor. That certainly wasn't part of your persona when we first started our chats."

"You're probably right, Greg … all in all, I have a much lighter attitude about life in general, now that Maria and Duffy are part of it. Coincidentally I'm not traveling as much either. I don't feel as though I need to run away from anything."

Mendelsohn felt that he could now bring up a topic that they had not discussed in many months. He believed that this might be the right time. "Do you ever think much about Anne Mohr these days?" He was careful how he worded the question but Al Moses was very direct in his answer.

"I don't think that much about her anymore. And the answer to the question behind your question is 'No, absolutely not.' Besides it would be highly inconvenient to be talking to Anne with Maria in the room." Al Moses laughed at his own answer, and it was very reassuring to Dr Mendelsohn to observe that his patient had crossed a reality bridge that had seemed so troubling in the past.

"There's that new humor again. Good to see."

Mendelsohn seemed to be mulling something over for a few seconds, and Moses watched him closely to see where he might lead the conversation.

"Do you and Maria have any plans to marry?"

Moses took his time answering the question and when he did so he was speaking in a much softer tone. "No. Currently, we have no specific plans along those lines."

"Not currently? But what about in the future? Is it something that you would like?"

Al looked directly at his therapist and offered a light hearted response that may have guised his true feelings. "What was that old Doris Day song? 'Que sera, sera.' Whatever will be, will be."

****

It was now 3:30 in the afternoon and the executive team had been working diligently throughout the day. Lunch was brought into the conference room around 12:30 and the team had taken a 45-minute break and then started in again.

"Let me start by going through a quick synopsis of our current achievements that have led us to our position of financial surplus at the midyear point." Ben Hui Zhang spoke clearly and confidently. He was unmistakably self-assured in his role as CFO.

"Sales are off to a terrific start in 2010. We are now approaching a total of 4000 memberships, at an average initial membership rate of just under $50,000 per membership." Ben was pointing at the PowerPoint chart on the screen that pulled down along the wall at the end of the conference room. He used a laser pointer to draw tight circle around the membership line. "From memberships alone we have recognized revenues of nearly $200 million. But let's break that membership number down a little bit finer. During the fourth quarter of 2009 we hit our goal of five hundred Cornerstone Memberships. I know many of you believe we could have done better, but that was our target and we didn't want to exceed it drastically, while we were still piloting some of our services. Between January 1st of this year and the end of March, or just before the opening of our center in mid-April we sold an additional hundred memberships. If you are doing the math quickly in your head you realize that we have sold an additional 2400 memberships in the last 2 1/2 months. All of these numbers are ahead of plan, so the near-term financial picture that I am showing you is quite rosy."

"Just a point of clarification, Ben ... we did give away a certain number of memberships during the pilot phase ... are you counting any revenue in these numbers for those memberships?" The question was asked by Maria Cardoza who was beginning to get involved in many more aspects of the business, beyond just her leadership with respect to the spa concepts.

"The revenue from those memberships is counted in the top line on these charts and then subtracted out as contra revenue a couple lines below. In this way we will be able to show our top line trends over a period of time in the clearest manner. Naturally as the anniversary of those cornerstone memberships comes about, we will be looking at renewal revenues and the contra revenue line should begin to zero out. Does that make it clearer?"

"Yes, thank you."

"Okay then, getting back to the positive top line growth, it should be clear to everyone that we will blow beyond the original projections for members in 2010. If it's not clear to us based on the projections for the center here in New York, it should be very clear to everyone, when we add in the projected numbers for the London center that we will be opening in the fall."

"Let's stop there for a second, Ben," said Abby. "Although this membership revenue is wonderful on the one hand, it is certainly causing us some consternation on the delivery side, as we saw from the many issues that we put on the table this morning. We will want to keep a close eye on these trends, so that we don't over promise and under deliver with respect to service."

"Excellent point, Abby… As you can see, later this year we will begin seeing the impact of renewals, or retention memberships if you will, on the top line. Regardless of how many initial memberships we sell, if we don't hit our target of an 80% retention rate, much of the business plan will suffer significantly. It goes without saying that our retention rate will be highly dependent upon the service rendered to the members."

Just as Ben was about to make another point, the conference room door opened and Abby's secretary came in and handed her a short printed note. Abby looked up from the note and said to the team, "It appears that we have the first utilization of our air ambulance service by one of our Diamond Key Members. As you may have heard on the news earlier, Congressman Powelson from California, has suffered a mild stroke while on vacation in Ireland. One of our at-large GPS physicians saw him at a Dublin Hospital, but he wants to be flown home. Apparently our air ambulance partners are arranging for the flight as we speak. The process is working. That's good to know. I hope the Congressman is doing well. He is a heck of a nice guy."

The team got back to work and concentrated on Ben's presentation of the numbers. The chart they had up in front of them was more like a vision test. They all squinted and peered at the column of expenses that Ben was now highlighting with a laser pointer. In many cases they were well under budget, but that was not necessarily good news. It simply signified that certain things were yet to get done. Again it all came back to utilization rates for various services, and they were learning some of this on the fly. There were many questions back and forth until the executive team was satisfied that they at least understood the numbers, even if they didn't have a handle on exactly what to do about some of the projections.

At the end of an hour and a half of presentation and discussion about the operating financials, the team took a short break before coming back to discuss several upcoming strategic decisions. Included among these decisions would be a determination about a more rapid deployment of centers.

"Okay let's get everybody settled back in here. We should be getting a call momentarily from Sun Feng. As some of you are well aware, Sun has been a strong advocate for putting a center in Beijing at an earlier date than we had originally planned. Both he and Bob Johnstone are in Beijing now and have been talking to friends and colleagues about Rhapsody."

"If I may be so bold as to ask, exactly what is our current financial arrangement with Feng?" Zoë Mansfield asked the question.

"In order to answer that appropriately, we should acknowledge a couple of facts. In early 2009, Mr. Feng provided us with $5 million in bridge funding that was basically unsecured. He showed a lot of trust in us. As you are undoubtedly aware, we repaid the bridge funding with proceeds from our line of credit with the Louisiana Group, as soon as that facility was made available to us. We currently have no direct financial arrangement of any sort with Mr. Feng. However his close friend Bob Johnstone, as the principal of the Louisiana group, is our principle debt holder. In addition Mr. Feng has shown a great deal of ongoing interest in Rhapsody Holdings, and has been a key advisor to me directly over the past eighteen months or so, since I first met him in Paris. Twice we have offered him a seat on our board and twice he has declined for personal reasons. I have assumed that these personal reasons are mostly reflective of the rigors of his own portfolio of businesses."

Abby was giving an elaborate answer to Zoë's straightforward question. She was doing this for the benefit of the group as a whole not just for Zoë. Just as her answer was settling across the group, the phone rang.

"Hello, Dr. McDuffee?" The intonation was the unmistakable.

"Hello, Mr. Feng. This is Abby. I am here with many members of our senior management team and we have you on a speaker phone." Abby didn't bother acknowledging each of the team members by name. She expected this to be a two-way conversation for the most part. "Is Bob Johnstone with you as well?"

"Mr. Johnstone is here with me in Beijing, but he has not yet risen for the day. Last night we discussed the fact that I would simply update you on our mutual perspective about progress on the Rhapsody concept here in China."

"Thank you Mr. Feng. When we last spoke you indicated that there was some significant interest in the possibility of putting a center in either Beijing or in Tianjin, following our plans to put a center in Hong Kong. Would you care to characterize the continued interest since our last discussions?"

"There is considerable interest in health and wellness concepts for all markets in China. This is especially true of some of the government officials in Beijing. However, there is some concern that the Rhapsody approach will not be broad enough to impact large groups of people. Having said that, there is substantial support in the private sector and even enthusiasm amongst the senior Communist Party members, for the opening a Rhapsody Center in the capital city."

"That is very good to know."

"What you should also know is that the greatest appeal for your concept in the private sector is your personalized physician program … I believe you call it your PAL program … it is very exciting amongst the wealthy community in China. They sometimes have found it difficult to get the correct answers to their health issues, and they frequently get conflicting directions with respect to wellness and dietary concerns."

"All of these things are matters that are addressed in the context of the *Rhapsody Lifestyle*," said Abby.

"Yes, of course," said Sun Feng. "And many of the political and industrial Chinese leaders have a significant interest and curiosity about longevity. They are fascinated by the possibility that a business such as yours could actually help them live longer more fulfilling lives. I would count myself amongst those who think this way."

"Have you discussed with them the fact that we will soon be putting up Asian centers in both Hong Kong and Singapore?"

"Yes, Dr. McDuffee. These plans have been well documented. Part of the attraction for prospective Chinese members would be their ability to access services in other ports of call throughout the Pacific Rim. There is simply one matter of contention."

"And what would that be, Mr. Feng?"

"Those with whom I have discussed the Rhapsody concept here in China, all speak with a single voice on this one matter of contention. We all believe that the very first Asian center should be here in Beijing. We are prepared to discuss very favorable financial terms to see that that occurs. There are several people here in Beijing, with whom Mr. Johnstone and I have been discussing these potential financial terms and the ability to get a center in place in less than nine months. They are quite anxious for you to come to Beijing personally, Dr. McDuffee. They have asked that I relay a request to see you within the next few weeks. Their request also is for you come to Beijing, so that those discussions can take place in a meaningful context."

"Based upon our earlier discussions, Mr. Feng, this request does not surprise me. However our plans for Singapore and Hong Kong are well underway and have been for quite some time."

"Dr. McDuffee, I would consider it to be a personal kindness to me, if you will favor us by coming to Beijing to discuss this further."

Abby recognized fully that she had no choice but to accept Mr. Feng's invitation. She also believed in Feng's sincerity and integrity. She answered exactly the way Mr. Feng had intended her to answer: "I would be most honored to join you and your colleagues in Beijing shortly. I will have my staff adjust my calendar and make travel plans accordingly."

"Thank you Dr. McDuffee." There suddenly was a loud dial tone that indicated that the call was complete.

****

Sales were underwhelming for Fundamental Health Resources and their Manhattan-based medi-spa. After a strong start, new sales had stalled to just a trickle. Jason Tobin and the other management leader, Eric Mallory, had been trying to execute a strategy in downtown Manhattan where they would pick up potential members where they worked as well as where they lived. Even though the financial community had been rocked to the core over the last two years, there still was a great deal of activity in the Wall Street area.

During the past month there had been a significant change in the FHR leadership command. Although Tobin and Mallory were still the titular heads of the business, they were responding to significant input from John Brady, from Chipper Geld, and from Paul Pritchard. The three-headed monster was all the more ominous because it possessed three different outlooks on the right direction of the business. One of those heads was now sitting in Jason Tobin's office, across the desk from the FHR leader.

"We need to have a good bit more focus on our main competition here in New York City," said Chipper Geld. "They are getting far too much favorable publicity for a business that doesn't address the needs of society as a whole. Where the hell are our public relations people? And what the hell are they thinking? It's not enough for them to put out some positive press on us, they need to help us differentiate ourselves from Rhapsody Holdings. It should be easy enough to shed some doubt on what they're doing. They named a damn center after some dead Russian dude and it looks to me like they cater to a lot of rich snobs, who can afford to pay their outrageous prices, while the bulk of the people, that is to say, most of the middle class, can't get in to see a doctor in a timely fashion. That's the rap that we have to pin on those people."

"The problem, Chipper, is that we are chasing the same market that they are. But we need to face facts. We have an inferior product." Jason Tobin had been making this same succinct argument for more than a year. He was growing more frustrated every day. The "oversight" that was provided to the business by Brady and Geld had been driving marketing and advertising dollars toward the prospect of selling memberships in the center. There was very little being spent on developing an overarching, and differentiating, concept that would enable FHR to better compete against the likes of Rhapsody Holdings. Tobin continued. "Rhapsody is selling memberships in the concept that they refer to as a *lifestyle*. We seem to be selling memberships to a high-end fitness center with available medical assistance. These just aren't the same product. We are not competing with Rhapsody appropriately."

"Let's be straight here with one another, Tobin. If you can't get the job done, I think it's time for you to step down. I know JB has been very supportive, but with all the things that are on his mind these days, I don't believe he understands how out of touch with the team you are."

"I think that the by-laws of the firm require a vote of the board to have me replaced. Are you suggesting that I resign and forego any of the benefits that I would receive as a result of a forced resignation?"

"No. Not at all. However if we can come to a gentleman's agreement here, I think I can they ensure you that the board will agree to give you your full severance benefits with your resignation."

"There is only one gentleman in the room, Mr. Geld. I'll have my attorney call you." With that Jason Tobin got up from behind his desk and walked Chipper Geld to the doorway. "Until we have a new contractual severance agreement in place, or the board, as a whole, tells me that I am no longer in charge, I intend to discharge the duties of my office to the best of my ability. Good day Mr. Geld." He stopped and then added, "You should also know that Rhapsody named the center after a Ukrainian dude not a Russian dude."

"What the fuck's the difference?"

"That's the problem with you, Geld. You're twenty years behind the times. Grow up!"

"Don't plan on coming back in the morning, Tobin. I'd use the rest of the afternoon to pack your things if I were you." Soon after he left the building, Geld was on his cell phone talking to Paul Pritchard and telling him that he needed his vote to oust John Brady's puppet, Jason Tobin, from the lead management position at Fundamental Health Resources. With some reservation, Pritchard gave Geld his support. When Pritchard later called JB to give him a synopsis of what had transpired, John Brady's retort was truncated but very direct.

"That bastard, Geld, will wish he never met me." Even though his voice was just an oxygen-aided rasp over the phone, it sent a chill down the spine of Paul Pritchard and Pritchard was beginning to wish that he himself had never met John Brady.

****

Gina entered the conference/consultation room on the third floor just outside the personalized drug and medication compounding area. Mark Candu was already speaking with two other Rhapsody members.

"Come on in Gina. Jedediah said that you might be joining us. My name is Mark Candu and I'm not sure if you've met Tom Garrett. And Caitlin Browning, works here in the city at Rhapsody HQ over on Lexington Avenue. She heads up corporate sales."

Gina came fully into the room and greeted the three other occupants. Ironically she had met both Garrett and Browning before, but she had never met Candu until just this moment. As always, she lit up the room when she entered.

"I'm pleased to meet *you* Mark. Caitlin and I met in April for the first time at the grand opening. Of course I know her sisters Abby and Alison quite well. And Tom and I are old acquaintances. I did an interview with Tom shortly after my tour with the Lay D's concluded, the Christmas before last, or sometime around then."

"Hi Gina, Darling, How have you been?" Tom Garrett got out of his seat and walked over and gave Gina a peck on the cheek. He was much more effusive in person than his staid stage personality as a network news commentator. Caitlin Browning also rose to greet Gina, and also gave her a friendly air-kiss somewhere near her cheek. Candu stuck out his hand in greeting and Gina shook it. Then they all sat down on a quadrangle of comfortable couches that surrounded the slate topped mahogany coffee table. The room itself was quite comfortable and the walls were adorned with some newly selected art pieces that were imported from an art gallery in Venice.

"Just before you came in, Gina, I was explaining to Tom and Caitlin some of the things that our scientific community is aiming to do in support of the *Rhapsody Lifestyle* concept. We're all very strong proponents of the belief that we are on the verge of a major breakthrough with respect to genetics and their impact on longevity."

"Yes Jedediah Miller told me a little bit about it when I saw him earlier today. Thanks for letting me sit in on your discussion."

"Well as we were just saying," Mark Candu continued, "longevity is not solely determined by an individual's genes. Lifestyle issues certainly are influential. Smoking, drinking, eating, sleeping, exercising and other routine activities certainly play a role in longevity. However if Dr. Zoë Mansfield were here she would tell you that a healthy sex life also has a positive impact on longevity. There is no doubt that other factors, such as stress have an influence as well. But all these lifestyle issues don't detract from the fact that genetics play a major role in longevity.

"And now that people are able to see genetic evidence of a predisposition toward a certain disease, they are beginning to take preventative measures in increasing numbers. For example, women with a genetic predisposition toward a particularly aggressive type of breast cancer are having prophylactic mastectomies even before the appearance of a tumor. In other cases where a familial strain of a particularly lethal stomach cancer was genetically evident, people are having their natural stomachs removed before the onset of the disease." Candu said all of this in a rather matter-of-fact way. By nature, he was not very animated individual, but the actual words he spoke were ponderous.

"I'm not sure whether this is good news, or bad news," said Gina, as she crossed her hands in front of her chest in a subliminal gesture of protection. "If such aggressive surgical intervention becomes the norm as we discover more and more genetic disposition towards disease, we might simply become a species of aging amputees of sorts."

"You're absolutely right. And I selected some rather radical examples to make a point. Fortunately surgery will not be the only solution for treating these problems. Over time, alternative treatments will be an option. And of course doing nothing medically is also an option."

"What are we talking about here in terms the numbers of genetic diseases that are being discovered?" Tom Garrett asked. He had a clear way about asking the question. It was almost as though he knew the answer and was putting Candu to the test. Gina was beginning to remember why she never cared for Garrett. He was a rather pompous sort who appeared to be wearing makeup even while off-camera.

"As I'm sure you know the human genome project was completed about a half dozen years ago. What this amounted to was a definition of some 30,000 genes that make up the recipe for a typical human being. More recently scientists have delineated which genes are on which of the 23 chromosomes, and began making associations and correlations with various genetic diseases. More than 6000 genetic disorders have been identified to date. Some of these are very serious, and others are less critical.

"One very intriguing area of research that continues to get a lot of attention is the association between genetic disorders and infectious diseases. It seems there are many cases where a given genetic disorder may, in fact, have a positive impact on a person's resistance to certain infectious diseases. This whole line of inquiry only underscores the simple fact that there is an enormous amount of work yet to be done."

"I've received an increasing number of questions on genetic screening from our clientele," Caitlin Browning continued. "In fact I think we also should talk about the ethics of all of this. It certainly is a factor in the way I try to do my job."

"What kind of questions, Caitlin?" Mark Candu looked at the tall redhead sitting in on the meeting who bore some resemblance to her twin sisters. Although Caitlin was three inches taller, fifteen well-placed pounds heavier, and sixteen years younger than her sisters, many of her mannerisms were reminiscent of those of the older McDuffee sisters.

"In the process of making group sales to major corporations, we often meet with the HR directors of the firm. Besides being very interested in providing a *Rhapsody Membership* as a perk to their executives, they often ask questions about the advanced genomic screening that we do for our members. One particular HR director, wanted to contract with us separately, just to do these kinds of screenings for prospective employees. Of course we told them we were not in that business, and that the purpose of our screenings was simply to serve our members. But the question itself certainly raises some ethical issues about using these technologies to evaluate and screen potential employees, or to deny insurability, or a host of other questionable uses of the science."

"You bring up an extremely important point, Caitlin. The fact that matters is that the pace of scientific discovery is making it more difficult than ever to keep abreast of the ethical issues that coincide with those breakthroughs. To be quite candid about it, these issues are part of the reason why I have become involved with the *Rhapsody Lifestyle*. I think we have a great opportunity here to bring together some great minds around some of the significant issues of the 21st century. You can be sure that they will have an impact on not only health and wellness, but also on education, politics, morals, ethics and the general world order. In a word, it will impact every aspect of life as we know it today. That is not an exaggeration in any way whatsoever."

****

Later that same evening in early June, Tom Garrett, the network news commentator, left the *Tkachuk Center* and went to a familiar watering hole 20 blocks further uptown. It was an upscale spot where the outrageous price of the martini kept clientele limited to the few who are willing to pay exorbitant prices for mediocre service just to stay out of the public eye when they drank.

Garrett had a secret or two that he had never intended to let see the light of day. Garrett had no idea how Paul Pritchard had discovered his secret lifestyle but Tom fully intended to do everything he could to ensure that Pritchard would keep his information to himself. They had known one another for about ten years or since Garrett originally began investing with Pritchard's old firm Cromwell Parsons

Resources. Garrett moved his money to the Pritchard Fund after Paul Pritchard had left CPR. But he had never been close enough to Pritchard to understand how he operated. He didn't know about Pritchard's wide network of electronic surveillance, and he didn't know that it was the mechanism that first tipped Pritchard to Garrett's secret life. It was only quite recently that Pritchard began to exploit the fact that Garrett was involved in a long term sadomasochistic relationship with a prostitute from the meatpacking district. Obviously news of this relationship could have ended Garrett's network news career, and he would then be whipped in more ways than one. He needed to do whatever he had to do to keep his "friend," Pritchard happy.

"So Tom, tell me. How is the new Rhapsody Lifestyle member doing?" Paul Pritchard had a way of getting right to the point when he had a mission in mind.

"It was an interesting day. I think I got the ammunition I need. Everything about Rhapsody flies in the face of universal health care. Basically, Rhapsody is an uppity club for rich snobs. They use their wealth and position to access healthcare in ways that the man in the street can't possibly do. We will run an exposé on these people to put them in their place. Not a problem. It's just another blatant example of rich bankers and financiers, coupled with a bunch of air-headed celebrities, taking advantage of a very broken system. I think that the public is sick and tired of hearing about multimillion dollar bonuses for Wall Street types. They will be even more pissed off when they hear that these people are getting assistance with their own healthcare needs, when the same programs are not available to the general public."

Pritchard knew that he and his friends at FHR would gladly have accepted the same clientele into their business, but so far they had not been able to get to this market, so he chose to condemn Rhapsody's efforts instead, and he knew that Garrett was the perfect foil for the job at hand. "I think you're onto something, Tom." Pritchard ordered himself a very dry Grey Goose martini, with a blue cheese stuffed olive garnish. He paused for a few seconds to make sure that the bartender recorded his order correctly and then continued. "So tell me Tom, what is it about being stretched on 'the rack' that floats your boat?"

"That's not a question that I feel compelled to answer. Do we have a deal, or not?"

"We have a deal. Just make sure that your exposé lives up to my expectations."

Chapter 17: *Money, Money, Money –* February 2011

*T*he *Struben Center for the Rhapsody Lifestyle* was up and running in the Mayfair section of London in October of 2010. Both Stephen and Josh had felt honored when Abby told them that the Board had decided to name the center after their family. Now, four months later it continued to attract wealthy *Diamond Key Members* at a rapid pace. Memberships at the *Struben Center* had sold at a much faster tempo than sales for the original Rhapsody location, the *Tkachuk Center* in New York City. However the *Tkachuk Center* had also surpassed its goals for 2010 including achieving a significantly higher retention rate for memberships than had been originally anticipated.

Danielle Dubonet Struben was an active *Rhapsody Lifestyle* member at the new *Struben Center.* She truly loved the fact that she had a single place where she could go for the many services she desired to maintain her youthful feeling and her beauty. She was not afraid to admit that a certain amount of vanity was a good thing. She knew herself well. She knew that if she looked good, she would feel good. She also knew that if she felt good she would be more prone to do good things for others. And at this stage of her life she was becoming more and more convinced that what was important, was to do good things for others. Rhapsody was helping to make that wish possible.

Beyond the many spa and beauty treatments that Danielle took advantage of, she was also happy to feel confident and secure in the health care treatment she was receiving. Although her breast cancer scare was almost two and a half years behind her, she never forgot the anxious feeling of uncertainty and doubt it had caused. She also never forgot the shock and anger that came with her misdiagnosis. She wanted to make certain that the likelihood of another woman suffering through the same trauma would be greatly reduced. Over the past two years, Danielle had come to know more about her personal health than she ever believed possible. She was truly practicing the Rhapsody mantra "own your own health."

What drove Danielle's backing of the *Rhapsody Lifestyle* more than anything else was the company's persistent pursuit of longevity. She believed that her best years were yet to come. She also wanted to make certain that her husband Stephen would not begin to show signs of advanced aging anytime soon. Danielle believed that the time to do something about their prospective longevity was right now. Danielle knew that her daughter-in-law Gina believed that Mark Candu, head of Rhapsody's scientific community was a great resource for inquiries about longevity. Danielle had met him only one time, and that was briefly at the opening of the Struben Center. She was happy that Mark had agreed to have lunch with her so that they could get to know one another better. She was meeting him at 12:30 PM over at the nutrition corner at the Struben Center. They were going to be joined by the Rhapsody nutritionist, Lettie Potter.

After Danielle completed her visit to her esthetician she went back into a locker area of the women's spa to freshen up before going to meet Mark Candu and Lettie Potter on the fifth floor of the building. Twenty minutes later she arrived feeling refreshed, happy and looking forward to their discussion.

"Here she is. We were just talking about you, Danielle," said Mark Candu as Danielle approached.

"*Notheeng* I shouldn't *'ear*, I *'ope*."

"Of course not." responded Lettie Potter. "I was just telling Mark how wonderful it is that you and your daughter-in-law get along so well. It's nice to be associated with you and your extended family."

"That's kind of you, Lettie. Gina *ees* much more *meteeculous* about what she eats than I am and she seems to know so much more about *nutreetion*. Frankly, I get confused on *thees topeec* rather *easeely*, and that's why I'm *lookeeng* for some *'elp*. I know Gina believes that a good diet *ees* essential for longer life and she *'as* been trying to reign *een* Josh on *thees topeec* also. *'Owever* Stephen *ees* another matter entirely. *'E* just eats whatever *'e* feels like eating."

"Your husband is still in very good shape. He must do some things right to maintain his health. He's a very good looking man." Lettie was simply trying to make conversation. She was in awe of Danielle but was trying not to show it. Her words came out a little awkwardly, but she was trying her best to maintain her professional decorum.

"I *well 'ave* to tell Stephen that one of the prettiest young Rhapsody staff members *theenks 'e ees 'ot*. *Eet weell* be good for *'ees* ego." Danielle laughed, but changed the topic when she noticed Lettie redden a bit. "So Mark, *'ow* was your flight over to the UK? *Weell* you be *een* London for a while?"

"Only for a few days. But I am hoping to make it over to the openings in China next month. Are you going?"

"No, *eet* was very nice of Abby to *eenvite* me, but I *'ave* been *runneeng* around so much lately that I *theenk eet* would be nice to spend a *leettle* more time back *'ere een* London for a while. Of course, Stephen says that *'e ees goeeng* to go and *'e 'as* tried to *conveence* me to come *weeth* him. But I *theenk* I'll just relax a *leettle*." The simple exchange of pleasantries went on for a few more minutes before Danielle asked Lettie about some of the diet recommendations that she had made the last time they sat down together.

"As we have been discussing," Lettie began her commentary. "Nutrition is one of the most effective methods of disease control. If you can consistently have a half dozen servings of fruit and vegetables on a daily basis your cancer risk is mitigated, as is the probability of stroke. Other research shows that low-fat dairy products in your diet can be even more effective as an alternative to medication in lowering high blood pressure. Certainly it will have at least a complimentary impact. There are also some articles that I have sent you about the impact of reducing cholesterol on lowering your risk of heart disease. But all of these items are what I refer to as the nutrition basics. If they were so simple to adhere to, we would not have the obesity problems that are so widespread today."

After a while Danielle asked Mark Candu about the scientific community's views on the relationships between dietary adjustments and longevity.

"Mark, *'ow* do you feel about all of these things we *'ave* been *deescusseeng*? *Eet's eenteresting* that the research *ees demonstrateeng* that a good diet can *'elp* avoid diabetes, cancer, heart disease and strokes. But apart from disease avoidance, *ees* there a body of *eveedence* that shows that certain dietary measures *weell defeeneetively 'elp* us *leeve* longer *'ealthier* lives?"

"I'm not quite sure what you're looking for Danielle." Candu tried to look through the eyes of the actress/singer and into her soul. She was a beautiful woman, who did not look to be in her fifties. He wondered how he himself would view the aging process in another twenty years when he was her age. He respected her experience as well as her intelligence and did his best to answer what he believed to be a question beneath the question. "There are certainly some indications that dietary modification may delay the commencement of the neurodegenerative process. Alzheimer's disease, among other neurodegenerative disorders seems to be hastened or triggered by a buildup of insoluble proteins as well as by increased levels of oxidative pressure. In short, many of the cognitive negatives that are sometimes associated with aging, such as memory loss, can be positively affected by diet."

"Thank you for adding that Mark. When I *theenk* of what I *'ave accompleeshed een* my life so far, I *theenk* of myself first and foremost as a wife and a mother. After that I *theenk* of myself as a *performeeng arteest*. I want to be able to *fulfeel* these roles *effecteevely* for many years to come."

****

Even before her 25th birthday Gina Struben recognized that celebrity has its drawbacks. In fact, for several years she had been feeling captive to her own celebrity. She was recognized everywhere she went. She used to feel that this was her own choice and that she could take her foot off the accelerator at any time and slip into relative oblivion, if she so chose. However that was hardly the case. Gina's fame seemed to be growing every day. She no longer did interviews or appeared on talk shows. The one exception was the publicity events, the previous September, surrounding the opening of the *Struben Center for the Rhapsody Lifestyle* in London.

Gina's celebrity had taken on a slightly different character of late. She was still the sexy pop/rock icon to the music world. This was underlined by her chart topping smash hit "Kiss Away," which was a remake of the mid 90s version of the song that was popularized by her mother-in-law, Danielle Dubonet. Gina's marriage to Josh Struben had helped transform her image. She was now being referred to in some circles as the, "Princess of Pop." Together with Danielle, they were also being referred to as the "Royal Family of Pop." The fact that she was spending more and more time in London, added to this new blue-blooded aura. The more Gina tried to avoid the media the more it simply fanned the flames of her mystique.

It was now mid-February, 2011, but it was summertime "Down Under." Josh and Gina Struben were heading to Bondi Beach in

Sydney Australia. They had earned the respite. They left their hotel in a taxi heading towards Bondi Beach just before noon.

Josh rented an umbrella from a shop along the walkway and they made their way down onto the sandy beach. They were still within 20 yards or so of the long arching walkway, and now they were also within 20 yards of the surf. Josh quickly set up the umbrella and put down the two blankets. Gina crawled under the umbrella before removing her coverall. She grew up on a Caribbean beachfront so she always loved the sun, but she was aware that her fair skin could not risk overexposure. She also modestly kept her black bikini top in place, and replaced her hat and oversized sunglasses after briefly removing them when she stripped off her sundress.

Josh and Gina settled on their beach blankets and were undisturbed by any of the beach crowd, although there were sunbathers within 30 feet of their spot on the sand. They talked to one another in soft tones as they reclined on the supple white sand.

"It certainly is bit easier to get away from it all than I might have thought," said Gina. "I'm hoping that we can really relax for a change."

"We just have to take it nice and easy. This is the first time I've ever been to Australia and I'm glad we selected it as our getaway."

Gina took a couple of paperback books out of her beach bag and handed one to Josh. They both loved to read and found it to be an excellent way to escape and relax. The young couple lapsed into silence for a while. Josh was rapidly paging through a mystery novel, and Gina was reading Alison McDuffee's book about the founding of *Rhapsody Holdings*. As close as she had become to Rhapsody and the McDuffee twins, Gina had never read the bestselling book that described its modest beginnings. The book had now been in print for more than 18 months and had facilitated several appearances by Alison on the Omar Show as the business grew. Gina found it fascinating to read about how the three principal founders, Abby and Alison and Dao got together with Ben and Sandeep to form the "band of five" that brought their concept to life. She wondered if they were surprised by the scope of their success and she also wondered about whether or not they were prepared for the avalanche of opportunity that was in front of them. Gina turned to Josh and asked, "Are you happy with success that you have had on Wall Street? People are beginning to recognize you as one of the new 'good guys.' Does that make you happy?"

"I don't know about the 'good guy' thing. I've been successful during a very tough economic period. I don't know if that makes me a 'good guy' or just lucky. I'm not foolish enough to think that my popularity is not related to the success of my investment strategies. The list of former 'good guys' is now lining the hallways of the Federal Court House in Manhattan." Josh sounded sarcastic. He had gradually developed distrust as well as a dislike for some of his fellow members of the financial community.

"Fair enough. But do you like what you're doing?" Gina was leading the way toward her idea.

"Things have certainly changed a good bit lately. We have some new young people coming into the firm on a regular basis. The day-to-day management of the fund is going well, and in another six months, I think I'll be out of Cromwell Parsons entirely. It's been a good run, but I'm just looking for some new challenges." This had obviously been on Josh's mind for some time and Gina was well aware of it. She had simply waited for the appropriate time to probe his restlessness in more detail. After a few seconds Josh inquired, "Why do you ask?"

Gina sat up on the blanket and pulled her knees up towards her chest, effectively folding her body in half. She pushed down the tops of her sunglasses, with her right forefinger so that they rode out over the tip of her nose. She then peeked over the top of her lenses directly at Josh and smiled. He looked into her big blue eyes as she spoke, with their faces no more than a couple feet apart.

"I have my reasons. And what do you want to do when you leave Cromwell Parsons?"

"I'm not yet sure. But so far in my career, all I've done is make a lot of money. Now I want to make a difference."

"Well that's how I feel too. I feel like I'm always making money. Every call from Carl or from Seth seems to be about a new opportunity to make more money, almost to the point of boredom. That's a part of why I wanted to come to a public beach like this. There are real people around here. I can feel it. Don't get me wrong. I love our friends and our homes and the fact that we can fly anywhere in the world, anytime we want, on our own Gulfstream. But here we can just blend into the scenery. There's a lot to be said for having a certain degree of anonymity. Life can't possibly be all about fame and money." Gina tightened her grip on her calves and continued to peer over her glasses. Her lips parted into soft smile and she playfully stuck her tongue out at her husband and then retracted it and listened as he spoke.

"But this money thing....it's not quite the same for you. You are an artist. Your performances help people. They bring them happiness and joy. The fact that you're making a lot of money is in some ways incidental to who you are." Josh wasn't quite sure where they were going with this conversation, but he knew that he was speaking from either his brain, or from his heart or from his soul. He wasn't sure which, but he at least knew what he was feeling was unfiltered. It made him feel better just to talk about it.

"I'm not as sure about that as you are." Gina now relaxed slightly. "It's true that I enjoy myself when I am performing. It hardly seems like work, at all. And I have to admit that I get pretty turned on by my audiences. But other than the concerts themselves, the rest of it is a lot of work. I'm not complaining, mind you. Overall I enjoy what I do. But I'm almost certain that I would do pretty much the same things, regardless of how much money I earned. The money is nice. However it's about much more than just money."

"I understand perfectly. My job is much more directly about the money. I'm not complaining either. I'm grateful for the fact that I have been as fortunate as I have been. But we both sit here saying that it's not about the money, and yet we both realize that we most likely would never have met one another if it weren't for our financial success."

"I hear what you are saying. But I disagree. I believe that what was meant to be was simply meant to be. We would've met anyway. I'm sure of it. Your mother is a performer just like I am. We could have met through her." Gina decided that she didn't want to talk about money anymore. She still hadn't sprung her idea but she was coming around to it slowly. She pushed her glasses back up once again covering her eyes, but she whipped off her broad hat and stood up. "Let's go for a swim."

Gina didn't wait for an answer. She simply jogged quickly across the sand and splashed into the edge of the water. She took off her sunglasses and clutched them with her right hand as she dove headfirst under an oncoming wave. They gradually moved in the surf to a spot that was almost shoulder deep for Gina but that was more of a bobbing spot than a ducking spot.

"You know what I think you might want to do?" Gina went back to their earlier conversation. She was determined to get her idea across to Josh.

"To do, about what?" asked Josh.

"To do about a job… didn't you just tell me that you wanted to leave Cromwell Parson?"

"Yes I did say that. But I don't want to venture a guess about what you think I should do. But I know you're going to tell me anyway. So, go ahead. Advise me. What were you thinking?" As he said it a high swelling wave followed a series of low cresting waves, and once again Gina was forced to grab her glasses and duck under the wave. They both reemerged on the other side and Gina finally responded.

"I think that you might want to get more directly involved in the management of Rhapsody." Her suggestion was now out in the open.

"And why would that occur to you?"

"I know that you would be able to help Abby and the team a lot. When I saw her last, she looked like she needed a vacation. I have an awful lot of respect for her and for the kinds of things that she's trying to achieve. But I also think she needs a lot more help than she knows. To begin with the business is top heavy with women and there needs to be more young vibrant males in the business."

"What she's going to need is a lot more Asians. Rhapsody is opening up three Asian centers in the next few months. No wonder Abby needs a vacation."

"No I think she needs you. And I think you need the challenge that Abby can give you. What do you have to lose?" Gina's question went unanswered, as the young couple made their way back toward their blanket. Along the way they overheard one of the oceanside sun worshipers saying Gina's name, in recognition, but they kept walking steadily toward their spot on the sand.

They settled back down under their umbrella, and Gina changed the topic once again. "We have a few other things that I'd like to talk about." Gina said this in a manner that got Josh's rapt attention.

"I'm listening," said Josh.

"Remember last summer when I was concerned about the possibility that I might have a genetic predisposition towards developing Huntington's disease?"

"Of course I do. And you took the test and it was determined that you do not have those CAG repeats on the gene on the fourth chromosome that indicate the likelihood of the disease. We went through all this in great detail. And because of your genetic makeup you are no more likely to develop Huntington's Chorea than I am. Correct? Is there something else I should know about this?" Josh's tone now sounded a little worried, but Gina alleviated his concerns.

"Yes, you got it right. And there is nothing new with respect to my own health in that regard. However, I'm still intrigued about my father. Other than the fact that he had Huntington's disease, I know very little about him. I think that I want to find him, if in spite of everything, he is still alive. Who knows I may have some other siblings that I just don't know about. And each of those siblings would also have a 50 percent chance of suffering from Huntington's disease. It's been in the back of my mind for a few months now, kind of, well … haunting me."

"I see and I guess I can understand that. You just need to be prepared for what you find." Josh was leaning on his left elbow with his left hand up against the side of his neck. He was gesturing with his right hand as he spoke. When he finished talking, his right hand was turned upward in a supplicating manner, encouraging Gina to speak more.

"Well regardless of whether or not I have siblings, who may or may not have Huntington's Chorea, I still have a keen interest in the disease. After reading everything that I could, I have come to realize what a horrible disease it is and how much people who have this problem, suffer. And for that matter how much their families suffer along with them. We have so much money ourselves. Maybe we ought to do something about it. I don't mean just donate a lot of money. I think that maybe we could start a research foundation focusing on this particular disease."

"If that's what you want to do I am with you."

"And I think it's a good idea for us to work with the Rhapsody Foundation. Their approach is to fund study efforts that focus on preventative and promotive research rather than remedial approaches. It is not sufficient to treat diseases only. There is much that we can do to prevent the occurrence of disease as well."

"Huntington's Chorea is inherited and not acquired, so prevention would be difficult."

"Mark Candu said that some of the stem cell research work that is being done may have a direct impact on the treatment of the symptoms of the disease. Who knows where this will lead." Gina was quiet for a second or two, and her natural smile disappeared briefly. "And regardless of all of this, I would still like to find my father if he is still living."

"He might not want to be found."

"I've gone back and forth about that. It's a risk I'm willing to take."

"But is it a risk that *he* is willing to take?"

"I don't know. But I don't want to talk about this anymore." Gina changed the topic rather abruptly and this surprised Josh. He knew that there were several things on her mind that she wanted to explore with him and the themes kept changing rapidly.

"What do you want to talk about?" Josh tried not to allow any frustration creep into his voice, but Gina sensed an impending impatience. So she smiled coyly and said, "I have a surprise for you."

Josh stared into his wife's eyes for a brief second and then Gina leaned forward and gave him a short but loving kiss on the lips as she whispered softly, "I'm pregnant again."

****

Abby McDuffee was up to her elbows in alligators. The operating results for the first two years of Rhapsody Holdings showed excellent progress. However if the team wasn't a bit more cautious it risked suffering from its own prosperity. While the financials were good there was a host of operating issues that presented significant challenges to Abby and her executive team.

During 2010 the team had successfully opened its first two centers in New York and London. But the plan for 2011 had now expanded from four new openings to a total of six new openings. Beijing and Paris had been added to the 2011 plan. The good part about all of these new openings was Rhapsody was no longer playing with its own seed money. Their original line of credit was still in play but it was underutilized and frankly unnecessary. Ben Hui Zhang and the finance team were actively working to restructure the terms of LOC. Meanwhile as each new center was conceived, Rhapsody opened the opportunity for local investment through regional joint ventures that allowed Rhapsody Holdings to retain 50% of the equity and the profit in each of the centers. Abby entrusted the negotiations for the financial structures of the new centers to her financial staff, assisted by her legal team. Ben Hui Zhang was demonstrating superior leadership in all of the negotiations.

All of this financial prosperity however yielded a different set of monetary concerns. The rapidly growing cash-rich firm needed to find appropriate interim treasury/depository opportunities that wouldn't burden the company with inordinate financial risk and that would allow significant appropriate operational liquidity. While many multinational corporations would salivate for such problems, Abby was smart enough to realize that the financial issues were real. They had not set up the business for the purpose of being a financial superpower. However if the treasury functions were mishandled, the company could suffer from its own prosperity. And while Ben Hui Zhang was a terrific operational CFO, Abby had come to rely more and more on the investment and development acumen of Sun Feng. In many ways, Feng had more influence on the global direction of Rhapsody Holdings than any of its directors or officers. His personal fortune had continued to aggregate, even throughout the global economic downturn of 2009 and 2010. Feng was now generally considered to be one of the twenty-five wealthiest men in the world, and his influence throughout the global political and financial powers of the world was growing proportionately. The good news for Abby and her team was that Sun Feng was a strong believer in the Rhapsody vision and mission, and acted almost like a guardian angel to the investment interests of the company.

One area of concern for Abby was that the new Asian centers were projecting a significantly different service mix from the services that had been most popular in New York and London. For example the Asian centers projected a significant volume of "skin lightening procedures." There had been very little demand for these services in the *Struben Center* in London and almost no demand at all in the *Tkachuk Center* in New York City. And although alternative medical procedures such as acupuncture and ayurvedic medicine were on the rise in New York and London, the demand for these services in Beijing, Hong Kong and Singapore was projected to be much greater. Abby always knew there would be regional differences in demand for different services, but she didn't believe that they had adequate data to project that demand.

Another major concern that sometimes kept Abby awake at night was the fact that their rapid growth of personnel at the center level, was far outstripping the number of hires that was taking place in the headquarters complex. On one hand she was happy that the business was able to hire effective service personnel at each of the centers who would be able to service their client/members. On the other hand it was becoming difficult to hire the appropriate headquarters resources needed to ensure continuity, similarity and quality of service. They were getting by, but the headquarters team was being worked to the bone.

Abby also had some personal things to think about. Her family life was out of balance with her business. Her husband, Bo Blanchard, had been throttling back on his work at his law firm to spend more time with their daughter Mindy. It was difficult for Abby to believe that Mindy was now thirteen years old! It had not been as difficult for her to realize that she and her sister Allie had celebrated their 50th birthdays together the previous summer. Nevertheless Abby knew that life was coming at her fast! She knew that Rhapsody Holdings already had a ten figure market value and that her personal stake in the business was worth more than $100 Million. She didn't want to think about a Rhapsody exit strategy. They had only just begun.

****

Things had come unglued quickly for Maureen Brady after her 45th birthday. She still hadn't gotten over her long past run-in with Chipper Geld and his Russian friend. Her lawyers had done some background checking on Geld for the sake of her sanity, and it had only confirmed her suspicions and made her feel more dirty for ever having trusted him in the first place. She kept these findings to herself and didn't share them with JB because she believed that JB's business relationship with Geld had nothing to do with the sordid and seamy set of commercial endeavors to which Maureen's lawyers had alluded. The asinine Fundamental Health Resources project was her husband's problem.

For the first time in her life Maureen began to pay attention to the family finances. It wasn't that she dug into them in great detail. She simply wanted to ensure herself that she could continue her lifestyle if her husband passed away.

For the past six months she had begun to pay attention to some of the details of her own net worth. She managed to do this without alerting JB. In fact, Brady himself was always keenly aware of the performance of every investment and every asset that he owned. Over the years he had frequently encouraged Maureen to learn more about their family portfolio, and he was mildly disconcerted when she professed very little interest in the subject. So when Maureen finally demonstrated some interest in the topic, JB encouraged her interest. John didn't consider it in any way unnatural for Maureen to be planning her own financial vitality if he predeceased her. When Maureen came to realize that the combined net worth for JB and herself was now nearly $150 million, she began to worry about why her husband would be making significant investments in such foolhardy endeavors as Fundamental Health Resources. In truth, Maureen had very little understanding of the risks and rewards that went along with any business endeavor. She didn't understand her husband and his addiction to playing to win.

As Maureen learned more about the Brady family assets, she began to realize that she didn't know where all of the assets were. They had literally hundreds of accounts in various financial institutions in multiple parts of the world. It began to fascinate her that her husband was able to keep track of it all, particularly now that he was so significantly handicapped. However there was a never-ending parade of business and financial advisors who came to the house to visit John in the study, and JB also made frequent excursions into the city in the specially outfitted Cadillac that Fernando drove for him. The one thing that JB did not do at all anymore was travel on planes. His world had been reduced to New York, Kings Point and an occasional car trip to the Hamptons. His world also no longer included Maureen. They barely spoke at all other than about money. Oddly enough, it was the one topic that they had never discussed prior to his operation.

Maureen also didn't go to the club much anymore. She didn't need or want the pity that was usually served up. So she simply stopped going. Unfortunately Maureen did come across an old acquaintance and she didn't know what to do about it. The old acquaintance was booze. The relapse had started shortly after her reckless driving arrest on her 45th birthday. The police had administered a somewhat embarrassing field sobriety test, followed by her refusal to take a breathalyzer test at the police station. Although her lawyer arrived promptly at the station house and advised her to take the test or risk losing her license anyway, she steadfastly refused because she hadn't been drinking. The legal mess was straightened out but the damage had been done. When Maureen returned home later that evening, she celebrated her birthday in solitude with her only true friend, an ice cold Cosmopolitan. The ensuing months became a blur of disjointed mistakes.

Although she had never cheated on her husband during their many years of marriage, that would-be virtue also went by the wayside when Maureen started drinking again. She simply asked her personal trainer, Grant, to do a little overtime. Following their normal workout one morning, she took him into the steam bath with her and shortly thereafter Grant began to grunt. After that threshold was passed, Maureen dispassionately dismissed her trainer only to hire him back a few days later. And although the passion returned, it was never accompanied by any genuine emotional attachment. Grant simply and dutifully scratched her itch. He also tripled his personal training fees.

Maureen was most disturbed by the deterioration of her relationship with her children. Mark and Megan had always been very independent from the time they started college. However, Maureen was most distressed by the fact that Kenneth had also now become quite distant. She knew that he had a new male companion at school, but she knew very little more than that. His previous lover, Rickie Van Dorfan was now a part of his past.

Although Maureen made no effort to hide the fact that she was no longer abstemious when it came to alcohol indulgence, there was no one around her who cared enough to make an issue of her addiction. Not only was she unsure about whom she could call for help, she was unsure about whether or not she wanted help in the first place. One thing she knew for sure was that she would never be able to return to Solace in the Sun, as long as SIS was still owned and operated by Chipper Geld.

Early one afternoon, following her double-header session with Grant, Cara, her housekeeper, found her in her bedroom and said there was someone on the phone who wanted to speak with her.

"Hello, this is Maureen"

"Hi Maureen. It's Mike Kelvey. It's been such a long time since we've spoken. How have you been?" Maureen recalled Dr. Mike Kelvey. He had been JB's personal physician when he was CEO of ICD. Kelvey had also accompanied Maureen when she first went down to Solace in the Sun, two and a half years ago. She hadn't heard from him since right before JB's operation. She immediately wondered why he was calling and why he had asked to speak with her, rather than with JB. Maureen wished that she had fixed herself a drink before taking this call.

"Well hello Dr Kelvey! You're right. It *has* been a long time, hasn't it? I've been just fine. How have you been?"

"Not too bad. In fact, not bad at all. I haven't been doing much at all with our friends over at ICD since JB left. However my practice certainly keeps me busy. In some ways I'm much happier now than I was a few years back."

"That's good to hear. How have your wife and family been doing?" Maureen couldn't remember Kelvey's wife's name, having met her only one time, and she wasn't even certain whether or not the Kelvey's had children. She was simply making small talk and making no real effort at getting it straight.

"Well, I got divorced about a year and a half ago, I think it was the best thing for both of us. We didn't have children. So no one got hurt unnecessarily." Kelvey was obviously trying to be friendly and sociable, but Maureen had no inkling as to where this conversation was headed so she simply put the conversation into focus.

"So Dr. Kelvey, what can *I* do for you? Have you spoken to John?"

"No I haven't talked to JB in quite some time. I did send him an e-mail a couple of weeks back but I haven't heard back from him. Actually I was simply looking for JB to provide a reference for me with respect to a group I'd like to join. When I hadn't heard back from JB for a few days, it occurred to me that I might ask you for the same kind of reference."

"And what kind of reference would that be?"

"I want to join something that's called a GPS or a *Global Practitioner Society* that is associated with *Rhapsody Holdings*. Have you heard about them?"

"Yes. Yes I have. That's the company that was started by two twin sisters. Right? One of them has appeared on the Omar show a few times. I know who they are."

"That's right. That's the group. In fact one of those twin sisters, Abigail McDuffee, used to work at ICD. I didn't know her, but I'm sure JB knows her well."

"Oh he knows her alright. In fact, he can't stand her. Apparently they were rivals back in the ICD days, and JB still considers her the enemy. John and a couple of his business colleagues have a business that is competing with Rhapsody in some way."

"I didn't know that."

"Well, I'm not sure exactly what I can do to provide an effective reference for you, but I certainly will be happy to try. It's totally up to you. However I would give up on using John for a reference, because of the conflict with Abby McDuffee."

"Thank you for your candor, Maureen, and for your willingness to help. Let me think about what's best, if I might, and get back to you. Would that be all right with you?"

"Sure."

"You know what? I have a better idea. Would you consider joining me for lunch one day this week? I could tell you a little bit more about Rhapsody, and we can catch up on a few other things as well."

"That would be nice. I'd like that." Maureen Brady said to Mike Kelvey and they made some plans to meet later that week. Maureen wasn't totally certain whether or not she liked Kelvey, but it quickly crossed her mind that he was a few years younger than she was and he was could possibly represent an upgrade from Grant, the grunt.

****

Dr Al Moses' life had been more or less resurrected from the scrap heap of depression over the past two years. He was eating differently and he was thinking differently. Maria Cardoza had embraced yoga at his suggestion, and now he himself was following her lead. His group of personal relationships had grown along with his interests. Maria had stopped seeing Dr. Lefebvre for therapeutic help but Maria and Al now counted Angelique Lefebvre and Yogi Vijay among their close circle of friends. Increasingly Dr. Al was spending more of his life learning the simple fact that his best days were yet in front of him. Yet time did move rapidly. Duffy was already a year and a half old and was toddling around their homes in a precocious pursuit of tactile information gathering. She was already talking a bit, or at least naming the objects around her. She called Al, "Dah, Dah," without any encouragement and for no readily apparent reason. Al was simply thrilled with the recognition.

Al and Maria, and Duffy, all spent a fair amount of time at the Tkachuk Center. Maria had moved her office from the Lexington Avenue headquarters building to the administrative area of the Tkachuk Center on the fifth floor. Al had now narrowed his practice down to the point where 80% of his clients were *Rhapsody Lifestyle* members, whom he saw at the Tkachuk Center's facilities. Several days a week for multiple hours at a time, Duffy played and learned at "Rhaffies" on the fourth floor of the center. Al was very happy with the way his life was becoming structured. He was even finding time to begin a fitness regimen, geared towards regaining a more youthful physical outlook to go along with his reinvigorated intellectual and emotional conventions. The renaissance of Dr. Al Moses was remarkable. The only difficulty with the current arrangement was that Maria was working long hours. He wished that Maria had a bit more time to spend with Duffy.

Al and Maria had a grand plan for the upcoming openings scheduled two weeks apart in Beijing and then Hong Kong. They were going to take a much-needed vacation first and make European stops in Spain and then in Rome. Maria would introduce Al to her old friends at Poco Pedazo de Ciela in Spain and then Al would introduce Maria to his med school friend and classmate, Paolo Grassani, in Italy. They were also going to visit Maria's home town just south of Venice. She hadn't been there since her parents died several years back.

Dr. Al was already at home when Maria arrived back at the apartment after work. He had already put Duffy to sleep for the evening and was waiting to share a bottle of wine with Maria to discuss their upcoming vacation plans. As soon as she came to the door Al took out a corkscrew and opened a bottle of Cakebread Cabernet Sauvignon. He poured two glasses of wine and handed one to Maria as she sat down in the living room and kicked off her shoes.

"I am glad to see that you finally made it out of there. Were you at the center all this time or did you go back over to the headquarters building?"

"I almost never get to HQ anymore. After I moved my office to the center, I've been able to stay out of the headquarters stuff. If Abby or Alison wants my opinion on anything, they usually just pick up the phone and call. But the center is getting a bit hectic. The members all seem happy, but the staff is feeling the pressure. We are getting more and more traffic from members who live outside of the US."

"Most of the members I see live here in the city."

"Well that's sort of goes with the nature of your specialty. Wouldn't you say?"

"Yes, to a large degree. But I actually have three cases now for London members, where I'm coordinating treatment with their OB/GYN back in the UK. So I guess I am starting to see some of the same trends. This is a good thing. Our members are starting to see the value in the global coordination of their healthcare."

"I think the biggest challenge that globalization presents to us in spa services area is the wide variety of treatments that people are looking for. Abby has asked me for some service specific estimates about what to expect during the next quarter, and I'm hard pressed to give accurate estimates. But I'm sure we'll figure it out." Maria began to relax as she sipped her wine. She unbuttoned the top button and reached inside her blouse and massaged her own shoulder. She took a deep sigh and changed the topic. "Is Duffy already asleep?"

"Oh yes. She's been out for a couple hours already. It's the nanny's night off so I keep walking in to Duffy's room just to look at her sleeping. She is just so beautiful, so very very beautiful, just like her mother."

"That's sweet of you to say, Al. But to be honest with you, I am so darn tired that I feel anything but beautiful. But I think I'll go inside and check on Duffy." She put down her glass of wine and wandered into the baby's bedroom and came out a few minutes later smiling. "You're so right Al. Just looking at her makes me happy. She sleeps so peacefully. When I bent over to kiss her, I could feel her little breath. Otherwise I would barely know she was breathing. So peaceful ... she is just so peaceful."

"Isn't it amazing how one small human being can bring out the best in us?"

"And when she smiles at us, I can feel that the love is reciprocal. Can't you?"

"Yes absolutely. I love her as though she were my own daughter."

"You're the only father she has ever known, Al."

"It's very nice to hear you say that, Maria. I certainly feel like a father to Duffy."

"Why don't you adopt her, Al? I will sign whatever papers are necessary to make you her adoptive father. Then we can be her parents together."

"How is that done? Do I need John Brady's approval? Can Duffy have more than one legal father? Wouldn't it be a lot easier if you and I were wife and husband?" Although it was proposed in a very different way, this was at least the fifth or sixth time that Al Moses had asked Maria Cardoza to marry him.

"Everything is going so well for us now, Al. I am perfectly content with the current arrangement between the two of us. I love you and I don't need any piece of paper to make that official. However I'm not quite sure how Duffy will react to all of this when she is older. She already calls you 'Dah, Dah,' which is close enough to 'Da Da.' If it means a lot to you; I am willing to become Maria Moses."

It was not exactly the most romantic acceptance of a marriage proposal, but Al Moses was pleased anyway. He knew that Maria treasured her independence, and he took her acceptance as a trusting acknowledgement that he would continue to honor her autonomy within their marriage. There were no further promises made and they decided that they would have a small private wedding ceremony when they went to Italy the following month.

****

John Brady's driver Fernando had become much more than just a chauffeur, over the past two years since JB's ill-fated operation. In addition to driving Brady's car, Fernando was by his side twelve to fifteen hours a day. He didn't just help him get in and out of his vehicle; he also assisted Brady in moving about in his high-tech wheelchair. In many ways Fernando became Brady's arms and legs, and was allowed to remain silently in the room during many business meetings that his boss presided over.

Fernando had worked for Brady for half a dozen years when both were in the employ of ICD. With overtime, Fernando was still being paid nearly $60,000 a year by ICD as part of the contractual severance arrangements with John Brady. ICD also took care of Fernando's healthcare, vacation pay and other employee benefits. But Brady wanted a good deal more from Fernando and he was willing to pay for it. He paid Fernando an additional $10,000 a month to ensure his presence and loyalty at all times and in all matters.

Although Fernando had only a high school education, he was innately a very bright and "street-wise" young man. His experience growing up in a very tough area of the South Bronx taught him the value of keeping his mouth shut. He managed to avoid allegiance with any of the street gangs in the city, while at the same time maneuvering to have his nonpartisanship be overlooked by the leadership of these neighborhood gangs. He moved to Queens County at the age of sixteen, and worked after school in a local garage. He learned to drive and after getting his initial drivers license, he began working for a car service, and answering every job ad that he could find for private drivers, because he realized that the money would be much better.

Fernando was 23 years old when he began working for John Brady at ICD. Brady regarded him as very dependable and very loyal. However beyond that JB never wanted to know that much about Fernando. This arrangement worked well for both JB and for Fernando during their ICD days together. Fernando was privy to the philandering of John Brady during his days of episodic cohabitation with Maria Cardoza, often dropping Brady at Cardoza's Manhattan apartment and/or driving both of them to work the following morning. An occasional dalliance or two with other women also took place while Fernando drove, and kept his musings to himself.

Brady's wife, Maureen, also remained personally remote from Fernando, while he chauffeured her from one event to another, as an adjunct responsibility to his duties for JB. Keeping his personal distance had been tantamount to keeping his job. There never was even the least concern on John Brady's part, that his chauffeur would breach his confidence.

The relationship began to evolve and change after Brady fell victim to the wayward knife of Dr. Thomas Madison. Once Brady was confined to a wheelchair, complete with oxygenated breathing apparatus, and some waste removal facilities, the nature of his association with Fernando was redefined and, by necessity, it became more intimate and dependant. Although Brady had a full-time staff nurse, Fernando often attended to some of Brady's simpler hygienic needs. Gradually John Brady learned more about Fernando. He learned that Fernando still lived with his mother in the Hollis section of Queens. He knew that Fernando's mother worked as a hospital porter and made enough money to make an annual trip back to her native Mexico. Fernando never accompanied her when she went to Mexico. He was native to the Bronx. Besides, Fernando was always too busy working overtime, determined to one day lead a prosperous lifestyle, like the people he drove around town. He knew he didn't have the education to facilitate the attainment of these goals in a conventional manner, so he purchased a daily number, bought lottery tickets and occasionally played the horses in the hopes of getting lucky one day. He also went to church and prayed.

Fernando was grateful for the additional money that he made taking care of John Brady. At the same time, he was astounded by the fact that Brady could still make people cringe even though he couldn't make a fist. Fernando fully realized that JB's only weapon was his wallet. He also realized that it was a sizable weapon.

One of the significant perks of his job was that Fernando was able to commute between his home in the middle class, mixed racial community of Hollis Queens and Brady's Kings Point home on the North Shore of Nassau County using Brady's stretch Cadillac. Although the door-to-door distance that he commuted daily was a mere twelve miles each way and a half an hour in the usual traffic, their homes were worlds apart.

Fernando wondered what it was that John Brady wanted to speak to him about this morning. Brady had asked him to come to his house at 9 AM, but he didn't indicate a destination for the day. He was worried that his days as John Brady's chauffeur might be coming to an end and this concerned him greatly. He knew that ICD had an obligation to provide Brady with a chauffeur for a few more years, but he knew his selection as John's driver was strictly subject to Brady's own whim. He didn't believe that he had done anything to annoy Brady, and he rarely drove Maureen Brady anywhere these days. But you could never be sure what these rich people believed. You never knew what they were thinking. But Fernando's own thinking was very clear. He knew that it be extremely difficult to find another job that would pay him nearly $180,000 a year with the limited skill set and experience that he possessed.

"Good morning Mr. Brady." Fernando was finding it difficult to hide his nervousness, as he walked around the wheelchair to sit in a chair that faced the door.

"Good morning Fernando. There's something important that I want to discuss with you this morning." In typical John Brady fashion, he didn't inquire about anything personal with respect to his driver's family, or the weather. He was, as always, direct and to the point. "I am having some significant problems with my so-called business partners, Geld and Pritchard."

"I'm sorry to hear that Mr. Brady." Fernando was alarmed at where this might be leading. If business was bad for JB, what did that say about his own future?

"You don't have to be sorry. It has nothing to do with you, at least not yet." Having been around Brady in his current condition for almost 2 years, Fernando was familiar with the ugly rasp that had become JB's voice. He was also not disconcerted either by the immobility of Brady's limbs or by the floppy vacillating of his neck and head, as JB's eyes flashed the only body language that could possibly underline his words.

"Yes Mr. Brady." Fernando knew that basic affirmation was the simplest response and the word that Mr. Brady wanted to hear.

"Let me tell you some things." Brady's voice was labored and he tried to limit the words he uttered. "Pritchard told me that Geld has obscene pictures of my son Kenneth and the prissy bitch boy, Rickie

Van Dorfan, who used to work for me." Brady was now sweating profusely down both sides of his face. Fernando took a throwaway wet wipe cloth from a bookcase on the side of the room. This was not an isolated incident. Fernando had performed this task many times in the past. He kept the sweat from Brady's brow, while JB caught his breath and started again. "He claims that these pictures were taken in Costa Rica when my wife was in rehab down there. Pritchard also told me that Geld was sleeping with my wife, Maureen."

"I don't believe that about Mrs. Brady, sir." By his omission, Fernando was indicating that he thought the liaison between Kenneth and "prissy Rickie" could possibly be true.

Again trying to conserve his strength Brady used few words to convey his concurrence. "I agree with your assessment … precisely."

Fernando was now less than 2 feet from JB and was looking directly into his hot liquid eyes. He didn't answer Brady. He just waited for Brady to speak again.

"I want those fuckers out of my life once and for all. Geld should rot in hell, right next to Pritchard. Do I make myself clear, Fernando?"

Fernando was now not as sure, but he at least started his response with the right word. "Yes Mr. Brady. I understand that you don't want to be involved with them. But …"

"No fucking butts Fernando. I want them out of my life. I pay you well but I never asked you for real help. You grew up in the South Bronx. You can give me real help now." He stopped for about fifteen seconds to catch his breath but it was obvious he had more to say. "I know life is cheap in the South Bronx. I know it is not cheap everywhere. There are some things money can't buy but I have yet to find out what they are." It was nearly as painful for Fernando to hear, as it must have been for Brady to speak.

"You can help me Fernando. Money is not an object. So I'm only going to ask you one more time, Fernando. Do I make myself clear?" It took almost one full minute for Brady to get this entire message out. There was only one answer to give.

"Yes Mr. Brady."

"Go over to the bookcase near the window, and roll back the rug." JB's breathing was now extremely labored.

Under the floorboard was a small steel door about 30 inches square. The door had two imbedded circular combination locks and Fernando realized that he was looking at the top of a safe of unknown depth and capacity.

Although the safe had not been touched by anyone in more than five years, JB did not have difficulty recalling the combination numbers. He managed to pass these codes along to Fernando without losing his breath entirely. Fernando punched in the codes as JB instructed on the dual safe locks and swung open the heavy steel door to the safe. Below the floor level and inside the safe Fernando saw four shoe box-sized cartons. Following instructions from JB he took one out and removed the lid. Inside he saw many stacks of US currency, all with the photo of Ulysses S Grant. Each stack contained $100 notes and each stack was wrapped together by a thin paper belt. The bills were non sequential. There were 25 of these stacks inside the box that Fernando opened. It was more money than he had ever seen in his life. The one box alone held $250,000 in cash. And there were four boxes in the safe. If the contents were the same in each box, John Brady had been hiding $1,000,000 in cash under his floor. That certainly was a tidy little nest egg.

The things that JB had previously coveted in life were now no longer nearly as important as they once had been. While his wealth had continued to grow, his health continued to deteriorate. Where he had once stood a robust 6'3" tall and 235 lbs, his two years in a wheel chair had caused him to lose more than seventy-five pounds. He simply couldn't feed himself. He needed help. And now he was simply asking Fernando for help.

"There's an oversized brief case behind the desk. It should hold all of the money. Take it." Brady's eyes widened as he tried to catch his breath to speak some more words. They weren't coming easily, and he was perspiring once again.

Fernando was truly dumbfounded. John Brady was asking him to kill two of his business colleagues, Chipper Geld and Paul Pritchard. And he was offering him a million dollars to do it! Fernando thought that this was the kind of thing that only happened in the movies. He couldn't possibly be serious. But then again maybe he was! And then it hit Fernando like a ton of bricks. Brady was definitely serious! JB was a very diminished man, who could in actuality control very little. How dare he think that he could control Fernando with his money!! Fernando grew angrier and angrier. He now moved very rapidly, and went behind the desk and retrieved the fat legal sized brief case. He stuffed all of the money into the briefcase and it actually fit..... a million dollars in one hundred dollar bills!

Fernando walked over to the stack of wet wipes and once again mopped the perspiration from Brady's face, carefully avoiding any accidental dislodgment of the cannula that fed oxygen to Brady through his nostrils. He did manage to turn the wheelchair so that Brady was no longer facing the shelving and the now empty safe. He also subtly turned the oxygen valve clockwise slightly without Brady noticing his action. He didn't want it off entirely, at least not yet.

"Mr. Brady, what exactly do you want me to do with Mr. Geld and Mr. Pritchard?"

"They're scum. They're taking my money and conspiring against me. And they're also laughing at me behind my back." The words came painfully and with maximum effort. "I don't care how you do it."

Fernando moved away from Brady but not before turning the valve a little tighter. He went over to the safe area and wiped the lock and handles cleanly with more of the wet wipes. He then did the same thing with the floorboards after he closed the safe and replaced the flooring. He then kicked the rug back in place over the floorboards. As he was doing this he heard Brady's rasp one last time. "Just tell me when you've finished the job. Tell me when they're dead."

Fernando had heard enough. He walked back over and turned the oxygen valve off, so that the alarm would not go off. He then sat down across from Brady and waited as JB's lungs fought to extract oxygen from the air in order to feed the brain. The struggle wasn't visibly violent. But neither was it immediate. Brady lost his mind before he lost his life. Many weird expressions crossed his face as his oxygen-deprived brain gradually became dysfunctional like the rest of his body. Somewhere along the line during the 45 minutes that it took for Brady to expire, JB learned that not everyone "had a price."

****

There were lots of talk show hosts and then there was Omar! Omar was a person who asked all the questions that real people wanted answered. His relationship with his audience was stunningly personal. They all loved him. Although Omar had become extraordinarily wealthy over the past 20 years he still seemed to have much in common with his audience. His common man approach to topics of significant public interest enabled him to bond with his audience like no other television personality. He always seemed to be slightly in front of every trend and social change, and in fact sometimes he even appeared to sponsor these changes.

Alison McDuffee had made her first appearance on the Omar show in the late summer of 2009. The appearance had been arranged through Seth Silverstein, but Omar took such a liking to Alison that a few subsequent appearances were done at Omar's request and facilitated by Omar's in-house physician/consultant, Dr. Zoë Mansfield. Omar had a genuine interest in the direction that Rhapsody Holdings was headed and he made an effort to keep his audience informed of its progress as well. But a recent problem had emerged and Omar wanted to explore it at its roots.

"For those of you unfamiliar with the *Rhapsody Lifestyle*, I will attempt to characterize it as a health and wellness business whose mission is ensuring that its Members lead a longer and healthier life. Is that a fair characterization, Alison?"

"Yes, Omar. I think you've captured the essence of what we are looking to achieve, and you, yourself, are a member, so we hope that you are personally seeing the value of what we have to offer."

"Let's talk a little bit about those memberships Alison. Is it fair to say that there has been more than a little controversy stirred up about your memberships over the last few months?"

"If you're referring to the piece that was done by Tom Garrett, I have to tell you I think that it was grossly unfair and quite frankly I was surprised by Garrett. I believed him to be a responsible reporter from things that he has done in the past."

"So that our studio audience and our viewers at home recognize the issue we are discussing let me lay out some of the allegations made by Garrett and get your response to them. As I understand it, Mr. Garrett purchased a Rhapsody lifestyle membership and has used a number of services at Rhapsody's New York Center, which is called the *Tkachuk Center for the Rhapsody Lifestyle.*"

"Normally I wouldn't even acknowledge who is a member and who is not a member of the *Rhapsody Lifestyle*. However, the reporter, Mr. Garrett, is quite forthright in telling everyone that he had purchased a membership and also expressing how he has employed some of the services we offer. Beyond that I really don't think it's appropriate for me to comment on how Mr. Garrett uses his membership."

"But Alison, let's be straight up about this. Tom Garrett has alleged that Rhapsody members are … and I quote … 'an elitist group of wealthy snobs, who believe that they deserve better healthcare than the rest of Americans. They could care less about the healthcare of the man in the street.' How do you answer that allegation?"

"Well Omar, let me say right away that it's totally off the mark. Our total membership is currently only fifty percent American. Our business is a global business, and our membership is a global membership. While it's true that our first center was set up here in New York City and had a high concentration of Americans, our London center, named for the Struben family, has less than a fifteen percent American membership. So to begin with Garrett's assertion about some kind of American elitism is misguided.

"In addition, I think it's grossly unfair to characterize our members as snobs. They are anything but snobs. They are leaders. They are innovators. And these are people who are very progressive thinkers. It shouldn't surprise anyone, but because of these traits, they are also quite frequently people with ample means."

"Isn't it true however, Alison, that a $50,000 annual membership is beyond the reach of the common man. So *all* of your members are from an elite group simply by a financial definition. And if this is true, how do you justify making services available to your members, that aren't available to the general public?"

"Although our memberships are geared toward a more affluent market, the products and services that we are developing will have a significant benefit for a much wider market over time.

"The healthcare bill that was signed into law last year in the US calls for groups to be formed that are called 'accountable health organizations' and talks about 'bundled payment' approaches. Whenever these methodologies do finally get enacted for the large number of middle-class and working class Americans, we will have the appropriate products and services to offer in these markets as well.

"Meanwhile our members, by virtue of their endorsement of our products, processes, procedures and protocols, are actually setting the stage for the way health and wellness will be administered across all markets in the future. One of the key tenets of a Rhapsody lifestyle membership is that the member is called upon to *own* his or her own health care. We believe that this paradigm shift will enable our members to live longer and livelier existences. Over time these benefits will also filter out into the mainstream markets. We also believe that variations of our membership or subscription model will also be offered in other markets at other price levels over time."

"Yes Alison, but Tom Garrett's criticism was that the elite Rhapsody Members were getting pampered personalized treatment while the majority of Americans are struggling with a healthcare system that is underfunded and underserved by an overworked and understaffed group of professionals. How would you counter that argument?"

"Let me start by saying once again, that this is not just about Americans. Our membership is a global membership. Healthcare is a global concern. Frankly, all Americans have a much better system than most other people around the world when it comes to healthcare. Many Americans simply don't realize that the level of professionalism amongst practitioners in this country is much higher than it is in other parts of the world. American medical schools are the envy of other countries. People from around the world come to this country to get educated in the medical arts. Having said all of that, I will also tell you that western medicine is not the end all and be all for everyone. That is why it is so important for our members to make their own choices, and to be guided in those choices by our global network of PALs. At Rhapsody, we believe that our eclectic approach to healthcare will be the standard practice of the future.

"With respect to the issue of financial facilitation, I want to point out that five percent of Rhapsody's profits each year go to the *Rhapsody Foundation*, which in turn funds the kinds of research that underscores the *Rhapsody Philosophy*. This funding goes toward research that prevents disease rather than simply treating disease. So in a way, it could be said that the very members that Garrett is criticizing, are actually those who subsidize the development of substantial new medical breakthroughs, that will be good for everyone in all markets. My belief is that Garrett is erroneously calling targeted philanthropy by the misbegotten label of elitism. And I have no idea concerning Mr. Garrett's motivation for doing so."

"Those are very strong words, Alison. But as you indicated earlier, I myself am a Rhapsody member, and I concur strongly with your opinions and your approach...."

"One other thing," Alison interrupted Omar's endorsement. "The tenets of the *Rhapsody Philosophy* that we have discussed several times on your show pertain to everyone. They are effective guidelines to a longer, better life and there is nothing exclusive about them."

Omar was up against a commercial break, so he ended a bit awkwardly. "Yes I agree Dr. McDuffee and thank you for joining us today and good luck. Okay let's go to break."

When they were off camera Omar, Zoë and Alison all relaxed a bit. However they were still in front of a live studio audience, and so they shut off their microphones altogether for a moment or two while a couple of staffers canvassed the audience for those who would care to ask questions on camera when they went back live. They all seem satisfied that they had successfully aired Alison's defense of Garrett's criticisms and looked forward to changing the topic during the audience Q&A that would be upcoming. But all three of them knew that Rhapsody would eventually need to have a much better message. They were at the stage in the business wherein they were no longer simply required to satisfy the membership, but they were also required to be effective civic-minded corporate citizens.

****

It had been a while since JB had been in church. But this time would be the last time. The pallbearers were not family members. They were not former coworkers. They were not friends from childhood or from Brady's adult life. They were simply employees of the funeral home that was located four blocks from the church. As the pallbearers rolled John Brady's body out of the church in front of the procession of mourners, there was a sense of perfunctory ritual, rather than a sense of profound loss. Brady's three children were accompanied in their mourning by three other young adults who doubled respectively as their significant others. None of the three of them had ever met Brady. And for that matter, Brady's three children were not so sure that they knew their father that well either. They seemed to feel an opportunity loss instead of the personal loss that they should have felt. The church was crowded with people who knew John Brady from his business career; from the clubs he belonged to; from the charities he supported; and from the people he employed. There were not that many people who truly regarded him as a friend. And there were not many in the church that shed a tear for his demise.

As the casket was removed from the church and put in the back of the hearse to head out to the burial ground, there was an odd collection of mourners that made their way up to Maureen Brady and her three children to pay their respects. The comments were all very brief and to the point. They simply paid their respects and moved on.

Paul Pritchard and Chipper Geld walked together up to speak with Maureen, and simply said they were sorry for her loss. Maureen simply nodded and didn't even make eye contact with Geld.

Alice, JB's longtime secretary at ICD, was off to the side talking with Fernando, JB's driver. They had not seen one another in more than a year and were quietly exchanging stories of years past.

A few feet from where Maureen stood, Jeannine and Cara from the Brady family household staff were standing together and talking quietly to Maureen's youngest son, Kenneth and his new friend, Brett. Nearby her daughter, Megan, and her boyfriend were getting acquainted casually with her brother, Mark and his girlfriend. Each of the conversations was subdued but genial.

Maureen looked up across the crowd and spotted, Dr. Mike Kelvey, whom she had spoken to five days earlier. She had left a message for him that she would have to postpone their luncheon because of the unfortunate passing of her husband, but she hadn't heard back from him. Kelvey was standing next to another former ICDer, Maria Cardoza. And they were joined in conversation with a nondescript balding man, and a young toddler. Maureen always liked Maria, when she was John's EA, but oddly she had not heard John mention her even once since he left the company. Maureen walked away from her children and over towards the Kelvey/Cardoza group.

"Hello Maria, Hello Mike, so nice of you to come," said Maureen.

"I'm so sorry for your loss, Maureen," Maria responded. "I'd like you to meet my fiancé, Al Moses."

"Hello Mrs. Brady. Nice to meet you, but so sorry about the circumstances," said Dr. Al somewhat uncomfortably. "I never had the pleasure of meeting your husband, but Maria has mentioned him often."

Maureen looked at Maria Cardoza quizzically. Maria was every bit as attractive as she remembered her to be. She didn't believe that Maria had ever been married and she was interested to see that Maria was now engaged to a much older man. It didn't seem to quite add up, but Maureen realized that it was difficult thinking rationally at her own husband's funeral. So she just allowed the words to flow freely from her lips as her thoughts moved fluidly from her brain to her consciousness. "And who is this young lady?" She inquired as she gazed down at Duffy, who was sitting in a stroller but was dressed in a dark navy coat.

"This is my daughter, Duffy," said Maria. She didn't bother to explain why she had brought her eighteen-month-old daughter to the service. In truth, Maria was unsure of the rationale herself. Meanwhile Maureen tried to compute whether or not the baby was Al Moses' daughter as well, but her brain was simply not clicking that fast. She simply turned her attention to Dr. Mike Kelvey.

"Thank you for coming also Dr. Kelvey. I assume you received my message the other day. We'll have to reschedule our meeting." She noticed that Kelvey had seemed to age a bit since she last saw him. He was still in his late thirties or maybe early forties. Maybe she was wrong about him being younger than she was. Odd things crossed her mind at odd times.

"I know it's a difficult time for you Maureen. Would it be better if I gave you a call sometime early next week?"

"That will work just fine," said Maureen. Then she paused in private reflection for a moment and said to no one in particular. "It's so sad how quickly things changed for John. One moment he was on top of the world. The next moment he was so dependant. And now he's gone." She hesitated once again and no one interrupted her thought process. Then she completed the reflection. "And so much of what he seemed to really care about in life was just so much bullshit." She listened to the words come out of her mouth, but they were atypical and it was almost as if they were uttered by someone else. "I guess no one gets to live forever." An hour later she buried him.

****

The life and death of John Brady was chronicled in great detail in all of the New York newspapers as well as many national and international newspapers. Most of the media lionized the business leader as a resourceful, independent-minded fighter, who was a pluperfect role model for the great American Dream.

Over the next several weeks only a few newspapers in New York caught an unusual story that seemed to be unrelated to the death of John Brady. Numerous churches throughout the boroughs of Brooklyn and Queens as well as Nassau County were receiving very large cash donations in their collection baskets and poor boxes. These donations were reported to be as much as $10-$20 thousand in cash and were curiously bestowed in wrapped sets of non-sequenced $100 bills. When two separate ministers reported the unusual donations to the police after suspecting that the money might have been crime related, the New York City police began inquiring about similar "donations" that might have been made to other churches and synagogues in the city. They were able to document more than $230,000.00 in cash donations that were made to various Christian Churches in the city, mostly in the Borough of Queens. They were now cooperating with the Nassau County Police Department who had reported similar large donations to two north shore Churches. Their investigation showed that all of the donations were made on a single Sunday and there was no evidence of any crime related activities … bank robberies … money laundering … kidnappings … ransoms … that might have spawned such unusual largesse. Because of the large sums of money involved and the ongoing nature of the investigation, the police did not leak the exact details or amounts to the press. They hoped that they would be able to "nail Robin Hood," as he made subsequent donations, over the upcoming weeks. But as it turned out the so-called "Phantom Philanthropist" had completed his mission in a single day.

Chapter 18: *Spirituality* – August 2011

Chipper Geld and Paul Pritchard were at the offices of the Pritchard Fund in downtown Manhattan. Three attorneys who represented the interests of Maureen Brady joined them. Attorneys for the corporate well-being of ICD were also at the meeting. They were discussing the bankruptcy proceedings for Fundamental Health Resources. The situation wasn't pretty. The venture had been a disaster almost from the outset. Pritchard, Geld, ICD and Maureen Brady's now deceased husband John Brady, had all lost a good deal of money in a short period of time trying to get Fundamental Health Resources to create a niche of business in New York and San Francisco.

Oddly enough the group had been able to come to a relatively amicable settlement of the dissolution of the business. This was mostly due to the fact that Maureen Brady had instructed her attorneys to extricate JB's estate from the mess as rapidly as possible and to liquidate its claims on any of the assets of FHR, even if it meant significantly diminishing the return of capital that had been invested by JB personally.

During the life span of FHR the constant management change had allowed a good deal of wiggle room for Chipper Geld. Although FHR was now insolvent, Chipper Geld had done quite well with the venture in a very different way. As the primary supplier of spa products to FHR, Geld's Costa Rican based company, *Solace in the Sun,* was able to quadruple the costs of these products and add on service charges as well. It was an outrageous arrangement, but one that was accounted for legally if not ethically. The other scam that Geld had been working was neither legal nor ethical, but right up to the time of the bankruptcy filing for FHR, Geld believed that he was getting away with it. Geld had placed a couple of his operatives in the accounting department at FHR and they were using the FHR assets to facilitate a money laundering operation, on behalf of Geld's titty-bar flesh peddling business. Even though Geld had annoyed several government agencies in the past, he felt as though he was immune to government scrutiny, because he felt he had been exonerated for income tax evasion a decade earlier and in the interim he had made a lot of important friends in a lot of important places. Besides the FHR scam was just too easy. He was taking money from a paraplegic's widow, Maureen Brady, and from one of Wall Street's biggest losers, Paul Pritchard. They deserved it anyway. They were weak.

After a couple of hours of working on details of the dissolution of the business, the group took a break. Pritchard walked out of the conference room and back into his private office. Geld followed him into the twenty-foot square chamber.

"This is going a lot smoother than I anticipated, Paul. What do you think?"

"It depends upon what you mean by smooth. It depends upon what your expectations were going into the negotiations."

"Unless I'm grossly off-base about the nature of what has transpired in this meeting this morning, I believe that both Maureen Brady and ICD are willing to take a quick and diminutive settlement that will leave the Pritchard fund in a much more attractive position than we may have anticipated."

"That's quite true, Chipper. But even in an asset liquidation which gives us some meager return for the properties here and in San Francisco, we will still be recognizing a substantial loss."

"Could've been larger."

"Listen, Chipper, I am not totally naïve. I know a little bit more about what goes on between FHR and SIS than you think. And I'm not happy about it. Just so you know, I'm not the only one who feels cheated. But I'm glad I now have this opportunity to mention an old adage to you, 'what goes around comes around.' Do you get my drift?"

"What the fuck is the matter with you, Pritchard? You screwed me over once or twice in your day and you know it. So remember your own words 'what goes around comes around.' And for the record I have no idea what you're talking about with regard to Solace in the Sun. We have a very effective supplier relationship with FHR. It wasn't the fault of SIS that FHR failed. It was the miserable management team that you and Brady assembled. I tried to put some of my guys into strategic positions, but I guess it just wasn't enough. You screwed yourself, Paul." Geld was more than a bit surprised that Pritchard seemed to know as much as he did. He had underestimated his adversary. The question that ran through Geld's mind was exactly how much did Pritchard know and what if anything was he going to do with that information.

Geld left the offices of the Pritchard Fund and made his way to the elevator bank. He got into the last elevator to the right and another man dressed in a dark suit and yellow power tie followed him into chamber, while apparently completing a text message to someone, somewhere. When the elevator got to the ground floor, there were two other men in dark suits waiting directly across from the elevator. The taller of the two men opened a wallet size credential that read Federal Bureau of Investigation. The man in the elevator grabbed his hands and cuffed them behind his back while the third man looked directly at Geld and said, "Mr. Geld, you are under arrest and you are once again charged with income tax evasion. You are also charged with money laundering and RICO violations for the interstate trafficking of females for the purpose of prostitution."

As he was reading Geld his Miranda rights, the FBI agent noted a sense of surrender on the part of the former fugitive. Geld knew that the RICO charges came with an added burden that meant that it was illegal for racketeering-influenced businesses to profit from any legitimate business enterprises as well, and that any such profits were subject to confiscation and seizure by the federal government. Chipper realized that this time the government could make the charges stick. They walked out into the sunshine and across the street where two federal vehicles were parked. As he was placed in the back of one of the vehicles Geld began to sweat profusely and he knew that on this hot summer day in New York City, there was no solace in the sun.

****

It was now four days before the opening of the seventh Rhapsody Center. This would be the second US-based Center and the first one to grace the great state of California. Rhapsody was already operating in New York, London, Paris, Beijing, Hong Kong and Singapore. One more center was planned for 2011. The opening in Rome was scheduled for November.

This evening was somewhat of a family reunion for the McDuffee women and their families. Alison McDuffee and her husband, Tom, were hosting Abby McDuffee and her daughter, Melinda at their new west coast home in the Bel Air section of Los Angeles. Abby's husband, Bo, did not make the trip. In fact, he wasn't making many trips at all of late, and unbeknownst to her sisters, Abby was now formally separated from her husband. It seemed that his legal career and Abby's work at Rhapsody were not meshing well for family life, and neither Bo nor Abby knew what to do about it.

Meanwhile Caitlin Browning was the real rising star of the family. She was leading the sales force at Rhapsody to record volumes of new sales while at the same time maximizing renewals. She was now in charge of corporate and retail worldwide sales. Caitlin's husband, Scott, had quit his job, in order to travel with Caitlin. They had spent the last year traveling extensively to all parts of the world to work with Rhapsody's diverse sales force. Caitlin knew that as the company expanded there would be an opening in Europe for the Regional Senior VP job that was responsible for all of the operations for Europe and the Middle East. It was a job that she felt that she had earned, but she knew that her credentials would need to be extra impressive in order to avoid the allegations of nepotism. Caitlin and Scott were now also at Alison and Tom's Bel Air home.

Another of the prominent female leaders of Rhapsody, Maria Cardoza-Moses was also at the gathering in Holmby Hills. Maria and her toddler daughter Duffy were staying at the Beverly Hills Hotel just a short distance away. Maria had left her young daughter with her nanny back at the hotel and came to the party alone. Her husband, Dr Al, was visiting with Stephen Struben in London. When Maria arrived at the party Tom Singleberry greeted her.

"Hello Maria, you look fabulous as usual." The ex-baseball player smiled and allowed his eyes to take in every detail of Maria's tight body. He did it in the approving way that happily married men tend to do, with a 'look-don't-touch' reservation. It was effective in conveying admiration of a good-looking woman, in a sensual but not salacious manner. "What can we get you to drink?"

Maria returned Tom's smile and said, "Something summer-ish would be nice. What are you drinking?" She nodded toward the glass in Tom's hand.

"Pina Colada, the specialty of the evening,"

"Looks good to me…" The two of them walked together toward the poolside bar, where the three McDuffee sisters were gathered in conversation with Zoë Mansfield.

"The members in our Asian centers have really taken an open ended approach to theories about intuitive healing, energy transference, habit harnessing and meditative medical makeovers. We think that the California market will also embrace many of these same approaches, to health, wellness and beauty." Alison was leading the conversation.

"I know a little bit about most of those concepts, but one that you mentioned – 'habit harnessing' – is something that I have never heard of before. What's that all about?" Maria jumped right into the conversation as though she had been there for hours.

"It was formerly known as 'Habit Harvesting,'" Alison continued. "It's a conceptual approach to wellness that is being promulgated by Dr Etan Everson. Dr Everson believes that habits are the residual effect of the human need for rest. He does this whole thing about conformity versus creativity and rest and regeneration as part of his theory."

"And he does this in the context of spirituality?"

"Yes, interestingly Everson differentiates between spirituality and theology in the same way that he separates creative energy from constructive energy. He doesn't dismiss theology. He just says that it is a construct of the human mind and the human need for rest. He believes that the major theologies of the world were constructed by a group of so-called prophets, including Buddha, Jesus, and Mohammed, but that those who follow these religions sometimes sacrifice their creative energy and merely use their constructive energy to embellish on the teachings of these prophets."

"Sounds to me like Everson wants to be thought of as a prophet himself." Caitlin commented in a contrarian way.

"I don't know about that," Alison offered. "I've been to two of his workshops. He is a very humble sort of teacher. And he is a fabulous listener. He somehow motivates people to work with their own energy to help create their own futures. One of his fundamental precepts is that man is a creature of habit. Man understands relativity, and then uses constructive energy to create habits and norms, some of which are good habits and some of which are bad.

"Whether habits are good or bad they can be collected and codified and addressed. This is what Everson referred to as 'habit harvesting.' In and of themselves habits have very little to do with creative energy. Forming good habits does however allow for the deployment of positive constructive energy. However when people move from habit harvesting to habit harnessing, they are able to neutralize the constructive energy for a period of time and release creative energy, which Everson regards as a pathway to a higher form of understanding of the human spirit."

"So then you said that Everson thinks that the organized religions of the world are a product of constructive energy. Correct?"

"Yes, but that doesn't make them wrong or bad or anything negative. It's just that they are a format for collective thought that allows the theologies of the world to be tied up in a nice neat bow. The package in the bow houses the doctrines of the given religion. The gap between these doctrines and the unknown mysteries of life is simply referred to as faith." Alison seemed very enthused at this juncture and was gesturing with her palms facing up and open. "These theologies don't allow creative energy to expand our understanding of the spiritual world. That's all."

"It all sound very interesting. And our new California Members will find this intriguing? Right?" Maria asked this question even though she herself found the topic enthralling.

"Yes, more than 80 per cent of our members believe that spirituality plays a significant role in longevity. That's why we are using the Spirituality Conference as part of the kickoff events for the center out here in Beverly Hills."

"Besides Everson, who else is speaking at the conference?" Tom was still standing nearby and posed the question. Generally Singleberry stayed out of the business aspects of Rhapsody, but having attended a couple of Everson's sessions along with his wife Alison, he was curious as to the makeup of the conference speakers and participants.

"We have an excellent set of speakers. Etan Everson is actually co-chairing the event for us with Mark Candu. In that way we have an interesting balance of spirituality and science. Mark is normally a bit skeptical about spirituality in general, so in a way it's a tribute to Everson that he and Candu have managed to get along well enough to chair this event together for us"

"That's good. Mark is a native Californian. He knows how we think out here."

"You know what I find interesting," Abby broke her pensive silence to join the conversation. "I think that there is a very relevant crossover between Candu's work in genetics and Everson's work in spirituality. More and more we are hearing about genetic susceptibility to disease. This genetic vulnerability seems to go hand in glove with some predestination theories that underpin many religious beliefs. Both Candu and Everson are looking at ways to alter any negative manifestations of a predetermined future. Everson uses his energy theories and Candu uses his scientific research to understand where we might be heading as individuals and then they try to create alternatives and options that would allow us as humans to make changes in our lives."

"This is all getting a little too heavy for me," Tom said. "For tonight let's just kick back and enjoy each other's company."

****

Earlier in the spring of 2011, Stephen Struben had made a stopover in Italy to serve as Al Moses' best man when Moses had married Maria Cardoza. They all then headed off to China for the openings of the Rhapsody Centers in that part of the world. Stephen had even convinced Danielle to accompany him, and she agreed to go with him to the wedding and then on to the Far East. Danielle had taken a liking to Maria, but it was not a close friendship like it had been with Anne Mohr. However Stephen and Al were as close as ever.

They hadn't seen each other since their trip to China but Al Moses and Stephen Struben were about to get together for another of their long standing "catch-up dinners." But this time it would be just the two of them. Stephen thought that Al simply wanted to shoot the breeze, but Al had something more important in mind that he wanted to discuss with Stephen. Al was set to meet Stephen at the Struben family townhouse in London for a cocktail before dinner. Neither of their wives was in town. Maria was in LA for the Rhapsody opening and Danielle was on her way to New York to meet with her son Adam who had recently become engaged to his long time girlfriend Celine.

Soon after arriving at Stephen's residence, Al was shown into the study by the Struben family butler. Stephen was already comfortably seated with a martini in hand.

"I guess I must be late if my friend Stephen Struben has started drinking without me."

"It's not that I was drinking without you. I was just testing the gin to make sure it would meet with your approval..... So tell me, do you feel much different now that you're a married man, Al?"

"No, not really ... as much as I enjoyed my extended bachelorhood, I really have grown accustomed to married life rather rapidly."

"It's hard for me to think of you as a married man and a father." Stephen took a healthy sip of his martini and nodded in Al's direction as if to encourage him to imbibe along with him. He decided to needle Al a bit so that he would recognize things hadn't changed between the two of them. They could still joke and talk about almost anything. "So are you going to tell me what it is that a beautiful young woman like Maria sees in an ornery old man like you? I know she didn't marry you for your money. Although rumor has it that she has more dough than an Italian bakery. Tell me, Al, what is your secret?"

"I don't know Stephen. Maybe it's because I just sit around licking my eyebrows." Stephen tried to suppress a laugh but couldn't help but at least snicker.

"I'll try not to remember that you said that the next time I see Maria." He paused for another sip of his martini and then said, "Anyway I'm glad to hear things are going well. I wondered whether or not you folks were ever going to tie the knot after you moved in together, with the baby."

"You are aware that Duffy is not my biological child?"

"No I was not aware of that fact. And as close as we have always been, I still would never have presumed it was my prerogative to ask. But in light of the fact that you brought it up, is there something else that you wanted to tell me about Duffy? Who is her father anyway?" Stephen felt wrong about asking the question the moment he had put it out on the table.

"Duffy's biological father is unimportant to me. He has since passed away and he never played a role in her life." Stephen was curious about Al's pronoun. Did 'her' refer to Duffy or to Maria? However he allowed his friend to take the topic in whatever direction he wanted to go. Al continued, "I have formally adopted Duffy, and I spend more time with her than Maria does. She certainly thinks of me as her father. Duffy just turned two years old last week and Maria has taken her out to California on her business trip. I miss them both already."

"I'm sure you do. Why didn't you go with them?"

"Frankly I wanted Maria to have more time alone with Duffy, some mother/daughter time if you will. Hopefully she won't be too busy, but the nanny went along anyway."

"Maria really likes her job. I guess."

"Loves it! She has got to be one of Rhapsody's best ambassadors. She never stops glowing about *the Lifestyle* as she calls it."

"That's not a bad thing, Al. We are *all* wrapped up in Rhapsody these days. Danielle, Gina and lately even Josh are very actively supporting the benefits of membership in Rhapsody. Of course, what do I know? I'm only a member of the Board of Directors." Stephen shrugged with an air of complicity and it was apparent that his aloof remark was meant sardonically.

"Don't get me wrong. I'm not complaining about Rhapsody at all," Al continued. "As you know my practice is now entirely within the confines of the *Rhapsody GPS*. It's Maria that I'm concerned about. She eats, sleeps and breathes Rhapsody. She even named Duffy out of respect for Alison and Abby McDuffee." It wasn't apparent to Stephen where Al Moses was going with this line of discourse. He knew that Al was also fond of the McDuffees.

"So what's the point, Al?" Stephen recognized that sometimes a direct question was best.

"Well it brings to mind a question I've been asking myself and that I want to bring up to Maria." This time Al took more of a gulp than a sip of his martini. "Do you think it would be selfish of me to ask Maria to have another child? I mean, of course I love Duffy. In fact, it's because I love Duffy so much that I am even thinking about this. Wouldn't it be great for her to have a sibling? Maybe, a little brother? What do you think?" Al just blurted it all out.

"That's a lot to think about, Al. This conversation has gotten pretty heavy, pretty quickly. Are you sure you still want to go out to dinner? We could just as easily order something in." Stephen walked back over to Al, opening the lid of the humidor as he did so and simply asked, "Cigar?"

"You didn't answer my question, Stephen."

"And you didn't answer mine, Al"

"What do you mean … about dinner? Yes I do want to go out to dinner. And yes I will have a cigar. So now answer my question. Do you think I should ask Maria about having another child?"

Stephen cut the tip off his cigar, while he made sure that Al made a selection from the humidor. "You know Al, these things aren't so easily answered … like say … a seven letter word on a crossword puzzle. You yourself are now a family man. Granted this has occurred much later in life than it has happened for 99% of the world, but one way or another you are now a family man. If you and Maria want to have another child, I think that that would be wonderful. But what I think doesn't really matter. Do you know if Maria wanted to have a child, when she became pregnant with Duffy?"

"That's a complicated question. Just realize this for a second. When I first learned that Maria was pregnant, she was my patient. We did not have a personal relationship at the time, although it grew very rapidly thereafter. Maria then made many decisions in a short period of time. She decided to keep the baby. She decided that it was okay to have a personal relationship with me. And then finally she decided that it was okay for us to live together. The one decision that she did put off for a little while, was the decision to become my wife. And, of course, Maria also eventually made that decision. We have not yet had a serious discussion about the possibility of having another child. However, Maria had said to me more than once, that Duffy was an absolute blessing, and one that she never expected."

"In that case, Al, why don't you just go for it? Why don't you just ask her flat out? And for the record, Al ... I'm very impressed that this is even a viable option for you." Stephen was totally unaware of the fact that part of the Al's motivation for fatherhood, was his insecurity with respect to his relationship with Maria. This insecurity was emanating from Maria's captivation with her work at Rhapsody, and the corresponding sporadic inattentiveness at home. Al never answered this last question on the topic.

By this time both Stephen and Al had lit their cigars and the smoke was circling in the direction of the overhead fan.

"Before we go to dinner, are there any other problems of the world that might be worth solving?" Stephen was a little eager to change the topic, but that didn't mean that they would drop their interpersonal agenda and begin to discuss the weather. Their friendship was much deeper than that.

"There's something else that I wanted to ask you about, Stephen. Even though you and I got married at different stages of our lives, there are a few similarities. For one we both married much younger women. And secondly we are both Jews who married Christians. How important is all of this religious stuff to you?"

"I'm sure you have a personal reason for asking. Given that, I will tell you that neither Danielle nor I consider ourselves religious ... at least not in the traditional sense. Early on, Danielle wanted to have the boys baptized and we did that much ... that was about it. The denominational thing never became an issue until Gina and Josh wanted to get married in a Catholic Church. They got over that and got married by a Christian minister. Now they are more into the Rhapsody philosophical approach to spiritualism than they are into any specific religion."

"That's them. How about you and Danielle? Do you practice your religion at all?"

"Not really. Why do you ask?"

"Well I don't either. And I didn't think that Maria cared much about religion, but lately she has begun to talk more and more about spirituality. Maria also had Duffy baptized, soon after she was born, but didn't make a big fuss about it."

"Okay, that all makes sense. So what is it that you are worried about?" Stephen knew that his friend Al was working his way around to some kind of personal disclosure, or some sort of telling question. He noticed that Al was a bit more fidgety than his normal fidgety self. He thought that the conversation would go more smoothly as Al began to sip at his martini faster.

"I don't know what it is exactly. Maybe it's just that I want to stay on the same wavelength with Maria. We lived together for more than a year before we got married, and I didn't expect things to change much at all once we were married. But as I said she is much younger than me, and I want to be sure that I stay interested in the things that interest her. Maybe I should be more interested in her religious or spiritual side. You have managed to do that so well with Danielle over all these years."

"I am fourteen years older than Danielle. You are more than 30 years older than Maria. Your respective interests are more likely to be at variance with one another, especially at the beginning of a marriage. Is there a problem, Al?"

"No, not really. I just had hoped that once we were married, Maria and I would begin to pursue some common goals, maybe work a little less and travel a lot more. It will be harder to do when Duffy gets a little older."

"But you and Maria are traveling a lot now, aren't you?"

"Yes, but when we travel, she is always busy with Rhapsody stuff. I want us to travel more just to enjoy ourselves, to relax and slow things down, to get a handle on life."

Stephen stared at his friend for a second or two and attempted to put the disjointed meanderings of the conversation with Al in context. He drew on his cigar and spewed a circle of smoke toward the ceiling and then attempted to summarize.

"Let me see if I have things right. I'll work the issues backwards. A – You are concerned that Maria is working too hard to pay attention to common goals for your marriage. B – You're worried that Maria and you are not on the same spiritual wavelength, what with you being a Jew and her being a Christian and C – Even though there is a significant age difference between you and Maria, you feel that you are doing the lion's share of the parenting and want to have another child. Do I have the whole list?"

"Almost, I forgot to tell you the part where I think Maria is cheating on me."

****

Maureen Brady had stopped wearing black the day after she buried JB. Now, six months later, there was a lot of color in her life. She had begun dating Dr. Mike Kelvey within weeks after John's death. Maureen realized that this probably caused all kinds of whispers in the North Shore social circles, but she didn't care. In fact she rather enjoyed the fact that her pseudo friends at the club were probably calling her a "cougar," because she was sleeping with a man who was nine years younger than her.

Maureen was also cautiously optimistic that she had gotten her drinking back under control. She was no longer totally abstemious like she was right after her sojourn at Solace in the Sun a few years back, but she felt as though she were drinking a lot less than she had been a few years earlier. In fact Maureen believed that she had a lot of her life back under control. JB might not have been the most attendant husband to ever walk the planet, but he did leave her a fabulous portfolio of financial assets valued at nearly $140 Million even after the write off of the ill-fated investment in Fundamental Health Resources. This portfolio was independent of the three multi-million dollar trust funds that had been set up for her children, Mark, Megan and Kenneth.

Another area of Maureen's life that was coming into focus was her relationship with her children. Maureen didn't believe that she was that much closer to her children than she had been in the past, but at least the communications channels were clearing up. She didn't think this had as much to do with a change of heart on her part - she had always desired a closer relationship with her offspring - but it was clearly an indication that her children now all wanted a little more of her time. She never doubted the motivation for this adjustment, but was simply satisfied that it represented a step in the right direction. The children were even very accepting of her relationship with Mike Kelvey. They had all spent some time together this summer out at the Brady's summer home in Southampton on a few occasions.

Although Cara moved quickly to open the front door, Maureen greeted Mike Kelvey at her door personally. It was midweek and they were planning to drive to the Southampton together. It was a gorgeous late summer day and there was a lot less traffic in the middle of the week. The noontime sun was high overhead and they planned on taking Kelvey's new Lexus rather than Maureen's new Benz. Kelvey was going to drive because Maureen was tired of being hassled by the police. She had been stopped three times in the last year and had been ticketed twice for the same infraction of not having a current inspection sticker.

Maureen hated cops. She believed that the stereotype about them being more interested in donuts than justice was accurate. Nassau County cops were also curious about her 'dating' her doctor friend so soon after the death of her husband.

In the first few days after John died, the police had begun asking some questions. They were curious about a few mundane issues at first. Maureen herself had requested that an autopsy be performed before John was buried. She knew that John had been interested in stem cell research and what it might have eventually been able to do for his paralysis or the similar plight of other people. She also knew that he had a living will and although no usable organs had been harvested from his body, the physicians at the hospital managed to do a fairly thorough analysis of the cause of death. And there was one outstanding oddity with respect to JB's passing. No one could find any clear evidence of a malfunction of the oxygen unit that was supporting his breathing. Brady had life insurance that had been purchased for him as a perk while he was at ICD, and while the $2.8 Million face value would hardly make much of difference in the size of his estate, the insurance company was also slow to pay out the proceeds, but had relented after about two months of making its own inquiries.

The chronology of John Brady's last moments on earth was rather simple. Fernando had merely found Maureen's husband dead after first believing that he was sleeping. The poor chauffer was really spooked by the whole episode and had a hard time talking to the police when they came to the house that day after he called 911. She certainly could understand why Fernando was upset. The stupid cop-bastards asked so many questions. Fernando didn't know anything. He simply found JB. But they asked him a lot of questions about JB's personal life and for that matter a lot of questions about Maureen's personal life as well. They also queried the rest of the house staff as part of their so-called investigation. They were not the kind of professionals that the television episodes depicted. In Maureen's mind, they were just a bunch of nosy assholes trying to act like the guys they also saw on TV.

"Now don't you look nice and sporty," Maureen said to Mike Kelvey as he stood just inside the front door to the Brady mansion. Kelvey was dressed casually in light tan linen shorts and a white linen shirt. He also was wearing a white Nike baseball cap, and had the appearance of being ready for a relaxed afternoon garden party.

"It's a beautiful summer afternoon and I'm ready for a nice ride out into the countryside. I noticed a couple of your guardian angels sitting up the street on my way in. What is it that those guys want anyway?"

"I have no idea. The problem goes back about a year. It started with the jackass cops in Suffolk County, who wanted to give me a breathalyzer during the days that I didn't drink at all. I might say that I wasn't exactly cooperative. They weren't happy with the way my lawyer berated them in court. I think that the Suffolk PD is in cahoots with the Nassau County guys. And so they thought it would be cute to cause trouble when John died. They also asked a million questions and harassed my house staff for several days after we found John dead. It seemed like all they wanted to do was make my life miserable. And then they've stopped me for a few minor things over the last few months, so some times when I pass them in town I give them the finger. It's now a full blown love affair, as you can imagine."

"You can't win those battles, Maureen. They'll just continue to make your life miserable."

"That's what irks me most about those people. They finish in the bottom half of their high school class, can't get a real job and so they become cops. They're pissed off at the world and jealous of everyone who has a decent education and they take out their frustrations on honest citizens." Maureen vented her venom without regard to the fact that she herself had never held a serious income-earning job since her college graduation. She was content in the belief that she somehow earned her lifestyle while the cops who tormented her did so out of resentful envy.

Down the road from the Brady estate in Kings Pont, an unmarked car stood out like a raisin in a bowl of macadamia nuts. Seated in the dark blue Mercury Marquis, the two Nassau County detectives waited for the return appearance of Dr. Michael Kelvey's Lexus. One of the detectives was a flabby fifty year old who sat in the passenger seat sipping his coffee and hounding down a bacon egg and cheese sandwich dripping with runny ketchup. He was a veteran of many of these "observances," that didn't quite add up to a full scale "surveillance." He was wearing a cheap suit, but had a paper napkin tucked up under his chin to avoid getting coffee or ketchup on his already stained tie. His younger partner sat behind the wheel and listened as the older detective rambled on about the logic of their stake out.

"I don't know why we're here. We've been watching this rich bitch off and on for months on end and all we do is clock her in and out with her boyfriend. If our boss, Captain Numb Nuts, really believes that Brady whacked her husband, why doesn't he just pick her up?" The fat cop didn't wait for an answer. He just continued his blather. "I'll tell why. He has no fucking evidence. That's why. He thinks that the Brady bitch snuffed her old man so that she could play hide the baloney with this Kelvey guy. But you know what … he can't prove a fucking thing. This bitch is too sharp for Numb Nuts and yet he makes us sit out here and watch her come and go. Tell you what. She's not a bad looking head. I wouldn't mind getting a piece of that action myself."

The pause in the soliloquy allowed the younger detective a moment to snicker and shake his head without making a comment. Having finished his sandwich, the fat cop removed the napkin bib and the continued his sermon.

"Numb Nuts figures that the Brady Bitch wouldn't off her hubby for the money because she has it all anyway. And she can't be pissed off at him for bopping the office talent, because the poor bastard can't even wiggle his hands and feet much less doodle with his noodle. So that leaves only one reason why she would off her husband. It seems like she wanted to get serviced by this limp-wristed dickhead Kelvey." The portly policeman was more than capable of stringing together four or five hyphenated adjectives in a single sentence, when he was on his game. However the corpulent cop was toning down the number of expletives from his normal narrative because he correctly sensed that his partner was developing a headache from listening to his derisive diatribe. Nonetheless, after each brief pause he then fired up his logic machine.

"What I don't understand is why she decided to wait so long to get rid of the guy. If appears that she was fucking her personal trainer, Grant, before she started doing Kelvey. She fired him right after the guy told us that he was balling her in the basement steam room right about the time that old man Brady went south. None of this shit makes any sense anyway. The poor bastard's oxygen unit just went out of whack on the guy and he croaked….that's all there is to it. Numb Nuts is watching too many cop stories on TV. There's no murder here. El Capitano just wants us to harass the bitch so that he can tell his friends in Suffolk County that he's got their back."

"Here comes the Lexus. Should we follow it?"

"All we're supposed to do is see if she is in it or not. But I guess it wouldn't hurt to follow it for a little while if she's in it." The fat cop shifted uneasily and splashed some remnants of now cold coffee onto his uncovered tie. "Fuckin' A." He looked down at his tie as the car approached.

At the wheel of his Lexus Mike Kelvey rounded the corner and passed the Mercury Marquis at a deliberate speed. He turned to Maureen and said, "we're now about to pass your guardian angels."

"What a waste of tax dollars," she responded. "What a bunch of dimwits. They don't contribute a damn thing to society. A couple of months ago they were out trying to find someone who was making large donations to the church and now they're spending a fortune in tax dollars trying to see if I have paid my registration and inspection fees. What is this world coming to?" As they passed the Marquis she rolled down her window and gave them the finger.

"Christ, Maureen, what are you doing?"

"Just saying hello…."

The young cop behind the wheel noticed that his fat partner had missed the salute from Mrs. Brady as he was busy wiping his tie with the paper napkin. He himself chose to ignore her greeting and decided not to follow closely. He turned the car around slowly and followed at a distance for a short while until the car passed through Great Neck and was on its way to the LI Expressway.

"They're not behind us anymore." Kelvey said. "Let's just chill out and enjoy the ride," He drove down the ramp and entered the expressway heading east, a ride that Maureen had taken hundreds of times in the past.

"I agree. Let's change the topic."

"Fine by me… What would you like to talk about?"

"I don't know … anything but cops … how's your medical practice going?"

"Actually, it could be a little busier now that you ask."

"Weren't you hoping to have some kind of tie up with that company that John always hated…What's it called? ….Rhapsody?"

Kelvey frowned as he moved his vehicle toward the center lane. "Yes I was. I'm not sure what actually happened. I was going to become what they call a 'PAL,' a personal advocate for longevity. The compensation was generous. The hours were good and you could make great contacts. I thought that I had all of the right credentials on my resume, and I certainly was familiar with the kind of clientele that they have as members, but I never got offered a position. They gave me some aptitude and psychological tests and I thought I did well enough on them. But I'm not quite sure what they were looking for. Eventually I had a half hour interview with a young woman, who heads up the PAL group, and she told me that they didn't have any current openings that fit my profile, whatever that meant. From there it was simply a 'don't call us, we'll call you' ending to the application process. Why do you ask?"

"I don't know. I was just curious. One of my financial guys told me that there was a rumor that they might put out an IPO before the end of the year. And as I told you once before, John and Chipper Geld and the clowns that started FHR somehow believed that Rhapsody was its competition. If so I guess it's clear by now that Rhapsody won that skirmish."

"I'd say you're right about that for sure. I read somewhere that after Paul Pritchard attempted to cooperate with the government in its case against Geld, that Geld also had some pretty incriminating information about Pritchard's financial maneuverings as well. Now they have both been indicted."

"I don't understand how people can get so screwed up over money."

"It's not the money with those two. It's the power." Maureen responded.

"What power?" Kelvey inquired.

"I'm sure by now they are asking themselves the same question."

Maureen and Kelvey then lapsed into silence for a while and merely enjoyed their early afternoon drive.

****

Chapter 19: *Changes* – August 2011

"You know I've just about had it with Carl Gordon," said Gina. "Sometimes I think he just doesn't get it. You can't recapture the past. I'm not the same woman that I was when I sang with the Lay D's, and partied with the band at night."

"So what's the problem with Pepper?" asked Josh. "Frankly I like the guy a lot. I think he's a pretty decent chap."

"He wants me to be more sociable. He thinks that I need to be at more of these so-called A-list parties that he is always going to. He says I should be more visible. He doesn't understand that I am six and a half months pregnant and nearly twenty-seven pounds overweight. How much more visible could I be?" Gina was waddling around their east side townhouse in Manhattan uncomfortably. She was nervous about doing too much of anything that might put any stress on her pregnancy, and Josh realized that the biggest risk was her nervousness itself, and so he was constantly trying to calm her down.

"You look great! And guess what! You're supposed to gain weight when you're having a baby. That's part of the deal. Besides I think you look sexier than ever and I'm really excited that you are having our son."

"So am I. That's why I can't understand what Carl expects of me. I'm having a baby. I don't need to party every night of the week."

"Well it's hardly every night of the week. People just want to know more about you and our baby. That's all."

"Let's not talk about it now. Maybe you can handle Carl and Seth for me. I'm not sure I want to deal with anything until after our son is born."

"As you wish, darling." There was an ever so slight derision to Josh's tone. He meant to be supportive, but he also wanted to convey the message to Gina that everything was under control. In an odd way, this was a new role for Josh. Until this pregnancy, Gina's self-confidence was extraordinary. No matter how exciting life got for Gina, she had always been in control. However now she was shaken a bit by the fact that certain things were slightly beyond her control. She was following the directions of her obstetrician closely and she was also meeting regularly with a dietitian. Gina also maintained a healthy, but slightly less rigorous, workout regime with her personal trainer, who was now *Rhapsody Certified* even though his only client was Gina.

"Don't you have a session scheduled today with your PAL, Jedediah?"

"Yes I do. Besides you, Jed is the only one that I can talk to who keeps me calm. On second thought, I would add your mother, Danielle, to that list. But even when I talk to my *own* mother, she gets me very nervous. She says things like she wants to have a grandchild before she dies. The woman is in her 50s for God's sakes." Josh realized this was typical Gina-talk of late.....multiple topics in the same breath.

"Our son is going to be just fine, as long as you stay calm, Gina. You need to simply relax and enjoy the oncoming role of motherhood and not worry about what your mother, or my mother thinks."

Gina thought for a moment and her reflection led her to understand that what she loved most about Josh was that he was so calm about everything. Nothing ever seemed to bother him.

"You know, we still have to agree on a name." Gina said.

"I thought we agreed on Travis. Have you changed your mind?"

"No. I just want you to really like the name. You said that you wanted Scott."

"I like Scott, but I like Travis also."

"But which do you like most?"

"As I said before, I thought we already decided this. Our son will be named Travis."

"But do you really love the name or are you just humoring me? I know that you wanted to name him Scott."

"It's Travis, Gina. T-R-A-V-I-S, Travis. That's all there is to it." He hesitated after spelling out the name and noticed that Gina still didn't look entirely convinced as she paced in front of the couch where he was sitting. Then he added as an afterthought, "And yes, I truly love the name Travis."

"That's what I wanted to hear." Gina plopped down next to him on the couch and threw her arms around him and gave him a big kiss. Gina then threw her right leg over the top of both of Josh's legs and sat spread eagled across his lap, with her bulging stomach between them, and her swollen breasts looming in front of Josh's face. She added softly. "I love you. We are going to be so happy. Aren't we?"

"I thought we already were so happy." Josh teased her in a soft voice as he looked up into her smiling visage, radiant with the pink glow of impending motherhood.

"We're going to be even happier." Gina was staring down into her husband's eyes and her long blond hair was now hanging slightly in her face.

"Impossible," he continued to tease her. "How can I possibly be any happier?"

Gina bent her neck and pulled her chin to her chest so that her forehead was touching Josh's forehead as they whispered to one another. Her lengthy flaxen tresses were now tenting around both of their faces. "Oh, I think I know how I can make you happier, in the short run."

A half hour later Gina was singing in the shower, doing an unimpressive imitation of Fats Domino's "Blueberry Hill." Josh was lying down in the adjacent bedroom wondering why his wife always chose throaty male crooners to imitate when she was showering. He laughed out loud. It was truly funny to him. He was happy, very happy.

Over the past five months Josh had become very involved with the financial operational aspects of Rhapsody Holdings. After resigning his position as a Fund Manager with Cromwell Parsons, Josh immersed himself in working with Rhapsody. At Gina's urging he had had several conversations with the McDuffee sisters, who were thrilled to have Josh join them as part of their executive team. As a sort of internal financial consultant, Josh spent most of his energies working with Rhapsody's CFO, Ben Hui Zhang, and with one of Rhapsody's other investors, Sun Feng. The three men were similar in many ways. None of the three men had an ego that required a high profile within the business. Josh Struben and Sun Feng had become major investors in Rhapsody by buying into the centers in Europe and Asia respectively.

As Gina got dressed and made her way to the doorway she blew a kiss in Josh's direction just as Josh heard his phone ring. It was Sun Feng.

"Mr. Struben. It is Sun Feng." Josh never could quite get over the formality of Mr. Feng. He knew that the rigidity that was always in Feng's voice belied the subtle caring nature of Sun's character. Josh had grown to like and respect Feng and was constantly amazed by his ability to be in so many places seemingly at the same time.

"Where does this call find you Mr. Feng?"

"I am in Macau but I am leaving shortly for Los Angeles and I have several significant issues with respect to capitalization of the expansion program that I would like to discuss with Dr. McDuffee. Is it possible that you would be able to join us in LA? Dr McDuffee holds your opinions on many issues in high regard and I would also find it helpful if you could join us."

"I hadn't planned on being out at the opening. I'm trying to respect my wife's wishes about keeping a low profile lately."

"Yes, I understand. How is Gina doing by the way?" It was very rare for Feng to use a first name reference, but Gina was Gina to almost everyone.

"She is doing quite well thank you. In fact, she just walked out the door, heading over to the Center when you called."

"Good. Please give her my regards."

"I will."

"With respect to my trip to LA, I am not planning on attending the opening ceremonies either. I just need to discuss some significant investment interest from one of Rhapsody's partners."

"Who would that be? Is it STRX?"

"Yes, of course I'm not surprised that you would know this. Have you spoken at all to your father about their interest?"

"Not in quite some time. And we have never discussed an influx of capital from STRX. And to set the record straight, I know nothing directly of their interest, other than they are a very valued supplier to Rhapsody. I'm just not at all surprised that they would want a more direct financial involvement. It makes sense. Rhapsody has become one of their five largest customers almost overnight and we will probably be their single largest customer by this time next year. It's almost as if Rhapsody has single-handedly spurred the growth of the STRX Medical/Healthcare business unit."

"Well I can tell you this much, their interest is significant and they want to act quickly."

"Okay, I'll fly out to LA in the morning and meet you there. My mother is actually on her way here to spend a few days with Gina and me, so I won't stay in LA more than a day or so. Mom and Gina get along fabulously so they won't miss me for a couple of days."

"Good, I have already talked with Mr. Zhang. He has too many schedule conflicts to make the trip to LA, but we will be able to conference him in, if necessary, when we meet with Dr McDuffee."

Josh hung up the phone and looked down at the floor for a second. He was still sitting in his briefs on the edge of his bed in their bedroom. He wasn't sure how he felt about the call from Feng. He believed that STRX might want to buy Rhapsody Holdings, but he for one, was not thrilled with the idea of selling out. Rhapsody was just hitting its stride. STRX was one of the largest multinational corporations in the world. How would they co-exist? Josh and Gina had some holding company stock but most of their investment was in the Struben Center franchise in London. While both investments were substantial winners, it was not about the money for Josh. It was more about the *Lifestyle*. What would happen to the *Rhapsody Lifestyle*? It might be several years before he would find the answer to that question.

****

Ben Hui Zhang was looking forward to Dao Diskul's visit to Rhapsody's Singaporean headquarters. He was very fond of Dao, and although the physical intimacy of their relationship had cooled off considerably over the last year, they remained good friends. They also had a healthy respect for the business skills that they knew each other to possess.

Ben was very interested in what Sun Feng had recently disclosed to him about STRX's interest in Rhapsody, and he almost certainly would have accompanied Feng on his visit to LA if he hadn't already planned to spend several days together with Dao in Singapore.

Recently Ben was feeling much better about himself and about life in general. He was spending as much as two to three hours a day of late in meditation. He was beginning to see the meaning of his life in a whole new way. He was looking forward to discussing this with Dao, because she was one of the few people in his life that he felt truly understood him. Oddly it was Dao's constant search for "peak sex" that had originally spurred Ben's own introspection. He had come to the conclusion that pervasive satisfaction was a multi-dimensional pursuit and could not be obtained through physical and intellectual means alone. There needed to be a spiritual dimension as well. Ben was also getting feedback from many of the Asian members of Rhapsody that indicated that the company should be exploring the dimension of spiritualism in greater depth and he had given this feedback to the McDuffee sisters as well as to other members of the executive team.

Through his personal efforts at spiritual cognition, that were explored through yoga as well as through his readings of the great prophets, Ben had come to reevaluate his life and the direction it was taking him. Although on paper he was now an extremely wealthy man, money itself had become somewhat irrelevant to him. He lived simply, in a midsize two-bedroom condominium and almost never entertained. When he wasn't absorbed in his work at Rhapsody, Ben read extensively. His particular interests ran to the works of the ancient Chinese philosophers. He took particular interest in noting how many of these philosophies later morphed into religions and eventually had significant impact of Chinese politics, right up to the modern day.

Ben waited outside of the Rhapsody office building while the cab pulled in front and Dao got out. He put his hand out to help her out of the cab, but did not offer a more affectionate greeting. The driver removed Dao's one bag of luggage from the trunk and the moon-faced dermatologist paid for the ride from the airport as Ben pulled her bag up onto the walkway.

"I'm glad you called from the cab, so I could meet you down here. I just needed to get out of the office for some fresh air. Care to go for a walk? I'll have someone bring your bag up to the office and you can bring it to the hotel later."

The doorman to the building overhearing the conversation, looked at Ben and asked, "Should I have Dr. Diskul's bag sent up to your office, sir?" The doorman didn't bother to ask Dao what she felt he should do. However Dao answered for Ben.

"Yes please bring my bag upstairs." Then she turned to Ben and said, "I think I'll take you up on your offer to go for a walk. I'm still a little stiff from the plane ride over."

Ben turned and began walking next to Dao, a short distance down Orchard Road toward Fort Canning Park. He knew that Dao's idea of a good way to discuss anything was to take a walk in the park. She didn't like confined spaces and Ben respected that and often made the effort to spend time with Dao outdoors, even in the hot summer along the equator. He also always made it seem like he was the one who wanted to go for a walk.

"I'm happy that you were able to come to town for a few days. We need to catch up on a lot of things. And your travel schedule seems to be never ending."

"I guess that comes with the job. However you should be happy that we have more GPS practitioners in Austral-Asia than in either of the other two regions. So you can't accuse me of under developing Asia while I spend all of my time in the US and Europe. The fact of the matter is that I split my time relatively equally amongst the three regions. I've told Alison that I need a lot more help. Zoë helps a bit, but her time is consumed in the PR aspects of the GPS. In fact I told Alison and Zoë both that the Austral-Asia region is probably enough work for me as it is. The larger we grow the more people we will need to truly develop this business to its full potential. If we don't do a lot more hiring at the executive level relatively soon a lot of us could just burn out."

"I've been worried about that a little bit myself. I know in the past I have always managed to balance my time and take stock of what was important in life. I think I have been able to do that while we have been developing Rhapsody as well. However, in some ways Rhapsody has become my life. I enjoy what I do immensely and I believe that we have just scratched the surface on what we can achieve as a team."

"I had similar thoughts, but I have to confess that I am growing weary of all the traveling. It will be nice to spend a few days here in Singapore."

Ben was happy to be having this discussion with Dao and to have her as a trusted colleague, and a kindred spirit. He moved their social discussion onto a more practical matter.

"I want to talk to you about Sun Feng, and what he is thinking about."

"Yes, he seems to be a fascinating person. I haven't had the opportunity to work with him like you have, but I know Abby holds him in high regard."

"Just so you know, Feng plans to discuss Rhapsody's exit strategy with her later this week. It's actually a bit awkward for *me* to be telling *you* this, when you are one of the Founders."

"Not at all…by virtue of forming the business concept with Abby and Alison, I may own more equity in the business than you and some of the other senior leaders, but I know my role. When the time comes to talk about an exit, I'm sure I will have my say. Besides there's an awful lot to do before we can logically consider an exit." Dao didn't want to talk about an exit. She wanted to discuss the here and now. "Let's go back to talking about Singapore."

Dao started walking at a slower pace and seemed somewhat contemplative, as she asked Ben, "What do you see as the long range plan for Singapore as the regional hub for Rhapsody?"

"I think we made the absolute best decision with respect to Singapore as our eastern hub. As you would know better than anyone, throughout Asia medical tourism continues to grow. I see some natural synergies between what we are doing at Rhapsody and the major medical institutions throughout the region. These are exactly the things I need to discuss and have a precise strategy for, before we go to Abby and the board to make some logical suggestions for additional growth. As successful as we have been over the last couple of years I am thrilled and excited about the opportunities that are yet in front of us."

"I share your enthusiasm, Ben. I'm sure we'll continue to bring things together as a team. There's plenty of room to do a lot of good in this world."

****

As CIO of Rhapsody Holdings, Sandeep Mehra was experiencing constant demands on his time. Not only were all of his systems required to be up and running 24/7, but also it seemed like he himself was running 24/7. Besides maintaining stewardship over all of the IT Systems throughout the Rhapsody enterprise, he was also called upon to be the executive interface with many of Rhapsody's key suppliers. Like all of the other Rhapsody executives, Sandeep had made a great deal of money in a very short time frame. Sandeep was also the youngest of the "band of five" that had started Rhapsody, and the second executive that the Founders had hired.

Whether it was a fair assessment or not, Sandeep Mehra was given credit for developing the *Rhapsody HealthPort* into the best-known electronic medical record in the world and successfully implementing *Rhapsody HealthMap*. Ironically it was not Sandeep's IT expertise that helped him develop the *HealthPort* and *HealthMap* as rapidly as he did. The real secret to the quick deployment of the *HealthPort* was the pervasive cooperation that he received from members of the *Global Practitioner Society* in developing the applications that were needed to make both the *HealthPort* and the *HealthMap* as robust they were.

The interesting part of Sandeep's success was that his leadership skills were so well honed. His mentor Ben Hui Zhang was instrumental in challenging Sandeep to be a leader of people first, and a leader of technological development, second. Unlike many of his fellow Indian entrepreneurs, Sandeep Mehra was able to leverage the leadership ideas of others as well as his own industriousness.

Maybe it was the fact that Sandeep was constantly on the go 24/7, or maybe it was because he still regarded himself as a very young man with much of his career yet in front of him. Either way the fact of the matter was that Sandeep saw no end in sight to the hustle and bustle of the Rhapsody workload. He now had more than 2000 employees in his shop and he was responsible for another one thousand IT consultants. The pace was frenetic and the challenges were many.

During the first year that Rhapsody was in business Sandeep had rejected overtures from the world's largest software companies to leave Rhapsody and to come over and lead major healthcare related projects within those businesses. The money was irrelevant. Through his equity ownership in Rhapsody Holdings, Sandeep was assured that extreme wealth was inevitable. However some of the offers that came his way had a high degree of early liquidity, which he was not in a position to recognize at Rhapsody. Nevertheless he shunned these offers and still managed to learn a good deal about business along the way.

Sandeep believed deep in his heart that eventually Rhapsody would be offered a liquidity event via a tie in with one of the global software giants. He was surprised to get a call from his mentor Ben Hui Zhang that he needed to stay focused on delivering the upcoming software releases on time and on spec, because it might have an effect on warding off an unsolicited takeover offer. Sandeep thought that such an offer would not be a bad thing, considering the fact that the stock was tightly held, and the founders were in control of its destiny. It never hurt to listen to these kinds of offers, and Sandeep worried that there might be a rift growing among the founders. He resolved that he would soon fly to Singapore to have discussions on this topic directly with Ben Hui Zhang.

****

Danielle Dubonet Struben sat across from her daughter-in-law, Gina Alvarez-Struben at a rear table in Michael's Restaurant. It was one of Seth Silverstein's favorite haunts and he had invited his two clients to lunch. They agreed to go as long as Seth would be discreet about meeting them. They sat at a rear table instead of Seth's normal mid-room meet and greet table location. Silverstein was late getting to the restaurant and the maitre'd seated them and brought them some water and iced tea while they waited.

"So my son stood us up by leaving for *Caleefornia* before I even got here. What's that say about *'ow* he feels about *'ees* mother?" Danielle was making the inquiry entirely in jest. She knew that it must have been an important meeting if Josh was willing to run out to California at the last minute.

"He said that he would only be gone for a day and a half, and that he isn't going to stay for the opening party at the Beverly Hills Center."

"By the way, do they *'ave* a name for that place yet?"

"Yes, after all the hemming and hawing about not wanting the center named after themselves, the McDuffee women finally gave in and are allowing it to be called the McDuffee Center. However Alison, Abby and Caitlin agreed that they were naming it for their parents, John and Mary McDuffee, who both passed on many years ago. Apparently they both died very young – in their early fifties, in fact." Gina wrinkled her nose in a way that expressed curiosity or at least uncertainty, and then continued her thought process. "Ironic isn't it that Alison and Abby would form a business dedicated to longer better lives, when their genetic make-up seems to suggest that longevity may not be in the family cards."

"You never know about those *theengs*. Maybe their parents' short lives were the *eenspiration* for the business *een* the first place."

"Could be … who knows?" Gina answered. "Lately I've been thinking a lot more about the beginning of life than the end of life. I feel like I've been pregnant for about a year and a half. Did you feel that way when you had your sons?"

"More so *weeth* Josh than *weeth* Adam, because every *feeleeng* was new and *deefferent*. *Weeth* Adam, I more or less knew what to expect. I *weell* tell you *thees* much *'owever*, once the baby *ees* born, you *weell* forget all about the pregnancy *een* a hurry. Besides the joy and the *'appiness* there *ees* a lot of work. You'll love *eet* though. I can tell. You're *goeeng* to be great Mom."

"Thanks, Danielle. Coming from you that means a lot to me."

Just then Seth Silverstein entered the room. Sometimes Silverstein seemed even more popular than the celebrities he represented. He made his way back to the table where Gina and Danielle were seated but not without first shaking hands with people at two other tables. When he finally arrived at the table he was as effervescent as ever.

"Hello ladies. I'm terribly sorry that I'm late. I haven't seen either of you in a while. How you feeling Gina? How is the baby doing? Rumor has it it's a boy. Or am I overstepping my bounds?"

"No. That's okay. We're thrilled. Not for publication just yet, Seth, but yes Josh and I are having a son. And of course Danielle is having a grandson."

"And Danielle also *ees threelled*," said Danielle.

"Great … great … absolutely great … it's so wonderful to see the two of you together. You make such a great team."

"And how have you been, Seth? Has business been good? How is the family?" Gina had always had a fond feeling for Silverstein. She enjoyed the fact that he always seemed happy and upbeat. Nothing ever bothered Seth. In some ways he was one-of-a-kind.

"The family is fine. Business couldn't be better," he answered. "I must tell you that I do have a bit of a hidden agenda for lunch today, however. I have been talking to our mutual friend, Carl Gordon, and Pepper says he's a bit worried about you Gina. He thinks you're maintaining too low a profile. He knows, what I know, that everyone *wants* to know; 'what's new with Gina?'" He said this in an emotional whisper. He had the uncanny ability to paradoxically shout softly. Meanwhile his trademark wide eyed smile of excitement blazed across the table as though he were delivering the most important news of the year. He then shifted his head slightly to turn the same high-beamed smile onto Danielle. "The public has grown accustomed to loving the mysterious personality of Danielle, and now they are attributing the same air of mystery to their beloved Gina. And together the two of you represent an inscrutable enigma that they can't wait to learn more about. Not only that, Pepper tells me that your music has been selling better than ever - in both of your cases. In fact, both of your versions of 'Kiss Away' are in very high demand."

"Thank you for saying all of that, Seth. You know I really do love my work. Right now, I am purposely keeping a low profile. There's nothing really mysterious about it. I just want to have as much privacy as I possibly can, so that I can enjoy the upcoming birth of my son. I'm sure you know that Carl has asked both Danielle and me if we would consider doing a special together. Did he ask you to push us on this?"

"Damn, caught red-handed. You got me." In spite of the obvious, neither Gina nor Danielle could express any malcontent towards Seth. He was simply too nice a guy, too straightforward, and too sincere. That's what made him such a talented public relations giant.

"Okay Seth. At least you're honest about it." Both Gina and Danielle laughed a little bit at Seth's blushing countenance, and then

Gina continued, "You can tell Carl that Danielle and I have discussed the topic, and we agreed that we would consider it but not until after the baby is born." Danielle nodded her concurrence silently.

****

Sun Feng made a slight concession for the fact that he was dining in the laid-back informality of Southern California. He wore a pale blue sport jacket instead of one of his normal dark colored tailored business suits. And it was the first time Abby had ever seen Feng without a tie. Josh Struben had gotten off a plane less than two hours earlier and didn't wear a jacket at all. Abby herself wore a simple straight lined flowered dress that hung on her rail thin physique.

Feng had arranged for the three of them to be served dinner in a private wine cellar, so that they could discuss their business dealings without concern about being overheard. The restaurant had an Asian-Fusion style menu but had apparently been cross-bred with California wine snobbery. The outcome was a relatively popular bistro conveniently located just outside Santa Monica. The wait staff was mostly Chinese and had little understanding and no interest whatsoever in the content of the business conversation as they came and went from the wine cellar.

They all arrived at about the same time and after they were seated and exchanged cordial greetings and pleasantries, Sun Feng started down the path that would lead him to the real purpose of this business dinner.

"In two more days Rhapsody will be opening its seventh major center and in another three months, the center in Rome will make eight centers. The plans for eight additional centers next year seem to be well on their way. Dr. McDuffee, you and your team have very much to be proud of. You are ahead of schedule, even though many business people would have considered your original business plan to be wildly optimistic."

"Thank you for acknowledging our success. And of course as you know, I consider you to be a major part of that team you are praising."

Sun Feng waved his hand slightly but in a dismissive gesture nonetheless. "You're success is remarkable and your continued achievement is now highly predicted by those same business cynics, who had previously viewed you as overly confident. As you can imagine, there is no shortage of people who want to be associated with such a renowned triumph. We are all well aware that investors are already lining up to co-capitalize the new centers along with Rhapsody."

"Yes. The financial model that Josh and Gina started with the Struben Center and that we continued with your investment team in our Asian Centers is working quite well. Interestingly, every investor to date is also a Rhapsody Diamond Member."

"Of course they are. What's not to like about the Rhapsody proposition?" Sun Feng smiled ever so slightly as he said this. "My understanding is that the executives at some of your supplier/partners are also members. It shows how highly they value your product."

"Frankly it is very challenging to keep up with the wish list of our members for what they want out of their memberships. For example they now expect security briefings from Rhapsody when they travel to exotic places. This is a bit off course from our health and wellness beginnings, but there are those who believe that we need to look out for every aspect of their longevity, including security."

"Yes, yes. I understand. Far be it from me to say what is right and wrong to have in your product offering. But I didn't want to get together with you this evening to discuss selling your memberships. I came here to discuss selling your company."

"Of course this is no surprise. You have often cautioned me to be ready for such an event. Who is it that wants to buy our company?"

"I have had several conversations with board members of STRX about Rhapsody and they want to engage in a much more strategic set of discussions with you about the relationship between the two firms. These discussions are not meant to be about operations but about investment. These discussions can go in many different directions, but in the end all of them will be aimed at having STRX obtaining a substantial ownership stake in Rhapsody."

"In the past we have had some discussions about their willingness to co-venture with us on the establishment of centers in Germany as well as in our European cities. But I gather, this is not the type of ownership that we are discussing here tonight."

"Exactly, having an ownership stake in a few centers is not what is of interest to a major corporation like STRX. The centers generate profits only after paying Rhapsody Holdings for a variety of products and services, and they hold no intellectual property that is distinctly their own. They lease all of that from Rhapsody Holdings. STRX wants a more strategic relationship. They want to acquire a stake in Rhapsody Holdings. They certainly realize that Rhapsody Holdings is entirely privately held and that all of the equity is also tightly held. Through some mutual business associates, they have asked me to inquire whether you would entertain a discussion of a significant equity investment at the Holding Company level."

"That would include up to 100% of the company. Is that correct?"

"Yes. The original discussions will posture multiple different equity scenarios, I'm sure. But in the long run they want to own the company. They believe they have only a short window of time before some of their strategic competitors might approach Rhapsody as well. And I believe that they are one hundred percent correct on that issue."

Josh Struben was listening as Abby and Sun exchanged thoughts and ideas and then he commented about the direction the discussions might flow.

"If Rhapsody does decide to entertain an early exit for the founders, there are multiple ways to achieve that goal. The structure of the company allows for a wide variety of scenarios. For example, strategic assets, like the *HealthPort, the HealthMap* or the *GPS* could be sold off with an attractive long term lease back arrangement for Rhapsody Holdings to have access to these assets, while the buyer can expand their utilization in other markets. Rhapsody only addresses the high-end market today. These products can be adapted to serve other markets as well. The founders and other equity owners need to decide how they want to monetize some or all of the value they have created. As you have said Abby, the capitalization model that we're working with right now seems to have a lot of appeal to investors, just as it has for Gina and me in London, and for Sun and his group in Asia."

Josh listened to his own words as he spoke them and then without waiting for comment, he turned to Sun Feng with a question, "Do you think that STRX has considered multiple investment scenarios that they might propose, or do you think they have a very specific agenda."

"Of course all of these things are open to negotiation, and it is true that there are multiple possibilities for Rhapsody – including an IPO – which we haven't discussed and that I personally wouldn't recommend. Consequently, Rhapsody has begun to repay the first round funding to the Louisiana Group ahead of schedule. The business is in excellent shape and therefore Rhapsody is in a position of strength for any equity negotiations."

"I agree," said Josh.

"And a lot depends upon that lady sitting across the table from you." Feng was not normally as flip with his rejoinders and he certainly meant to convey an 'all business' demeanor. However he was uncertain as to the intentions of Abby McDuffee and her sister. Together with Dao Diskul, the McDuffees owned controlling equity interest in the firm. This, in effect meant that whatever Abby wanted she would get. It was an unusual position for Sun Feng to be in. He was a businessman who almost always understood motives and incentives. To Feng, the rest was merely details. Both Sun Feng and Josh Struben simply watched Abby's lips to see what she would say.

"You realize that this year we will achieve more than $800 million in gross profit and next year we will rocket past the $1 billion mark. This is an extremely profitable business that is still in its infancy," Abby said.

"We all realize that of course. But next year for the first time we will also have to discuss the practical limit to memberships on a worldwide basis, and what do to about market expansion and broadening the product line. These measures will also attract some viable competition for the first time. We have just about exhausted the benefits of first mover advantage. The question really comes down to where you want to take the business Abby, and do you have the staff and resources to get it there?" Josh had never run a big business himself but he was astute enough to see how businesses could stumble if they weren't careful.

"Frankly I have been thinking about all of those issues nonstop lately." Abby spoke deliberately but not cautiously. She trusted Sun and Josh unequivocally. Sun had been a mentor to Abby during the last two years, and Josh had become a trusted sounding board during the last six months or so. She spoke candidly about some of her own self doubts. "The challenge that concerns me the most is my own personal competence in being able to lead this business through the next three or four years of growth. Candidly I have asked myself if I am really up to the task. Do I really want to work this hard at this stage of my career? These are really important questions and I haven't answered them to myself yet and I know I am discussing these with you for the first time. Last night I had a long discussion with Allie about just this topic. We agreed to take up the topic of succession planning for the executive team at our next board meeting. For the most part we've just scratched the surface on this topic at previous meetings."

"Thank you for being so candid with us Dr. McDuffee. Obviously your doubts and concerns would need to stay below the surface in any merger and/or acquisition discussions. There is an appropriate time for such concerns to be aired. If you were to leave the business anytime soon it would certainly have a material impact on the value of the business." Feng gave his opinion matter of factly.

"Yes I realize all that. And I apologize for airing my self-doubts so blatantly, at a time when you came to dinner, praising our success, and telling me that the marketplace values our accomplishments in such a significant way."

"There is no need to apologize. You have created multiple billion dollars of value in a very short time. You have been heralded as one of the most powerful businesswomen in America, and for that matter throughout the world. Everybody wants to know more and more about Rhapsody all of the time. The simple decision for you is whether you want to continue that path or whether you want to make way for others to follow you. And as it so happens, if there is acquisition interest from a major corporate player such as STRX, then you may be able to achieve your personal goals on multiple fronts, and still achieve what is best for Rhapsody in the long run. However we should realize any significant financial investment that results in a change in controlling ownership will likely require an 'earn-out' on the part of certain members of the executive team. The length of the earn-out could be negotiated, I'm sure. Eventually new ownership would want their own team in place."

"Well I'm sure it couldn't hurt to talk to these folks. What do you see as the next steps, Mr. Feng?"

"I think it would be a good idea for us to set up an exploratory meeting between you and Kurt Gutfreund, the CEO of STRX. He may want to bring one or two other people to the meeting and you will have to think about whom else you would want to bring from Rhapsody. I see this as a very high level meeting where you get to know one another as people before discussing any of the details of a more progressive partnership between Rhapsody and STRX. I know you have the opening of the Center here in LA on Saturday. I'd like to be able to give them a call sometime next week to set up a meeting within the next fifteen days. I think they have a strong bias for action and I'm happy that you agree that it's at least worthwhile listening to what they have to say."

"Okay. Let's do it."

****

It was Al Moses' first appointment with Dr. Mendelsohn in many months. He had come to believe that he had reached the point of diminishing returns with these sessions. In the beginning he had found Mendelsohn's insights to be helpful and constructive. But over time he now believed that he could fend for himself. This perception changed after visiting with his friend Stephen Struben in London.

His longtime friend had recommended that he get help as soon as he got back to New York and Al followed the Stephen's advice and set up a session with Mendelsohn. After relaying some of his paranoid fears and phobias to both Struben and Mendelsohn, Dr. Al Moses had gotten the same feedback. Neither of them believed that Dr. Al's wife, Maria, was cheating on him. Additionally Dr. Mendelsohn expressed grave concern about the re-apparition of Dr. Anne Mohr in his life. Maria and Duffy had been on the west coast for the last ten days and when Al returned from London to his Manhattan home, the silent voice of his late lover, Anne, had returned to fill the void.

Al Moses' appointment with Dr. Mendelsohn wandered over a number of different topics but halfway through the 50-minute session they narrowed the focus down considerably.

"What exactly is it now that makes you believe that Maria has someone else in her life?"

"There isn't anything specific. Nothing that I can hang my hat on … it's just a feeling that I have and I know that it's true."

"You mentioned earlier that you had expressed the same concerns to your friend Stephen Struben, and that Stephen wasn't accepting the validity of your concerns. Correct?"

"Yes, that's true. Stephen thinks that I am suffering from some sort of paranoia. To be honest about it, he was the one who pushed me to come back to see you. But I believe that my concerns about Maria are real. I'm not sure why she married me. Maybe it was simply because she needed someone to help her with the parenting of Duffy."

"That may have been a contributing reason. However that still doesn't mean that she doesn't love you. And it is certainly not an indication that she is seeing someone else. Didn't you tell me that Maria was happy? Didn't you say that she has told you often that she loves you?"

"Yes, but I have a feeling."

"Is your relationship with Maria still physically affectionate?"

"Yes, on the occasions when we are home together we are still sexually intimate."

"Doesn't that tell you something?"

"No. It is much more perfunctory than passionate."

"And that is much different from when you first started seeing each other?"

"No. Not really. I guess it's always been about the same."

The dialogue between Al Moses and his therapist, Dr. Greg Mendelsohn, wound around in circles as the psychiatrist attempted to get his patient to accept the fact that he may indeed be a bit paranoid about his relationship with his wife Maria. However as the session was drawing to a close Al's frustration only increased. Why did everyone think that he was paranoid? Why was he the only one who believed Maria might be cheating on him? Why was he simply feeling so sad?

Al Moses left the Tkachuk Center after his session with Mendelsohn and took a cab back to his apartment. Inside the empty apartment he wandered around for a minute or two before taking a bottle of water from the refrigerator. He suddenly felt quite thirsty. Al then walked back into his bedroom sat on the edge of his bed and began his conversation with Dr. Anne Mohr.

"Good evening Anne, my love. How are you this evening?"

"That's nice. That's very nice. Oh by the way, I went to see Dr. Mendelsohn this evening."

"It's not that important. Not something you need to know about."

"No he doesn't believe I need any meds whatsoever. He thinks I can alter my behavior. He thinks I can work through my issues."

"I told you. It's not that important. And it's not something you need to know about."

"No, of course not....you are my one and only true love."

"She means nothing to me. And I think I mean nothing to her as well."

"Well yes. She wants us to move out of this place. She thinks it's too dreary."

"Below our station in life, I think."

"We need more room for Duffy, and we need to have the nanny live with us."

"But, of course, Duffy is not my daughter. Sarah was my daughter. Sarah was *our* daughter."

"Duffy is not here. Duffy is with her mother in Los Angeles."

"That's a different topic altogether."

"Sex is only sex. It doesn't always have meaning."

"Maria is *not* the only woman with whom I've had sex since you left me. She's no different from the others."

"Okay I will never mention her name again. But you brought her up. I didn't want to discuss her."

"Okay. Okay. I agree. As I said, I will not bring her name up again."

"But Anne, my love, my time has not yet come. No. I don't want to think about that. I don't want to think about that at all."

"No. No. No. As I told you, *you* are my love. I just don't want to think about it."

"Good night, Anne, my love. There is nothing more for us to talk about."

Al Moses got up from the edge of the bed. He was perspiring mildly. He was also still very thirsty. He finished his bottle of water and walked into the kitchen to retrieve another bottle. He drank about half of the second bottle but didn't realize that his hand was shaking while he was drinking the water. He was still amazingly thirsty. He then finished the remainder of the second plastic bottle of water and crushed it nervously in his hand.

Al continued to wander around his apartment. He went to the bathroom to relieve himself. Then he walked over to his television set, clicked it on and clicked the remote more than a dozen times changing channels, before rapidly turning it off as suddenly as he had turned it on. He walked around past the bed to the pastoral oil painting on the wall. The painting had been a wedding gift from his med-school friend Paolo

Grassani and Maria absolutely loved it. It had been placed in a spot that had previously housed the large framed picture of Al and Anne, which had been taken when they were in Acapulco together. *That* picture was now on a shelf in the closet. Moses removed the newly positioned pastoral oil painting and exposed the wall safe behind it. His wife, Maria, had never shown any interest in the contents of the safe and had never seen it opened. After spinning the combination lock to its familiar settings he withdrew his loaded Smith and Wesson 38 caliber handgun. Moses knew that there was something familiar about the unfolding drama. However there was more a sense of dread than a sense of déjà vu that came over Dr. Al Moses. Some of the setting had changed slightly. In addition to the painting on the wall, Maria had replaced Al's antique chair and table, with a white leather love seat. And the walls had been painted in a light blue hue.

Dr. Al sat down on the love seat and once again put the 4" barrel of the loaded Smith and Wesson 38 in his mouth and cocked the trigger. The same scenario had played out three or four times in the past. This time was different. This time he fired.

****

The resort strip in Cancun, Mexico was lined with oceanside resorts and lagoon side restaurants. The young man waded ankle-deep in the pristine waters of the Gulf of Mexico, and wandered north on the beach past the procession of high rise hotels He carried his shoes in his right hand and reached back with his left hand to grasp the hand of the older woman. He was wearing a fanny pack around his waist and was careful not to wade too deep into the water, lest he risk getting soaked in salt water before attending the noontime church services. Although both the young man and the older woman were Mexicans neither of them had ever been to Cancun until relatively recently. They came to Cancun as tourists, but only vacationed for a week before getting employment at one of the local resorts. The resort city was a far cry from their ancestral home in Mexico City, but it suited them well.

The young man and the older lady had been to Sunday Mass at every Catholic Church in the greater Cancun area during the past several months, and rumors had begun to circulate that the young man who worked as a bartender was also responsible for leaving substantial donations at each of the churches. No one seems to know where in Cancun, Fernando and his mother were living, but most believed that they were simply staying in the resort where they worked. They didn't know that Fernando and his mother had purchased a small 1500 square foot home on the outskirts of the city, and traveled to and from work in a twelve-year-old Ford Escort.

As Fernando and his mother continued to stroll along the beach they kept an eye on the time, so that they wouldn't be late for Mass, which on this particular Sunday was being celebrated by a local parish priest in a conference room at the Marriott Hotel midway along the strip. As they got closer to the Marriott, Fernando and his mother began to walk across the sand to the beach side entrance to the hotel. They then went up to the main floor and sought out the location for the services that would be said in Spanish.

There came a time for the collection and most of the Catholic vacationers contributed a variety of nominations of cash into the wicker basket. Fernando took an envelope out of his fanny pack that had been imprinted with the name of the different hotel on the strip. Inside the envelope Fernando had placed his usual Sunday offering of ten $100 bills. There were only 35 people at the noontime Mass and the collection basket had only one envelope in it among the other naked currency.

As Fernando and his mother left the conference room where Mass had been celebrated, he made some broad calculations in his head. When JB died, Fernando still had two years to run on the agreement for services as Brady's chauffer. With his compensation at $180,000 a year that left him with $640,000 to dispose of appropriately. He made this calculation after he deducted his self arranged severance package from the cash that he had received from Brady's safe. His severance package had been carefully deposited in more than a dozen different banks stateside before he and his mother left for Mexico. It took him almost 3 weeks and more than 50 visits to the various banks and bank branches to deposit all the cash that he deemed to be his. That coupled with the numerous visits to churches throughout New York had kept him quite busy before he told his mother that he wanted to bring her back to Mexico. His only risk had been the huge amount of cash that remained in his possession when he left the United States and went to Mexico. His mother never knew the risk that she was taking with the contents of her bags. Once they reach Mexico Fernando carefully unpacked everything and his secret was preserved. Over the next five months, Fernando had managed to distribute the rest of the cash that he believed belonged to God.

Chapter 20: *The Rhapsody Victory –*
March 2012

It was astounding the difference seven months could make. In August of 2011, Rhapsody Holdings was experiencing significant success within its targeted market segment of the rapidly expanding global health and wellness industries. However much was unknown about the future direction of the business, and even less was known about the motivations and desires of the founders and leaders of the business. In August of 2011 Rhapsody was still a private enterprise, and so there was not a tremendous amount of public disclosure required for the business to continue to flourish.

Even the most optimistic insiders could not have predicted that by March of 2012, Rhapsody Holdings would be recognized as the most astonishing business success story of the 21st century. They were now opening centers at an electrifying pace with a new center being established every two months. There were centers in the United States in New York, Los Angeles, Chicago and Seattle. European centers were up and running in London, Paris and Rome. Centers were flourishing in Asia in the cities of Hong Kong, Beijing, Singapore and Tokyo. Eleven centers in all were up and running and five more were planned for completion by the end of the year. These included the first center in Australia in the city of Sydney as well as the first center in South America in the city of Rio de Janeiro, Brazil. Centers in San Francisco, Washington DC and Miami would all be opened before the end of the summer. Negotiations were ongoing for 2013 for additional centers in Moscow, Geneva, Dubai, Bangkok, Athens, and Caracas, Venezuela.

The most daunting challenge for Rhapsody Holdings was not its expansion of centers but its expansion of staff. The executive team for the holding company now numbered 24 people. The operating company now employed more than 3,500 people and the centers themselves employed another 13,000 people. In addition there were more than 8500 health and wellness practitioners who were either employed by, or associated with, the *Rhapsody Global Practitioner Society, (GPS.).* This included a little more than 1175 PALs, deployed around the world. Training programs for Rhapsody personnel were ongoing and everywhere. The desire for Rhapsody to have a ubiquitous presence in all the major cities of the world had once seemed to be a wildly optimistic vision. However the unprecedented demand for *Platinum and Diamond Rhapsody Memberships* on a worldwide basis gave the company the cash and liquidity necessary to make that dream come true.

Another hallmark of Rhapsody's phenomenal pace of success was that medical schools throughout the United States, and for that matter, around the world were now commonly offering courses in longevity assistance. This was a direct tip of the hat to the success of Rhapsody's PALs, and the recognition of the importance of patient-centered (or in Rhapsody's case, *Member Centered*) medical approaches. These same educational institutions were also stretching to encompass a curriculum that reflected the worldwide interest in *Healthness*, Rhapsody's term for its holistic medical treatments and processes.

Of course the biggest difference of the last seven months was the acquisition of controlling interest in Rhapsody Holdings stock by STRX. The STRX shareholders had approved an $11.7 billion USD purchase of 80% of the outstanding equity in Rhapsody Holdings in early December of 2011, and had agreed to run the company as a separate business unit headquartered out of NYC. The complex terms and conditions of the deal included a fifty percent payment in cash and a fifty percent payment in STRX parent company stock. This left the Rhapsody founders and other shareholding executives with a significant incentive to make sure the change of control went flawlessly.

The most unusual part of the agreement between STRX and Rhapsody was the agreement surrounding the composition of the new Executive Management Team. There was very little conflict. Both Abby and Alison McDuffee had agreed to step down from their positions, but STRX didn't want to put one of its own executives in-charge. Instead the new CEO was slated to be Ben Hui Zhang. In addition, several other Rhapsody executives maintained positions on the new EMT including Dao Diskul, Zoë Mansfield and Mark Candu. Maria Cardoza-Moses opted to take a severance package and leave the business citing personal reasons. She had been on an extended personal bereavement leave for most of the last seven months anyway. The youngest of the McDuffee women, Caitlin McDuffee-Browning was being promoted to head up worldwide business development including all of sales and marketing for the firm. Each of these appointments was scheduled to be announced in the next few weeks.

Meanwhile Josh Struben had begun working closely with Sun Feng. They had formed a new business alliance together and were working on ways to provide funding for a variety of health and wellness business initiatives that were outside the scope of Rhapsody but definitely not in conflict with Rhapsody either. For the most part these businesses were centered on medical devices, surgical tools, process improvements and the like. The businesses would more than likely work well with Rhapsody in the future. Their business interests also included significant interest in the growing insurance industry throughout Asia. The two financial tycoons were also still helping Rhapsody directly as the merger into STRX unfolded.

The STRX CEO, Kurt Gutfreund, was careful to place experienced managers and leaders from other parts of STRX into Rhapsody, so that the blend of the two businesses would go smoothly. He had also taken a personal liking to Sandeep Mehra, and had offered him a position in the parent company leadership team so that Sandeep's skills could be more broadly used throughout the firm. Sandeep discussed the offer with his mentor, Ben Hui Zhang and they both recognized it as an opportunity for Sandeep to demonstrate his leadership skills outside of Ben's shadow and so he took advantage of the opportunity and became the CIO of the entire STRX conglomerate.

All of these changes were taking place at the speed of light. The changes would be profound. Plans and meetings had gone on incessantly from the beginning of the New Year and now on the last weekend of March, the spring weather was finally beginning to replace the long cold winter. It was time for a break and a few of the female members of the executive team at Rhapsody were taking a well-earned respite from the rigors and challenges of day-to-day life in running the Rhapsody enterprise. Abby McDuffee had invited her sisters, Alison and Caitlin to join her on a leisurely horseback jaunt through the Western New Jersey countryside. The recently widowed Maria Cardoza was also invited to join the three sisters for what was meant to be a simple afternoon of recreation.

Abby and her husband, Bo, had reconciled the differences in their marriage and were once again living together with their fourteen-year-old daughter, Mindy, in their Scarsdale home. Bo had come to grips with his wife's success. Their common love for their daughter, Mindy, had proved to be the blowout patch that was needed to get them back on the same page. Abby had purchased a horse farm in New Jersey as a weekend getaway. Family life was now looking rosier for Abby and Bo.

Abby McDuffee was still was in the process of transitioning her responsibilities to her successor, Ben, who was still living on the other side of the world. Her sister, Alison McDuffee was now living full time in California. Alison and Tom sold their longtime east coast home in Bernardsville, N J. and Alison was beginning to spend more of her time with her west coast friends. Her trips east were becoming more infrequent, now that she was in the process of stepping down as Rhapsody's Chief Strategic Officer.

Whereas her older twins sisters, Alison and Abby, were getting ready to leave the business, Caitlin Browning, was looking forward to being part of the new executive management team for the restructured Rhapsody business unit. Rhapsody was to be operated separately from the STRX medicals/healthcare business, with its own P&L and its own set of operating imperatives. Kurt Gutfreund had indicated to Wall Street that the company could take advantage of synergies with other business units within the conglomerate, without actually being merged into one of these entities. However numerous members of the STRX management team were being transferred into the new Rhapsody business unit. Caitlin was widely recognized as the driving force behind worldwide sales of *Rhapsody Memberships*, and although her original desires were to run the European region for Rhapsody, she was now thrilled to be promoted to be a member of the Executive Management Team for the newly created business unit of STRX.

The McDuffee sisters were glad that Maria Cardoza had accepted Abby's invitation to join them out at her new horse farm. They were all deeply saddened at the sudden death of Dr. Al, at the end of the previous summer. They all liked Maria very much and wanted to do whatever they could to help her overcome her loss. Actually Maria had adjusted quite well to her husband's suicide. She had thrown herself into her role as mother of her daughter, Duffy. Rather than returning to work after a lengthy bereavement leave, Maria told the new management team that she would like to take advantage of the executive buyout program, at the same time that the McDuffee sisters stepped down from their roles as leaders of the business. Maria certainly didn't need the money. She was already wealthy before joining Rhapsody, and the exercise of her Rhapsody shadow stock options had merely added to her vast portfolio.

Maria, however, intended to maintain one strong business connection to Rhapsody Holdings. About two months before Al Moses died, Maria had acquired controlling interest in Poco Pedazo de Ciela where she used to work on the Mediterranean coast in Spain. She had hoped that one day she would be able to convince Abby and Alison that resort locations would make good additions to the portfolio of cities that contained Rhapsody Centers. She believed that the new management team might look more favorably on such expansion.

Maria was confused by Al's suicide. He hadn't bothered to leave a note. However his therapist, Dr. Mendelsohn, spoke with Maria in private and indicated that Dr. Al was suffering from acute paranoia and may have misinterpreted Maria's occupational industriousness for matrimonial disenchantment. Maria found that odd, because throughout her relationship with Dr. Al, she had remained faithful to him and was even gratified by the constancy that this fidelity had seemed to bring to their marriage. Another irony that kept Maria wondering was the fact that she had originally gone to Dr. Al complaining about her own depression. It never dawned upon her that Al Moses himself could also be suffering from depression.

The four women who set out on a horseback in Western New Jersey were all very well off financially. Even Caitlin Browning, who was the youngest of the group, had managed to accumulate a good deal of personal wealth through her ownership of Rhapsody stock. If anyone were to take a snapshot of the four riders they would see a picture that appeared to be right out of an exclusive equestrian magazine.

Abby and Alison rode next to one another, while Caitlin and Maria trailed about 25 feet behind. The twin sisters rode at a very deliberate pace as they clomped their way through town along Route 29. Caitlin and Maria followed. The goal was to ride in a broad loop and eventually reach Abby's farm where her staff had prepared a picnic lunch near a cluster of maple trees at the western edge of the farm. No one was in a hurry.

"Remember when we used to ride horses when we were growing up in Ohio?" Abby reflected.

"Sure absolutely. We used to go over to the ranch with the 4-H club every couple of weeks. That was a lot of fun then. I was just thinking about those days. I am enjoying the ride today. Thanks for inviting me."

"I agree, those were good times. However as much as I loved riding the horses, I don't really miss those days at all for other reasons.

Remember how much we used to get teased about being the 'string bean sisters.' That sort of thing never let up."

"How many times could you hear the same stale quips about wearing skis when you take a shower so you don't go down the drain?" Alison made light of the memories.

"We were both just skin and bone I thought I'd never grow breasts."

"Yea, I think Caitlin had the right idea. We should have just *bought* them." She laughed quietly so that their sister would not hear their banter.

"Yes, those were crazy days, but I did miss the horseback riding and that's why I bought this place last September."

"I wanted to ask you about that. What made you buy this place?"

"Right after I got back from Germany and our preliminary discussions with STRX, my head was spinning. There was an awful lot going on and Bo and I were trying to make our marriage work. It was starting to have an impact on Mindy. I just needed to get away. I remembered what my childhood was like and how comfortable I felt when I was riding, so one Saturday afternoon Mindy and I came out here for some mother-daughter talk. It was the first time that she had ever been on a horse and we had such a great time together that I wanted it to last much longer. There was a sign out in front of the house indicating that the horse farm was for sale and so I talked to the owners for a few minutes when we returned and impulsively I made an offer."

"Really ... it was all that simple?"

"Yes it was."

The two women who were trailing Abby and Alison had something in common. Both Maria Cardoza-Moses and Caitlin Browning had at different times held the position of executive assistant to the now deceased John Brady. Later, each of these women had come over to the employ of Rhapsody Holdings. They then worked closely together and formed a lasting friendship. This kind of relationship was new for Maria, who could count her close female friends on one hand. Caitlin was very much the opposite when it came to social engagement. She had made many friends throughout her school years and on into her business life, and had continued to expand her relationships throughout her tenure at Rhapsody.

After the sudden death of Al Moses, Maria found herself searching for someone to confide in. She spent some time talking with

Dr. Angelique Lefebvre, her therapist, but the sessions became too painful to maintain. For the first time in her life Maria realized that she needed friendship more than she needed anything else. Maria looked up to both Abby and Alison but they were many years older than she was. Caitlin Browning was actually a couple of years younger than Maria, and their personal backgrounds and values were somewhat different. Maria still remained somewhat introspective and obsessed with art, beauty, longevity, and the meaning to life. Caitlin was far more impulsive and was driven by a desire to try new things and enjoy every moment of her day. However the two women had enough experience in common, both from their days at ICD and well as their time with Rhapsody, to serve as the basis for a good friendship. At Abby's urging, Caitlin reached out to Maria on multiple occasions following Al's death to make certain that Maria knew that the whole Rhapsody team was supportive in her hour of need.

"You ride like this isn't your first time on a horse," said Caitlin to Maria.

"Actually it's been quite some time since I've been around horses. However I used to live with a man whose whole life was about horses. He was an Arab gentleman, and he also dealt in the global oil and munitions businesses. But his true love was horses. He was my Arabian horseman." Maria opened up a bit to Caitlin. She wasn't used to being so approachable.

"Do you ever still see him?"

"No unfortunately he passed away many years ago. But he was very good to me." Before too long Maria added, "He was an older man, like Al, and he died suddenly of a heart attack."

"Oh, I am so sorry, Maria. I didn't mean to pry. It sounds as though you've had quite a string of bad luck." Caitlin couldn't help but think that it was a bit odd that Maria had such an attraction for older men, but she didn't comment on that particularity. She knew, from an earlier conversation, that Maria's stint at Poco Pedazo de Ciela included a live-in relationship with an art dealer who was also a good bit older than Maria.

"I'm not all so sure that I have had such bad luck. Some people would think that there has been quite a bit of good fortune in my life. For the most part, the men in my life have treated me quite well. I have nothing to complain about really."

"Al was your first husband. Wasn't he?" Caitlin's curiosity made her pry anyway.

"Yes he was my first and only husband. Before I became pregnant, I never much felt the need, or for that matter, the desire, to marry. Even after Duffy was born, Al and I lived together happily. He wanted to get married and I had no objection. I loved him." Maria gazed down over the right side of her horse, away from where Caitlin was riding on her left. Then she looked up again and added softly, "And I miss him."

Maria was unusually talkative and so Caitlin just let her continue to speak.

"I have had my share of older men in my life, but that was by choice. I have never paid very much attention to how old a person is. I pay more attention to the experiences they have had and the kind of people that they are. I can't say I have made all the right choices in men either. But I have always been faithful to the men I love, and in return they have taught me many things. In addition to learning about horses, I have learned about art, about health and about business.....and I have learned about love."

As they rode, Caitlin listened to Maria and wondered if there had been any truth to the old rumors that Maria and John Brady were lovers. She dismissed the thought somewhat quickly because she could never see someone as sensitive and cerebral as Maria, falling for someone as crass, cruel and callous as her former boss. However she did wonder how such idiotic rumors get started. Was it just because of the nature of a close working relationship? And then the thought occurred to Caitlin that maybe people said the same thing about her and JB. Just then the mare that Caitlin was riding made a sniffling shiver and shook its head as it exhaled. The horse's shake and shiver moved to its whole torso in a way that seemed humorous to Caitlin. It was almost as though the horse was also disgusted by the thought of John Brady as a lover.

****

Maureen Brady knew that she needed change and she was fortunate to find a modicum of help from her companion, Dr Mike Kelvey. They had discussed the fact that there seemed to be a pall over everything that they did in and around Maureen's Kings Point home, and so Maureen had decided to sell the Brady family's long time residence as well as their vacation home in the Hamptons. That was going to be step one. Step two entailed finding a new place to live.

Maureen had more money than she could ever hope to spend in several lifetimes. However to this point in her life, happiness had been somewhat elusive. She had come to the phase in her own self-awareness, where she recognized that the only true relationships that she had in life were those with her children. She also accepted that even those relationships did not have the depth of emotional bonding that normally accompanies parent-child relationships. Regardless, it was these relationships that she viewed with a hope to capture true happiness in the future.

For now, Maureen was still living in her Kings Point home. Her friend and lover, Mike Kelvey, didn't live with her, but managed to sleep over at the house several nights each week. On a Friday morning following such a sleepover, Kelvey was sitting in the large kitchen area reading the New York Times and having a cup of coffee. He looked up from the newspaper and stared for a second or two at Maureen before asking her about a news item in the business section of the newspaper.

"Did you see this article about Chipper Geld? Apparently this time the Feds really got him. He has been trying to work a plea bargain and it looks as though the government isn't giving in. They seem to have an airtight case and your friend Mr. Geld could be looking at some serious jail time."

"Couldn't happen to a nicer guy ..."

"It also says that he has been forced to liquidate almost all of his personal assets to pay for his legal fees. The government has seized all of his US based business assets. But it looks as though they are having some trouble getting their hands on some of his foreign assets. Apparently there has been a buyer for Solace in the Sun. I know that you liked that place, regardless of the fact that Geld owned it."

"Yes. The people who worked at SIS were all very good to me when I was there." Maureen said this with a secretive smile. She had been fighting with her alcohol issues off and on for a long time, and had intermittent relapses on several occasions over the last forty months. However she currently viewed her problem in much the same way that she did when she was leaving SIS in December of 2008. Alcoholism is a disease.

Maureen's belief that she would be able to simply drink less had proved to be an illusion. Every time she tried to "cut down" on her drinking she only delayed the inevitable binge drinking that would ensue. Recognition of her problem would be the key to her successful quest for happiness in the future. Her current situation had her at 187 sober days in a row and counting. She was hopeful once again.

Maureen's attempts to conquer her alcoholism had the positive impact of allowing her to understand that life itself was a countdown of sorts. With that in mind she had resolved to enjoy her life and to search for new horizons, which probably included some new people. And even though she had left Solace in the Sun almost three and a half years earlier, she was still grateful to the practitioners there. Through an intermediary corporate entity that was set up by her financial advisor, Maureen had actually purchased the property and business in Costa Rica from Chipper Geld just two months earlier. She managed to make the acquisition for less than 35 cents on the dollar. She resisted the opportunity to contact Geld and inform him about the new ownership that was controlling Solace in the Sun. She believed that she would just wait until he found out in hell.

Maureen didn't share the information about her acquisition of SIS with Mike Kelvey either. Although she liked Kelvey, the relationship did not seem to have much of a future. Kelvey served a purpose in Maureen's life, but she had come to the realization that he was not someone that she wanted to spend a significant part of her future with. She knew that she would get around to telling him that she wanted to move on, but she was just taking her time doing so. For now Kelvey served the purpose of keeping the tongues wagging at the club.

"I was thinking that I might acquire some property in the Caribbean. I'm going to talk it over with the kids. They are not overly happy about the idea that I will be selling this place and our place in the Southampton. But they'll get over it. In fact before this past summer they were all spending less time at both places."

"But they did enjoy the Southampton home last summer. Maybe you want to think twice before you sell the place. The market has taken a while to rebound and property is finally beginning to appreciate once again."

"Don't worry Mike; you'll get over it too." Maureen's sarcasm gnawed at Kelvey a bit but he didn't respond.

They sat in silence across the table from one another. Kelvey returned to reading the paper and Maureen reflected upon her relationships with her children. They were now all living in New York City. Her oldest son Mark was working with a small Wall Street firm and living with a very pretty young girl, who didn't seem to have a meaningful job, didn't read much, and couldn't carry on a meaningful conversation. Maureen hoped it wouldn't last. Her daughter Megan was now in graduate school pursuing a degree in molecular biology. She had been in and out of several relationships over the last few years, but Maureen believed she had her head on straight. Moreover Maureen believed that Megan was happy and had a direction in life.

And then there was Kenneth. Kenneth was extremely handsome. His physique had filled out during his college years to the point where he was the spitting image of his father, John Brady. Kenneth had transferred after his sophomore year and was now in his senior year at NYU. He had continued writing poetry and was now in the process of co-writing a play with one of his professors. He was pursuing a degree in the theatrical arts and was living in what he described as a 'marriage triumvirate' with another young actor and actress. They all seemed to be happy and gay.

Maureen excused herself and returned to her boudoir. She walked over to the sitting area near the unlit fireplace and retrieved copies of some of the poems that Kenneth had sent to her since he started in college. The first one that she picked up was about four pages long and seemed to be some kind of a discussion between a bar tender and a patron at the bar

> *Red vested smile, come pour my blood,*
> *And I will tell a tale,*
> *About the drops that start the flood,*
> *And turn my complexion pale.*
> *So fill me quick and fill me full,*
> *Before I go aquiver*
> *And I can keep the talk from dull*
> *With just another jigger.*

After reading just a few lines of this particular poem she put it aside remembering the entire text was a bit too painful to read. Besides there was another piece of poetry that Kenneth sent to her that she wanted to re-read. She searched around for a while remembering that it was something that he had written to her a couple years back when he returned to school after the holidays. She remembered it as the moment in time when she thought she would have to stop worrying about her son. He had entitled the piece *Autonomy*. She found it and picked it up and read it aloud to herself once again.

I really don't care what you think,
And much less what you say.
I am totally autonomous
Growing more so day-by-day.

Your thoughts are fine, for your own mind,
Maybe even quite correct.
But you don't know, should I think so,
On each precise subject.

So play it smart and just don't start
To try and understand
The things for me to have to see
To be the perfect man.

So call me 'fool' or call me 'cool,'
It really doesn't matter.
I am into 'me.'
That's all you see. The ego just gets fatter

What should you do? How should you act?
Why should you even listen?
Just embrace, 'auto no me'.
Then see what you've been missing.

Maureen was uncertain whether her son was being sarcastic, sardonic or sadistic when he wrote this piece, but somehow she saw the temperament of her husband JB entwined in the personality of their son, Kenneth. However she recognized the fact that Kenneth was not destined to be a business leader like his father; she realized that he would probably make a different use of his God-given tools. She also realized that as a mother, she would never stop worrying.

****

Kurt Gutfreund, the CEO of STRX, was very happy that his Board of Directors approved the acquisition of controlling interest in Rhapsody Holdings. He believed that his company made an excellent deal. Including the assumption of Rhapsody Holdings' debt, STRX was paying $11.7 Billion in the acquisition deal. For that sum they received eighty percent of the Rhapsody Holding equity as well as one hundred percent of RH's equity interest in its subsidiaries. Also included was the subsidiaries' respective interest in the eleven Rhapsody Centers that were already in operation as well as the four that were currently under construction. In the business world there were some who believed that Gutfreund and STRX overpaid for Rhapsody Holdings, and there were others, who like Gutfreund, believed that STRX was making a fantastic deal.

Gutfreund readily acknowledged that the deal had a relatively complex set of terms and conditions with respect to the ongoing involvement of the Rhapsody founders. However he also believed that this acquisition had the potential to make STRX the single strongest public corporation in the world. STRX had a market cap that exceeded $150 Billion (USD) and encompassed more than a dozen different industrial business units.

The process of sorting out the leadership responsibilities for Rhapsody was going smoothly. Several of the original founders and executives had expressed an interest in leaving the company after the buyout by STRX. After a good bit of discussion and negotiation Rhapsody and STRX came to an agreement that the company would best be served by retaining Ben Hui Zhang and promoting him to the position of President of the Rhapsody business unit, a position comparable to the CEO role that was formerly held by Abby McDuffee. Another of the original founders, Dao Diskul would also be staying on in prominent management position after the buyout. And Zoë Mansfield had accepted significant financial inducements to make a full time job out of her position as head of the *Rhapsody Global Practitioner Society.*

Kurt Gutfreund invited Sun Feng and his new business partner, Josh Struben, to join him for a celebratory dinner. They had agreed that Nice, France was a good place to meet. There was a beautiful hotel directly across from the beachfront on the Cote d'Azur that was both stylish and sedate. The Hotel Negresco was the class of the French Riviera and had the added advantage to Sun Feng of being a short distance from Monte Carlo, where he was spending more of his time in recent months. The building itself has the feel of an art museum with expensive original pieces by Salvador Dali, Niki de Saint Phalle and many others on display in the hallways of the luxury hotel. There were five centuries worth of French Art located within the confines of the hotel that was now celebrating its 100th anniversary.

The trio of businessmen dined together at the Chantecler restaurant, at the Negresco, amid a carrousel-like décor complete with painted wooden horses in the middle of the eatery. After dinner, Feng, Struben and Gutfreund decided to take a stroll along the Promenade des Anglais, the stone walkway that arched along the sand, which abutted la Baie des Anges (the Bay of Angels) section of the blue Mediterranean Sea.

"Mr. Gutfreund you have to make certain that your team acts swiftly to consolidate the working relationships of your businesses," said Sun Feng. "I know that you have long term plans to merge the interests of your other business units together with the interests of Rhapsody to achieve greater success for all of STRX. However it is my belief, as well as the belief of many who invest with me, that STRX will be best served by having many of your business units be supportive to the ultra-rapid growth of the Rhapsody business unit."

Feng continued, "Healthcare will be by far and away the fastest growing industry segment for the next ten to fifteen years, and possibly well beyond that. Rhapsody has one foot in the door due to what it's achieved at the high end of the market, but it has yet to realize its ultimate vision of serving all markets with the opportunity to achieve a longer better life span and lifestyle."

"I appreciate your perspective Mr. Feng. So let me give you an oral progress report. I know that you are well aware STRX acquired the world-renowned Casa Celestiale hospitality chain three years ago. Not only is the CC Brand well known throughout the world, but is well established in multiple markets. We have luxury hotels that compete effectively in the five-star market and we have properties that are comfortable stopovers for the mid-level business travelers as well. We have properties in large cities as well as in suburban and rural locations. And we also have Casa Celestiale Resorts in forty-seven resort city locations around the globe. We see an opportunity to put a Rhapsody Center in all of our resorts and in another 250 locations within the next 5 to 8 years. Some of these will be conversions of existing spas and some of these will be new build-outs entirely.

"In addition we have already begun working on a Rhapsody-lite product. Obviously we will select a different name to avoid cannibalizing our existing market. But we expect to leverage our intellectual property and begin to offer many of the benefits, like the *HealthPort* and access to the *GPS* to a broader based clientele."

"So this planning process is underway already?"

"Yes we began this process immediately after the merger. And although I have appointed an STRX lifer to head up the strategic effort, he is working very closely with Dr. Alison McDuffee on all of the strategic implications for the future. This will be Alison's last major contribution to our business before her retirement. As you would imagine she has been extremely cooperative and incredibly insightful."

The three businessmen had walked for about a half a mile and finally slowed their gait to a near stop pace. Although Struben's native language was English; Gutfreund's native language was German and Feng's native language was Chinese, the three men were conversing in heavily accented English as they walked along the French Riviera. In reality, this was a testament to the global nature of their joint business interests. Their backgrounds and experiences spanned the globe

"How is your relationship with Ben Hui Zhang working out?" Josh directed his question to Kurt Gutfreund?"

"Very well … very well indeed. Ben was absolutely the perfect choice to lead Rhapsody. He is very much a team player and a very strong leader. I think we were absolutely correct in selecting an Asian American to run the business. Ben has also been most helpful in convincing Sandeep Mehra to stay with STRX. We are going to give Mehra the responsibility for running IT across the whole STRX franchise, and he will report directly to me. He has been a tremendous asset to Rhapsody in the rapid development and deployment of the *Rhapsody HealthPort* as well as the Rhapsody *HealthMapping* process. I have challenged him with the idea of bringing the same sense of urgency and speed to the many other businesses within the STRX family."

"Both Mr. Struben and myself are glad to hear such positive support of Mr. Zhang. Your plan to expand the market for Rhapsody's products and services is going to need a very strong leader. The market that Rhapsody has exploited so far is one where 100,000 or so of the wealthiest people in the world are willing to pay for substantially all of their health and wellness care as long as they have access to the right physicians, practitioners, medicines, procedures and facilities. Cost never enters into the equation for *Rhapsody Platinum and Diamond Members.* However there still needs to be a mechanism to get similar services into the broader market at a much more affordable rate."

Josh took up Sun Feng's leading comments. "Mr. Feng and I have set up several different insurance businesses in Asia over the last year. We believe that there is a need for a global payer in order to be able to process insurance claims at the low end of the market. We have already begun to look at a trans-European payer model. We know that in the US, the Obama administration has been struggling for several years to get this right. The typical American political process has slowed the adoption of a national payer approach. And when we look at Asia we have even more work to do. Insurance has been a new and growing phenomenon in Asia. However we believe all of these parts of the world are heading in the same general direction. In short we believe that within the next five years we will be able to put together a global payer system that will facilitate the ability of Rhapsody to expand its markets and compete ably against the competition that will eventually emerge."

The three businessmen continued their discourse as they meandered back along the Mediterranean beachfront in the early evening. The various security personnel maintained their distance in the background. Eventually they crossed the street and went back into the lobby of the Hotel Negresco. Gutfreund took the lift directly up to his room while the other two men decided to walk the wide staircase toward their third floor rooms. As they went their separate ways, Josh Struben turned to Feng and asked him. "Do you think Gutfreund understands what it will take to realize the full potential of Rhapsody?"

"If I didn't believe that he could do it, I would never have given my support to the acquisition. I think that the next few steps for Rhapsody will be gigantic steps for mankind."

****

A slimmer version of Omar than had been seen by viewers in many years appeared before the camera to start his Friday show. Omar had lost nearly seventy-five pounds from his 6'2" frame over the last year as he was finally beginning to take his Rhapsody Diamond Membership seriously. Through a combination of diet control, personal training, meditation and health and wellness vigilance he had returned muscular definition to his 195 pound frame and looked ten years younger than he did merely a year earlier.

"Good morning ladies and gentlemen. We have some very special guests with us here today. As you all are aware, we have been very close to our friends at Rhapsody Holdings for a few years now, and we have had numerous members of their *Global Practitioner Society* on the air with us on an intermittent basis. In fact our very own colleague, Dr Zoë Mansfield, has been an integral part of Rhapsody's growth over the last couple of years. Now that Rhapsody has new ownership, I have asked

Zoë to come back on our show along with Dr Dao Diskul to discuss what this means for Rhapsody in the future and more importantly what it means to our own healthcare. Welcome back ladies."

"Thank you Omar. As always it's great to be here on your show." Dao responded.

"Where do you ladies see the future of Rhapsody heading? Is there a plan that will allow the working men and women of the world to avail themselves of the same level of medical attention as the *Rhapsody Diamond and Platinum Members* have enjoyed for the last three years?" Omar went back to a familiar topic that had been aired frequently in his discussions with Rhapsody executives over the years. Although Omar himself was a *Rhapsody Diamond Member*, he clearly saw the need for some of the services that he received to be offered to the general public as well.

"Yes Omar. The time for market expansion for many of our products and services has arrived. Frankly, I believe that this opportunity is exactly why STRX found our business to be so exciting. They will certainly help us grow. We are now all pulling in the same direction." Zoë answered.

"I know that among many other businesses, STRX owns the second-largest hotel chain in the world. There has been some speculation that Rhapsody intends to put centers in many of these hotels in different parts of the world?"

"You are absolutely right, Omar. There's a fantastic opportunity for expansion of our concepts through the existing infrastructure of the Casa Celestiale chain."

"Speaking about the Rhapsody philosophy, I realize that these values have continued to evolve over time. However when you folks first began down this pathway you had five basic principles that your team provided as guidelines to your Membership. Am I right about that?" Omar directed this question to Dr. Dao Diskul as one of the original founders, rather than towards his longtime friend and colleague, Zoë Mansfield. "We have discussed these principles several times on our show in the past. However for the benefit of those who may not have heard about these values on our prior shows would you just quickly tick them off for us?"

"Sure, Omar … I'll just list them one through five as they appear in our Membership handbook. "The principles are straight forward: #1 'Own your own health': #2 'Practice a holistic understanding of your physical, mental and spiritual lifestyle and lifespan.' #3 'Observe preventative and prophylactic approaches to disease detection, deterrence and management.' #4 'Recognize that regardless of age, race, gender, or socio-economic position, all men and women share the common gift of 24 hours in a given day.' And Principle #5 'Accept the possibility that near-perpetual life may be achievable." Dao ticked these off as she had many times over the last few years. She was well aware that the fifth principle was the most controversial and she was prepared to discuss this in detail if that was the way that Omar wanted to orient his interview. The moon-faced physician simply shone her ever-present smile and waited for Omar to proceed.

"I don't want to trivialize any of the work that you and your teams have done in developing the Rhapsody philosophy, but my take away from all of this has simply been captured in your very first principle, the one about 'owning your own health.' I think all of us can relate to the fact that over many years we became comfortable with outsourcing our own health care to a variety of different medical specialists. Personally speaking, once I understood my own responsibility in caring for myself, I have been able to do a much better job of it."

"Yes Omar. We are proud to have you as one of our diamond members. And I might add that you look absolutely fabulous. You have reduced your weight, increased your muscle mass, and you are now sexier than ever." Zoë Mansfield teased Omar a little bit with a flirtatious smile that the audience found humorous. They all knew that there was a strong business friendship between Omar and Zoë, but everyone recognized that there was nothing more intimate than that. However now that Omar was bouncing his dialogue back and forth between Zoë and Dao, he couldn't resist the opportunity to tease Zoë a bit as well.

"That's just like you Zoë. Everything seems to begin and end with sex." Omar put on a false frown to underline his jab.

Dao then chimed in. "Sex is an extremely important part of a healthy lifestyle."

"Oh....you too, Dao? Someone told me that you two ladies were kindred spirits. Now I understand why." They all laughed a little more as Omar crunched up his face in mock surprise. He too believed that a healthy sex life was an important aspect of overall healthiness; he simply found it more entertaining to allow his lady friend physicians to be the ones who emphasized this attribute.

"On another note," Omar clearly wanted to go back to a discussion of the overall Rhapsody philosophy. "What can you tell our audience about the Rhapsody philosophy that has made the biggest difference from the standpoint of your original platinum and diamond members?"

"Thanks for getting us back on course, Omar," said Dao

"Don't get me wrong. We can talk about sex all day if you would like, Dr Diskul, or maybe I can just shut up and let you and Zoë talk about sex." Omar made a wide-eyed twist of his facial features and the audience laughed approvingly. Dao waited until the noise level settled a bit before finally answering Omar's question.

"Our members have reacted very favorably to their ability to understand their own health, wellness, beauty, intelligence, spirituality … and yes, sexuality, in a common context. And more than anything they like to be able to get answers to their questions, from experienced practitioners."

Omar accepted this answer studiously by slowly bobbing his head in an up-and-down manner. When he stopped moving his head, he changed gears and asked another probing question.

"Let me ask you ladies about something that I have been wondering about personally as a Rhapsody Member. Your literature and marketing material talks about longevity and the ability to live a 'longer healthier lifestyle.' With all of the data that you folks collect, do you have any evidence that indicates that practicing the *Rhapsody Lifestyle* will, in fact, elongate my lifespan?"

Zoë jumped on the challenge. "It is still somewhat early in our history as a company to be able to demonstrate the definitive impact that practicing the *Rhapsody Lifestyle* has on each of our personal lifespan potentials. Over time we will be able to demonstrate a strong correlation, I'm sure. But right now we have to operate with purely 'anecdotal evidence.' Now I do recognize that that phrase is somewhat of an oxymoron. But Omar, each one of us is an example of one. Just look at yourself." Zoë then appealed to the studio audience and asked, "What do you think people? Doesn't Omar look fabulous? Don't you think that he will be living a longer better life?"

Zoë Mansfield had become a bit of a media maven herself. She knew how to use the tools at her disposal. The audience erupted in loud applause and cheers for their beloved Omar. They could see right in front of them that Omar looked healthier. By extrapolation they believed that he was also happier and that he would lead a longer life. The cheers went on and on.

****

Gina Alvarez-Struben was now quite happy with the way that her life was progressing. She could now add the title 'Mommy" to the other titles that defined her in the past. Her son, Travis Scott Struben, was now four months old. He was blonde and blue-eyed like his mother rather than dark featured like his father, Josh. But Gina was totally captivated by his cute and innocent smile, which reflected his father's genetic makeup right down to the dimpled cheeks and cleft chin. She couldn't resist tickling the baby by rubbing her forefinger across his chin or rubbing her nose against the baby's nose. Gina was also thrilled to know that her son was the picture of health. Before and after the baby's birth, Gina and Josh had run a wide variety of tests to ensure that they knew everything there was to know about the health of Travis Scott Struben. They were now confident that he was free from any preordained vulnerability to diseases that were defined through any genetic susceptibility. These tests included a chromosome analysis that would have detected Huntington's disease, if any such proclivity were present. She loved introducing her newborn son to her friends and business colleagues. He was her joy.

Gina was expecting an interesting visitor to her home. She hadn't seen Marilyn Mitchell since Travis was born, and she looked forward to sharing her excitement with her friend from the Lay D's. The Group had agreed to do a mini reunion tour with half of the profits going to the Rhapsody Foundation. There were going to be some interesting twists to the upcoming five-city tour. The show was also going to feature a lead off act by Gina's mother-in-law, Danielle Dubonet and a grand finale that had all of the performing artists on stage together.

Until recently The Lay D's had not enjoyed anything near the spectacular success that they had when Gina was their lead singer. However the group was now doing well and Gina's break from the original Lay D's remained amicable. Marilyn Mitchell and Gina had stayed friendly even after their careers had gone their separate ways. Karen Buffet had recovered from her eating disorders and was now a Rhapsody Platinum Member. Sophia, who had filled in for Karen on the world tour in 2008, stayed on with the group as the trio was reconstituted after Gina went out on her own. After a mediocre start the *new* Lay D's had once again gained in popularity. As the new lead singer, Marilyn gave the Lay D's a bit of a Motown makeover, and their music was now more reflective of a soul sound than the pop/rock that had been so very popular with Gina as lead singer. The ironic part of this was that Gina now loved the new sound of the Lay D's, but confined her rendition of their music to her shower stall. She was thrilled for her former partners and in particular for her friend Marilyn.

Following her pregnancy Gina had worked very hard to recover her rock hard rock star shape. She spent a good bit of time working with her personal trainer, and the results were evident. In less than four months she had gotten her weight back to pre-pregnancy levels and this made her feel very good about herself. It was quite apparent that motherhood had done nothing to diminish Gina's physical attractiveness. She had no concerns whatsoever along these lines and the fact that her husband Josh continued to physically express an ongoing and aggressive lustiness, simply contributed to her self-esteem both as a mother and as a lover. Knowing that her friend would soon be there, Gina checked quickly on her sleeping son and then slipped into a very tight pair of jeans and a thin formfitting sleeveless knit top.

The only domestic help that Gina employed in her expanded Greenwich Village loft was Travis' nanny. However Gina spent so much of her time with Travis that the nanny morphed into the role of a major domo for the residence. The nanny went to the door to allow Marilyn Mitchell to come in and visit her old friend. Marilyn also wore skintight jeans. The faded denim was torn at mid thigh of her right leg. There was another designer rip high on the outside of her left thigh, just below her panty line. She also wore a light yellow fabric top.

"Hey, Girl. Where you at? You lookin'good, girl!! Or should I say, girl you're a woman now? So tell me how does it feel to be a mama?" Marilyn sashayed into the loft as though she had just been there every day for a week. Gina got up from where she was sitting and threw her arms around her friend.

"You look absolutely wonderful, Marilyn. I couldn't wait to see you. How are the rest of the girls doing?"

"Everybody's doin' just fine. Karen looks wonderful. Wait to you see what that girl did to her body!!! She put on weight in all the right places and she now eats like a human being instead of like a bird. Still mostly keeps to herself, but she has a thing goin' with our drummer. He's only twenty-one years old but built like Adonis. Hot stuff!!!"

"What about Sophia? How is she getting along with Karen?"

"She acts like she's been there all along. She's got her groove goin' now and a lot of our fans get a kick out of our Roman girl singing soul. Somehow it all works. But we miss your sexy self, Girl. You gotta give us the 'hot mama' instead of the 'cool mama' when we be all out there together."

"What do you mean 'cool mama'? I'm looking forward to us doing our thing together."

"I am too. And I certainly won't be telling you how to do your thing, Girl. I was just commenting that you are now a mother, and that is so co…ooool !!! That's what I mean by a cool mama!!!"

Gina took that as a cue. She curled her finger at her friend in a way that said "Follow me. I've got something to show you." They walked to the rear of Gina's residence and into the nursery. Gina picked up her son and cradled him in her arms. The baby wore a one piece navy blue stretchy and was wrapped in a light blue blanket. He was sleeping peacefully. Even as Gina picked up Travis, he continued to sleep softly and quietly. However Gina was making no effort to speak quietly herself. As Marilyn moved closer to Gina and her baby, the former lead singer of the lay D's introduced her son. Still hugging him tight to her chest, she said, "Let me introduce you to the new love of my life, Travis Scott Struben."

Gina held Travis at a slight angle so that Marilyn could get a much better view. Marilyn walked right over to within a foot of Gina and her baby. She leaned her head down towards the child and with a wide toothy smile made a couple of inane googley noises. Then she pulled back and looked into her girlfriends face and said, "He's wonderful! He's very very wonderful!!"

Gina rested her index finger on the tiny cleft in Travis' chin and lightly wiggled it back and forth. The baby didn't open his eyes, but the ends of his lips turned upward ever so slightly, in what Gina accepted as a smile. Gina had always taken personal complements and accolades in stride, but she positively beamed when Marilyn complimented her son.

"Can I hold him?" Marilyn asked.

"Sure," said Gina. She carefully handed her son with both of her hands into Marilyn's arms, but didn't move more than a couple feet away. Marilyn received the child in her hands and clutched him high and tight, staring down into his sleeping countenance.

"Doesn't he look just like a little prince? I'll bet he grows up to be a king. What does your 'Hedgie Hunk' husband, Josh, think about all of this? Is he cool being a dad?"

"He is thrilled, simply thrilled, to be a father. He is still working a lot, but he returns from his trips as quickly as possible to spend time with Travis. You wouldn't believe how he acts around the baby. It is very precious to watch."

"And how about all the grandparents? How are all of them doing?"

"Stephen and Danielle have been wonderful, and my mom just left to go back to Detroit last night. She also believes that Travis is the most beautiful baby she has ever seen. She has also gotten herself into tip-top shape. She wants to be dancing at her grandson's wedding. I told her she'd have a while to wait. Right now Travis' heart belongs to Mommy."

"What about your father? Last time I spoke to you, you were trying to track him down even though you hadn't seen him since you yourself were a baby."

"You are right. I was very curious and really pushed hard to find out what happened to my father. We were able to track him down and find out a little about him, but not too much. Apparently he died more than seventeen years ago. He was an only child and his parents predeceased him by many years. He never married and I was his only child. After he was diagnosed with Huntington's Chorea, he left Puerto Rico and was institutionalized in a hospital in Miami shortly thereafter. His condition continually worsened until his death in 1995. The doctors believe that, for our family, the genetic predisposition to this disease died along with him."

"I guess that qualifies as a sad story with somewhat of a happy ending. I'll bet you're at least very happy that Travis won't suffer from the same problem."

"Yes in many ways that's true. But let me tell you something about my little man here. He's going to live forever. He's going to learn how to fly!!!"

****

Stephen Struben walked hand in hand with his wife Danielle through a section of the ruins in Rome. Two beefy Italian security guards shadowed them, so that they could enjoy some privacy without being interrupted by a gaggle of tourists the likes of which they had encountered earlier in the day while walking near Trevi Fountain. Stephen had managed to quickly procure two large cups of pistachio gelato from San Crispino, before they hurried over to the area of the city where the ruins stretched out in front of them.

They had already passed by the Colosseum, and the Arch of Constantine and were now near the top of Palatine Hill, the most famous of Rome's seven hills. They were looking across two millennia of history and down upon the Roman Forum and Nero's Circus Maximus, viewing the exact locations where the chariot races were held. Although the Strubens had visited these sites a couple of times in the past, the view was still breathtaking and thought provoking in an awesome way.

"I *'ave* always been amazed by the ruins of Rome. You can stand right here and look down on history. *Eet ees* almost as though you can see the ghosts of the gladiators *rideeng* around on their armored horses ready to do battle." Danielle lingered on this thought for a second and then added, "You *'ave* to wonder whether or not *eet* was appropriate for archaeologists to unearth the ruins here and *een* Greece and *een* South America and *een* other places around the world. It feels like they are *deeggeeng* up the graves of *ceeveeleezations*. We don't normally exhume people from their graves, why should we do *eet* to *ceeveeleezations*?"

"I understand your perspective, Danielle. However that's how mankind makes progress. We learn from the history of our fore fathers. The Roman civilization that is laid out in front of us is more than 2000 years old. Some aspects of the Roman Empire go back even further, nearly 2500 years. It was an empire that lasted for the better part of a millennium. There's nothing like it in today's world. The United States is not even 250 years old yet and it's the closest thing to an empire in the modern world."

"I don't usually *theenk* about the US as the 'American Empire.' When I *theenk* about empires I *theenk* about countries that stretched their influence through geographic expansion *een* various parts of the world. That was what *'appened weeth* the Roman Empire as well as *weeth* the British Empire, the Chinese empire and others."

"Empire, superpower, what's the difference? Really? It's still all about one group of people trying to superimpose their lifestyles on the views and ideologies of others. The US may not be trying to convert other countries to its Judeo-Christian moral ethics. However it has very blatantly attempted to export its views on democracy and capitalism. In many ways it is much more of a secular society than some of the other empires have been."

The Strubens were walking slowly hand in hand. And the pace of their conversation was similar to their gait. Each of their perspectives was met with a thoughtful interlude before the other person responded. Danielle began to trek down along the broken stairway into the ancient

Roman Forum. She led Stephen by the hand down to a new landing where they were able to get a different visual perspective. She then replied to his viewpoint.

"I don't want to make *thees* a *poleeteecal deescussion. 'Owever eet* seems that *poleeteecs* and *heestory* are always *eentermeengled*." Again there was a lengthy silence as they both looked out across the Forum. Finally Danielle completed her thought process. "I guess *ceeveeleezations* don't *leeve* forever…….and for that matter neither do people." She turned and looked to the left and then back to the right and the finally added, "But I find *eet eenteresting* that the lifespan of people *ees* getting longer while the lifespan of *ceeveeleezations 'as* begun to atrophy."

"I'm not sure whether your comments are meant to be positive or negative in nature."

"Neither. *Eet's* just that sometimes the world seems to be *speenneeng* out of control. I *'ave 'ad* the same conversation *weeth* Gina recently. *Eet's* so *eenteresteeng* what a different perspective younger people *'ave*. Gina really believes that she and Josh, and now Travis, *weell* live for a long long time. I *'ave* to confess that even though I'm a big fan of protracted *longeveety*, I know that we all *'ave* just so much time to *leeve*. And I really want to make the most of the time I *'ave*." Danielle took her hand out of the interlocking finger grip that she had been maintaining with Stephen and turned to face him looking directly up into his eyes. She then said softly, "And I love you very dearly Stephen. And I want to make the most that we can out of the rest of our lives together."

Stephen Struben looked down on the pursed red lips of his wife, paused for a second and then bent down and kissed her warmly. They remained with their arms around each other and their lips together for the better part of the minute, but neither one of them was keeping time.

Two young Italian tourists passed them on the steps. One of them offered his assessment. "Devono essere i newlyweds."

* * * * * * * * * *

Abby, Alison, Caitlin and Maria arrived at their luncheon spot near the three massive maple trees at the western end of Abby's horse farm. The staff had set up an exquisite picnic lunch for the four women while they were on their ride. The wrought iron picnic table was covered with an embroidered tablecloth. The wrought iron chairs that surrounded the table had been softened with fitted cushions that took some of the rustic flavor away from picnic lunch. However the cushions were meant to cater to the comfort and convenience of the four horsewomen. The staff had also placed a large bouquet of fresh cut flowers in a low flat centerpiece that adorned the middle of the table.

There were two large wicker baskets placed on the table. A short distance away six or seven large blankets were open on the grass in order to provide an alternative lounging spot for any of the women who cared to recline in a more relaxed fashion. And when they arrived at their destination three members of Abby's staff were there to greet them and take their horses back to the barn. The staff also brought hot and cold wet towels and a small container of liquid soap so that the women could clean up a bit before sitting down to eat. The staff stood in front of each of the women and offered them the towels and soap while they relieved them of their riding helmets, gloves, crops, and other unneeded riding accessories. They placed the equipment in the back of the larger of the two horse trailers that they had driven over to the western part of the farm. The staff then packed up the horses and left the ladies alone to enjoy their luncheon together.

After her staff had driven off with the four horses Abby walked over to one of the picnic baskets and grabbed half of a turkey sandwich, an apple and a bottle of water. She didn't bother sitting in one of the cushioned seats but rather she extended her body across a couple of the blankets and kicked off her shoes. Her two sisters and Maria soon joined her. None of them opted to sit at the table, so Maria grabbed the bouquet of fresh flowers and placed it near the center of the blankets. Alison sat down close to her twin sister and stretched out her legs as she placed the palms of her hands in an inverted position above her hips so that her finger tips were allowed to grip at her lower back.

"That was a lovely ride. An absolutely beautiful day … not too hot … not too cold … just perfect." Alison was actually stretching her voice as well as her back as she made her comments. "What I would like now, is a nice strong good-looking young masseur to rub my back for about an hour and then I could just take a nap. Sounds great … doesn't it?"

"Sorry Allie the young men who work here on the farm are much more adept at massaging horses than humans."

"Too bad we don't have a center out here in the suburbs," Maria said as she knelt down on the blankets and sat back over her heels.

"You never know. I am sure it will be a while before we have full-blown centers out here in rural areas. But Gutfreund and the gang are looking to license out elements of the Rhapsody brand to centers that are located at hotels in suburbia. So there could be a small center close by, sooner than you think. There's so much yet to do." Caitlin made her comments as she stood next to Maria. She was the last of the women still standing as they spoke. The twins had already stretched out on the blankets. Caitlin kept one of the cool wet towels and was wiping some of the trail dust from her forehead. When she finished she too removed her riding jacket, and her chest pushed out against her thin white blouse. Abby and Alison exchanged silent smiles with respect to the humor they shared earlier regarding their sister's purchased corpulent cleavage. They kept the joke to themselves.

"I thought we agreed that we were not going to talk about Rhapsody all afternoon," Abby said.

"Sorry about that," Caitlin said. "It's just that by the Fall I'll be the only one of us still working for Rhapsody."

"Don't worry. We will all still have plenty of interest in its ongoing success." Abby responded. She then looked over at Maria and asked, "What will you do when you leave, Maria. Will you spend most of your time in Spain at Poco Pedazo de Ciela?"

"Duffy and I will go over to Spain for a few months anyway. I really want her to have a good deal of exposure to the arts in a more casual atmosphere than what it's like in New York City." She took her time and answered the question deliberately as she began to munch on her sandwich. "I intend to keep my home in Manhattan anyway because I want Duffy to attend preschool in New York this coming September. After that, who knows? I think that we will just play it a month or so at a time."

"You know what I'm going to be doing, and Maria just outlined her plans for us. What about you Abby? What are your plans for the future? So now that you have successfully deployed this business for living longer better lives, what are you going to do next?" Caitlin inquired.

"That's a good question, Caitlin. And it's one that I have asked myself many times over the last six months or so. As you might imagine riding horses out here on the farm is a nice respite but it certainly doesn't constitute a significant contribution to society. Allie and I have been talking a lot about what we accomplished in our first few years at Rhapsody. And, as you indicated earlier, Caitlin, there is still in an enormous amount of progress yet to be achieved before the healthcare revolution is completed. But we now have passed that baton to you and Ben and Dao and Mark Candu and Gutfreund and all of the others that will carry on. So Allie and I have decided to tackle something completely different."

"So don't keep us in suspense. What is it that you two want to tackle next?"

"Education of course. Do you realize what a mess our educational system is in? Allie and I have just formed a new company called 'BOOOM,' which stands for 'Been Out Of Our Minds.'"

"Tell us about it."

"Well that's another story altogether. I'm so glad you asked."

****

And so it goes in the continuing saga of the Rhapsody Players. Each of their days is a snapshot in time. Each of their lives has crossed at a common overlapping juncture in history. One hundred years earlier each of the Rhapsody players was yet to traverse Planet Earth. Another one hundred years from now most, if not all, of the Rhapsody players will be planted in Planet Earth. Before then however, some will have learned how to fly.

THE END

ACKNOWLEDGEMENTS

The idea for writing <u>The Rhapsody Players</u> emanated from a business discussion with publicist Richard Rubenstein with respect to the real life business of Rhapsody Holdings. Richard encouraged me to put many of our concepts into a story that would help our membership comprehend the breadth and depth of what *we* were hoping to achieve.

The *"we"* that I refer to above is the real life Rhapsody Holdings team. The four founders of the business include Jeff Moskowitz, Gurinder Shahi, Art Thompson and me.

Jeff Moskowitz is a physician and businessman based in New York. His original idea of developing women's centers in various parts of the world grew into the concept of Rhapsody Holdings as it is today, a corporation ready to embrace and develop every aspect of the business as it is fictionally represented in the novel. Jeff and I have worked together on a daily basis to broaden the Rhapsody Holdings business and Jeff was the first person to read this book. I am grateful to Jeff for his selflessness, as well as confidence, encouragement and boundless intellectual curiosity.

Gurinder Shahi is a physician, a business consultant, an educator, and an author. His many talents were vital in the furthering of the Rhapsody Holdings business concept as well as in the initial editing of <u>The Rhapsody Players</u> manuscript. Because of Gurinder's enthusiasm for an eclectic approach to the issues surrounding health and wellness he is recognized as one of the visionaries that will help shape the future of global health.

Art Thompson, a Manhattan based businessman, has served an effective sounding board throughout the development of Rhapsody Holdings. We have reviewed much of the concept development with Art over multiple lunches near his midtown Manhattan office. His faith in our collective success has been unwavering.

I am grateful to these co-founders of Rhapsody Holdings for their encouragement to pursue my "night job" of writing <u>The Rhapsody Players</u>.

Several other members of the Rhapsody Holdings executive advisory group also deserve thanks for their patience and perseverance during the concept development stage of the Rhapsody project. Their contributions are immeasurable and their insights are invaluable. These business leaders have allowed me to create the notion of "reality writing," as an enabling medium for business development. I list these individuals in no particular order other than an approximation of when I first began discussing the Rhapsody project with them: Everett Lang (former CEO of National Discount Brokers); Judy Campbell (former CIO of New York Life); Susan Kurland (EVP at CB Richard Ellis); Marlene Roth (Director, Service Operations, Time Warner Cable); Tim Gilfoyle (Former Sr VP of Siemens) Bill Newman (Partner, Sullivan & Worcester); William Bangert (EVP of TeleTech Inc); Mark Kelley (CEO of Henry Ford Medical Group); Jane Smith (CEO of Spacesmith); Scott Carcillo (COO of Ambrose Employer Group); Karen Walker (CEO of OneTeam Consulting); Barbara Kaczynski (former CFO of the National Football League); Loren Wimpfheimer (Atlanta based attorney and entrepreneur); Ken Price (Former VP of Marketing for Compaq Computer.) All of these individuals have provided insights and perspectives that have helped formulate the basis of the fictional story of The Rhapsody Players, but more importantly will play a prominent role in the development of the real-life saga of Rhapsody Holdings. For their ongoing contributions to each of these efforts I am eternally grateful.

I am also sincerely grateful to Betty Kelly Sargent, my editor for teaching me a lesson that every first time writer must learn: "less is more." A truly talented professional, Betty, was able to bring me closer to my prospective readers. What more could a writer ask for? Thanks also to Jan Colby, Jane Smith, and my brother Mike for some early editorial help and commentary.

Finally I am grateful to my wife, Debbie, who has stood by me throughout this effort. She has been my partner in life, throughout nearly 35 years of marriage. We have raised eight wonderful children together, and no matter what else we accomplish in life, I recognize our children as our enduring legacy.

ABOUT THE AUTHOR

The Rhapsody Players is the first book written by Jim Lynch. The story is a fictionalized account of a real life broad-based business initiative (Rhapsody Holdings).

Jim is a visionary business executive who has spent more than 35 years leading other professionals in both entrepreneurial pursuits as well as big business initiatives. He started his career with eight years experience in a family business as an investigator for James J. Lynch Investigation and Security Services. He then spent the core of his business career (22 years) as an executive with AT&T. After retiring from AT&T he founded a thriving sales consulting business and co-founded a successful IT outsourcing business. Then he was one of four entrepreneurs who co-founded Rhapsody Holdings in 2007.

In addition to his career as a business executive, Jim is a member of the Board of Trustees for the Hunterdon Healthcare System and the Hunterdon Medical Center. He is also a member of the Board of SOAR, based in Washington DC, a group that assists aging members of the clergy.

Jim is currently working on his second novel, The Twenty-Twenty Players, which is a sequel to The Rhapsody Players.

Jim and his wife Debbie reside in western New Jersey, where they have raised eight children together.

TRP@RhapsodyHoldings.com

High Praise for The Rhapsody Players

"Lynch's characters are so real that I miss them the moment I put the book down. He combines a wealth of experience with compassionate human insight to create people and situations that feel comfortable and familiar. The author weaves together individuals, places, intrigue, fame and fortune into an exciting and thought provoking narrative. His ability to humanize far flung destinations and political, financial, social, corporate and national cultures allows the reader to experience the world from the comfort of their personal environment. The Rhapsody Players superbly employs fictionalized fact to create a fascinating story that will be embraced and enjoyed by many who, like me, will be anxiously awaiting the future when life imitates art."
Jeffrey Paul Moskowitz, MD – Clinician, Entrepreneur, Strategist, Co-Founder Rhapsody Holdings.

****

"Jim Lynch has done an outstanding job of integrating fact and fiction in this engaging "factionalized" novel that brings the Rhapsody vision to life. This is an enjoyable read with memorable and engaging characters. Their experiences powerfully illustrate the opportunity and need for Rhapsody's revolutionary approach to managing health and well-being. I eagerly anticipate the movie version!"
Gurinder Shahi, MBBS, PhD, MPH - Co-Founder, Rhapsody Holdings, author of BioBusiness in Asia.

****

"Riveting reading; a fun filled plot with characters who represent the realities of today's financial and healthcare industries."
Everett F Lang, Ed.D and former CEO and President, National Discount Brokers; former Chairman & CEO, BT Brokerage.

Breinigsville, PA USA
13 October 2010
247269BV00002B/53/P